THE GATECRASHERS

By Alexander Fullerton

SURFACE!
BURY THE PAST
OLD MOKE
NO MAN'S MISTRESS
A WREN CALLED SMITH
THE WHITE MEN SANG
THE YELLOW FORD
SOLDIER FROM THE SEA
THE WAITING GAME
THE THUNDER AND THE FLAME
LIONHEART
CHIEF EXECUTIVE
THE PUBLISHER
STORE

THE ESCAPISTS
OTHER MEN'S WIVES
PIPER'S LEAVE
REGENESIS
THE APHRODITE CARGO
JOHNSON'S BIRD
BLOODY SUNSET
LOOK TO THE WOLVES
LOVE FOR AN ENEMY
NOT THINKING OF DEATH
BAND OF BROTHERS
FINAL DIVE
WAVE CRY
THE FLOATING MADHOUSE

The Everard series of naval novels
THE BLOODING OF THE GUNS
SIXTY MINUTES FOR ST GEORGE
PATROL TO THE GOLDEN HORN
STORM FORCE TO NARVIK
LAST LIFT FROM CRETE
ALL THE DROWNING SEAS
A SHARE OF HONOUR
THE TORCH BEARERS
THE GATECRASHERS

The SBS Trilogy
SPECIAL DELIVERANCE
SPECIAL DYNAMIC
SPECIAL DECEPTION

The Rosie Quartet
INTO THE FIRE
RETURN TO THE FIELD
IN AT THE KILL
SINGLE TO PARIS

THE
GATECRASHERS

Alexander Fullerton

LITTLE, BROWN

A *Little, Brown* Book

First published in Great Britain in 1984
by Michael Joseph Ltd
This edition published in 2002
by Little, Brown

A CIP catalogue record for this book
is available from the British Library.

ISBN 0 316 85760 2

Typeset in Palatino by
Palimpsest Book Production Limited
Polmont, Stirlingshire
Printed and bound in Great Britain by
Clays Ltd, St Ives plc

Little, Brown
An imprint of
Time Warner Books UK
Brettenham House
Lancaster Place
London WC2E 7EN

www.TimeWarnerBooks.co.uk

THE
GATECRASHERS

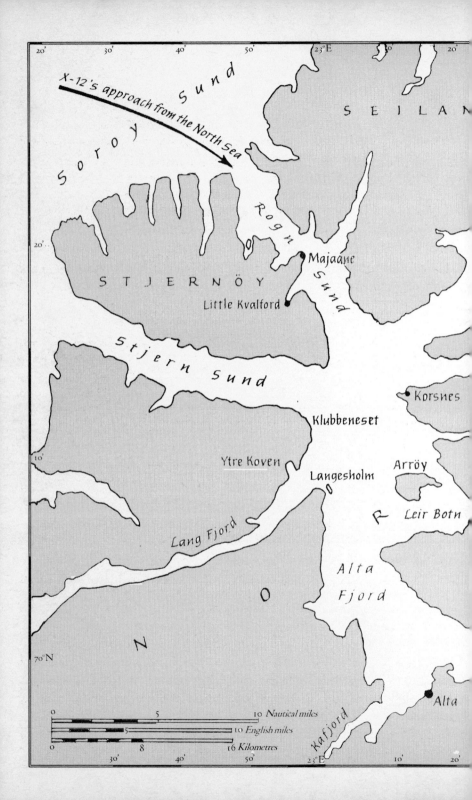

The Norwegian lair of the
Tirpitz, Scharnhorst and Lutzow

ENLARGED AREA

ARCTIC OCEAN

Alta

Narvik

NORTH
SEA

NORWAY

SWEDEN

FINLAND

Gulf of Bothnia

Trondheim

Bergen

OSLO

BALTIC
SEA

USSR

USSR

varg sund

D

Rafs
Botn

1

God Almighty, he thought, this is impossible! X-12 pounding, thrashing her thirty-nine tons around like a whale having an epileptic fit! Paul Everard, his hands clamped to solid fittings and muscles straining to hold himself in place against the midget submarine's frantic porpoising, saw Jazz Lanchberry, the engineer, open-mouthed and wide-eyed as he fought the wheel and tried at the same time to stay in his seat. His left shoulder had slammed against the end of the storage locker, and he was dragging himself back into place now, a snarl of anger taking over from the shock in his dark face: he'd momentarily lost control of the wheel and the boat's wild cavorting had acquired a lateral component as well as the plungings and soarings. At sixty feet she was fighting the tow-rope like a huge fish with a barbed hook in its mouth instead of a very, very small submarine with a steel coupling in her snout. Not a damn thing you could do about it, for the moment . . .

Well, there was. In fact there were two things. One, you could release the tow-rope – it could be done from inside, by winding a handle in the bow compartment – and start the motor, surface. But that wouldn't achieve anything except short-term relief, because this exercise did have to

be completed and you'd only have delayed it. With annoyance to a lot of people, since the practising was just about
finished now, the operation imminent . . . The other option
– Paul didn't like it, in fact all his submariner's instincts
were against it, but he'd have to try some damn thing
before she shook herself to death. He looked round, met
Dick Eaton's sideways glance from the first lieutenant's
seat a few feet aft: Eaton looked desperate, the violent
motion too savage for his hydroplanes to cope with – and
X-12 shooting upwards with a steep bow-up angle on
her. You couldn't blame him for not having countered it;
the upward lunge had been caused by the towrope, slack
or at any rate unstrained at one moment and then in the
next tugging upwards at the midget's stem. Paul yelled
over the noise of the sea and thumping steel, 'Flood
for'ard!'

Eaton's head turning: then he was hesitating. He couldn't
not have heard. Presumably he was wondering if he'd
heard right, knowing this was a manoeuvre Paul had sworn
to avoid. Paul was opening his mouth to repeat the order
when the sub-lieutenant acted – pushing the trim-lever
forward to pump ballast from the after trimming tank to
the bow one, shifting weight into her forepart so she'd lean
on the tow and maintain an even strain on it.

That was the theory, how it was supposed to work. The
price was to be trimmed heavy for'ard, which in professional terms was unseamanlike, in plainer language bloody
dangerous. Other X-craft COs had made a practice of
it: Paul realised that until now he'd just been lucky, had
had no worse than moderate weather for his own towing
exercises.

Stench of diesel, and wet salt smell from the bilges, a
slight odour of disinfectant from the wet-and-dry compartment – known as the W and D – which also contained the
heads, or lavatory. Bomber Brazier, the man crouching in
there with a vaguely startled expression as the boat threw

herself around, was this crew's diver . . . The flooding of
the bow tank was already taking some effect, though,
leaving her light aft, so the stern had a tendency to float
upward; to counter this, Eaton pulled the lever back and
shoved it over to port to admit seawater from outside into
the midships trim-tank. Sweat gleamed on Eaton's narrow,
intelligent face, and Paul was remembering that split-
second delay in carrying out his 'Flood for'ard' order. If
he was given the operational command of this boat, he
wouldn't have Dick Eaton on the team. And he would –
please God – get the operational command. He couldn't
exactly count on it for certain, but—

If the medical gentry had rumbled him? If they knew
about the nightmares?

Christ . . . But they couldn't. He'd have been told. At
least, given some indication . . .

It was working: the shift of ballast had taken all the
viciousness out of her motion. Midget submarine X-12 – she
was forty-eight feet long (internally, more like thirty-five)
and had a maximum internal diameter of five-and-a-half
feet – was riding quite comfortably, now. You could feel the
tugging surges of the tow, but the weight being permanently on the tow-line was cushioning it, dampening-down
the jerking around which only a minute ago had been
frightful. The towing ship – in today's exercise it was HM
Submarine *Scourge* – was on the surface, and with the sea
kicking up as it was this afternoon she'd have a lot of
movement on her, which was what imparted that violent
upward snatching routine. It would be a lot better when
Scourge herself dived and got under the surface turbulence.

He thought, touching wood – this end of the storage
locker – Oh, not the passage-crew chore . . .

There was a chance he'd draw either passage or operational. Most of his training had been for the operational
job, but there was still no certainty about it. Passage crews

would man the X-craft for the long haul to the target area, and then operational teams would take over for the actual assault – which was likely to be short, sharp and frightening, but considerably less of an ordeal, Paul thought, than eight days of towing – eight days like this. Three men elbow to elbow, with so little space there was hardly anywhere they could squeeze past each other. Right here amidships, at the CO's position near the periscope, a small man could just stand upright under the dome of the main hatch; but Paul wasn't all that small.

She was towing quite easily still. Eaton had adjusted the trim – her bodily weight in the sea, and her fore-and-aft balance. Balance was easily upset in these midgets: you could move a tin of baked beans from the storage for'ard to the gluepot, which with an electric kettle comprised the boat's cookery equipment, and see an immediate shift of the bubble in the spirit-level . . . But a trim that produced this milder reaction to the rough handling from above still went dead against the grain, against all submarine training and experience and common sense. The reason was that if you ran into trouble when you were heavy in the bow, the boat could go down like a stone before you could do anything to check her.

Ten knots showing on the log. Porpoising a little still, but depth only varying between about fifty-five and sixty-five feet. Eaton was using as little hydroplane-angle as possible, so as to encourage her to settle down. There was a varying list as well as depth, a slight rolling as she gently porpoised. Paul watching points carefully all the time – watching Eaton's work, just a few feet aft in the first lieutenant's position, and Jazz Lanchberry's on the helmsman's seat. Lanchberry stolid, silent, rock-like: and Brazier watching from his crouched position in the W and D.

A sharp buzz and a flashing point of light: Paul grabbed the telephone.

'Everard.'

'All right down there?'

It was Vallance – captain of *Scourge*. The telephone wire was enclosed in the centre of the tow-line, which was 600 feet long and made of heavy Manilla rope. Nylon rope was infinitely better – stronger and less heavy – but nylon came only from the USA and was hard to get. Whatever the material, each rope had to be specially made, built around the central telephone wire. A few of the other X-craft did have nylon tows, but X-12 was not one of those lucky ones.

She'd jerked hard to starboard. Lanchberry countering with rudder. That would have been a sudden yaw on the part of *Scourge* . . . Paul had staggered, grabbed at an overhead pipe for support: he told Vallance, 'Not too good when you do that to us. It was very lively for a while, but easier now I've weighted her for'ard. It's the way your stern tugs at the rope that makes for problems. But we're surviving.'

'Good show . . . I'll make the ninety-degree turn to port now – OK?'

'All right.'

'Then I'll dive. Putting Scutson on this line now.'

'Aye aye, sir.' He told the others, 'About to turn ninety degrees to port.'

A nod from Eaton. Lanchberry lifted a hand, without looking round. He was an ERA, engineroom artificer. He'd steer her round, as he felt the pull developing, and Eaton would watch for the tendency to angle upwards on the swing, resulting from the flow of water sliding in under her forepart. But the weight for'ard might be expected to counter that, on this occasion. Some course and speed alterations were part of the drill for this exercise, and in themselves they presented no problems, but on the new course *Scourge* would be battling directly into wind and sea – wind force four, sea rough. There'd be a lot more movement on her, and it would be inflicted on X-12 too, via the tow-line from that heavily pitching stern. Might need a few more gallons in the for'ard tank . . .

But the weight in the bow was already a danger. If she went out of control for some reason – for instance, if the tow parted – she'd be in a nosedive heading for the sea-bed.

He decided he'd use human ballast instead of liquid. Quicker to shift back in an emergency: and self-propelled, at that . . . 'Bomber' Brazier, sub-lieutenant RNVR and X-12's diver, weighed close to 200 pounds, and if Brazier moved from the W and D into the bow compartment where the battery was housed, that considerable weight would be shifted about twelve feet.

Paul warned him that he might be required to transfer for'ard quickly. Brazier raised a thumb the size of a banana. 'OK, skipper.'

A voice over the telephone announced, 'Ten degrees of port wheel on!'

That was the voice of *Scourge*'s navigator, Willy Scutson. Paul acknowledged, 'All set, Willy.'

'Bumpy, is it?'

She'd lurched again. Lanchberry spinning his wheel back, muttering soft curses. Paul told Scutson, 'Be easier if you kept your bloody ship still.'

In a minute *Scourge* would be head to sea.

A number of full-sized submarines, S and T class and all of them fitted with the special towing gear, had visited Loch Cairnbawn for exercises like this one and for more elaborate rehearsals as well. Then they'd departed, to continue their natural warlike functions elsewhere. But now the whole group was assembling – eight of them, and each would sail with a midget in tow and a thousand miles to cover. Originally the plan had allowed for only six, and the whole team had trained on X-5, 6, 7, 8, 9 and 10. X-11 and X-12 were recent deliveries, and HM Submarines *Setter* and *Scourge* had been added to increase the towing flotilla equivalently.

X-12 turning now, the Manilla dragging her round. It was becoming a jerky, erratic pull, though. Getting worse . . . She was behaving like a hooked fish that had been lying doggo for a while and was now starting a fresh attempt at breaking the line.

'All right, are you? X-12?'

'So far.'

He gestured to Brazier, who turned to move for'ard, like a big dog in a small kennel. He was built like a heavyweight wrestler. The W and D was a closet-sized compartment with a hatch in the top of it and flooding and pumping controls inside. The diver, wearing a rubber suit and oxygen mask, could shut its two doors and flood it – by a pump working to and from number two main ballast – then open the hatch and go outside, usually to cut through anti-torpedo nets and let the boat slide through to its target. When she'd passed through, the diver would climb back in, shut the hatch and drain the W and D down again.

Jazz Lanchberry glanced round. 'Be all right if it don't get worse, skipper.'

Compared to that earlier knocking-about, the motion wasn't too bad – thanks to one displaced body and the shift of ballast. But you could still feel the towline snatching at her as *Scourge*'s stern swung up and down.

'You OK, X-12?'

'No problems at the moment.'

'We'll be diving in a minute.'

'Roger.'

'Thirty feet for five minutes, then sixty. Captain suggests you go to a hundred.'

You wouldn't want to be towed right in the larger ship's slipstream. He told Dick Eaton, 'She's about to dive. Periscope depth for five minutes, then sixty feet. We'll stay where we are for the time being, then go down to a hundred.'

The first lieutenant's position was an aircraft-type seat a few feet aft, set transversely and surrounded by controls for the hydroplanes, main motor and trimming pump. He could even steer from there as well, if the ERA happened to be busy with some other task. Paul told Eaton, 'You'll have to be quick to pump as soon as the motion eases. Normal trim quick as we can get it.'

'Aye, sir.' A sideways jerk of the narrow head. Eaton was dressed in serge battledress trousers and white submarine sweater. Paul was in similar gear except he had on waterproof over-trousers; he'd dumped the waterproof jacket near him. It was very essential protection for riding on top of an X-craft if the sea was anything but dead smooth . . . The telephone warned, 'Stand by. Diving.' He repeated it to Eaton, who was watching his hydroplane position indicator and the depthgauge and the bubble in the spirit-level – which would be a couple of degrees aft of the centreline, because of the bowdown trim. The hydroplanes – just one pair, right aft behind the single propeller which was now idling, with no power on it, out there in the dark water about twenty feet from where Paul crouched with his backside against the warm casing of the gyro-compass motor – were in effect horizontal rudders. The murmuring, moving sea was all around you – within just inches, this steel cocoon like a bubble in it, held and compressed by its enclosing weight. Paul crouching, peering through the W and D, through the open doors in its two bulkheads, to where Bomber Brazier's hunched body seemed to fill the whole of the bow compartment.

Brazier grinned. 'Wotcher, skips.'

'*Scourge*'ll be diving now. When I beckon, move back.' Brazier nodded. Paul asked the ERA, 'OK, Jazz?'

'Lovely grub.' Eyes on the gyro repeater inches from his face, hands resting on the wheel. It was like a car's steering wheel, about that size too. There was no other kind of ship in which an engineroom artificer would double as helmsman. But Jasper Lanchberry also had the blowing panel – high-pressure air valves to numbers one and three main ballast, and main vent levers, and the pump for emptying number two main ballast, which was a kingston tank and had no high pressure blow – right at his elbow. Besides which his province was the entire boat, the whole complicated bag of tricks tightly packed into the tiny space.

Paul was edging back into his position amidships, when it happened. Simultaneously with the squawk from the telephone – 'Diving!' – a very strong jerk, upwards, at the midget's stem. Then recoil, as the tow-rope slackened and the weight of her bow took charge, forepart slamming down, bow-down angle growing fast and depthgauge needle beginning to swing round its dial: sixty-five feet, seventy, seventy-five, eighty . . . Brazier was heaving his bulk into the W and D: and Eaton had the pump running – the trim-lever pushed right back, aft, switching the pump to suck on the for'ard tank. Too little and too slow, to have any useful effect on the immediate crisis. Paul shotued at Lanchberry over the din of external sea-noise, 'Blow number one main ballast!' Then into the telephone as X-12 snouted downward – 'Willy?'

Silence.

He'd only been checking, confirming that the tow had parted, the Manilla rope and its wire core snapped. X-12 standing on her nose, and rate of dive increasing – 120 feet now, steep and aiming for the sea-bed, which wasn't so far away by this time, maybe 160 feet, or less . . . High pressure air was blasting into the for'ard main ballast tank, though – Lanchberry turning his head to see Brazier emerging on this after side of the W and D bulkhead. Paul ordered, 'Shut the shallow gauge.' A reminder to Eaton – who'd have done it anyway, since the shallow depth-gauge would have bust a gut if it hadn't been shut off pretty soon. But the blowing was taking effect – that, and Brazier's move: she was levelling, and the needle's swing was slowing. Bow finally coming up . . . None too soon, in fact: the seabed might be soft here but you might have had the bad luck to find a rock-patch too, and X-12's forty tons of deadweight had been heading for it like a truck driving into a wall.

'Stop blowing. Main motor full ahead, group up.'

There'd been nothing to be gained by using the motor while she'd been bow-down; a forward thrust would only have driven her deeper. But now she had her snout up, that screw at full power would combine with the effect of the hydroplanes to push her up.

Eaton had slammed the field-switch shut and turned the hand-wheel clockwise to its full extent. Those main motor controls were sited close to his right hand.

'Motor's full ahead group up, sir.'

'Periscope depth.' She was acquiring a pronounced bow-up angle now, and the trim-pump was still running. Paul told Lanchberry, 'Open number one main vent.'

You heard it bang open, and the rush of escaping air. Eaton meanwhile pulling the trim-pump lever back, then pushing it over to starboard, which would start it sucking on the midships tank. It was a four-position lever, a very neatly arranged control; the first part of each movement opened or shut the necessary valves, and the second part started or stopped the pump.

'Back in your hutch, Bomber.'

That too would help to level her. Paul realised that his pulses had been racing, that he was slightly breathless. Until now he'd been too busy to know it. Lanchberry muttered, craning round, 'Nasty. Highly insalubrious, you might say. *Scourge* must've stuck her arse up like a bleeding duck, and . . .'

'Right.' X-12 was quivering under the motor's thrust. Paul told Eaton, 'Group down. Half ahead.'

It was a lesson learnt, a lesson mostly for *Scourge* and for

Vallance her captain, primarily that in anything approaching rough weather he had to take care to dive in slow time when he had a midget in tow. *Scourge* had been head to sea, she'd been diving into a lot of turbulence, and – well, Jazz Lanchberry had summed it up well enough . . . Lanchberry added a minute later, when X-12 was lifting slowly, in excellent control again and not as yet high enough to come into the influence of the waves, 'No bloody stopping her, I reckoned. Could've hit the putty, smashed up good an' proper!'

'Still had about forty feet under us when we checked her, Jazz.'

The ERA's head turned. Crewcut dark head, blue-black jaw, a derisive slant to the thin, wide mouth. Paul added, pressing the 'rise' button of the periscope and watching as the tube slid up to its full nine-foot extension, 'Thirty, anyway.'

Lanchberry let out a snort of amusement, and winked at Brazier. Brazier's head poking out of the W and D like a tortoise's from its shell. Eaton reported, 'Periscope depth, sir.'

Eaton was a fairly new sub-lieutenent, and he used the word 'sir' a lot. Ordinary, full-sized submarines were less formal than surface ships – no less well disciplined, but not as pompous about it – and X-craft crews were slightly more relaxed still. More socially relaxed than *Scourge*, for instance, could afford to be. Paul didn't want to embarrass Eaton, and he hadn't said anything about it yet; left to himself, he'd catch on, soon enough. Paul had his eye at the periscope, scanning grey-green wave slopes. 'Bring her up to eight feet, Dick.' Nine feet was all right in flat conditions, in harbour conditions, fjord conditions such as they'd expect to have on this operation. In truly smooth water you'd only need an inch of glass showing above it. Now he needed an extra foot or so, to see over the waves. No higher than necessary, because the shallower you were the more you got slammed around, but he did need to see where *Scourge* was before he surfaced.

Shortly after that, passing a new tow, he'd be getting very, very wet, despite the waterproof suit.

Lanchberry muttered as he turned back to his wheel and gyro display, 'I dunno . . .'

Referring, presumably, to Paul's equanamity over X-12's recent dash towards the sea-bed. But it truly hadn't worried him. The accident had been foreseeable, and he'd accepted the risk of it when he'd told Eaton to shift the weight for'ard. Then it had happened, and he'd been ready for it and dealt with it, with no more hesitation than a man driving fast on a wet road would have in reacting to the beginning of a skid. Afterwards, there was time to be scared.

And for dreams. The nightmares were bastards. He'd never suffered from anything of the sort before: and they did, frankly, worry him. It was the suspicion that they had to mean something, that there could be a canker of fear inside you. The theory of 'no smoke without fire', and dread that some day it might show itself – in waking hours.

Bloody silly. He'd been a submariner long enough to know he didn't have even the slightest tinge of claustrophobia. The nightmares recurred, he told himself, only because he allowed himself to think about them. It was tantamount to inviting them back. And if people got to know about it – in view of the strict medical and psychiatric supervision of all the X-craft personnel – well, if the medical department realised it, he'd be out of this operation like a dose of salts!

He told himself, Forget it.

That was the one good answer. The basis of the worry was that old spectre, fear of fear. You could only beat it by ignoring it.

Jane knew. Since the night he'd woken screaming in her arms . . .

Scourge had just surfaced, emerging streaming from the suds a couple of hundred yards away, her stern towards X-12's periscope – which was about as thick as a walking stick. A sharp underwater thud, followed by two more, was Vallance's three-grenade signal telling Paul to come on up. Vallance was no doubt anxious, scared that X-12 might not be capable of coming on up . . . Paul pressed the other periscope-control button – they were both enclosed in a rubber bag on the end of a wandering lead, and you had to select the right one by feel – and sent the tube sliding down.

'Stand by to surface.'

She was rolling now, feeling the waves. And there was a very strenuous and uncomfortable half hour or so to come, getting a new tow passed and secured. All good practice, because it could become necessary on the way to the target area too. When the balloon went up, the eight midgets would be setting off with their towing ships on the surface and themselves at forty or fifty feet, but closer to the target area – which was in the Arctic Circle – the whole outfit would duck out of sight. Closer still, the tows would be slipped and the X-craft would go in under their own power.

A thousand miles of underwater tow was an astonishing thing to contemplate. You just had to accept the fact you were going to do it. Then, penetrate nets, defended anchorages . . .

Plugging in towards Loch Cairnbawn four hours later, following *Scourge* but no longer in tow from her, X-12 was more in the waves than on them. Paul, standing on his boat's flat top – the midgets had no conning towers – stood upright, swaying and bending to the rise and fall, with one arm wrapped around the raised induction trunk. The trunk was a man-high pipe that hinged at deck level and when raised acted as a conduit of air for the diesel engine intake, also as the communication link between himself up here and the dry, warmer people down inside. The hatch was shut: it had to be, or the boat would have filled, since the sea was sluicing right over her, swirling around Paul's legs. All that mattered was that the top of the pipe was clear. Diesel pounding throatily, exhaust spluttering through the froth astern, fumes unpleasant on the following wind. The engine was a four-cylinder, forty horsepower Gardner diesel, the same one that drove London buses.

Any crofter on that headland, as X-12 approached the entrance to the loch, would either have sworn to give up the malt or rushed straight home for a restorative dram. All he'd have seen, with the midget's low, flat top hidden in the waves, would have been a man not only walking on the water but gliding over it at a smart 10 knots . . . Not, in fact, that there could have been any bemused shepherd to have seen it. Security was tight, Loch Cairnbawn and its surroundings a restricted area. Precautions had been intensive right from the start, but from the first day of this month – September of 1943 – the clamp-down had become total. No leave was being granted, no private telephone calls were allowed, and no mail was being taken ashore. You could write your love-letters but they wouldn't be posted – for a while.

So Jane could write – he'd had a letter from her only yesterday – but she wouldn't be hearing from him. He'd warned her it would happen, that for a certain period he'd be incommunicado . . .

'How long?'

'Absolutely not the faintest.'

She'd frowned. 'That's exactly what Louis said.'

Louis being the man – Louis himself believed – who really counted in her life.

'What is it all about, Paul?'

She didn't know anything at all about the X-craft, didn't even know such things existed. Only a small handful of people did know anything – that they'd been designed for breaking into enemy harbours and anchorages, destroying major warships that couldn't be got at any other way. For a long time Paul and his friends hadn't known in any detail what their objective was to be: there'd been guesses and assumptions, but no certainty. They knew they'd been training for one specific operation, and that it had originally scheduled for March, then postponed for six months. Training had continued: and now they all knew that their primary target was the *Tirpitz* – 43,000 tons, 800 feet long, ten decks deep, clad in armous plating fifteen inches thick, carrying a devastating punch and currently lurking – with *Scharnhorst* and *Lützow* and a big pack of destroyers – in a deep fjord in the remote north of Norway, out of range of bombing or any other kind of attack.

Except by midget submarines – if they could gatecrash the anchorage. One part of her that was not armoured was her belly: and this was where you'd hit her. But – a thousand miles away, and in a narrow fjord approachable only through other narrow fjords, guarded by minefields, steel nets, accoustic detection gear, patrol craft, shore guns and probably fixed torpedo batteries.

Paul's father, Nick Everard, had asked him – in a London restaurant, about eight weeks ago – 'What are you up to now? You're not standing-by *Ultra* in her refit, are you?'

Ultra was the submarine Paul had served in, in the Malta flotilla. She'd been near-missed by a bomb off Sfax on the Tunisian coast last November, a fortnight after the 'Torch' landings, and she'd been sent back to the UK for major refit. In the week that she'd reached the Clyde there'd been an invitation to junior submarine officers to volunteer for 'special and hazardous duty', and having no idea what his next job might be, Paul had rather casually put his name in. At about the same time his promotion to lieutenant had come through.

He'd answered that question of his father's, 'No, I'm in – another flotilla, up there.' He'd hesitated. The secrecy surrounding the X-craft had a capital S on it: the message had been driven home a dozen times, secrecy was total. So, even when you were talking to Captain Sir Nicholas Everard, Bart., DSO*** DSC* RN . . . An older, heavier version of himself, gazing quizzically at him across the table. Paul had mumbled in some embarrassment, 'Careless Talk – all that stuff?'

Kate, Nick's new Australian wife, had laughed. Nick told her, 'But he's right. In fact I shouldn't have asked, in a public place like this.'

'My, can't we be stuffy!'

She'd said it to Paul, teasing Nick. Paul shook his head. 'I never thought so.' Hesitating again: 'In fact, all things considered' – he'd glanced at his father's medal ribbons – 'I'd say rather amazingly un-stuffy.'

'And bully for you.' Kate's hand patted Paul's, on the white table-cloth. 'I quite like him too, would you believe it?'

Kate was very attractive, Paul thought. His father had told him in a letter ages ago that she had a look of Ingrid Bergman, and it was a fact, the resemblance was striking. Paul remarked on it, and saw that she liked it; he liked her . . . It had been a happy lunch, with an air of celebration about it – despite a certain background tension – and there was reason for celebration, too. Earlier, walking to the restaurant through a light summer drizzle, he'd asked his father whether he was on leave now.

'No. Just playing truant.' Nick had told him, 'They've given me a cruiser. She's finishing a bottom-scrape at Chatham, and I've dragged Kate down here just for a couple of days. From my point of view it's a bit of a pier-head jump. The ship's *Calliope* – *Dido* class.'

'Well, congratulations!'

Kate said, 'Wait till you hear the rest of it.'

'It's supposed to be a temporary appointment only.' Nick explained, 'I'm really just filling in. Hence the short notice, etcetera. The fact is – look, this is a secret now—'

'OK'

His father drew a breath. 'It suits Their Lordships to keep me busy for a few months, because after that I'm in line for a cruiser squadron. Taking it east.'

'Squadron . . .' Paul did a quick double-take. 'My God, you mean—'

Kate nodded proudly. 'Promotion.'

'Rear-Admiral?'

'Isn't it incredible?'

Kate objected, 'Not in the least!' They all laughed. Paul began, 'Well, double those congratulations. And I agree, Kate, it's not at all—'

'But it is.' Nick Everard shrugged. 'Hasn't happened yet, anyway – I'll believe it when it does. But considering I left the service between the wars – with consequent loss of seniority, plus the fact Their Lordships never entirely forgive a man for walking out on them . . .'

'Obviously you've made up for it.'

'More than made up for it.' Kate had broken in. 'Exactly what I've been telling him. It's time they let him take a rest!'

Her eyes were on Nick, and she meant it. Paul was surprised. A moment ago she'd been proud of Nick's achievement, and now she'd have rather seen him shunted into some desk job?

Nick told him, 'Kate has some loony idea about my luck running out.'

'Oh. Well . . .'

'Don't you agree he's been through enough, Paul?'

He nodded. 'I couldn't disagree with that. On the other hand I can't imagine him putting his feet up. Even if they'd let him.' He could see she was seriously concerned; he tried to make light of it. 'Anyway, cats have nine lives, Kate.'

'Miaow,' Paul's father said, 'He's right. I'm a survivor. Case-hardened. Believe me, I have more reason now to stay alive than I ever had before. Another thing – very few flag officers get drowned. So really all I have to do is last out the next few months, and I'm home and dry.' He too, Paul realised, was trying to allay Kate's fears by sounding as if he didn't take them seriously. Then explaining – by way of changing the subject: 'But the delay, Paul – this is the secret you have to keep – is because there's a plan to send a contingent of ships to join the Yanks and Aussies in the Pacific. We can't do it right away, partly because we have to keep powerful forces up north – in Scapa and so on – to guard against any break-out by the *Tirpitz* and others into the Atlantic. Presumably there's some expectation of eliminating that threat before long. Don't ask me how . . .'

Paul hadn't enlightened him, although he had a pretty good idea of at least one answer. It was intriguing how the various factors meshed, forming a cohesive and logical pattern which had a surprising simplicity to it. Destroy the *Tirpitz* and you'd free major fleet units which could then be sent to the other side of the world to add their weight to a different struggle against another enemy. In the same blow you'd be removing the major threat to the Arctic convoys – which were vital to the whole strategy of the war – and to the transatlantic supply routes; and the trick would have been pulled by a handful of submersible bathtubs manned by young amateurs like Paul Everard . . .

He shouted down the induction pipe, 'Starboard ten!'

Loch Cairnbawn's afforested northern slopes loomed to port against grey sky. Entering sheltered water, at last. Ahead, farther up, lay the cluster of moored ships which included the X-craft depot ship *Bonaventure* and the other one, the old *Titania*, who'd arrived more recently to mother the towing submarines. Around them, dotted about in the rippling grey water of the loch, were smaller ships of various shapes and sizes, the rest of the Twelfth Flotilla's entourage.

'Midships!'

The quiet, mist-shrouded scene was fascinating – when you knew what it was for, how carefully the secret had been guarded and what a far-reaching effect the operation's success would have.

2

From *Norway Pilot*, Volume III:

Altafjord. General Remarks. Altafjord is entered between Klubbenes (70 12′ N, 22 58′ E) and Korsnes light-structure about 4½ miles eastward; together with Kafjord and Rafsbotn, its continuations, it is the largest fjord in the western part of Finmark and indents the mainland for about 17 miles . . . The shores are irregular, forming several large bays and small inlets . . . Altafjord is accessible for large vessels.

Even for the largest afloat, for a 43,000-ton battleship . . . Which had put to sea – slipped out and vanished, during the dark hours!

The man on the church tower stared for a few more seconds through his binoculars. Focussing on Kafjord, the main waterway's southwestern extremity and innermost recess. It was barely daylight yet – dawn came at about 02.00 here, at this time of year – and visibility was tricky, but of one thing there was no doubt: where yesterday at dusk the *Tirpitz*'s great bulk had lain at rest in the flat, reflective water, now there was nothing except a rectangular enclosure of buoys supporting steel anti-torpedo nets. The monster was no longer in her lair.

One floating object which the observer could make out was an anchored battle-practice target; and against the far shore he could distinguish the shapes of a lighter and a tug at the landing place just north of the empty nets. If *Lützow* was still in her berth she wouldn't have been visible from here in any case, since her box of nets was hidden by a spur of land on the inlet's southern side.

Pushing the glasses inside his coat, the Norwegian turned away, hurried to the belfry stairs and down them spiralling to street level. Emerging, he crossed the churchyard and turned right into the street: then stopped abruptly, drew back into the shadow . . .

A blacked-out saloon came racing. Brakes squealed as it juddered to a halt. His mind racing too, providing answers to questions he'd be faced with now: what he was doing in the street at this hour, where he'd been, where he was going, what for . . .

He told himself, Calm down, now. There's no problem . . . A visit to the church: a private prayer. Even a German would accept that – he hoped – as damn-all to do with the Master Race . . . The car halted just across from where he stood motionless with his back against the grey stone wall, rigidly defensive. Then he saw the face at the window as the driver wound it down and peered out at him: his breath fogged the air in a whoosh of relief.

'I'll be damned. That old bus of yours looked like a Mercedes Benz, for Christ's sake! It's the light, I suppose.' He was at the car, stooping to the window. 'What if you're caught on the road at this hour?'

'I had a job. Official. Little diversion here, is all . . . You got the message, eh?'

The driver's home was on the shore of Kafjord, he ran this old banger as a taxi and regularly drove *Tirpitz* officers into and out of town – this town being Alta, at the south end of the main fjord. The other man asked him. 'Where's she gone?'

'God knows. All I know is what I see. Or rather, don't see. But your question should be where have they gone.'

'The others too?'

'*Lützow*'s still here, but *Scharnhorst*'s out and so are ten destroyers.'

'How do we know that? *Scharnhorst*, I mean?'

The 26,000-ton *Scharnhorst*'s berth was in Langefjord, ten miles away. The driver said, 'Young Wielding Christoffersen. He was crewing in the Ellefsens' boat. Played truant yesterday – his mother's furious, but—'

'He's a fine kid. But he'd better be damn careful . . . Listen, does Torstein know?'

A nod. 'Just left him. He'll be putting the news out – right away, not waiting for the routine time.'

'Dangerous.'

'Well. It's an emergency, if ever there was . . .'

'Funny we didn't get even a whisper of this in advance, isn't it?'

'Last-minute orders, maybe. A convoy at sea, or something. The girls surely didn't know a thing, they were on their way down to the landing-stage before they realised.'

By 'the girls' he meant some local women whom the Germans employed on board their battleships as cleaners and cooks. They made sure of hearing whatever was being said, they read every notice that was pinned to the bulletin boards, and whatever they picked up went off to London over clandestine radio the same night. The wireless was operated by the man these two had referred to as 'Torstein'. A couple of years ago the Gestapo had been getting close to him and his underground activities, and he'd escaped to Sweden and from there to London, where he'd been trained, equipped, and sent back. Now he lived in Alta and had a job in the Highways Department; he'd set up his transmitter in that building, linking it before each transmission to a German officer's private receiving aerial. His sources of information included the taxi-driver and the women workers, and also some crew members of boats which supplied *Tirpitz* with fresh provisions. The bits and pieces, when they were strung together, added up to a substantial flow of valuable intelligence, and in recent months London had absorbed every single item and still begged for more. Even the smallest detail of shipboard routine in the German squadron seemed to be of profound interest to the British.

He straightened from the taxi's window. There'd be a Bosch patrol along at any minute, and there was no point in hanging around now.

'See you this evening?'

'Yup.' A gloved hand lifted. 'Maybe we'll have had news.'

'Only that single fact, sir – that *Tirpitz* and *Scharnhorst* have sailed from Altenfjord.'

Mid-forenoon in the Admiralty building in London. The news from Norway, a very unusual daytime transmission, had compelled the man at the table to switch his mind from the Italian surrender – news of which hadn't been generally released yet – and the imminent landings at Salerno, codenamed 'Avalanche', to events in the cold north.

'PQ 19 is now – where, precisely?'

'Here, sir. Best estimate – not precise.'

An arm with a mere three stripes on it had stretched to tap the chart with a pencil. The position of convoy PQ 19 was marked, and so was another to the west of it. This was only an updating brief before the man sitting at the table joined the team on duty in the Operations Room; before he got in there he wanted to be au fait, have his own perspective as clear as his subordinates' would be.

Clearer. Because the picture he'd have in mind would be much broader.

The commander cleared his throat. 'That's if the convoy's

up to schedule, sir. And this is the position – again, only
estimated – of the fighting escort. They'll be altering course
from north to north-east about now, to overhaul the convoy
before dark.'

'We had reason to discount the possibility of any surface
attack on this convoy on its way north, did we not?'

'That's so, sir.'

It had been a very convincing intelligence appreciation,
asserting that there'd been a decision at the highest level
– meaning Adolf Hitler and Admiral Dönitz – that the
German surface units based in northern Norway would
only be used against southbound convoys – meaning
against Arctic convoys on their way back to Iceland and
the United Kingdom.

'So the escort's somewhat light. And those cruisers are
too far away to be any use to us if *Tirpitz* is steering directly
to intercept. It would be rather too much of a coincidence
that she'd have sailed at this juncture for any other purpose,
so – well, I suppose we have to expect the worst . . .'
Impassive: like a man studying a chess-board. 'Battle
squadron still in Akureyri, of course.'

'They're raising steam, sir. C-in-C Home Fleet's signal—'

'But screened only by Hunts.'

To provide a fighting escort of fleet destroyers, at the
same time as a climactic battle on the North Atlantic convoy
routes was drawing every small ship that could be whipped
in – as well as all available escort carriers – the Home Fleet's
battle squadron at Akureyri in north Iceland had been
robbed of its escort of fleet destroyers and provided with
a temporary screen of the smaller, short-range Hunt class.
This imposed drastic limitations on the movements of the
big ships: effectively they could only operate to the west
of Jan Mayen Island, which meant that in support of the
Archangel-bound convoy they could hardly be seen as
anything but a very long-range bluff.

On the other hand if this was subterfuge, if the enemy

were only using PQ 19 as an excuse for putting to sea, with the real intention of making a dash out into the Atlantic and joining in the convoy battle – well, the British battle squadron would be well-placed west of Jan Mayen.

'We've had no sighting reports at all – from aircraft, submarines, anyone. We haven't any clues at all, no idea what they're up to.'

It had sounded like a statement, but the upward flicker of the man's blue eyes made it a question.

'No clues at all, sir,' the commander added, 'and visibility up there is bad. Sleet-showers, and fog on the ice-barrier.'

That last piece of information would have come from the Norwegian weather station on Spitz-bergen, relayed via the W/T station at Seidisfjord in Iceland. Wireless links were far from reliable in those latitudes . . . The man at the table was silent, deep in thought as he leant over the chart. He asked, finally, 'Has Admiral Barry been told his birds have flown?'

'Indeed he has, sir.'

Rear-Admiral Barry was Flag Officer, Submarines. His target date for an attack on the *Tirpitz* by midget submarines was 20 September. One might guess that the enemy ships would be back in Altenfjord by then, but until their return could be positively confirmed Operation Source and almost a year's training and preparation were in the balance.

But here and now, that was a side issue. The immediate concern had to be for the convoy.

'Would you consider turning them back, sir?'

PQ 19 was already 250 miles north-northeast of Iceland. So any German ships looking for it could just as easily be to the south of it as anywhere else. Turning it back, therefore, might amount to turning it into danger. It was only a small convoy, northbound, the main object of the operation being to bring back merchantmen who'd been marooned up there all through the summer; the 'empties' were badly needed, in view of a general shortage of shipping as well as Churchill's promise to Stalin of regular Murmansk runs during the winter months. In fact there was a slight complication just at this moment – a Churchill-Stalin row brewing; and the nights weren't yet long enough for operations in those northern waters. The go-ahead had been given despite these factors, and the timing was planned so that the southbound convoy would sail from North Russia after the X-craft operation should have eliminated *Tirpitz* as a danger to it.

Further considerations in the mind of the man at the table were one, that the First Sea Lord, Admiral Sir Dudley Pound, attending the 'Quadrant' conference in Quebec at which Churchill and Roosevelt were approving outline plans for an invasion of the European mainland next year, had suffered a stroke and was returning to England as an invalid. You had a feeling of vacuum at the top, a sense of flying blind . . . And two, that convoy PQ 17, which had been thought to be under threat of surface attack very much as PQ 19 seemed to be now, had been thrown to the wolves as the result of a panic decision here in London. One of the lessons of that tragic episode was that tactical decisions should be taken by the commander on the spot, not by 'chair-borne warriors' hundreds of miles away.

'Who's commanding this fighting escort?'

'Captain Sir Nicholas Everard, sir. In . . .'

'*Calliope* Yes, of course . . .'

Motionless, gazing at the chart, like a clairvoyant staring into a crystal ball.

Calliope, at twenty-two knots, plunged and swayed over the long following swell. A string of flags at her yardarm whipped multi-coloured in grey, cold air over a sea that was grey-green slashed with white where the ships' hulls carved and split it. Nick Everard, on his high seat in the starboard for'ard corner of the bridge, had a pipe in his mouth and binoculars intermittently at his eyes, examining the surrounding wilderness of grey Norwegian Sea enclosed by an horizon that was hazy at best and in the north obscured by what looked like cotton-wool. At this moment, though, his attention was on the screening destroyers, ahead and on both bows – low, thrashing hulls with white bow-waves curling, mounds of foam boiling under their pitching sterns. At each of the five destroyers' yards now a blue and white Answering Pendant had been hauled close-up, indicating that *Calliope*'s flag signal had been read and understood.

Moloch dead ahead, *Laureate* and *Legend* to starboard, *Leopard* and *Lyric* on the other bow. *Moloch*'s captain, the senior destroyer officer, was Tommy Trench; he'd been Nick's first lieutenant in *Intent* in 1940, when they'd survived a fairly hair-raising adventure in the Norwegian fjords and wound up by taking a hand in the second battle of Narvik. Trench was now a commander, with a DSO as well as the DSC he'd won in *Intent*.

'Captain, sir?'

The short, pink-faced character at Nick's elbow was Instructor Lieutenant 'Happy' Bliss. A sheet of signal-pad – it was about the shade of pink to match the schoolmaster's complexion, thus indicating secrecy, a cypher as opposed to an ordinary, unclassified signal – flapped in his hand, and he seemed to be flapping too. But whatever was so exciting would have to wait a minute: Nick swung round to tell the navigator, Bruce Christie, 'Executive'.

'Haul down!'

The signals yeoman of the watch yelled the order to his minions on the flag deck, the hoist bellied outward on the wind as it came tumbling down, and at the same time the officer of the watch ordered *Calliope*'s wheel over to starboard. The hauling-down of the flags signalled the order to act on their message, and destroyers were racing – one ahead and two to port, while the other two cut their speed and angled outward – to take up positions that would leave them in proper station when the squadron steadied on its new course.

Calliope heeled to the turn as her rudder gripped the sea and hauled her round. Nick turned to the schoolmaster. 'Now, then.'

'Secret Immediate, sir, from Admiralty!'

Bliss's excitement was slightly irritating. Behind him the officer of the watch – Halcrow – ordered, 'Midships . . .'

SECRET IMMEDIATE
FROM: Admiralty
TO: AIG311
            SBNO N. Russia

Tirpitz and *Scharnhorst* reported to have sailed from Altenfjord with 10 destroyers approximately midnight. No indications of intentions or present position yet available.

Glancing at a three-quarter profile of *Laureate* sheeted in foam as she raced to adjust her station, the first reaction in his thoughts was We're for it, then . . . Then eyes down again, re-reading, and noticing from the signal's time-of-origin that it had been drafted nearly two hours ago. The next reaction was to ask, What help can I count on? – and the quick and easy answer was, None at all – you're on your own. Because surface attack had been virtually ruled out of the likely contingencies, and consequently the battle squadron temporarily based on Akureyri wouldn't be able to play any part at all in whatever was about to happen. The German force – according to this signal – had been at sea since last night, and Akureyri was nearly 300 miles astern; in any case those Home Fleet battle-wagons' range was strictly limited by their lack of a fleet destroyer screen.

The distance-and-time factor also applied to Rear-Admiral Kidd's close-support cruiser squadron. It was a safe bet that C-in-C Home Fleet, from his flagship in Scapa Flow, would be ordering Kidd out of Akureyri at about this moment; and as the cruisers would already have had steam up, they wouldn't take long to put to sea. But they wouldn't be of much use either, if the *Tirpitz* and *Scharnhorst* were steaming directly to intercept the convoy.

Turn the convoy back?

He nodded to Bliss – who with Marcus Plumb, the chaplain, had the job of cyphering and decyphering all secret signals.

'Don't tell us much, do they.' He was talking to himself as much as to the schoolmaster. 'Ask the commander to join me in the chartroom, will you?'

'Aye aye, sir!'

But Bliss, poor fellow, seemed disappointed – no doubt at his captain's impassive acceptance of the dramatic news. It was dramatic, too: *Tirpitz*, sister to the late and unlamented *Bismarck*, was the most powerful fighting ship afloat in the Atlantic Ocean, and at close quarters with a lightly-defended convoy she'd be like a great white shark in a school of mackerel. Bliss would be looking for a more electric reaction now from Commander Treseder . . . Nick, on his way to the rear end of the forebridge, saw that his ship had been steadied on her new course – 064 degrees, up the convoy's track so as to overtake it from astern – and that all five destroyers were in station. Trench had a well-drilled team, there. He told Bruce Christie, his navigator, 'I'll need you too, pilot.' He rattled down the portside ladder: one level down, he slid back the chartroom door. There was a chart-table at the back of the bridge too, but with no chance of sighting land for several days now they weren't using it.

Christie had followed him down. Nick passed him the signal.

'*Tirpitz* and *Scharnhorst* putting in some sea-time.'

He saw the navigator's slow blink. Christie was a tall man, long-chinned and with deep-set, pale eyes. A Scot, and a mad-keen fisherman. Studying the message with one bushy eyebrow cocked, and no doubt resisting, Nick guessed – he was doing the same himself – an initial impression that massacre might be imminent. Taking this report at face value, assuming the worst . . . But as far as Nick had been able to assess his navigating lieutenant in a comparatively short acquaintance, he had him down for one who was as quick-thinking as he was calm and slow-moving. Thumb-nail sketch of the perfect dry-fly man?

Nick's pierhead jump into this command had landed him among a host of strangers. He thought he knew Christie reasonably well by this time, and a few others, but the great majority of his officers and ship's company were only faces to which one had constantly to make the effort to pin names.

'Want me, sir?'

Jim Treseder, *Calliope*'s second-in-command, wasn't tall, but he was broad enough to have to turn sideways to pass through the narrow doorway. Duffle-coated, and with his legs straddled for balance against the ship's pitch and roll, short arms akimbo and his eyes on the pink sheet of signal-pad . . . 'Something about *Tirpitz* being out?'

Christie handed him the signal. Nick bent over the chart, reaching for dividers and parallel rule. With no hard facts or even indications, the only way to approach this was to accept possibilities at their worst – assume the German battle group was informed of the convoy's position and steaming to intercept, that it had been steaming to inter-cept ever since putting out of Altenfjord.

In which case the prospects were – well, inauspicious . . .

Plotting it. Hearing Treseder mutter to Christie that after months of harbour time, with any luck the Huns would be as sick as dogs . . . Nick said, seeing one result in advance, 'They could get to the convoy before we do.'

Conceivably the two battleships and their powerful escort could intercept PQ 19 – approaching it from ESE, its starboard bow – by about 1800 this evening. The convoy had its own close escort with it, of course, but that consisted only of two rather old destroyers, four minesweepers, an AA ship and a pair of trawlers. *Calliope* and her six fleet destroyers weren't expecting to overhaul the convoy until about the same time. This of course could be adjusted easily enough by an increase in speed . . . He worked it out: increasing from twenty-two knots to twenty-eight would advance the rendezvous time by three hours.

Bruce Christie's mind was operating on the same wavelength. He suggested, 'Come up to about thirty knots, sir?'

'Something like that. But wait a minute.'

You had to think beyond it, first. For instance, whether to change the convoy's route now, signal the close-escort commander to swing the whole circus northward, steer them closer to the ice. Or even to reverse the convoy's course, bringing them back into the protection of this stronger escort more quickly. But doing either of these things would involve breaking wireless silence – which would give away this squadron's position and perhaps also provide an indication of the convoy's, which might not yet be known to the enemy.

Guesswork was about all one had to go by: the Germans could only intercept PQ 19 this evening if (a) they already knew the convoy's position, course and speed, and (b) had steered the appropriate interception course directly and all the way from Altenfjord at no less than thirty knots. On several counts this seemed unlikely. First, there'd been no sign of the convoy's having been reported either by U-boat or long-range aircraft. PQ 19 had sailed from Loch Ewe in northwest Scotland, instead of from Seidisfjord on the east coast of Iceland which was the more usual assembly point,

primarily to reduce the chances of being spotted early on
– enemy reconnaissance had been concentrated on the
Icelandic east coast area. *Calliope* and Trench's destroyers
had set out later from Akureyri, in north Iceland, steering
to pass west and north of Jan Mayen Island – which now
lay about forty miles to starboard as the force pushed
northeastward to catch up with the convoy . . . But second,
one might question the German squadron's ability to maintain high speed for such a length of time. *Tirpitz* would be
capable of thirty knots, according to latest information, but
the 26,000-ton *Scharnhorst*'s best speed had been estimated
as twenty-eight. Another part of the equation was the
known fact that German surface ships were hamstrung by
an acute shortage of oil-fuel, and this cast doubt on whether
those two monsters, with their huge consumption of fuel,
would be allowed to burn up so much of it.

Particularly when one saw – as Nick did now, startled
by the simplicity of it and annoyed with himself for not
having seen it before – that they didn't need to!

Because if they knew the convoy's position, course and
speed they'd also know it could only be making for North
Russia. So by steaming north from Altenfjord at economical revs they'd only have to cover about half the distance
in order to intercept it east of Bear Island, inside the Barents
Sea, a day later. Saving fuel, and staying much closer to
their base. It was so obvious – and as good as certain they
wouldn't have come steaming out northwestward. So there
was no need to break W/T silence, or slow the convoy's
progress by diverting it. Not at this stage, anyway. In the
longer term, by the time the surface threat could be close
at hand, Admiral Kidd and his cruisers could be close, too.

Nick straightened from the chart.

'Revs for twenty-eight knots, pilot. Go up and see to it.
It should bring us up to the convoy at about 17.00. Before
that we'll shift to line-abreast and . . .' he shrugged, . . .
'trust to luck.'

Slight frown on Christie's hawkish face. Navigators didn't believe in trusting to luck – or at least, to admitting they sometimes had to. In point of fact there'd be a considerable element of chance in making this rendezvous, however well he'd done his sums. There'd been a spell of foul weather further south, and no opportunities for sextant fixes, starsights or sunsights. Nor had there been any position reports exchanged, because of the need for strict W/T silence and the hope of slipping through undetected. On top of these factors was the overriding one that navigation in these northern reaches was never as accurate as you'd have like it to be.

The door slid shut behind Christie. Nick looked at Treseder.

'Something bothering you?'

'Well, sir,' a snort of humour, '*Tirpitz*'s fifteen-inch guns do bother me, a little. And *Scharnhorst*'s – what, eleven-inch?'

Nick thought, looking at him, that Treseder knew damn well what calibre of gun the *Scharnhorst* sported. The commander added, 'And ten destroyers, with five point nines? Even they out-gun us!'

He was right. The Narvik-class destroyers were more like light cruisers in terms of armament. *Calliope*'s guns were 5.25s.

'So what's your conclusion?'

'Well, sir,' Treseder looked uncomfortable, 'if they're out looking for us, and we hold on as we are . . .'

Nick sighed, turned away. He said quietly, '*Tirpitz* isn't within 300 miles of us, Jim.'

'H'm . . .'

Puzzled; and hoping for an explanation. Nick let it ride. He believed totally in his assessment, and Treseder hadn't bothered to work it out. So – leave it at that, be proved right, and next time one might hope for this man's trust.

Trickery? Perhaps it was. But expertise in any field might

be described as an amalgam of tricks, and leadership didn't have to be any exception. Nick was aware of his newness to this job, and that it was in the ship's best interests as much as his own that her officers and men should have confidence in him.

'But incidentally . . . You're right – if those destroyers are Narvik-class, they out-gun us. And compared to *Scharnhorst*, let alone *Tirpitz*, we're a sprat . . . But off Sirte in March last year – just bear this in mind, as a point of reference – Philip Vian had three ships of the same class as this one to defend a Malta convoy, and he drove off the battleship *Littorio*, three heavy cruisers and eight destroyers!'

'Yes.' Treseder nodded. 'Italians, though.'

He had a point. But Germans, too, tended not to put their big ships at risk if it was possible to avoid doing so. And half the value of actions like that one of Admiral Vian's was that it demonstrated to others what could be achieved by the resolute handling of a small force against less resolute larger ones.

Whistling in the dark?

On his way back to the forebridge, a new thought kindled. It was a question: if his analysis of enemy movements was correct, why should they have sailed from Altenfjord thirty hours earlier than they need have? When (a) they were safer in those heavily-protected anchorages, (b) all the time they were at sea they were burning oil, and (c) by putting out so early they were giving advance notice of intention to attack?

It didn't make sense.

Able Seaman Tomblin, Nick's servant, asked him, 'Be taking your dinner up 'ere, sir, will you?'

'Yes, please. But I only want a snack. Tell Parker, will you.'

'Corned dog an' beans, sir?'

Parker was his PO steward, and Tomblin was a three-badger, a seaman with three chevrons on his arm indicating that he'd completed at least twelve years' service. He was a man of about Nick's own height, with a seamed, weathered face and slitted grey eyes. One of a particular species, quite distinct from the type who rose to Petty Officer and then Chief PO and eventually Warrant Officer. The Tomblins of the Royal Navy were unpromotable because they'd have regarded any suggestion of promotion as insulting.

'I'll have coffee with it, please.'

The watch had changed. It was Ferrimore at the binnacle now instead of Halcrow. Ferrimore was an RN sub-lieutenant: tall, fair, and in the process of growing a beard. Crossing the bridge towards his high chair, Nick thought it must be about ten days since the boy had requested 'permission to grow'. If the fuzz didn't shape up pretty soon, he'd be told to shave it off. He got up on the seat and put the strap of the binoculars over his head. There was one logical answer to that question of the premature sailing of the enemy battle group: that they'd put to sea for some purpose that had nothing at all to do with this convoy operation. Only one such purpose came to mind – a break-out into the Atlantic.

'Captain, sir. Another signal.'

Bliss seemed to have control of his excitement this time.

'Let's have a look.'

Again the prefix was SECRET IMMEDIATE. But it was from CS 39, to the same addressees as the previous one. CS 39 meant 39th Cruiser Squadron, which consisted of *Nottingham* – flying the flag of Rear-Admiral Kidd – *Rhodesia* and *Minotaur*. Kidd was informing all concerned that his squadron had cleared Akureyri and was steering 055 degrees at thirty-two knots.

'Cavalry to the rescue, Schooly.'

'Sir?'

Bliss was a rather humourless young man, Nick thought. He re-read the signal. It had been originated only twenty-eight minutes earlier, and he guessed it would have been transmitted from the shore W/T station at Akureyri after the cruisers had sailed. Kidd wouldn't have broken radio silence from sea. In present circumstances none of the participants in this game of hide-and-seek would let out a single peep unless an enemy was already in contact – air, surface or sub-surface – in which case there'd be nothing to lose, with the cat out of the bag already. When it happened, you'd transmit all the signals you'd been holding back.

'Pilot.' Christie approached, and Nick gave him the signal. 'CS thirty-nine's cutting the corner to the south of us. Put it on the chart, will you.'

He could visualise it – courses, relative bearings and distances – roughly, but well enough. If the cruiser admiral stuck to his present course and speed he'd most likely be something like a hundred miles south of the convoy by breakfast time tomorrow. A 'close-support' cruiser force, in this kind of set-up, wasn't supposed to stay in sight of the convoy it was protecting; convoys attracted air and submarine attack, and the cruisers' function was to ward off surface interference, not to get themselves bombed or torpedoed. Kidd's aim would be to put himself between the convoy and the attackers, but with nothing yet to tell him which direction an attack might come from he'd be keeping his options open. And meanwhile – this new truth struck suddenly – if he held on as he was steering now he'd be taking his ships well into the range of bomber-strikes from the enemy airfields in north Norway.

So, he wouldn't. He'd make as much distance east as he could by dusk tonight, then turn up northwards to put himself nearer the convoy. Astern of it or on the quarter, perhaps thirty or forty miles away, to shadow until the enemy showed their hand.

You could bet on it. But would the German admiral have the nous to bet on it too? One guess you could hope he might make was that the British battle squadron would not be far behind the cruisers.

The air threat was a very real one, as previous Arctic convoy experience had proved. Passing around that high shoulder of the world and entering the Barents Sea – where PQ 17 had been torn to shreds – convoys and escorts had to run the gauntlet of all those airfields. Nick wished, sadly, that he'd been given an escort carrier on this jaunt; some fighter cover would have made all the difference in the world. One carrier had in fact been allocated, but then turned out to be not available; there'd been no replacement. There was a make-or-break battle raging at this moment on the Atlantic convoy routes, to which the U-boats had returned in strength after their heavy defeat in May and a few months of licking their wounds and some redeployment; also there were large-scale operations in progress in the Mediterranean, in support of the battle for Italy. Against that background of high employment for all available ships, this operation had been mounted at short notice and provided with only as much as could be spared.

Rear-Admiral Kidd had told Nick, on board the cruiser-flagship in Akureyri: 'There's a steaming row between Winston and Stalin. Mostly because Winston's very properly reading him the riot act over the bloody awful way they treat us up at Murmansk and Archangel, all their damned restrictions and red tape – and lack of any decent medical facilities. He's proposed sending a hospital unit of our own up to Vaenga – as opposed to a couple of doctors in a wooden hut – and the buggers won't allow it! So we're to fetch these empty ships back now, but Winston's not promising any more convoys until his points are satisfied.'

The Russians certainly were inhospitable. Particularly so to men who risked their lives to bring them the material they needed. Perhaps the convoys weren't quite as vital to them now as they had been earlier, but late in 1941 when the Germans had got to within thirty miles of Moscow, this flow of war supplies had almost certainly tipped the scales and saved Russia from defeat. Which admittedly had been in the British interest too, but might still have inspired some gratitude – especially in a country which, until it had itself been attacked, had been quite happy to see Britain and all Europe ravaged by the Nazis.

Tomblin, with a covered lunch-tray and an odour of rum – natural enough at this time of day . . . He whipped the covering napkin off, revealing corned beef, baked beans, beetroot, a slice of buttered bread and a cup of coffee.

'Splendid. Thank you, Tombin.'

'We in for a dust-up, sir?'

'Your guess is as good as mine.'

But one of the perks of Tomblin's job as Captain's Servant was to acquire snippets of information. To be in the know enhanced his status vis à vis the rest of the ship's company. Respecting this, Nick added, 'My guess is that if we run into them it'll be by chance. We know they're at sea, but I don't believe they know we are. Not yet, anyway.'

'Any 'elp near if we do fetch up with 'em?'

'Yes. Thirty-ninth Cruiser Squadron's chasing up astern now at thirty-two knots. They'll be in shouting distance by first light tomorrow.'

Tomblin nodded approvingly.

'It's all in 'and then, sir.'

Alone again, forking corned beef into his mouth, he marvelled at Percy Tomblin's bland acceptance of cruisers as a shield against two of the most powerful warships afloat. Tomblin's confidence contrasted with his own self-doubt, the disturbing question, What if I've got it wrong?

Chewing, glancing round and noticing Jim Treseder's preoccupied expression as he listened with contrived patience to a monologue from Fountain, the diminutive Captain of Marines; Treseder plainly did have doubts. He could be right, too. If – a new theory now – if enemy Intelligence had learnt that PQ 19 was on the way, and

Admiral Dönitz – Hitler had sacked his former Commander-in-Chief and appointed the U-boat admiral in his place – had been really well informed, suppose Dönitz had decided to strike at the convoy before the fighting escort joined it?

At 14.00 he ordered the destroyers into lineabreast at 6000-yard intervals. The move had been prearranged, a minor item in Nick's briefing of Trench and the other destroyer captains back in Iceland. As the flag-hoist dropped from *Calliope*'s yardarm all the destroyers' helms went over; his own destroyer-man's heart warmed to the sight of them fanning out at high speed to their new stations. Trench was putting three of them on *Calliope*'s starboard beam and two to port, he himself in *Moloch* taking the centre starboard billet. The total spread of ships as they advanced, zigzagging, in search of the convoy which should now have been about fifty miles ahead but might easily be closer, was fifteen miles – plus the range of the wing ships' radar.

Half an hour later Nick increased the speed from twenty-eight to thirty-two knots. It was a measure of his anxiety – unrecognised, he hoped, by others. It was extremely important to link up with the convoy before dusk. Even if he'd been only half-wrong – or half-right . . .

He lit a pipe. Two of *Calliope*'s three radar sets were in operation: the 281 air warning set with its aerial at the fore-masthead, and the Type 273 surface warning set on the leading edge of the gunnery director tower. Also, up on the tripod foremast, a seaman lookout in the barrel-shaped crow's nest had binoculars constantly sweeping. Swaying in great arcs against grey sky as the cruiser rolled and pitched: to tolerate that motion demanded a cast-iron stomach.

Visibility was still variable. Not bad in some sectors, worse in others.

14.40: Another Secret Immediate . . . This was from

C-in-C Home Fleet, to the effect that the battle squadron had sailed from Akureyri and was steering 076 at twenty-eight knots. Bruce Christie took it down to the chartroom and came back to confirm what Nick had already guessed: that course would point straight across the Norwegian Sea at Altenfjord, and would be intended to make the enemy believe the battle squadron was aiming to cut them off from their base. But with only Hunts to screen them, the big ships wouldn't cover even half that distance.

15.00 . . . Treseder, back on the bridge after lunching down below, was smoking a post-prandial cigarette and adding his binocular effort to the search. During the past hour the gap should have closed by eighteen miles. If all estimates were correct, there'd be at least an hour to go before you'd expect to make contact. Nick had shifted to the line-abreast formation early because the convoy was as likely to be astern of station as ahead of it. More so, in fact.

Treseder moved over to Nick's corner.

'Too bad we don't have an escort carrier with us, sir.'

'Yes. The point was made, in Akureyri.'

The carrier that had been included in the original orders had suffered either machinery breakdown or action damage. They'd said, in Iceland, 'Forecast is you'll slip through to Archangel without much trouble, anyway. The U-boats are concentrating in mid-Atlantic and between Gib and the Azores, and we hear a lot of the northern bomber strength has been sent south too. Italy, you see. Then southbound, your main worry would have been *Tirpitz* and co, but we've reason to believe they'll be – well, taken care of.'

'What does that mean?'

'It's not entirely clear, actually . . . But – apparently – inshore mining of some sort, backed up by a strong picket of submarines. We have no details, but that's the inference. You can take it that surface attack is – unlikely.'

There'd been no U-boats piping up yet, either. But a patrol line somewhere in the area of Bear Island wouldn't come as any surprise. Even if most of their strength was deployed in the mid-Atlantic air gap in a last gasp struggle for supremacy over the convoys. After the beating they'd taken earlier, if they lost this battle, you could reckon the U-boat threat was on the wane.

Calliope rocked across the swell, dipping her graceful bow to toss white sea streaming on the wind. From this viewpoint Nick was looking down over the tier of three forward turrets – three twins, two guns to each turret, and with two more aft she had an armament of ten 5.25-inch. They were dual-purpose guns, with a high elevation that suited them to anti-aircraft use – ideal for convoy protection when the main threat was expected to be from the air. Beyond the three turrets with their jutting barrels only a small triangle of foc'sl was visible from this angle – foam-washed, plunging . . .

Air attack would come, for sure. Whatever else might happen, you could count on bombers and torpedo-bombers east and south of Bear Island.

Treseder muttered as he moved away to the other corner, 'Long as we find 'em before dark.'

At 4.00 pm when the watch changed for the First Dog there was still no sighting, and nothing on any radar screen. Not that this should have been surprising: after days at sea and the bad weather they'd been through you couldn't expect pinpoint accuracy. Even if Christie the perfectionist did aim for it. He'd brought a chart up to the bridge table – it was at the back of this forebridge, close to the asdic cabinet and the entrance to Nick's sea cabin – and he was fiddling around, checking one theory after another. Christie was a professional as well as a perfectionist, Nick appreciated; only the amateur believed in his own infallibility.

17.00: Tomblin brought tea and biscuits. He asked, 'Mislaid 'em, sir, 'ave we?'

'What?'

'Convoy give us the slip, 'as it?'

Harvey-Smith had the watch now. He was senior watch-keeper and also *Calliope's* first lieutenant, which in a cruiser gave him responsibility for anchors and cables, seaboats and other upper-deck gear. He looked old for his two and a half stripes – and he was. He'd been passed-over for promotion a few years before the war, and retired, but he'd come back for war service – complete with a drink problem, on which Treseder was keeping a baleful eye.

One might have hoped for some more information by this time. Some damn thing . . .

Something did come in just after 18.00: another Secret Immediate from Admiralty, announcing: Air reconnaissance this afternoon confirms only *Lützow* is now in Altenfjord and no heavy units are in Narvik or Trondheim.

All one learnt from that was that the two heavy-weights were definitely at sea, hadn't just moved to one of their other Norwegian bases.

Christie murmured a few minutes later, 'I suppose we could have gone past them, sir, just out of radar range. In which case . . .'

'It's possible.'

Christie was talking about the convoy, of course. But the German battle group could be just as close. There were still a couple of hours of daylight left, anyway. A month or two ago there'd have been no darkness at all: and in two months' time, in November, darkness would last round the clock, the sun never lifting itself above the horizon. That was the best time for running convoys north, from the point of view of cover from the bombers; the snag then was the weather, the constant gales and above all the ice – ships deep-laden with it, spray freezing as it came aboard, and the constant hard work of getting rid of it – chipping, shov-elling, steam-hosing . . .

Haselden, Engineer Commander, came up – ostensibly for a smoke and a chat, but Nick allowed a silence to grow until he was obliged to come out with it.

'Bit worried about fuel consumption, sir, at these revs several hours now.'

'So am I,' Nick pointed at *Lyric*, a low, racing profile three miles on the beam. She was turning at this moment, as *Calliope* was too, to a new leg of the zigzag. 'Particularly for them. But we have two oilers with the convoy, so they can all top up tomorrow.'

Haselden seemed a pleasant-enough fellow, and he'd been quite right to raise the matter, but at that moment, with other things on his mind, Nick could have done without him.

If the convoy was as little as thirty miles to the north or south of its prescribed track, Christie was right and they could have passed it already, overhauled without making contact. On the other hand it could be thirty miles ahead, still: so if you turned now to try a sweep to the north or south, you might miss it, lose it completely . . . It would be best to hold on, he decided. At least, as good a bet as any . . . When the light went, of course, it would be real needle-in-haystack stuff . . .

A decision he'd have to make soon was the question of a night cruising formation. Enemy ships were at sea, and night encounters tended to be sudden, their outcome decided by speed of reaction; and this was no fighting formation he had his ships in at present. On the other hand he was reluctant to reduce the width of the line-of-search before he had to.

'Captain, sir?'

The chief telegraphist – CPO Tarrant – was offering him a clipboard. The plain white signal-pad sheets on it told him that whatever this was, it wasn't classified.

'If it's bad news, Chief, I don't want it.'

'I'd guess you'd enjoy this lot, sir.'

'Well,' he nodded, 'I'll buy it, then. What is it?'

'BBC bulletin, sir. Eyeties've jagged in. Armistice signed, the lot!'

Italy – surrendered?

After – how long? Putting memory to work . . . June of 1940 – when Mussolini had felt sure he was joining the winning side. Russia hadn't been in it at that stage, because Hitler hadn't yet ratted on his Soviet ally. When the Nazis had invaded Norway, and Nick and Tommy Trench had been trapped in a fjord in a broken-down destroyer, Molotov, the Soviet foreign minister, had broadcast: 'We wish Germany complete success in her defensive measures.' As when France fell, the Nazi ambassador in Moscow was offered the Soviet government's warmest congratulations on the Wehrmacht's 'splendid success'. The Italian jackal and the Russian bear had been eager for whatever pieces of the carcase they might snatch.

The dark age seemed more like thirty years ago now, than three.

'Sir,' Tarrant pointed: 'Flashing, sir—'

A port-side lookout was also reporting it. An Aldis clashed as a signalman jumped to answer the winking light. Nick swung round to read the message for himself: it was *Laureate* reporting surface radar contact on bearing 358, seventeen miles.

'Yeoman – twenty-inch, port and starboard – *Six Blue*.'

'*Six Blue* – aye aye, sir!'

Yeoman of the watch PO McLoughlin bawled to that signalman as he acknowledged *Laureate*'s report. 'Shift to the twenty-inch, 'Arris. Make to *Laureate* and *Legend*, *Six Blue!*'

Leading Signalman Merry was taking the other side. The twenty-inch lamps were powerful, signal searchlights more than lamps, and the most distant of the destroyers would see them easily, with no need for the intermediate ships to relay the message down the line. The order 'Six Blue' would turn all ships simultaneously sixty degrees to port, leaving them in a slightly staggered line-ahead formation but steering more or less directly at that radar contact.

It was probably a wing ship of the convoy's close escort. In which case it had been a lucky chance they'd picked it up, at long range from their own wing ship. If it had been just a few miles farther north, you'd have scraped by without knowing it.

On the other hand, this could be an enemy. The only safe way to play it was to assume exactly that.

'Message passed, sir!'

'Executive.' He told the officer of the watch, 'Bring her round to oh-oh-four.' The big lamps' shutters clashed again, passing the executive order to carry out the turn. *Calliope*'s wheel was over now. It was the quickest way to get the whole force pointing in the right direction: now he'd adjust the course as might be necessary and also reorganise his ships into an attacking formation, on lines which he'd explained to the destroyer captains at the conference in Akureyri.

'By light to *Moloch*, Yeoman. "My speed twenty knots. Destroyers form line astern six thousand yards on my port beam. Executive."'

'Twenty knots, sir?'

'Yes, please.' The reduction in revs was to allow the destroyers to gain bearing on *Calliope*, in the process of forming the squadron into two divisions, the five destroyers in their primary role as a torpedo force and the cruiser on her own as gunship. As they moved in closer to the enemy, Trench would have the option of keeping his flotilla together for a combined attack of the classic kind, or splitting it into two subdivisions; his decision would depend on the number of enemy ships and their formation. On the way in, Trench or his subdivision leader would also act as flank-markers for *Calliope*'s gunnery, reporting their observations of fall-of-shot over the talk-between-ships telephone.

Calliope was steadying on the ordered course, vibration and fan-noise lessening as engine revs decreased.

Destroyers racing out to port: a sight of sheer beauty, if you'd had time to watch it . . . He told Treseder, 'Get the hands up, please.'

'Aye aye, sir.' Treseder swung to face aft. 'Bugler!'

Action stations . . .

3

The Italian surrender announcement had been received in 'Port HHZ' – codename for Loch Cairnbawn – as an excuse for a party. Broadcast the night before, it had been followed that morning by news of landings around some place called Salerno, and a glance at a map had been enough to show this had to be aimed at capturing Naples. As for the surrender, everyone realised that the German armies in Italy wouldn't be laying down their arms. The tide had turned, with a vengeance – North Africa had finally been cleared in May, the landings on Sicily in July had resulted in the island's capture last month, and now Anglo-American armies were advancing in Italy while Russian forces progressed westward and, in New Guinea, American and Australian troops had just re-taken the Huon Gulf ports. But there'd still be long, hard roads to travel, and lakes of blood would flow before the end of it.

In fact it was likely to get tougher, as the beasts were cornered.

This morning the X-craft men's party spirit had been dissipated in drizzle and also anxiety over the whereabouts of the *Tirpitz* and *Scharnhorst*. RAF recce flights from North Russia had confirmed that only the tiddler of the group – *Lützow*, so-called 'pocket battleship', 10,000 tons and eleven-inch guns – still lurked in her berth in Altenfjord. All three of those ships were listed as targets for the X-craft.

'Ace up, king towards.' Spinning the dice to decide who would start . . .

Not that anyone was all that keen to play; but there was time to kill and a few of them were hanging around, waiting for news. Soft drinks on the table: this was mid-forenoon, 'standeasy' time in the wardroom of the depot ship *Bonaventure*. Paul Everard, Dan Vicary, Johnny McKie and Tom Messinger . . . McKie won it with a jack, and scooped the dice into their leather pot. Vicary, a South African, growled, 'Trouble is, man, the bastards might pitch up in some hole we never heard of. Some new anchorage, nets and stuff we don't know about?'

From the trots of X-craft alongside floated the rumble of Gardner diesels charging batteries.

'I wouldn't think it's likely,' Tom Messinger mumbled, 'RAF'll have been flying recces all over those fjords, won't they. At least—'

'Three nines, in two . . . Surprised the Russkis allow it. Seeing they wouldn't let the RAF use those same airfields for bombing attacks on *Tirpitz*.'

'Wonder why the hell . . .'

'Bloody-minded, aren't they . . . *Tirpitz* might have gone south d'you reckon?'

'Then she'd be in bomber range from this end, and the RAF could look after the whole issue!'

'God forbid.' Paul shook the cup. The thought of bombers doing the job – after all this training and preparation and with all of them now keyed-up and ready . . . A voice behind him suggested, 'Someone shove up, so I can honour you with my company?'

'Hello, Louis.' McKie asked him, 'Nice outing?'

'Except I'm developing a chronic dislike of towing.'

Louis Gimber had been out in X-12 on a night exercise,

and he'd missed the party. His brown eyes rested on Paul as he slid in behind the table. Gimber had regular features and gleaming black hair that seemed always to have just been combed. He was the 'tall, dark and handsome' kind that girls were supposed to like; but not all of them found him as irresistibly attractive as he thought. Paul had reason to know this, and to feel guilty – as well as some quite different emotions – when he thought about himself and Jane. Which he did, a lot. But he was probably the only man in Loch Cairnbawn who did not suffer from the delusion that Louis Gimber was every woman's dream.

Gimber asked him, 'If they'd let us decide it between ourselves, would you take the passage job and let me have the fjord end?'

'Hypothetical question.'

'Would you?'

'Would I hell.'

Messinger's nines were still the highest throw. Paul threw two pairs and failed to make it a full house. Gimber persisted, 'Think of the happy ending you'd be in line for. Coming back to my girl, with a clear field?'

'That's a bloody silly remark, Louis.'

Vicary, the Springbok, had a reddish face pitted with old scars, either smallpox or acne. His rough-hewn features were in total contrast to the decidedly film-starish Louis Gimber's. He shook his head. 'Stow it, would you mind?'

It wasn't the taunt about Jane he minded, which was Paul's business and Gimber's, and at that probably intended to be mildly humorous, since Gimber had no idea how far things had gone. What annoyed Vicary was the assumption that operational crews were unlikely to get back. He was right, too.

Gimber suggested evenly, with his attention on the dice, 'I think you might consider minding your own business, Dan.'

They didn't like each other. Resentment from Vicary's side

was the primary cause. It emerged as contempt, from a rough diamond to a smoothly polished one. He envied those good looks and disliked Gimber's awareness of them, and was jealous of his reputation as a Don Juan. Gimber's family was rich, too. On the subject of the alleged success with girls, Paul knew he could have delighted Vicary and doubtless softened his attitude considerably, by imparting certain private truths; but it was out of the question, obviously.

He'd first met Jane when a group of X-craft men on weekend leave from Fort Blockhouse at Gosport – where the initial training had started – had got together in London to celebrate someone's twenty-first. It had been a long, hectic evening, culminating in a wild party in the Bag o' Nails. Louis had let them all know that he was serious about this girl, really serious, so although Paul had been strongly attracted to her he'd behaved himself, even tried to discount the encouragement she'd seemed to be giving him whenever Louis wasn't in close attendance.

Gimber was a romantic. He lived up to his own appearance. He was also sure of himself, of his own appeal to women in general and to Jane in particular. So much so that he'd actually asked Paul to telephone her and ask her out for a meal, a few weeks later: little knowing that by this time the stable door was already wide open.

'How about it, Paul? Seriously? Passage CO?'

'You're nuts. Anyway, what d'you think Jane is – one of your harem, to be handed over as a quid pro quo?'

'You misunderstand me, old boy. I'm not making you an offer, I'm simply pointing out that if you took the passage-crew job it would be a natural result – whatever view of it Dan here may care to take.'

Vicary suggested, 'Why don't the pair of you go down to a cabin flat and bash each others' heads in?'

'Nothing to fight about. She's Louis' girl. I've taken her out a couple of times, that's all.' He jerked a thumb towards Gimber, 'At his instigation.'

'Nice cosy arrangement . . . Whose turn is it?'

'Mine.' Gimber rattled the pot. Nobody was taking much interest in the game, though. Certainly not Paul, who was thinking about Jane.

She was flattered – or comforted – by Gimber's adoration. He was a very useful escort, too, when he happened to be in London. Plenty of money – family house in Oxfordshire and another one in Town. Recalling some of those early conversations, Paul could hear her now, telling him, 'And he's so nice looking: and he knows his way around . . .'

'Aren't you in love with him – or supposed to be?'

She'd shaken her head. 'I've never said I was, either. He just assumes that whatever he feels must . . .' He'd had to wait again, until she said 'Really, it's like being with a brother. Someone one likes, but—'

'Honey – the way you dance together . . .'

'You mean like I dance with you?'

'Not in front of him, you didn't.'

'Well, what d'you expect? I don't set out to hurt him, for God's sake! Paul, he's sweet to me!'

'So?'

'Well, for instance, where do I come in?'

'You know darn well where you come in! Here!'

He'd laughed. She was fairly outrageous: unless it only seemed that way to him, from his own rather limited experience . . . By this time he was too deeply involved with her to be sure of his own clarity of vision, or wisdom. He was in no doubt she lied about some things – perhaps they all did, to their boyfriends – and he thought she was probably a good actress. She was certainly two-timing Louis Gimber – who loved her, or thought he did; so you had to be aware that two-timing was perhaps to be expected.

Rather extraordinary, really. In his own case it wasn't love. Infatuation was the other thing, the other word people used: so, infatuation, and difficulty keeping his hands off her. Hands or mind. He thought this amounted to infatuation. It couldn't be love, he guessed, because he could see through some of her tricks too clearly and detachedly. Could you look at anyone that analytically and love them?

His father had asked him, when Kate had been away in the ladies' room at the end of that lunch, 'How's your love-life?'

He'd hesitated; then admitted, 'Exciting.'

'Lucky man. One or more?'

'Just one, right now.'

The first one who'd ever meant anything much to him. Until he'd met Jane he'd thought he might be different from the other Everards – including his own father – in that respect. Now he knew he wasn't. He was hooked. Just as a girl called Fiona had had first his father and then Jack Everard hooked: Jack who'd been a prisoner of war in Germany and had been reported 'shot while attempting to escape'. The news had come through last Christmas.

Rough luck on Fiona. One dead, the other married . . .

But Jane had been married – for a matter of months only, to a fighter pilot who'd been shot down over Dieppe. She cried quite often, especially in bed.

'Hey! Four kings!'

Paul came out of his thoughts – with Jane's sexy, tear-stained face in his memory and, right across from him, her would-be fiancé pointing accusingly at Johnny McKie. 'Did I not hear the click of a finger turning up the fourth?'

'No, you bloody didn't!'

'Hi, Don . . .'

Donald Cameron had just walked in. Cameron, skipper of X-6 and the senior sea-going X-craft officer, had been the original of the species, the first recruit. He'd carried out the trials with the prototype, X-3, in the Hamble River, before any of the rest of them had even heard of X-craft. Don was twenty-six, married, and he had a four-month-old son.

'Anyone know where Godfrey might be?'

'Ja.' Dan Vicary jerked a thumb. 'Over in *Titania*, man. Was, anyway . . . Hear anything yet, Don?'

'Not a whisper.'

'We were . . . speculating. Suppose the buggers have shifted to some other fjord – some new place could've been got ready for them?'

'Wouldn't think it's likely.' Cameron paused. 'But I did get one buzz. Seems there's a Russian convoy operation in progress. That character from London mentioned it. The plan is we tie in with it, in a way. They're expecting that by the time the home-run gets under way we'll have nobbled the opposition. How's that for supreme confidence in us?'

'So it's still on, anyway.'

'Of course it is, you silly bastard!'

'Glad to hear it.' Vicary shrugged his heavy shoulders. 'Just the timing seemed so bad. As if the Bosch knew—'

'Forget it.' Cameron shook his head. 'It'll be the convoy that's drawn them out, and in a day or two they'll be tucked up in that fjord again. Meanwhile I'm told crew lists will be going up today, and X-11 and 12 will be getting their side-cargoes tomorrow forenoon – right, Paul?' Paul nodded. Cameron put a hand on Vicary's shoulder. 'Any other reassurance you want?'

'Well. I take it someone's told the bloody Germans to be back there in time to welcome us?'

Cameron turned away. 'Anyone wants to know, I'll be over in *Titania*. If I can get a boat over.' *Titania*, first in service in 1915 and still going strong, was the depot ship for the towing submarines – for *Thrasher*, *Truculent*, *Syrtis*, *Sea Nymph*, *Stubborn*, *Sceptre*, *Scourge* and *Setter*. Cameron asked from the doorway, 'Towing exercise satisfactory, Louis?'

'Except I'm not wild about the Manilla towropes.' Gimber frowned. 'I had balsa-wood floats on mine today, and even then the damn thing's far too heavy. Care to swap?'

'Likely . . .'

He'd gone. Don Cameron had one of the three existing nylon tows. Not, of course, that he'd be passage-crew. He was operational CO of X-6, just as Godfrey Place, the man he was looking for now, had X-7. Place was the only RN officer in the seagoing X-craft force; he was twenty-two, an experienced submariner, and he was married to a Second Officer in the Wrens. During the months in which he'd helped Cameron in training the other crews, Place had lived through some nasty moments. He'd lost one diver, a sublieutenant, during a net-cutting exercise, and had another man washed off the casing and drowned. On that occasion the fore hatch had been open and the wave that swept the lad away had also flooded the W and D compartment, leaving the boat bobbing vertically with her artificer isolated in the fore end and Place himself shut in the engine-room. Houdini himself might have been proud to have got out of that one.

'You've a heap of ideas for swaps, Louis. Girls, jobs, ropes . . .' McKie said it. He was Dan Vicary's first lieutenant in X-11, almost certainly her operational crew. Vicary muttered facetiously, 'Give him enough rope, he'll hang himself.' He pushed his chair back. 'Don't know about you bums, I've work to do.'

Setter, last of the eight towing ships, entered the loch soon after noon and secured alongside *Titania* with the others. Cameron told Paul at lunch in *Bonaventure*, '*Setter*'ll be your towing ship, I gather.'

Paul knew *Setter*'s officers reasonably well. She'd made several training visits to the loch at earlier stages, joining temporarily for exercises of one kind and another. The dress-rehearsal exercise had involved the midgets attacking the battleship *Malaya*: with a submerged tow first, then a solo approach, a long, fjord-like loch to negotiate and nets

to cut through, and finally success, surfacing right alongside the old battleship inside her box of nets, having simu-
lated a drop of side-cargoes on the sea-bed under her. The
side-cargoes were the X-craft's only weapon, carried like
contoured blisters on the sides and fitting from bow to
stern. Each had two tons of Torpex high-explosive in it,
and could be released from inside the boat after time-fuses
had been set.

Paul asked Cameron, 'Crews been detailed yet?'

A nod . . . 'Lists will be up any minute now.' The
Scotsman added, 'Can't be any doubt you'll have X-12 for
the attack.'

'I'm hoping, Don.'

'You can count on it.'

Finishing lunch, he got his coffee from the urn and went
through to the anteroom. He was about to sit down beside Brazier when Claverhouse, Surgeon Lieutenant-
Commander RNVR, touched his elbow and asked whether
he could spare a few minutes.

'Brief chat? Would you mind, Everard?'

Cursing inwardly, Paul allowed himself to be led aside.
In recent weeks he'd managed to steer clear of this character.

'Let's sit here. I shan't keep you long. A matter of
completing the final records, you know. I'm supposed to
– er – take soundings, from time to time?' He sipped at his
coffee. 'Well. How's life?'

'Not bad, sir.' The 'sir' acknowledged that extra half-
stripe, but one use of it would now have to see the conversation through. Claverhouse was a psychiatrist, and a
comparative newcomer to the medical staff. The others
were all right, but there was something leech-like about
this one. Paul added, 'Except our birds have flown.'

'Ah. Yes . . . And I suppose you'd be very disappointed
if the operation had to be cancelled?'

'Of course. We all would.'

'But – why, Everard?'

This was really silly. At such a late stage, and with nerves already on edge through the disappearance of the targets. It would have to be Claverhouse's private initiative – none of the other medicoes would have been so ham-fisted. Paul told him, patiently but with effort, 'We've been training for a long time. We're ready for it.'

'Do you look forward to the attack itself? To the – er – action?'

'Yes.' He did, too. Despite natural qualms.

'I find that curious.'

Paul stared at him. The only thing that seemed curious, to him, was to have to put up with this nonsense. He explained patiently again, 'We're ready, we know we can do it, and it happens to be a job well worth doing. I can't understand your even questioning it, frankly.'

'You aren't worried – at all?'

'If you mean do I get butterflies in the stomach at times – yes, of course I do. You'd have to be bone-headed not to. But as I said – we know we can do it, we're trained right up to the eyeballs, so why shouldn't—'

'Rather begging the question, surely.' The smile was irritatingly donnish. 'You're trained because you offered to be so trained. Eh?'

In a much earlier session, part of the selection process down in the south, another head-shrinker had tried to suggest that Paul's motivation might be a desire to emulate his distinguished father. It wasn't so – except in so far as any leader set a standard, and Nick Everard was no exception to that generality. Paul had come to the conclusion since then that it wouldn't have mattered a damn if this had been his motivation.

'I only wondered' – Claverhouse's tone was ingratiating, now – 'entirely for my own interest as a psychologist, how you'd feel about it now, as it were on the eve.'

'It's only the eve if those bloody ships reappear.'

McKie, passing, had just winked at him. Claverhouse was frowning, brushing that off as an irrelevance.

'They'll have to reappear somewhere . . . But a point of interest in your case, Everard, is you surely have nothing to prove. I'm aware of your background, naturally, and as I recall it you were in a destroyer that was sunk at Narvik? Ordinary Seaman at that time, and a Mention in Despatches for saving lives? Then more latterly you won a DSC,' he nodded at the ribbon on Paul's battledress jacket, 'in the Malta submarine flotilla?'

'Place has a DSC, too. D'you hold that against him?'

'By no means against him or you – I only . . .'

'I've never tried to prove anything at all. At sea in wartime you can find yourself in certain kinds of situation, and—' he heard his own voice rising – 'well, for Christ's sake—'

'Everard – please . . .' Claverhouse embarrassed now . . . 'You seem to be – if I may say this without further offending you – well, wound up, rather. Under some degree of stress?'

'Wouldn't you be?'

'You're conscious of stress?'

'If I am, it's because our targets have vanished. That makes me anxious, sure. But . . .'

'What about dreams?'

He'd been reaching to put down his coffee cup. A muscle tensed: he'd fumbled, cup and saucer rattling as he just managed to lodge them on the table. Claverhouse's interest was sharp: 'You have been worried by bad dreams, have you?'

There'd been nightmares, all right. And he had been worried by them, was worried by them. They were none of this clown's business, though. They were his, Paul Everard's, to live with, deal with as best he could. He had an urge to use one short, four-letter word, then get up and walk away: then out of the blue – or desperation – a better way out of this occurred to him. He told the psychiatrist confidentially, 'Wet dreams.' The man's expression changed dramatically: he was blinking, stupid-looking, like a parrot being poked off its perch. Shocked? Could a trick-cyclist be a prude? Paul added in that same confiding tone, 'If you call wet dreams bad ones?'

Actually he did quite often dream about Jane. Deliberately, sometimes: in the process of dropping off to sleep he'd concentrate his mind on her, try to dream about her instead of about being suffocated or falling over cliffs, crushed under heavy rocks . . .

But something was happening, beyond the double doorway. Crew lists?

He asked Claverhouse, 'Excuse me now, please?'

'Well, if we could just . . .'

'I'm sorry. There's really no point, you know.'

It was a stir of movement, a general flocking towards the notice board. Crew lists, for sure . . . He remembered, as he went to join the gathering crowd, briefings they'd been given on how to cope with German interrogation techniques, and wondered if this might have played a part, helped him to block that dream question despite its having thrown him for a moment. Then he forgot Claverhouse. He was edging into the scrum, getting close enough to the board to see it was a list of X-craft crews. Then reading it – over Louis Gimber's shoulder . . .

His eyes skimmed down to the lower section of the type.

X-11, towing ship *Scourge* (Commanding Officer Lt M. S. Vallance)
Passage:

Commanding Officer	T. F. Messinger
Crew	J. W. Hillcrest
	C. E. J. Amor

Operation:

Commanding Officer	D. V. Vicary

Crew	J. McKie
	T. N. P. Maguire
	T. Brind

X-12, towing ship *Setter* (Commanding Officer Lt E. A. MacGregor)
Passage:

Commanding Officer	L. W. Gimber
Crew	O. T. Steep
	A. L. Towne

Operation:

Commanding Officer	P. H. Everard
Crew	R. S. Eaton
	H. A. J. Brazier
	J. Lanchberry

Louis Gimber swung round, tight-lipped with disappointment; although he must have known this was how it would be. He brought up short, finding Paul – of all people – right there in front of him. Paul said, quite genuinely sympathetic and knowing how he'd have felt, 'Sorry, Louis. We couldn't both have got it.' His eyes went back to the list. It had been inevitable, anyway; it was only because he'd wanted the job so much that he'd had any doubts of getting it, whereas Gimber had been trained primarily as a passage CO.

Gimber smiled. 'You know the saying, old boy. Lucky in war, unlucky in the only thing that really matters?'

'Well,' emerging together from the throng, 'perhaps you have a point.'

And perhaps I'm a bastard . . .

But not necessarily. Wasn't it more that Louis had the wrong end of the stick, about Jane?

'Louis, the passage command's the toughest. The fact they picked you for it shouldn't make you feel done-down.'

'Balls.'

'We don't know how they decided, do we. Maybe they

spun coins. But now look – we have work to do. Quite a lot, and not too much time. For starters, since she has to be hoisted out at sparrow-fart . . .'

'Lighten ship, etcetera.' Gimber nodded wearily. 'Ozzie has the preliminaries in hand.'

X-12's tanks had to be pumped out, every moveable weight taken out of her, so that the depot ship's crane could swing her up on to the well-deck for side-cargoes to be fitted. The other six boats had already been fixed up; there wouldn't have been space for the two late-comers on that deck as well, and in any case their side-cargoes hadn't arrived on the fifth, when the others had had theirs fitted. But there were other things to see to as well, and this afternoon there was to be a briefing on the subject of an overland escape route, then a COs' meeting to recapitulate on the alternative target-area plans, those for Narvik and Trondheim.

Dan Vicary, who was one of two South African X-craft COs, slammed a meaty hand down on Paul's shoulder. 'Just the job, man, ay?'

Gimber, throwing the Springbok a frigid look as he departed, clearly disagreed. Then Dick Eaton joined them – diffident, as always, but more cheerful, like everyone else who'd had his billet in an operational crew confirmed. Brazier too – looming like a man-mountain through the thinning crowd . . . 'Arf, arf!'

It was a Popeye expression, which he used to express pleasure or enthusiasm. He added, 'But we've lost the sods, haven't we?'

'They'll turn up, Bomber.'

'Hope you're right.' Brazier snapped his fingers. 'Had a message for you, skipper. SDO sent it down, while ago. RPC drinks on board *Setter*, eighteen hundred, operational and passage crew – OK?'

'Fine.' Paul nodded. 'Tell the others. Louis's gone down to the boat, and Steep's down there too, I think.'

'Right. Poor old Louis, eh?'

'Yes. We're lucky.'

To an outsider it might have sounded crazy – and it would to Claverhouse – to think of yourselves as lucky, in being picked to transport four tons of high-explosive through miles of narrow, defended waters – and minefields – and get it through nets designed to be impenetrable, then deposit it precisely under the belly of the most vital naval target in the world; and to do it in some expectation – hope, anyway – of remaining alive, even getting home again!

The overland escape briefing was at 1430 in the recreation hall down aft.

The briefing officer, a Norwegian expert sent up from London, told the assembled submariners, 'An overland trek might prove to be the only escape route available to you. I say might . . . Obviously it's hoped you'll do the job successfully and then get out to sea, make the planned rendezvous with your parent submarine and come home in triumph. Or say, in comfort . . . But since many factors are not predictable, we can't count on it. So this overland exit is just an extra string to your bow, and despite the very limited stowage space in your X-craft you'll be taking certain escape gear with you. But first, before we discuss the equipment – here, on this map, bare as it is, what you see is as much as anyone can tell you about the terrain you'd be crossing.'

A blackboard easel supported a map that was, indeed, unusually featureless.

'First, right from the shore of Altenfjord, you'd have these mountains to climb. Definitely a climb, not a steep walk. Then if you made it that far, you'd find you were facing several hundred miles of plateau – which I can't describe in any detail because it's never been properly mapped. The simple fact is that to reach the Swedish border, which would have to be your destination, you'd have no option but to cross this expanse of – nothing . . .

And you see – well, we're in autumn now, early autumn; but that area might with a little poetic licence be called the roof of the world, and it won't be long before it's deep in snow. There'll be snow up on the tops there already. Once the winter sets in, it'll become more desolate, more hostile, than ever. In fact – I'm being straight with you fellows – it'll get to be bloody horrible.

'There are some features, and some of them are shown on the maps we're giving you – maps printed on parachute silk, very pretty, your girls'll love 'em and I dare say that could be the best use for them, because I wouldn't swear they're accurate or show enough to be worth having. Once the land's under snow, mark you, this won't matter in the least – you wouldn't find any of those topographical features anyway. Even without snow covering them, you'll find it very difficult to identify any one – er – landmark positively. The features, those that exist, tend to be repetitive and very much alike. The only people capable of navigating by them, effectively, are the Lapps. And this, please note, is very important to you – by far your best chance would be to make contact with Lapps and have them guide you. They're nomads, as you may know, and they know this territory like you know Piccadilly. They migrate right across it twice a year, driving bloody great herds of reindeer, so they have to know it pretty well; and they'd be perfectly capable of steering you over the Swedish border – which otherwise you probably wouldn't see even if you were standing on it. Just a stone marker here and there – buried in snow, of course . . . Yes?'

'Excuse me, sir.' The questioner was Toby Maguire, X-11's diver. 'Would the Lapps be likely to co-operate?'

'I was coming to that. And – well, you'll find them reasonably well-disposed. Not hostile, anyway. But in any event you'll have the where-withall, in your kit, to bribe them. No – let's say reward them. You'll have Norwegian and Swedish cash, and blocks of chewing tobacco – most Lapps'd sell their mothers for it . . . Apart from that, you'll have to rely on your natural diplomacy, charm and bullshit.'

Maguire muttered, 'I'll be all right, then.'

He got a laugh. The lecturer warned, 'Don't be too sure of it. I'm giving you a rough idea of the terrain, but remember there's a hell of a lot of it – and it tends to be swept by snowstorms, sometimes for weeks without a break. All right, so you'd be starting around September twenty-first, twenty-second – and you're thinking that's early in the year, you'd make it before the really heavy snows? But listen – you won't climb those mountains and then get yourselves over hundreds of miles of the hardest going in the world in just a week or two. You'll be into winter, sure as eggs. I have to emphasize this – you'd be crossing a frozen wilderness, temperatures way below zero, storms that last weeks and snow continuous for days. You'd have to contend with frostbite, snow-blindness, hunger, crevasses to fall into and sheer cliffs you won't have the strength to climb, nights when you daren't sleep because if you do you can't be sure of waking up again . . . Now, why am I painting this in somewhat stark colours?' He pointed. 'Let me check your agile brain. Sublieutenant . . .?'

'Hillcrest, sir.' He was first lieutenant of X-11's passage crew, and known as 'Bony' because of an alleged resemblance to Napoleon. 'I'd imagine you were advising us not to attempt it.'

'You'd imagine right. Except that it might, in some circumstances, be your only way out. You'd have the choice then, but obviously you have to know what you'd be taking on. The hope – as I said – is you'll do your stuff, extricate your boat from the fjords and make the prearranged rendezvous with your towing ship, and Bob's your uncle. But we have to accept that it may be easier said than done. An alternative, which has been discussed before, of course, is to surrender; scuttle your boat, first destroying anything inside it that could help enemy intelligence if they got at it later, and turn yourself in. This may simply happen to you, without any question of choice. But in case you can't get out and you're in a position to choose between the alternatives, we're providing you with certain basic equipment that would allow you to try the overland route home . . . Point taken?'

He went on, 'Don't imagine that because you're in peak condition now, those physical difficulties won't bother you. Try to imagine how you may be after a couple of weeks. Those conditions, iron rations, no certainty of survival, and starting right after a spell of action that's liable to drain a lot of the stuffing out of you . . . But all right, you've been warned. Now I'll tell you about the gear we're giving you. First, the obvious things – protective clothing, boots suitable for climbing as well as walking, ropes for the climb, compasses, and the silk maps. Plus the other things I mentioned – pack-rations, money, tobacco. But also first-aid kits, which include small surgical saws for amputating frozen toes or fingers. That item may help to underline some of the points I've been trying to make. And in addition – this is as important as anything, because you could have Hun patrols chasing you – you'll have Luger pistols.'

He moved over to the table.

'Gather round, now. I'll show you this stuff and how it works. I dare say you've been wondering where you'll find room to stow it, but in fact it packs into a very small kit, as you see here . . .'

Later in the afternoon, Paul and the other COs and flotilla staff conferred again over the alternative target plans. Whatever *Tirpitz* and *Scharnhorst* were doing now, they might well turn up in Narvik or Trondheim, where they'd spent certain periods before.

'If there's still no news by the day after tomorrow, all things being equal you'll be sailed on schedule and you'll get your orders later by W/T. As you know, moon and tides are right for 20 September and for a few days after, but if we're forced to miss this chance – well, with short days, winter darkness and iced-up fjords coming shortly, there'd have to be another long postponement. To next Spring, in fact.'

Groans. They were ready to go now.

'No word of attack on the PQ convoy, sir?'

'None. No sighting, no sound.'

By 18.00, when X-12's operational and passage crews went along for drinks on board their towing ship *Setter* alongside *Titania*, a fresh RAF reconnaissance report had been signalled from the Admiralty. There'd been no change: *Lützow* was still in Altenfjord, and the other berths were still empty.

There were seven X-craft guests. Passage crews consisted of only three men, since there was no job for a diver en route. About a dozen submariners packed the tiny wardroom, with some overflow to and from the artificers' mess where Messrs Lanchberry and Towne were being entertained.

MacGregor, *Setter's* lieutenant-in-command, raised his glass.

'Welcome. Glad to have you aboard.' He glanced at Louis Gimber. 'Or as the case may be, on the string back there.'

Paul said, 'I'm afraid we'll crowd you. But if I may, sir, I'd like to stand a watch.'

Eaton said he'd like to, too. Brazier had no watchkeeping experience, and offered to stand watches as a lookout. Towing ships would be on the surface for the first few days of the passage.

Brazier said at one stage, 'Beats me how there can be a convoy on its way, and those battle-wagons out hunting for it, and not a sound out of anyone!'

'It's a big area. This time of year the ice barrier's as far north as it ever gets.' MacGregor stubbed out a cigarette. 'And visibility's often zero. Plus the fact all parties will be maintaining wireless silence.'

Massingbird, *Setter's* red-bearded engineer lieutenant, reached for the gin bottle. 'My guess is the bastards have sneaked down south, to some German port. Into the Baltic, very likely.'

MacGregor said, 'Rubbish, Chief.' Crawshaw, the first lieutenant, shook his head at the engineer. 'Bloody old Jeremiah.'

The beard jutted: 'Want to bet?'

'Certainly. Five bob that we'll sail with X-12 in tow day after tomorrow.'

11 September, that would be. Eight days on passage would lead to arrival off the fjords on the nineteenth. Attack, 20 September.

4

Before noon on the same day, the German battle squadron, having demonstrated their destructive power, had been turning their sterns on Isfjord, in Spitzbergen. *Tirpitz* increased to twenty-eight knots and *Scharnhorst* took station astern of the flagship, while the escort of ten powerful destroyers disposed themselves into an arrow-head screening formation across the big ships' bows. Astern, smoke rose thickly and widely enough to fill half the sky, billowing from the shattered and still burning weather-station and wireless shack, accommodation huts, stores, other collapsed, smouldering structures. Nothing has been left standing or intact, and there were dead Norwegians sprawled among the ruins, as well as live prisoners in the ships. But no word of this had got out, yet. The squadron had made its approach at dawn, the ships growing like huge phantoms out of the mist and skirting the loose ice which, despite the Gulf Stream's northerly flow along this west coast of the island, cluttered the offshore approach. At first sight of the enemy, the operator on duty in the W/T station above Barentsburg had begun tapping out an urgent message, but *Tirpitz*'s radiomen had been ready for it and they'd jammed the transmission. Then the monster's guns had made that wireless station their first target, reducing it to a blazing wreck in one devastating salvo.

The destruction and rounding-up of defenders had continued for five hours. Then the destroyers had re-embarked their landing parties and transferred Norwegian prisoners to the battleships. Well pleased by the easy triumph – although *Scharnhorst*'s captain, Hoffmeier, was critical of his own ship's gunnery performance – the battle group under Admiral Kummetz was now on its 500-mile journey south, steering to pass about twenty miles west of Bear Island.

'Green one hundred – angle of sight five!'

Bruce Christie – as well as the lookout who was yelling his report of it – had picked up the approaching aircraft in his glasses. It had been on the 281 air-warning screen for several minutes, and several pairs of eyes and binoculars had been concentrating on that hazy southern horizon. It would almost certainly be a snooper, and Nick was hoping it might swing away before it sighted them, might decide it had come far enough north: against the murky northern background, it didn't have to have seen the convoy, at this range . . . But – sadly – it would close in now, close enough to see all it wanted while still keeping outside gun-range; its crew would count the ships and note their shapes and sizes, the strength and dispositions of the escorts, and one of the airmen's priorities would be to check whether there was an escort carrier here. The Luftwaffe commanders would be tickled pink to hear there wasn't. The snooper's report would of course start with the convoy's position, course and speed; the zigzag wouldn't fool him, because he'd hang around long enough to see the pattern of it. In fact, mean course was 065 degrees, speed twelve knots – making good about ten, since zigzagging reduced the actual rate of advance – and at this moment Bear Island was about 145 miles due east. Time – 18.20. The report

which that snooper would send out would be the first intimation to Luftwaffe bases on the Norwegian coast that this
very worthwhile target was now entering the radius of
bomber strikes.

'Send that signal, sir?'

Calliope's ready-coded signal to Admiralty, Christie
meant. Among the recipients of it would be Admiral Kidd,
whose cruisers couldn't be far away. Kidd would be glad
to know exactly where the convoy was – although it would
be less good news that the enemy had the same information.

'No. Not yet.'

A minute or two wouldn't make much difference, and
it would be as well to make sure this was a snooper. There'd
be another decision to make, too. If for the time being one
stayed silent, and if the German flyer waited too, didn't
send his sighting report out while he was making his full
assessment and meanwhile came into reasonable close
range, it might be worth using this convoy's one and only
catapult-launched Hurricane, to shoot the intruder down,
if by doing so you could be sure of gaining a few more
hours' privacy. It would be dark soon, so you'd be starting
tomorrow still undetected, a hell of a lot better than having
the bombers swarming over at first light . . .

But with only one shot in your locker, you didn't want
to waste it. If you launched that fighter too soon, and the
German was about to send out his report at just that
moment – well, there'd be very small dividends from
shooting him down after he'd sent it.

Nick had the approaching aircraft centred in his own
glasses now: like a very small mosquito stuck on a dirty
window. It was the visibility, the surroundings, not the
lenses . . . He still hesitated: not from indecision, but from
a stirring of doubt.

'It's a seaplane, sir.'

Exactly. He was sure of it now, as the image hardened.

A float plane, and a small one: certainly no Focke-Wulf or Blohm and Voss long-range reconnaissance . . . *Tirpitz* carried four seaplanes, and so did *Scharnhorst*. But he didn't think this was one of them. If he had thought so, that Hurricane would be belting off by now. The seaplane was flying directly towards the convoy, coming from the south; *Calliope's* helm over at this moment as she, along with the solid block of ships surrounding her and the perimeter screen of escorts too, swung to a starboard leg of the zigzag – which put the unidentified aircraft on the bow instead of the beam. The convoy was in five columns of three ships, with *Calliope* in the centre of the front rank leading column three, and the anti-aircraft ship *Berkeley* astern of her. To port and starboard of the AA ship were the two oilers – *Bayleaf* as centre ship in column two, and the Russian *Sovyetskaya Slava* in column four. Tommy Trench's five destroyers were spread across the convoy's van with his own ship *Moloch* as its spearhead and the two older destroyers, *Harpy* and *Foremost* – who'd brought the merchantmen up from Loch Ewe – integrated with that screen. All destroyers had fuelled during the day, Trench's ship from *Bayleaf* and the other pair from the Russian – which had taken much longer, because the Soviets were new to the refuelling drill, and clumsy at it . . . Then on each flank were two minesweepers – *Redcar* and *Radstock* port side, *Rochdale* and *Rattray* starboard – and astern the two trawlers, *Arctic Prince* and *Northern Glow*. It wasn't too bad an escort for just ten freighters, two oilers and a rescue ship – except for that serious omission of an escort carrier – but the return convoy of empty ships would be a lot bigger.

Examining that slowly-growing but still miniature aircraft image, Nick had become fairly sure he was recognising an almost domestically-familiar shape.

'Swanwick!'

'Sir?' Swanwick, an RNVR lieutenant, was ADO, Air

Defence Officer. Nick asked him, 'Are we certain there's no IFF?'

'Operators say not, sir.'

IFF was a radar device: 'Identification Friend or Foe'.

'Then this fellow's isn't working, or it isn't switched on.' He was sure he was right. He looked round, for Christie, and found the commander, Treseder, beside him. 'What d'you make of it?'

'Beginning to look rather like a Walrus, sir.'

'That's exactly what it is!'

At the same time a spark of light appeared on it, grew into needle-point focus and began to flash short-long, short-long . . .

'Aircraft signalling!'

And no doubt at all now – it was a Walrus from the cruiser squadron. From Kidd's flagship, probably – which might not be far over that hazy southern horizon. The flying-boat – its shape was entirely clear now as it turned – was flying parallel to the convoy's course, its rather slowly winking light drawing acknowledgement word by word from an Aldis clacking sporadically in *Calliope*'s bridge. Nick turned away to sweep all round, checking on the other side where visibility was worse; turning again, he saw the signing-off group, and PO Ironside, yeoman of the watch, scrawling a time-of-origin on his pad as he came for'ard.

'From CS 39, sir. I intend holding my present position forty miles south of you until 0600/10. Thereafter I shall cover your approach to Archangel from the south and west, if enemy air permits. Walrus reconnaissance this afternoon drew blank between your present position and Bear Island.' Ironside looked up. 'Message ends, sir.'

'Make to him, "Many thanks. So far so good".'

Really, very good. The signal he'd had cyphered-up and ready for transmission wouldn't be sent, after all; wireless silence could be maintained. It meant at least another twelve hours' immunity. To have reached eight degrees east longitude without being detected wasn't a bad start at all: and it was very satisfactory to know where Kidd's ships were and to know he knew where the convoy was.

And still no U-boat reports . . .

He glanced up at the sky. In about a quarter of an hour the hands would be called to action stations, the routine sunset precaution, and at the same time he'd take *Calliope* and Trench's five destroyers out ahead, leaving the convoy in the hands of the other escorts. His own ships would then have freedom of movement and be in a position to engage any enemy encountered during the dark hours. For enemy, read *Tirpitz*, *Scharnhorst*, ten destroyers . . .

Where the hell were they?

The Walrus dwindled, vanished southward; after a few minutes it was off the radar screen as well. The convoy was turning back to its mean course, *Calliope* heeling to starboard, graceful as a dancer as she swung, her slim length dipping to the swell. On her beams as she steadied were the *Tacora* – the commodore's ship, to star-board – and the *Carrickmore*, the CAM-ship, with its Hurricane perched on the catapult gear on her foc'sl. Beyond her, leading column one, was the *Plainsman*, whose American master was vice-commodore. Four of the ten freighters were Americans, and on the decks and in the holds of the ten were 1600 trucks or other military vehicles, 200 battle tanks, 50 fighter aircraft and 70 bombers, 18,500 tons of aviation spirit and about 75,000 tons of ammunition and other war material. This was probably the smallest convoy, Nick thought, that had ever been brought to North Russian ports, but the Soviets should still be glad enough to take delivery.

As glad as the Germans would be to stop it.

The commodore was signalling, How nice to know we have company.

He'd have read that message from the Walrus, of course.

He was a former Royal Navy captain by name of Insole; Nick had never met him or heard of him before this trip. Politeness demanded some kind of answer; he told the yeoman, 'Reply, "We may yet have need of it".'

Kidd's report of clear seas ahead at some time in the afternoon was no guarantee for the coming hours of darkness. *Tirpitz* and comapny might well have been lurking somewhere to the east of Bear Island – having sailed from Altenfjord much sooner than they'd needed, and decided to lie in wait?

Night, now – and cold, as the convoy and its escort drew closer to the ice. Radar aerials circling, binoculars probing darkness that was thickened by the mist like flour in clear soup. *Calliope*, plunging rhythmically across the swell, was eight miles ahead of the convoy, with *Moloch* ahead of her and two others on each bow. All of them with asdics pinging, pinging . . . The convoy had ceased zigzagging at dusk, largely because for the merchantmen in close formation the dark made it too dangerous; a small error of judgement or a quartermaster putting his wheel the wrong way near the end of a tiring, boring watch, could easily lead to collision. But the fighting escort still wove to and fro, with slightly increased revs to allow for the convoy's greater speed of advance. *Calliope*'s 271 radar kept its eye on the ships astern – primarily on *Foremost* and *Harpy* in the van of the close escort.

Calliope was at the second degree of readiness: all quarters closed up, but some gun, torpedo and director crews sleeping at their stations. The ship could be brought to instant readiness within seconds.

Nick dozed under an oilskin in a deckchair behind his high seat. It would take only about one second for him to be up and on his toes, but meanwhile it was in the ship's interest as well as his own that he should get some rest while things were quiet. You could hope they'd stay quiet,

but certainly not count on it. The staff officer who'd said
in Akureyri, 'You'll slip through without any trouble, if my
guess is right,' had never himself been up here with a PQ
convoy; he was the kind of theorist who'd read an intelligence summary stating that the enemy's bomber squadrons
had all been moved south, and believe it . . .

By dawn, they'd be well inside the bombing zone. This
quite apart from the chance that just east of Bear Island
might be where *Tirpitz* and *Scharnhorst* were patrolling. At
slow revs, conserving fuel, one might guess.

He reminded himself, Remember Vian.

'Captain, sir?'

'Yes, pilot.'

Christie told him, 'Coming up for one o'clock, sir, and
Bear Island will be abeam. We should alter to oh-nine-oh.'

'Go ahead.'

He'd use TBS – talk-between-ships – to pass the course
alteration to the destroyers. The VHF telephone system
wasn't detectable over any great distance – over more than
the radius covered now by the type 271 radar, for instance
– and it was by far the best way of communicating quickly
with a number of ships at once.

'Rabble, this is Thief. Course, zero nine zero. I say again
– course, zero nine zero. Over . . .'

Christie was using the set himself. Rabble was the collec-
tive callsign for the destroyer force, the five here and the
pair fifteen thousand yards astern. *Foremost*, back there in
the darkness and identifiable only as a blip on the 271
screen, would pass the order to the commodore, who'd
promulgate it to the other merchantmen by fixed signal-
lights at his masthead. Meanwhile the Rabble had a routine
sequence in which to respond. *Moloch* first, with her callsign Tinker: then *Laureate*, *Legend*, *Leopard*, *Lyric*, *Foremost*
and *Harpy*, identifying themselves as Tailor, Soldier, Sailor,
Richman, Poorman and Beggarman.

Nick went aft to the chart-table, to light his pipe under

the cover of its hood. He heard the acknowledgements coming in; and he could visualise Tommy Trench – six foot four in his socks and broad in proportion, looming over *Moloch*'s jolting, swaying bridge as he listened to the same sequence of replies. Trench who in Akureyri had wrung Nick's hand, beaming in delight at their reunion . . . 'Heard you got spliced, sir. In Australia?'

He'd nodded. 'Yes, Tommy. Kate's in England now, though. And we have a son, getting on for a year.'

'Well, that's splendid!' Trench's broad, infectious grin . . . 'Bit late for congratulations, sir, but all the same—'

'Thanks, Tommy. And how's your family?'

'Two sprogs now – boy and a girl!'

'Don't you ever put in any sea-time?'

He had the pipe going: he ducked out from the chart-table cabouche. Christie reported, 'They've all acknowledged, sir. Executive?'

'Yes, please.'

Course would become due east now, rounding Bear Island and leaving it about fifty miles to starboard. That course, with the edge of the ice roughly thirty to forty miles north of their track, would be held until dark tomorrow evening. Then there'd be a turn southwards for the run down to the White Sea.

Barring prior interference, of course.

Kate had begged him, the last night they'd been together, 'Please, be careful?'

He'd kissed her. 'I always am.'

'Like hell you are!'

'Nowadays. I have a wife and child, you see.'

'Just keep us in mind, huh?'

He'd had no answer to such an unnecessary instruction. But she'd burst out again – later when he'd been dozing and woken abruptly with her voice in his ear – 'I'm scared, Nick! I hate it, I'm not used to being this way!'

'What?' Half asleep still, having to struggle to make

sense of it – not only with waking, the blurred mind and sense of alarm, but with Kate's panic, startlingly out of character . . . 'Darling, what are you talking about?'

'All I can say is it's real, and I'm frightened, and . . .'

'I don't know what you're telling me.' Drawing her closer, tight against him. By this time she'd woken fully and so had he. She was crying – wet-faced, his shoulder damp from it. 'Kate, darling what's this nonsense?'

Some dream she'd had? Intuition?

He'd told her, 'You must have been dreaming. Forget it, now. Everything's all right, my darling . . .'

Calliope was under helm, carving a bright curve of white in black, ice-cold sea.

Dawn: radar screens still empty.

He'd slept and dozed, hearing the watches change, the murmur of night-watch routines, the roar of the ship's fans and the slamming and creaking of her motion as she zigzagged eastward. Now, with her company at action stations as the light grew and no enemy showed up, he was about to turn her back to the convoy to resume the day cruising formation, which was designed for countering air attack.

To port, at some indefinable distance, fog lay like a rolled blanket along what would be the beginning of the ice, the loose litter of its fringes perhaps twenty miles away. Fog was to be expected, where air warmed by its passage over the long northerly drift of the Gulf Stream suddenly found itself on ice, and reacted in white vapour. It might hang there all day, or you might come to an edge where it abruptly ended. Or you could run into and through patches a hundred miles deep, slowly drifting.

It looked fairly clear ahead and to the south. Daylight entrenched now, and in *Calliope*'s bridge wind-whipped, stubbled faces were clearly visible to each other. Nick slid off his seat, and stretched. Glancing round, seeing bridge staff at their action stations – Treseder with his glasses up, feet straddled against the roll, Swanwick the ADO farther aft near the port target-indicator sight and his panel of communications to the close-range weapons. Harvey-Smith was at the binnacle: an unhappy man, ambitions disappointed years ago. Pennifold the torpedo lieutenant – roundfaced and double-chinned despite the fact he wasn't thirty yet. The tin hat on his head made him look even rounder: and Pennifold might be persuaded to take some exercise, Nick thought. Not that he was going to be able to do much with this crowd, as a new arrival and expecting to stay no more than a month or two . . . Bruce Christie had binoculars up and sweeping the blind side, the fog-bank to the north: close to his elbow was the chief yeoman, CPO Ellinghouse, squat and frog-like with that wide, heavy jaw.

Nick told Treseder, 'Fall out action stations. Better send them to breakfast right away.'

So as to get the meal over quickly, while things were quiet. This peace couldn't last much longer. If it lasted the whole day, so that tonight PQ 19 would be starting the southward run still without having been detected, that simpleton of a staff officer in Akureyri would have been proved right – which seemed, to say the least, unlikely.

At 07.40 there was an 'Immediate' from CS 39 . . .

Am being shadowed by Focke Wulf. My position 74° 12' North 18° 40' East, course 060 speed 15. Convoy is approximately 60 miles to the north. Intend turning south and west if air attacks develop.

That 'if' was somewhat superfluous, Nick thought. If Kidd was being shadowed, it wouldn't be long before he came under attack. The message ended with a weather report and was addressed to Admiralty, repeated AIG 311 – meaning all ships and authorities concerned with PQ 19 – and to SBNO, North Russia.

'I'm going down for a shave. Who's PCO?'

'I am, sir.'

Spalding, the gunnery officer. 'PCO' stood for Principal Control Officer: he, Treseder and Christie shared the job, when Nick himself was off the bridge.

The cruiser squadron's position was twenty miles southeast of Bear Island. Kidd's present course of 060, northeasterly, was bringing him up closer to the convoy's track. He must have passed well south of Bear Island during the night, but his intention as indicated in this signal was to turn away from the convoy rather than draw attackers up towards it.

The wild card was still the *Tirpitz*.

'Ready for your breakfast sir?'

Percy Tomblin, back again. The ship's company had already fed, but Nick hadn't wanted it, earlier; he'd been conning her back into the convoy formation when Tomblin had last suggested it.

'Yes, please.' Wiping foam from the razor. 'Up here, right away.'

But he needn't have rushed it. It was an hour and a half before CS 39's next signal came in . . .

Under attack by Ju 88s. My position 30 miles SE of Bear Island, course 130.

Evidently Kidd had changed his mind about altering to south and west; he must have decided that the battle group was still potentially a threat to the convoy. He was increasing his distance from PQ 19, but in fact only cutting the corner of the convoy's planned route, so he was keeping his squadron in the general area where he could hope to take a hand in any surface action that did develop.

Nick thought about it, and arrived at two conclusions.

One, the Admiralty was unlikely to sanction CS 39's continued presence in such extremely dangerous waters, not for much longer or unless there was some solid expectation of a meeting with the battle group. Two, the air activity down there would surely extend itself northwards soon, at least in terms of reconnaissance initially; the Germans weren't all stupid, they'd realise that a cruiser force wasn't subjecting itself to air attack for no purpose. He told McLoughlin, yeoman of the watch, 'By lamp to the commodore – "In view of enemy air activity in the south, propose altering mean course to north for about two hours".'

Use of the word 'propose' was a courtesy to the commodore. 'Intend' would have been more accurate. As escort commander he, not the commodore, was responsible for PQ 19's defence, and whether Insole liked the idea or not he was going to get closer to that fog, close enough to make use of it if he needed to.

Insole concurred.

'Right. Yeoman – by TBS to Rabble . . .'
Time, 0920.

At 10.19, CS 39 signalled:

Large formation of He 111 torpedo bombers and Ju 88s approaching from south. My course 290 speed 18.

Kidd shouldn't have been allowed east of Bear Island, Nick thought. Hindsight, of course; but that message reminded him of Crete in 1941, when such alarms had been commonplace and as often as not the preliminaries to much worse news. Ships operating without air cover, close to enemy air bases – it was an old, old story. That signal said it all: and having been there oneself, on occasion, no description of what it would be like for those ships was necessary.

Treseder murmured, 'Afraid they're in for it.'

At least the convoy was ten miles farther from the bombing than it had been an hour ago. Pretty soon they'd catch a sight of the ice: then he'd turn, head east again. He asked Treseder, 'You were in the Crete thing, weren't you?'

'I was sunk in *Fiji* sir.' The commander nodded. 'Picked up by *Kandahar*. At least we had a warmish sea to swim in.' He nodded again, catching Nick's meaning. 'Yes. There's a familiar ring.'

It rang worse at 10.34.

Minotaur hit on 'B' turret. Attacks continuing, mostly high-level Ju 88s. Two He 111s and one Ju 88 destroyed.

Ice was visible ahead at 10.50. A blue-green, fiery shimmer under low-lying haze; but the fog had rolled back, piled and driven by a freshening southwest wind. The ice-edge was farther south than one might have expected at this time of year. It meant the fog wasn't going to be quite the ally he'd been looking for – except as an obscuring background against which these ships would be less easily visible from the south.

'Yeoman – make to the commodore, "Propose resuming mean course 090". And by TBS to Rabble, "Stand by to resume mean course east".'

The Aldis began to stammer out the message, while Clark, signal yeoman in this forenoon watch, passed the stand-by order over the radio-telephone. Nick asked Christie, 'What's our distance from the cruisers?'

'Plot makes it ninety miles, sir.'

Better than he'd thought. And as Kidd was now steering west, convoy course of due east would widen the gap fast. And then of course, if you ran into the *Tirpitz* you'd be sorry . . . But PQ 19 might stay lucky, for a while . . . The W/T office bell rang: Christie answered the voicepipe, and listened grimly.

'Very good. Send it up.'

He came over to Nick's corner. 'Signal from CS 39, sir. Simultaneous bombing and torpedo attacks in progress. Four more aircraft destroyed and further minor damage sustained by *Minotaur*. Then he gives a position, course still two-nine-oh and speed eighteen.'

PO Clark suggested, 'Executive, sir?'

'Yes, please.'

The executive order was being passed, and that signal was arriving in the bridge; destroyers were racing to adjust their stations. Swanwick the ADO called from the after end of the bridge, 'Bogey on one-six-oh, range fourteen, closing!'

'One single aircraft?'

In other words, a single reconnaissance plane, or an attack on its way? For just a snooper, he wouldn't call the ship's company to action stations . . . 'Yeoman – hoist "aircraft bearing" – whatever it is . . . Pilot, have the W/T office stand by with a position and "am being shadowed by aircraft".'

Christie kept Bliss and the padre – who did their cyphering job in the plot – supplied with regularly updated position, course and speed data. It was to the plot he was talking now, through its voicepipe. And that flag-hoist was whisking up – the aeroplane flag, a red diamond on white background, surmounting the bearing pendant and three numerals – one, six, zero.

Swanwick had confirmed this was a single aircraft approaching. You'd know when the pilot sighted the convoy, because the right-to-left movement – which he'd also just reported – would cease as he turned towards.

A new range now, new bearing. The ADO's communications were to the radar offices, the director tower, guns and close-range weapons; and his target-bearing indicators, one each side of the bridge, could put either the director or the guns on to a target first spotted from the bridge. It was a very flexible system.

The convoy was steadying on its course of east. Nick moved from one side of the bridge to the other, checking around and astern to see whether any of the ships might be letting out enough smoke to catch a German observer's eye. There was a slight leak from *Papeete*, the long, low-built freighter leading column five, on the commodore's starboard beam. But the *Papeete* was about a cable's length astern of station, with the *Galilee Dawn* treading on her heels, and very likely the reason for that smoke would have been a terse order to her engineroom to speed up. Astern of the *Galilee Dawn* was the American *Caribou Queen*, her upperworks visible over the Soviet oiler's tank-tops. No tell-tale smoke-trails there, anyway; even the *Papeete*'s had cleared now. On the other side the *Carrickmore* and the *Plainsman* beyond her were both angling outwards, adjusting for having closed in too far during the turn. The oiler *Bayleaf* steamed in the *Carrickmore*'s wake, and the rescue ship *Winston* trailed the oiler. A whisp of greyish smog swirled from the *Earl Granville*'s tall stack – she was next-astern of the *Plainsman* – and he focussed his glasses on it, but again it was hardly enough to make a fuss about. Astern of the *Granville*, the third ship in column one was the American *Ewart S. Dukes* – with the minesweeper *Radstock* veering out across her stern . . . Nick leant out, turning his glasses back to where the AA ship *Berkeley* had finished the turn very neatly astern of *Calliope*; astern of her the *Republican*, another of the US contingent, was nosing into station.

'Nine miles, sir, true bearing one-five-five!'

Still closing, and still moving slightly from right to left. He went back to his tall chair. Treseder, Christie and the yeoman were all on the starboard side with their glasses up. *Calliope*'s motion was a combination of pitch and roll, with the long swells lifting under her quarter.

'Range eight miles!'

'Aircraft in sight.' Treseder had got it. 'Green six-oh,

angle of sight – zero. It's a Dornier two-one-seven, sir.'

Nick was on it too. Very low to the horizon – and even with that slight degree of profile it was easily recognisable, the 'flying-pencil' shape of the long-range Dornier . . . Swanwick called form his ADO position, 'Turned towards, sir!'

No element of profile at all now. The Dornier was a darkly hostile intruder lifting very slowly against pearl-grey sky.

'Two-eight-one continue all-round sweep. See the look-outs do the same.'

Otherwise they'd be watching the approaching recce plane instead of looking out for newcomers. Who would undoubtedly be along, by and by. Perhaps not quite immediately – since they already had one target closer to them and already damaged – but they'd be coming.

'Tell them to get that cypher away, pilot.'

The Dornier spent about fifteen minutes limping around the convoy in its characteristic nose-down position, the posture of a wounded dragonfly. It stayed carefully out of range while it completed its inventory of merchantmen and escorts and then turned south, dwindled, finally vanished from the radar screen.

Treseder said grimly, 'Matter of time now, sir.'

But it always had been. Nobody could have believed in that prediction of getting through unscathed.

At 11.44 there was a new and worrying signal from CS 39.

> *Nottingham* damaged by near-miss. Speed temporarily reduced to 14 knots.
> Large formation of Ju 88s closing from southeast. My position . . .

The position was twenty miles south of Bear Island, and Kidd was still steering 290. He was obviously in bad trouble, and the Luftwaffe's interest in the cruiser squadron explained why they hadn't yet moved against this convoy. Having hit *Minotaur* and now damaged the flagship, you could guess they'd be encouraged to keep up that effort.

In the interim he'd altered the convoy's mean course again, slanting up thirty degrees to port. Two hours on this northeasterly course would bring them as close to the ice as might be reasonably safe at present speed. It would add a few miles to the distance between the convoy and the Luftwaffe, and put them closer to the area of uncertain visibility; there was even a chance of fog spreading southward, providing real cover.

'Cooks to the galley' and then 'Hands to dinner' were piped earlier than usual, on the heels of 'Up spirits', in the hope of getting another meal over before the bombers came. Nick had his own lunch tray on his knees when at about 12.15 the chaplain, the Reverend Marcus Plumb, came up with a freshly decyphered signal from the Admiralty.

Plumb's appearance didn't match his name. Far from 'plummy', he was quick-eyed, brisk and muscular – a Welshman, and a rugger player of renown.

'This'll remove one of your headaches, sir.'

SECRET IMMEDIATE
FROM: Admiralty
TO: CS 39
REPEATED TO: AIG 311 and SBNO North Russia
   Tirpitz and *Scharnhorst* are reported to have returned to Altenfjord. Withdraw to the west at your best speed.

Astonished: reading it over twice . . . 'I'll be damned.' Glancing round – 'Here, pilot . . .' Then, 'Thank you, padre. If you haven't lunched yet, I suggest you tuck in while the going's good.'

'I shall indeed, sir. Soon as my oppo's back from his repast.'

By 'oppo' he meant Happy Bliss. Nick wondered where the German battleships had been. Up in this area, searching ineffectually for the convoy? Given up, sneaked home again, running out of fuel? Whatever the answers, for the moment you could forget them: and it did simplify the tactical problem. The snag was that as Kidd's cruisers pulled out westward now, increasing their distance from the enemy airfields, the bombers would feel free to switch their attentions to this convoy.

He asked Bruce Christie, 'How far has CS 39 to go before he's out of their range?'

'On his present course, about eighty miles, sir.'

At fourteen knots, six hours. But *Nottingham*'s engineers might improve on that, of course.

A luminous streak underlying the northern haze was a reflection from the ice. Nearly 12.30 now. He decided he'd hold this course for about another hour or an hour and a half. Loose ice couldn't do anyone much damage, and if there was a chance of getting into fog up there it might be a lifesaver.

The watch had changed at noon, and now with the midday meal finished various individuals came up to the bridge, hung around for a while, wandered off again. Pitcairn, the paymaster commander, came to talk to Treseder about new arrangements for action messing, and the gunnery officer, Keith Spalding, came to confer with Swanwick. At one stage the PMO – Francomb, surgeon commander – brought Nick some quandary about medical stores they were carrying for the so-called 'hospital' at Vaenga, the base settlement in the Kola Inlet, the approach to Murmansk.

As this convoy was destined for Archangel, not Kola, the stores would have to be trans-shipped, and Francomb's concern was that the Russians shouldn't get any chance to steal them. The obvious solution, Nick suggested, was to transfer the stuff to one of the four minesweepers, who'd be staying in North Russia, relieving others who'd be returning with the convoy of empties; sooner or later the sweepers would call at Vaenga and be able to slip the stores ashore – surreptitiously, perhaps, to avoid entanglement in Soviet red tape.

At 13.45 Christie suggested they'd come far enough to the north and should alter back to 090. Nick agreed, and a few minutes later the six-mile-wide block of merchantmen and escorts swung back to point east. It was getting on for three hours since the Dornier had fingered them.

A lookout's yell came just after the convoy had settled on the new course . . .

'Aircraft, green one hundred, angle of sight ten, closing!'

He'd beaten the radar to it . . . All around the bridge binoculars sought and found the oncoming attackers – midge-like objects, a scattering of them approaching from the south.

They were Ju 88s: nine of them, flying in and out of cloud now, at about 7000 feet. Swinging left, cloud swallowing them . . .

Radar and the director control tower were on target – had been, but now only radar held the contact. The tower, above and abaft the bridge with its rangefinder behind it, pivotting this way and that as its crew strained to pick up a fresh sight of the bombers, resembled some seamonster's stiffly raised head with eyes out on stalks. When it found the target, the guns would follow, pointers in electronic receivers lining-up, with additional calculations thrown into the circuits by the TS, transmitting station, deep in the ship's bowels where Royal Marine bandsmen and others laboured, locked in a cavern of armoured steel. All guns elevated, ready, and all personnel in this bridge and other exposed positions were in tin hats and anti-flash gear. Close-range weapons – Oerlikons, pompoms and multiple point-five machineguns – manned, sky-searching . . . An answer from Tommy Trench crackled over TBS: Roger, Thief. Out. Then Trench was calling Tailor and Sailor – meaning *Laureate* and *Leopard* – ordering them to take up new stations in the convoy's rear while *Foremost* and *Harpy* spread outward to cover the sectors they'd vacated.

Nothing to do but wait and watch now. Eyes on the clouds, fingers on triggers, ships plunging, ploughing white furrows in grey-green sea.

'Bogeys closing from astern, sir!'

That was a report from the 281, 'bogeys' being radar talk for hostile radar contacts. The Junkers would attack by diving from astern. Some might drop a bomb or two through cloudholes overhead, but the main weight of the attack would come from aircraft diving over the convoy's wakes. *Laureate* and *Leopard* had wheeled and were racing back between the outer columns of merchantmen with guns cocked up, bow-waves high, ensigns whipping, the two sleek-looking ships sheeted in foam as they rushed to their new stations. Without them, there'd only have been the two trawlers astern, where most of the action was bound to start. Unfortunately their armament of four-point-sevens wouldn't be as effective as one would like, since they were low-angle guns and couldn't elevate enough for overhead attackers. *Moloch*, one destroyer class later, had dual-purpose guns, as did *Calliope* with her 5.25s. Those L-class destroyers did have one high-angle four-inch, in fact, and of course their close-range weapons could fire vertically, like everyone else's.

Astern, someone had opened fire . . .

Three Ju 88s, emerging from cloud and in shallow dives aimed at the convoy's heart. Almost certainly they'd be going for the oilers – for *Bayleaf* and the *Sovyetskaya Slava*. Nick had already passed the order to open fire when ready. Tracer was rising from several of the merchantmen: and now *Leopard*, almost on her beam-ends in a high-speed turn as she fell into station astern of column two, opened up with her four-inch. *Laureate* too. *Calliope*'s two stern turrets joined in, the ship's steel ringing to the crashes, the entire convoy at it now like a great percussion band with ship after ship coming into it, sound thickening from individual explosions into a solid roar, and the sky around the diving Junkers – two other sections of three in sight now, all nose-down and on their attacking runs – pock-marked with brown and black shellbursts, streaked with the garish tracer that seemed to curve as it rose ahead of them then bend sharply to whip away astern. Noise deafening, composed not only of the large-calibre guns but also the Oerlikons' harsh snarl, pompoms' thudding, the Bofors' distinctive barking too, and the metallic clangour of point-fives. Bombs separating, slow-looking, from the first group of planes as they swept over – one with an engine trailing smoke; the trio splitting now their bombs had gone, two banking left and the smoker pulling out southward – the smoke was darkening and the machine looked as if it was having trouble staying up. Bucketing upwards . . . Gunners' aim shifting to others, two threesomes merging into one rough echelon of six roaring over the columns at about 2000 feet, everyone deaf by this time, bomb-splashes lifting here and there, destroyers under helm dodging bombs while their guns blared. The merchantmen's close-range weapons were lacing the sky overhead so thickly that it was amazing any of the attackers could fly through it and not be hit. He saw a near-miss on the *Bayleaf*. The sight of it – a column of sea leaping right on her quarter, too close not to have done some damage – was frightening: *Bayleaf* being the one ship you couldn't afford to lose. The second bomb of the same stick raised a spout on *Calliope*'s beam, midway between her and the *Carrickmore*, and two others splashed in ahead, in the space between the convoy and the destroyer screen. Noise diminishing as the last of the attackers droned over; a voice over the wires from the director tower was intoning 'Check, check, check . . .'

A bomber had nose-dived into the sea ahead; *Legend* was going out in search of survivors.

'The *Bayleaf*'s in trouble, sir.'

As he'd guessed she would be – but still hoped . . . He went to the other side and looked astern. The oiler was falling back, and the rescue ship, *Winston*, had put her helm over to pass clear. The trawler *Arctic Prince* was standing by the *Bayleaf*. There was a lot of smoke right astern, out of his sight from here, and he guessed at a ship on fire on the other quarter.

'Chief,' talking to the chief yeoman, Ellinghouse, 'to *Laureate* by TBS – report on damage to the *Bayleaf*.'

Swanwick told him, 'That's the *Springfield* on fire astern, sir.'

The *Springfield* was next-astern to the *Sovyetskaya Slava*. One of the bigger ships in this assembly, she had a deck cargo of tanks and trucks, and a between-decks load of explosives.

But it was the *Bayleaf* he was most concerned for. She was indispensable – not so much for now, because at a pinch the Russian oiler could serve the destroyers' bunkering needs, but for the return trip when she'd be the one and only source of replenishment.

He was waiting for a reply from *Laureate*. About half a mile astern, she was closing in towards the damaged oiler. Her captain would confer with the *Bayleaf*'s master by loud-hailer.

Time now – 1417.

The *Springfield* had also dropped astern, gushing smoke more thickly than before. The other trawler, *Northern Glow*, was forging across the convoy's rear towards her, and *Leopard* was also there.

'Rigging hoses . . .'

Commentary by Treseder, with his glasses up and muttering to himself. That activity on the destroyer's foc'sl was hidden as she turned sternto, following the *Springfield* round. She'd be turning head to wind, Nick realised, because the fire was on or in her after-part and this would make it less likely to spread forward. The *Northern Glow* was turning to catch up with the convoy. He heard *Laureate*'s report coming in over TBS: there'd been something, garbled by atmospherics, about a fractured oil-feed and repairs in hand, then the voice broke through the static and he heard clearly, Maximum of five knots for at least half an hour. Over.

It sounded less bad than it might have been.

'Tell *Laureate* to stay with her.'

Dense smoke drifting from the *Springfield* hid whatever was happening there. *Leopard*'s captain would have his hands full with the attempt at fire-fighting, though, and there was no point bothering him with questions. Except perhaps whether he wanted help: and the idea of detaching another escort, when a new attack might develop at any moment, was unattractive. If he wanted help, he could ask for it. Every pair of glasses in *Calliope*'s bridge was sky-searching: the air-search radar hadn't been any help last time.

'Swanwick – what happened to the 281?'

Legend was reporting she'd picked up two German airmen, one wounded.

The ADO came over. In the summer of 1939 he'd been starting a career as an actor in repertory at Bexhill-on-Sea; he was a good-looking young man in his mid twenties, but the tin hat with its stencilled letters 'ADO' looked too big for his rather narrow head – like the top of a mushroom. He said apologetically, 'They tell me the set's all right now, sir, but—'

The *Springfield* blew up. A muffled roar built into a thunderclap: flame shot vertically, snuffing itself out in black smoke through which a second explosion lobbed a fireball – crimson, disintegrating in its turn into oily-looking smoke. Swanwick with his mouth still open, goggling; Nick focussing his glasses on what was now a foggy mess extending for several hundred yards across the convoy's wakes. He couldn't see *Leopard*: but she'd have been right in there, close enough to have been reaching the freighter's deck with her hoses. A glance to the side showed the *Bayleaf* well clear and *Laureate* leaving her, heading for the new disaster area. The *Arctic Prince* was still with the oiler. Then, where the *Springfield* had been, he found *Leopard* lying stopped and shrouded in thinning smoke which was coming from the destroyer herself, from a fire on her port side. A seaboat – a whaler in its davits – was blazing, and there were other burning areas, while that side of her bridge superstructure had been blackened by scorching.

'Chief – general signal, "Speed five knots".'

Still no bombers. Everyone expecting them, surprised by every minute that passed with the sky still empty.

By three o'clock the *Bayleaf* was back in station astern of the *Carrickmore* and speed had been worked up to twelve knots. Allowing for the zigzag this gave a true rate of advance of a fraction over ten. Five badly burnt survivors of the *Springfield* had been picked up and they and eleven wounded from *Leopard* had been transferred to the *Winston* – which had a doctor, wards and even an operating theatre. *Leopard*'s wounded included her captain, and the first lieutenant had assumed command. Her damage was superficial; that whaler and some other upper-deck gear had been destroyed, but very little else. The casualties, suffering from burns and blast, concussion, had all been in her bridge and for'ard guns' crews.

Column four had only two ships in it now instead of three. The empty billet, which had been the *Springfield*'s, was astern of the *Sovyetskaya Slava* and between two Americans, the *Republican* and the *Caribou Queen*.

Worsening visibility on the port side suggested fog might be extending southward. If so, it would be welcome. Binoculars caught the glint of ice as they swept over that sector: but only a suggestion, a gleam underlining the soupy haze.

The *Bayleaf* seemed to be all right now. During the half-hour wait when he'd had only her engineer's relayed promise – therefore no guarantee at all – he'd considered what might be done if they failed to improve on her five-knot speed. One possibility would have been to send her to Spitzbergen, perhaps into Bell Sund in the island's ice-free west coast where she could have holed-up to work on the repairs and then been picked up again somewhere north of Bear Island in about ten days' time. An alternative might have been to start her back towards Iceland and request support that would have needed to include another oiler with a destroyer escort. But this would have been tantamount to asking for the moon: Spitzbergen would have been the best answer. Even though you'd have had to leave a destroyer with her . . . One had to think ahead, be ready with solutions, alternatives . . .

He'd put out a signal to the Admiralty – wireless silence being unimportant for a while, with the Luftwaffe knowing all it needed to – reporting the attack, damage to the oiler and the loss of the *Springfield*. There'd been nothing new from CS 39, and he guessed Kidd's squadron would be out of range of bombing by this time. Touch wood . . . But the corollary was that here, soon, one might expect the enemy's full weight.

'Cup o' char, sir?'

Tomblin had brought tea and biscuits.

'We're still at action stations, Tomblin. Where's your tin hat?'

'Ah.' A surprised look suggested this was a completely novel idea. 'That's a point, sir.'

'Fetch it, and don't appear on this bridge again without it. And anti-flash gear, for God's—'

'Bogeys, one-seven-five, fourteen miles, large formation!'

'All quarters alert!'

Voicepipes and telephones were suddenly busy again. A flag-hoist ran up to the yardarm, drawing other ships' attention to that bearing. Two minutes later, radar reported a second wave of attackers coming in behind the first. Bearings were unchanging, indicating a direct, purposeful approach. Treseder said. 'At least the two-eight-one seems to have pulled itself together.'

Count your blessings . . .

But sparing a thought, another one, for the idiot in Akureyri who'd been so sure PQ 19 would get through unopposed – by way of a let-out, of course, for failure to lay on an escort carrier. Nick would have liked to have had that man here now, to watch – as they all did, a few minutes later – the first group of bombers sliding round astern, high enough to be flying in and out of the lower extremities of cloud, and dividing into three sections of respectively four, four and five aircraft – these were Ju 88s again, thirteen of them.

'Large formation green eight-oh, angle of sight five, flying right to left!'

That was the second bunch . . .

One quartet of Junkers had turned, to start their approach from astern. The group of five still circled on towards the port quarter. The third section had climbed into cloud and were out of sight.

'These are Heinkel 111s, sir!'

Torpedo bombers . . . Swanwick had his glasses on them. He added, 'I make it two batches of nine Heinkels in each, sir.' They were circling from right to left, out there to starboard, and they'd be likely to attack from the bow either in two waves or all together. Simultaneous attack would be preferable from the convoy's point of view, and with any luck it was what the Germans would put their money on. But there'd be the Junkers to contend with at the same time, of course.

The first group of them was droning in now. Looking

like blood-thirsty black bats. Not quite as poisonous as Stukas, the Ju 87s, but still foul enough. Quite a distance astern, as yet, and high.

Nick spoke to Trench over TBS.

'Tommy – with your armament, *Moloch* would do better astern. Put the other two up front to frighten the Heinkels?'

Aye aye, sir! Trench added, Out . . . Then he was calling the two astern. He might have thought of this himself: there was barely time now to make the switch before the attack came in. *Laureate* and *Leopard*, with low-angle four-sevens, were equipped to counter the low-level torpedo bombers, while *Moloch*'s high-elevating guns could be used against the 88s. *Moloch* was already under helm, and before Trench had finished passing his orders the other two were beginning to move up, cracking on full power to pass up between the columns; they'd have been prepared for it by hearing Nick's call to Trench.

Leopard seemed to be handled well enough by the first lieutenant who'd assumed command.

Waiting again. Gun barrels lifted, ready. Eyes at binoculars or over sights watching the enemy deploy for an assault in which they must have known some of them would die. The group of Junkers that had crossed astern was circling back, to swing in behind four that were already on their way in. And there was another group up there somewhere, above the clouds. While out on the bow the two parties of Heinkels had joined up to form a single line-ahead; when they turned to start their attack, there'd be eighteen of them in line-abreast, so you'd have an echelon of thirty-six torpedoes raking in on that bow. But the long straggle of them was still in profile, snaking up . . . *Moloch* swept past at about thirty-four knots, all her guns jutting skyward, tin-hatted seamen clustered at each mounting. There was an exchange of waves – and the large bulk of Tommy Trench, towering in the front of that bucking swaying bridge, lifted a hand in salute. Astern, the *Berkeley*'s high-angle four-inch

opened fire, and the 'ting' of *Calliope*'s firegongs was just
audible before her after guns came in on the act. Her three
for'ard turrets and the two after ones could be used and
controlled as two separate batteries, when targets prolifer-
ated so that a division of her fire-power was needed. Now
the racing *Moloch*'s for'ard turrets opened up. *Leopard* and
Laureate still lancing up to the convoy's van, one each side,
each in a welter of flying foam, and the first black-brown
shell-bursts opening like puffballs under the diving
Junkers' noses. Oerlikons in action, and pompoms – at an
88 roaring over on a slanting course, diving, coming from
the direction of the port bow and bombs already in the air
– two, three, four – and another on the tail of that one, two
others a few hundred feet higher and coming from right
ahead. *Calliope*'s five turrets thundering: firing, recoiling,
firing, smoke belching away and the reek of cordite heavy
in the wind. Bedlam as guns of many calibres and types
engaged both the attackers from astern and these
ambushers, queue jumpers, whom nobody had seen as
they'd broken cover, diving out of the cloud-layer more
like 87s than 88s – and thank God Swanwick had caught
on to it just in time. A bomb whacked in fifty yards off
Calliope's port bow, a second between her and the
Sovyetskaya Slava, and the next one hit the *Galilee Dawn*
amidships. Other bomb-splashes leaping: the rescue ship
had been near-missed – Nick saw the mushroom of sea
dumping itself across her quarter. Every ship in the convoy
was using every gun it had: the *Galilee Dawn* included, on
fire but holding on.

Then the noise-level was falling. The change came
suddenly, as the last two 88s swung southward, climbing
out of shellbursts. Nick had seen one go into the sea, and
he thought a second, just before that hit on the *Galilee Dawn*,
and at least one German had been trailing smoke as he
departed. But there were still four to come, this last section
already boring down from astern: there'd been a lull, a

good half minute with no guns in action, time for gunners to clear away some of the litter of empty shellcases and for ammunition-supply parties to build up stocks and refill the ready-use lockers, Oerlikons to change ammo drums, pompoms to fit new belts. *Moloch* had opened up again. The *Galilee Dawn* was still burning, a squad of fire-fighters visible in her for'ard welldeck, hoses gushing, and the mine-sweeper *Rochdale* was nosing in to help. The *Berkeley* opened fire, and *Calliope*, the whole deafening orchestra at full blast again. Shellbursts opened all around the leading bomber: bombs falling away only seconds before it was hit, flinging over as a wing buckled, bits flying off and the machine vertically nose-down streaming smoke. Numbers two and three coming in together, the fourth a long way astern. The *Winston*, rescue ship, was listing to port and falling back, alone, losing way – result of that near-miss . . . He had his glasses on her and on the *Arctic Prince* who'd turned to stay with her, the trawler part-hidden under a haze of smoke from her own close-range weapons which had only that moment ceased firing, when Treseder – unable to make himself heard – touched Nick's arm, pointing out on the bow to where the eighteen torpedo-bombers had swung into line-abreast, low to the sea and racing in.

5

The Heinkels were about sixty yards apart and thirty feet above the water and the destroyers were deploying to meet them in a line slanting across the convoy's van – *Lyric, Leopard, Foremost, Harpy, Laureate, Legend* . . . Nick would have taken *Calliope* out to join them, but there were still two 88s to come – from astern, where *Moloch* had just started banging away again. With those six destroyers out of the close AA defence, *Calliope*'s guns were needed here, for the moment.

One Junkers was turning away – banking to port, exposing loaded bomb-racks as it tilted. No reason clear, so far . . . *Berkeley*'s guns had opened up, after the briefest of breathers. Now he heard *Calliope*'s fire-gong, and her after turrets thundered, the vibration rattling her hull. There was no close-range in it yet; that 88 was still high, and its turn had taken it out to the convoy's quarter.

Another coming over now . . .

The one who'd swung away had done so in order to go for the *Winston* – the rescue ship, well astern and alone except for that trawler standing by her. Listing hard to port: that nearmiss must have holed her, or opened a seam, or seams. *Arctic Prince* opening up with all her close-range weapons – and *Moloch* shifting target, throwing up a defensive barrage under the bomber's nose.

Bombs slammed in between the *Berkeley* and the Russian oiler. The *Galilee Dawn*'s upper-deck fire was out, but she was still leaking smoke, and there might be fire below decks. The second bomb of that stick fell close to the *Tacora*'s stern, and a third just over her bow on the other side. Some of the destroyers ahead opening fire; and as if he'd taken that as a reminder of the torpedo threat, the commodore's siren blared for an emergency turn to starboard.

Time for *Calliope* to move out . . .

'Full ahead together. Starboard fifteen.'

AA fire from the merchantmen died away. The action was astern now: and ahead, all six destroyers were engaging the Heinkels. The emergency turn – the convoy's helms all over to starboard as *Calliope* also turned but speeded, drawing ahead – would leave the ships' sterns pointing straight at the attackers. Harvey-Smith reporting from the binnacle, 'Fifteen of starboard wheel on, sir, both engines full ahead.'

'GCO' into the director telephone, 'I'm moving up between *Foremost* and *Harpy*. When your range is clear, use the for'ard turrets against those Heinkels.' Over the wire, as he pushed the telephone back on to its hook, he heard the control officer shifting target and ordering red barrage – red meaning long-range fuses, as opposed to white and blue for medium or short.

'Midships, and meet her.'

'The *Winston*'s sunk, sir. Direct hit from that . . .'

'Steady as you go!'

'Steady, sir . . .'

Steering her into that gap. All the destroyers' for'ard guns in action, the whole wide front of the torpedo attack plastered in shellbursts. But it wasn't stopping them: they were dodging, bucketing up and down, but still coming. *Calliope*'s three for'ard turrets about to join in: just for the next few seconds as she lunged forward, thrusting across the swell, her range was still obstructed by *Foremost*. He saw a Heinkel hit – flung on its side, cartwheeling into the sea. Calling over his shoulder, 'Two hundred revolutions!' She was in the gap now: he heard the tinny clang just before her 5.25s crashed out – brown haze rushing over, with the reek of cordite – and rapid fire, barraging: left barrels fired, recoiled, right barrels fired, recoiled. Noise, flash, smoke, and the jarring concussions ringing in her steel, through your feet and bones. In his memory's ear, under the racket, was an echo of a report from Christie – the rescue ship, sunk. With those survivors in her. Her loss was serious, for now and also for later, in Russia and on the way home with the bigger convoy. The *Winston* hadn't been just a ship detailed to act as rescuer, she was specially fitted and equipped to look after survivors . . . A Heinkel climbed, pulling up steeply and banking away: two others followed suit. They'd have fired, their torpedoes would be on the way, and all the others would be dropping their fish about now.

You could see them, splashing in. But others were holding on: getting in close to make more certain of their shots. It would take some nerve, he thought, to hold on into that barrage.

'One-sixty revolutions.'

Leopard and *Lyric* diverging to starboard – countering a diversion by a group of Heinkels at that end of the line . . . Another one hit – the third he'd seen – on fire before it hit the water in an eruption like a shallow depthcharge. Torpedo exploded there, he realised. The attack was breaking up – two still coming, but the others splitting away right and left, some climbing as they turned, others at sea-level . . .

'Torpedo tracks port side!'

But the torpedoes themselves would already have passed: the tracks rose to the surface astern of them. Some would be getting to the convoy any moment now: and not a damn thing anyone here could do, except hope.

'. . . starboard, sir!'

It was all he'd heard of a strident yell. An open mouth, pointing arm – and a single white track ruler-straight, converging: and too late, too bloody . . .

A clanging impact, from somewhere aft on the starboard side.

Nothing else. He'd felt that jar as well as heard it. Faces tense, breath held . . .

No explosion, though. *Calliope* dipping her shoulder into greenish sea and digging out white foam. That torpedo's warhead had not exploded. Treseder shouted, 'Glanced off us, sir!' Arms spread – and a guffaw of a laugh picked up and echoed by others – 'Bounced off her!'

An explosion farther astern, though, wasn't anything to rejoice in. It was the semi-smothered but hard, knocking thump one had heard all too often. Christie shouted with his glasses trained back on the convoy, 'I think that was the *Papeete* . . .'

A second hit came like a duplicate of the first.

Guns falling silent, seeping smoke. A telephone buzzed, and the chief yeoman was there answering it – listening . . . He reported, 'Engineer Commander says something walloped the ship's side abreast the after boiler room, sir, but no damage.' And that would be *Calliope*'s full ration of luck for this trip, Nick thought. It was the glancing angle of the impact that had saved them. The quiet, as gun-fire ceased altogether, was startling: you'd been living in noise, encased in it. The sound of yet a third torpedo finding a target was shocking – like a dirty punch after the bell had rung to end a round.

No aircraft targets now. Two Heinkels had flown down the convoy's starboard side but they'd been circling away, getting out of it.

TBS calling: and it was Tommy Trench's voice . . . Thief, this is Tinker. Minesweeper *Redcar*'s gone, sir. Blown to bits. *Arctic Prince* is looking for survivors. I'm standing by the *Caribou Queen*: doubt if she'll float much longer. *Papeete*'s crew is abandoning her: *Northern Glow*'s with her. I have fourteen survivors from the *Winston*. Over . . .

17.10. The *Caribou Queen* and the *Papeete* had both gone down. Survivors from them and from the *Winston* were on board *Moloch* and the two trawlers. When time permitted he'd get some transferred into *Calliope*, who had more room for them. There'd been no survivors from the minesweeper.

In the past forty minutes, in this lull which was still lasting, Nick had conferred with the commodore and then re-formed the convoy into four columns. *Calliope* was leading now, on her own between the block of merchantmen and the destroyer screen, which as usual was spread across from bow to bow in an arrow-head formation. He'd put two of the minesweepers into vacant billets at the rear of columns one and four, while the third, *Rattray*, was astern between the two trawlers guarding the assembly's rear. The two oilers were in the middle, well surrounded and with the AA ship right astern of them.

Fog a few miles to the north looked dense, but there'd be ice there too. His prayer was for the fog to spread south. But to be of any value it would need to happen quickly: the Luftwaffe would be as aware as he was himself that there were only a few hours of daylight left, and they'd be keen to take advantage of the light and of these calm conditions while they lasted.

Some sort of mix-up developing astern. He swung round, with his glasses lifting . . .

Bayleaf, in trouble again?

Focusing on the oiler's stubby, rather old-fashioned shape – bridge superstructure separate from and some distance for'ard of the upright, solid-looking funnel –

which at this moment was leaking black smoke. The *Bayleaf* was no juvenile: she'd been launched in 1917, with triple-expansion engines to give her fourteen knots – which was more than most currently available oilers could claim, and would explain her inclusion in this convoy. He remembered that bomb bursting within a few feet of her side: and plainly the repair job hadn't lasted, so here was a major problem back again . . . Swanwick the ADO chose this moment to present him with another one as well.

'Radar has bogeys on bearing one-eight-four, sir, nineteen miles, closing!'

'Flag-hoist, Chief.'

'Large formation, sir – fifty to sixty aircraft!'

He murmured, 'Better and better.' Watching the *Bayleaf* still dropping back, smoke coming out of that funnel in black gushes that would be visible for miles.

Flags rushed bright and fluttering to the yardarm.

'Chief yeoman – make to the *Bayleaf*, "What speed can you maintain?" And to the commodore, "Request speed reduction to five knots to keep *Bayleaf* with us. Large formation of aircraft approaching from south".'

That number of bombers against so small a convoy would be hard to cope with. He was also aware that a lot of ammunition had already been expended. With about two hours of daylight left, and then from dawn tomorrow something like 400 miles to cover – forty hours if you could make-good ten knots, but twice that long on the *Bayleaf*'s present showing.

'From *Bayleaf*, sir, "About seven knots. Regret funnel-smoke temporarily uncontrollable".'

'Range sixteen miles!'

'By light to the *Bayleaf* – "Convoy speed five knots. Resume station before arrival of bomber formation now fifteen miles south". Then TBS to Rabble: "Speed five for *Bayleaf* to catch up. Radar indicates incoming bomber strength fifty to sixty".'

Convoy speed was already falling, and there was some bunching in the columns. The last thing one wanted was confusion just as an attack came in. *Calliope*'s guns were cocked up to starboard and inching round as they followed the radar bearing. Treseder grumbled, with his glasses up, under the rim of a tin hat which had three short gold stripes on it, 'One escort carrier. Fighters'd be scrambling now. All the difference in the world.'

He was right – although it wasn't much use moaning about it. If they'd had a carrier with them, her fighters would be airborne and winging out to break up that attack before it came anywhere near the convoy.

'Bearing one-nine-five. Range fourteen . . .'

Bayleaf, shepherded by *Arctic Prince*, was creeping up past the AA ship while the *Earl Granville* edged over to port to give her more room. If she was making seven knots to the convoy's five, the 400 yards she had still to cover would take – mental arithmetic – six minutes . . . Anyway she was pretty well in the fold, close under the umbrella of the *Berkeley*'s guns and with the sweeper *Radstock* on her port quarter. The minesweepers each had two four-inch AA guns, as well as Oerlikons.

He thought, Five minutes: then we can increase by two knots . . .

'Captain, sir.'

Swanwick: looking puzzled. 'Range has begun to open, sir!'

Nick thought, Impossible. Radar's getting it wrong again . . . Then he saw a possible explanation. 'Probably circling away to come up astern.' Treseder was staring critically at Swanwick. Nick guessed the attackers might be making a wider sweep now because they might not be sure of the convoy's exact position. But once they caught sight of the *Bayleaf*'s smoke-signals . . .

'Range sixteen miles, sir!'

'Bearing?'

'Two-oh-three, sir . . .'

So they'd be flying northwestward, roughly. Circling clockwise, they'd come to the ice and then turn east, ending by coming up astern. One factor was they'd be at the limits of their fuel-range; they wouldn't have much margin in hand for hanging around, up here.

Treseder said, '*Bayleaf*'s almost in station, sir.'

Things were better than they might have been. But in the back of his mind was a sharp awareness of losses incurred already, depleted ammo stocks, distance still to cover, possible fuelling problems if *Bayleaf*'s troubles got any worse.

'Bearing two-oh-oh, range eighteen, opening!'

Bruce Christie said, quietly but with an air of certainty, 'They're pushing off, sir.'

A bit too soon, he thought, to jump to that happy conclusion. He told Ellinghouse, 'Ask the *Bayleaf*, "Can you maintain seven knots now?"'

Leading Signalman Merry jumped to the ten-inch lamp and began to call the oiler.

'Bearing one-nine-four, sir, twenty miles!'

They might still turn back: might realise their mistake and make a cast in this direction. He guessed they'd decided they'd been heading too far east: but whatever the reason, it seemed to be the second miracle of the day.

'Radar lost target, sir . . .'

So – all right. For the moment, count your blessings. But he couldn't imagine the Germans not having another try, while daylight lasted. Three quarters of an hour later, when he was in the chartroom and Treseder came to tell him that radar had picked up a new incoming bogey, he was only surprised they'd been so slow about it. Drawing at a newly-filled pipe, he went up the ladder to the forebridge. He'd been studying the chart, working out how the convoy route might be altered to cope with the speed-reduction *Bayleaf*'s problems had forced on him; her master had said he could maintain the seven knots, with any luck, but he needed a few days with the machinery shut down, to make a proper job of it.

Seven knots meant a thirty per cent longer exposure to bombing between here and Archangel.

'Where are they?'

'It's a single aircraft this time, sir. Bearing one-seven-three, range nineteen miles.'

He got up on his seat. One fast all-round look showed convoy and escorts all in station. He'd come up here expecting an attack to be coming in, and it seemed this must be a recce flight, a scout sent to check on how that last expedition had gone wrong.

'Radar confirms one single aircraft, sir. Bearing one-seven-four, range seventeen.'

An idea kindling . . . With the chart in his mind's eye, and this convoy's position on it, and the rough line of the ice and this snooper nosing up towards them from the south . . . Time now being 18.07: about an hour of daylight left, say. Hardly time, therefore, for a new bomber strike to be launched – unless one was already on its way, this snooper out ahead of it as guide.

'Bearing one-seven-eight, fifteen miles!'

He thought the recce flight would have been sent north – this one and perhaps others too – because that large strike had failed to locate its target. They'd hardly have sent off another full-scale strike without first locating the convoy. Fifty bombers burnt a lot of gas. This reconnaissance, he guessed, would be aimed at pinpointing the target so that new attacks could be launched at dawn.

He had his glasses on what looked more like cloud than fog. Sea-hugging murk with the ice somewhere inside it.

'One-seven-five, range thirteen!'

Drawing slightly left, but near-enough steady to be sure that unless the snooper gave up and turned for home in the next few minutes, he was bound to find this convoy.

So – make it worth his while? Make use of him?

There wasn't time to sit and think about it. You either did it or you didn't. And the passive line – waiting, and accepting punishment – never got anybody anywhere worthwhile.

'Chief yeoman – make to the commodore. "Request immediate emergency turn starboard".'

He saw Treseder trying to fathom it. He was a direct, rather simple man, and his thoughts – puzzlement, now – showed in his face. Ellinghouse had put his leading signalman on that job: Nick told him, 'Now to the *Carrickmore*. Tell him, "Hurricane stand by. Target a snooper closing on bearing one-seven-oh range twelve. Do not launch until further order".'

The *Tacora*'s siren wailed, ordering the turn. Nick told Harvey Smith, 'Bring her round.' Then to the chief yeoman, 'TBS to Tinker. Captain to captain.' Ellinghouse called *Moloch* and got Trench on the line, then handed Nick the microphone.

'Tommy, and Rabble, listen to this. This emergency turn starboard is for the benefit of a snooper coming in on bearing one-seven-oh. I want him to think our mean course is southeast. So move *Laureate* and *Legend* from the port wing to the starboard wing – now, passing astern of the convoy . . . Second point: this snooper is not to be fired on. I want him to get his report out, before I set our tame bird-man on him. D'you understand? Over.'

Shifting those two to the other wing of the screen would help to make the course look like southeast. The emergency turn wasn't as good as wheeling would have been; it was simply the quick way to get them round. It had to be done quickly because otherwise the recce 'planes pilot might see the bend in the convoy's wakes, and decline to be bamboozled.

Bruce Christie was wearing an enigmatic highland smile

as the convoy steadied on the course of 130 degrees. Treseder reported, with his glasses on the *Carrickmore*, 'Pilot's in his Hurricane, sir.'

'Good.' The commodore was flying the signal for 'Commence zigzag'. A lookout shouted, 'Aircraft – green four-oh, angle of sight ten!'

Zigzag recommencing now: the first leg would be to starboard, putting the convoy on a course of 170. The pattern of ships would be confusing to the airmen, but they'd be sure to settle for a southeasterly mean course. Nick watched the Dornier as it came in closer: it might have been the same one that had visited them this morning.

'Swanwick – tell radar to watch for any new formations.'

Because this might be a scout heralding the arrival of an attacking force . . .

He'd be transmitting now, anyway. Circling up towards the bow. Could they recognise a CAM-ship when they saw one, Nick wondered? The fighter on its launching gear was very noticeable – from here. Perhaps less so from the air than in this low profile view.

Treseder asked diffidently, 'Might have sent his message out by now, sir?'

'Yes. But I want him astern, where he won't see the launch.'

He wondered how the Hurricane pilot would be feeling. Sitting there waiting, knowing his flight could only end with a swim in ice-cold sea. It wasn't usual, to send CAM-ships with Arctic convoys.

'Pilot's got out. He's going aft to the bridge.'

'Chief yeoman. Make to the *Carrickmore*, "Dornier now bears – whatever true bearing is – circling anti-clockwise. I will order launch when target is astern. Following destruction of enemy, Hurricane should ditch close to starboard wing destroyer, who will be ready for pick-up".'

Ellinghouse scribbling it down on his pad, one shoulder

braced against the ship's side for support against the roll
. . . 'Give me the microphone, will you. What's *Lyric*'s codename?'

'Richman, sir.'

Zigzag bell again, for a swing back to port. Over TBS to
Lyric's captain, Nick suggested warm blankets and hot
whisky should be ready for the Fleet Air Arm pilot. He
watched the Dornier limping round the bow, thinking that
with any luck they'd be in for a much longer swim.

Long, icy-looking swells sliding in on the beam rolled
Calliope heavily as they ran under her. All ships in convoy
were feeling it – masts swaying like metronomes, and deck-
cargoes would be straining at chocks and lashings.

'Message passed, sir.'

The Dornier was flying from the port bow round towards
the beam. And the convoy was now steering 130 degrees.
The next leg of the zigzag would be to port, bringing the
German back from the quarter to the beam again; but the
turn after that, to starboard, would put him right astern.
With six minutes on each leg, say in twelve minutes.

He checked the time . . .

'Call the *Carrickmore* again. Make, "I expect to order
launch in about ten minutes. Good luck".'

The pilot would be on her bridge to take in that message,
and watching his target as it circled. Target so far unaware
that it was a target – or victim . . . The Hurricane's engine
would be ticking over, warming up. Leading Signalman
Merry had begun to pass that signal, and Nick ran over
the plan in his mind, looking for flaws in it . . . First, the
Dornier had to be shot down, having already reported the
convoy as being on course for Archangel or Kola: so at first
light the Luftwaffe would be out hunting for it a long way
south, perhaps only about 200 miles from its destination.
When they didn't find it, that would be the general area
they'd search. In fact, PQ 19 would have turned north –
into the ice and its attendant fog. The southern area of the

ice should be navigable, loose and patchy after the comparative warmth of the summer months. Up there he'd detach
the *Bayleaf*, with a trawler as escort and if necessary ice-
breaker, destination Hope Island, to anchor in the island's
lee and make those repairs she needed, while the trawler
kept her from getting iced-in. The convoy would meanwhile push on eastward at twelve knots, just clear of the
ice until daylight and then in it – in fog too, please God
– through the daylight hours. Then at dusk tomorrow, right
turn, for Archangel. If it all worked out, the enemy would
have mislaid their target for something like thirty-six
hours.

He explained these intentions, briefly, to Treseder, with
Bruce Christie bending an ear to the explanation.

'What about the *Bayleaf*, sir?'

'We'll rendezvous with her north of Bear Island on our
way west with the return convoy.'

Treseder nodded. 'And fuelling the destroyers?'

'Tomorrow. Under cover of fog, I hope. The Russians'll
have to improve on their performance quite a lot – we
might put a few stokers on board her to speed them up.'

Christie coughed. 'Might not get 'em back, sir. Half that
Russian crew's female.'

Nick had his glasses on the CAM-ship; he'd seen the
pilot walk for'ard and climb into his machine, and now
the convoy had completed its turn to port. Christie was
asking, 'One thing, sir – what if the ice is too thick for the
Bayleaf to make Hope Island?'

'She could simply lie-up. Stop engines. Weather and fog
permitting. The trawler would have to keep on the move,
circling her. Alternative would be to make for Bell Sund,
in Spitzbergen.' With an eye on the Dornier, which was
now limping round to the convoy's quarter, he checked the
time . . .

Zigzag bell. Helms would be going over to starboard
now.

'Chief – make to the *Carrickmore* – "Launch".'

He'd trained his binoculars on the CAM-ship's foc'sl again. *Calliope* rolling fiercely as she turned: and the Dornier would be astern now. He could hear the clack of the Aldis, identify each letter by the sound. Last letter, and now the signing-off group . . . He saw a lick of flame, bright in the fading light, as the launcher fired: the Hurricane shot forward, and was airborne. Banking to starboard, but still low, using the ships as cover as he picked up speed, throttle wide open and flying at wavetop height across the convoy's van: only seconds after the launch the fighter sped past astern of *Calliope*. The pilot wouldn't have seen those caps being waved at him: he'd have his mind on other things entirely, mainly the Dornier – still there, completing its circuit of the convoy. Out of gun-range, of course, feeling safe, doing its best to ensure the destruction of these ships and the deaths of the men who sailed them. That Dornier crew would have no legitimate grounds for complaint, Nick thought. The Hurricane pilot would want to get as close as possible before the Germans spotted him: he'd catch them easily enough, but he wouldn't want a longer chase than necessary. He'd swung around the *Galilee Dawn* and he was hard to see now, with other ships in the way. A glimpse, just for a second, as he flew across the space between the *Galilee* and the *Republican*: then after a moment he was in sight again – climbing, and heading westward. The Dornier was several miles out on that same quarter: it was turning, evidently preparing to fly up parallel to the convoy's course at a discreet distance off to starboard.

'They've seen him!'

Treseder was right . . .

The Dornier had rolled to starboard, swinging violently away. A panic reaction – but the Germans didn't have a hope. One young Fleet Air Arm man had them at his mercy – which in the next half-minute might not be exactly brimming . . . The Dornier was trying to run for it – low to the sea, but with the Hurricane already there, going down on his tail in a shallow, killing dive.

No sound. It was happening too far away, and the background sound was the roar of *Calliope*'s fans, the slamming of sea as she rolled. There was a flash, out there: the Dornier's nose came up in a convulsive effort to remain alive before it nose-dived into the sea. A leap of spray caught the dying light as the Hurricane swept over its kill; then it was turning, banking steeply round, perhaps looking to see if there might be survivors on the wreckage. But by the time a destroyer could have got there, any swimmer would have died of cold. A few minutes was all it took: you either pulled them out instantly, or you found Tussaud-like dummies with open, staring eyes, stiff in their life jackets, bobbing to the waves. He'd seen it, more than once: and he was thinking about the Fleet Air Arm boy now, who'd be the same age more or less as his own son, Paul.

Who was doing God-knew-what, to be so close-mouthed about it . . . His thoughts returned to the pilot as the Hurricane steadied on a course to fly back up the convoy's starboard side.

Nick reached for the microphone.

'Richman, this is Thief. Your guest is about to drop in. Get him out double quick, now. Over.'

He switched to 'receive', and waited. It was only seconds before the answer came.

Thief – this is Richman. Lieutenant-Commander Clegg speaking, sir. We're ready for him, and the whisky's warm. Out.

You couldn't see it from here – *Lyric* being about four miles away – but she'd have a whaler manned and low on its falls, ready to slip, a scrambling-net rigged and her doctor waiting with the rescue party.

'Chief.' Nick was looking for the Hurricane, but it was out of sight, down at sea-level and hidden behind the ships of the starboard columns. 'Make to the commodore, "Request alteration of course to zero-two-zero".'

He'd explain it all to Insole later, over the loud-hailer.

The Hurricane was in sight for about two seconds before it bounced into the sea close to *Lyric*. On the far side of her. A sheet of foam flung up, travelled with the skidding fighter and, then vanished. All you could see then was *Lyric*'s length shortening as she swung to starboard, losing way.

'They'll have him all right.' Treseder talking to himself, with glasses at his eyes. 'Can't see a bloody thing . . .'

TBS hummed into life . . .

'Thief – this is Richman.' It was Clegg's voice again. 'Sub-lieutenant Jones is in good shape and tucking-in to the refreshment. Barely got his toes wet, I'm glad to say. Over.'

Nick laughed. Out of relief, more than amusement. He thumbed the switch to 'transmit'.

'Richman, this is Thief. Well done. Give Sub-lieutenant Jones my congratulations. Out.'

And now – the ice . . .

6

⟨═══──◆═════⟩

From the railed Oerlikon deck at the back of *Setter*'s bridge, Paul watched X-12 as the Manilla rope took the strain, hauling the midget's bow around. Tow beginning now – and a thousand miles to go . . . Dusk was spreading over the lower slopes of the surrounding hills, shadowing the water of the loch, and the last glow of cloud-filtered sunshine was highlighting the depot ship's silhouette; from *Setter*'s bridge a bosun's call squealed in salute, and *Bonaventure*'s bugle – a nobler, rounder note – acknowledged the tin whistle . . . MacGregor, the submarine's captain, was at the salute, all hands in her bridge and on the casing at attention, *Bonaventure*'s high decks crowded with sailors. The bugle sang out again, signalling 'Carry on', and the pipe shrilled; then for the fourth time on this Saturday afternoon that crowd of men were cheering, waving their caps, shouting final 'good lucks'.

It was quite a moment, Paul thought. Conceivably, historic.

Jazz Lanchberry took a plainer view. He growled, 'We really gone an' done it, now.'

'Unless anyone wants to jump off and swim.' Brazier pointed astern, at Louis Gimber erect on X-12's casing with an arm hooked round the induction trunk. 'I wouldn't blame that poor sod if he did.'

Nobody envied the passage crews. *Setter* was quite a small submarine and her wardroom was going to be uncomfortably crowded, but it would be like living in the Ritz, compared to the eight days' close confinement facing Messrs Gimber, Steep and Towne in that tin sardine-can two hundred yards astern.

At least the weather forecasts had been good. At this time of year it was a toss-up whether you'd have fair weather or force ten gales, and the prospect of a tow across the Norwegian Sea at its worst, or even half-worst, was not a happy one. But for the next few days the outlook wasn't at all bad.

They were about to pass the other depot ship, *Titania*. It still wasn't quite sunset, so the piping ritual was starting all over again. After sundown, you didn't have to do it: but now – salutes, followed by more cheers, a sea of waving caps . . . That small, dark object astern – Gimber saluting with his free right hand as he faced the old depot ship's upperworks looming above him – looked ridiculously small, even in the confines of the loch. In open sea it would look and feel like a toy.

As lethal as it was miniature. But not necessarily lethal only to the enemy. Brazier murmured, as the 'Carry on' sounded for the second time, 'D'you think we're all nuts?'

Dick Eaton nodded. Beside Brazier he was like a whippet in company with a Great Dane. Paul said, 'Think how good it'll feel when we've done it.' He waved his cap for the last time, settled it back on his head; Lanchberry observed, 'Like banging your swede on a wall so it'll be nicer when it stops?'

Setter and X-12 were the third team to sail. First out had been Don Cameron's X-6, in tow of *Truculent*. Willy Wilson had the passage command. Then Kearon's X-9, behind *Syrtis*. Now X-12; and later – with the last of them not leaving until tomorrow, Sunday – would be X-5, whose operational CO was Henty-Creer and towing ship *Thrasher*; X-8 towed by *Seanymph*; Godfrey Place's X-7, passage crew commanded by the South African Peter Philip, towing ship *Stubborn*; Hudspeth's X-10 with *Sceptre*, and X-11 – Dan Vicary's boat – towed by *Scourge*.

Eaton said, 'You could shut your eyes and believe this was just another bloody exercise.'

Paul had the same feeling – difficulty in grasping that this was it, the real thing at last. After so long, the long period of training first at Blockhouse and then in the Firth of Clyde at Port Bannatyne and Loch Striven, and then finally up here in Sutherland . . . It had seemed at times like interminable preparation for something that might never happen.

Even until yesterday there'd been no certainty. Then the news had broken like a clap of thunder – *Tirpitz* and *Scharnhorst* back in their anchorages. A preliminary report of it had come early in the forenoon, from some intelligence source, and later it had been confirmed by Spitfire reconnaissance from North Russia. The Spits' photographs were being flown down from Russia by Catalina flying-boat, but in advance of their arrival the decision had been taken immediately by Flag Officer Submarines: Operation Source was to go ahead, on schedule and with departures commencing next day – today, Saturday 11 September. The admiral himself had flown up to Port HHZ to see them off.

Sunset now: from astern, bugles sounded as ensigns were ceremoniously lowered. *Setter* was passing various other Twelfth Flotilla craft now, and astern of her X-12 was towing easily in the sheltered, darkening water. There was some more waving and shouting: if you allowed yourself to feel it, there was a touch of emotion in this farewell – but not much to be heard over the rumble of the submarine's diesels. One last contact with the shoreside lay ahead, where Admiral Barry, accompanied by the two flotilla

captains, had put out in the *Bonaventure*'s motorboat to
bestow a final blessing on his children as they left home.
He'd given a dinner party for them last night, on board
Titania: it had been a lively evening, with a lot of shop-talk
but good food and drink as well, and the admiral on top
of his form, clearly delighted by the cheerful confidence
around him. The party had continued later – for some –
back on board *Bonaventure*.

A fly in the ointment was the non-arrival of those reconnaissance photos. They were needed for a final check on
the positions of the targets and of the nets enclosing them.
Without those pictures the final attack plan – choice of
certain alternatives, but including the allocation of the
various X-craft to this or that target – couldn't be decided.
Barry had ordained they'd sail without them, with final
details to be settled later by signal to the towing ships.

Crawshaw, *Setter*'s first lieutenant, called a warning
from the forepart of the bridge: 'Here's FOSM – port side,
chaps . . .'

Flag Officer Submarines, Claude himself, waving his
brass hat and shouting goodbye, good luck . . . MacGregor
saluting, and the X-craft men on the Oerlikon platform
responding too. The motorboat was nosing in close to the
tow, to within hailing distance of Louis Gimber – who in
this fading light could have been a scarecrow perched on
a half-tide rock. The admiral would be well aware that the
passage-crew assignment was going to be at least as
hazardous as the attack itself.

Voices carried across the water, over the rumble of diesel
exhaust; motorboat and X-craft were practically alongside
each other, with a lot of talk in progress. Brazier asked
Paul, 'Louis somewhat pissed last night, was he?'

'He wasn't the only one.'

Eaton smiled. 'Say that again. Old Dan, for one.'

Lanchberry said, 'You're a bunch of alcoholics. Opened
my eyes, this lark has, to wardroom antics.'

'Never saw you exactly abstaining, Jazz.'

'Well. When in Rome . . .'

After dinner last night Paul had gone to his cabin in the depot ship to finish a batch of letters he'd started earlier – one to his mother in Connecticut, one to his father, and the longest to Jane – when Louis Gimber had sloped in, distinctly under the weather.

'Writing letters, eh.'

He'd thought of answering no, feeling trees. But he had an inclination to be kind to Gimber. Because of Jane – which was at least partly a sense of guilt – and for the bad luck of drawing the passage-crew job. It certainly wouldn't have been a good idea to have Louis know he was at this moment writing to his girl – or the girl he thought of as his. When Jane wrote to Paul she used a typewriter and plain white paper instead of the violet-coloured stationery she used to Gimber. She was so good at this kind of thing, seemed to take it so naturally, that Paul sometimes wondered how much practice she'd had in the arts of two-timing. She'd certainly had some: for instance, talking about her dead fighter-pilot husband, she'd mentioned quite freely that the squadron's CO had 'had a thing' for her, that he'd more than once taken advantage of Tom's absence from the station to take her out dining and dancing. There'd been some bits of the narrative missing, non-cohesive, suggesting more to it than she'd cared to divulge: and whether her volunteering that much, so unashamedly, was an indication of amorality or innocence was hard to say. But she could tell that story, and still weep for Tom . . . One aspect Paul saw and understood was that since he had no thoughts of any permanent relationship with her, while Louis Gimber did at times propose marriage, she felt she could afford to share her secrets – or some of them – with him, but not with Louis; which might suggest she was taking a raincheck on the marriage idea?

'I've done all my letters.' Gimber leant against the

bulkhead – white-enamelled steel, and exposed piping, angle-irons; this was just a steel hutch for a man to sleep in and stow his gear. He added, slurring slightly, 'Left hers open so's to add a few famous last words. Give her your love, shall I?'

Paul turned the envelope which he'd already addressed to Jane over on its face, and left his hand on it.

'Jane?' He nodded. 'Please do.'

'Smoke?'

'No, thanks.'

'D'you have a few popsies to write to Paul?'

'A dozen or so regulars. Plus a few reserves.' He folded the letter to his father and slid it into its envelope, addressed to HMS *Calliope*, c/o GPO London. 'But that's to my old man.'

'Where's he now?'

Paul shrugged. 'Not the faintest.'

'Sent him your Last Will and Testicles?'

He shook his head. 'That's silly, Louis. We're going to pull this job off, and survive.' He saw cynicism in Gimber's dark-skinned face. 'I'm sure of it. And the others all feel the same. We know what we're up against, we've sorted out the problems – what the hell.'

'You're still writing letters.'

'I often do. Particularly when I know I'm going to be away on patrol or something for a while. A letter doesn't have to be a suicide note, you know.'

'Qui' a few of the others have made wills.'

'They must be concerned for their worldly goods, more than I am.' He pointed. 'Some dirty shirts in that drawer, and odds and ends, is all. They send that kind of stuff to your next-of-kin automatically . . . Anyway – I want to finish this letter, Louis, then get some sleep.'

'I'll give her your love, eh?'

'Thank you. Fine.'

'If you come back and I don't, Paul—'

'Oh, stuff that!'

'—would you see she's all right?'

'Certainly.' He shrugged. 'Although I imagine she'd survive pretty well without my help. But – sure, you can count on it.'

He thought it was much more likely to be Gimber who got back, if it had to be one or the other of them, and that Jane would survive the loss of either or both of them very well, even stylishly. He had no idea at this time, of course, how absolutely right he was.

'But,' Gimber pointed at him with a waving finger, 'what I'm saying is – look after her. Really look after . . .'

'Message received, Louis. Loud and clear. Wilco, out – because it's getting bloody late and we need to be fit tomorrow, and you're shall we say slightly—'

'Paul.'

He sighed. 'Yes, Louis.'

'You're a real bastard, aren't you?'

He smiled at him. Not really wanting to go into anything like that too deeply, here and now. He said, 'I suppose I could be. But you're as pissed as a coot, old horse.'

'So I am.' Nodding, as at a declaration of profound truth. 'So I am. But you hear this. If I get back, I'm going to marry her. Hear me? Marry her!'

'Delighted for you both. Marvellous. I'll be your best man, if you like. But now for God's sake, Louis, go to bed.'

'Bastard!'

'Louis – fuck off?'

You wouldn't have mistaken that object astern for a prospective bridegroom. In these last shreds of daylight it looked more like a palm-stump on a sand-spit. *Setter* and X-12 were emerging from the loch, pushing out into the loppy water of the bay. The light might last just about long enough for a sight of the midget when she slipped under, Paul thought.

The 'thing' between himself and Jane – 'thing' being her

word for an affair, possibly deriving from the currently popular song *Just One of Those Things* – had started in the first instant they'd set eyes on each other. Right at the start of the party, to which he'd taken a girl he'd met the day before. Jane of course had been with Louis. Later – it was a dinner-dance at the Dorchester in aid of some 'good cause' – he'd asked her to dance, and she'd moved into his arms as if she'd been wondering when he'd suggest it. Dancing together again much later, at the Bag o' Nails, he'd dated her for the following weekend. She was a WAAF, Women's Auxiliary Air Force, and was stationed at some secret establishment in Buckinghamshire where most of the personnel were Wrens; this in some indirect way was how she'd met Louis Gimber. Paul had proposed that she might come up to London next weekend: she'd told him with her head back, looking at him under those long brown eyelashes, 'One condition. Not a word to Louis.'

'You got it.'

'Sometimes you sound quite American.'

'My mother married one. After she and my father split up, when I was a kid. She lives in Connecticut, with her millionaire, and – well, I was at college over there.'

'What fun!'

'My father's more so. He's terrific. He has a new wife too now, an Australian army nurse. She was in a hospital unit in Crete and he snatched her from some beach under the noses of the Germans. How's that for romance?'

'You're an interesting bunch, you Everards.' She'd moved closer: not for long enough for Gimber to have seen it but long enough for Paul to know it and for the glow to brighten. 'Tell me all about them next Saturday?'

Then on the Tuesday of that week, at lunch-time, he was coming in through the hall of the wardroom block – at Fort Blockhouse, the submarine headquarters at Gosport – just as Gimber emerged from the glass-walled telephone kiosk. Gimber looked unhappy.

'What's up, Louis?'

'You can buy me a beer, if you like.' They went into the mess. Gimber told him, 'I just rang Jane. But she's on duty this weekend, can't get away. So—' he shook his head; he seemed surprised as well as disappointed. 'Too bad. I won't bother to go up, there's no point. But she never had weekend duties before – she told me, the WAAFS don't have to because the poor bloody Wrens do it all, for some reason.'

'Well, you better find yourself another girl.'

'There isn't another girl!'

'How about Betty?'

Betty lived in Southsea, on the other side of the harbour, and at one time Gimber had been more or less shacked up with her. At one time or another, quite a few submariners had been – more or less . . . Gimber muttered, as if that once familiar name hadn't been mentioned, 'Now I know Jane, there never will be.'

'Bad as that, Louis?'

'Don't you think she's a smasher?'

'Well.' He'd looked away. Feeling more like a heel than he'd have liked. But nodding: 'Since you mention it. She's really something.'

That Saturday he took her to the Gay Nineties, then dinner at the United Hunts Club in Upper Grosvenor Street; much later, it was her idea that they should go to the Bag o' Nails. For old times' sake, she suggested – 'old times' meaning the previous weekend. It was already foggy at midnight, but when they left the nightclub that Sunday morning London had been gripped in a really thick, traditional pea-souper, un-navigable without radar and a compass. It was also bitterly cold, and Jane was audibly whimpering, cat-like sounds emanating from the bundle of fur coat stumbling beside him, fur arms hugging one of his while they blundered in a mile-wide circle and twice asked directions from the same policeman who loomed up, at about one yard's visibility and after a half-hour interval, on the same street corner. The policeman was an elderly reservist, a 'special', and his attitude on the second occasion was paternal as well as humorous. He advised them to give up trying to get to where Paul had had hopes of finding a taxi; he directed them instead to a hotel only about one block away. There was a night-clerk on duty, and a room available – which was providential, because there were never any rooms to be had in London at weekends. From there on memory was confused but interspersed with moments of graphic recollection: then he'd been waking up in grey morning light, Jane's eyes slowly opening – those huge, thick eyelashes, eyes greenish in her pale, oval face with its surrounding heap of very soft, dark-brown hair. She'd been puzzled, trying to remember, the tip of her tongue testing sore lips. The green eyes wider then, fixed on his.

'Paul?'

He kissed her. 'Well done. Clever girl!'

Meaning she'd got his name right. She'd protested: 'I must've been plastered. All that hooch! You shouldn't've—'

'If you were stinko, how d'you know we did?'

'I—' she'd shut her eyes – 'I do know.'

'You were frozen. It was an act of charity.'

The green eyes slid open: surprise gave way to laughter which had to be smothered in the bedclothes because of people in the rooms on both sides; then they'd begun to make love again, conscious of each other and their isolation, the silence of London all around them – London fogbound, gagged and blindfold.

Six weeks later, after the training programme had been transferred to Scotland, he'd been planning a weekend in London. In fact he'd had to spend the following week at Vickers Armstrong at Barrow, where X-12 was being completed, and the duty trip was giving him the chance of a few days off which he'd spend with Jane. Before he'd left Gosport they'd met whenever it had been possible; she'd come down to a pub in Petersfield one weekend, and for another they'd met in Midhurst. But there wasn't much leave being granted from Port Bannatyne at this stage. Then Louis Gimber had astonished him by suggesting, 'Care to give Jane a ring? Take her out for a meal, or something? I'd like to hear how she really is – and you could explain why I can't get away for a month or so?'

'Well – I'd really planned to spend most of the weekend with Sally, but I suppose . . .'

Lying came easily, which it never had before. In fancy he wondered whether he could have been possessed by the spirit of the late Jack Everard, his half-uncle, to whom the ends – personal inclinations – had always justified the means . . . But another aspect was Gimber's own embarrassment, and recognition that what he was after was a check on Jane, on what other involvements she might have now Louis himself was so far away.

Paul had nodded. 'OK. Where can I get hold of her?'

Setter's casing party were climbing up into the bridge and dropping down into the hatch. Last to come was Bob Henning, the ship's gunnery and torpedo officer. He reported to MacGregor, 'Casing secured, sir.'

'Very good.' MacGregor raised his voice: 'Everard, want to talk to your pal, ask him if he's ready to dive?'

'Aye aye, sir.' He lowered himself on to the ladder and climbed down into the submarine's control room. The helmsman looked round, then turned back to his gyro repeater ribbon, and the PO of the watch – it was the coxswain, CPO Bird – growled, 'Evenin', sir. All right, are they?'

'Just about to check.'

This end of the tow-line telephone was in the wireless office, a cupboard-sized box between the control room and the engine-room. Paul edged in, nodding to the two operators, one of whom was reading *Picture Post*.

'I want a word with X-12.'

'Be our guest, sir.'

He pointed at a nude pin-up on a grey metal case of radio gear. 'Rather be hers.'

'Ah, well . . .'

'Hello, X-12?' He wound the handle again. 'X-12, d'you hear me?'

Ozzie Steep's voice came through thinly, under a lot of extraneous noise. 'Steep here. Hello?'

'Hello, Ozzie. Everard . . . All well there?'

'All fine so far, sir. Want the skipper?'

'Yes, please.' There was a loud thrumming, a fluctuating roar, and most of it would be the noise from the induction pipe, sea and wind. Gimber would be climbing down inside now; Steep could have passed the telephone up to him but over that racket at sea-level you wouldn't have heard much.

'You there, Paul?'

'How goes it?'

'No problems – yet. Time to dive now?'

'We're ready when you are.'

'OK. As soon as she slows, I'll pull the plug.'

'Communications check at twenty-two hundred, then every two hours. And you'll surface for a guff-through at oh-two-double-oh, right?'

He went back up to the bridge. The telegraphist on watch would answer any emergency calls from the X-craft. *Setter* would reduce speed for the actual dive, then work up to ten knots again. X-12 would tow at about sixty or one hundred feet – Gimber's option – depending on sea conditions, comfort and stability, and every six hours he'd surface for fifteen minutes to ventilate the boat.

He told MacGregor, 'They're ready to dive, sir.'

Setter's captain ducked to the voicepipe: 'One hundred revolutions!'

Back there astern you could see the white flare that was the midget's bow-wave, but not much else, even with binoculars. He wondered – as presently that white patch faded, disappeared, the sea mending itself over the tiny craft which would now be at the mercy of every tug and strain imparted via the heavy Manilla rope – wondered what Jane would think of it: her 'earnest' boyfriend on the submerged end of 200 yards of rope and her 'charitable' one – that adjective had stuck in her mind, since his 'act of charity' in the hotel – here at this end of it, with a thousand miles to cover, and then God only knew what outcome . . .

Gimber's chances depended on that rope and on the weather holding up. Paul's rested on a dozen or more factors, and the most important element might be luck.

'Nip down to the telephone, Dick, and let us know when Louis's ready for ten knots.'

The towing submarines would stay on the surface until they were much nearer the target area, because the rate of progress dived would have been too slow. Nearer the Norwegian coast they'd be dived for reasons of security – which was primarily why the midgets were to keep out of sight right from the start. One chance sighting by some recce aircraft or U-boat could abort the whole operation: the bases in Norway would be alerted, anti-submarine forces concentrated, quite likely the target ships moved elsewhere.

On his way to the wardroom for supper, Paul stopped for a look at the chart. The first few days' courses were already pencilled in. From Cape Wrath, course for all the towing submarines would take them through a point seventy-five miles west of the Shetlands, and from there they'd diverge, fanning out on to parallel tracks twenty miles apart for the long haul northeastward.

Soames, *Setter*'s navigator, paused beside him.

'Make sense?'

'More or less.' Turning his back on the chart, he was in the gangway but to all intents and purposes also in the small space known as the wardroom. 'What bothers me is how we're all going to fit in here.'

In fact there were five bunks; but one was always empty, its owner on watch, so one extra man could be accommodated by 'working hot bunks' – ie when you came off watch you got into the bunk someone else had just left. There'd be space for another body under the wardroom table – his head and legs would stick out at each end, so he'd be trodden on sometimes – and a hammock was to be slung in the gangway for a third. Jazz Lanchberry was being accommodated in the ERAs' mess, so that would do it.

Brazier pointed out, 'You'll be better off when we make the change-over. Only three in the passage crew, instead of the four of us.'

'But we've got to put up with you for a whole week, first?'

'Eight days, Chief.'

Massingbird, the engineer, shook his head. 'Bloody hell . . .'

MacGregor glanced at him. 'Hospitable little ray of sunshine, isn't he?'

Paul turned in early, using Soames' bunk, Soames having gone up on watch. He was taking the midnight-to-two watch himself, so he left it to Eaton to make the 22.00 communications check, and made another himself when the control room messenger shook him at ten minutes to midnight. It was Ozzie Steep who answered: Gimber was off-watch, he said, asleep in the fore end. That bow compartment was the only place in the X-craft where a man could stretch out full length, on top of the wooden cover of the battery. Steep said everything was all right: plenty to do, but no problems. From the background 'Trigger' Towne shouted, 'No problems yet, chum!' Paul said, 'Give Trigger my regards and tell him he should have more confidence in his own machinery.'

Steep repeated it. Then, 'I won't tell you what his answer is.'

'I can guess. Tell him to get stuffed too. Listen, I'm going on watch now, I'll contact you again just after two. You'll be due for a surfacing then, but tell Louis to wait for my call first, will you?'

The routines wouldn't have to be spelt out, after a day or two. But Towne was right, you did have to expect problems, defects, sooner or later. None of the X-craft had been run for a solid week, for instance, until now. Also, the passage crews were going to be kept busy – checking machinery performance, carrying out constant maintenance and keeping the boat dry. Condensation would be a problem, and damp would be a threat to insulation, and thus all the electrical equipment. There'd be a lot to do, all round the clock, for the two men on watch, and as well as maintenance and mopping up there'd be meals to prepare. The food was all tinned stuff and concentrates, and the cooking equipment consisted of one glue-pot for heating things in, and a kettle. But the maintenance, of course, would have one vitally important purpose – to have the boat in tiptop condition when they reached the Norwegian coast and switched crews.

Keeping his watch in *Setter's* bridge, alone except for the two lookouts behind him while the submarine drove northward at a steady ten knots, Paul was constantly aware of Gimber down there at the end of the tow-rope. Of the fact that they were friends – on the face of it – and also relied on each other for their lives . . . Feet braced apart against the submarine's jolting, wave-bashing motion: binoculars at his eyes in a constant lookout for enemies, searching the surrounding darkness, black sea and an horizon that was no sharp division, only a vague merging of sea and sky . . . One of the discomforting aspects of his involvement with Jane was that it would really devastate Louis Gimber if he ever found out about it. To start with it hadn't seemed so serious: there'd been the phrase 'all's fair in love and war' in mind, and the fact that wartime relationships had tended to be – well, transient; girls like Betty, for instance: nothing so very serious or long-term. But Paul knew he was hooked now, he couldn't have given her up, despite the fact that if Louis got to know about it, it would kill him.

He stooped to the voicepipe.

'Control room . . . Tell the W/T office to call X-12 and ask if they're OK.'

It was an hour since he'd spoken to Ozzie Steep. No harm in an extra check.

He'd asked Jane, a few months ago, why she didn't break it off with Gimber. Why not tell him she didn't love him, so there could be an end to pretence. Jane's answer had been, 'Because I'm really very fond of him. Don't you see? I don't want to hurt him, Paul, why should I?'

'But aren't you deceiving him? You've told me he wants to marry you – if you let him believe it's on the cards – when it isn't, is it? So he has to find out some time, you can't string him along for ever!'

'I can't just brush him off, either – when he's so kind, and . . .'

'But when it gets to a point when he's actually pressing you to marry him?'

'That's just him, it's not my fault. He knows very well that as far as I'm concerned marriage is out of the question. I've told him so – oh, fifty times . . . I've been married – and you know what happened.'

'Wouldn't it be less hurtful in the long run to let him know he doesn't stand a chance?'

'But why should I hurt him like that? When he knows I don't intend marrying anyone while this bloody war's still going?'

Round and round. Leading nowhere.

'Bridge!' He bent to the pipe. The helmsman told him, 'Lieutenant Gimber says all's well, sir!'

'Very good.'

Straightening, resuming the careful all-round search. Behind him the two lookouts, one each side of the bridge, pivotted slowly, each man sweeping from bow to stern and across the stern and then back again. Diesels rumbling through submerged exhausts while the sea rushed and boomed over the curve of the pressure-hull a dozen feet below the perforated platform that he stood on, and white foam seething, leaping, all along the submarine's slim, plunging length.

All Jane knew about Paul's job or Gimber's was that they were submariners and in the same flotilla. When they'd been down in Hampshire, and as often as not free for weekends in London, she'd asked him why none of them ever seemed to go away to sea. She'd said, 'You're like a fighter squadron. A crowd of you all part of the same outfit and – well, always around!'

His mind hadn't been on the question – war, fighter squadrons, X-craft, anything like that.

'You're sensational. Really absolutely . . .'

'So what's the answer?'

She'd been on top, looking down at him, her face in darkness because of the brilliance of the chandelier in the middle of the room behind her. They'd booked into the Savoy, that weekend. Jane's idea – the Savoy being one of a handful of places where you could be just about sure of not running into any of your friends.

'If you don't tell me, I'll just sit here, I shan't move!'

'That's all right. I like the view.'

'Please, tell me?'

'I'll do the moving.'

'About time . . .

'Submarine patrols can be quite short. And some people are what's called spare crew, not permanently in any one boat . . . Did I mention you're the most beautiful thing I ever saw?'

'Bridge!'

He leant down. 'Bridge.'

'Relieve lookout, sir?'

'Yes, please.' So it was now fifteen minutes to the hour. Lookouts and OOWS changed over at staggered times so there'd always be some eyes up here that were already tuned to the dark.

At ten past the hour he was in the W/T office and had Gimber on the telephone. X-12 was due to come up now, to 'guff-through' – meaning to get the stale air out and fresh air in.

'How's it going, Louis?'

'Like always – stuffy and damp. We're porpoising a bit, but not too badly. Any new met forecasts?'

'Not that I know of. Keep your fingers crossed, we might get this weather the whole way over. But stand by, now – we're slowing down.'

Engine noise, and the rush of cold air past the wireless office, lessened as diesel revs decreased. Gimber's voice distantly over the line, 'Stand by to surface', then the click as he hung up and the wire went dead. This was to be the routine for the eight days of towing: four times a day, so thirty-two surfacings and a total of eight hours up top during the whole period. The last surfacing would be for the change-over of crews, close to the entrance to the fjords. Thinking of that as he put the telephone down, Paul was looking forward to the moment, probably as much as Gimber would be: he wanted to get there, get it over.

'Excuse me, sir.'

The telegraphist was holding back an earphone, uncovering the ear on this side. 'Asking about weather forecasts, was he?'

'Yes. Why?'

'On the log, sir. Be on the chart table now, most likely.'

'Thanks.'

He edged out, slid the door shut and moved for'ard.

MacGregor was coming the other way, dressed for the bridge, and the helmsman was shouting up the pipe to Crawshaw, 'Captain coming up, sir!' MacGregor asked Paul, 'Been talking to them?'

He nodded. 'Surfacing now, sir.'

The signal log was on the chart, and the new meteorological report was the top sheet in the clip. At first glance, the first words he saw were bad enough: he began again, getting the detail, wanting that first impression to have been wrong. It had not, though. What this promised was a new weather-pattern approaching from west-southwest and reaching the Norwegian Sea by tomorrow night or the day after – a deep depression accompanied by south-westerly gale-force winds.

7

Light from a new day's dawn glinted on the crests of a lively, rising sea. Wind on the beam, and *Calliope* rolling hard; with his glasses moving slowly across the convoy's bows Nick heard Treseder's gruff report, 'Ship's at action stations, sir.'

He'd only just come out of his sea-cabin, having enjoyed a few hours' sleep. And how good or foul a day this might turn out to be would depend very largely on how soon the Luftwaffe located them. This was the main consideration, at the moment. The amount and height of cloud would be a factor in it and would reveal itself more clearly in the next half hour; but the rising wind might well break it up, however promising it might look to start with, so the wind was to the enemy's advantage.

Another factor was simply luck. And perhaps – recalling his own words of yesterday – no, day before yesterday – it might be unwise to count on more of that, when they'd had so much already. Torpedoes that didn't explode, for instance; and fog in the right place at the right time; and Kidd's cruisers taking the brunt of the Luftwaffe's ire . . .

Until dusk last evening the convoy had still been in pack-ice and its accompanying fog. In air like frozen soup, sea blotched white, a black-and-white surface rising and falling as regularly as if the ocean were taking long, deep breaths; a great ice-bound lung expanding and contracting, surviving in deep sleep, hibernation, blind to the double column of ships forging eastward through it from dawn to dusk, ghost-ships gliding through a mysterious, silent wasteland. *Calliope* had led the starboard column, with the commodore's *Tacora* abeam and the rest of the merchantmen and the AA ship in double file astern. Up ahead the trawler *Northern Glow* had cleared the way where necessary, her strong hull and stem being better suited to occasional arguments with floating ice than a destroyer's thin plating would have been.

From dawn onwards Nick had mentally kept his fingers crossed, dreading an end to the fog-bank where the convoy could, at very short notice, have found itself steaming out into clear, bright day. In fact it had thickened, if anything; then the night was coming and finally they'd finished with it, having taken maximum advantage of its shelter. With the darkness, PQ 19 had re-formed, and steered south.

Now, inevitably, the holiday was over. Or very soon would be.

Northern Glow was the only trawler with them now. *Arctic Prince* was escorting the *Bayleaf* to – or towards – Hope Island. Before they'd diverted, *Bayleaf* had fuelled three of the destroyers, while the *Arctic Prince* had gone scrounging around the convoy to collect as much white paint as could be begged from close-fisted bosuns. Nick had suggested that either at Hope Island or on the way there, or wherever they might have to heave-to, both ships should paint their upperworks white. Then if, or when, the fog lifted they wouldn't so easily be spotted.

The other four destroyers had fuelled during the day from the Russian. Practice had improved the performance of the *Sovyetskaya Slava*'s part-female crew, and it hadn't gone too badly. The *Slava* was back in the middle now, in the centre billet of three columns each of three ships; she had the *Tacora* ahead of her and the AA ship astern, and Americans – the *Plainsman* and the *Republican* – on both sides. *Calliope* was on her own, 400 yards ahead of the commodore, with *Moloch* another 1000 yards ahead and *Harpy* and *Foremost* almost abeam, on the convoy's bows. *Laureate* and *Legend* were close to port of the block of merchantmen, *Leopard* and *Lyric* to starboard, while the rear was covered by the minesweepers and *Northern Glow*. Course 170, speed twelve: Cape Kanin, guarding the entrance to the White Sea, was now about 350 miles ahead.

Improving light allowed him to see *Moloch*'s dark superstructure rolling crazily above the white froth surrounding her, while to port that very familiar H-class silhouette was *Harpy*, clearly outlined against the rising dawn. Nick's glasses swept past *Foremost*, and on round to the starboard quarter. That was the *Galilee Dawn* leading column three; beyond her, only just visible from here, was *Leopard*. That was the dark side and the dangerous one, where an enemy would be hard to see but would have any of these ships clearly in his sights. Although the only enemy one would have expected here would have been a U-boat, and there'd been no sight or sound of any. All busy down south. To that extent the intelligence appreciation seemed to have been right. Much less so when it came to the shifting south of air-strength: German airmen would be watching this dawn, too – impatiently, with search 'planes ready for take-off, eager to seek out this target for the bomber squadrons.

The last news they'd have had of PQ 19 would have been thirty hours ago, when that Dornier would have reported it as 200 miles west of here and steering south. Since then they'd have realised it could only be hiding in the northern fog, but not necessarily that it had been pushing east. If they'd been fooled by that southerly course they might even be panicking now, imagining their target might have eluded yesterday's searchers and practically reached its port or ports of destination. Which they might assume to be Murmansk, the Kola inlet.

'Anything on the screen, Swanwick?'

The ADO said no, the 281 screen was clear. Not that one could rely on that set entirely.

In London, admirals would be worrying, wondering where PQ 19 had got to. The last they'd have heard would have been when the convoy was under attack and losing ships.

'Pilot.' Christie moved up closer. Nick told him, 'Draft a signal to SBNO North Russia, repeated to Admiralty and AIG 311. Give him an estimated position for dawn tomorrow, and request rendezvous with local escorts, ditto fighter cover. Let me see it before you give it to Bliss to code.'

He'd hesitated over this one. Mostly because to predict where they'd be by this time tomorrow seemed like a twisting of the devil's tail. But chances of getting some help from Soviet destroyers and some fighter cover might be improved by putting the request in early. Also it would be as well to get everything off your chest at the first contact with an enemy, get it out when you had the opportunity and if necessary amend it later if things went badly.

Tomblin brought breakfast to the sea-cabin. While he ate it he thought of the day ahead, his dispositions, orders to the escorts and arrangements with the commodore. Whether there might be anything he'd overlooked or that could be improved. By this time he'd already shifted *Moloch* to the convoy's rear . . . He'd finished eating and was lighting the first pipe of the day when Tomblin came to collect the tray.

'More coffee, sir?'

'No, nothing else.'

'Is it right we're for Archangel this time, sir, not Kola?'

He nodded. 'Because that's where the empty ships are,

that we're collecting. Moved there to be further from the German airfields.'

The anchorage at Vaenga in the Kola Inlet was a frequent target for bombers.

'So now it's bring on the dancing girls, sir, eh?'

'Except they have to find us first.' He added, 'When they do, don't let me see you without a tin hat on.'

It would have been a shorter trip to Kola, the Murmansk approach. Better therefore from the fuelling angle too – which was partly why it had been essential to have the *Bayleaf* available up there – but in any case a shorter period of exposure to the bombers as the convoy ran south. But Archangel was where the empties had congregated, and bringing them home was the main purpose of this operation. Archangel being ice-free still, which in a month's time it probably would not be.

Radar picked up its first contact just after five in the morning. The bearing was 224, range eighteen miles.

'One aircraft, or more?'

'Single bogey, sir.'

It was too early in the day to be found – with fourteen hours of daylight yet to come, and the enemy only about 300 miles away, flying-time lessening every minute.

'Drawing left. Bearing two-two-one, range sixteen.'

A minute later the bearing steadied. Indicating a direct approach. Then it began to draw right. Christie murmured with his hands together as if in prayer, 'Turned for home. Please God.'

'Tempt not the Lord thy God.' Treseder growled it, with his glasses up on that bearing. Swanwick reported, 'Bearing two-two-five – bearing steady – range fourteen!'

Treseder said, 'Warned you, pilot.'

A minute passed. Two minutes. The German was still coming straight for them.

'Aircraft – green five-oh, angle of sight ten!'

It was Merry, the leading signalman, who'd made the

sighting, but suddenly everyone else could see it too. Treseder looked round at Nick. 'Seems to be flying left to right now, sir.'

'Yes, I'm on it.' It was a Blohm and Voss this time. And no Hurricane left to deal with it. Very shortly it would be delighting the Luftwaffe commanders with the information they'd been waiting for: and there wasn't a damn thing you could do about it.

He saw the thing's profile shortening, as it swung towards the convoy.

'He's spotted us.'

'Yeoman – flags – aircraft on that true bearing.'

You could only sit and wait now. With a fair idea of the likely pattern of the next fourteen hours. It would start quite soon, he guessed; the bomber squadrons would almost certainly be lined up and ready, they'd only need to get the snooper's signal and take off, fly 300 miles . . . One thing you could do now was get that signal away.

The first attackers appeared at 07.28, and the red air-warning flag, which had been bent-on and ready, rushed to *Calliope*'s yardarm. Radar tracked bogeys coming in dead straight from the southwest, obviously knowing exactly where they were going, this time. By the time they came in sight the bearing was shifting to the right; it was a force of a dozen Ju 88s and it was deploying to attack from astern, as usual.

Cloud-cover was patchy, wind-driven at about 6000 feet. The ships were rolling heavily, bedded in foam, the destroyers in particular finding the going hard. Bombers like black insects against the patchwork of grey and blue; they were flying in and out of cloud, which was wide-spread enough to provide them with cover but not so thick as to impede their frequent viewings of the convoy.

They'd be chatting among themselves. Schultz and Muller go for the cruiser, Schmidt and Braun take the oiler . . . Guns like pointing fingers following them round, gunners' eyes slitted through the white cotton anti-flash masks under the rims of tin hats.

Nick used his telephone to the control officer in the tower, to remind him not to waste ammunition. 'Shoot at incoming aircraft only. This is likely to be a very long day.' He hung up. Glancing round astern, checking that all ships were in station: and they were, Commodore Insole had his mob well disciplined. The view had some of the quality of a panorama in oils: the bright colours of the day, the warships' slim lines, plunging hulls and waiting guns, and the stolidly advancing merchantmen. There was a look of doggedness about them: they were ignoring the approaching enemies, simply getting on with the job that mattered, the delivery of their cargoes.

The leading pair of Ju 88s were turning to come up astern.

'Attacking, sir . . .'

'Tell radar to keep all-round watch.'

There'd be more coming behind these. Probably some already on their way. The best you could hope for would be reasonably good intervals between assaults – time to draw breath and tidy up. Off Crete, he remembered, there'd sometimes been no intervals at all; the enemy bases had been so close that the Stukas had run a shuttle service – some attacking, others flying back for new bomb-loads, the fresh waves always coming in. Day-round bombing: Crete had been about as bad as it could get.

Except, as Treseder had said the other day, the water had been warm enough to stay alive in.

Moloch opened fire, at two 88s coming in at about 2000 feet with their snouts down. Two more behind them, doubtless attempting to slip in unopposed while those front-runners drew the flak. Another pair, higher and farther back, banking round to tag on to the queue . . . All the rear part of the convoy was in action by this time, the sky dirtying rapidly with shell-bursts and the haze from disintegrated bursts, tracer soaring red and yellow through it. A lot of that was the sweepers and the trawler, who were very close to the rearmost ships – *Moloch* crossing astern of them, weaving and with her four-sevens cocked up and spitting. The *Berkeley* had opened up: she'd be barraging over the Russian oiler. Now *Lyric* and *Legend* from the beams – with the Junkers down at about 1500 feet, one slightly astern of the other and both going for the centre, straight into the defensive barrage over the *Sovyetskaya Slava.*

Bombs starting, in slow-motion . . .

The one astern flared like a match being struck. Pieces flew off: then it was a black nucleus plunging seaward, trailing smoke and flame: the sea on the *Berkeley's* port side received it in a sheet of foam. Bombs were going in astern of the Russian and off her bow and abeam of the *Galilee Dawn.* First brush, and so far the only blood spilt was some of their own. Second pair coming and a whole day of it stretching ahead, about as forbidding as a day could be.

'Captain, sir . . .'

Bridge messenger: red-faced, about eighteen, the look of a farm-boy, tin hat seemingly resting on his ears. 'Yes?'

'From the ADO, sir – new formation two-three-oh, sixteen miles!'

He was looking up at two Junkers flattening from their dives over the rear of columns one and two: they were wing-tip to wing-tip, and their bombs were falling away together, twisting slowly as if suspended on elastic but then accelerating so you quickly lost sight of them; two more attackers were in their shallow-dive approach paths. A bomb smacked in within yards of the stem of the *Earl Granville* – so close that she was steaming on into its splash, a shower of white rain sprinkling her deck cargo. The second exploded on the *Plainsman's* stern: he saw the flash, flame and smoke in the split second before another went in amidships and she blew up – splitting open, gushing skyward, flame and smoke and a thunderous roar from the explosives that had been packed into that midships hold. The *Earl Granville* vanished into the wide mess of it and came out again on this side: she'd have had no room even to put her wheel over, she must have scraped past as much of the American as was left – no more than wreckage, burning still, while the sweeper *Radstock* nosed in to look for survivors. Not that you'd expect any. *Legend* tearing in, barraging with her close-range weapons in the face of another German slanting over from the quarter.

'Aircraft green six-oh, angle of sight ten, closing!'

This would be the second wave. The Luftwaffe would be determined to make a job of it now, make up for the day they'd lost while PQ 19 had been hiding in the ice. And there was to be no pause this time. The fellow coming over now was, like his recent predecessors, going for the Russian oiler. Oilers were always priority targets, coming second only to escort carriers . . . *Calliope*'s guns thundering as she rolled from beam to beam under a sky plastered black and brown and that 88 banking away, baulking at it, nose coming up and the pilot getting the hell out, funking – but the bombs coming, too – less aimed than ditched. Nick was wanting to turn away to look at the new formation coming in, see what they were and how many. But with those bombs in the air and every ship in the convoy shifting target to greet the next comer – from astern again, this one straight and purposeful . . .

The first of the stick of four randomly sprayed bombs went into the sea abeam of the *Tacora*, a second farther out, a third off *Calliope*'s port quarter, and the last – *Harpy*.

It hit amidships. Seeing it was like feeling it: a kick in your gut, or brain. He saw a flash, a gout of smoke breaking out with things flying in it: as she rolled back to starboard he thought the hit had been in her engineroom. But – she'd broken in half. The urge to get over there was countered by the need to stay exactly where he was, where *Calliope*'s guns in combination with the *Berkeley*'s were of the greatest use, barraging above the merchantmen. *Harpy* was hidden in what looked like smoke but was more likely steam: the bomb-burst had been in her belly and it would have been a boiler exploding that had torn her apart, he guessed. *Calliope* barraging over the *Tacora* and the *Sovyetskaya Slava* as this 88 levelled at about 1200 feet and its bombs began to fall away in a straight line right over the middle of the convoy. Looking back at *Harpy* again he saw the bow section on its own and the *Carrickmore* swinging inward to pass this side of it; beyond was *Laureate*, like everyone else ceasing fire as that last enemy swept over, roaring over astern of *Calliope* and banking right, beginning to climb but with smoke coming out of its starboard engine. He was aware of a fleeting prayer in his heart for the damage to worsen, flames to spread, engulf, fry . . . Astern of *Carrickmore* the bow section of the wrecked destroyer was vertical in a blossoming of white foam: he could see figures still clinging but others leaping off, and *Laureate*'s whaler in the water, *Laureate* herself within yards and stopped, *Legend* passing on her far side – and the *Earl Granville*, rolling ponderously and with a large area of empty sea ahead of her where until about eight minutes ago the *Plainsman* would have been. *Moloch* was moving fast across the *Earl Granville*'s stern and engaging another bomber: a bomb-splash went up to starboard of the commodore, and that attacker was removing itself, now, climbing, *Calliope* therefore shifting target – *Berkeley* too, at an 88 peeling to starboard to go for *Laureate*. *Moloch* coming to help, Tommy Trench having seen this danger, his ship under full rudder, on her beam ends as she turned at flat-out revs, all her guns blazing . . .

Time: 08.04.

In the second wave there were only seven aircraft – Ju 88s again – and they'd gone by 08.30, leaving one of their

number in the sea. There was a lull then, and by 09.00
there was still nothing on the radar screen. Nick had taken
the chance of relaxing his ship's company from action
stations; it was a chance that might not come again all day,
and therefore worth taking. Not that 'relaxing' was quite
the word: you watched the minutes crawl by, knowing
that the enemy would be back, and soon. Every minute
that passed meanwhile was of value, not only recupera-
tive, but a fractional erosion of the long hours of strain
that lay ahead.

Five survivors of the *Plainsman* had been picked up by
Radstock, and *Laureate* had fifty-three on board from *Harpy*.
There was too much of a sea running now for wounded
men to be transferred from ship to ship and all those five
in *Radstock* were in bad shape, so *Legend* had put her doctor
into the minesweeper by seaboat. *Laureate* had taken
Harpy's position on the convoy's bow, *Legend* had moved
up and *Radstock* had joined her on that port side.

A signal had gone out to Admiralty, repeated to AIG 311
and to the rear-admiral in North Russia, reporting the new
losses. It would also alert the rear-admiral to the possibility
of delay in making the proposed dawn rendezvous with
locally-based escort forces.

The *Plainsman*'s master had been vice-commodore, the
man who'd have taken over as commodore if Insole in the
Tacora had come to grief. Insole had appointed Captain
Hewson of the *Carrickmore* to replace the American, who'd
been lost with his ship.

09.10 now. It felt more like noon. Nick wished to God it
had been noon.

Visitors, taking advantage of the lull, came up to the
bridge for various purposes. Surgeon Commander
Francomb, the PMO, was one of them, reporting on the
state of the wounded men among the survivors who'd been
transferred into *Calliope* two nights ago from the trawlers
and from *Moloch*; they were survivors in fact from the

Winston, the *Papeete* and the *Caribou Queen*. Francomb had had to operate on one American, a radio operator from the *Caribou Queen*, to remove a piece of metal from his ribcage, and the patient was apparently in good shape.

Next came Mr Wrottesley, Commissioned Gunner.

'Ammo state, sir.'

He accepted the piece of paper. 'Thank you, Mr Wrottesley.'

'Not much to give thanks for, sir.'

Studying the figures for ammunition expended and remaining, and knowing these levels would apply equivalently in the other ships, was like considering a list of unavoidable expenses for which you didn't have the cash in hand. If attacks continued at this rate, by dawn tomorrow there'd be very little to fight back with.

He passed the list to Treseder, and told the gunner, 'We'll last out, I expect.'

'I expect we better, sir!'

Pink, smooth face, freshly shaved. Small, bright eyes, and a nose like a dab of putty. Mr Wrottesley was president of the warrant officers' mess, and he was always dapper, brushed and polished. Nick guessed he'd have shaved specially for this visit to the bridge. Asking now, 'Four of 'em downed, was it, sir?'

'Three and—'

'Bogeys bearing two-four-oh, eight miles, sir!'

'– and a probable, Mr Wrottesley.'

Eight miles was very close for the radar to have picked up a new attack. He glanced at Treseder: 'Action stations.'

'Radar lost contact, sir!'

Treseder, with his mouth opening to pass that order and one hand simultaneously reaching to the alarm push-button, hesitated, looking back at him; Nick nodded, and the commander shouted 'Action stations!' That was for the Marine bugler, whose station was at the back of the bridge near the tannoy broadcast system; the buzzer duplicated the urgent message and also specified the nature of the emergency by sounding repeatedly the morse letter A, standing for air attack. Nick meanwhile guessing at the reason for close-range detection and then immediate loss of contact – they'd be low-flying aircraft, most likely torpedo bombers, approaching under the radar loop, with one or more of them climbing for a better view when they'd known they were somewhere near their target. Having spotted the ships, dipping down again – and the next contact, as likely as not, would be visual.

All hands were rushing to their stations, putting on anti-flash gear and tin hats as they ran, climbed or flung themselves down ladders, the ship's rolling adding to the hazards. The red warning flag was hoisted, and an Aldis lamp was clashing, to flash a message to the commodore: a loudspeaker boomed over the general racket of the process of closing-up, 'Director target! Torpedo bombers, true bearing two-six-oh, range seven miles, angle of sight zero, flying right to left!'

He picked up the telephone. That broadcast system was an emergency way of overriding the routine communications links, which tended to be cluttered at moments such as this one, to alert all quarters to a new threat.

'What are they?'

'Heinkel seaplanes, sir – one-one-fives. About fifteen of them.'

'Right.' Decision took about two seconds. 'When they start to turn in, I'll take her out to meet them.' He hung up. He'd try to break up the attack before it got in close. 'Pilot, give me the TBS.' He told Treseder, 'Fifteen Heinkel one-one-fives, this time.' Then: 'Tinker, this is Thief. Captain to captain. Over.'

Moloch piped up: Trench here, sir. Over.

'Tommy, these are Heinkel one-one-fives – now green sixty-five, range about five miles. When they show which way they're coming from, I'm going out to head them off.

Whatever birds get past me will be yours. You'd better come up this way now. Out.'

'Ship is at action stations, sir.'

'Aircraft green six-oh, seaplanes, angle of sight zero!'

That had been a lookout's yell, and Nick had his first sight of them at about the same moment. Studying them, he realised that unlike yesterday's 111s these would have only one fish each. They were slower too, and should be easier to hit.

The loudspeaker warned, 'Enemy turning towards! Bearing green five-eight!'

Time to move out, then . . . 'Three hundred revolutions. Starboard ten.' He'd scrape out under *Foremost*'s stern.

'Ten of starboard wheel on, sir. Three hundred revolutions passed.'

Moloch was pounding up between columns two and three, passing in a welter of suds between the *Republican* and the *Sovyetskaya Slava* as *Calliope* swung to starboard, heeling as she pitched bowdown, her foc'sl buried in the sea, for'ard turrets lashed by the flying spray: then her bow was rocking upwards and her four propellers, gripping in deeper water, thrust her forward. He shouted back to Harvey-Smith, 'Midships – steady her on two-three-oh!'

The sad-looking, greyish face dipped to the voicepipe: 'Midships . . .'

From the Heinkels' cockpits *Calliope* would be just one grey fragment of a jumbled crowd of ships. In these sea conditions she wouldn't easily be distinguishable from a destroyer, at that distance and to a flyer's untutored eye, so until she'd passed astern of *Foremost* and pulled herself right away from the convoy they wouldn't know what was being prepared for them.

'Course two-three-oh, sir!'

She'd cut through *Foremost*'s wake about thirty yards astern of her. Christie had checked that the destroyer's bearing was changing, drawing left, so the anxious look on Harvey-Smith's face was hardly justified. He wasn't a destroyer man, of course – and Nick was handling *Calliope* like a destroyer now. Not getting much of a view of the seaplanes at this moment because of the sheets of spray that she was flinging up . . . Cutting astern of *Foremost* now: the destroyer's X and Y guns' crews and depthcharge team huddled in shelter, watching the cruiser race by: she'd be quite a sight, too. He put his glasses up again. Not wanting to open fire too soon and waste shells, nor leave it too late either. Thinking of the ships lost in that first torpedo attack, the sense of defeat he'd suffered from then, and also remembering the experience of the previous convoy, PQ 18, in similar circumstances: in one assault by Heinkel 111s, out of seven ships in the two starboard columns six had been hit – and sunk – and another two in the centre of the convoy as well. It wasn't a form of attack to be treated lightly. His tactic now was to leave the convoy well defended by its destroyers and at the same time carry the attack to the enemy at some distance from it.

He'd adjusted the course to 225. The convoy was well astern now, and the Heinkels in plain sight ahead. Low, wave-hopping, looking like clumsy birds with legs down ready for a landing. Torpedoes ready between those legs . . .

'Open fire, sir?'

'Yes. Open fire.'

The gongs chimed: and the for'ard turrets roared, *Calliope* quivering from it as she plunged. Rising – and another salvo, smoke and cordite fumes rushing over. With his glasses on the attackers and the three turrets falling into a rhythm of steady barraging he saw the bursts opening, seaplanes bucking as if to bounce over the stuff exploding in their faces. Guns in faster rhythm and in triplicate – fire, recoil, fire, recoil – alternatively left and right barrels in each turret. It was having its effect too: he saw two bombers collide and a third in the sea on its nose, tail up and somer-saulting over. Some were turning away and another, pouring smoke, light glinting on its torpedo dropping askew, before the seaplane burst into flames and went into the sea. About seven were still coming – three of them circling away to their left. The guns were still concentrating on the larger group: of which another had gone down . . .

'One-four-oh revolutions!'

Sea flying, wind whipping, familiar stench of battle acrid in eyes and nostrils. High speed was no longer necessary or desirable; slowing down would reduce the pitching and make the gunners' job easier. There were four attackers still coming, that he could see. One of them turning – another's wings slanting as it banked to follow. Three had split away earlier on their own, but Trench would be taking care of them. Nick was deaf, by now, from the guns' noise: Treseder's shout came so faintly that it might have been from fifty yards away instead of six feet: 'Convoy's altering to starboard, sir!'

To comb the tracks of an attack by that trio, he guessed. A quick glance astern showed destroyers in action. Turning again, focussing his glasses on the last two Heinkels – which were close, now, slanting over from the port bow like droning, jinking moths – they must have swung right and then left, he realised, manoeuvring for an attack not on the convoy now but on this ship herself – he saw one fish splash down: then the other . . .

'Port fifteen!'

'Port fifteen, sir . . .'

No problem – it was just a matter of turning her head-on to the torpedo tracks, to let them pass harmlessly each side of her. Oerlikons and pompoms were in loud action: he thought suddenly, Wasting ammunition – imagining they'd be shooting at the pair whose torpedoes he was now avoiding. He hadn't realised, at that point, that there'd been a third Heinkel coming in at *Calliope* from the other quarter.

Explosion, right aft . . .

It had been a crash so unexpected that for a second you

couldn't believe in it. Then you were hearing its echo deep in the ship's bowels, a jolt that shook her hull and frames: pure shock, under the roar of a seaplane banking away to starboard, turning and climbing for safety.

'Torpedo track starboard side, sir!'

He'd centred the wheel. But engine vibration had ceased – engines stopping. Guns silent: the only enemies were tail-on, departing. Gunfire from the direction of the convoy was also petering out. About thirty seconds might have passed since he'd given that helm order. She was still swinging, but with her screws stopped the swing was slowing. Wind and sea were on the port quarter: looking aft, where seas were breaking over, his mind registered that fact that she was down by the stern and taking a list to starboard.

09.25. A fine time and a fine place to have been crippled.

8

Calliope, with no power of her own to resist the forces of wind and sea, rolled helplessly from beam to beam, slowly turning. Treseder had gone down to take charge of damage-control; Nick told Christie, 'Ask Trench whether he has anything to report.' He had his glasses focussed on the convoy, where Insole was in the process of turning his ships back to the mean course of 170: they'd have been fully occupied with the Heinkels who'd got through to them, and probably wouldn't have seen what had been happening here. Nick's primary requirement was a report from *Calliope*'s engineer commander, but knowing what things would be like below decks he was restraining himself from asking for one: when Haselden had time to pick up a telephone, he'd do so. Nick raised his voice over the sounds of wind, sea and the battering of his ship: 'Swanwick, what's on the two-eight-one screen?'

'Screen's clear, sir!'

That was something. And something else that the set was even working, had power on it. He picked up the director tower telephone to ask whether the stern turrets were functioning – this telephone was working, too – and the answer was affirmative: communications and circuits had been tested and found correct, ditto magazines, shell-rooms and

ammo hoists. So there was a bright side . . . He heard Tommy
Trench's voice over TBS informing Christie that there'd been
no torpedo hits in either convoy or escort, and one He 115
had been shot down by *Leopard*. The message ended, Do
you require assistance? Over.

He took the microphone.

'Tommy, I've been torpedoed, on the starboard side aft.
No assessment of damage yet. Send one destroyer to stand
by me, then push on and I'll catch up later. Out.'

The damage-control telephone was buzzing, its pinpoint
of blue light flashing. Ellinghouse answered it, and passed
it on to Nick as he left the TBS. You needed at least one
hand free for holding on, with this savage roll . . . 'Yes?'

'Treseder here, sir. All the damage is right aft. It's a big
hole and we have extensive flooding on the hold and platform decks, and either both the starboard shafts are bent
or the screws are damaged – or A-brackets – or the lot . . .
Haselden's about ready to try again now with port screws
only – he stopped everything because she was shaking
herself to death. They're checking the shafts first. The
flooding's contained well enough, I'd say, and we're
strengthening those bulkheads.'

'All right. Keep me informed. Tell Haselden the priority's
to get her moving.'

Christie told him as he put the phone down, '*Lyric*'s on
her way to us, sir.'

He wondered about the rudder. Stopping on his way aft
across the bridge – he'd been going to the tannoy to let the
ship's company know what was happening – he joined
Harvey-Smith at the binnacle. Clinging to the binnacle –
to the compensating spheres – because dead in the water
as she was now, she wasn't just rolling so much as
performing acrobatics. Recalling that the tiller flat was well
abaft the screws, which were set on her flanks – so there
was a chance the steering could be intact.

'Check the steering.' Shouting, above the wind. 'Every

five degrees all the way to full starboard rudder, then same the other way, wheelhouse checking against the rudder-indicator – all right?' Harvey-Smith nodded dumbly, lowering his face to the voicepipe, while Nick began to think about what he'd do if she was unsteerable. With the starboard screws out of action, you'd need to carry port wheel: if you couldn't do that, there'd be no way on her own of steering a straight course. One of the minesweepers, perhaps, with a wire to *Calliope*'s stern – if necessary another at the bow – the two of them holding her straight, or when necessary turning her. Hand-held flags from this bridge to tell them what was wanted . . .

When the bombers attacked again, she'd be an easy mark for them . . . Harvey-Smith said into the voicepipe, 'Midships . . . Seems to be answering normally, quarter-master?'

'Nothing wrong far's we can tell, sir.'

Harvey-Smith shouted, straightening, 'Seems to be answering, sir!'

He nodded. Reminding himself that he'd brought ships out of worse predicaments. 'They'll be getting the port screws turning, in a minute. Then we'll see.' Because the gear could be working normally – conceivably – even if the rudder had gone . . . He reached the tannoy now, switched it on, began, 'D'you hear me – Captain speaking . . .' Men trapped below decks and sticking to their jobs now as they had to do – if the ship was to survive or have any chance of surviving – were entitled to know what the situation was, and primarily that she wasn't in any danger of sinking, that the damage had been contained and that it was hoped she'd soon be on the move again. Christie was taking a call from for'ard engineroom at the same time. Both enginerooms would have to be in use, since one drove the inner screws and the other the outer ones. Nick felt it start while he was still speaking – vibration first, its quality changing as revs built up, and the change in her motion as the screws began to take effect: it allowed him to finish with 'There – as you can feel now – we're under way . . .'

By 10.15, when the next incoming air attack was picked up on radar, they'd got her moving at a steady ten knots. Vibration was excessive, but this had to be accepted. Repairs would have to be made in Archangel – or dockyard facilities might be better in the Kola Inlet . . . She seemed to be carrying about eight degrees of wheel: steering would be affected not only by the fact the starboard screws weren't useable, but also by her list to starboard and sterndown posture in the sea.

A cyphered signal to Admiralty, repeated to others including SBNO North Russia, was being transmitted at this moment: *Calliope reduced to 10 knots by torpedo hit aft. Maintaining convoy course and speed. New bomber formation approaching from southwest.*

'Bearing two-three-two, range seventeen – large formation . . .'

Calliope was steering the convoy's mean course of 170 but she wasn't zigzagging. He'd brought her into the position astern of column two which had been *Moloch's*. If mechanical problems worsened, or her clumsy steering put her off-course, she'd be in no other ship's way here. *Moloch* had transferred to *Calliope's* former station, in the van with *Foremost* to starboard of her and *Laureate* to port. *Calliope* was on her own, much of the time, as the convoy zigzagged ahead of her, but *Northern Glow* and the sweeper *Rochdale*, making independent zigzags, stayed fairly close.

'Bearing two-three-oh, fourteen miles . . . Second formation on two-three-five, nineteen!'

He told himself, There've been worse times. Plenty . . .

And a drubbing today had been inevitable. Put yourself in the Luftwaffe chiefs' shoes – an easy target only about 250 miles away, and their ears ringing with the Fuhrer's insistence that Allied convoys to North Russia must be stopped . . . He thought, We should have had an escort carrier with us. We really should . . . Glancing aside, he found himself under the somewhat hawkish scrutiny of Bruce Christie. Not for the first time, in recent days. Christie's expression was less questioning than analytical – no questions to ask, but his own mind to be made up, through observation of how his new commanding officer was reacting or would react to this heightening of the risks . . .

He told Ellinghouse, 'Chief yeoman – TBS to Rabble. "Second bomber formation is approaching five miles behind the first. *Moloch* inform commodore".'

Moloch was close ahead of the *Tacora*, but from here, depending on which way the zigzag was going, there were always others in the line of sight – usually the *Berkeley* and the *Sovyetskaya Slava* in the middle column.

'Coffee, sir?'

Percy Tomblin: properly dressed in a tin hat.

'Good idea. Thank you, Tomblin.'

'Left these in your cabin, sir.'

Matches – Swan Vestas . . . He took them, slid them into a pocket. Life's trivia – in present circumstances faintly ridiculous. So much in the balance – lives, ships, and a war cargo worth risking them for: but essentially men's lives – and in the middle of it they brought you cups of coffee, boxes of matches . . .

Treseder, back from another inspection of the damaged area aft, appeared behind Tomblin. He was trailed at a respectful (or wary) distance by his 'Doggie', an ordinary seaman by the name of Wilson. Nick said, playing the game of trivialities, 'The commander might appreciate a cup of your coffee, Tomblin.'

'Aye aye, sir.' Tomblin eyed Wilson, obviously thinking he might have been sent for whatever sustenance his master wanted. Treseder murmured, 'Most kind, sir.' He added, with a glance at Tomblin, 'Coffee that tastes like coffee

being as rare as it is on this bridge.' Tomblin, mollified by
the compliment, glanced again at Wilson as he left them.
Nick told Treseder, 'We have a second attack coming in
behind the first bunch.'

Treseder nodded, pursing his lips as he turned his eyes
south-westward. Swanwick's communications number
called, 'Bogeys on two-three-oh, ten miles, and two-three-
one, sixteen miles, both formations closing, bearings
steady!'

Treseder said, 'The old one-two again, perhaps, eighty-
eights and bloody Heinkels.'

Binoculars were all trained on and around that bearing.
Calliope plunging, soaring, rolling. The violence of her
motion worried the damage-control people, of course,
because there was added danger of bulkheads splitting
under the constantly shifting, uneven strains.

10.19. Minutes crawling by so slowly that clocks and
watches might have had treacle in their works.

'Bearing two-two-nine, eight miles, sir!'

But no sighting yet?

'Above the cloud.' Treseder muttering to himself.
Lowering his glasses, cleaning their front lenses but with
his eyes still on the sky. Christie pointed out, 'Cloud is
lower than it was, sir. If it'd thicken up a bit, now . . .'

Looking for another miracle?

'Aircraft – green six-oh – angle of sight—'

'Where?'

It had appeared and gone again: flown into cloud . . .
Swanwick questioning that lookout – which way had it
been flying, what height, what type . . . Christie was right
about the cloud-layer being lower, Nick realised. If it hadn't
been for the wind that was tearing holes in it for bombers
to see through, it could have been an ally.

Pray for the wind to drop, he thought. Wind drop, cloud
thicken. Better still, ask Marcus Plumb to do the praying,
since he presumably would have a direct connection . . .

'Aircraft in formation green eight-oh, angle of sight one-five – eighty-eights, sir!'

In the open, suddenly. Strung out in groups of six to eight: but more cloud there again now, so appearing and disappearing. Flying from left to right: ships' guns elevated and following them round although they weren't in range yet. *Calliope* rolling as hard as ever, ensign whipping in bright colour against grey sky; the black, twin-engined bombers were below the cloud now and coming round astern. Treseder announced, 'I count thirty-six.' Back into cloud – but before they were swallowed in it one group had been separating from the mainstream, turning right, this way. The whole lot were hidden in cloud again.

'Second formation bears two-three-oh, nine miles . . .'

DCT telephone: 'We have a group of them coming in on the quarter, sir. Permission to engage when . . .'

'Open fire when you're ready.'

In effect, this meant immediately. Before he put the 'phone down he saw them coming in – nose-down, already in their dives – and heard the ritual war-cries from the team up there in the tower: 'Green one-four-oh, angle of sight three-five!'

'Cut!'

'Have height, have plot!'

'Range oh-two-six!'

'Ready!'

'Range oh-two-four!'

'Open fire!'

Fire-gong's clang, and the turrets' ringing thunder. The *Berkeley* joined in, and *Rochdale* . . . *Calliope*'s ten 5.25s plus the *Berkeley*'s six four-inch amounted to a lot of barrage when it was all directed at the same piece of sky, a barrier of explosive no pilot in his senses would choose to fly through if he had any option. The noise of gunfire combined with the ship's erratic motion made for an impression of confusion, bedlam: if you came through this you'd work out afterwards what had happened, how you'd performed, but while it lasted it was a matter of second-by-second action and reaction and a fast-moving picture buried in noise – as if vision were indistinct and under-standing fogged as well as hearing deadened. Bomb splashes lifted between *Calliope* and *Northern Glow*: they hadn't come from the 88s that were attacking from the quarter, but from others overhead at higher level, releasing bombs through cloud-gaps and out of sight in cloud again immediately. Another splash, on the *Berkeley's* quarter: he looked astern, at those four coming in steeply, ranged back at intervals but aiming themselves directly at this ship, shellbursts opening under them and in front and all around them, close-range weapons in it too – and one of them hit, pulling upwards after the explosion, smoke like black blood streaming: then it was spinning, falling, but bombs slanting from the front-runner now . . .

The killed one had raised a tower of blackish sea. Second bomb-stick releasing and the first well on its way. He shouted at Harvey-Smith, 'Hard-a-starboard!'

The first lot had begun slanting away to port before he'd lost sight of them, hadn't looked like hitting or even like falling close, but the second batch had appeared to be dead right for line. He wouldn't have taken this avoiding action if it hadn't seemed essential since it would take an age, in *Calliope's* wounded state, to get her back in station: the convoy needed the protection of these guns and *Calliope* needed to be close to the collectively defensive barrage as opposed to being stuck out on her own. But he'd had to do it. She was turning fast: a starboard turn was easy, with the port screws to drive her round. Two bombs thumped in just off the bow: he shouted, 'Midships, and meet her!' His own voice was barely audible to him: he'd never been able to wear ear-plugs in action, and consequently was quite used to ending up five-sixths deaf. In old age he'd regret it, but this wasn't old age yet. Another thought there, but there wasn't time for thought. Harvey-Smith had heard the order, anyway. Two splashes astern of the *Berkeley* – and others in a line right up the centre of the alley between columns one and two. There'd have been a lot one hadn't seen, of course: those two that had gone in close to her bow would have been hits if he hadn't put the wheel over, there wasn't any doubt of it. The swing had been checked now: he ordered, 'Port thirty.'

The third and fourth members of that Junkers group had refused to be put off when *Calliope* had turned, they'd held on as they'd been going, only saving their bombs for the *Sovyetskaya Slava*. She was answering the full port helm, but slowly, and she'd lost several hundred yards of distance on the convoy. The gap was still opening as she dragged herself around: it would have been quicker, he realised now – too late, of course – to have let her complete the circle to starboard, the way she'd been fairly whizzing round. There were Ju 88s in all directions and at all levels now, like a swirl of mammoth crows. Two more coming at *Calliope* at this moment, and bombs in the air over the middle of the convoy – then a near-miss on the *Ewart S. Dukes*, rear ship in column three. This was a painfully slow turn – the ship's wounds handicapping her, wind and sea not helping either. He saw an 88 belly-flop into the sea over beyond the *Rochdale*, skidding in a sheet of spray for a hundred yards or so before it turned up on its nose and sank. *Northern Glow* was off *Calliope*'s bow to port, her close-range spouting tracer at the pair attacking now, *Calliope* blazing at them too: every time her steel shuddered to the crashes of her guns the damage-control men down below would be expecting seams to open, bulkheads to collapse. By dropping back they'd lost the protection of the AA ship: the *Berkeley* was busy enough half a mile away, barraging over the Soviet oiler.

Treseder shouted, something like 'Take cover' – pointing, a stab of one of his short arms towards a Ju 88 approaching at what looked like masthead height – probably twice that height – but pulling out of its shallow dive now, and bombs leaving it, black eggs turning in the air: he didn't see how they could miss. But the pilot now paid the price of having pressed in so close: his port engine exploded, the wing flew apart, bombs smacking into the sea close to *Calliope*'s port side – one abreast her second funnel, the other close to her foc'sl – the twin explosions as close and jolting as if she'd been hit by some giant sledgehammer. It was probably the swing still on her that had spared her from direct hits. Nick shouted to Harvey-Smith to steady her on 170: acknowledgement was a mouth that opened and shut but emitted no sound. Nothing audible, over the total enclosure in noise. Two more splashes went up ahead. Another attack coming from the quarter – this one also low – Swanwick getting the pompoms and Oerlikons on to it, a cone of multi-coloured fire with its apex on the German's snout, *Calliope* back on course, aiming up the convoy's wakes. Close-range guns racketing in that attacker's face while the three for'ard turrets added their quota to the barrage above the convoy's rear. And that 88 was suddenly one of the good ones – meaning harmless, dead, a carcass in a mass of smoke and upside-down, on its back as it hit the sea.

Bomb splashes to starboard, and Treseder bawling in Nick's ear – having been aft to talk to Swanwick during some flurry of alarm there – 'The second wave is another lot of eighty-eights, sir!' Pitching his voice high at a range of two inches and at the same time pointing at the procession of small groups, a total of something like twenty aircraft approaching from ahead. A lull in the action at this juncture was giving an illusion of respite; Nick had his glasses on the convoy, to check on what was or had been happening there, and the guns up ahead were already increasing the density and rate of fire, engaging some Junkers approaching at about 1200 feet from the beam, *Radstock*'s Oerlikons hosing tracer that curled in coloured streamers past the bombers' noses as they swept over ahead of her – going for the *Earl Granville* perhaps – one lot of bombs starting down, but the *Berkeley*'s guns concentrating on them now and the second German banking away out of it – to starboard, this way, across the convoy's rear towards *Calliope*. *Northern Glow* acting as if she felt this was her bird – but the *Earl Granville* had been hit, amidships, smoke and a fire there – and the second one had survived the trawler's attempts to stop it, had swept on over and was aiming at *Calliope*, close now, nose-down. A wing-tip sparked, became a flaring trail of smoke with glowing objects in it but the bomber extraordinarily holding on dead straight, the dive steepening a little and bombs appearing now . . .

He knew they'd hit. He was seeing it about to happen, and nothing he could do could prevent it. Too close, too late, too every bloody thing, the 88 smoking and diving, a long incline towards the sea, towards certain death for its crew, while the bombs had started then blurred into the background of pockmarked, smokestained sky. He was aware of the bomber hitting the water close to his ship's stem but also that those bombs were going to hit. Guns deafening, and a roar of aircraft engines thickening the sound like new instruments joining in the orchestral thunder: it was an 88 flying down the starboard side so low that from this bridge you saw the white crosses on the tops of its wings as it blasted past. Then *Calliope*'s for'ard funnel split, flamed, blew to pieces, the starboard strut of the foremast tripod kinked, and the launch in its davits on that side was fuelling a fire whose flames shot up the after part of the bridge superstructure. Those had been the visible and immediate effects of one bomb: another – Haselden the engineer commander was telling him about it a few minutes afterwards, over a sound-powered telephone from damage control headquarters on the main deck aft – had burst against the ship's side below the waterline and abreast the after boiler-room. All he'd known of it from up here had been the crash of the impact booming through her, a jarring thump powerful enough to send men flying and stop her engines – and, just about, your heart.

'It's very bad generally, I'm afraid, sir. After boiler-room's filling, and there's been a lot of casualties – concussion, and steam—'

'The for'ard boiler-room's still intact?'

But he recognised the sum of it before the engineer had finished his catalogue of damage. Other telephones were buzzing, reports arriving from all quarters while Haselden explained that the flooding aft, result of earlier damage, couldn't now be controlled for long; and with that boiler-room gone – it was a very large compartment . . . 'Even if we got her going, sir – one boiler-room, one engineroom and probably the port outer shaft – you'd get two or three knots, no more – and not for long, because . . .'

'All right.' He was right, of course. If you didn't accept it, all you'd be doing would be throwing away good men's lives. There were men wounded down there, the survivors of other ships, and you had to work for what could be saved, namely those lives and the convoy . . .

The broadcast boomed, 'Main armament in director control!'

So they'd got those circuits working. The guns hadn't ceased firing so they must have been temporarily in local control. He told Haselden, 'Prepare to abandon ship. Is Treseder there with you?'

'Yes, sir, he's . . .'

'Give him that order. And tell the PMO I want his patients brought up right away. Under the foc'sl deck port side, and the launch's davits can be used for lowering them in Neill Robertsons. But we'll take this step by step: we can't abandon yet, and the guns have to be kept working until we're ready.'

Bombs were separating from that Junkers. And from the other too. *Calliope*'s three for'ard turrets pounding at them.

What he'd meant in that message to Treseder via Haselden, a point Treseder would take immediately, was that as long as there were living men on board this ship she'd have to be defended against the bombing, and to use her main armament involved the manning of the complete turrets. What was often referred to as a turret was in fact only the gunhouse, the turret as a whole extended deeply into the ship, through upper and lower decks, platform deck and hold deck, with magazine and cordite-handling room in its base, shellroom above that, then the ammunition hoist feeding projectiles and charges straight up into each gunhouse. But when you cleared lower deck in order to abandon ship, all those positions would be evacuated and the guns would be starved of ammunition . . . The ship was still swinging, wind acting on her superstructure as on a sail. Splashes to port – that Bosch had held on to his bomb too long. He didn't see where the second load went: Christie was shouting in his ear, 'Commander Trench asks do you require assistance, sir!'

The sky over the convoy was heavy with shellbursts and the dirt of battle. The *Earl Granville* was on fire but seemed to be maintaining her station. The convoy's tail end – where *Northern Glow* and *Rochdale* were barraging over the *Ewart S. Dukes*, which was putting up a bright canopy of tracer of her own – seemed a long, long way off.

'Tommy. When you can spare her, I'd like one destroyer to stand by me, and if possible a second when things ease off a bit. I intend abandoning ship, then one of them can put a fish in her. Meanwhile the convoy's in your hands. Good luck, and out.'

Four 88s, one trio and one 'plane on its own, were boring in on widely separated bearings. Swanwick leaning over from the starboard-side lookout bay and yelling to the Oerlikon gunners down there to engage the enemy coming from that quarter. His telephone links with the close-range had failed, presumably. A voice on TBS now: 'Richman, this is Tinker. Stand by *Calliope*, prepare to take off her ship's company and then sink her. Over.' It came in the same tone of voice that had passed a thousand other messages: and now *Lyric* was acknowledging in the same flat tone, as if this were no more than routine or perhaps an exercise. It heightened the sense of unreality, while Nick dealt with dozens of points of detail – just as if these proceedings were real, were actually in progress. Points such as the ship having no motive power or steerage way, so the steering position could be evacuated. The job of OOW had also ceased to exist in practical terms, so Harvey-Smith could be sent down to organise the preparation of Carley floats for launching, also any boats that might be intact, and the davits of destroyed boats to be made ready for lowering wounded men. There was a signal to be coded and transmitted, and Christie was to put his 'Tanky' and another couple of spare hands on to the job of destroying all CBs – confidential books – and classified documents. The TS – transmitting station – was to be evacuated too. The kind of gunnery that was called for now was barrage work, and the intricacies of the HA control table were superfluous, so the Marine bandsmen could now be brought up from the steel cell in which for some hours they'd have been listening to the sounds of battle. An 88 roared over, passing it seemed only yards above the bridge, and behind it an explosion and a shoot of flame told of a hit somewhere on her starboard side, somewhere amidships. An object – a ready-use ammunition locker, something that size and shape – rose spinning to more than masthead height. A second bomb splashed in twenty yards clear of the bow to port, and there were three more 88s approaching from ahead; the chief yeoman's voice bawling in Nick's ear, 'There's four men 'urt on the flagdeck, sir.'

'Get a stretcher party if you need it, but get 'em down to the foc'sl break port side quick as you can. You'll find other wounded there. You plus one signalman will be enough to leave up here, so send all the rest down too. Rig the loud-hailer, will you?'

For talking to *Lyric* – who was on her way, ploughing northward up the convoy's starboard side, her guns lifted and in action as she came. There was some distance still to cover: the gap between *Calliope* and the convoy was wide, now. A line of splashes – from high-level bombing, he guessed, since no enemies were in sight there at the moment – fell near that starboard column, but not near enough to worry anyone. Here, gunfire mounting in intensity again as those three droned in, in echelon'd line-astern and diving . . . Treseder appeared: 'I've started the hands coming up, sir, mustering 'em under cover both sides. I've put officers and POs in charge of various parts of ship and routes to the assembly areas. All the sick and wounded are up already – and I know exactly which parties are still below, so . . .'

A bomb burst on the roof of number three turret, which was about thirty feet for'ard of the bridge and slightly below it. Wind deflectors on the bridge's leading edge deflected the blow-torch flame from the explosion too, but it blistered paintwork on the front of the director tower. *Calliope* bow-down, rolling to port, but more sluggish now with the huge weight of water in her. A second bomb hit somewhere aft, and splashes went up to starboard. Christie, just back from clearing out the safe for the destruction of CBs, pointed and yelled, 'Heinkels, sir!'

Heinkel 115s. And their target was going to be *Calliope*. They were in loose formation on her bow, spreading themselves outward as they flew in. Slow-looking, moth-like – and tracer was lobbing out to meet them. *Calliope*'s for'ard turrets shifting target, gun-barrels lowering swiftly as they swung. *Lyric* had put her helm over; obviously she'd spotted them and decided to meet them head-on, putting herself between them and *Calliope*, which had been his own

earlier tactic and was basically sound enough – to take the
offensive, carry the attack against the attackers and possibly
even stop them attacking effectively at all – but not such
a good idea in present circumstances because in a minute
she'd foul the range and *Calliope*'s own heavier armament
would be silenced, for fear of hitting her. *Lyric* on her beam
ends as she turned at high speed under full rudder, half-
buried in foam, sea streaming over and away from her on
the wind, pendants of clear white against green background. *Calliope*'s guns were making themselves felt: with
any luck *Lyric* might wake up and see it and scram out of
the light. Two Heinkels had swung away, to fly up the
convoy's wake, and one of the others had been hit, trailing
smoke. *Lyric* had put her wheel over the other way – having
caught on to the facts of life. Two Heinkels still threatened:
and a torpedo dropped, down-slanted, gleaming, splashing
in . . .

Nothing you could do about it, in a ship that couldn't
move. If it ran true, it would hit.

Now the other. A splash, the Heinkel's wingtip almost
touching the water as it banked to get away. The guns were
shifting again – swinging round and lifting swiftly – to
meet an 88 coming from the quarter at about a thousand
feet, flying straight and level. *Lyric*'s pompoms and
Oerlikons had drawn attention to it – a bit late, with bombs
already spilling from the racks – two, three, four . . .

Moloch's guns were still at maximum elevation but silent,
lacking a target as the last of those attackers climbed away
southwestward. She was forging up between columns one
and two, overhauling the *Tacora*, who'd had some of her
deck cargo blown overboard. Trench was aiming to pass
within half a cable of her; he had his loud-hailer rigged,
and a group of tin-hatted men were waiting in the wing
of the *Tacora*'s bridge, watching the destroyer plunging up
from astern. Trench talking meanwhile to Poorman,

Foremost, telling her captain, Batty Crockford, to join *Lyric* in standing by *Calliope*.

From as much as Trench had been able to see, in glimpses during recent minutes and with a lot of other action in all directions, *Calliope* with *Lyric*'s support had beaten off an attack by Heinkels, two of which had turned away to make a pass at the *Berkeley*; *Rochdale*, *Northern Glow* and *Radstock* had blocked this, destroying one of the pair and driving the other away. Only minutes earlier *Radstock* had been trying unsuccessfully to get in close enough to the *Earl Granville* to help fight the freighter's upperdeck fires. The *Earl Granville*'s crewmen had been losing the battle, by the looks of it; her master couldn't turn his ship to minimise the effect of the wind without isolating himself from the convoy and its escort – which would have guaranteed the bombers concentrating on him. *Moloch* had been in the centre of the convoy at the time, practically alongside the *Sovyetskaya Slava*. Trench using his loud-hailer to talk to the English-speaking woman radio operator. The oiler had had a hole punched in her side by a technical near-miss; she was leaking oil and her speed was down to eight knots, but her captain had been adamant he'd keep going. His ship's upperworks were filthy from an earlier fire which they'd fought for a long time and finally put out; at that time there'd been comparatively little wind.

Now he had to tell the commodore that the speed reduction was to be permanent. He lifted the loud-hailer: '*Tacora*, ahoy . . . commodore, sir!' *Moloch* pitching violently, Trench swaying on his high seat, long legs wrapped around its struts. Looking astern, seeing *Calliope* as a grey smudge in whitened sea: binoculars showed that she was down by the stern and listing heavily. She'd lost most of her for'ard funnel, one of her foremast struts had gone and the mast itself seemed to be swaying independently of the ship's rolling. A single Ju 88 beyond her, flying south, was momentarily in sight between a gap in the clouds.

Insole's voice came on the wind: 'What can I do for you, commander?'

Lifting the loudhailer again, facing to starboard where the *Tacora* butted stolidly through the waves, but at the same time throwing a quick glance back to see what might be happening around *Calliope* – and not wanting to plague Everard with questions over TBS . . . Attack might be resumed at any moment, the loss of *Calliope*'s guns and now of two destroyers' as well was a serious reduction of the defensive strength: it wasn't a situation you'd want to prolong if you could help it . . . He began to tell the commodore about the Soviet oiler's damage, the need to accept a four-knot cut in speed. This in itself was a serious handicap, increasing by one third the convoy's period of exposure to attack. It was Everard's business as escort commander to make this kind of decision, but in the first place there wasn't much option and in the second it wasn't practicable to consult him; in any case he'd said, 'Meanwhile the convoy's yours.' The only alternative to slowing the convoy would be to abandon the oiler and sink her: discussing this – Insole agreed that the Russians would most likely refuse to accept that decision anyway – Trench looked back towards *Calliope* again just as a Heinkel's torpedo struck her, a pillar of sea shooting vertically on her father side; in the next blink she was hidden in a rain of bombs.

She'd been hit by three of them while the geyser of upthrown sea from that torpedo had still been hanging in the air, the cruiser making a slow roll to starboard, her stem lifting, and sea flooding across her quarterdeck. Sam Clegg, captain of *Lyric*, had had his eyes on the foremast as it carried away completely, crashing down in a tangle of wreckage on the other side. He'd thought she was going, there and then; then the bombs fell in a tight pattern – one in the sea, one on the flooding quarterdeck, one (he thought) down the second funnel, but possibly into the boiler-room with a subsequent explosion up through the funnel, and the fourth on her starboard side abreast 'B' turret. Clegg ordered, 'Away seaboat's crew. Slow ahead together. Starboard five.' To nose in closer. *Lyric* already had scrambling nets down, Carley floats ready to be dropped, and parties mustering for rescue work; also medical and other preparations – piles of blankets and hammocks warming on the engineroom gratings, and hot soup in preparation – all of which could help to save men's lives, if you got any alive out of that freezing water. He'd ordered the whaler to be manned because *Calliope*'s suddenly worsened predicament had impelled him to do something: but how much use the boat could be, in this sea and with the large number of men there'd be to cope with, was questionable. But *Calliope* herself could have no boats: you could see at a glance that her upper deck was a shambles.

'Stop together. Midships the wheel.'

Smoke hung over her, thickest where she was on fire amidships. Her bridge was a scorched mess, but men were moving in it, including one in its forefront who, Clegg guessed, must have been Everard. Stench of burning . . . He'd brought his ship up in the cruiser's lee, thirty to forty yards of tumbling sea between them, close enough for survivors to have a chance . . . Some Carley floats – *Calliope*'s – were already in the water, and stretchers were being lowered on boats' falls at the two pairs of davits on this side; men in the floats waiting, handling lines dangling from the stretchers – Neill Robertson stretchers, the kind that strapped around a man's body, converting him into an object that could be slung around like a stoutly-wrapped parcel. There'd been an attempt five minutes ago to use the crane, but electric power must have failed because they'd abandoned it, transferred to the falls. The floats alongside were tossing and crashing about, despite being in the cruiser's lee: and her side was stripped completely bare of paint all along the waterline, where ice had scraped.

There'd be more wounded than they'd have stretchers for, now – or floats for.

'*Foremost*'s joining us, sir.'

Clegg had made his mind up that despite the sea, and the fact *Calliope* might turn turtle at any moment, he was going to risk getting right in alongside her. It was the only way, now, to save those people's lives.

'The whaler's manned, sir!'

'Get 'em out of it. I'm taking her alongside. Starboard side-to . . .' He called down, 'Slow ahead port, slow astern starboard.' He'd had her lying broadside-on, so he had to turn her where she lay before he could move her in closer . . . 'Is Cramphorn ready?'

'Yessir.' Cramphorn was *Lyric*'s doctor. 'Your day-cabin and the wardroom—'

'Stop starboard. Starboard twenty-five.'

'She's going!'

Clegg saw it himself, at that same moment. She'd resumed the roll to starboard which had checked at about the same time as the bombs had struck. There might have been some counter-flooding at that time. Now the resumption was at first slow, but by the time you'd seen it happening the momentum was increasing, becoming swift, unstoppable . . .

'Stop port. Midships. Slow astern together.'

Wash and suction from the roll were capsizing the floats, turning them on end, spinning them like leaves in a whirlpool. Most of them empty now, some with men clinging: but bodies in Neill Robertsons couldn't cling . . . *Foremost* – Clegg had seen her moving up but had not had time to take her movements into consideration – was backing off, too: she'd been approaching gingerly, stem to stem with the cruiser, her captain – Batty Crockford – aiming to put his bow alongside *Calliope*'s foc'sl, and there'd been a crowd of men gathering there, ready for the chance to jump over.

Gunfire beginning again, swelling from the direction of the convoy . . .

'I'll need the whaler, after all.'

'Aye aye, sir!'

'Stop together . . .'

Roar of aircraft engines mingled with gun noise. *Lyric*'s after four-sevens were engaging some attacker, and now her pompoms and Oerlikons had joined in. Clegg had to leave all that to his control officer in the tower: his concern was *Calliope*, and the darkening that wasn't dusk or doomsday but the cruiser's forepart lifting to shadow the space of sea between them: she was on her side and the roll seemed to have stopped again, stern buried and the long foc'sl lifting completely out of the water now, rising towards the vertical and displaying her scarred body naked to the day for these last agonising moments *Lyric* and *Foremost* both in action; *Calliope*'s raised forepart alive with men – some holding on, some jumping into the seething foam. Bomb splashes shot up on her other side, then one off *Foremost*'s port bow as she drew away, and a fourth exploded in the sea between *Lyric* and the dying cruiser. A scream of fury from a sailor on 'B' gundeck, harsh as a seabird's shriek, cut through the petering-out of gunfire: 'Christ, lay off, you bastards!' Guns had ceased fire: a new sound was the rush of escaping air as *Calliope*, vertical now, slid stern-first into littered, convulsing sea.

Trench said into the TBS microphone, 'All right, Sam. Resume your previous station. Out.'

Tone as flat as he felt. Clegg had just reported that seventeen of the bodies who'd been dragged on board *Lyric* might be kept alive: but none of them was Nick Everard. Before that, Crockford of *Foremost* had reported having picked up fifty-three men of whom twenty-two had died or had been dead before they'd arrived on board – leaving thirty-one, many of them in very poor shape. Here again, no news of Everard.

'The *Earl Granville*'s in trouble, sir.'

He swung round on his high seat. McAllister, his navigator, had binoculars aimed through the space between the *Tacora* and the *Carrickmore*. The *Earl Granville* had been on fire for the last couple of hours. She was down by the bow, after an explosion in her for'ard hold which her master had claimed would not prevent him maintaining the present eight knots – and now she was turning out to port and seemed to be losing way.

In fact she'd stopped her engines. There was no bow-wave at all.

Radstock was closing her, and *Northern Glow* was only about six hundred yards astern. There were no bombers overhead, and nothing on the radar screen either, at this moment: Trench suspected there might not be many other moments like it, between now and sunset. The idea of putting the *Earl Granville* in tow – perhaps of the *Berkeley* – entered his mind; but it would slow the whole convoy by several knots, prolong the exposure to attack still further, as likely as not cause further losses. Better, he thought, to cut those losses – especially as she looked burnt-out, had flooding for'ard and fires in 'tween-deck areas elsewhere, was hardly worth risking other ships and lives for.

He reached for the TBS again, and called *Legend*, told John Ready to close the *Earl Granville* and talk to her master. If she couldn't keep up she was to be abandoned and sunk. He slid off his seat. 'Hold the fort, pilot. I'll be in the chart-room.'

One of the things he'd learnt from Nick Everard was that as long as options were open, a wise man kept them all in mind. The most dangerous thing was to act like a tram on tracks, unable to re-think a plan or intention when changing circumstances demanded a new approach.

Everard had taught a lot of people a lot of things simply by demonstrating that objectives which might seem unattainable could often be reached by varying the route to them. This was exactly what he was thinking about now – and he was motivated not only by the natural and proper desire to get as much of these cargoes into North Russia as could possibly be fought through, but also by what felt like a personal obligation to Nick Everard to do so. In Trench's mind it was still Nick's convoy, his own position that of caretaker.

Everard had been Trench's CO at Narvik, where their performance in the destroyer *Intent* had – well, had been highly productive, after a thoroughly forbidding start. Nick had subsequently given Trench a boost in his own career with a glowing personal recommendation. It was one of the characteristics of the man that he'd always stood by the people who'd served under him.

Trench leant over the chart table. He was escort commander now, and he didn't want to be off *Moloch's* bridge a moment longer than necessary. But the plain fact was that the distance between here and Archangel – he set dividers against the latitude scale – was, say 350 miles to get to the White Sea, then another 160 or so through to Archangelsk, as the Russians called it. Roughly 500 miles. A hell of a long haul at eight knots and under this intensity of attack.

Suppose PQ 19 diverted to Kola. From dusk this evening. Hold this present course for five or six hours, then at sundown alter course for Kola. That would be a run of only two hundred miles.

It was probably the only way to get most of the remaining cargoes through. It was also – Trench thought – most likely what Nick Everard would have done. In fact the more he looked at it, the more obvious it became. He pulled a pad towards him, and began to rough out a signal which could be put into a more complete form presently . . .

To SBNO North Russia, repeated to Admiralty and AIG 311, from *Moloch* . . . *Calliope* sunk by torpedo and bomb attacks in position—? – as—?. 48 survivors including wounded picked by *Lyric* and *Foremost*, but commanding officer is missing.

He poised the pencil over that word 'missing'. Then he decided, scowling, that it was as good as any other word for it. He wrote, *Earl Granville*, and left a space for a mention of this new loss, which surely was imminent. McAllister could fill in all the blanks – positions, times etcetera. Trench scrawled swiftly.

Oiler *Sovyetskaya Slava* holed by near-miss and reduced to 8 knots maximum. This and continuing air attacks make diversion to Kola Inlet essential. Course will be altered at dusk to 220 degrees. Request fighter cover and early rendezvous with local escort. Estimated position of PQ 19 dawn 13th—?

McAllister could fill in the missing bits. You didn't keep a dog and do your own barking. He left the signal on the chart, and ran up to the bridge.

'Slow together.'

McAllister passed the order down. Trench's intention was to drop astern for a loud-hailer chat with the commodore, tell him about diverting to Kola. McAllister told him as he straightened from the voicepipe, 'The *Earl Granville*'s abandoning, sir.'

Cramphorn took the stethoscope from his ears and told Sick Berth Attendant Bowles, 'Don't bother.'

Bowles had been wrapping a pre-warmed blanket around a lanky, ginger-haired body, the ninth of eleven hypothermia cases and the second to die after being brought down here. This was the captain's day cabin, inter-connecting with sleeping cabin and bathroom. Officers' cabins which led off the flat outside had also been comman-deered. *Lyric* rolled suddenly and powerfully to starboard, sending camp-beds and stretchers sliding . . . Cramphorn said, 'Get him up to the lobby.' He was checking the list. 'No identification?'

'Got 'im on this one, sir.' Bowles had it. 'Name of Keeble – torpedoman. No identity disc, but that Killick knew 'im – bloke with the duff left 'and.'

Cramphorn had been operating on a leading seaman – he'd finished the job only a few minutes ago – an amputation at the wrist of a hand that looked as if it had been chewed by a shark but in fact had been caught in the block of a boat's falls and crushed. Cramphorn had been using the officers' bathroom as an operating theatre, an advantage of the cramped space being that he could jam himself in between his patient and the bulkhead and thus avoid being flung off his feet during the course of the operation. While he'd been doing that and another job, Leading SBA Murchison with Bowles and two wardroom stewards as assistants had continued the treatment of hypothermia cases, a production-line system devised by Cramphorn and involving immersion for ten minutes in water at a temperature of 45 degrees – sea water, in the skipper's bathroom, which connected with the adjoining sleeping-cabin – then a rubbing-down with warm towels, and finally enclosure in blankets, also prewarmed. Cramphorn had studied the experiences of others, mainly of doctors in small ships on Arctic convoys, and he'd trained this team, making the best use he could of limited facilities. He'd impressed on them that too much warmth would be as fatal as too little: but he'd still been worried, having to leave them at it on their own while he was operating, that their enthusiasm and anxiety for the patients might run away with them, so they'd overheat the bath-water . . . But what really determined success or failure – meaning life or death – given reasonably good treatment and men who hadn't been in the sea more than a few minutes, was the individual's physique. They were all unconscious now, of course, knocked out by the cold, and the questions were firstly, whether consciousness would be regained in time, and secondly, whether there might be brain damage, which could be either temporary or permanent.

Only two to go, now. Murchison and the others had put three men through the defreezing process while Cramphorn had been performing his two operations. They were the only surgical cases he had, although he'd expected dozens. The reason, of course, was the cold water: badly wounded men had simply not survived. And this was the best time of the year: in January, one minute in that sea would be as effective as a bullet in the brain.

'This lad's for an 'ammock, sir. Carry on, shall we?'

'Hang on.' Cramphorn went over, with his stethoscope. All bunks were now occupied, and this next patient, and then one other, would go into warmed (body-temperature) hammocks slung in the wardroom flat. The two stewards were carrying the red-headed torpedoman through there now, and up the ladder to the quarterdeck lobby; Bowles had gone next-door to give the last man his towelling. Staggering like a drunk as *Lyric*, under helm and heeling, pitched to a head-on sea.

'Be better off in an 'ammock, I'd say.'

Less likely to be thrown out, he meant. But all the bunks had lee-boards on them, and bedding strapping the patients in tight. Cramphorn asked, applying his stethoscope, 'Got this one's name and rate?'

There was a heartbeat, thank God. Faint enough, and breathing so shallow you'd only detect it by vapour on a glass, but there was life – despite an appearance of death, dead-pale complexion which emphasized a puckered scar running from the left eye to the corner of the mouth. No beauty now, this fellow – but largeboned, deepchested, and Cramphorn had no doubt he owed his life to that powerful constitution. His life so far – and to have survived even this long, after at least several minutes in that sea, was fairly miraculous. Wonders never ceased; and David Cramphorn, who'd been a medical student when the war had started four years ago, marvelled at them all.

Murchison had answered that he didn't know this patient's name or rate.

'Weren't no disc on 'im, nothing.' checking his own list again. 'Yeah, I'm right. We 'ad to cut the suit off of him. It 'ad a label sort of thing saying *Everard* . . . 'ere, flaming 'ell!'

Reeling – he'd been squatting on his heels – and grabbing as he fell at the camp-bed, to stop its slide across the deck. On the new course the motion was worse than it had been. Cramphorn checked his own notes. 'You did say *Everard*?'

'Yeah, but didn't seem to be 'is name, like, more just . . .'

'On a suit, you said?'

'Sort of – well, flying suit, might've been. Zipfastener, an' all. Couldn't shift it, so Lofty Smith pulls out 'is pusser's dirk an' . . .'

A pusser's dirk was a seaman's knife. Cramphorn had looked round as the stewards came back in. One of them came over to help with this patient, the nameless man who'd worn a flying suit, and the other went through to help Bowles. Mention of a flying suit had confused Cramphorn for a moment; he'd thought of Jones, the young Fleet Air Arm pilot they'd picked up and who was still on board – how anyone in *Calliope* could have been in his suit . . . But there was no connection – except Jones had also been in the drink, for about ten seconds . . .

He'd found that name in his notes now.

'Parrot.' Addressing the steward. 'I'll lend a hand here. You nip up to the bridge, give the skipper a message. Tell him we have an unconscious hypothermia case down here who I believe may be Captain Sir Nicholas Everard.'

'Cor, stone the crows!'

Staring down at the pallid, lifeless-looking features . . .

Cramphorn added, 'Be bloody careful how you go.' He'd jerked his head, drawing the steward's attention to the pounding of heavy seas across the deck above their heads.

Trench had been talking to the commodore by loud-hailer, explaining his intention of diverting to the Kola Inlet. He finished, 'Then we can collect the homebound lot from Archangel – or they might sail with a local escort and we'd meet them at sea. How does it strike you, sir?'

He lowered the hailer. On the far side of the strip of lively sea that separated them, Insole raised his.

'I agree – it's the best thing, in the circumstances. Mind you, Trench, the Russkis won't like it.'

Trench said, not into his loud-hailer, 'Bugger the bloody Russkis!'

'Hear, hear.' A grin from Willy Henderson, *Moloch*'s first lieutenant. Trench had the hailer up again: 'Have to like it or lump it, won't they?'

There'd been a call on the radar voicepipe, and McAllister had answered it. Trench told Henderson, 'Two-eight-oh revs, Number One.' McAllister reported, 'Radar has aircraft formation closing on two-five-three range seventeen miles, sir.'

'Red flag, yeoman.'

'Red air warning flag – hoist!'

Moloch was surging forward . . . Trench's thumb on the alarm buzzer to bring his ship's company back to their action stations. The respite – he checked his watch – had lasted three quarters of an hour. Focusing his glasses now on the smoking hulk of the *Earl Granville*: she was a long way astern, and *Legend* was still there with her. They should have got all her crew out of her by this time, and with a new wave of bombers coming in they'd better be told to get a move on. He looked round, to tell his yeoman, Halliday, to call *Legend* on TBS, but someone else piped up on the radio-telephone at that moment. It was *Lyric* calling, Sam Clegg, her skipper, wanting to speak to Commander Trench.

9

'So where is he now? I mean, where's *Calliope*?'

Setter was plugging through a choppy sea, this evening, in a rising wind that promised badly for tomorrow. The weather forecast had been right, it seemed. Up to now the going hadn't been at all bad, but at this halfway point it looked as if Messrs Gimber, Steep and Towne were in line for some discomfort.

Paul told Crawshaw, 'I've no idea. Last time I saw him was in London, and his ship was at Chatham. In dock, bottom-scraping or something. By this time she could be anywhere.'

'They might have sent her down to the Med.' Massingbird, the engineer, eased the lid off a tin of fifty Players. He was a graduate of the Royal Navy's engineering college at Keyham – Devonport – but after these few days at sea he looked more like a recent escaper from Devil's Island. He added, 'Salerno, all that malarkey.'

MacGregor brought the conversation back to where he'd started it in the first place – the Everard family.

'What about Admiral Sir Hugh Everard? I know he'd retired before the war and went back to sea as a convoy commodore – but is he still doing that?'

'No. On the beach again, much to his annoyance.

Arthritis – he can hardly move. He's my great-uncle; nice old guy.'

'He's more than that. What about his part in the Battle of Jutland – when he commanded the battleship *Nile*, right?' Paul nodded. MacGregor told the others, 'He turned her out of the line – positively Nelsonian, and what a sight it must have been! Poor old *Warspite* was getting really bollocked by the entire Hun battlefleet, and he turns *Nile* straight towards them and draws their fire!' MacGregor wagged his head. 'Not a doubt he saved *Warspite*.'

'My father was at Jutland too. He was in a destroyer. He'd been in a battleship's gunroom in Scapa Flow, in the Grand Fleet. Hated it – he was "under report", supposed to be a failure. Then he got this break – I think his uncle Hugh pulled a string and got him the draft-chit to this destroyer – *Lanyard*, her name was . . . Anyway, she was in the thick of it, and he finished up as the only officer left alive – he was a sub-lieutenant then, not quite twenty-one – and he brought her back, three-quarters wrecked, having torpedoed a Hun destroyer en route.' Paul smiled. 'Then promptly got into hot water over something else. I forget what – but he was never what anyone would call orthodox.'

'Your mother's a White Russian?'

'Well, she's American now. But yes – he married her in the Black Sea in 1919, when we were trying to help the Whites against the Bolsheviks. But they split up when I was still a child. He has a new wife now – a real honey.'

'Might say he has it made, then.' Crawshaw could have been envious. 'Terrific reputation, a honey of a wife, you say, a title, medals by the yard, big house, land in – Yorkshire, you said?'

'West Riding.' Paul accepted one of Massingbird's cigarettes. 'Thanks, Chief.'

Henning, the navigator, was on watch, and Dick Eaton was up there with him. Brazier was sitting next to Paul, but he hadn't contributed a word to the conversation. He'd never been exactly talkative. Crawshaw asked. 'Mind a personal question, on the subject of your family?'

'No, I don't mind.'

'Are you in line for the baronetcy? I mean, are there any other Everards ahead of you?'

'No, there aren't. So if I survived my father – yes, I am. But that's a toss-up, really, in present circumstances.' He lit the cigarette, in a general silence. No-one wanting to agree with him, when that would imply that chances of survival from the X-craft operation were slim. Which they were, of course – and knowing it was good enough reason not to mention it. Paul added, 'My stepmother's had a baby son, a year ago. Named Hugh, after the great-uncle. So if my father was knocked off and I was too, that's who'd inherit.'

'I'm sure we all hope that neither your father nor you will get *knocked off*, as you call it!'

'Thank you, sir.' Paul glanced up at the electric clock. 'But if you'd excuse me now, I have to go and make a 'phone call.'

X-12 and the three men in her were never out of his mind. Particularly now, with the weather turning bad. He went aft through the control room, through the cold rush of air which the pounding diesels drew in from the hatch; he slid back the wireless office door, pulled it shut again behind him to keep out the noise and cold.

'Evening, Colbey.'

The telegraphist moved over. He was grey-headed, unusually old-looking for a submariner. Paul sat down in the spare chair, pulled the telephone closer and cranked its handle. All he got was static: he waited, anxious, remembering a dream he'd had last night. He'd been doing this, trying to get through – but no sound at all, the wire had gone dead, towrope parted, X-12 lost . . . Then Gimber's face and staring eyes seen through a film of water, Gimber's body floating on its back – inside the craft, and the realisation suddenly that he, Paul, was also inside it with the corpse and trapped, water-level rising swiftly, roaring as it always did when it jetted in under pressure . . . He remembered too the psychiatrist, Claverhouse, asking him 'What about dreams?' A truthful answer would have been, I have them quite often, and they're terrifying . . . He'd cranked the handle again, and now Gimber's voice came through loud and clear: 'What's for supper in the Grand Hotel, then?'

'You sound cheerful, Louis.'

Gimber adopted the voice of Mona Lott, a character in Tommy Handley's ITMA programme: he whined, 'It's being so cheerful keeps me going . . . Actually I have an unpleasant feeling that things are becoming bumpy. Any worse than this, we'll have to trim her heavy for'ard. What's the forecast now?'

He could visualise them, in that cramped space a hundred feet under the sea, the other two with their eyes and ears on Gimber, dreading the answer to that question. Paul told him, 'It's not too good, I'm sorry to say.'

'So what is it?'

'Force four, southwesterly.'

Actually the forecast had been for winds force four and five, sea rough to very rough. There didn't seem any point in laying it on thicker than you had to. It would happen anyway, you couldn't do anything to stop it . . . Paul added, 'We've coped with a lot more than force four on exercises, Louis.'

'Exercises lasting a few hours, not whole bloody days on end . . . Anyway, don't wet your pants, we'll make out . . . Any news from FOSM?'

'Not yet.'

The news they were waiting for would be the reconnaissance photos of Altenfjord, the details of the targets' positions and net protection. When the photo-intelligence experts had completed their analysis of the pictures there'd be a signal from Admiral Barry spelling it all out and ordering one or other of the alternative attack plans.

Gimber grumbled, 'I thought we'd've had it cut and dried by now.'

'Maybe the Catalina developed more pigeon problems.'

They'd been flying the pictures down from Russia by Catalina flying-boat; and this was a reference to Soviet red tape. The Catalinas up there had carrier pigeons in them for life-saving purposes, to carry SOS messages back to base in emergency. Soviet customs officials had impounded the birds, on the grounds it was illegal to import livestock. There were jokes now about the pigeons having to be Party members to get in.

'How's the routine going, Louis?'

'OK. Except if you take Benzedrine to stay awake it's bloody impossible to sleep when you come off watch. Also your mouth tastes like a garbage pail . . . What's the news from Italy, if any?'

'The Bosch are said to be pulling back, above Salerno, and the Eighth Army's linked up with the Fifth. Us and the Yanks, that means, I suppose.'

'Of course that's what it means, and Eaton told me the same thing two hours ago.'

'It's good news, anyway.'

'Tell you what I'd call good. A hot bath, some big eats, a night in clean sheets, a first-class warrant down to London, Jane there to meet me.'

'She will be, Louis. In due course.'

'I wonder.'

'What's that mean?'

'Would you give a damn, anyway?'

'I'm not quite with you, Louis.'

'Say that again, old boy . . . But now listen. If the weather gets worse – when it does – might be sensible to check communications every half-hour instead of hourly. Can do?'

*   *   *

The air stank inside the midget. It was one of the things you just had to live with. 'Trigger' Towne asked Gimber as he replaced the telephone, 'What's that weather news?'

'Force four's expected.' Gimber looked at Steep. 'I'll take over, Ozzie. Get some rest.'

'But it's your turn.' Steep looked harassed as well as ill. 'I'm OK, honestly.'

Pale, dull-eyed; sweat gleamed on his face and forehead. In the last twelve hours he'd developed chronic seasickness; he was very far from 'OK' and he didn't seem to be getting any better. X-12 was porpoising on her tow-rope, depth varying all the time between about seventy and ninety feet in more or less regular undulations; she'd been doing it for two days, except for the six-hourly breathers on the surface. Steep was on his seat at the after end of the control room, with a bucket beside him which he'd been using since last night; it did nothing to improve the atmosphere, despite his emptying it into the heads – the lavatory, in the W and D compartment – at frequent intervals.

Gimber told him, 'That wasn't a suggestion, Ozzie. It's an order. Go for'ard, get your head down.'

X-12 launching herself downward now. A fifty-foot steel cylinder weaving up and down like a kite on a string. Towne winked sympathetically at Steep as the sub-lieutenant climbed out of his seat and went for'ard, squeezing past Gimber under the dome, pausing in the W and D for his own purposes and then crawling through into the fore-end, on to the wooden pallet that covered the top of the boat's battery. All Gimber could see from this end now, looking for'ard through the openings in the two transverse bulkheads of the W and D, were the soles of his tennis shoes. He was lying on his face, head pillowed on crossed arms: he'd just crawled into that position and stopped moving. He'd left the bucket in the Wand D.

Gimber said quietly, 'Trigger – be a good bloke, put a lashing on that bucket?'

'Eh?' Then he caught on. Before the bucket started flying around, Gimber had meant. Towne slid off his seat and crept into the W and D. Gimber was settling himself at the controls, on the first lieutenant's seat. Before the telephone conversation with Everard he'd been doing some mopping-up, a chore which Trigger Towne would now continue when he'd secured the pail. It was one of a number of routine chores that had to be done for several hours each day, to keep the dampness under some kind of control.

Gimber murmured, as Towne came back, 'Poor sod.'

'Wouldn't have thought it.' Towne wrung out a swab. 'We had worse than this, training, and I never saw him puke.'

'It never went on this long. It's either that or it's the Benzedrine affecting him, some sort of reaction to it.' Gimber was moving the hydroplane control very cautiously, aiming to reduce the amount of porpoising but careful not to overdo it. A little too much 'plane angle could make this worse instead of better; and if you had her fighting the drag of the tow, you could easily snap it. He shook his head: 'He'll get over it. By tomorrow, I'd guess.'

'You didn't think to tell Everard.'

Gimber shrugged. 'Wouldn't be much point.'

'Except if it goes on – or he gets worse—'

'Odds are he'll have his sealegs by tomorrow.'

'Bloody hope so.' Towne scowling: he was on his side with his legs drawn up and his bearded face against the casing of the trim-pump, one arm reaching down into the bilge and the other doubled out of the way behind him . . . 'How long before the next guff-through?'

Gimber checked the time. 'About an hour.' He'd found the optimum angle for a permanent setting on the hydroplanes: she still porpoised, but slightly less, in slightly flattened curves. By 'permanent' he meant of course in terms of present sea conditions: wind and sea were getting up, so it wouldn't last for long. By morning, in fact, life might be distinctly less than comfortable. Still, he had his hands free now, so he could keep an eye on the depth-gauge and the bubble but at the same time do some drying-out maintenance, wiping moisture off the inside surface of the hull, off pipelines and machinery and exposed wiring. Most of the dampness – and actual water, gathering finally in the bilges – came from condensation, and its main threat was to equipment, particularly electrics. The prime symptom would be reduction in insulation values, but electrical gear generally was at risk. The creeping damp also affected human beings – wet clothes, wet skin inside them, hair that remained wringing wet as if you'd been swimming . . .

Well, nobody had been expecting a joyride.

Towne was wriggling backwards, as a preliminary to getting himself into an upright or partially upright position. You couldn't just sit up or lie down or turn around: you had to look first to see what was where and how best to fit around it. With the whole bag of tricks swooping up and down all the time. Towne swearing softly to himself as he extricated his long legs, then folded them the other way; he muttered, 'I better take a shufti at the compressor. Right?'

They'd thought it was noisy when it had last been running. It was driven by the main engine, the Gardner, and its function was to compress air into steel bottles from which main ballast tanks were blown, for surfacing. High-pressure air was a precious commodity, since it was basically your ticket to the surface, and the machine that provided it was therefore a vital item of equipment. Not that any single item was superfluous: if any had been, the designers would hardly have wasted valuable space by including it. And as every single piece of gear had to be in the best possible running order when the operational crew took over in a few days' time, maintenance was a very important part of the passage crew's duties.

Only two of them to do it all, if Ozzie was going to be kaput for long.

Gimber frowned, remembering the end of his conversation with Paul Everard. It had just slipped out: result of the strains of the recent days, he supposed, but no less unfortunate for that. He'd have liked to have wiped it out of his own memory and Paul's: and it was a reminder that, under pressure as they were, you needed to watch out: he hadn't realised that the rot had already set in, to that extent . . .

Trigger Towne, having extricated himself from his recent Houdini-like entanglement, broke into Gimber's thoughts.

'Compressor, then – OK? Got an hour, you said?'

He nodded, waking up. He'd been staring at the depth-gauge in a sort of daze. You could get hypnotised, gazing at its shine for hours, literally. Seeing nothing, or seeing – everything. Jane, for instance, and Everard's relationship with her. If any. Her sweetness and her ambivalence, his own patience out of consideration for the dreadful hurt she'd suffered. Jane as one of the walking wounded of this war . . . He transferred his eyes from the bubble to Trigger Towne. 'Say fifty minutes.'

'I'll do it in more like thirty.'

Towne began to squirm aft. The compressor was in the engine compartment, the after-end. To run it – when you were on the surface or at least had the induction trunk up, because the diesel couldn't run without air – you clutched it in at a point between the engine-clutch and the for'ard end of the main motor. It was a hell of a spot to get at; the designers didn't have to.

By daylight it was blowing force four, as promised. *Setter* pitching hard with the blow on her port quarter, and Paul was scared about conditions down there in the midget. Gimber wasn't saying much on the telephone; only that it was 'much as you'd expect'. Then: 'For God's sake, do I have to describe it to you?'

'Not if you don't want to, Louis. But keep your wool on.'

'Yeah . . . And if you want to know, I'll tell you – it's fairly bloody!'

'Anyone seasick?'

'Of course we're seasick!'

'All of you?'

'Trigger's all right. He's got no more belly on him than an eel has, he doesn't know how to be sick.'

Paul heard some muttering in the background. Towne's voice. He said, 'I didn't know you did, Louis.'

'Well, this motion is somewhat exceptional.'

MacGregor commented, when Paul told him, 'I can't imagine much worse. Seasickness on its own is bad enough – but in that tin can . . .'

On the surface during her last ventilation period, X-12 had hardly been visible in the waves sweeping over her. But the change of air would have more than compensated for such a minor discomfort as getting soaked. From what Gimber had said, their clothes were permanently sodden anyway, just from condensation.

Paul had been wondering about Gimber's cryptic but hostile remark over the telephone the previous evening. It might have meant very little – a very minor undercurrent of jealousy or suspicion exacerbated by conditions. Gimber might have been having some problem with Jane and imagining she'd have discussed it with Paul. But it had sounded like more than that – like smoke indicating fire. Ordinarily Paul might have shrugged it off, thought All right, so he's caught on, we can play it in the open now. He'd have been glad of that – ordinarily. But this was no time for emotional complications.

They were having breakfast in *Setter*'s wardroom when FOSM's signal arrived. Part of the table was cleared, and Brazier and Eaton did the decyphering. Jazz Lanchberry, who'd got the buzz that the all-important message had come in, shuffled aft from the ERAs' mess and sipped at a mug of wardroom coffee, leaning against the bulkhead door while he waited for answers. Brazier muttered, as they started work, 'Could be they've taken off again. Fjords empty, no bloody targets – turn round, come home . . .'

Massingbird said from his bunk, 'Then you'd be lucky.' They ignored him. Eaton said, 'First word is "reconnaissance".'

The aerial photographs had been analysed. *Tirpitz* was in her protective box at the end of Kafjord, and *Scharnhorst* was similarly penned nearby. *Lützow* was in Langfjord, in her own private enclosure; the system of nets and barriers was as it had been before. FOSM's order to the X-craft flotilla now was 'Target Plan 4'.

MacGregor was standing on one leg in the gangway, pushing the other into waterproof trousers in preparation for a visit to the bridge. Hopping on the one leg as she rolled, Lanchberry backing out of his way. MacGregor asked Paul, 'What does that mean for you, Everard?'

'We go after the tiddler.'

'*Lützow*?'

He nodded. It was disappointing. All right, to destroy a 10,000-ton 'pocket battleship' would be a good day's work, but one had hoped to get a crack at the big one, *Tirpitz*. Under Plan 4, *Tirpitz* would be attacked by X-5, X-6 and X-7, *Scharnhorst* was allocated to X-9, X-10 and X-11, and Paul would share *Lützow* with X-8.

MacGregor said, reading Paul's mind, 'Hardly a tiddler. I'd call that a very worthwhile target.' He added, into a silence – Brazier and Eaton were looking glum too – 'I wouldn't mind.' Meaning he'd be glad to get *Lützow* in his sights from *Setter*. It was a point well made: and at least the thing was fixed now, they could get on with it. Paul got out his chart and large-scale diagrams, and settled down with the others to check over the approach route, distances and timing. X-12 and X-8 would be the last to go in, as their target was the closest and the entire attack needed to be synchronised. Otherwise if you were in the fjord when someone else's charges went up, you could be blown to kingdom come: or a premature attack could spoil all the others' chances. Routes for different craft were varied, but there was a minefield to be crossed to start with and for most of them the last part of the approach to Altenfjord would be through a narrow channel called Stjernsund. But X-12 was to use Rognsund – a narrower passage, somewhat trickier.

It would be an extraordinary moment, getting there. Being there, inside, with those enormous enemy ships in reach. Other enemies too, no doubt. He couldn't guess, now, how he'd feel – mainly excited or mainly terrified. And in any case you had to get there first.

Eaton murmured, 'I'd have liked a shot at the Beast.'

'The Beast' was said to be Winston Churchill's name for the *Tirpitz*. Churchill was personally very keen to see her put out of action. The Germans, taking a different view, had nicknamed her 'the Queen of the North'.

Nobody had ever given *Lützow* a pet name. She'd been laid-down in 1931 as the *Deutschland*. 'Pocket battleship' was a meaningless term: effectively she was an exceptionally powerful heavy cruiser.

'I'll be back.' Paul slid out from behind the table. 'Have to tell Louis.'

Gimber said, 'So you're the third eleven.'

'Thanks. How's the boat, Louis?'

'Christ. What a question.'

'I mean electrics and mechanics – defects, if any.'

'One or two little things. Had a leak on the periscope gland, was the latest. We took it down, and I've just put it together again. Seems OK, at the moment, but I'll watch it. Trigger did a job on the compressor – but I told you about that. Most of the little things have been electrical, caused by the damp. Which is the worst – no, belay that, second worst thing's the damp.'

'Seasick, still?'

'Ozzie is. He's really bad.'

'Well.' Paul hesitated. 'I suppose one of us might take over – if he's really sick, and we could make a transfer. I'd ask MacGregor, if . . .'

'Wait. I'll ask Ozzie.'

He heard Gimber and Steep talking – thin, distant voices. Then Gimber was back on the line.

'Ozzie says he'll stick it out, thanks all the same. Says he's getting over it. He doesn't look like it, and every few minutes he doesn't sound like it, either. Tries to puke, but all he can do is make revolting noises . . . But we'd better accept his word for it – the aim is for you lot to be all bright-eyed and bushy-tailed when the day dawns, isn't it.'

'Meanwhile you and Trigger are sharing all the work?'

'Most of it. But we can handle it.'

'All right. But let me know if . . .'

'Yeah, yeah. Paul, what I would ask for is a call from you every fifteen minutes. Possible?'

'Well, of course it's possible, but . . .' He thought, Must be worse than he's admitted. He asked, 'You mean, in case the tow parts?'

'Or in case Trigger and I both pass out. But we've parted tows before this, haven't we, I mean it can happen, and being trimmed heavy for'ard as we do have to be now.'

'Yes, I'm with you.'

'It might be nice for you to know we were still with you. Every quarter-hour?'

'All right. I'll set it up.'

'Very kind.'

'Is that sarcasm?'

'Could've been . . . Question now, though – where are we? How far to the target area?'

'We're a hundred and twenty miles west of the Lofotens. About three hundred and twenty miles to go.'

'So we've covered about seven hundred already . . . Afford to slow down a bit, couldn't we?'

'Not really, Louis.'

If he'd been in better shape he wouldn't have suggested it, Paul thought. You had to remember how desperately uncomfortable – and unnerving, at times – it must be, down there. He heard Gimber argue, 'But three hundred miles at ten knots—'

'Louis, it won't be ten knots for more than another day or so – day and a half, say. Towing ships are to make the last part of the passage dived, remember?'

Dived, *Setter* would make-good three or four knots, not ten. The lapse of memory was extraordinary, and it showed how right the planners had been to decide on having separate crews for passage and for action. The passage men would be mentally and physically exhausted by the time they reached the Norwegian coast. Paul reminded Gimber – appreciating the enormous strain he was under at this moment, and that his mind was already clouded to some extent – 'Besides which, old horse, we can't risk falling astern of schedule. The last-quarter moon's on the twentieth, which is the day we start in, and if we didn't take advantage of that waning moon—'

'Paul.'

'Huh?'

'Teach your grandmother?'

They'd need some moonlight for the passage of the outer fjords, after getting across the minefield, and also a high tide to take them safely over the moored mines. Those were the basic essentials for the kick-off, and such conditions would prevail in the few days starting on 20 September.

Gimber had hung up the telephone, muttering angrily to himself. Trigger Towne asked him, 'Problems, skipper?'

X-12 bouncing, jerking, her porpoising movement

three-dimensional and with sharp, sudden angles in it now.

'They'll make contact every fifteen minutes. Bit of a bloody nuisance, but – well . . .' He knew Towne hadn't heard him. You got sick of asking for repetitions, when someone didn't shout loud enough over the constant noise. He yelled, 'I'll take her now.'

'If you want.' Towne hadn't moved, didn't seem to be about to move.

'You've been on at least three hours, Trigger.'

'So what?'

Gimber tapped him on the shoulder. 'Change round. Get your fat head down.'

'Nah.' There was no point trying to sleep, when you knew the Benzedrine wouldn't let you. You needed the pills in order to stay awake, and sleeplessness was the price of it. In any case, there was plenty of work to be done, and only the two of them to do it. He shouted, easing himself off the first lieutenant's seat, 'Job or two first.' Turning, coming face to face with Louis Gimber: Towne's face bearded, sunken-eyed, the eyes inside there bright and glaring, crazy-looking. He kept one hand on the hydroplane control wheel until Gimber had reached to it: then they were sliding around and past each other, each needing a spare hand for steading himself against the bucking motion of the craft. Trim would have gone to pot, with two men's weights shifting around like this and no immediate adjustment, but the trim was all to hell anyway, bow-heavy and entirely dependent on the tow's drag. Towne bawled, 'You're looking better, skipper. Like a corpse half warmed-up. Hour ago you looked like one on the slab.'

'Charmed!'

'It's me old-world courtesy got me where I am . . . Take a shufti at the Sub, should I?'

'No. Let him sleep it off.'

Rest was probably the best medicine for Ozzie. Until

he'd passed out he'd been as bad as he had yesterday – retching, groaning . . . He'd slept, finally, because the effects of the Benzedrine had worn off; Gimber had suspected the pills might have been making his sickness worse, and he'd told him to stop using them. The drawback was that he and Twone were now entirely reliant on them, since they had all the watch-keeping and maintenance chores to share between them.

'W and D pump motor,' Towne was crouching behind Gimber, yelling into his ear, 'claims me attention, like. Want to compensate?'

To work on that pump in the wet-and-dry compartment meant a big shift of weight, one that would make her even heavier for'ard than she was already. As things were now, you had not only extra ballast in the bow trim-tank, but also Ozzie Steep in the fore-end. Some heaviness for'ard was necessary, to reduce the boat's tendency to dance like a cork in a waterfall, but if you overdid it you'd be increasing the strain on the Manilla rope to such an extent that it was almost bound to break. Then the weighted bow would drag her down – plummeting, as likely as not very difficult to stop in time. There was a vicious circle in this hydrostatic problem, too: the deeper a submarine dives the heavier she becomes, and even in normal circumstances you had to be alert to this, ready to pump ballast out as depth increased. With the bow-heavy trim, circumstances were a long way from normal and a lot more dangerous.

Gimber had two other things in mind, when he thought about it. One, that his own reactions and Towne's might not be as fast as they should have been, now, and two, that X-12 had something like ten thousand feet of water between her and the ocean floor – which would make for a long, long dive.

He nodded to the ERA 'Right!'

Left hand on the pump lever. Glancing round, seeing Towne move to wait amidships, under the dome. Gimber pulled the lever aft: visualising the valves opening and then the pump motor starting; then he was counting, with his eyes on the bubble in the fore-and-aft spirit-level, while seawater flowed through the trimline from the bow tank to the stern one.

Enough . . . He pushed the lever back to its central position, neutral. This movement would first have stopped the pump, then shut the valves. They had to be shut, obviously, or water would be sloshing through from one tank to the other as the midget plunged around. Then you'd have had no control over her at all. Gimber turned his head, saw Towne already crawling into the W and D, dragging a bag of tools.

X-11, in tow of HM Submarine *Scourge*, surfaced at noon for her routine period of ventilation. The sea was rough: standing on the midget's casing was like riding a surfboard. But Tom Messinger, X-11's passage-crew skipper, was enjoying the fresh air too much to give a damn about getting soaking wet in freezing Norwegian Sea. (Not quite freezing: but bloody cold.) The hatch was shut, of course – if it hadn't been the boat would have filled and sunk within about two minutes – and the induction trunk raised, Messinger with a rope's end securing himself to it and his arms wrapped round it too: there was an enormous expanse of wildly tossing sea around him, and if you were washed off you knew you'd have no hope of being seen alive again. The pounding Gardner diesel was sucking air throatily down the pipe and through the boat, filling her with fresh, clean air in place of the putrid fog they'd been breathing for the last few hours.

Two hundred yards ahead, *Scourge* had reduced speed to five knots: she was still towing, because the diesel was running at its lowest revs, entirely for air-change purposes. Messinger's watery view of *Scourge* was end-on – swaying bridge and periscope standards, two lookouts in black silhouette, sea heaping white, the submarine's after casing alternately engulfed in the white mound of it then rising shiny-black as her forepart plunged. That after casing was a lot higher out of the water than this midget's casing: the seas sweeping over X-11 were waist-high, at times. He shouted aloud – addressing only himself, sea, sky, and the cutting wind – 'This is a hell of a way to get around!' Then laughed – crazy, happy, which left no doubt you had to be pretty far gone – filling his lungs with the air, revelling in daylight and the brilliant seascape under scudding grey. Enjoying too the fact of being part of this truly extraordinary adventure – three men in a boat and the boat a tiny, highly-explosive one at that, and seven other identical rigs out there, each as solitary-feeling as this one. To starboard and ten miles away there'd be X-12 with *Setter*, while to port the line-up was *Sceptre* with X-10, *Thrasher* with X-5, *Stubborn* and X-7, *Seanymph* and X-8, *Syrtis* and X-9, *Truculent* and X-6. Spread like chariots in a race, in distant line-abreast advancing east-northeastward . . .

But it was time to go down now, so that *Scourge* could increase to ten knots again. Joy faded at the prospect of return to cramped confinement, the continuous banging around and the steadily deteriorating air. Messinger shouted down the induction pipe, 'Stop the Gardner. Tell *Scourge* we're about to dive. Shut off for diving.'

A last look round: and another at *Scourge*, where Dan Vicary, Johnny McKie, Toby Maguire and Tommo Brind were lolling in the lap of luxury. Comparatively speaking . . . Messinger had got the rope off the induction pipe and was holding on with one arm locked round it; he was giving Hillcrest time to pass that message by telephone and Charlie Amor a moment to shut the induction pipe's hull-valve. It was only the action of a moment – a lever-operated valve on the port side at shoulder-level to the helmsman, he had only to stretch out and yank it shut. He'd have done it by this time. Messinger lowered the pipe on its hinged base, crouching and holding to the casing itself with one hand while he forced it right down, horizontal. The pipe's top end was sealed by a flap-valve which tripped shut when the pipe was fully lowered – as it was now, flat to the deck. And the diesel had stopped. Crouching, still hanging on with one hand, using the other to open the hatch at a time when she'd risen to a wave and was well clear of the water: Messinger slid in feet-first and fast, pulled the lid shut again over his wet head and forced the central handwheel round so that the securing dogs engaged under steel lips around the rim.

'Sixty feet.'

Water running off him puddled on the deck boards. Bony Hillcrest, on the first lieutenant's seat, repeated the order and swung the hydroplane control wheel to 'dive'; Amor had opened the main vents and she was already going down. He'd been as sick as a dog, day before yesterday, but he was all right now; they'd all been under the weather for a time.

Forty-five feet. Fifty . . .

Hillcrest was holding the dive-angle on her. Messinger would have been easing it by now, starting to level her. But he didn't want to seem to be breathing over the shoulder of a number one who knew his job as well as Bony did.

He'd begun to take the angle off now, anyway.

Messinger noticed that the bubble was still well aft. In other words, his boat still had a pronounced bow-down angle on her. Of course, Hillcrest would have put some extra weight in her bow, but—

Telephone. Messinger reached for it.

'Yup? That you, Dan?'

The Springbok's voice assured him, 'It's not Adolf Hitler. Might be, if you didn't have an unlisted number . . . You all happy there?'

'Could be happier. Say if we'd brought some bints along.'

He meant girls. Mediterranean service had injected a lot of Arabic into the language. Vicary said, 'I'll make that point to FOSM, man, suggestion for the next op . . . Call you in an hour, ay?'

'Don't you mean half an hour?'

'Oh, ya, half—'

'Dan, I meant so they'd cook hot meals for us.'

He hung up. He'd been watching the depthgauge all the time, and she was at seventy feet now with a three-degree bow-down angle. He said, 'Let's have her at sixty, Bony.'

They called Hillcrest 'Bony' because he was supposed to look like Napoleon. Messinger saw him ease the trim-pump lever aft, to suck some weight out of the bow tank. Just as he was doing it the tow-rope snatched upwards so violently that it felt as if she'd hit a rock. Her bow shot up: if Messinger hadn't been holding on he'd have gone flying. Everything happening in one second, as if in one movement, connected parts of the same event: Hillcrest falling sideways against the lever, pushing it forward – he was on top of it, Messinger frantic in the effort to pull him up, only too well aware that ballast was flowing into that bow tank now. Bow-down, diving. Seventy-five feet – eighty, angle and rate of dive increasing. Hillcrest had got himself off the pump lever: he pulled it to neutral and then aft, to the pump-from-for'ard position. Messinger shouted, 'Blow number one main ballast!' He should have ordered this before, but he'd been preoccupied with Bony's predicament. The needle was swinging past the one-hundred mark: she was steeply bow-down and accelerating in her dive. One-twenty; one-forty . . .

Blowing. Charlie Amor had wrenched open the high-pressure blow to number one main ballast. But it wasn't making any difference – yet. One hundred and sixty feet. One-seventy-five. Hillcrest shouted at Amor, 'Blow one and three!' Amor agleam with sweat, teeth bared in a snarl as he twisted open the other HP blow. You couldn't blow the

midships main ballast tank, number two; it didn't have an
HP airline to it. One and three were blowing all the stored
air gushing to them from the bottles, but – incredibly – it
was having no effect at all. Two hundred feet: she was
nose-down, diving very fast indeed. Hillcrest turning to
stare at Messinger, face contorted: 'Christ, skipper . . .'

Messinger saw it. He flung himself towards the half-
dazed ERA's blowing-panel. He screamed, 'Main vents!'

Too bloody late. Knowing it, there and then, in those
seconds before perdition. Main vents were still open from
the act of diving and all that air had been blowing straight
out into the sea.

A bunch of *Setter* and X-12 officers were playing poker dice,
the variety of the game known as Double Cameroon, that
evening, when Brazier took his turn to go along and make
the routine telephone-call. When he came back, squeezing
his large frame on to the bench, he said, 'Louis's
complaining he can't get any work done when we inter-
rupt him every few minutes. He wants to make it half-
hourly again.'

'Fine. But that was his own idea . . . Now there's the
high straight I needed . . .'

Gimber must be feeling better about things, he
concluded. Sea-sickness on top of all the other discomforts
would be fairly shattering to morale. He wished the
weather would ease a little.

After supper, a signal from *Stubborn* was picked up and
decoded. She was reporting having come across X-8 loose
and wandering, having parted her tow from *Seanymph*
earlier in the day. *Stubborn* gave the midget's position,
course and speed, so that FOSM could arrange for
Seanymph to rendezvous with her and re-establish the tow.

'Darned lucky finding her.' MacGregor was turning in.
'Odds against must've been in thousands.'

'And I wouldn't like to be in Jack Smart's wet socks.'

Paul scooped up the dice. Smart was X-8's passage-crew CO. 'A whole night on the surface, in this sea?'

At midnight there was another urgent signal. X-11's tow had parted, and *Scourge* had reversed course in the hope of finding her.

Nobody made any comment. But you couldn't rest easily, either, after that. It was all too obvious that X-11 might not have had X-8's luck. Luck, or skill, or whatever combination of the two you'd need, in whatever the circumstances might have been . . . Paul went to the wireless office to call X-12, and it was a relief to hear Gimber's voice over the wire, even though the tone of it was peevish.

'I had Eaton on this thing only about twenty minutes ago!'

'So, I've warmed the ball a bit . . . But you're OK, are you?'

'You might say so, at a pinch. Ozzie's still out for the count.'

'Oh, is he . . . Well, d'you want someone to . . .'

'No, I don't!'

Paul waited a moment. Then he tried again. 'I was about to ask—'

'I know, I'm sorry, I don't want any bloody thing at all. Ozzie'll soon snap out of it, and meanwhile we're coping all right.' There was some distant mumbling: Gimber talking aside to Towne, he guessed. Then the voice came back: 'Trigger agrees, we're all right as we are. Benzedrine's the answer . . . Any news?'

There was no point telling him about X-8 and X-11. Paul said, 'Nothing worth repeating. You'll be up for a guff-through at two, right?'

'If our luck holds out, we will.'

He certainly wasn't his normal self. Perhaps one shouldn't have expected it. Paul told him, 'I'm turning in, now. Talk again later.'

'Ha. Sleep tight. Pleasant dreams.'

'In four days' time, Louis, you'll be doing the sleeping-tight routine.'

'D'you ever dream about her, Paul?'

Hanging up, Gimber stared grimly at Towne. He muttered, 'Four days . . .'

10

Trench leant over the bunk, staring down at him. Looking for something he didn't find. Outside, the sounds of work in progress were loud and constant – from the deck above, and from the jetty and from *Foremost* who was secured on the other side – while in this semi-dark cabin the tranquillity was an illusion, a phoney quiet in which Trench's deep concern for Nick Everard's life was at odds with his need to be elsewhere – in about half a dozen other places, at this very moment. He asked *Lyric*'s doctor, Cramphorn, 'Is there really a chance he can take in what's said to him?'

'It's quite possible, sir. And probably best to assume he can. I mean, for his sake.'

Trench didn't know what he'd meant by that. *Foremost*'s doctor – also an RNVR two-striper – saw the frown, and explained quietly, 'Sort of to keep him in touch, sir. By engaging his attention, getting the brain back into gear, as it were. Could make a lot of difference.'

Trench's eyes rested for a moment on this other doctor. He didn't look much more than twenty years old, but of course he had to be more than that. He nodded. 'I see.' Turning back to the man in the bunk: wondering what it would be like to hear things that were said to you but not be able to answer or even signal that you'd heard.

'Are you hearing me, sir?'

To be asked a question would be even more frustrating. But it might be like hearing a voice in a dream, he guessed. He was still looking for reaction – for the movement of an eyelid, the twitch of a muscle – and not seeing any at all. Trench wasn't enjoying this – either the situation itself or the charade of addressing someone who was so deeply unconscious that it felt like talking to a corpse. He had no confidence in being heard, or of doing any good at all: it was simply a matter of taking these quacks' word for it, accepting that they'd have to know more about it than he did himself . . . 'It's Trench here, sir. I expect you feel bloody awful, but the doctors say you're doing well, so there's nothing for you to worry about. Just prove them right, get better – and I'll handle the trip home, you've nothing to worry about at all.'

Rubbish. He told himself, If he's hearing me, he's thinking, 'What a load of codswallop!' He'd glanced round again, at the two doctors. Feeling idiotic . . . This cabin belonged to *Lyric*'s first lieutenant, or had done until it had been commandeered to become Nick Everard's sickroom.

Trench forced himself to start yacking again . . . 'Everything's under control, sir. We're at Vaenga, in the Kola Inlet. I diverted because if we'd stuck to the Archangel plan there might not have been much left of us by the time we got there. You're on board *Lyric* – they picked you up when *Calliope* went down. You're in what the doc calls a coma, as a result of hypothermia – that's a technical term for too long in cold water. It's like a bang on the head, apparently – knocks you out . . . But you're in good hands, sir, and they tell me you'll be sitting up and taking notice before much longer.'

Lyric was alongside Vaenga pier, and *Foremost* was berthed outside her. Some of the survivors had been moved into the AA ship, the *Berkeley*, while fit men or those only lightly wounded were being distributed among the destroyers. Only men who were considered unlikely to survive the journey home were being left ashore, but whether they'd survive here was something of a toss-up; the hospital was little more than a shack, with inadequate lighting, heat or sanitation and only the most basic equipment: the medical stores which had been on board *Calliope* were now at the bottom of the Barents Sea.

Trench had brought the remnants of PQ 19 into the Kola Inlet soon after dawn this morning. The last hundred and fifty miles had taken twice as long as he'd expected, mostly because the *Sovyetskaya Slava* had been hit again, on the afternoon of the day of *Calliope*'s loss, and her speed reduced from eight knots to four and a half. Then the *Carrickmore* had also been hit and a fire started in one of her holds; she'd still been smouldering internally when the merchantmen had gone to their berths for discharging cargo. But yesterday there'd been only one attack, high-level and ineffectual. They'd owed this mercy to the wind having dropped overnight and the cloud thickening, pressing down towards the sea, providing cover which must have been infuriating to the Luftwaffe. So this morning Trench had delivered the *Tacora*, the *Sovyetskaya Slava*, *Carrickmore*, *Republican*, *Ewart S. Dukes* and *Galilee Dawn* and their more or less intact cargoes of war material. The Soviet tanker, as she'd plugged slowly on up the inlet with a tug to help her, had gone so far as to signal a 'thank you', which in Trench's experience was unprecedented.

He described these events to the unresponsive patient. There was some coming and going behind him while he was talking, and when he paused and looked round he found Sam Clegg, *Lyric*'s captain, at his elbow.

'Crockford's waiting in my day cabin, sir. D'you want him in here?'

'No – we'll go through.'

Crockford was captain of *Foremost*, and Trench had sent for him to come over. Saving time, while he was here – two birds with one stone . . . Cramphorn was telling Clegg he'd stay with the patient; Trench asked him whether Nick would need to have someone with him all the time.

The doctor nodded. 'Within sight and sound, anyway. When he comes-to,' he added more quietly, 'or if he does . . . It could happen soon, or not for days . . . When he does, he probably won't have any memory – for events or people, may not even know his own name, for some time . . . We'll be keeping him here in *Lyric*, will we, sir? Home to the UK?'

'Home to the UK, but I think not in *Lyric*. Although it might be an idea for you, Cramphorn, to stay with him.'

Clegg asked, 'Stay where with him?'

'In *Foremost*. If these chaps will agree he can be moved. But I'd also suggest Cramphorn here might move over with him. Change places with your own doctor.' He'd glanced at Kingdon. 'Simply for continuity. Cramphorn started with him, might as well carry on?' Trench beckoned to the two doctors. 'Couple of minutes, he won't come to any harm.' He asked them outside, out of earshot of the patient who might or might not have heard, 'You do agree he shouldn't be left ashore?'

'Yes.' Cramphorn said, 'Same with all the hypothermia cases. There simply aren't the facilities.'

'But you think,' he nodded to Crockford as they filed into Clegg's day cabin 'you're confident he can survive the trip home?'

'No, sir.' Cramphorn shook his head. 'At this stage, it's a toss-up. But he'll have a better chance coming home with us than he would have if we left him here. If we have a reasonably quiet passage.'

'Nobody can promise that.' Trench lowered himself into an armchair. He told *Foremost*'s captain, 'I'm arranging for him to be moved over to you, Crockford, because being close escort you're less likely to be dashing around, and the ride shouldn't be as bumpy. Also – we've just been talking about this – I think it would be as well if Surgeon Lieutenant Cramphorn moved over to you with him, having looked after him up to now, d'you see. Sam here could have the loan of your doctor, a temporary swap?'

Crockford asked, 'D'you mind, Kingdon?'

Cramphorn excused himself, to return to the patient. Kingdon also left, to put in hand arrangements for Everard's reception on board *Foremost*. Trench talked to the two destroyer captains now. He was glad the doctors had agreed to change places. It had been his own instinctive preference, a choice of Cramphorn as the man most likely to keep Nick Everard alive. Trench was to admit, later, that it had been no more than a hunch. He'd simply wanted to give Nick Everard the best possible chance of survival that could be provided, and Cramphorn had seemed the best bet.

He told Clegg and Crockford, 'I can't tell you exactly how soon we'll be sailing from here, but I want to be ready to go as soon as we get the word. Fuel and fresh water's laid on. You'll have had that signal, I suppose?'

They had. Clegg put in, 'But no answer yet about four-seven ammo, sir.'

'That's being taken care of, don't worry. And tomorrow forenoon I want all commanding officers on board *Moloch* for conference at 11.30 sharp. I've no idea why we have to wait for permission to sail: the thing is to have everything on the top line so we can get cracking as soon as possible. In principle it's been agreed that QP 16 can be sailed from Archangel with an escort of Soviet destroyers plus minesweepers who'll be coming all the way with us. The ones we brought will be staying here as their reliefs, of course. But there'll also be a small Russian oiler with the convoy – she'll turn back to Archangel with their destroyers after we've fuelled from her. That'll see us through until we meet the *Bayleaf* somewhere near Bear Island – thanks to the good sense of that man in there.' He jerked a thumb towards the sickroom. 'But as I say, we may have to wait a day or two, or even several days. SBNO doesn't know the reason – or isn't divulging it, anyway.'

Crockford asked him as they got up, 'What's made the Russkis so co-operative?'

'I suspect they've been persuaded that until we get these empties home we won't be bringing them any full ones.' Trench said, 'While I'm here, I'm going to take another look at him. No need for anyone else to hang around, though.'

Cramphorn was beside the bunk: he'd been talking quietly. Trench shut the door. 'Any sign he might be receiving you?'

'There couldn't really, at this stage, sir.' The doctor got up, and pulled his chair out of the way. 'But it's worth trying.'

'He could stay like this for days, you said.'

'Yes.' The doctor opened his mouth to add something: then shut it. Trench crouched at the head of the bunk: the size he was, it was the only way he could get down to that level, without breaking his back.

'It's Trench here, sir. We'll be moving you over into *Foremost*, before long. You should have a more comfortable passage in her, and I've arranged that you'll keep this same sawbones with you. His name's Cramphorn – poor fellow . . . He'll take good care of you until we get you home. Then you'll be surrounded by all the experts and specialists, and I shouldn't be surprised if one of the nurses was Australian . . . So just hang on, sir, take it easy, and don't worry. You can leave all the worrying to the rest of us, for a change.'

Cramphorn came with him to the doorway. Trench thoughtful as he looked at him. The doctor was a smallish man with steady eyes and a direct, take-it-or-leave-it manner. Scrawny little bastard, and he looked as if he could have used about twenty-four hours' sleep. But then, who couldn't have . . . Anyway, Trench had a good impression of him. He warned, 'This man's worth his weight in diamonds. Believe me, he's one we can't afford to lose.'

Cramphorn said, 'They all are.'

Paul said into the telephone, 'OK, Louis. We'll reduce to five knots now. I'm due on watch, I'll be up there when you surface.'

'Wow.' Gimber's voice was thin over the line. 'The very thought makes my heart go pit-a-pat.'

He'd got over his own seasickness, he'd said, although Ozzie Steep was still out of action. You couldn't blame a man for getting sick, but Paul was still glad he hadn't taken Ozzie for operational first lieutenant in Eaton's place, which at one stage he'd considered. He went into the control room and addressed the helmsman: 'Relieve officer of the watch, please.' Henning replied 'Yes, please,' and Paul climbed up through the wind-tunnel of a conning-tower into the dark, swaying bridge.

The weather hadn't eased at all. *Setter* was making eight and a half knots, lurching clumsily through a whitened sea, rollers sweeping up from her port quarter. Spray burst in bathfuls across the bridge, flung up by her butting, slog-ging progress. He told Henning – ducking spray as he yelled it – 'Revs for X-12's surfacing routine, please?'

Straightening, he got a faceful. Henning calling down for two hundred revolutions: then shouting as he turned to Paul, 'I wouldn't like to be surfacing that little object in this lot!'

'You would if you'd been under for the last six hours with one of your crew puking every five minutes. I'll take over, if you're ready?'

There wasn't much to hand over. The course, the revs, when he'd last 'blown round', the captain's night orders – which in any case were in the night-order book on the chart table, and no different from last night's or the night before. The main difference on this jaunt was that if you ran into an enemy – a U-boat being the most likely variety – the orders were not to attack, but to evade and remain unseen. It was obvious, however, to anyone with experience of night encounters on the surface that the odds were you'd see each other at roughly the same moment, so secrecy could best be preserved only by the quick destruction of the U-boat.

But it would depend on the range and bearing of an enemy when you sighted him. The X-craft had all been warned of the possibility of sudden dives by their towing ships.

X-12 duly surfaced, spent fifteen minutes impersonating a half-tide rock while she 'guffed through', then slid under again. Five minutes after she'd disappeared Paul told the W/T office watchkeeper to call through and check that all was well; confirmation of this came up the voicepipe at 02.28, and he increased to revs for eight and a half knots again.

He wished he'd been able to tell his father about this business. On the face of it, it was silly that he hadn't. As if Nick Everard, of all living men, would have gone around talking about it! But the security angle had been stressed so hard, had been dinned into all participants so vehemently and regularly all through the training period, that you'd have hesitated to have whispered about it even to yourself. There'd been fatuous gags about security – like, 'These orders are to be burnt before being read'.

He swung the binoculars slowly across the bow, intently following the indefinite curve of dark horizon. Mountains of sea, white flashes like bow-waves everywhere you looked: the only comfort was that a real bow-wave would look different. When you saw it, you'd know it . . . His father would hear all about this Operation Source eventually, of course, and he'd understand the need there'd been for secrecy. Despite this, Paul still wished they'd been able to talk about it together.

*   *   *

Gimber had been doing his first lieutenant's job, taking her down to ninety feet and – in a manner of speaking – levelling her there. If you could use the word 'levelling' when she was being flung around like an old boot in a mill-race.

Ozzie Steep yelled, 'Take over, shall I?'

Gimber looked round at him. He also noticed an expression of alarm on Trigger Towne's now fully-bearded face. Towne had that blue-black, silky-looking growth that made the brightness of his eyes seem like a madman's. Ozzie Steep's eyes, in contrast, were as dull as if he was looking at you through dirty water. He looked weak, and – despite that offer – unsure of himself.

'You're not fit yet, Ozzie. Maybe tomorrow, if the weather eases – or when *Setter* dives.'

'But I'm fine now, skipper!'

'So you can do some wiping-up.' Gimber pointed. 'There, to start with.'

Towne had got out of his seat; he put a hand on Steep's shoulder as he squeezed past. The other hand latching on to an overhead pipe for support. He shouted to Gimber, 'After end. Tail-clutch.'

Wherever you looked, condensation gleamed, trickled. Keeping her almost dry was a full-time job, and there was plenty of other maintenance as well, so if Steep could lend a hand now it would make life a lot easier.

Every time *Setter*'s stern rose, X-12's bow was wrenched upward. But *Setter* was rolling as well as pitching, so the imparted motion was lateral as well as vertical. As it continued hour after hour, day and night after day and night, it caused a degree of strain and discomfort that made you hate that thing up there – to a point where for an interval of peace you could have crawled for'ard and wound the handle that would slip the tow . . .

Ozzie Steep's conflicting feelings showed in his pale, ginger-stubbled face. He wanted to be doing his job, and it shamed him that he was not, but he also knew Gimber was right. Gimber guessing, meanwhile, at how anyone would be after such a period of chronic sickness: you'd feel hollow inside, weak and shaky . . . He shouted, with his eyes on the depthgauge and the bubble, 'She'll be diving tomorrow. It'll be smooth-going, then, and you'll be stronger, too. It's not your fault, Ozzie, nobody's blaming you.'

It would be a lot easier and far less uncomfortable once *Setter* was dived for the approach to the Norwegian coast. But Gimber doubted whether he'd let Steep have charge of the boat even then. Not unless he got himself together very rapidly. This was no job for a man operating at half-strength. In the immediate situation, this crew's lives depended on the man in the first lieutenant's seat, and in the longer term one eighth of the operation's chances of success rested in the same pair of hands. Just as much as in the boat's commanding officer's.

Gimber didn't know about the loss of X-11 yet, of course, or about X-8 being motherless.

Steep was mopping wet surfaces on the starboard side, behind Trigger's vacated seat. Trigger, back there in the after end, was in the midget's narrowest, tightest space while he lubricated the tail-clutch mechanism. It would be like lying in a pipe that had uncomfortable projections in it, and so constricting that you'd have problems with your elbows as you worked. When she turned her snout up – which she was doing now, a surging bow-up swoop – he'd be head-down, as good as stuck until she levelled again. But she'd been dragged up and then pulled hard to port – a solid jar right through her as the tow-rope stretched bar-taut. You could visualise the movement out there in the black water: it didn't exactly soothe the mind to do so, but imagination tended to operate on its own, didn't ask permission, the pictures simply flashed in there, matching the gyrations . . . Bow falling now. There'd been a compensating jerk to haul her back on course; Gimber had seen

Steep's apprehensive glance for'ard at the same time as in his mind's eye the Manilla tow had slackened and then sprung rigid again: the downward swing of the bow had checked, but then continued. *Setter* was tormenting the midget like a child dragging a puppy on a string. The tow-rope came up all-standing for a second time: mentally he saw it quivering-taut, stretching ruler-straight through black turbulence. That jerk had been powerful enough to have wrenched her stem off. Gimber had felt it in his own body, like the hideous jar a man might get from the rope as he drops feet-first through the trap.

Christ, imagination . . .

Quiet, suddenly. He was waiting for the next upward drag, the cycle of violence to recommence.

But it didn't. Hadn't. She was bow-down, and the needle was beginning to swing slowly around the face of the depthgauge. Ninety-three feet – ninety-five . . . Three degrees bow-down: ninety-eight feet. He felt it, then – a sensation of drift, of idling in the water without steerage-way or any grip from the hydroplanes.

Gimber leant sideways, reached for the telephone.

Nothing. No jerking from the tow-rope either. X-12 was in a smooth glide: and the telephone line was dead. A hundred and four feet on the gauge, bubble six degrees aft of centre. Downward movement accelerating: a hundred and ten feet. Gimber snapped, 'Blow one main ballast!' Steep throwing himself into Towne's seat and reaching to the HP air valve. The hollowness in your gut might have been fright but there wasn't time to take notice of it, and another precious moment passed while he reminded himself, No use using the screw until she's got her bow up . . . A hundred and twenty feet. Gimber had seen Ozzie check that the vent-levers were in their shut position before he'd wrenched that valve open. One-twenty-five feet. Air was scorching through the pipe to the for'ard main ballast tank. One-thirty feet, bow-down angle eight degrees, a minute object sinking through a vast surrounding mass of sea. In spite of the bow-down angle Trigger Towne was appearing feet-first, wriggling backwards out of the engine-space, panting like a dog.

Levelling. Gauge showing one hundred and thirty-nine feet. Gimber's left hand had pulled the trim-pump lever aft, and now with his right he closed the main motor field switch – to start the motor – and then span a twelve-inch hand-wheel through the positions for slow, half and full ahead grouped down, on through slow and half to full ahead grouped up: this was maximum forward power, the two battery sections linked in parallel to put full power on the motor. As he'd begun to throw the speed-control wheel round he'd ordered, 'Blow number three main ballast!' Steep had opened the valve, and now he and Towne were changing places. Gimber knew he'd have to take a chance on Steep now – let him take over here at the controls so that he, Gimber, could be in the CO's position for surfacing, opening the hatch and then getting out on to the casing. But first things first . . . He beckoned to Steep, and he'd stopped the trim-pump. He shouted to Towne, 'Stop blowing one!' She'd been taking too much of a bow-up angle. The midships tank was still blowing, though, to give her overall bodily buoyancy: it wasn't a time for half-measures, and he'd be wanting her well up, when she surfaced, as high in the waves as she'd ride. He was getting out of the seat, to let Ozzie in. Telling him – because he was already out of reach of the rheostat control – 'Half ahead grouped up.' Then he tapped Trigger on the shoulder: 'Stop blowing three!'

Theoretically he should have stopped her at periscope depth, not taken her straight up. He should have held her there while he took a look to make sure he wasn't surfacing her right under *Setter*'s bows – *Setter* perhaps having guessed the tow had gone, and turned back to search. But (a) this wasn't likely, (b) even at periscope depth – nine feet, or even less in this sea, *Setter* would still have run her down if she'd been there to do it, (c) you wouldn't see much anyway, in this weather, and (d) at eight feet she'd be unmanageable. So you could forget the drill book.

Ozzie was doing all right. Something rather odd about him, but he wasn't making any mistakes.

The next telephone check was to have been at 03.00. In sixteen minutes. They wouldn't know the tow had parted until they found the 'phone was dead. In sixteen minutes at eight and a half knots *Setter* would have covered just over two miles: two sea miles – well, 4250 yards. It would take her about the same time again to get back to where the rope had snapped: or a bit longer, if MacGregor reduced speed, which he probably would do, because spotting the X-craft with her low freeboard in this wild sea wouldn't be at all easy. All they'd know in *Setter* was that the tow had parted at some time between 02.30 and 03.00, and they wouldn't know with any certainty that X-12 hadn't done a nose-dive to the bottom.

Gimber told Steep, 'Soon as I'm up there and the induction's open, start the donkey, half ahead.'

'Aye, aye, sir!'

Fifteen feet. Twelve . . . At nine she was rolling like a barrel.

'Officer of the watch, sir!'

Paul swung round. The lookout told him, 'Tow may have gone, sir. Saw an end washing loose. Least, I think . . .'

He'd dipped to the voicepipe, 'Control room – tell the W/T office, check communications with X-12 – quick!'

'Aye aye sir!'

'Time?'

'Oh-two-four-nine, sir.'

May Louis Gimber have been wide awake and on his toes . . .

'Bridge – telephone line's dead, sir!'

He'd expected it, and was ready for it. 'Stop port. Port twenty-five. Shake the captain, tell him the tow's parted. Shake the X-craft officers too.' It was up to MacGregor who else got shaken.

The casing officer – Henning – and the second coxswain, surely; but that was his business. *Setter* was swinging, taking green seas over as she turned across the wind.

They won't see us . . .

Teeth clenched, eyes slitted against wind and salt water, muttering to himself, desperate . . . X-12 battling through waves more than over them. Not even the sharpest-eyed lookout would spot her, except by pure chance.

All right, he told himself. All right. Calm down. It's up to me to do the spotting!

And in fact – getting used to it now – the motion wasn't as bad as he'd expected. Waves were crashing over her but she was riding it well, forging ahead at about three knots; it was a quartering sea and she was rolling, naturally. He spoke to her, told her that she was doing marvellously, that he was pleased with her. He had no rope lashing, but both arms wrapped around the induction pipe. At this stage he could spare both hands for his own safety.

He was reckoning on an interval of twenty to thirty minutes before he'd have much chance of seeing *Setter,* but he still searched for her, straining his eyes through the flying spray in case his calculations were wrong. He was doing this, and going over the figures again in his mind, when he did see her. He couldn't believe it, at first, thought he'd imagined it – but that was her, all right! To port – a white flurry of broken water, and in the next blink the black loom of her conning-tower above it. Two or three more blinks, to make certain it wasn't his imagination playing tricks. It hadn't been. He estimated that she was between two and three cables' lengths away.

'Aldis! Quick, now!'

He'd warned Ozzie to have it ready under the dome.
The price of getting it up on to the casing was a few bucket-
fuls of salt water sloshed down into the boat. Then he had
the lamp out and the hatch shut again, he was rising to his
feet with both arms round the induction pipe and the Aldis
in both hands.

During that gymnastic feat, he'd lost sight of her.

Fright was sharp, breath-stopping. He knew that if they
passed each other without contact, it might never be
regained. This was no sheltered loch or bay X-12 was floundering in. The effort now was to steady his mind as well
as his body and the lamp; hugging the pipe while the craft
under him bucked, rolled and pitched . . . He had the lamp's
pistol-grip in his right hand, its weight on his left forearm:
he pressed the trigger, swung the beam slowly left, scything
horizontally across the wavetops.

And – he bellowed it into wind and sea – 'There!'

So pleased that he told X-12 again, 'Good girl!' Although
she was still trying to fling him off. Like talking to a crazy
horse, trying to placate it . . . *Setter* was on the beam to
port. They'd seen Gimber's light, obviously. He watched
her, saw the turn she was making – slowing, and turning
about forty degrees to port, putting herself beam-on to the
sea. It was an invitation to him to bring X-12 up into that
lee, into the small amount of shelter to be found there.
MacGregor had swung her into that position, and he'd be
working his motors as necessary to hold her there: motors,
not diesels now, because diesels couldn't be put astern,
either in *Setter* or in the midget.

Setter must have reversed course quite soon after the tow
parted, he realised. Paul Everard was, on the whole, fairly
clued-up. Gimber was turning X-12, to get her up close and
in *Setter*'s lee: *Setter*'s own Aldis on him like a searchlight.
Throwing herself every which way as she turned: and he
was passing the lamp down, Ozzie snatching it from him
and the hatch banging shut, after some more sea had burst

in. Rising, clinging to the pipe, relief still enormous but subsiding somewhat in facing up now to the business of passing a new tow. It was an exercise that had been practised often enough, and it would be done without any exchange of signals – nobody needed to explain to anyone else what to do.

When he had her in *Setter's* lee and bow-on to her, about fifty yards clear of her port side, he called down the pipe to Steep to stop the Gardner, take out the engine clutch and put the electric motor to slow ahead. This gave him the manoeuvrability he needed. *Setter*, broadside-on to the weather, was rolling like a cow. It wasn't much of a weather break, for all that. Better than nothing. Lying bow-on to her, X-12 was both stemming the sea and in the best position to accept the new tow. *Setter's* Aldis lit activity down on her sea-swept fore-casing, near her gun: men in waterproof clothes and lifebelts were inflating the rubber boat and coiling down the Manilla rope. Two men moving aft now with its inboard end – clambering cautiously around the catwalk, clinging one-handed to the rail surrounding the tower. That inflatable boat would be used again in a few days' time for the change-round of passage and action crews.

Slow-ahead speed on the motor was just about keeping her where he wanted her, countering the sea's drift and providing enough steerage-way for Trigger Towne, as helmsman, to hold her head on the ordered bearing. Ozzie Steep, meanwhile, ready for orders to reach him through the pipe – slow down, speed up . . . Steep seemed to be functioning, more or less. Give it a day or so, Gimber thought – watching the work on *Setter's* casing, waiting for the new tow to be floated down to him – and Trigger and I might get some rest. Have to cut out the Benzedrine intake first. You couldn't keep going for ever on bloody pills, anyway . . . The rubber boat was being launched over *Setter's* side. A cluster of men on the casing there, some standing and some kneeling: one of them was climbing down into the boat while others held it alongside. The one climbing down – he recognised that man-mountain easily enough. They were passing the end of the Manilla down to him: the whole evolution floodlit by an Aldis from *Setter*'s bridge, and going exactly as they'd rehearsed it, in Eddrachillis Bay. It hadn't seemed real, there, more like a game, an exercise to keep them all busy: but it was real now, and he was very glad indeed they had rehearsed it. The tricky part – which would be coming during the next few minutes – was beginning to look more dangerous and difficult than it ever had before. Because he could only hang on here, watch the thing develop: he wasn't going to leave the induction pipe until he had to. When the time came, he'd be flat on his face on the midget's bow, with the sea washing right over him: and he'd need both his hands to work with, with no spare for holding on.

The only sense in which he was eager for it was to get it over.

The boat was clear of *Setter*'s bulging saddle-tanks. Men behind her gun – they had a small degree of shelter there as well as a curve of guard-rail for security – were paying out a light line attached to the boat, and also the Manilla. The man in the boat, rubber-suited and – when the Aldis flickered over him – larger than life, was Bomber Brazier.

X-12's bow was drifting off to port. Quite a long way off. Now, of all times . . . Gimber shouted down the pipe, 'Watch your steering! Half ahead, main motor!'

It was all right. She was coming back on course. Half a minute, and he was able to order slow speed again.

Brazier was such a mild, placid sort of individual that in the early stages of the training programme there'd been a tendency to pull his leg. The way he so seldom spoke – just listened, smiling . . . Then one evening in a pub an RAF character made one taunt too many, and Brazier, as usual, laughed: but he did a double-take, then, and knocked the flight lieutenant across the bar and through a door which had looked quite solid until he hit it and went through it. It had been generally agreed afterwards that any of the Bomber's friends could have made the same remark and got away with it: from a stranger, Brazier had considered it de trop.

Time to move. The boat was more than half-way over. Tossing about, with Brazier kneeling in the middle with the end of the Manilla in his big hands. From *Setter*'s casing they were paying it out yard by yard, not feeding him more weight than they had to. In that fragile, cavorting boat, keel-less and extremely unsteady, having to keep his balance while keeping both hands free for handling the rope, it wasn't by any means an easy job. Not even for Bomber Brazier.

Gimber eased himself down to casing level. There was a low enclosure of rail to cling to here: it protected the night periscope, which was a fixed protuberance set in a stub above the casing. When you made use of it you'd have the boat only just covered, that stub like an eye just breaking surface. Gimber crawled forward over the well containing the fore hatch – the outlet from the W and D – and down a step to the narrowing section for'ard. There were holes in the casing for fingers to hook into. He was already soaked through to the skin, crawling not through foam but at times through solid water – having to hold his breath as she dipped, stopping, just hanging on while the sea dragged at him. He got a hand to the mooring cleat on her bow: this was fine, enabling him to haul himself right for'ard. Waves breaking in his face and right over. You had to enclose yourself in the immediacy of the task, never see yourself as it were from the outside or think of the risk or the forces involved, the performance – your own – as breathtaking as any high-wire artist's. If you'd let your imagination loose to that extent, you might easily discover that you were terrified. Then you'd fumble, hesitate,

doubling the chances of failure – failure here being synony-
mous with disaster. Lifting his head and shoulders clear,
he saw the boat with Brazier in it a dozen feet away, tilting
on a crest. Brazier yelled something but he didn't hear it:
he was holding on with one hand, reaching over the
midget's snout with the other, groping for the towing-slip.
The old tow should have dropped clear, since Trigger had
released it from inside and then reset the gear to accept the
new one. It was a simple-enough device: the towing pin
was locked by an interrupted ring; by turning this until
the gap in the ring coincided with the position of the pin,
the pin hinged away and the tow was released. Gimber
heaved himself for'ard until his head and shoulders
projected well over the bow: as she lifted, exposing her
whole stem, he could see as well as feel that the slip was
clear. One step at a time . . . But lifting again now, and
ready for Brazier: through a film of salt spray he had a
bird's eye view of him while the rubber boat was in a
trough. Still a yard too far to reach . . . Brazier with the
end of the tow gripped under one arm, pointing this way
and ready to be passed over. From *Setter's* casing they were
inching out both the tow-rope and the boat's securing line,
knowing he was almost in the right spot, that a bigger
wave than usual could lift him and the rubber boat and
dump them right on top of the X-craft – if they let out too
much slack at this stage. But from their angle and in the
dark it would be extremely difficult to judge the distance,
despite *Setter's* Aldis being on the boat and on X-12,
blinding in Gimber's salt-washed eyes. Reaching: the tow's
shackle dangling . . . Brazier for some reason howling like
a wolf as Gimber reached towards him. Brazier continued,
not howling, but bellowing, a gale-beating volume of sound
out of those huge lungs so that Gimber caught a few words
of it – '. . . for a life on . . .' The wind's howl and the waves'
crashing drowned it, while Gimber's hand grasped the
shackle: the rubber boat rocked sideways, spinning, Brazier

nearly ejected but swaying his weight back in the nick of time, yelling the last words of what had evidently been a question: '. . . the ocean wave?'

Gimber had his boat's sharp stem under him, between his elbows, while his hands clawed at the end of the Manilla – most of its weight across Gimber's boat, but even this yard or two of it extremely heavy: he was forcing the shackle towards the towing slip. Choking, coughing out salt water, and blind . . .

Bow down. Crashing down. A glimpse of Brazier silhouetted against the light's beam, tottering: Gimber holding on, but half over the side – drowning . . . Coming up, at last. Catching a lungful of air with sea in it: life itself consisting solely of the need to complete this – now . . .

Connecting!

Screw-threaded pin one-handed into the shackle. The two pins at right-angles but not much weight on them yet, so turning this was – was feasible, even with numbed fingers . . . Bomber Brazier's shout as the rubber boat shot upwards: 'Not me for one!' Brazier howling with crazy laughter: a happy man, delighted, in his element and loving it, turning with an arm up and waving to the men in *Setter*'s bridge to tell them, 'all fast – heave in . . .'

Gimber told the others, when X-12 was at sixty feet, on course and under tow at eight and a half knots again, porpoising as before, 'Brazier's round the bend. I hadn't realised.'

Thinking as he said it that he'd never seen the Bomber in such a state of exuberance. Towne nodded, crawling aft. 'I reckon. He's a good hand, though.'

Ozzie Steep nodded. Expressionless. He was functioning all right, but in the manner of a zombie. He was in his first lieutenant's seat, he'd handled her competently in the dive, caught a trim with just about the optimum weighting for'ard; now as Trigger Towne moved aft he moved the trim-pump lever again, sent a few gallons from stern to bow in compensation for the shift of one man's weight. But there was a goon-like quality about his movements and manner. Gimber thought it would be unsafe to trust his reactions in any new emergency: therefore, that he mustn't be left unsupervised. But since the principle was to have two men on watch and one man resting, a private word with Towne, a warning to him to keep his eyes open, might answer the problem.

Which might in any case be imaginary.

There weren't any more tow-ropes. *Setter* had been carrying one spare. And in submarine emergencies, reactions had to be immediate and right. Delayed action or the wrong kind . . .

He thought, I can't risk it . . .

Hang on until tomorrow, when *Setter* would be dived and the tow smooth, emergencies far less likely to arise?

Steep looked round at him. Gimber had been checking bilges. Steep said, reaching for his mug – Trigger had heated a can of soup after they'd dived, and as usual poured his own straight down his throat scalding hot – 'Skipper, you ought to get your head down. I'm perfectly all right now.'

'I doubt if I could.' Gimber wondered if Ozzie had been reading his thoughts. He explained, 'Up to here with bloody Benzedrine.'

'Oh.' Ozzie turned back to the depthgauge. Gimber slipped another tablet into his mouth. First one for several hours: he'd been thinking of cutting them out, so as to be able to get some sleep, but – glancing at Ozzie again, still unsure of him but also unsure of his own judgement . . . Then he saw Trigger Towne – he'd turned his head like a man on guard, afraid of being caught out doing something illegal, like surreptitiously taking that pill, and there was Towne, this side of the after bulkhead, glaring at him. He had his hand on a canvas roll of tools he'd left there behind Ozzie's seat, and had now come back for. Crouched with his head half-turned, eyes burning out of dark holes in his head, he looked like some wild animal ready to dive back into its burrow. He shouted, lifting that hand to point at Gimber, 'Oughter get in some zizz-time, skipper!'

'So ought you, chum.'

The ERA gestured dismissively, as the midget's bow slammed down and brought up hard on the new tow-rope: Gimber heard, 'Got jobs waiting, Christ's sake . . .' Gimber pointed at Ozzie's back – grimacing, waggling a hand palm-down to convey his doubts; Trigger watching the pantomime, frowning, working out what it was he was being told. Then he nodded, made a gesture of helplessness before he turned away and slithered back into the engine-space. Gimber crawled for'ard to the W and D to fetch a bucket and a cloth.

Brazier told Paul confidentially, 'Louis G did a good job. He's not bad, when he gets his finger out.'

That had been a long speech, for the Bomber. He'd have given it some thought before he made it, too. Paul reflected, looking at him across the wardroom table, that if Gimber had made a hash of it Brazier wouldn't have commented at all.

The quick recovery of X-12 underlined one's fears for X-11. The last news of her had been that *Scourge* had turned back to look for her. One whole day ago – and it felt like a week.

Crawshaw said at supper, '*Scourge* couldn't break W/T silence now, though, could she. Now we've got this close to the target, don't we have to go right up almost to the Pole if we want to transmit?'

'Where we are now, yes.' MacGregor pointed out, 'But *Scourge* turned back. She'll be a long way south still.'

The restriction applied within a certain radius of the target: wireless silence inside this area was to be total. The last thing one could risk was for the enemy to be alerted to the presence of submarines of their battle squadron's doorstep. But *Scourge* would still be outside the restricted area: so if she'd found her baby, she'd have piped up.

Good news arrived just before Paul was due to talk to X-12 at ten o'clock: X-8 was back in tow of *Seanymph*. Paul told Gimber this, over the telephone: 'X-8 did the same as you did, apparently. Tow parted, but she's back on the lead now.'

'What happens when the second rope busts, with no spare?'

'Just make sure it doesn't, Louis . . . No, actually I've been talking to MacGregor about that, and we'd improvise with a two-and-a-half-inch wire. If we had to . . . How are you three now?'

'Ozzie's back in shape, more or less. Trigger and I are so stuffed with pills we're pretty well on automatic.'

'Can't you lay off the Benzedrine, now he's fit?'

'Tomorrow. When you dive. To which event we're counting the minutes, believe me . . . No news of any of the others?'

Paul told him falsely, 'Only that X-8's back in tow.'

Lying to Louis Gimber was becoming a habit.

He wondered what Louis had meant by those remarks about Jane. He couldn't remember exactly what had been said, now, only that he'd sounded snide and that it had been unexpected and disturbing. But time itself was becoming confused, the days telescoping, and 20 September seeming constantly to recede. It would be worse still for the passage crew, he realised, especially under the influence of those pills.

A signal was coming through. Colbey, the grey-haired telegraphist, was taking it down when Paul finished his chat to Gimber and hung up the 'phone. He left him at it, and went back to the wardroom.

'Signal coming in.'

Heads lifted from books and magazines. Massingbird's

eyes, from the recess of his bunk, gleaming like an old fox's before they shut again. Eaton with a copy of *Men Only* open at one of the famous 'Ladies out of Uniform'. He turned it face-down, and slid off the bench. 'May as well get the book out.'

The signal turned out to be from *Scourge*. Twenty-four hours' searching had yielded no trace of X-11, who had now to be presumed lost. *Scourge* was proceeding to her patrol billet off the target area.

Brazier muttered, 'Bloody hell.' Eaton scowling as he took the code-book back to the control room safe. MacGregor muttered from his bunk, 'I'm very sorry.'

The picture had been developing in Paul's mind while the message had been taking shape on Dick Eaton's signal-pad. Three faces clearly defined: Tom Messinger's, Bony Hillcrest's, Charlie Amor's. There was also a vision of an X-craft interior split open and under 1600 fathoms of Norwegian Sea: it would be still, by now, at rest, those bodies sprawled . . . The stuff that dreams were made of – and there were enough of those already, God knew. He wrenched his thoughts back to practical considerations – such as the fact that Dan Vicary's X-11 had been one of the three boats detailed to attack the *Scharnhorst,* and only X-9 and X-10 were now left for that job. He guessed there might be a switch now, that either he or X-8 might be re-directed from the *Lützow* to the *Scharnhorst*.

He was in the process of turning in, on the camp-bed under the wardroom table, when the next instalment of bad news arrived. He lay still, listening to Henning and Massingbird decoding it, the engineer doing the looking-up while the torpedo officer read out the groups and wrote down the translation. It was from *Syrtis* to Flag Officer Submarines, repeated to all concerned in Operation Source: X-9's tow had parted, and *Syrtis's* captain had reason to be certain the midget had gone to the bottom.

X-9's passage crew had been Kearon, Harte and Hollis.

It was hard to accept as fact, at first. Right on the heels of the other one. But it had happened, it was real – and you had to accept that there might be other losses too, before the attack itself went in. Paul thought of Gimber, Steep and Towne, whose chances were exactly the same as those other teams' had been . . . Also, that with such a high incidence of loss on passage, FOSM probably would not order any variations to the attack plan until he knew for sure how many X-craft he had surviving.

11

—▷·○·◁—

As long as the bloody rope held . . .

Gimber prayed with his eyes shifting between the depth-gauge and the bubble, Please don't let it part?

Setter was on the point of diving, so as to be down and out of sight before daylight exposed her to any wandering German aircraft. She'd dived for the first time yesterday, but come up again last evening to spend the night on the surface; this was necessary both to maintain the scheduled progress northward and to charge her batteries. So for X-12 there'd been another seven hours of acute physical discomfort exacerbated by the tension of knowing the two-rope could snap at any moment.

Yesterday the hours with *Setter* dived had been marvellous. Hour after hour of smooth running. Gimber had slept for two hours, then taken over from Towne, who'd been unconscious for nearly four.

Towne muttered now, 'Get on with it, get bloody under!'

Longing for a resumption of that peace and quiet. Also to get the act of diving over – and for MacGregor to handle it carefully, take his ship down gently, in slow time . . . X-12's bow jerking upwards and to port: then the strain was off the rope and she was hanging, drifting with her bow falling quite slowly. The two could have gone already,

could have been broken by that last tug. But it hadn't –
there was a yank to starboard, just as he'd been beginning
to think she might be on her own . . . She still carried the
slight list to port, oddly enough. Gimber looked at the
transverse spirit-level, the one on the deckhead that
showed angles over to port or starboard. She was in her
gliding state again – the tow slack, no pull on her nose,
but the bubble still showing the two-degree list to port.

There was no obvious reason for it. Towne was in his
seat – which was on the starboard side – and Steep was
flat-out, asleep, in the fore end. The battery and its wooden
cover which served as the off-watch sleeping berth was
also, as it happened, on the starboard side. Nothing had
been moved from one side to the other, so far as Gimber
could see or recall, and an X-craft had no port and starboard trimming tanks. Most of the food and drink was
stored on the port side of the bow compartment, so as the
cans were emptied the tendency would be for her to be
lightened on that side – the opposite to what seemed to be
happening.

The telephone buzzed; Towne stretched out a long left
arm to pick it up.

'Yeah?' He listened for a few moments. Then: 'Roger.'
He was half-turned on his seat, looking like a first cousin
to Rasputin – gaunt, bearded, with those deepset, gleaming
eyes. He told Gimber as he hung up the 'phone, 'She's
diving now. Brazier, that was.'

Everard would have his head down, no doubt. *Setter*
diving quietly on the watch. Gimber would have preferred
to have known Paul was awake and looking after X-12's
interests at a time like this. At this moment she was on an
upward swoop with the needle in the gauge swinging past
the sixty-five-feet mark. But no jerk: there'd been a long,
steady pull angling to starboard, and now it had ceased.
She felt loose again, drifting, bow slowly sinking as the
forward motion slowed.

Adrift again?

About once every two minutes, that was how it felt. Imagination, of course, yet another of the coward's thousand deaths. But there'd been no jar, no sudden wrench. And in point of fact the imagining part wasn't so much fear as the need to anticipate, to have a mental picture of what was happening ouside the hull so you could be ready to cope with an emergency when it struck. Like having worked out in advance that if this new tow did part they'd replace it with the two-and-a-half-inch steel wire rope which *Setter* was carrying lashed inside her casing. He'd discussed this again with Everard; the wire's weight would make it a hell of a thing to handle, from this end, but at least it existed – another accident wouldn't necessarily remove X-12 from the operation.

'I'm taking her to one hundred, Trigger.'

'Aye aye . . .'

Setter would go to sixty. Gimber's intention was to be well below her, out of the wash from her screws. These were all new techniques, history in the making; despite the facts that his mouth tasted like the bottom of an old dustbin and that he'd rather have been in Wimbledon.

Autumn – first signs of it, the trees beginning to change colour . . . Except it would be pitch dark there at 02.00 . . .

Going quiet now. The pull was steady, all in one direction. She'd already be under, he guessed, below the surface turbulence. The time being 0200 and the date – 18 September. Concentrating harder still, Gimber concluded that it had to be a Saturday. With seventeen hours of tranquillity ahead, and his own turn to take a rest.

Except Eaton probably needed that sleep.

He had her levelled at a hundred feet when the telephone buzzed again. Brazier informed Towne that *Setter* was now in trim at sixty feet.

'How is it with you now?'

'Better 'n it was, chum, I'll say that . . . Might even get some shut-eye later.' Towne was frowning, looking around like an animal suspecting danger while he listened to whatever Brazier was saying. He'd craned outward to see the depthgauge and the hydroplane indicator. Nodding: rasping into the telephone, 'That soon?'

Brazier said something else. Towne nodded. 'Yeah. Right', and hung up. Gimber said, 'You've noticed it, have you.'

'What is it – three degrees?' Towne got out of his seat and moved a few feet aft, to check on the position of the bubble in the transverse spirit-level. 'Just under.'

'So what's doing it?'

'I'll look around.'

'Checked the bilges lately?'

'Yeah, course. But I will again. Mind you, I've a feeling . . .'

'Well?'

'Tell you in a mo' . . .' Rasputin jerked a stained thumb in the direction of their towing ship. 'Tomorrow night', he said. 'Crews change over. Big eats and all night in – what about that, then?'

'I'll believe it when I'm inboard . . . Trigger, see if you can trace this list.'

Butterflies, Sub?'

Massingbird, stroking his red beard, grinned at Dick Eaton across the table. Eaton was refusing breakfast: he'd drunk some tea, but declined all offers of food. His voice was thin as he told the engineer, 'If a sharp pain in the guts can be caused by butterflies – yes.'

Massingbird's implication had been that Eaton's digestive problem might be connected with the imminence of action. Which wasn't either far-fetched or insulting. Paul was aware of the flutter of those abdominal insects, at times, and Jazz Lanchberry had admitted to it readily.

Brazier muttered now, 'You're lucky if it's only butterflies. I've got bloody great pterodactyls in my gut.'

'Well,' Crawshaw smiled, 'you've got room for them, in there.'

'Is it really bad, Dick?'

Eaton told Paul tightly, 'Bad enough to hope it'll stop soon.'

'When did it start?'

'In the night. I was OK on watch, so it must have started after I turned in.'

MacGregor suggested, 'Perhaps the cox'n had better take a squint at you.'

Submarine coxswains did some kind of medical course as part of their training. *Setter*'s CPO Bird would have a kit of drugs, and some implements, and a handbook of symptoms and treatments, but apart from first-aid it was likely to be rough-and-ready medicine. Eaton's glance at MacGregor made it plain he was well aware of this.

'I'll be all right, sir. I'll turn in, wait for it to wear off.'

'Anyone else got stomach trouble?'

Nobody had, so you could say it hadn't been last night's canned pilchards. Whatever it was, Paul thought, it had certainly chosen its moment, with the changeover of crews scheduled for tomorrow evening.

MacGregor commented, 'Your first lieutenants seem to be out of luck. First Steep, now Eaton.'

'Steep's back on the job, Louis says.'

'So will I be, skipper, by tomorrow.'

'Well, let's hope.'

'I'm sure of it. It's just a belly-ache, nothing serious.'

But he was barely able to haul himself up into the bunk – the upper one, against the curve of the pressure-hull – which Crawshaw had recently vacated. The pain was probably worse than he'd admitted, Paul guessed. In fact if it hadn't been pretty bad, he wouldn't have mentioned it at all. One had now to face the fact that he might not get over

it, whatever 'it' was, in time to move over to X-12: there'd
be no question of taking him along in this state.

Over the telephone at 08.00, Gimber reported that the
midget had a list of six degrees to port.

'It's the side-cargo, a slow leak on one of its buoyancy
chambers. That's Trigger's assessment, and I agree with
him. There's nothing else it could be.'

The side-cargoes had buoyancy chambers so that their
weight wouldn't throw the X-craft out of trim. All the
banging around they'd be subjected to must have damaged
this one.

'Is the list increasing?'

'Well, it was, but I'm not certain, it could have got to
where we are now and stopped.'

One thing after another . . . He said – thinking aloud –
'We may have to ditch that one.'

She'd still have one two-ton egg to lay underneath the
Lützow. Gimber hadn't commented. He had enough on his
plate with the passage job; what happened afterwards
would be Paul's headache. Paul asked him, 'How's Ozzie
now?'

'Oh – he's OK. Sleeping it off.' Gimber dropped his voice
somewhat. 'To be honest, he isn't really a hundred per cent
yet. Be a bit much to expect he would be, after several days
of all that.' He'd paused . . . 'Anyway, it's hard to judge,
we all look like rats and feel like—' He checked the splurge
of words. 'Well. Every two hours from now on, right?'

'Yup. And you'll surface to ventilate at midday – so take
the noon call first, will you? Tell Ozzie I'm glad he's better.'

Because he might need him as a replacement for Dick
Eaton. It wasn't a happy idea, to start with one member of
the team already played-out; but maybe a dose or two of
Benzedrine . . . There'd be no option, if Eaton didn't make
a quick recovery: and it wouldn't be enough to have him
claim to be all right, then maybe collapse at some crucial
moment. The first lieutenant's job was a very complicated

one, requiring a lot of experience and skill: you couldn't put just anyone on that seat. You couldn't do without him, either. Jazz Lanchberry would have his hands full, Brazier's task as diver was something else altogether, while Paul's business was at the periscope, conning the midget and her high-explosive cargo through whatever obstacles lay between her and the target. Under, over, or through the nets, and the man who did the trimming had to be one hundred percent sure and right in every move he made.

Paul wondered whether he could possibly take the boat in with a heavy list – accepting some clumsiness in the boat's handling as the price of taking her in fully armed.

Gimber asked him, 'What time tomorrow do we change round?'

'Soon as it's dark. Which would mean about nineteen-thirty . . . Is it nice and quiet for you now?'

'It's quiet. I wouldn't call it nice.'

'What, because of the condensation?'

'Mostly.'

Like water trickling down your face and neck as you hung up the telephone. They were too busy keeping the inside of the boat and her essential equipment dry to bother much about themselves. Human bodies, fortunately, didn't rust or get insulation problems. But clothing clung damply to cold skin: and Gimber's beard felt like a wet cloth around his jaw.

With *Setter* dived, it was almost too peaceful. Sitting and gazing at the depthgauge – which did have to be watched – it would have been easy to doze off, now one had less Benzedrine in the nerve system. The yellowish gleam from that circle of glass was mesmeric: and the constant thrum of water-noise was only background, the basic structure of the silence.

There was this list to watch, as well. Still six degrees. Just one buoyancy chamber flooded, he guessed, and the flooding now complete, so that this was as far over as she would lean, unless it began to affect another chamber too. If it did get worse, the boat might become awkward to handle, and it was going to be tricky enough inside those fjords without having a craft that wouldn't do what she was told. It would be for Everard to decide, anyway.

Gimber was humming – running through it for (he thought) about the second time, 'A Life on the Ocean Wave'. It was the Marine bandsmen's signature tune, but it was on his mind because that lunatic Brazier had been bawling it out when they'd been passing the new tow. But he was also humming to keep himself awake. Trigger Towne meanwhile checking hull-valves: one of his routines, crawling through the boat from stern to stem, stopping wherever his mental check-list told him to. In the control room now, he suggested mildly, 'Mind changing the record, skips?'

Gimber looked round at him. Two long-term prisoners in a deep, damp dungeon, staring at each other like men about to come to blows.

'Have I regaled you with that ditty more than once?'

'You been bloody torturing me with it ever since we dived.'

'I hadn't realised. Sorry. If it starts again, tell me.'

'Yeah.' Towne said, 'Why not give us a renderin' of 'Eskimo Nell'?'

'Oh, I doubt I'd remember it well enough to—'

'Garn! I heard you do it, word perfect!'

Months ago. Some jaunt ashore when they'd been at Port Bannatyne. He remembered now: they'd been stuck in Gouroch and had to spend a night at the Bay Hotel. He began to run the verses through his mind, checking whether he could still manage it. Silence, meanwhile – except for Towne's heavy, dog-like panting as he crawled towards the W and D.

Ozzie Steep screamed in his sleep.

Gimber jumped, his gut tightening with the shock of it. Towne froze – like a pointer. The scream echoed in the steel enclosing them. As it died away, an echo only in your mind now, Ozzie began to snore. Regular, pig-like honks.

Towne said to Gimber, 'Some lucky lass'll have that for life . . . Shake him, shall I?'

Steep choked: then yelled stridently, 'Get her up! Christ's sake, up!' He screamed again. Gimber shouted – while the noise still reverberated and Towne was already crawling forward, furious-looking, virtually trotting on all fours – 'Wake him up!'

Setter surfaced at seven-twenty that evening, by which time it was pretty well dark.

Eaton had only toyed with supper, sipped at a mug of soup and then turned in. He'd been dozing in his bunk. MacGregor had heard him groan, and sent for the coxswain.

Chief Petty Officer Bird seemed to be embarrassed at having to play the part of doctor. Theoretically he'd been taught how to deal with any more or less ordinary kind of injury or illness, but there was very rarely any opportunity to practise his art, beyond handing out a few asprins or bandaging a cut.

'Where's it 'urt, sir?'

'There.'

Setter pitching, slamming through the waves, diesels hammering away and the boat full of cold Arctic air.

'I'll 'ave to – er – exert a slight pressure on that spot, sir. If you don't mind . . .'

'Oh, bloody hell!'

He'd twisted away, in agony.

'Sorry, sir.' Bird glanced at MacGregor. 'We won't do that again.' His chuckle was entirely forced, as he edged out around the table; there was hardly space between it and the bunks for a solidly-built CPO like Bird to slide through sideways. He shook his head, unhappily. 'Well, I dunno. Proper turn-up, this is. Strike a light . . .'

MacGregor asked him, 'Are you trying to tell us something, cox'n?'

Bird was in the gangway, with a hand on the latched-back water-tight door for support.

'Rather not 'ave to say it, sir. Let alone bloody do it.'

'Come on, let's hear.'

'Captain, sir.' This was Garner, the PO telegraphist, pushing past Bird. 'Cypher, sir.'

'Thank you, PO tel.' MacGregor looked back at Bird. 'Go on.'

'I better check in the manual before I – er – confirm the diagnosis, sir.'

'Appendix?'

Bird winced. 'I'll just 'ave a little read, sir.'

'All right. But make it quick.' He passed the cypher to Massingbird. 'Sort this one out in your book, Chief . . . Ellis, let's have some coffee in here!'

The wardroom flunky's head appeared round the bulkhead from the galley.

'Tea do, sir? I just wet some.'

'All right.'

Massingbird growled, 'Can't tell the difference anyway.' Brazier helped him with the decoding of the signal: they'd discovered, by the time the coxswain came back, that it was from *Seanymph* to Flag Officer Submarines, repeated to forces and authorities concerned in Operation Source. Decoding work ceased now: Bird was staring gloomily at Eaton, who was on his back with his eyes shut. Bird looked at MacGregor and raised his eyebrows, gesturing towards the control room. MacGregor got up, and they went aft together.

Seanymph's signal was to the effect that X-8 had been forced to jettison her side-cargoes, and had been badly damaged by the explosion of one of them at a range of several miles. She had now been abandoned and scuttled.

Brazier muttered, 'Leaves us on our todd.'

X-8 was to have been X-12's partner in the attack, each with a half-share in *Lützow*. Now X-12 would have that target to herself; just as X-10 would be the only boat attacking *Scharnhorst*. *Tirpitz* would still be honoured by the attentions of three boats – Cameron's X-6, Place's X-7 and Henty-Creer's X-5.

The messenger of the watch appeared in the gangway and asked Paul, 'Step aft just a minute, sir?'

MacGregor and Bird were waiting for him, near the diving panel. MacGregor told him, 'Bad news, Everard. Cox'n says there's no doubt at all, it's his appendix. Which of course means he must be operated on.'

'When?'

CPO Bird suggested, 'Sooner the better, sir. Playin' safe, like. Not that safe's the word for it.'

'Don't under-estimate your own abilities, cox'n. Even more important, don't let Sub-Lieutenant Eaton think you're anything less than confident. But as to the timing – it can wait twenty-four hours, can't it?'

'Depends, sir. But I'd sooner . . .'

'After the crews change, we'll have one less body in the wardroom. We'll also have time on our hands. Will you do the job in the wardroom?'

'Well – if that's all right, sir.'

'He'll be laid up for the rest of the patrol, won't he.'

Bird nodded. 'Best if he could be in your bunk, sir.'

'Why the hell?'

'On its own, sir, no bunk above nor below it, so there's access like, and a light right over it. I could stand on the bench – that way I'd be right on top of the job, like.'

MacGregor nodded. 'All right. When the time comes, I'll take over the first lieutenant's bunk . . . But we'll do it tomorrow night, cox'n, after the transfer. I'll go deep, so it'll be quiet and steady for you.'

'Aye aye, sir.'

Paul was wishing it could have been done immediately:

Bird was obviously worried. But this surface passage tonight was necessary, in order to keep up to schedule, and as long as *Setter* had the X-craft in tow, with the possibility of some emergency at any minute, you couldn't guarantee there'd be no interruptions . . . MacGregor asked Bird, 'He isn't going to die on us before tomorrow, is he?'

'Well – if it turned what they call *acute*, sir, I reckon he'd let us know. I mean he'd sing out, like. Then we'd need to look lively, no matter what.'

'All right. You'd better read-up your manual carefully, cox'n. I'll break the news to him, and I'll tell him you've taken out an appendix before and you say there's really nothing to it. Purely for morale.' He turned to Paul. 'What are you going to do about this?'

'I'll take Ozzie Steep, sir. There's really no option.'

A highly unsatisfactory solution, none the less. Everything seemed to be going wrong, at this point. Three boats out of the running, X-12 with a duff side-cargo, and now she'd have a first lieutenant who'd be decidedly below par right from the start.

'Better warn your friend Gimber. Perhaps he could make sure Steep gets a lot of rest between now and change-over time . . . Make sense of that cypher, did they?'

Paul nodded. 'X-8 abandoned and scuttled. Had to ditch her side-cargoes, and the explosion wrecked her, apparently. Leaves only five of us in it now.'

On his way to the wireless office, he was wondering whether X-8 had had to ditch her charges for the same reason that his own boat might have to get rid of one of hers. But he'd hang on to it if he could – as long as the list didn't get completely out of hand. It was Ozzie Steep who'd be coping with whatever trimming problems might arise . . . In the W/T office, he called through to Gimber.

'How's that list now, Louis?'

'No worse than it was. Hard to tell, though, when you're being thrown all over the bloody shop!'

'Yes, I dare say. Second question – is Ozzie completely fit now?'

'Well,' Gimber was shouting, over the noise surrounding him down there, 'up to a point, yes.'

'What does that mean?'

'Look – Trigger's got his head down – he and I have stopped taking pills – and Ozzie's on watch with me.'

'So you can't talk about it.'

'My God, you're quick, Paul!'

'Is he really on top of the job, is what I want to know.'

'Well – I'm *on top* of it, so—'

'You mean you wouldn't trust it to him alone?'

'Right. I may be wrong, but . . .'

'Listen. Dick Eaton's out of it. Appendix. As soon as we've swapped over tomorrow evening *Setter*'s going deep while her cox'n operates. See? I need Ozzie. And you say you could be wrong, so . . .'

'Not that wrong. Not for the action job. Just making out until tomorrow evening's one thing, but . . .' There was a pause. Gimber finished, 'No. Out of the question, Paul.'

There was a longer silence. You couldn't argue with that degree of certainty. Paul asked him, 'Is he still sick, or—'

'Washed-out. It was very bad for several days, you know. You can't imagine. It leaves a man – well, drained.'

Paul said, 'And that leaves you, Louis.'

'I thought it might. About ten seconds ago, I thought—'

'There's no alternative.'

Roar of the sea drumming around hollow steel . . . Then Gimber's voice grating through his teeth and over two hundred yards of wire, 'Jesus Christ Almighty . . .'

He'd been dreaming – re-dreaming, that old one about being crushed under rocks. Every detail was the same, and no less frightening for being familiar. He'd woken, struggled to shake it out of his mind, and he'd succeeded, but only to have it replaced by nightmarish reality – Eaton's appendicitis, for a start. Remembering it, Paul got out of his bunk and took a look at him. Eaton was asleep, but twitching and murmuring to himself, the actual words indistinguishable under the hammering racket of the diesels and the noise of seas crashing against the casing and guntower overhead. *Setter* was inside the Arctic Circle now, and the air inside her had a bite to it; it would be knife-like on the bridge, but none of the X-craft men was standing a watch tonight.

Eaton had been appalled by the decision to put Gimber in his place. Disappointment had seemed as bad as the pain in his stomach. He drew plenty of sympathy: the others knew how they'd have felt – even without the prospect of being operated on by CPO Bird. As Jazz Lanchberry observed, out of Eaton's hearing, Bird would be deft enough with a marline-spike, but splicing rope and wire didn't make for a surgeon's hands. And Bird himself looked about ready to jump overboard.

Paul turned in again. The object was to get in a sound night's sleep, since once you'd embarked in X-12 there wouldn't be much, if any. Tomorrow, there might be some restful periods, of course . . . Thinking about the procedure for the change-over, the rubber boat and who'd go first in it, and so on, he dropped off to sleep. His father, glad to see him after so long a break, asked him, 'What are you up to now, old chap? You're not going on this crazy attempt to nobble the *Tirpitz*, are you?'

Paul told him yes, he was. His father was wearing rear-admiral's stripes on his sleeves, he noticed. But Operation Source was supposed to be highly secret. He made this point – a little stiffly, considering it was his father he was talking to – and Jane burst out laughing.

'Secret, my foot!'

Tossing her hair back – a warmly familiar gesture . . .

But Jane – with Nick Everard? She was Paul's girl or

Louis Gimber's, or both, but – his father's? She could see how shocked he was, and she was amused, enjoying it. He wondered where Kate was, and whether she knew about Jane. Jane telling him, with a hand squeezing his father's arm, 'Even the Germans know all about it. They'll have the welcome mat down for you!'

He woke again, feeling as if it was her laughter that had woken him. It was an enormous relief, this time, to be awake, to know it hadn't been anything but a dream. He could see how Jane had got into it: he'd had Gimber in his mind a lot, naturally, and if you thought about him long enough you were bound to get round to Jane. As to his father, and the question he'd asked – well, he'd been thinking about him too, wishing he'd told him about this X-craft business.

MacGregor had said he'd be diving *Setter* on the watch, so the X-craft team's sleep wouldn't be interrupted. But Paul didn't feel like sleeping any more. He was lying there thinking about the attack plan, and the trimming of the boat with that list on her, when a new signal came in.

He checked the time while the control room messenger was shaking Massingbird, and saw it was just after 1.30 am. So they'd be diving in not much more than half an hour. Massingbird was cursing softly as he climbed out and went to fetch the code book; when he came back and slumped down at the table, under the dim red light that was supposed to be good for bridge watchkeepers' eyesight, Paul slid out and joined him.

'I'll give you a hand.'

Massingbird stared at him. 'Thought you chaps were supposed to be getting your beauty sleep?'

'Ah, but I'm lovely enough already . . . You read out, I'll look up?'

The signal was from Admiralty, to practically everyone under the sun, and it conveyed an intelligence report to the effect that *Tirpitz*'s crew would be changing her gun-barrels and also dismantling her A/S detection gear for overhaul between 21 and 23 September.

Massingbird read the message over, combing his beard with his fingers. He asked Paul, 'How in hell would we get to know a thing like that?'

'Haven't a clue. Unless we have spies in Norway. Which we do, of course.' But the information could have been obtained from intercepted signals, too. 'Doesn't really matter, long as it's reliable. If it is, it's good news – guarantees she'll be there and won't stir during those three days.'

They decided not to wake MacGregor, as there was nothing urgent about it and in any case he was due for a shake at 02.00. Massingbird put the signal in the clip and turned in again; he seemed to have an unlimited capacity for sleep. Paul went to the wireless office and buzzed X-12; he'd intended to give this news to Gimber, but Ozzie Steep answered and said the skipper had his head down.

'Resting up for stage two, sir. I wish you'd let me take Dick's place.'

'You've been under the weather, Ozzie. That's the only reason. It's bad enough having to take Louis, after a week cooped up already, but what you've been through's something else again. I just can't take chances – not ones I don't have to take.'

Steep said yes, Gimber had explained all that . . . 'But the fact is, I'm now as good as new. I mean, really.'

'I know how you feel, Ozzie. Dick's fed up too. But the decision's been taken, so let's leave it . . . How's the list, still the same?'

'Yes. Six degrees exactly, still. I've got used to it, now.'

'No trimming problems?'

'Not since we lightened her to compensate for the flooded buoyancy chamber.'

There was a copper strip between each side-cargo and the X-craft's hull. When you dropped them – by turning a wheel on each side – the strip was detached and this flooded the side-cargo's buoyancy chambers so that it lost its neutral buoyancy and sank to the bottom. This one must have lost some of its buoyancy already, and this was giving X-12 her list.

'D'you think she'll handle all right, in the fjords?'

'No indication that she won't. Apart from the problems you'll have there anyway.'

The problems would be from variations in salinity and therefore water density, arising from fresh-water patches where streams or mountain ice entered the salt-water fjords.

'What other defects d'you have?'

'Defects?'

Paul frowned at the telephone. 'Yes, Ozzie. Defects.'

'Oh. Sorry . . .' As if he was waking up. Gimber had been right, Paul thought. Steep said, 'We had that leak on the periscope again, but Trigger fixed it. Twice. He had some trouble with the heads hull-valve too – didn't you, Trigger, when I was . . .'

'Ozzie, put Trigger on now, would you?'

'Right.'

'*Setter*'ll be diving at about a quarter past. You'll get some comfort then.'

'We'll be ready for it. Here's the mechanical genius.'

'Hi, skipper!'

Defects, it turned out, had been only minor. The periscope-gland leak was a nuisance and would be likely to recur, and the list was something that one would have to cope with, one way or another. The head's outlet valve had been only a temporary problem, which had been cleared by a lot of blowing. Towne and Steep were now hard at work to get on top of the problems of condensation.

'We'll have her on the top line for you, don't worry.'

'That's fine, Trigger. See you this evening.'

Back in *Setter*'s wardroom he found MacGregor at the

table drinking kye. He asked, pointing at the signal log, 'This makes no odds to you, of course.'

'None, sir. Doesn't tell us anything about *Lützow* or *Scharnhorst*. Very nice for the three who've been given *Tirpitz*, of course.'

It was quite a coincidence the main target of the operation was to have her teeth drawn, so to speak, right in the period chosen for the attack. Almost too much of a coincidence, that the enemy should have picked on that stage of moon and tide – and let the news out?

The dream – Jane, and her red carpet?

He told himself, Ridiculous . . .

Eaton groaned as he rolled over on the bunk. MacGregor, about to go up to the bridge for a look round before he dived her, stopped, staring at the blanket-wrapped figure. Paul could sense his anxiety. In the interests of Operation Source the decision to get the crew-change done with before anything else was surely right; but if the delay cost Eaton his life . . .

It wasn't a good day for CPO Bird, either.

Setter was in trim at sixty feet by 02.30. And X-12 surfaced for her routine ventilation at six. The midget simply planed up against the pull of the tow, spent a quarter of an hour bouncing about on the surface, while the upward tugging at her stern affected *Setter*'s trm making it hard work for the control room watchkeepers, and then planed down again.

At eleven in the forenoon, since this was Sunday, MacGregor conducted a short religious service in the control room. He included a special prayer for X-craft crews, for the success of the operation and a safe return; Paul, head bowed and eyes on the toes of his own plimsol shoes, with Brazier's on one side and Lanchberry's on the other, couldn't remember ever knowingly being prayed for before. He wondered how God would see it. After all, they were preparing to take four tons of high-explosive and plant it under a crowd of people who had no idea what was coming to them, and not all of whom could be entirely villainous. The strategic requirement was obvious, the Germans were not in Norway to help old ladies cross the streets, and equally plain was the inevitability of fighting this entirely defensive war; but if the Almighty was primarily concerned with the souls of men, might he take a different view? This occupied Paul's thoughts for the next minute or two; when he surfaced he was hearing the end of another special prayer, for Dick Eaton's recovery. In MacGregor's place, he thought, he'd have said one for the coxswain, too. But praying was done with: they were singing *Eternal Father Strong to Save*.

It was a restless day, more than restful.

Louis Gimber took X-12 up for another breather at noon. He told Paul after he'd dived her again that the weather was improving, wind and sea moderating; if this trend continued, tonight's change-over should present no problems.

X-12 was still carrying her list of six degrees to port.

'Will you guff-through again at six, Louis? Or stretch it for the extra hour or so?' Because they'd be surfacing for the crew-change soon after seven.

'Might as well stay down. The air's perfectly OK after six hours, now nobody's being sick. Condensation gets heavier, but what's one hour?'

'All right. When the time comes we'll do it in two boat-trips. Jazz and I in the first one, and the boat brings Ozzie and Trigger back here, then the Bomber can be wafted over on his own. You getting plenty of rest, I hope?'

'Hell, yes. It's bloody luxury, down here.'

Old Louis was feeling sorry for himself . . . But the words and tone must have jarred in his own ears too. He added, 'I've had as much sleep as I can take. Tell you the truth, quite looking forward to seeing your repulsive faces this evening . . . How's Eaton?'

*   *   *

Setter broke surface at 19.20 and X-12 materialised 200 yards astern of her a few minutes later. It was about half to three-quarters dark. The rolling as *Setter* wallowed up had seemed to give the lie to Gimber's theory of improving sea conditions, but as she rose to full buoyancy one realised that wind and sea had eased. MacGregor manoeuvred his submarine to put her to wind-ward of the midget, both to provide a lee and so that the rubber boat could be floated down by wind-power.

Leading Seaman Hallet, second coxswain, and two sailors came up with the boat and a coil of hemp line, and climbed down on to the fore casing, to the gundeck where there'd be room to inflate the boat. MacGregor called down the voicepipe, 'Ask Lieutenant Everard and his crew to come up.'

Without binoculars, X-12 was only a black smudge in a patch of white: she wasn't in sight all the time, and as one's eyes adapted to the darkness the figure of Louis Gimber on her casing could be made out, apparently riding the waves.

Hallet called, 'Boat's ready, sir!'

'Very good.' MacGregor turned to Paul and the others. 'It's been a pleasure having you on board. Good luck now, all of you.'

'Thanks for your hospitality, sir.' They shook hands. This wasn't quite a final farewell, as there'd be telephone contacts between now and slipping time tomorrow night. Paul and Lanchberry climbed down the rungs and cutaway footholds to the cat-walk, and around it to the gundeck. Hallet saw them coming: he and his assistants had already launched the boat and were holding it alongside.

'Trip round the 'arbour, sir, 'alf a tanner?'

'Worth every penny . . . Go on, Jazz.'

Lanchberry climbed down. When the boat had steadied again, Paul followed, with a heaving-line coiled over his shoulder. The casing party wished them luck and began paying out the hemp securing line. All that was necessary was for the boat to drift along the lie of the tow-rope – which was where the wind would take it anyway. Within a few minutes the X-craft loomed up ahead – narrow, bow-on, sawing up and down on its tether. Gimber was standing, holding on to the induction pipe and now ready for Paul's line; he'd also have an infra-red torch tied to his belt for signalling to MacGregor – for instance, to tell them to stop paying out any more hemp. Paul waited until only a few yards separated them before he tossed his line, lobbing its weighted Turk's Head high over that plunging, end-on black shape. He saw Gimber's arm reaching for it: then Lanchberry bawled, 'Owzat?' A minute later Gimber was hauling them alongside – bumping, the boat tilting dangerously, Paul finally scrambling up and crouching in cold wave-tops to hold it alongside – Jazz out too, and steading the boat's other end. Gimber had the hatch open and figures emerging – Towne first, slithering down into the boat with shouts of 'Wotcher, Jazz!' and 'Best of British, mates!' Ozzie, close behind him, contrastingly silent.

'All set?'

'Let her go!'

Gimber flashed his torch at *Setter*'s bridge, signalling for the boat to be hauled back. Lanchberry meanwhile sliding feet-first into the hatch, Paul close on top of him. A glimpse of Gimber's pale face and black beard, face screwed up against the weather, a face like a Halloween mask lit by the glow thrown up through the hatch. Inside now, in the small, yellowish-lit cavern that was X-12's belly. He'd forgotten how small: Jonah might have had more elbow-room. But at first sight it didn't look bad – considering this tub had been dragged through a thousand miles of rough sea, inhabited by three men for – however long it was . . . Jazz was on his helmsman's seat, checking over the controls surrounding it. Paul called up the pipe, 'Louis, I'll look after the trim until you've dived her, OK?'

It seemed tactful, as well as practical. Gimber shouted down, 'Make yourselves at home!'

Lanchberry got off his seat, crawled for'ard into the W and D. Looking around, checking the gear, inspecting this and that. Examining the hatch for seepage. X-12 was hurling herself around like an unbroken colt on a lunging-rein. Paul making his own inspection at this stage by eye; he needed to stay close under the hatch in case Gimber wanted help. He tried – since it was one of the things within reach – the starboardside viewing port. There was one each side, a thick glass window set in the pressure-hull at head-height, with external steel shutters that could be opened or closed from inside. He slid this one open as a first step in a preliminary check on moving parts; during the next twenty-four hours, before finally parting from *Setter*, he meant to test every single fitting and piece of equipment. Through the uncovered port there was nothing to be seen except breaking sea, white explosions and the rush of foam along her flank: he cranked the shutter closed again, and he was checking on the starboard-side one when Gimber yelled down, 'Boat's alongside *Setter*. I can see the Bomber getting in.'

There'd be about five or ten minutes to wait, then. Despite the roll, the list to port was easily discernible: the transverse bubble centred itself on six degrees right of centre instead of on the centre mark. Paul decided that another job for tomorrow, the last day in tow, would be to work out what stores might now be superfluous and ditch them to lighten her. Most of the consumable stores, cans of food and drink, were carried on the port side, and every pound of weight removed from there would help.

'Boat's on its way. Looks like there's an elephant in it!'

Lanchberry smiling his sardonic smile as he passed, crouching double, on his way aft. Using the interval for a very quick inspection. Paul stayed where he was: the boat with Brazier in it had to be getting fairly close now, to explain that shout from Gimber, a wolf-cry into the wind. If there'd been an answer it wasn't audible. He had to squeeze aside to let Jazz get past again, the ERA returning to his helmsman's seat just as the dinghy thumped along-side and Brazier hauled his bulk aboard.

Colossal legs in wet trousers descended through the hatch, in a pattering shower of spray. 'Hi, skipper. OK, are we?'

'No problems yet.' Gimber dropped inside and pulled the hatch shut, reached up to wrench the handwheel round and secure it. Paul was moving to the first lieutenant's seat, to let him dive her before he himself assumed command, but Gimber grabbed his arm, pulling him back.

'That's my job. Thanks all the same.'

X-12's bow soared, crashed down . . . Paul checking that Lanchberry had shut the valve on the induction pipe. Gimber confirmed, as he slid into what had been Ozzie's seat, 'She's shut off for diving.'

'Thank you.' He had to wait for about two minutes, until the tow had got under way again, on course and battering through the waves. Looking round, seeing Gimber's back view – shaggy and spray-soaked but relaxed, waiting for the order to dive – and Jazz Lanchberry's crewcut head and square shoulders over the back of the helmsman's seat, Bomber Brazier peering from the W and D like some great St Bernard in a kennel . . . The telephone buzzed, and he answered it.

'Yes. Diving now.' He hung it up. 'Open main vents. Sixty feet.'

12

I asked Tommy Trench, 'How was it QP 16 set out from
Russia before the X-craft boys had done their stuff? Wasn't
the idea that *Tirpitz* and Co. would be knocked out before
you sailed?'

He nodded. 'That had been the intention. Not that I knew
it at the time. We were supposed to wait for some damn
thing – that's all – but not even Nick Everard had been
told about X-craft. He didn't even know his own son was
in it.'

Now in his seventies, Trench was a stooped, gaunt man,
with more bone to him than flesh. He still did a full day's
work though – seven days a week, he'd told me – and his
grey hair was thick, a lot bushier than he'd have worn it
in his service days. This was Captain Thomas Trench, DSO
and Bar, DSC, RN (Retd) – in corduroys and a patched
tweed jacket, the left sleeve of it empty, pinned into a
pocket. I'd run him to earth on his mink farm in Norfolk.
It was the second time we'd met; the first had been in
London about eight years before, when he'd helped me
with detail of Nick Everard's adventures on the Norwegian
coast in 1940. And I do have reason for going behind the
scenes, as it were, at this stage. First because, approaching
the end of a story in nine episodes covering more than a

quarter of a century, I think a change of perspective may give a more realistic view of the climax and its aftermath; and more particularly because when I'd last consulted him, and we'd touched briefly on these later events, he'd offered, 'When the time comes, look me up. I may be inclined by then to give you the real facts of it.'

Over the years he'd kept his mouth shut whenever he'd been invited to comment on his action in defence of convoy QP 16. I doubt if anyone else had ever suspected there might be 'real' facts behind the known ones, and I only knew of such a possibility myself because of that half-promise he'd made.

He'd been lighting a pipe – managing the job one-handed with a dexterity that had to be seen to be appreciated – but he had it going now, and he continued with his answer to my question about the convoy's departure from North Russia.

'At the time, all I knew was they were keeping us waiting – which I didn't go much on, mostly because I wanted to get Nick Everard into a proper hospital as soon as possible – and then suddenly came this order to sail. "With all dispatch" – meaning "Get a bloody move on" – after what seemed to me a quite unnecessary delay. This was a signal from Admiralty, of course. Later it transpired that the reason behind it had been a Norwegian report of *Tirpitz* having her gun-barrels changed, and some other incapacitating thing. London assumed this meant she wouldn't leave Altenfjord whatever temptation might be offered. The change of gunbarrels, incidentally, was because she'd worn them out bombarding Spitzbergen a week or so before – the only time she ever used them in anger, as it happened. Net result was our lords and masters decided it behoved us to scram out of the Barents Sea while the going was good.'

'Which in the event it was not.'

I added that the report from the Norwegian resistance

group, about *Tirpitz*, had been signalled to the X-craft force as well, as an indication to them that at least their major target would be there when they arrived.

Trench stared out of the window, puffing smoke. He mused, 'I've often wondered who actually drafted those signals. I mean the ones with "From Admiralty" in the address heading. I've asked myself how long such characters would have been left gibbering around that august building before people in white coats came for them.'

I laughed, but he didn't crack a smile. He said, 'Those Norwegians were extraordinary, you know.' He glanced at me, and nodded. 'Well, of course, you do know ... The really sad thing about it is one of 'em was caught, some weeks after the X-craft attack, by the Gestapo. Did you know that?'

I let him tell me, anyway.

'They tortured him, in Gestapo headquarters in Tromso. He jumped out of an upstairs window and killed himself, having told them bugger-all despite having had all his fingernails pulled out. I'd say chaps like that were the bravest of the brave, wouldn't you?'

I admitted I agreed entirely.

'Rasmussen, his name was. Karl Rasmussen.' Trench shook his grey head. 'If they haven't put up a statue to him by now, they ought to have their nails pulled out ... What else d'you want to know about my convoy?'

The truth was that I knew most of it; I had the facts from the official history and from papers in the Naval Historical Branch of the Ministry of Defence and in the Public Record Office. But there was some new angle he'd hinted at.

I prompted, 'When you joined up with the convoy off Cape Kanin, QP 16 consisted of twenty-six empty ships plus the AA ship you'd brought up with you, and the escort comprised your five fleets, plus *Foremost* and the trawler, whose name for the moment . . .'

'Northern Glow?'

'Yes. And two sweepers. *Barra*, and – *Duncansby*.'

'You've done your homework.'

'And the commodore was Insole again.'

Trench nodded. 'He flew from Vaenga to Archangel in a Catalina and installed himself and his staff in a ship called the *Lord Charles*. She was one of the two we lost to U-boats, and he went down with her, poor old bugger. U-boats were my main concern, when we were heading north. I was worried for the *Bayleaf*, the oiler Nick Everard had salted away for us up in the ice. She was coming down to meet us in the vicinity of Bear Island, and we were getting reports of U-boats mustering to form a patrol-line there. She had only the trawler *Arctic Prince* to look after her, and her oil was extremely important to us. A lot of eggs in that one basket, you see.' He frowned. 'But the most delicate egg of all was the one in *Foremost*. I stationed her at the rear of the convoy, after we'd made the rendezvous and fuelled and settled down. She and the trawler, *Northern Glow*. I had my five destroyers spread across the van, one sweeper each side, and the merchantmen in seven columns, four to a column – with one empty billet after the Soviet oiler left us. Centre column was led by the commodore and tailed by the *Berkeley*. We had good, solid cloud at low level, and although we had aircraft on the radar screens often enough and quite a few times heard them overhead, they didn't find us. Well – there were a couple of half-hearted attacks by eighty-eights on the second or third day, which did us no harm – just happened to stumble on us by accident, lost us again at dusk, and by morning the cloud was thick again . . . I suppose we were lucky. But I knew we had U-boats waiting for us.'

He'd let his pipe go out. He paused now, putting a match to it. The sleight-of-hand was as impressive as before. I remembered him telling me, at our previous meeting, that to inquisitive strangers his story was that he'd had that arm bitten off by a giant mink. He glanced at me as he flicked the matchstick towards the fire.

'I had a very strong ambition indeed to get that convoy home intact. One always did hope and try to, of course, you could say this was one's raison d'être; but in practical terms one knew how the odds lay – certainly with the Murmansk runs. Down in the Atlantic, in quieter periods and then later when we'd broken the back of the U-boat threat, we did bring a very high proportion of convoys through unscathed. But we were at the climactic point of that Atlantic battle, just at the time we're talking about. In fact we were about to turn the tables very decisively, but for those few weeks it was – a close-run thing. And – here's what I was going to say – since it's states of mind and so on that interest you, my determination to get QP 16 through without loss was all the stronger for the notion that it was Nick Everard's convoy, that I had it as you might say on trust from him. And by that time he was talking all sorts of gobbledegook, didn't know where he was or why, or recognise anyone, or remember anything he was told for more than a few seconds – so Cramphorn told me, over TBS.'

'He'd come out of his coma, then.'

'Yes, he had, but he was ga-ga. I mean his mind was wandering. Cramphorn said this was to be expected, and he hoped memory and mental processes generally would return to normal quite rapidly. But it could take months; and the worst possibility of all was permanent brain damage. The very idea of this – for Nick Everard of all people . . .'

'He'd sooner have been dead.'

Trench looked at me. Silent, for a moment. Then: 'I was also concerned for his wife. There was a certain horror in the idea of bringing home a man who mightn't recognise her, or make sense . . . I was – I suppose the word's involved. I was a devotee of his, you see. I still am.' He fell silent, staring into the fire so absorbedly that he might have been reading the answer to his own question in it. I was assuming that such a question would be in his mind, just as it was in mine.

'Where was I?'

'Heading north towards Bear Island.'

'Yes. Thanking my lucky stars for the cloud-cover and praying for it to last. Rather counting on it lasting, in fact, at any rate until we ran into foul weather, which was enough to ground the Luftwaffe anyway. The one threat to us, as I saw it then, was the U-boat line ahead of us.'

'You never suspected there might be a surface threat.'

'Well, I'd been given reason not to!'

Paul asked Ozzie Steep, 'If he's still unconscious, how can anyone know he's OK?'

'Cox'n says things like pulse-rate and temperature are all right by the book. He followed the instructions precisely – despite some nasty moments, one frightful panic-stations – and – well, he cut it out, and it all looked like the book said it should. He's keeping him drugged now because otherwise he'd be in pain, he says.'

'When he comes round, tell him we're all delighted. And give CPO Bird our thanks and congratulations, would you?'

'Right.' Steep asked, 'How's your first lieutenant?'

'He's fine. Going off watch, about to crash his swede.' Gimber was staring back at him, from a range of about three feet. Lank, blue-black beard, complexion greyish white. Jazz Lanchberry was in the first lieutenant's seat, and he was due for relief as well – by Brazier, who at this moment was making tea. Paul intended to spend the next hour checking insulations, but tea would be the first thing. They'd had corned beef hash for lunch, broken up in the glue-pot and mushed with beans in it, but it had been very salty and everyone had a thirst although Gimber, who'd been duty cook, denied having added any. Paul told Steep, 'Nice easy ride now. Even up top. Low swell, is all.'

'Yes, the improvement's well timed.' Steep sounded perfectly normal now, Paul thought. 'Will you guff-through at six?'

'If we decide to, I'll let you know. Otherwise we'll stay down until dark.'

Until it was time to surface, release the umbilical cord and set off to cross the minefield. *Setter* had made her landfall accurately during the night and was now paddling in towards the slipping position.

'That list still at five degrees?'

'Yes. It needn't worry us, I hope,' Ditching some stores and shifting some engineroom gear had reduced the angle by one degree. A lot of work for very small results, but if it made her any easier to handle they might be glad of it later. Paul said, 'All right, Ozzie. Give us a call at sunset.'

'Right.' But he seemed disposed to chat. 'That panic-stations in the middle of Dick's operation – Christ almighty, he started coming-to, right in the middle of it, when the cox'n had both hands inside his gut! So Colbey here – you know Colbey, telegraphist?'

The grey-headed one. 'Yes. What?'

'Cox'n had Number One as his theatre sister, as you might say, and Colbey as anaesthetist. Chloroform, on a pad. He moved like lightning, sloshed a lot more on, nearly asphyxiated himself and Bird as well!'

'I'd sooner have this job than that one.'

'Who wouldn't!'

Hanging up, it occurred to him that if Eaton died now, MacGregor wouldn't let the news out. He'd veto bad news, just as Paul himself had kept from Gimber the news about X-11 and X-9. Gimber had been told now: he'd taken it in silence, abstractedly – Paul had guessed that he'd been seeing it, guessing at those last few minutes, the shape of the catastrophe you'd always known was on the cards. He'd told him about X-8 too, of course, so that only five boats would be crossing the mines tonight, out of the original eight. And without X-11, X-12 would be the only one using Rognsund, the narrower of the two approach fjords.

'Here, skipper.' Brazier handed Paul a mug of the tea he'd been brewing. He put another within reach of Gimber, and leant over to pass one to Lanchberry.

Gimber swallowed some tea. His eyes, fastening on Brazier, looked like mud-holes. 'What did you put in this? French letters?'

Brazier nodded. 'Been saving 'em for you.'

Lanchberry growled, 'You're a dirty bastard, you are.'

Brazier was shifting his bulk into a less cramped position. 'Discipline's gone to pot already, skipper, did you notice?'

He was chattier than usual. He'd actually spoken several times without being spoken to; for the Bomber, this was the equivalent of anyone else having hysterics. There was a tension in them all, which they were trying to hide, or ignore. Nobody was looking more than they had to at Louis Gimber, either. Despite the rest he'd had in the last day or so, he seemed like a creature from some other world: you could sense his own awareness of the gulf between himself and them, and his resentment of it.

'You ready, Bomber?'

'Why not, indeed.'

It was a gymnastic feat, Jazz edging out and Brazier having to make room for him but still be close enough to get into the seat quickly as soon as it was empty. There were trimming adjustments to be made as the weights shifted, and the hydroplanes couldn't be left untended. Brazier's size and strength were fine for his own specialised job of diver, but less so for acrobatics in confined spaces. Lanchberry made the change-round possible, doubling himself around the back of the seat: Brazier told him, 'Quite handy, being a herring-gutted greaser, sometimes.'

Gimber offered, from five or six feet for'ard, 'Want to toss for the battery cover, Jazz?'

Lanchberry shook his head. He'd persuaded an amateur barber in *Setter*'s crew to tidy him up, before they'd made the change-over, and the sides and back of it had literally been shaved. He said, 'I'm not bothered. Better off aft, in fact.' On top of the fuel tank in the engine space, he meant, with his feet protruding through the opening in the after bulkhead. Gimber repeated, 'I'm quite prepared to toss for it.'

'Too bleedin' late, old son.' Lanchberry was crawling aft. 'I'm 'ere.'

Paul had put them into two watches – himself and Brazier, and Gimber with Lanchberry – each pair on watch for two hours at a time, and the two on watch could take turns at the controls and on maintenance chores. For the next two hours it would be himself and the Bomber working while Lanchberry and Gimber rested.

Brazier had the trim-pump lever pushed forward, shifting ballast to the for'ard tank to compensate for his own move and for the ERA having moved further aft.

Paul glanced for'ard. 'While you're there, Louis, pass me the bucket and a swab?'

Gimber grunted, as he turned himself around. The bucket clattered. He complained, 'Some lazy sod didn't wring this thing out. Here . . .'

'Thanks.' On his knees, reaching for it. 'You could have four hours off now, instead of two – if you like, Louis. I'm not tired at all.'

'Nor am I. Thanks all the same.'

'OK. Change your mind if you want to.'

'Look.' Gimber stared at him. 'Let's get this straight. I don't need – don't want – any bloody privileges. I'm perfectly all right.'

'If you say so, Louis.'

'You wanted a first lieutenant, you've got one. Huh?'

Paul returned the angry stare. 'Absolutely.' He pointed. 'And first lieutenants don't argue with their skippers. So get your head down. I'm not offering privileges, anyway, I simply want you fit and rested.'

'All right.' Gimber nodded: framed in the doorway of the W and D. 'One thing, though. With only five boats going in now, couldn't we all go in through Stjernsund?'

Stjernsund, the passage between Stjernoy and the mainland, was the most direct approach to Altenfjord, and it averaged about three miles in width. Rognsund, which was to be X-12's route, was no more than two miles wide at any point, and had a much narrower bottleneck about halfway through. The reason this back-door approach had been allocated to X-11 and X-12 – in fact to whichever boats were ordered to attack *Lützow*, and they'd turned out to be Paul's and Vicary's – was that with eight midgets all entering at more or less the same time, sending the whole lot through one channel might have increased the chances of detection. And in fact Stjernsund, being the main entrance and the one normally used by the German battle group, might be more closely guarded and patrolled. This might outweigh the hazards of the narrower passage.

'It's a toss-up.' He told Gimber, 'We may be better off than the others, for all anyone can tell. Besides, there's the timing factor.'

Gimber hadn't taken that in. But he was on the defensive, unwilling to admit it. Paul remembered that he hadn't been briefed as operational crew, only for the passage . . . Behind him he heard Brazier mumble, 'About right . . . Let's hope.' Stopping the pump, he added, 'Give or take a cupful.' He was talking to himself about the trim; and he'd need to make another small adjustment to it shortly, when Gimber went through to the sleeping pallet. Paul explained to him, 'Our target's closer than the others. But we have to start off together because we all need this same tide and moon. High tide soon after sunset for instance, so that we'll float over the top of the mines.'

It was a longer route, through Rognsund. *Lützow* was in

Langfjord, which led off from the top end of Altenfjord, whereas *Tirpitz* and *Scharnhorst* were right at the bottom, in Kafjord. The difference was about fifteen miles, and the plan was geared to the ideal of a synchronised attack, all three targets being hit at about the same time.

Gimber nodded. 'I remember now.' He turned again, to crawl though into the for'ard compartment. Paul squeezed out the swab, and stood up, only slightly stooped because at this point the dome gave added head-room, to dry the deckhead around the hatch and periscopes.

Gimber's state of mind worried him. So – slightly – did the fact that Rognsund was much shallower than Stjernsund. If you were caught in Rognsund you'd have a lot less water to hide in.

Brazier said quietly, 'They were shut up in this for more than a week. And in rotten weather, plus sickness, must've been bloody awful. Have to make allowances, I'd think.'

'You're right, Bomber.'

Lanchberry muttered from somewhere near the after bulkhead, 'He'll settle down. Give 'im time, you'll see.'

'Get some zizz now, Jazz.'

'Aye aye.'

Brazier muttered, 'Sounds quite hopeful for old Dick.'

Drops of deckhead moisture dislodged by the swab, spattered down on Paul. The condensation had a sickly smell and taste, like sweat.

'Well, that's terrific!'

X-12 was at sixty feet, but *Setter* was up at thirty, her periscope depth. It was now just after sunset, and MacGregor was taking a look around. Or had been – he was on the other end of the telephone now, and he'd just told Paul that Dick Eaton was conscious and quite comfortable – except for pain when he moved, which according to the coxswain's medical handbook was par for the course.

Paul put his hand over the 'phone, and told the others.

They'd all had some sleep, and they were at their diving stations, waiting for the sunset surfacing. MacGregor said, 'Bird did a good job on him, it seems.'

Paul thought this was the truth. He didn't think MacGregor could have lied so convincingly, not even for the sake of this crew's peace of mind. MacGregor was telling him now, 'We'll stay down until nineteen-thirty. I want it good and dark. All right?'

He agreed. There was plenty of time in hand. He told them as he hung up, 'Seven-thirty now. MacGregor reckons it won't be dark enough until then.'

The only comment came from Gimber. 'Don't know about anyone else, but personally I'll be glad to get on with it.'

You wanted not only the next stage over, but to have the whole thing done. You wanted to have it finished – targets destroyed, and the X-craft out of the fjords, making their separate rendezvous with the parent submarines. And when you'd got to that point, you'd still be looking ahead – to getting home to Loch Cairnbawn: then London, and Jane . . .

Daydreams. But the thought of Jane took his eyes back to Gimber – who looked about ten years older than he had a week ago. A shave and a hot bath would have made a difference, certainly, but the change was deeper than that. You could see it looking at you out of those dark holes in his head. Paul had decided, thinking about it during the afternoon, that most of the trouble might be Gimber's self-consciousness – being on guard against inadequacies in his own performance, and sensitivity to others' view of him. As Brazier had pointed out, you were dealing with a man who'd virtually been in solitary confinement.

He said casually, 'It's astonishing how well you've come through it, Louis.'

'Huh?'

Head twisting sideways: muddy eyes narrowed, suspicious. The blue-black beard gleamed with the moisture in it.

'Well, my God, you've been shut up in this tub for a week, and apart from growing that repulsive face-fungus you don't seem to have been affected by it. To be honest, I was worried whether you'd be in good enough shape.'

Gimber blinked at him. Determined not to be fooled. Which sent the mind off at a tangent – the question of whether in another area he had been . . . Jazz Lanchberry helped, then, with a beautifully timed mutter of, ''Ear, 'ear.' And Brazier boomed from the W and D, 'He's not just a pretty face, is old Louis!' They were all laughing then; Paul felt as if the sky had lifted by about a mile.

Setter rose into the dark off shore night at exactly seven-thirty. A few minutes later Paul was on X-12's casing with the induction pipe up and opened: he called down, 'Main motor half ahead.' *Setter* was lying stopped, sternto, rolling sluggishly to the swell, and men were already climbing down the sides of her bridge and mustering on the after casing. Four of them – one would be the second coxswain. He called down the pipe, 'Steer three degrees to port.' Aiming her at *Setter*'s stern. The midget was moving ahead now, driven by her electric motor, plunging and soaring as the long swells ran under her. He called down again, 'Steady as you go!' On *Setter*'s casing they were already taking in the slack of the heavy Manilla tow; it was much easier to get it in yard by yard as the gap closed than to have a big, heavy bight of it to drag in later. There was no question of just letting it go, having it dangle, 200 yards of tough rope on the loose so MacGregor couldn't move his screws for fear of having them fouled.

'Slow ahead, main motor.'

Repetition of the order from inside was like an echo in a tin drum. The gap was narrowing fast, and his intention was to stop with a few yards between them, not so close as to risk the two ships being washed against each other, but near enough to make the evolution easy and quick. To lie stopped on the surface this close to an enemy-occupied coast was an uncomfortable experience; MacGregor would want to get under way as soon as possible.

'Stop the motor!'

Echo floating up: 'Stop . . .' Vibration ceased. Only sea-noise now, the rush of it along her sides and the swells breaking around her, sluicing away in foam. He had a feeling almost of disbelief in what was happening: to be here, on the targets' doorstep, after all the months of pre-paration . . .

'Slow astern.'

To stop her, keep her where she was. He had to leave this command position and go for'ard now, and he wanted to keep the gap as it was. When stern-power had taken all the way off her, he stopped the motor, waited to make sure it had stopped, then let go of the induction pipe and began crawling for'ard, through rushes of water that looked and sounded like fizzy milk and felt like ice. He crouched, right up on her snout – which was arcing through about eight or ten feet several times a minute – and let them see he was ready for the line to be tossed over. Coming now: the man nearest *Setter*'s stern leant back, and an arm scythed forward in a slightly round-arm swing: the heaving-line came soaring – well over, but falling across the midget's bow and over Paul's outstretched arm. When he'd gath-ered enough slack to double-up about a fathom of it, he leant over her beak and threw a rolling hitch of the doubled line around the much thicker Manilla rope. He could let go of the line now, and unplug the telephone connection. Hands near-frozen, but still functioning. Finally, with a wheel-spanner which he'd had on a lanyard at his waist, he banged twice on the pressure-hull, a signal to Jazz Lanchberry in the fore-end to release the tow.

He heard it go, and waved to the group on *Setter*'s casing.

'All gone!'

A yell of acknowledgement: then a shout of 'Good luck!', over the crash of sea. Another yell had the words 'bloody *Tirpitz*' in it. They were hauling in the tow itself and also the line bent to its end, getting the whole lot out of the water fast, while Paul cautiously reversed his position in order to return to the induction pipe. X-12 rolling like a drunken whale, the sea alternately thumping and sucking at her sides: but it was done now – the tow completed, communication severed, decisions taken and risks accepted. He called down the pipe, 'In engine clutch!' Half a minute later she was turning clear of *Setter*'s stern, the Gardner diesel pounding throatily as it drove her across the swells on course for the inshore minefield.

An hour later she was among the mines. Or rather, over them. He'd picked up the island of Loppen half a mile to starboard, and turned her due east. The other four X-craft would be ahead and to the north, aiming for the gap on southeasterly tracks, across X-12's bows; some of them might already have cleared the minefield.

It was bitterly cold. He'd dressed for the weather, with an extra sweater on, but having his legs and arms soaked through had turned those into vulnerable areas. Frozen areas: he had no feeling in his feet at all. You had to ignore such things, and it was better not to think about the mines either. The fact there'd been no explosions up ahead was comforting: and thank God the swell was much lower, lower all the time as she closed in towards the fjords. It was more than just a matter of getting a smooth passage; it concerned the mines, the fact that heavy pitching such as she'd indulged in earlier could have nullified the safety-margin of the few feet of water between her keel and the horned mines swaying on their mooring-wires like long-stemmed flowers. She could have been dropped right on top of one, in one of those long bow-down swoops.

If she had been – he'd told himself earlier – you wouldn't

have had time to feel sorry for yourself. You wouldn't have had time to feel anything at all. Just boom: four men in the explosion of four tons of Torpex.

He'd set a running charge, so that the Gardner was simultaneously driving her along and charging the battery, so as to have a full quota of stored ampères before they dived. Gimber and Lanchberry would be attending to other things as well – running the compressor, for instance, to top up high-pressure air in the bottles, and making final checks on all sorts of equipment. Brazier would be busying himself mainly with the W and D and his own diving gear and tools.

A dark mass forming now to starboard was Silden, an island shaped like a teardrop and running north to south, its sharp northern end adorned with a light-structure, black and skeletal, looming above a rocky headland which at sealevel was fringed white by the east-running tide. He'd memorised this approach – the distances, timings and landfalls – and had a chart of it in his mind; he knew for instance that when Silden had fallen back on the starboard quarter he'd have the southwestern extremity of a bigger island, Söröy, to port. There was a hill 1600 feet high on that point, and he was expecting to see it soon. There was also a lightening in the sky suggestive of moonrise: he had this impression, without stopping to think about it very hard, and he was surprised – slightly confused, in fact – because he hadn't expected any sign of a moon for another ninety minutes or so. It bothered him, but he let it go – there were other things to think about and he was keeping a careful all-round lookout for ships. Fishing trawlers being the most likely: but there might be patrols as well, with those valuable ships in there. He'd thought he'd seen steaming lights once, about twenty minutes ago, but they'd vanished – a trawler passing behind land, or into some fjordlet, he'd guessed. But when the hill on Söröy's southwest point was abeam, which would be a ten-mile run from the point when

Silden's light-structure was abeam to starboard, he'd turn her to a gyro course of 103 degrees, and then after another twelve and a half miles she'd be close to the northern entrance of Rognsund. She'd have dived before she got that far, to be out of sight before the sun rose a few minutes after 02.00.

The wind was down to almost nothing; inside the barrier of islands, he guessed, the water would be like the surface of a lake. Not too good from the periscope point of view: a ruffled surface would have been infinitely safer. He was thinking about that – about running deep whenever possible, and coming up when necessary for quick and cautious peeps, when he realised that he'd been stupid, that that brilliance had nothing to do with any moon. It was Aurora Borealis, the Northern Lights, flickering above the Arctic icecap. The first time he'd ever seen it. Not that there was time now to enjoy the spectacle – any enemy to starboard would have this little craft in silhouette against those rising, shivering streams of gold. Please God, there'd be no enemy to starboard or anywhere else close enough to see them, and no observer with high-powered optics on the Silden clifftop where the light-structure stood unlit and as unwelcoming and secret as the blank windows of an empty house . . . It was, however, abeam; he called down the pipe to Gimber to check the log reading and make a note of it, so he'd know when they'd run the next ten miles. Straightening from the pipe – using it for communication was hard work, as you were competing with the noise of the diesel and the rush of air it was sucking in – he saw the hilltop he'd been looking for, in silhouette against the polar fireworks. Which was fine. Especially so since he knew, from having it on that bearing with the Silden head-land just abaft the beam, that he had now left the mines astern.

He passed this news down to the others: among all the racket, he thought he heard a cheer. He felt good about things generally at this point: about progress so far, chances of success, and Gimber having adjusted – so it seemed – to new conditions. In which, incidentally, there was a lesson learnt – understanding of the doctors' preoccupation with individual psychology. Even that super-irritant Claverhouse . . . He shouted into the pipe again: 'Louis! Like to take over up here for an hour?'

'Right!'

He warned, 'It's bloody cold . . .'

It was no less cold when he took over again an hour later, but hot soup inside him acted as anti-freeze, and he'd restored circulation to his feet by pressing their soles against the warm casing of the gyro compass. By midnight he'd turned her on to the course for Rognsund, crossing the wide lower part of Söröysund; and soon after making this alteration a glimmer of brightness on mainland mountains confirmed that the moon was rising. Those heights were snowbound – even now, at the end of the months of summer. Remembering that briefing they'd had about the overland route to Sweden, the sight was daunting as well as beautiful.

Lights on shipping to the north, when he was out in the middle at about 01.00, worried him for a while. If they'd been overtaking, as at first he thought they were, he'd have had to have dived her until they'd passed. But they began to draw left, and eventually disappeared. He realised that they'd first appeared just outside Kipperfjord, which was one of several wide inlets on that south coast of Söröy, and they could well have been fishing craft who'd spent the night in there at anchor and were now making an early start. From this point Rognsund would be roughly six miles ahead; he reckoned to cover two thirds of that distance before diving. Then he'd have the day's first light by which to steer her into that narrow gap, and the whole day in which to conn her through. He'd creep through, dead slow on the motor, to make no visible disturbance and as little sound as possible for hydrophones to pick up.

At 01.40 he called down, 'Diving in five minutes!'

Still thinking about Rognsund – its shallow areas which he'd steer around, and the headland which jutted from the right-hand shore to form a bottleneck, just the sort of place they'd have installed acoustic gear. You'd need to be very very careful, all the way. You'd have to show some periscope now and then, because of the twists and turns and tidal complications which could make for navigational problems. The tide was ebbing now, flowing seaward, but low tide would come at about 05.00, and you'd have a slack-water period before it started again in the opposite direction. Even in Stjernsund the tidal flow would be something to be reckoned with, but in a shallower and narrower passage you might get something like a mill-race, at some times and places.

Stjernsund . . . Cameron, Place, Henty-Creer and Hudspeth would all be on their way through, by this time.

The entrance to the sund was a black hole about two miles ahead. Diffused moonlight washed the higher slopes of both Stjernoy and Seiland, but the gulf between them lay in deep shadow.

'Stop the engine. Out engine-clutch.'

The Gardner's pounding ceased.

Silence was dramatic. There was only the swish of sea along her sides. A faint breeze from the west was barely enough to stir the surface. To the east, the high ground on Seiland was a black frieze against sky lightening with the first intimation of a new day coming.

From the direction of Stjernoy, a dog howled.

'Engine-clutch out!'

They'd disconnected the diesel, so as to change over to electric propulsion. Paul ordered, 'Main motor half ahead.' With the Gardner's racket silenced, the induction pipe was a reasonably efficient voicepipe. His watch's luminous face showed 01.47 The motor started: he could feel its vibration and the renewed forward impulse. He called down, 'Shut the induction.' Shutting the valve on the pipe not only made it safe to dive, it also cut off his communications with the men inside her. He stooped, pulled the hatch up, slid in feet-first, dropped through; reaching up to slam it above his head and then swing the securing wheel round to dog it, he ordered 'Open main vents. Thirty feet.'

Ten minutes later, after Gimber had caught a trim and they'd put her through her paces – down to sixty, up to twenty, trim re-adjusted and no problems found – he ordered periscope depth.

'Take it easy, Louis.'

Gimber grunted assent as he put angle on the hydroplanes, to ease her upward. The gauge showed seventeen feet when he shifted the trimpump lever over to port, to flood water into the midships tank, ballasting her as she rose. Paul had the periscope-switch bag in his hand – thick rubber for insulation, and you had to feel for the right button to press: he watched the slow, carefully controlled ascent. The caution was vital – would be at any rate once it was light up there, and this was a matter of starting as you meant to go on. In that channel, you'd only need to make one slip, break surface once . . .

Twelve feet. Eleven. Ten. His thumb pressed the 'up' button in the bag on its wandering lead, and the periscope rose silently, stopping with a jerk at its upper limit as Gimber reported 'Nine feet.'

'When we're inside, Louis, we'll try nine-foot six. I'll make do with about an inch of glass.'

The gap between the two mounds of land was right ahead. He circled, checking all round, knowing there couldn't be anything very close but still doing it out of long habit, standard safety-drill. When they were in the fjord he'd put this 'scope up for just seconds at a time, despite the fact its top was no thicker than a walking stick. In that flat calm, anything that showed above the surface

– particularly anything that left a wake behind it – would catch even the most casual eye.

Gimber had stopped the pump again.

A worrying thing was a slight misting in the lenses. There wasn't enough light yet to be sure, but the edges of the land seemed blurry. You'd tell better in half an hour or so, by which time the sun would have risen. Meanwhile she was on course and it would be an hour before she reached the entrance. He felt for the 'down' button, and pressed it, sent the tube gliding down into its well, below the deckboards.

'Sixty feet.'

The hydroplanes tilted. Gimber's left hand on the pump lever, ready to make new trim adjustments as she nosed deeper. Brazier squatting in the W and D, watching Paul who was crouching over the folded chart, studying the detail of that entrance. You had to use the chart folded to the area you wanted, because there wasn't room to spread it out – no chart-table either, since there'd have been nowhere to put one.

Lanchberry yawning, eyes on the gyro reading, fingering the wheel. He yawned again. Brazier murmured, 'Bastard's either snoring or yawning. Born tired . . .' He had his netcutter beside him, and some tools he'd been using to service it. It was powered by water-pressure, so as not to send up bubbles.

At 03.45 she was at ten feet again, and in the entrance. He'd have brought her up sooner but they'd heard propellers chugging and waited until a trawler had passed overhead, coming out of Rognsund. It was in periscope-sight now – well astern, and about to disappear westward behind Varneset, the headland on Stjernoy. The periscope was slightly foggy, not as bad as he'd feared it might be but certainly requiring attention when there was time and opportunity – tonight, perhaps, when they'd be holed-up for a few hours. He took some bearings, to establish their exact position, and set a course of 155 degrees, which would be good for three miles.

'Sixty feet, Louis.' He told them, as the periscope slid down, 'Nice and peaceful up there. Smoke drifting from cottage chimneys, some chaps mending a boat on a slipway, one horse-and-cart going somewhere very slowly, no signs of anything military.'

Lanchberry said, 'I never did like the military.'

Paul decided that he'd come up for a check after two and three-quarter miles, measuring it by the electric log. At this low speed it would take about two hours. Slow movement not only made less disturbance, it also extended the life of the battery, and there was no certainty when it would be possible to run a change. He'd get one in if he could, because you had not only the attack to think about, but also the withdrawal to sea afterwards. Or the hope of it. Maintaining slow speed like this would stretch the battery life to one hundred miles, but the snag was that in any kind of emergency it mightn't be possible to maintain low speed.

He cranked open the shutters that had been covering the viewing ports, port and starboard. They'd been shut because of the foul weather, mostly. There wasn't anything to be seen here, at the moment, but there would be later. Things like the underwater hull of a pocket battleship.

'Sixty feet, sir.'

'Well done, Louis.' He was acknowledging that 'sir' as much as the report. It was right and proper – not Louis Gimber speaking, but X-12's first lieutenant – but not strictly necessary; Gimber's use of it had been intended to tell him something. Paul said, 'We don't need four on watch. One man at a time could get his head down. Excluding me, that is . . . Louis, old horse, this looks like being the easiest stretch ahead of us, and I'd want you to be on the job after the next change of course, so how about taking your stand-off now?'

*   *   *

He kept a log – detail on which to build the report he'd have to submit later – in a small notebook. Entries showed that when the tide was turning, around 5.00 a.m., he brought her up twice to take shore bearings and ensure safety from navigational hazards. Subsequent entries included:

06.10. A/co to 123, having passed Stoergrd, shallow patch. Rock awash ¾ mile stbd with iron marker.
06.14. Small vessel ahead. Dived to 60ft. (Minesweeper?)
06.22. Ship passed overhead. Turbines, 180 revs.

Gimber asked him, 'How far on this course?'

'One point eight miles. We'll take a shufti after one and a half, though. We'll have the headland coming up then.'

Jazz Lanchberry was off watch now, Brazier at the helm. They heard a ship's screws again just after seven – a reciprocating engine, this time – and after a while it overhauled them on the port side. It was probably a fishing boat. Then shortly afterwards:

07.17. Fast H.E. stbd bow. More than one vessel, prob. E-boats.
07.18. Dived to 100ft.
07.29. H.E. drawing right. Two fast turbine craft, believe E-boats. Returned to 60ft then 40.

In the direction from which those enemies had come initially the chart showed a good anchorage in an inlet called Kvalfjord; he guessed it might be a base for patrol-boats, and made a note of this in the book. Then:

07.46. Periscope depth. A/co 151 to clear Mjaanes Pt.
07.48. 60ft.

This course would have taken her clear of the headland and right through, all the way. But he was wary of tidal sets in the bottleneck, and at 08.20 when he estimated that Mjaanes Point should be abeam he ordered periscope depth to check on it. She was at twelve feet, rising very slowly under Gimber's cautious control, and Paul had pressed the 'up' button for the 'scope, when they were all startled by the sudden thunder of propellers – from around the point of land, but loud, close and fast, closer and louder every second: and X-12 in its path, still slightly bow-up, lifting with her periscope rising too.

'Hundred feet!' Agony of waiting – only seconds, but seemingly an age, while Gimber got bow-down angle on her. Paul snapped, 'Full ahead, group up!' Expecting the end at any moment: the crash, hull splitting open, finis . . . Then the wash hit her as she wallowed down: powerful as the blast of a depthcharge, enemy screws racing over and that huge thrust hitting her as she fought for depth, bow-down with twenty-four feet on the gauge but her stern higher than that, catching the major part of it. That sound – a destroyer's screws so close it had been touch-and-go whether you'd be ploughed open like a can ripped by the opener – he'd heard once before, in *Ultra* in the Mediterranean when an Italian had very nearly made it. X-12 flinging over, rolling right over on to her beam-ends, rammed not by the German's forefoot but by his wash: Paul had been thrown off his feet, the others almost out of their chairs: the ringing of the gyro alarm bell was subdued under a fresh crescendo of propeller noise, a second ship rushing over the top.

They'd come from behind the headland. That was why the noise had burst on them so suddenly, without warning. X-12 was at forty feet and rolling back. Loose gear had been sent flying – including the gluepot and the kettle, utensils, tools and buckets. Paul got to the gyro alarm switch and shut it off – remembering that the Brown's gyro would tolerate a twenty-five degree angle but no more. He told Brazier, as the second lot of screws receded, 'Set the course indicator to ship's head one-five-oh.' Near enough: their course had been 151. The course-indicator was aircraft-type equipment; it would be better than nothing for a while, until they could get the gyro working again. The magnetic compass would be useless in this fjord – or in Stjernsund, for that matter – because of local magnetic anomalies creating wild variations. The chart, and the Pilot for the district, emphasized it.

'Fifty feet, Louis.'

'Fifty: aye aye.' Swinging the 'planes to get her bow up. Paul was still thinking about – or rather, reacting to – the extraordinary power of that first ship's wash. Admitting that this was a very small submarine indeed and that she'd been right at the crucial depth for it to hit her, and at extremely close range – even then . . . He told Gimber, 'Group down, slow ahead.' He'd needed full power to get her down, but in the last minute he'd been wasting amps. He heard Brazier comment: 'Like going over Niagara in a barrel.' Lanchberry was taking over the helm from him, having set the course indicator.

But – still rolling?

Lanchberry enquired, glancing back over his shoulder, that slanted, typically sardonic look as he slid into the seat in Brazier's place, 'Anyone notice anything?'

Paul was checking the transverse spirit-level. His impression of a moment ago had been wrong: she hadn't been rolling, she'd been taking up a much more pronounced list to port than she'd had before.

He told Lanchberry, 'Guess.'

'Ten degrees?'

'Twelve.'

It was giving Gimber problems with the trim. With this much slant on her, the hydroplanes could hardly be expected to function normally, since one was now lower than the other – therefore, in denser water, having more effect than the higher one – and also the slant giving an element of rudder-action to them, because they were so far off the horizontal. It needed only a few comments to establish this, for everyone to recognise the problem and the difficulties it presented. You could also understand how it had come about: the side-cargo, already loosened on its sealing copper strip to the extent that one of its buoyancy-chambers had been flooded, had been jolted looser still by the impact of the destroyer's wash. In fact Paul was wondering at this stage whether it had been a destroyer; the second one certainly had, and in retrospect a comparison between the two suggested that the first had been enormously more powerful. Lanchberry still staring at him over his shoulder: he suggested, 'Have to ditch the port side-cargo, skipper. D'you reckon?'

The idea didn't appeal to him. He told Lanchberry, 'Watch your steering, for God's sake.'

Both those ships must have been destroyers, he decided. Recalling the sound of their screws – even though the leading one had seemed so extraordinarily powerful . . .

Gimber reported grimly, 'Fifty feet.'

'Make it thirty.'

After that, he'd take her up to periscope depth, get a fix and line up the course indicator more accurately. Then – well, just south of this headland there was an inlet three-quarters of a mile deep, called Lille Kvalfjord. Lille meaning 'little'. The chart showed that it shelved to as little as ten fathoms in there, and if it was empty or at least not crowded it might be a good spot in which to lie on the bottom and set the gyro to rights, square off whatever other defects might show up when one had time to look around.

Gimber muttered, working hard at the trim, 'This is damn near impossible.'

'You're doing well, Louis.'

Not all that well, though. And nearer the surface,

controlling her was going to be even trickier. Also, there'd
be a slant on the periscope and you'd get distorted bearings. It was quite probable that the periscope would have
flooded again, after that rough handling; he guessed the
leak would be either around the frame of the top glass, or
in the metal casing itself.

It might be wise – although it went against the grain –
to ditch the flooded side-cargo. Set it to 'safe' and release
it. At least you'd be in shape to carry out a successful attack
with the other one – which on the present showing certainly
couldn't be guaranteed.

It seemed such a waste. Having brought the thing all
this way . . .

Gimber reported, 'Thirty feet.'

'Nice work.'

'I can't promise to keep her within a yard of any ordered
depth, though.'

'Have to find a way to, Louis. Somehow. Try twenty, now.'

'Christ.' Gimber raised his voice to acknowledge more
formally, 'Twenty feet.' Shaking his head, as he tilted the
hydroplanes . . . Paul still thinking about it – and realising
that with trimming as it was now he wouldn't have dared
to bring her up any higher than twenty. If they bungled it
now, alerted the Germans to the threat of attack – giving
them time to move their ships out, mount a hunt in the
fjords, plaster the whole area with depthcharges . . .

And if it happened, it wouldn't have been Gimber's
fault. She was at twenty-two feet now and going down
again: he'd been nervous of letting her overshoot upwards.

'All right. Twenty-five feet. I'll have to ditch the bloody
thing.'

Lanchberry's head inclined in a nod of approval. Gimber
said, 'Yes. I'm sorry, but it's just—'

'Can't be helped.'

It still irked him to have to do it. Fifty per cent of her
offensive potential down the drain. Facing facts, however,

it could not be helped. And with six hundred feet of water here, it was as good a place as any to do it. He crouched at the port side fuse-mechanism. The pointer on the clock had to be turned through two stops to the left, to the one marked SAFE. Until it had been set there – or activated, set going with a delay-setting on it – the release gear couldn't be operated. He gripped the knob between fore-finger and thumb, and twisted.

It wouldn't turn the whole way. It clicked to the inter-mediate stop, but no further. He returned it to the starting point, and tried again.

'The pointer won't go to "safe".'

She was at twenty-eight feet, and Gimber was still having to fight the controls. Paul beginning to appreciate that the problems were real and cumulative. He told them – Lanchberry, who was staring round at him, and Brazier's wide, ginger-stubbled face framed in the circular opening of the W and D – 'It'll travel right, but not left. Not far enough.'

So – next alternative . . .

You could turn the knob to the right to the full extent of its travel, putting the maximum delay of six hours on the fuse, and then ditch it. The fuse would have to be acti-vated, and after six hours it would explode.

Gimber had had the same thought. 'Set a long fuse, and dump it?'

'Can't do that.' He'd seen the answer. 'Suppose we did it now. The bang would go off at three this afternoon. What chance would we – or any of the others – have of getting any attacks in tomorrow morning, d'you think? The Bosch wouldn't just say "Oh, something's exploded in the Rognsund", and do nothing about it, would they.'

Gimber admitted, 'No. You're right.'

'So we're stuck with it, until tomorrow. Preferably until we find our target . . . Louis – let's try a bow-heavy trim, holding her on the 'planes?'

He thought that might answer the trimming problem. Instinct, the 'feel' of her, suggested it. But even if it worked, you'd still have a periscope on the blink, a heavy list and a side-cargo malfunctioning . . . He was behind Gimber's left shoulder, studying the effects of the change of trim as it began to take effect. Thinking about that side-cargo – whether if it was defective in one respect it could be trusted in any other.

13

Trench told me, 'I'd arranged for the *Bayleaf* and *Arctic Prince* to divert to a new, closer rendezvous position. Two reasons: one, low cloud was giving us cover from the Luftwaffe and the forecast was for rough stuff ahead of us, the sort of conditions that make flying more or less impossible up there, so there was a good chance the bastards would be grounded. Normally I'd have gone right up to the ice and out of their range as soon as possible, but in these circumstances I thought I could take the risk of cutting the corner . . . Clear?'

It was not only clear, it was on the record.

'Second reason was we knew there were U-boats waiting up near Bear Island. I turned the *Bayleaf* to a southwesterly course – instead of southeasterly – and kept her clear of them. At the same time I altered the convoy's route so as to pass south of the island instead of north of it. We made the rendezvous, got on with fuelling the escorts, and altered again – to about two-five-oh degrees, leaving Bear Island sixty miles to the nor'ard.'

Mrs Trench said, 'If you leave your food alone much longer, it'll be stone cold.'

He began to eat. She smiled at me. Eileen Trench was a good-looking woman, with a beautiful skin and good bone structure; in 1943 she'd have been what we then called a 'smasher'.

Trench told me with his mouth full, 'As it happened, a U-boat on passage to join its chums ran into us by sheer chance. It dived well out ahead, *Leopard* thought she'd made asdic contact and pooped off a few salvoes of hedgehog, but – well, may or may not have been a sub contact, but if it was the Hun survived it. Within an hour or so we had him shadowing from astern, calling to his friends to come and join him. Some of them did – resulting in the loss of the *Lord Charles* and an American freighter – whose name I forget . . . Quite a lot of survivors, from the Yank particularly, thanks to a very quick rescue. But Martin Insole drowned. The vice-commodore who took over from him was also American – name of Claypoole, master of the . . .' he'd paused, with a forkful of mutton in mid-air: and got it '. . . the *Harriet Smith*. Odd how some names stick and some don't.'

Trench seemed to be staring at his wife across the table, but his eyes weren't focussed on her and his thoughts, certainly, were a thousand miles away.

'We only lost those two. At dusk I made a drastic alteration southward. On its own this might have thrown them off, but in fact a strong blow from the northwest got up during the night, and by dawn – steaming west again by then – we had roughish seas with sleet and snow showers.'

Trench continued, 'My object had been simply to get away from the U-boat pack. This had been achieved, and we'd lost our shadower too – which was extremely fortunate. If they'd maintained contact and known exactly where we were, later events might have turned out quite differently. But anyway – the signal from London told me that *Lützow* and nine destroyers had been reported as having sailed from Altenfjord. It felt very much as it had on the outward passage with PQ 19 when they'd told us *Tirpitz* and *Scharnhorst* were at sea. Except we'd had a cruiser with us then – not that that alone could make a jot of difference, but she'd had a man commanding her in whom I had a lot more faith than I had in myself. I looked around and saw my handful of lightly-armed ships, as against twice as many Germans with much heavier guns – that's just the destroyers, let alone *Lützow* with her eleven-inch . . . I can tell you, I thanked God for the bad weather and for the fact we no longer had our shadower. But I still thought we'd come up against them, because we were so damn close.'

'About – two hundred miles?'

'From Altenfjord?' He nodded. 'About that, after we'd turned down to the southwest. I didn't know exactly when the Germans had sailed, but it would surely have been the night before, so we could have expected to run into them any minute. Their notion of my convoy's whereabouts might have been somewhat vague, based on U-boat reports twenty-four hours old, and I wasn't sure the U-boats would know which way we'd turned – they could have expected us to turn up towards the ice, you see, as we'd done before – I mean as Nick Everard had done. I had these imponderables in mind, and bad weather with very poor visibility as the one thing in our favour. Also, a fervent wish that Nick Everard had been on his feet and making the decisions.'

'But he was still . . .'

'Yes.' Trench put down his knife and fork. 'C-in-C Home Fleet ordered the battle squadron out of Akureyri, and he sailed CS 39 as well – minus *Nottingham*, who'd been sent south to get her bomb damage patched up. Kidd had transferred his flag to *Rhodesia*. But they might as well have been on the China Station, for all the support they could give me from that distance.'

I asked him, later, 'The ship that nearly ran down Paul's X-craft and damaged her with its wash – would you agree that might have been *Lützow* on her way out?'

'Might've been. It's never been possible to establish for certain, largely because there's doubt about exactly when she did sail. We know she was at sea when the Admiralty made that signal – some hours before, in fact, because they'd had to take in and digest a report from our Norwegian friends first. And she certainly wasn't in the fjord when the X-craft made their attacks on the twenty-second: but Roskill in his official history gives her departure date as September twenty-third. So –' Trench helped himself to cheese – 'you pays your money and you takes your choice. Bearing in mind that only Allah is perfect.' He glanced across at me. 'You knew Paul quite well, didn't you.'

'Oh, yes.'

Eileen Trench asked, 'Were you and he contemporaries?'

'More or less. And we were both submariners.'

'You weren't in X-craft, though, were you?'

'No. At a late stage I volunteered for it, but by that time they had all they wanted . . . One thing does strike me, about the ship that hit him with her wash. When he identified her as a destroyer, before he realised it might have been something much bigger, he had nothing to go by except the hydrophone effect.' I explained to Trench's wife, 'We called it "HE". It was the underwater sound of a ship's propellers. The noise a turbine made – which is tantamount to saying a small warship, as distinct from a cruiser or battleship – was quite different from a big ship's reciprocating engines.'

She smiled at me as if she thought I was talking double Dutch. 'Do go on.'

'Well. That was the general rule, in 1943. But as it happened, *Lützow* was turbine-powered. Geared turbines, with diesels for cruising speeds. So turbine-driven screws is what he would have heard.'

Trench nodded. 'You could well have a point.'

'And she must have sailed at about that time. But nobody

had any sight or sound of her in Stjernsund. If she'd gone out that way, I think they would have, because X-10, commanded by Hudspeth, an Australian, was still in Stjernsund then, trying to make-good his boat's defects. He had no compasses, no periscope, several other major problems. In fact he had rotten luck altogether – in spite of the defects he got her right down to Kafjord, then had to abandon the operation. He spent a week hiding in the outer fjords, and eventually made a rendezvous with one of the towing submarines. If *Lützow* had steamed out through Stjernsund when he was there, he'd have heard her, for sure.'

Trench agreed with me.

'You said,' his wife broke in, 'that this Australian had to give up. So besides Paul Everard's there were only – what, three X-craft left operational, when the time came?'

'Yes. Cameron, Place, Henty-Creer. All targeted on *Tirpitz*. Paul was supposed to attack *Lützow*, and there was nobody now to deal with *Scharnhorst*. Of course, none of the four teams who were in there had any way of knowing X-10 had dropped out.'

The image of Louis Gimber sliding on to his seat at the hydroplane and main motor controls seemed to shiver, mirage-like. Paul blinked, to clear his eyes, and finished replacing periscope tools in their canvas roll. Jazz Lanchberry muttered, 'Air's not too bad, considering.'

He meant, considering they'd been shut down for nearly twelve hours now, and he'd only made the comment because the truth was that the air was extremely thin. It would have been intolerable by this time if they hadn't spread Protosorb on trays – Protosorb being Lithium Hydroxide, white crystals to absorb the poison with which four men's breathing was polluting the midget's damp, yellow-lit interior – and also doctored the atmosphere with guffs of oxygen from bottles stored in the engineroom. You had to go easy with the oxygen, because tomorrow might be a long day too. If you were lucky, it might be a long day.

Paul told Lanchberry, 'It'll get worse before it gets better. We have a way to go yet.' He gave the periscope a pat, and sent it down; he'd stripped it, dried its flooded lenses and reassembled it, but whether it would stay dry now, or for how long, was anyone's bet. He hoped it only flooded when she was banged around, as she had been in the ship's wash and before that by the bad weather. The leak, he guessed, would be either around the frame of the top glass or from a strained seam in the metal barrel that housed the optics, and by this time it might have opened up enough to make for a constant seepage.

Lanchberry and Gimber had got the gyro back into operation, and Brazier had attended to several minor items. The one thing nobody could do anything about was the flooded side-cargo, the list you knew she'd take up again as soon as she floated up off the bottom.

He held up the damp, discoloured chart. Its paper absorbed the moisture of the atmosphere, and there wasn't anything you could do about that either.

'Look here.' Pointing, with a pencil. 'If we find we have to do something about the air, at a pinch I'd surface her here.'

'In daylight?'

Gimber had his mouth slightly open, like a dying fish. Paul added, 'If we had to, is what I'm saying.' Pointing at an islet near the bottom end of Rognsund – about a cable's length from the western shore, and with a fringe of rocks and outlying reef. 'We'd have cover there. Otherwise – preferably – we'll carry on, come up about seven-thirty when it's dark, then hole up here – this island, Langnesholm – until about dawn. Shove off before sunrise, and you could be at work on *Lützow*'s nets by four a.m., Bomber. That'd give us plenty of time to lay the cargoes and sneak out again.'

Brazier nodded. 'Right.' Lanchberry said, 'Give him a job, at last.' Bristling crew-cut, blue-jowelled, eyes showing their whites as he glanced over his left shoulder. Brazier crouching like a caged but amiable Hunchback of Notre Dame. Paul wondered what he looked like. Certainly like nothing to please the eye.

Depthgauge static at the figure 132.

'One hundred feet.'

Gimber pushed the pump-lever over to starboard to open the midships tank and set the pump's suction working on it, lighten her so she'd lift clear of the seabed. They were in Lille Kvalfjord, and it was about four hours since those ships had nearly run them down. The adjustment to the trim, after they'd fiddled with it for a while, had worked quite well; she was clumsy, and Gimber still had to work at it, but she was manageable.

'Ship's head?'

Lanchberry told him, 'Oh-two-two.'

'Steer that.'

It would do well enough. He'd turned her before he'd bottomed her, so she'd be pointing the right way – out – in case a quick exit had become desirable. Movement now, heeling over. Like a whale starting to roll on the fjord's rocky bed. The deckboards angled under his feet: then she was floating up . . . 130 feet. When she reached 120, safely clear, he ordered the motor slow ahead group down. X-12 was leaning woundedly to port but was otherwise responsive to her controls as she paddled gently out to re-enter Rognsund.

Back in business . . .

Gimber reported, 'Hundred feet.'

'Make it eighty, Louis.'

The periscope leak worried him more than the list did, particularly as Gimber seemed to be managing the trim all right. To use the stub periscope, the short bifocal night one set like an alligator's eyes just above the casing, you had to be right up there, breaking surface, and with her slightly awkward handling now you'd be really breaking surface, off and on. So there could be no question of using the stub in daylight, and without the use of the main periscope you'd be blind. As for the list – well, the aim had to be to get rid of the flooded side-cargo as soon as possible. Once she'd shed it, she'd be back on an even keel. Safe withdrawal after the attack therefore wasn't compromised, except in the sense that a successful attack was the necessary first step in that direction and that the chances of completing an attack undetected had been reduced by the loss of manoeuvrability.

'Depth eighty feet.' Gimber was adjusting the trim again. Lanchberry began to whistle between his teeth, then caught himself doing it, and stopped. Paul checked the log. One nautical mile – 2000 yards – would take her far enough out into the sund, then he'd turn her to starboard to a course of 150 degrees on which a run of five miles would take her into fairly open water.

'Half ahead, Louis.'

There was a need to conserve battery power, but he also wanted to get down near that little island, Stjernovodd-holmen, so that if lack of air became a really immediate problem he'd be able to bring her to the surface with some hope of not being spotted. The foul air was already making him feel sick, and he was aware that his pulse-rate had risen. Brazier was sitting instead of squatting, with his head down between his knees, the accepted position for countering nausea . . . Problem followed problem: this whole thing was a gamble, and all you could do was press on, cope with each difficulty as it arose.

He was navigating by dead-reckoning now – using log-readings to get the distance run, and accepting the fact that the gyro was accurate only to within a few degrees one way or the other. He took her out to what he thought to be almost mid-fjord, and turned her to the southeasterly course before he could risk coming up and trying to get a fix. It would be a check on the state of the periscope, as much as on the boat's position; if the prisms had been flooded again, he'd get no more than a blur. He brought her up slowly, in stages, and at thirty feet he cut the speed from half to slow ahead – to reduce or even eliminate any 'feather' at the tip of the periscope when it pushed up through the surface.

'Set the course indicator, Jazz. I'll turn her down-fjord, and we'll call that one-five-oh . . . Fifteen feet, Louis.'

The hydroplanes tilted gently. There was no sound – which he was listening for, not wanting to be caught twice – of any other ship's screws. Only the purr of the main motor, and the water rustling along her sides. At fifteen feet Gimber seemed to have her in pretty good control.

'Ten feet.'

He had the rubber bag in his hand, thumb on the feel of the 'rise' button inside it. At ten feet the top glass would still be covered. His hope was to show no more than half an inch above the surface, if Gimber could hold her that steady – and in such calm water it would certainly have been possible if she had not had the list on her . . . He decided he'd order a depth just greater than the one he wanted, and use the upward variations, put up with periods of being blanked off.

'Depth ten feet.'

He pressed the button. 'Try nine and a half, Louis.' The tube slid up, and stopped. Lanch-berry looking back over his shoulder: Brazier with his head lifted, eyes slitted under the beetling ginger brows. Paul put his right eye to the lens. Bubbling, bright whorls, a kaleidoscopic medley of blues, greens and white, and diamond-like flashes through it all; the top glass was still covered when Gimber blurted, 'Nine and a half. Can't be sure of holding . . .'

'Just do your best.'

Rising now. He'd get some kind of a view, before Gimber forced her down again.

The prisms were fogged. But he could see enough to confirm that she was well out in the middle. The land-mass to port – a mountainous rise almost abeam, matched the same feature on the chart. To starboard, about thirty degrees on the bow, there was a higher one inland on Stjernoy. Between those features – ahead, beyond a vacuity of clear water – blurred heights with snow on them towered against a patchwork sky.

'Steer three degrees to port, and set the course indicator on one-five-oh.'

'Three degrees to port, aye aye . . .'

The top of the periscope had dipped under. Water swirled, bubbling, then darkened into stillness. He pulled his head back and pressed the 'down' button.

'Well done, Louis. Sixty feet.'

'Periscope OK?'

'Far from it. But we're where we ought to be.'

More or less. An accurate fix wasn't necessary anyway at this stage. He took a new reading of the log, from which to measure the run southeastward. Deciding at the same time that an emergency stop at Stjernovoddholmen wasn't really to be welcomed. To get in close enough to have cover from the island when you surfaced would require accurate navigation, to avoid the hazards of rock and reef around it. This thin, putrifying air was going to have to last until the sun was down.

'We'll treat ourselves to another shot of the oh-two, I think.'

Approving murmurs . . . Oh-two meaning oxygen. The midget was nose-down, paddling lopsidedly down past fifty feet. He decided he'd renew the Protosorb as well, since it might have absorbed about as much carbon dioxide as it could hold by this time. He told Gimber, 'Half ahead,' and Brazier, 'Scrape up the Protosorb, Bomber, and spread a fresh lot.' Lanchberry murmured, 'Might as well be comfy', and they all laughed – laughter coming easily, when you needed it. Paul crawled aft into the engine space for another oxygen bottle.

It got worse again, of course. Worst of all were the last twenty minutes – having to resist the temptation to take a risk and surface before it was really dark. They were all sick, feverish, breathing in short gasps. The Bomber was asleep, but a better word for it might have been 'unconscious'. Paul had kept her on 150 for two hours, logging three point nine miles in that time, then altered to due south. If tidal streams had matched expectations, they ought by now to be in the wide upper part of Altenfjord. About an hour ago they'd have passed southward between Horsnes and Klubbeneset, and her immediate destination – Langnesholm, a very small island close to the entrance of Langfjord – would now be about three and a half miles on the bow to starboard. Driven by the diesel after she surfaced, she'd get there in about half an hour.

A quarter of an hour ago he'd brought her up to nine feet, but a quick glance through the blurred lenses had shown it wasn't dark enough yet, and he'd ordered her back to thirty feet. Since then, every few minutes he'd found either Gimber or Lanchberry staring at him. Once he'd snapped irritably, 'No – not yet!' It was like being stared at by hungry dogs: and he didn't need their reminders, he'd been trying to keep his own thoughts away from that cold, fresh air. He was also worried about Brazier, but a man asleep used less air than the same man awake, and that one, being twice life-size, used a lot. So the temptation to see if he could be woken had also been resisted.

The needle was steady on thirty feet, motor slow ahead group down, time 19.35, the others' panting intakes of breath irritatingly loud although one's own – oddly enough – were not. He thought he'd left it long enough, now. At his sudden move – he'd been sitting with his back against the gyro – the others glanced quickly round. He nodded.

'Nine feet.' The hydroplanes tilted sharply: he warned Gimber, 'Take it gently, Louis.' Gimber muttered something. Paul ignored it, and told Lanchberry to wake the Bomber; Lanchberry leant sideways from his chair, grabbed one of the large feet that were projecting from the W and D, wrenched it to and fro. 'Wakey wakey, rise and shine!'

Bomber groaned. Lanchberry did it some more: there was another groan, and then a growl of 'Oh, piss off . . .'

'We're about to surface, Bomber. You OK?'

Gimber croaked, 'Nine feet.' In fact she was at eight and a half. Brazier was on his knees at the heads bowl, retching into it. The periscope hissed up: Paul put his eye to it, circled right around, peering into blurry darkness in which an enemy would probably have been invisible even a yard away. But there was no sound of any.

'Stand by to surface.'

Circling again – knowing the periscope was defective to an extent that made the exercise futile, and hoping to God that Brazier was going to be all right. Surprising it should have hit the strongest of them all the hardest. Bigger lungs having more room for poison in them, perhaps, bigger heart needing more oxygen to run on . . . He sent the periscope down and positioned himself under the hatch.

'Surface. Blow one and three main ballast.'

The relief of getting into fresh air, then hearing the rush of it down the induction pipe when the Gardner thumped into action and began to suck it in, was so overwhelming that in those first minutes he didn't give any thought to the dramatic quality of the moment – that he was surfacing his boat in a German harbour and the one that accommodated the *Tirpitz*, at that . . . He did think about it later, though, while he was conning her southwestward at six knots to find that island. He was closer to it, in fact, than he'd expected; the ebbing tide – it would be flooding now, low water about an hour ago – must have been stronger than he'd allowed for. Land outlines were clearly visible, sharp enough to fix by, using the gyro and finding the results quite good. He had binoculars on the casing with him – in this dead calm water there was no problem using them – and that opening about a mile and a quarter wide could only be the entrance to Langfjord and *Lützow*'s net-enclosed berth. Nets which Bomber Brazier would have to be fit enough to cut a hole in tomorrow morning. The feeling of nausea was wearing off: it was like beginning to feel better after a really terrible hangover.

He saw Langnesholm – or rather, a dark end to land that couldn't be anywhere else. His idea was to tuck X-12 in behind its southern end, so she'd be lying in the channel and in the island's shadow . . . He lowered the binoculars, and called down for an alteration of a few degrees to port: straightening from the pipe, his eye was caught by a flash of white – starboard bow . . .

He whipped his glasses up. It had vanished – but it re-appeared, and he was on it. A ship's bowwave . . . Small, but fast, travelling from left to right: he guessed it might be an E-boat, or some other kind of fast patrol craft. He called down to stop the engine. If necessary, he'd dive her, but by cutting out any motion through the water – and if the enemy held its present course – he crouched, knowing the midget would be virtually invisible, with so little profile . . . The patrol boat would have entered through Stjernsund, he guessed, and from its present course might be heading for Leir Botn, the destroyer anchorage on the far side and oppo-site the south coast of Aaroy.

It had gone on, out of sight. He called down, 'No problem. E-boat or somesuch, just passing. Half ahead main engine.' Visualising the Germans in that boat's bridge – if they'd known there was a fox here in their hen-run. Highly explosive fox. But it was nerve-tingling too, in some ways – the racket of the Gardner, for instance, as she gath-ered way again, pushing through a surface that was rippling from a newly-risen breeze: you could imagine

Germans hearing this from miles away. The new wind was knife-cold – it made his eyes run, turned his damp clothes into an ice-suit. He shouted down the pipe, 'Below – how's Brazier?'

Gimber answered that he seemed to be all right. It was a big relief. And there was a job for him, or would be in a minute . . . 'Tell him to put his rubber suit on.' Gimber passed that message, then called again: 'Get a hot meal ready, shall we?'

'Good idea!'

Hot anything . . .

He'd been watching in case the patrol boat turned back, but there was nothing to be seen of it. He moved the glasses on, sweeping up the port side towards the bow. Down there at the southern end of the fjord, where in its offshoot Kafjord *Tirpitz* and *Scharnhorst* would be lying – tucked up for the night and feeling safe – X-5, 6, 7 and 10 would also be in wait. Cameron and Place, he knew, had intended to spend the dark hours lying-up among the Brattholm islands, three or four miles from the Kafjord entrance. They'd quite likely be in sight and sound of each other, close enough to chat from boat to boat – just as X-12 would have had X-11 for company, if X-11 hadn't been at the bottom of the Norwegian Sea, with Dan Vicary and his crew kicking their heels on board *Scourge*, pretty sick with frustration, no doubt.

In another ten minutes he had her close to Langnesholm; an unlit light-structure on its southern end provided a good leading-mark. He nosed her in towards the opening between the island and the mainland coast – into deep shadow and a cliff's overhang. He called down, 'Stop main engine!' The diesel's pounding ceased, and the rush of air stopped too; he didn't need to shout now, with only the swish of water along her sides. Silence emphasized the loneliness and the need for stealth . . . 'Out engine-clutch. Main motor half ahead group down. Steady as you go.' He was crouching, with the tube at a slant, half lowered. The gap between the island and the mainland shore was too shallow higher up, and too rock-strewn, to be navigable, and since there'd be no possibility of passing through that way in the morning he was going to hide her at this southern end. It was also more remote down here – roughly seven hundred yards from the other shore – and it was necessary to run a battery-charge while they were here.

X-12 gliding in, only the soft thrum of her motor and the wash of ice-water around her. The rocky coast of Langnesholm loomed against the sky on the bow.

'Stop main motor. Port five. Tell Brazier to come up.' The gear Brazier was going to use was lashed inside the casing; he confirmed as he got it out that he was fully recovered . . . 'Slight pain in the nut is all.' There was a coil of steel wire rope and an anchor, and he was cutting the lashings off. Paul asked him, 'Nut, or nuts?' The Bomber chuckled. The island coast was so near that any sentry up there might have been wondering what the joke was: Paul wondered how he could possibly risk running the diesel here, for the battery-charge . . . 'Midships. Slow astern.'

In a few minutes he had her at rest and, to all intents and purposes, hidden. Brazier went over the side, jammed the anchor in a rock-cleft and came back. He muttered, 'You could have them aching soon enough in that stuff.' Paying out the wire until her weight was on it; the end was shackled to the bull-ring, and they'd leave it here, simply unshackle it when they left in a few hours' time. Meanwhile it would hold her forty tons of deadweight stemming the inflow of tide.

'Nice work, Bomber. Glad you're OK. You had me worried.'

'Took a little snooze, that's all . . . Skipper, there's corned dog hash below, when you're ready for it. Shall one of us eat first, then—'

'Listen . . .'

Music. From the mainland side.

It sounded like a fiddle. And voices now, singing. He concentrated – wanting to identify the language – there'd be all the difference in the world between a bunch of Norwegians having a hooly and some German garrison . . . Also, the question of how near or far, and the matter of the battery having to be charged – it was absolutely necessary. To move out into mid-stream to do it was an unattractive alternative, with likely interruptions by patrol boats or other craft . . . The singing and the accompaniment climaxed and stopped. X-12 moving to her wire, sea-movement loud among the rocks . . .

A male voice – making a speech . . .

It was drowned in clapping. Brazier said quietly, 'Sounded Norwegian.'

Paul thought so too; and the music hadn't sounded at all Germanic. A door slammed like a distant pistol-shot, and the fiddle struck up again, then quietened as a woman's voice rose – some kind of folk-song, solo. There was no glimmer of light in that direction, or anywhere else either.

'Go on down, Bomber. Tell Louis to put on a standing charge. First man to finish his scoff can come up and relieve me.'

The day's run south would have taken all the guts out of the battery, and they'd need all it had to offer tomorrow. With nets to negotiate you could expect to need bursts of full power; and having made the attack, the only way to withdraw would be dived, and perhaps at some speed, in the initial stages . . . He heard applause now, cheers and clapping and a general hubbub of party noise. With luck, the rumble of the Gardner wouldn't carry that high and that far; another hope was that if anyone did hear it and stop to listen they might think it came from farther out, in mid-fjord or even from the far side.

It still sounded menacingly loud when it started. The rocky cliffs enclosed the sound, magnifying it . . . Then

Gimber came up to take over. There was no chance of hearing any party noise now.

'Bomber tell you about the singsong?'

'Yeah. We had a listen in the hatch. Think they'll be listening to us, now?'

'Doubt it. It'd be muffled, anyway, could be coming from miles away.'

'Sounds bloody loud to me.' Gimber added, 'Plenty of hash left, you'll be glad to hear.'

'Good.' He pointed astern. 'That's the danger sector. We could dive if we had to – trim her down right here and use the induction as a snort. Wouldn't even need to break the charge – just dive, on the wire that's holding us.'

'That's a thought!'

According to intelligence reports, the enemy were developing a new class of U-boat that could run submerged on its diesels, using a tube called a 'schnorkel' for the air inlet. One or two of the X-craft men had tried a similar technique using the induction pipe, but it was slightly hazardous because there was no automatic shut-off when the top of the tube 'drowned', and the helmsman had to be quick to shut the valve by hand.

Paul slid into the hatch. Gimber asked him, 'Will you be coming up again when you've eaten?'

He'd stopped, halfway in. Diesel fumes acrid, more noticeable down at this level. The lop on the water was more noticeable too: if the wind held, it would be good cover for periscope work tomorrow. If the periscope worked . . . He answered Gimber's question: 'Expect so. Why?'

'Something I'd like to talk about. While there's time and—' he'd checked, and caught his breath: 'Christ, look!'

There'd been a flicker of light reflected in his eyes. Whipping round – to face into what he'd called the danger sector – Paul was looking into a blaze of it, just momentarily, then distant and changing, lengthening, the sword-like beam of a searchlight which as it swung round level with the sea had passed over them, illuminating and throwing a huge shadow from the light-structure above them: now it was silvering high ground on the island of Aaroy – which was four miles from here – and then, scything on clockwise, sweeping over the forepart and bridge superstructure of a warship. A giant warship. Immensely long, flared foc'sl, twin gun-turrets wide, flattish, powerful-looking; the fore-bridge behind them had a similarly squat look about it, and was dwarfed by the colossal director-tower.

Unmistakeably, it was *Scharnhorst*. At anchor, in the lee of Aaroy island.

'Is she under way?'

'No.' Paul was recovering from the shock of that sudden glimpse, that enormous enemy just across the water. It had almost literally taken his breath away. The searchlight's beam fingered a steeply slanted funnel-cap, then abruptly switched off and died back, leaving them blinded in the dark, the diesel banging away . . . Gimber asked, 'What's that island called?'

'Aaroy . . . Hudspeth's bound to have seen her there.' He was thinking aloud, more than talking to Gimber. 'At least, I'd guess he would have.'

'Not if he made the southward run deep like we did. He could be at the Brattholms with the others, expecting to find her in Kafjord in the morning.'

Pure conjecture. They might all four be there, or some of them might not have made it. And there was no way of knowing when *Scharnhorst* might have moved – when, or for that matter why – out of the protection of her anti-torpedo nets. 26,000 tons of battleship, in an unprotected berth . . . There was no shred of light now, where a minute ago the colossus had been floodlit. It was dark in all directions and there'd be enemies in most directions, X-12 in the middle of them with her diesel grumbling throatily to itself, ignoring all of them . . . As to that question 'why?'

– well, the X-craft had been on their own for most of the past twenty-four hours, and there could have been all sorts of developments they'd have no way of knowing about. The battle group might be putting to sea, for instance – the report of *Tirpitz* changing her gun-barrels might have been wrong, or the intentions might have changed. He couldn't imagine they'd leave *Scharnhorst* for long in such an exposed position: she'd have to be only pausing there, on her way either in or out . . .

Unless there'd been a scare, one of the other X-craft detected, and the Bosch at panic-stations?

'Give me a shout if anything looks interesting, Louis.'

Below, eating his supper and chatting with the others, he decided that before he went up to join Gimber he'd strip the periscope down again and dry it out. You couldn't hope to do anything about the source of the problem, the leak – which would have been an external job, and you couldn't show a light up there – so it would soon flood again, but at least he'd be starting this next vital phase with a periscope that worked.

'Best hash we've had yet. Whose masterpiece was it?'

Lanchberry's eyebrows hooped. 'Skipper, I'm amazed you'd find it necessary to enquire.'

Brazier had been checking over various pieces of equipment, including the packs of overland escape gear. He'd also examined and tested his own diving gear and the water-powered net-cutter – so Jazz Lanchberry said, staring meaningfully at Paul.

'Well, for God's sake, how many times is that?'

Brazier looked embarrassed. Lanchberry said, 'Every five bloody minutes, that's all. Right, Bomber?'

'Better too often than not enough.'

'Ah, there's wisdom for you!'

'Leaks can develop, Jazz, and valves can seize up, and . . .'

Paul asked him, 'How about our stuff?'

Brazier nodded. 'The DSEA sets are on the top line, skipper.'

DSEA stood for Davis Submarine Escape Apparatus, and sets comprising face-masks, harness, oxygen bottles etcetera were provided for the three non-divers. But all such equipment was in Brazier's care for maintenance purposes.

'What time do we push off, skips?'

He put down his coffee mug. The air was as bitingly cold down here, with the rush of night air feeding the Gardner, as it was up top. He told them, 'About one-thirty. We'll dive right away to eight feet and keep the periscope right up as long as the light's dim. The leak's most likely near the top, in which case if I can keep it above water long enough to get a bearing on *Lützow* before we go deep, we'll be on the right track.'

Lanchberry nodded. 'Good thinking.'

'Well.' Paul looked at Brazier. 'He's paying me compliments now.'

'Because you liked his hash.'

'Oh, that's it.'

None of them felt like sleeping. Camouflaging taut nerves was a full-time job. For Paul it wasn't only the prospect of tomorrow's action – complicated by his boat's two-fold disability – it was the possibility of there being no action, if the battle group were putting to sea. He didn't mention this possibility to the others.

Gimber, on the casing a bit later, began abruptly, 'Better talk about it, don't you think?'

'About what?'

'Her. Jane.'

'Oh.' There was a pause. The engine rumbling on, and the light-structure a black etching against paler sky. Moonrise would throw no light into this chasm. Paul thought that if Gimber knew about his own affair with Jane, he'd been nursing the secret very guardedly. He said, 'If you want to, Louis.'

'Remember what I asked you, that last night in the depot ship – about looking after her, if I bought it?'

'Yes, I do. But you're alive and kicking, so we can forget it, can't we.'

'I was pissed. And I knew it, and I was being careful. Particularly as we were just off. It wasn't exactly a time to pick a fight.'

He'd have been sitting up here rehearsing this speech. In the middle of an Arctic night, surrounded by enemies, with his mind on a girl who'd two-timed him. If he knew that much, and it had begun to sound as if he might.

'I wouldn't say this is much of a time for it, either.'

'It's the only time we've got, though, for talking.' Gimber added, 'I had an uncle who was terribly proud he'd "gone over the top" in the last war. He said you saw things more clearly, when you were waiting for the whistle, although at the time you might be practically shitting yourself.'

'So?'

'What I tried to say that night was – well, if I didn't get back and you did, would you please either leave her alone or – well, look after her.'

'I think you did say exactly that. But what exactly you meant . . .'

'You know damn well, Paul!'

'Sorry, but I don't. For instance, by "look after", d'you mean marry her?'

'If, as I said, you got back and I didn't—'

'Louis – we're in the same boat, the odds are that either we both get home or neither of us does. But supposing it did happen as you suggest, why on earth should she want anything of the sort? From me, I mean?'

There was a pause. Gimber was a black shape hunched against the standard of the stub periscope. He said, 'She's fond of you. Despite . . .'

'For God's sake, I'm fond of her, but . . .' He did a double-take. 'Despite what?'

'The fact you've spent the last six months trying to get her into bed?'

Trying . . .

'I – what?'

The diesel's steady rumble filled the darkness around them.

'When did you dream this one up?'

'She told me herself. So I know it. Every time you were with her on your own. You never stood a chance – but she's sorry for you, she thinks it's just because you're lonely. Lonely, for Christ's sake! But that's how she is, she's so – understanding, sympathetic. And she's dead straight, she doesn't make things up, Paul, so I do know. She's – decent, and loyal to the memory of her husband – all right, still in love with him, it's been my main problem. I can tell you, I've been learning patience . . . But you, Paul – all you ever thought of was getting her to sleep with you!'

'Wasn't it all you thought of? With all the others?'

If she'd told him – and she obviously had – there wasn't much point denying it. He asked Gimber, 'Wasn't it, until you got involved with Jane?'

'You admit it, then.'

'I suppose one does – make passes . . . But look here, if you've had some such notion, why on earth would you have wanted me to go on seeing her, whenever I was down south?'

'It was the last thing I wanted, after she'd written to me about it. You were seeing her behind my back, by then. Not realising that she and I have no secrets from each other. She told me everything, you damn fool!'

Not quite everything . . .

'I'm sorry. I didn't mean to be abusive. But I happen to feel very strongly about her.'

'I think I gathered that much.'

'And you had when you were doing your best to seduce her, too. You also knew she was still in a state of – I don't know, shock, perhaps – from her husband's death.'

'Well, I wouldn't altogether agree with you there. But can we cut this short now, Louis?'

'Just like that? Just . . .'

'I don't want to go over and over the same ground. Jane, as I saw her, was a very, very attractive girl, and very much a party girl. Think of that first time you produced her – that night at the Bag o' Nails?'

'She could give that impression, but . . .'

'Right. She did. You happened to take a different view, but my own was – is, I suppose – pretty well how it's always been, vis à vis girls at parties. Same as yours was too – and the fact you've fallen for her doesn't entitle you to call the kettle black, either. A year ago, if you'd taken a shine to some popsie I was nuts about, you'd have jumped in boots and all the minute my back was turned!'

'Not if I thought you were really, deeply . . .'

'Oh, balls!'

There was a stir below the hatch – one of the others coming up. Gimber began quickly, 'What I'm asking you – look, if I get back, OK, no problem, I'll look after her, and believe me you won't get a look in. But if I don't, Paul – well, I don't want her treated like some cheap floozie. Either leave her alone, or—'

'Skipper?' Bomber Brazier was speaking through the open hatch. 'Anyone want to get his head down? I'd quite like some freshers.'

'Hang on, Bomber. Give us room, and Louis'll be right down.' He told Gimber, 'All right. You have my word for it.'

'Swear it?'

'If that's necessary. But we're both going to get home, so it won't arise, anyway . . . Will you go below now?'

You couldn't have too many bodies on the casing at one time, in case you had to dive in a hurry. Gimber said, climbing into the hatch, 'I'm glad we've had it out. No hard feelings, Paul.'

'Of course not.'

Jane obviously had fed Gimber that line of bull. Perhaps to hide the less acceptable truth behind it? And having her cake and eating it – enjoying the physical affair while still presenting Gimber with the image he treasured. And of course, if at some later stage Gimber had discovered that she and Paul had been lovers, it wouldn't be her he'd have blamed.

Not bad, really. Watching the Bomber heave himself up through the hatch, he thought, Not bad at all . . . But it was also possible she hadn't thought it out as purposefully as that, that she'd have done it on impulse – being as mixed-up as Gimber seemed to think she was, still in shock from the death of the fighter-pilot husband whom it was fairly evident she'd also two-timed. Happy memories tinged with guilt – but some sense of achievement too, because otherwise she wouldn't have talked about it as she had!

He told himself, Forget it . . . In this time and place, it had been an extraordinary conversation. Louis, of course, must have had it churning around his head ever since they'd sailed from Loch Cairnbawn. On top of everything else, poor bastard . . . He looked round, at the vaguely defined bulk of his diver.

'Bomber, I'll tell you something. True love's a killer.'

'Ah.' There was a pause. Then: 'Are you in love, skipper?'

'Like hell I am.'

Brazier asked him, after another pause, 'Starting out at one-thirty, how will it go for the firing periods?'

The operation orders laid down a schedule of 'firing periods' and 'attacking periods'. The object was to reduce chances of X-craft blowing each other up. Attacking periods, which were for making the approach and placing side-cargoes under the targets, were from 01.00 to 08.00, 09.00 to 12.00, and 13.00 to 16.00, and the single hours in which charges could be set to explode were 08.00 to 09.00, 12.00 to 13.00 and 16.00 to 17.00.

He answered Brazier, 'It should work out all right. Slip from here at one-thirty, and it'll be an hour before the light's much good. By that time I'll have her round to the north of this island, and up to then it'll be dark or semi-dark enough to show a lot of periscope – amongst other things, keeping the wet out, I hope. By about two-thirty I'll have a clear view up Langfjord – I hope. We draw a bead on the target, go down to eighty feet, run in about two miles – so we'll be at the nets by half-three, roughly. Allow one hour for you to go out and cut a hole and get back in when we're through it, half an hour to lay side-cargoes, and another hour to get out . . . That's maximum, allowing for snagging in nets, and so on, and with luck we'll do better. But at the latest we should be clear by six o'clock, which leaves us two hours in which to bumble round the corner into Stjernsund. So we'll be on our way out, and we'll have the headland – Klubbeneset – between us and the whumpfs.'

'Just the job.' Brazier approved. 'More so for us than for the others down in Kafjord.'

'Yeah. But I'd sooner be having a crack at the *Tirpitz* . . . I'm afraid the wind's going down again.'

It had risen suddenly, and now it was dropping just as quickly. He'd had hopes of a broken surface, but by present indications there'd be another flat calm.

14

'There's a big oiler in that cove. But *Lützow* is not, repeat not, in evidence.' He pulled his head back, thumbed the 'down' button – for the first time in about an hour. Gimber had glanced round at him sharply, so had Lanchberry; there was a scowl of anxiety on Brazier's wide, stubbled face. As a highly-trained diver who'd never dived in action yet, he'd been longing for this day, and now like the other two he was shocked by the suggestion that their target might not be here. Paul told them, 'Too bright now. And last night's wind's gone completely.' Too bright for the periscope to be kept up any longer, he meant; he'd had it up ever since they'd left the Langnesholm hideout in the dark fifty-five minutes ago, and its prisms had so far stayed dry and clear.

So far, and probably no farther. And he had not made any sighting of his target. At this point he'd have expected to have taken a bearing and gone deep for the approach.

That cove – checking it on the chart – was called Ytre Koven. Half a mile wide, three-quarters of a mile deep. A mile southwest of it was where *Lützow* should have been.

Gimber suggested, without moving his eyes from the depthgauge and bubble, 'Could've been her we saw off Aaroy in the night?'

'That was *Scharnhorst*.'

'But she could be there too.'

'It's possible . . . Fifty feet.'

'Fifty.'

Paul took a log reading and made a note of it. That might even have been *Lützow*'s searchlight, for all anyone here could know . . . He decided, 'We'll run one mile in, then take another look. If she's not there we'll have to think again.'

X-12 nosed downward. The list didn't hamper this kind of depth-change, it only made her awkward to handle when as little as a foot or a few inches counted, when she was up close to the surface. One of the satisfactions of completing an attack would be that getting rid of the flooded side-cargo would put things back to normal. She'd be on an even keel, in proper control again, for the withdrawal through Stjernsund. It would indirectly affect one's state of blindness too: when she was in full control, in certain circumstances one might be able to ease her up to a position where she was just breaking surface, so you could use the bifocal stub periscope. You wouldn't do it in the open or close to enemies, but in bad light or where there was some sort of surrounding cover it would be something to fall back on. Escaping through the sund, for instance. In fact the stub periscope's most useful service was in net-cutting operations. You'd have the boat nudged up against the net, keeping slow-speed pressure on it while her diver cut a hole, and through the stub you could watch it happening.

Gimber reported, 'Fifty feet.'

'Half ahead.'

From here, even if one could have risked showing enough periscope – and had one that wasn't flooded – to see across to Aaroy, the western bulge of the island would have hidden the berth in which *Scharnhorst* had been lying last night. It was conceivable that *Lützow* could be with her. Leir Botn was a wide, well-sheltered bay, and if the two big ships were on their way to sea and had wanted a quick departure without the delay of net-gates having to be towed aside, it would have been a convenient anchorage, during some waiting period.

He checked the log again. Wondering whether there could be much point in continuing deeper into Langfjord. *Lützow* was much more likely to have moved to some new berth elsewhere. This could turn out to be a waste of time.

'Slow ahead. Twenty feet.'

He hoped to God that *Tirpitz* was still in her berth in Kafjord. But when one thing changed, you had to be receptive to the possibility of everything else having changed too. All the detailed planning could have been shot to hell.

If *Lützow*'s not here, go for the *Scharnhorst*?

There was no latitude in the orders for switching targets. On the other hand one wouldn't be going over to the other side of the fjord to attack *Scharnhorst*, one would be searching for one's own target, *Lützow*. It was a reasonably logical supposition that since *Lützow* wasn't in her own berth, and one of the others had moved into Leir Botn, then she might be there too.

From here to the south coast of Aaroy would be a run of five or six miles. Two and a half or three hours, say. You'd have to get there, make the attack and then get round to the other side of the island – for protection against the blast of the explosions – before eight o'clock, the start of the first firing period.

It should be easy enough. With no nets to deal with, it would be a quick and uncomplicated attack.

Touch wood . . .

'Depth twenty feet.' Gimber added, 'Main motor's slow ahead.'

'Let's have her at fifteen.'

Light from the surface was gleamingly visible through the viewing ports, the thick glass windows at shoulder height on each side. The light was brightening as she rose towards it. He picked up the folded chart again – limp as damp blotting-paper. The gap between Aaroy and the mainland, at the island's eastern end, was only about a third of a mile wide, but in the middle of it the depth was shown as nine fathoms. It would be possible to carry out an attack and then continue out that way, out northward through the gap.

If the target wasn't here in Langfjord.

'Fifteen feet.'

'Make it ten, now. Don't try to rush it, Louis.'

Gimber grunted acknowledgement, fractionally changing the angle of the hydroplanes. At the same time he pushed the trim-pump lever over to port, to let a few pints in amidships.

Use the flooded side-cargo on that oiler?

At first thought of it, he dismissed the notion of what seemed like a waste of two tons of explosive. But there was also an attraction in it. For one thing, while not even the largest oiltanker was a target to compare with a major warship, its destruction would be a lot more useful than simply ditching a defective charge. Which he'd have done earlier if it hadn't proved impossible. Also, in doing it you'd be ridding yourself of a handicap, returning to full efficiency and still with a lethal punch in reserve for a better target.

'Ten . . .'

Gimber cut the report short, muttered, 'Sorry . . .' She'd risen to eight feet, seven . . . A few more inches, and the stub periscope standard would have broken surface. In broad daylight and with coastlines less than a mile on each side. Hydroplanes hard a-dive: and he was flooding the midships tank again.

Seven and a half, eight . . .

She'd dip now, before he could get hold of her and bring her back up, in control. Passing twelve now, nose-down:

and he'd reversed the action of the pump, sucking out the ballast he'd just put in. Working like a mad organist: muttering, 'Bitch . . .'

Looking like a mad organist, too. And entitled to. He'd been resident in this tin drum nearly a fortnight.

'Take your time, Louis. No rush.'

He had her in hand quickly enough: she was rising towards the ordered depth then, with the fore-and-aft bubble amidships. Paul reached for the rubber bag on its wandering lead, and pressed the button to start the periscope sliding up.

'Let's have her at nine and a half, if she'll wear it.'

'Oh, she's learning who's boss.'

The organist was in a good mood, this morning. Having got that stuff off his chest last night might have helped. After such a long time cooped up and under stress . . . Ten and a half feet now, ten . . . He had his eye at the rubber-rimmed lens, watching the bubbling changing colours as the top glass rose: then the tip broke out, an inch of window above the flat surface, Gimber reporting, 'Nine and a half feet,'

'Brilliant.'

He could see through it, too. It wasn't perfect but it hadn't actually flooded yet. Gentle treatment was what it needed. He made a quick allround check, then began to search carefully over the area where *Lützow* had been when the Spitfires had last been over taking photographs.

She wasn't there now. Right ahead were the buoys supporting her net-cage, and there was a launch moored at its inshore end. Nets hanging empty like an unmade bed. That launch would be for opening and shutting the net gate, for letting the occupant or attendant craft in and out.

Nothing else. He dipped the periscope – down a couple of feet, then up again, standard drill that made it less likely to be spotted – then trained left for a look straight up the fjord. He could see about five miles, somewhat hazily, but apart from some fishing boats anchored inside a headland about a mile west of the unoccupied nets, there wasn't anything afloat or on the move.

'At least the periscope's behaving.' As he said it, bubbles frothed up to drown the top glass, cutting off his view just as he'd begun to train right, to find the cove that had the tanker in it.

'Sorry, coming back up . . .'

'All right.' Waiting for it, he told them, '*Lützow* isn't here. Her nets are, but she's gone.' He had a clear view again suddenly. And a need to come to a decision: you couldn't ruminate for long, you had to make up your mind and act . . . The bearing of the oiler in Ytre Koven was – 318 degrees. It was at anchor, and in quarter-profile: he'd be on her port bow if he steered directly into the cove from here.

'Come round to three-one-eight, Jazz . . . Forty feet. Half ahead.'

Studying the chart again. About one mile to go. He took a log reading . . . Plenty of water all the way in, except only fifteen fathoms off the western point of the entrance. You wouldn't want to be deep at that point anyway. But mental arithmetic, as one looked further ahead, revealed complications which at first sight looked bad. He put the chart down on the storage locker, and laid a parallel rule across it: he saw at once that the key to his problem was that gap between Aaroy and the mainland.

'Course three-one-eight, sir.'

Formality, from old Jazz . . . Crises affected people in odd ways. He explained to them – after Gimber had reported the depth as forty feet and the motor half ahead group down – 'Here's what we do. Our target having removed herself. She may be south of Aaroy, with *Scharnhorst* – we'll see. But meanwhile we have this large oiler in Ytre Koven – here.' He pointed to it on the chart. 'We'll move in there now and drop the flooded side-cargo under her. It won't be wasted, and our performance will be improved. Then we'll buzz over and see if our target's there, otherwise find some other good home for the starboard bomb, off Aaroy . . . Any better ideas?'

Gimber asked him, 'With a fairly long trip over, what about the firing period? Will we make it?'

'Should work out.' He explained, 'Ten to three now. We'll be in there and slipping the side-cargo in half an hour. Away again by, say, three-thirty. Five-hour fuse setting, the thing'll blow at about eight-thirty – right in the middle of the firing period . . . The run over to Aaroy – six miles, roughly, say three hours if we go easy on the battery, so we'll get there around six-thirty. There'll be no nets to hold us up – at least, I wouldn't expect any. *Scharnhorst* must be there just temporarily, and so would *Lützow* be, if she's there. If she is, we'll attack her – otherwise *Scharnhorst* gets lucky. Then we push on through the gap at the eastern end of the island – which'll give us protection from whatever whumpfs are going off. Also, we'll be on course for an exit via Stjernsund.'

He checked the log again. Less than half a mile to go.

'One last look now. Slow ahead, fifteen feet.'

Up by stages again, a few feet at a time. A complication was that you had to reduce to slow speed so the periscope wouldn't make more feather than necessary when it cut through the surface, but slowing made her less responsive to the hydroplanes just when you needed maximum control.

The gauge showed nine and a half feet when the periscope's top window broke out. Paul searched all round once, then settled his single eye on the oiler. She was about fifteen thousand tons, deep-laden, and quite modern.

'Steer one degree to starboard.'

'Three-one-eight . . .'

There was a lighter secured to the oiler's port side and some boats at a timber jetty on the shore, but nothing else afloat and no sign of watch-keepers. No line of buoys, either, from which an anti-torpedo net might have been slung. He sent the periscope down.

'Forty feet. Bomber, you're out of a job again. No nets.' Lanchberry murmured, with a glance at Brazier in his rubber suit and with the weighted boots beside him, 'All dressed up and nowhere to go.' Paul saw that she was nosing down past fifteen feet; he told Gimber, 'Half ahead'. Because she'd got down far enough for the wash not to show up on the surface, with her stern up-angled. He'd noticed cloud was gathering in the north and northwest, and he guessed the calm weather wasn't going to last long; it would still be reasonably sheltered inside the fjords, but the passage out to join *Setter* might be a bumpy one. If one made it that far. But it was pointless to anticipate: you simply had to press on, cope with each problem as it came up. Here and now it was a matter of running in blind, all the way to the target; she was too close in now to risk showing periscope.

He guessed the oiler would draw about thirty feet, so forty would be a good depth at which to run in under her. He checked the release-gear on the port side-cargo, making sure the wheel was free to turn, and the time-clock of the fuse mechanism. You had only to make the switch, set the clock to a delay of anything from one to six hours, then turn the wheel to release the charge, which would fall away from the side and sink to the bottom. Even if it hadn't already flooded – which it had – it would sink when it parted company with the boat's side, as its buoyancy chambers filled and weighted it. On second thoughts, he set the clock now, for a five-hour interval; it was one thing less to be done later when he might be busy, and the fuse wouldn't start running down until the switch was made.

Dark water outside the viewing ports was lighter when you looked upwards. Daylight shimmered there, through forty feet of sea.

When the log showed a hundred yards to go, he ordered

'Slow ahead.' Gimber's right hand moved to the control wheel, but he didn't take his eyes off the trim. She was porpoising a little, just a foot or two each side of the ordered depth, and entering the cove he'd be alert for freshwater patches from mountain streams. In the reduced density you could drop like a stone if you weren't ready for it. The motor's hum softened as she slowed. Paul was watching through the viewing port on the port side, and his first sight of the target was a dark cloud growing, obscuring surface radiance as the midget crept into its shadow.

'Target's right ahead . . .'

A clang – from the starboard side, for'ard. She jolted, lurched over . . .

'Stop main motor.'

Rolling back. There was a scraping sound from outside, and vibration – as if her plates were rubbing against rock. But – not rock, it was more metallic. It was moving aft, down the starboard side.

'Hard a-starboard.'

Four faces, and no expression at all on any of them . . . Paul had realised what it was. Lanchberry spinning the wheel. Her bow had begun to rise and Gimber was working to get it down again – which was essential, as the tanker's keel would be only a few feet above her now. He could see the curve of one bilge through the viewing port. It was the anchor cable they'd hit. He'd thought from the angle at which the ship was lying and the direction of his own approach that she'd pass well clear of it, but he'd miscalculated.

The scraping ceased. He'd turned her around the cable, swung her afterpart clear of it: which was desirable, since the projecting hydroplanes would have snagged on it. X-12 was sinking, meanwhile, as she'd lost way through the water and the 'planes no longer gripped.

'Slow ahead. Midships.'

The shadow was out to port now, and dimmed by

distance. This was the oiler's port bow they were on, of course; X-12 had slid inside the cable, between its long slant and the target's forefoot, and the turn to starboard had carried her away from where he had to put her.

Thirty-five feet on the gauge. Thirty-six.

'Port fifteen.'

'Port fifteen.' Lanchberry muttered, 'Cannon off the red.' He added, 'Fifteen of port wheel on, sir.'

'That was her cable we side-swiped. Let's hope no-one was looking.'

Brazier put his hands together as if in prayer, and murmured, 'Arf, arf.'

'Midships.'

Now she'd turned back towards her target; its shadow extended from right ahead to about thirty on the port bow, filling half the area of the viewing port when he had his face close up to it. He moved to the stub periscope, through which as they closed in he'd have a clearer view.

'Wheel's amidships.'

'Steady as you go.'

'Steady. Two-four-one.'

'Steer two-four-oh.'

The outlines of the cloud hardened, became curved steel encrusted with marine growth. This oiler wasn't as clean underneath as she was up top, but X-12 was about to save her the trouble of dry-docking. Coming in on the target's port side and on roughly a forty-degree track. He checked the time – it was 3.19 – and glanced from there to the side-cargo's fuse-clock, ensuring that he had it set right, to explode five hours after he activated it. Six hours being the maximum you could put on it, but five being right for the firing period. In a minute he'd need only to touch the switch, wind the handle of the releasing gear, and – away, the hell out, fast.

Well, not fast, exactly. This was a tortoise, no hare. And there'd be plenty of time to get over to Aaroy.

The oiler's shadow blotted out all the surface light. X-12 was right under her.

'Starboard twenty.'

'Starboard twenty, sir.'

'Depth's very important now, Louis.'

Because with that much rudder on her she'd have a tendency to rise, and he didn't want to bump or scrape her on the target's bottom. There'd be people in there with ears – and nerves. Nearly all of them sound asleep, but a resounding clang right under them could change all that . . . Lanchberry reported, 'Twenty of starboard on.' She was turning rapidly, as he'd wanted just about under the centre-line of the oiler. But he was going to release the side-cargo closer to her stern, where an engineroom might be the focal point for an upward blast into the ship's guts.

All those sleeping Germans: without the slightest notion of what they'd be getting for their breakfast.

'Midships. Meet her.'

'Meet her . . .'

'Steady!'

'Steady – two-seven-eight, sir.'

'Steer that.'

He was back at the viewing port, close to the release gear of the side-cargo; with his face close against the port, to cut out reflections, he could see the barnacled curve of the tanker's belly as X-12 passed slowly under it. Gimber, looking up frequently at the other port, had the boat steady and level at forty feet. Paul said, 'Here we go, then.' He put the switch to 'on': the light came on in the clockface. The fuse was now activated, and in five hours – eight twenty-five – it would detonate two tons of Torpex. He used both hands to turn the wheel, which was like a motorcar's steering wheel – anti-clockwise, to release the charge.

He'd turned it as far as it would go, and nothing had happened.

'Still there.'

Turning the wheel back a little, he jerked it over hard, putting weight on the last part of its travel. It came up short and hard, and wouldn't budge another centimetre, but the side-cargo was still attached, with its fuse running. He tried once more.

No bloody good . . .

Almost as if this was only confirmation of something he'd expected. Recalling the doubt he'd had yesterday, when he'd wanted to set it to 'safe', and a signal from *Seanymph* on the day before the crew-change: X-8 having had to ditch her side-cargoes, and one of them exploding and wrecking her. There'd have been some good reason for ditching them, and they'd surely have been set to 'safe' – and still exploded . . .

'Give you a hand, skipper.' Brazier, coming aft from the W and D. 'Sharp kick may be all it needs.' Gimber's left hand went to the trimpump lever, to compensate for the transfer of that not inconsiderable weight. At least Brazier had taken off his lead-weighted diver's boots. He began trying to make the releasing gear work, as if he'd thought he had some magic touch which Paul lacked.

'Might try the rod.'

It was a heavy bar with a screw-thread on it, which you could wind out through a special gland in the ship's side. It was stowed nearby, with a lashing on it, and Brazier was on his side, reaching between other gear to free it. X-12 was still under her target but about to run out under the target's stern.

Brazier got the rod free. He shipped it, fitting its end into the socket designed to receive it. It was a device intended for checking that the side-cargo had dropped away, not a tool for shifting it. Still, it might help – and God only knew what else . . . He was cranking it around.

'Main motor stop. Port twenty. Slow astern.'

To hold her more or less under the oiler's screws, and

turn her. The charge might release suddenly, and you wouldn't want it any farther away than this from the target. Taking a look through the stub periscope he could see the oiler's screws and the heavy black-painted rudder up there in shimmery, greenish water. It slid away to the left as the X-craft turned, stern-first.

'No joy, skipper.' Brazier had the rod in but he couldn't turn it any further. 'Won't budge.'

Lanchberry muttered, 'Bugger's bloody well got to budge.'

Gimber working desperately at the trim . . .

'Far as it'll go.' Brazier scowled at the rod, rubbed his head, as if to stimulate some alternative way of doing it. Paul told Gimber, 'Stop main motor. Slow ahead.'

'Thank God.' Gimber's mutter was addressed to himself, expressing relief at being able to put the screw ahead again. The stopping and going astern, turning inside her own length with the oiler's screws only a few feet above the casing and Brazier's weight shifting aft at that same crucial time, had not provided him with much light relief. Brazier was having another shot at moving the wheel of the releasing gear, perhaps hoping that with the disengaging rod wound in there now it might have some effect. You could see – looking back and up through the ports – the glint of daylight receding, the oiler's screws against the last crescent shine of it, wavery like a mirage. X-12 was now creeping the other way, towards her intended victim's bow, but under her port side instead of the centreline.

'Come two degrees to starboard, Jazz.'

'One double-oh.'

'Switch it off, skipper, d'you think?'

'God, yes.' He reached to the switch, and flipped it up. You couldn't turn the clock's fuse-setting back, but you could deactivate it by the switch. The fact you couldn't turn back the timesetting meant that whatever alternative plan you fixed on now, you'd be stuck with a five-hour delay on this fuse. Or six-hour: it could be advanced, but not retarded.

Brazier was still persevering with the wheel. Gimber, who'd been pumping ballast for'ard from the midships tank, had just pulled the lever back into its pump-stopped, valves-shut position, having compensated for the Bomber's move.

The Bomber said, 'You didn't switch off, skipper.'

But he had.

He'd also checked that she was middled under the oiler. 'Come back to oh-nine-eight, Jazz.'

The light still glowed on the fuse-clock's face. He flipped the switch the other way – to 'on' – then back to 'off' again. The light still burned; the fuse was still activated and running down. It was an enclosed circuit, you couldn't get at the wiring – which was just as well, because if you'd tried to you'd quite likely have short-circuited the clock and fired the charge.

Four hours, fifty-six minutes to run.

He announced, for the information of Gimber and Lanchberry, also as a start towards rationalising the situation in his own mind, 'We have a side-cargo that won't leave us, and its fuse won't de-activate.'

He'd had no nightmares since the crew-change. This was understandable, he thought: once you'd started, you were no longer projecting, anticipating. But this was the stuff of nightmares now – so much so that you felt there had to be some way of snapping out of it, waking up. Solutions ran through his mind like high-speed film. Bottom her here, set the other side-cargo to a shorter fuze, and abandon ship by DSEA. Well, you couldn't. You'd give the game away, wreck the others' chances – let *Tirpitz* off the hook. So – all right, drop the starboard cargo with a five-hour delay on it, get over to Aaroy with this port one still ticking, bottom under *Lützow* if she was there or *Scharnhorst* if she was not, and abandon – by DSEA, one at a time, through the W and D.

You'd have lost nothing, that way – except all four of you in the bag, POWs.

'Skipper.'

Brazier looked as if he'd had an idea. Paul was conscious of the others' eyes and ears on him: they were waiting for his decision, the way out. Conscious also of the oiler's bulk overhead, shutting out nine tenths of the filtered surface light. Gimber had more up-angle on the 'planes than she'd been carrying before; he'd overdone the flooding for'ard by a pint or two, must have decided to leave it alone until Brazier moved back to his kennel. Still dickering with that second plan, Paul was also troubled by his uncertainty about the gear in general: when so much of the system had gone haywire, should one trust in a five-hour fuse-setting giving you five hours before it blew?

He'd glanced at Brazier. 'Yes?'

'I'll go out, skipper – release it from outside. It'll only be hanging on by an eyelash, all I'd have to do is prise.'

'No.'

It was his first mistake.

Trench said, 'As everyone knows now, *Lützow* had avoided the submarines who were waiting just off those fjords by steering due west instead of northwest or north, which was what anyone would have expected. The submarines who'd towed the X-craft over were positioned in an arc designed to intercept a sortie aimed at interfering with QP 16 – which was the whole object of the exercise, naturally.'

He picked up a stalk of straw and drew it across the top of the wire cage. The mink dashed out of her nesting box, and the same hand that held the straw moved to insert a metal shield between the box and the wire run, thus shutting Mum away from her litter. You could see that this annoyed her. She was coal-black, with a glossy sheen to her slim, agile body, and small, furious eyes. Trench dipped his one hand into the straw of the box and brought it out full of what looked like very small chippolata sausages.

He was counting them. 'Eight.' He told the mother, 'There's a clever girl.'

'Eight's good, is it?'

This was May – kitting time for minks, worldwide. He nodded. 'We get as many as eleven or twelve in a litter occasionally, but the average is about five.' He'd put them back, and shut the lid. As he lifted the shield out, the mother whipped in like a streak of ebony. He made some cryptic note on the card above that box, and moved on through the shed.

'It's as well to bear in mind that one knows a lot more than one knew then. All I was aware of at the time was that *Lützow* and nine big destroyers were at sea and hunting for my convoy. Might run into them at any minute – or might not. As I've explained, the weather was deteriorating and visibility was rotten. One minute you'd see perhaps five or six miles, and the next perhaps not even fifty yards.'

'Oddly enough it was clear and calm that morning in Altenfjord. There'd been some wind during the night, but it had dropped again.'

'I dare say. Conditions are often highly localised, up there. But our weather was moving in towards the coast in any case . . . Oh, I did also know that our battle squadron had sailed from Iceland. The heavy mob's usual tactic, if they had nothing else to go on, would be to steer straight for the enemy's base – either to cut him off and force him to action, or scare him into thinking he'd be cut off if he didn't get the hell out fast. Which as you know he usually did – largely because Hitler's orders to his stooges effectively vetoed acceptance of any risk. They could attack only if they were in overwhelming strength. He hated his big-ship Navy, you know. Under the skin, anyway. Its commanders had always tended to be gentlemen – which Adolf so plainly was not. At the same time he was highly protective of it – any loss reflecting personally on him. The *Graf Spee* affair was a prime example, wasn't it – scuttle, so nobody could say they'd sunk her. And *Lützow* – I suppose you know, her name originally was *Deutschland*, but the dread of having his *Deutschland* sent to the bottom, and the ridicule that would follow – well, he had her re-christened.'

'She'd turned south, incidentally.'

'Yes. But I had no way of knowing it. In fact all I had opposing me were the destroyers. Nine, against my five, and much more heavily armed – but you know all that. The first real news I had of them – and bear in mind I'd no doubt *Lützow* would be behind them somewhere in the sleet-showers – was an enemy report from *Legend*. She was on the starboard wing of the screen – and as I was expecting any attack to come from the south, it was rather a surprise. It was less than an hour after sunrise, we'd fallen out from dawn action stations and redeployed into day cruising formation. *Legend*'s signal told me she had two ships in sight to the nor'ard – on a converging course, speed esti-mated as about eight knots.'

'No radar contact?'

'No. Conditions were bloody awful, of course. And within half a minute of that signal, *Legend* reported the enemy had turned away and gone out of sight. I told her captain – John Ready – to investigate and *Leopard*, who was the nearest to her, to support her. I stayed with the convoy, but had *Laureate* and *Lyric* form line astern of me on its other bow, and for the time being I left *Foremost* where she was, astern. There was a minesweeper each side, and the trawlers were on the quarters. I'd alerted the new commodore – Claypoole – to the situation, of course, and the tactics we'd adopt if surface action did develop were all cut and dried. Of course it had to depend on which way the cat jumped – the cat, as I believed then, being *Lützow*.'

He'd stopped at another nesting box. The whole of the

shed, which was about forty yards long, was noisy with the squeaking of baby minks, but somehow he could tell when he was passing a box that had a newly arrived family in it. He'd stop, put his ear to it for confirmation, then go through his counting and card-marking routine.

'Only three. Below par, you see. What we do is we take a couple of kits from one of the outsize litters and add them to the very small ones. If it's done in the first few days the mothers don't know the difference.'

Walking on. This was only the second of about a dozen sheds. He told me, 'It was three quarters of an hour before *Legend* established contact. I heard gunfire before Ready came through on TBS. Two signals – first his own saying he and *Leopard* were in action, engaging four enemy destroyers who were on a parallel course, range four miles; then a report from *Leopard* that a larger but unidentified ship astern of the destroyers had opened fire. Only its gun-flashes had been seen, from *Leopard*'s director tower. To me, this could only mean one thing – *Lützow*. In fact it must have been a destroyer who'd become separated from those others, but in the circumstances it was a natural enough conclusion to jump to. It left five enemy destroyers not yet accounted for, but I obviously had to move out and join in. I told Crockford of *Foremost* to act in accordance with previous orders, and invited Claypoole – the American vice-commodore who'd taken over Insole's job – to make a ninety-degree diversion to port. Crockford knew what his job was – as the convoy turned away, if there was an enemy in sight he'd lay smoke between them. The sweepers were also to make smoke, but they were to stay with the convoy, chivvy the lads along and see they hung together. *Foremost* would hold the middle ground – and she had the speed, of course, to put herself and her smoke wherever it might be needed. One thing I ought to tell you. Crockford had talked to me that morning, over the radio telephone, when we were all at dawn action stations. Around two a.m. that would have been. He told me Nick Everard had been up and dressed and wandering about the ship. He still didn't know what was happening, or why. He had some impression that he was taking passage in order to take up a new appointment – a cruiser squadron, Crockford said he'd mentioned, and he was disturbed by a belief that he hadn't been able to say goodbye to his wife. Anyway, they'd got him back to his cabin and persuaded him to turn in, and so on. That young doctor I'd had transferred into *Foremost* to look after him, unusual name, but – oh, Cramphorn – got it rather heavily in the neck from me for having let it happen. He was as shocked as anyone, I think; he'd fallen asleep or gone to the heads, I don't remember. He was responsible, but – well, I gave him hell, I'm afraid. It wasn't fair – he couldn't have slept for about a week, poor fellow. But Nick could have gone over the side, you see, in the state he was in – that was what made me tear Cramphorn to shreds over TBS. I'd told Crockford to put him on. Crockford was rather a quiet, easy-going sort of man – I made up for that.' He shrugged. 'You know how I admired Nick Everard. And it was his life I was concerned for.'

Pausing near the door at the far end of the shed, Trench was obviously deeply concerned about the way he'd treated the young doctor. I could well understand his anger: he'd picked Cramphorn himself, as one who'd do a good job conscientiously and keep his – Trench's – hero alive for him. I liked Trench already, but I found myself liking him the more for this display of a nagging conscience over what was really quite a small thing. Cramphorn would surely have accepted the blame, and he'd have seen the rebuke as justified, particularly so from Trench; and he'd soon have forgotten it altogether. Whereas Trench had never forgotten, and still blamed himself for having been too harsh.

As a matter of fact I've encountered this kind of thing before. Old men's pigeons coming home to roost, and in their transit of the years changing into vultures.

I said, 'Cramphorn would hardly have expected congratulations.'

Trench pushed the door open. He said without looking round, 'I was tearing a strip off him at two-thirty. By seven he was dead.'

I caught on, then. Like a punch on the nose. Astonished that I'd been so stupid. Because obviously. I'd known . . .

'Where was I . . . Oh, yes. Belting out north-westward, *Laureate* and *Lyric* astern of me, thirty-four knots across a long, flattish swell and with a gusty snowstorm in our faces. Impossible to use binoculars – half the time you couldn't even see your own foc'sl. I had *Legend* and *Leopard* on radar by that time, I think – must have had – and I was getting frequent reports from John Ready over TBS. His exchange of gunfire with the four Huns – or five, counting the one astern of them that was supposed to be a heavy cruiser and which I was intending to attack with torpedoes if I could get into position to do so – well, those exchanges had been brief and sporadic, just a couple of salvoes snapped off between snow-showers. Well, you can imagine.'

I could, indeed . . . *Moloch*, *Laureate* and *Lyric* in line-astern, thrashing across the long rolling swells with spray sheeting back from high-curving bow-waves, their stems plunging and then soaring, tossing green sea back across the guns; snow blinding, driving horizontally, the ships racing directly into it and into the icy wind carrying it. Guns' crews and torpedo crews, oilskinned and tin-hatted at their weapons, needing to hold on and to watch footing and balance on steel decks often awash and constantly tilting, lifting and dropping through thirty feet or more a dozen times a minute. Trench was on his high seat, in the port for'ard corner of *Moloch*'s bridge, with – behind him – his first lieutenant and torpedo officer, Henderson, at the torpedo director sight, navigator Jock McAllister at the binnacle, Sub-Lieutenant Cummings taking reports from plot and radar, yeoman of signals Halliday and other bridge staff – a signalman, lookouts, messengers, communications numbers – crowding the pitching, jolting, spray-swept platform. Abaft and above their heads the director tower trained slowly to and fro, searching out gaps in the surrounding curtains of foul weather – Gareth Williams, gunnery officer, with his rate officer beside him, presiding over director layer and director trainer in the front seats. If and when there was anything to shoot at, all the guns would be aimed and fired from here.

Cummings had answered a call on the radar voicepipe. He reported, his voice pitched high over the racket of ship and sea, 'Radar has three surface contacts, oh-two-one to oh-three-seven, six point five miles, sir!'

Trench leant against a supporting pillar, doing his one-handed pipe-stuffing act. He told me, 'They could only be Germans, of course, split off from the bunch who'd been in action with *Legend* and *Leopard*, I presumed. I had them – John Ready's two ships – fine-ish on the bow, on the radar screen and liable to come in sight any moment if the visibility lifted. They'd lost contact with their Germans at that point. I was trying to get some more detailed information out of radar when John piped up on TBS; he was in action again, with two destroyers who'd appeared out of a snowstorm ahead of him, crossing his bows – steering something like south, in fact. So it was obvious this enemy force had divided. And there were still some who hadn't shown up at all. My guess was they'd be screening *Lützow*, and I had a nasty premonition: half the enemy destroyer force, *Lützow* with them, attacking from the south with nobody except *Foremost* and those tiddlers between the convoy and annihilation, I and my lot having been lured away northward, distance between us increasing every minute . . . But the enemy were here, you see, and what's more at least one group of them was steering south towards the convoy, very clearly couldn't be ignored. I had no evidence of attack coming in from any other quarter, remember: in fact I still reckoned *Lützow* was somewhere up on this side . . . Anyway – two lots of Germans, *Legend* and *Lyric* sparring with one team, and the other – radar now informed me, or the plot did – also steering south. I did about the only thing that seemed to make sense and answer obvious requirements – told John Ready to drive his pair away from the convoy, close the range and either sink them or force them to turn away but for Christ's sake not to let them work round to the south of him and get at the convoy – and I turned away to starboard to intercept the others. In fact I turned my three ships into line abreast – a Blue turn, happened to be a convenient way of doing it, and also put me in a position to attack with torpedoes if these contacts should happen to include the *Lützow* – which seemed possible, even likely, in view of that earlier report from *Leopard*. Radar range had come down to something like eight thousand yards, we were closing fast and I knew we might suddenly find ouselves looking right up the barrels of those eight-inch guns.'

Tubes were turned out and ready, with depth-settings of sixteen feet on the torpedoes. In each of the three British destroyers one quadruple mounting was turned out to port and one to star-board, allowing for immediate reaction either way, depending on when and where the enemy appeared. All three ships beam-on to the swell, and rolling – Trench said – 'like buggery'. Guns as well as tubes were ready – shells in the loading-trays, layers' and trainers' pointers following the director's. Below, in the transmitting station they were waiting for information from the director tower and radar, figures for enemy course, speed, range and inclination; one's own ship's course and speed were fed automatically into the computing system, and already in it were such factors as wind direction and velocity, atmospheric pressure and temperature, all the things that complicate the problem of translating the sighting of an enemy into straddling him with your shells.

Trench observed – breaking into my mental reconstruction of a scene he'd just lightly sketched – 'All be over by Monday. As you'll have noticed, only a very few haven't kitted yet.'

We were talking about minks again. It took a moment to readjust. I said, 'They seem very efficient, reproductively. Don't you ever get any that are sterile?'

'Well, they get weeded out, you know. But ninety per cent of it's simply a question of diet. And at mating time every female gets covered twice, by two different males.' He shut that box, withdrew the shield, and marked the mother's card.

'Your records have to be kept very accurately, I suppose – which ones have bred with which, and so on?'

'Certainly.' He turned, and moved on down the aisle; a big, shambling figure, ears apparently tuned to the squeaks even when he was talking. But it was only the cages with unmarked cards that caught his attention, I realised. He told me, pausing again, 'When I was just starting in this business, an old mink hand told me that if a pair of his animals didn't react too enthusiastically to each other, his method was to put 'em together in a sack and whirl it round his head for a minute or two. When he let 'em out, they'd be at it hammer and tongs.' He checked a card, put it down again. 'Don't know if that's ever been tried on human beings. For impotence or frigidity, what have you.' He glanced round at me as he started off again between the ranks of boxes and cages. 'Where were we?'

We were in the Barents Sea.

'Visibility opened up as suddenly as drawing curtains, and we were about three thousand yards short of a line-ahead formation of Narvik-class destroyers steering south at about ten or twelve knots. Three of them. No sign of *Lützow*, of course. We opened fire and turned to starboard, parallel to them – I'd no thought of wasting torpedoes on such a chancy target as destroyers, even big blighters like these, when I had reason to believe there was much bigger game in the offing, but it must have looked to those Krauts like a torpedo attack, and they turned away and increased to full speed. At least I imagine it was torpedoes they were scared of. They heeled away, cracking on full power and opening fire a few seconds after we had. Our first salvoes were only from A and B guns, of course, and one reason for turning was to open the A-arcs, get X and Y guns into action. The range was close, and I saw a hit almost immediately on one German's stern; I was told afterwards there'd been two or three, just from the for'ard guns before we'd got ourselves round. Most of the enemy's splashes went up short – very large splashes too, compared to our own – but I heard a few whistle over, and *Laureate* took a direct hit on her A gun. It wiped out the gun's seven-man crew and of course wrecked the mounting. Those five-inch bricks played hell with a destroyer's light armour – as we were to see demonstrated much more clearly very soon afterwards. But it was over almost as soon as it started, this phase. The Narviks could easily have out-run us, and they were running, and I wasn't prepared to be drawn any farther away from my convoy. I was in the process of turning my three ships back, then, when Batty Crockford of *Foremost* came up on TBS rather excitedly to tell me he was in action against another four enemy destroyers who'd come belting up from the southeast. Very close to that premonition I'd had, you see. Except no *Lützow* – this far. I was still expecting her to show up at any moment, and the likely place for her to appear now seemed to be in the south, behind these newcomers. I remember thinking I should have backed that hunch . . . Anyway, Claypoole had turned the convoy ninety degrees to starboard, now. Back to its original course, in fact. *Foremost* was laying smoke and from time to time nipping out through it to loose off a few shots at the enemy – one of which might even have been *Lützow*, for all I knew, and in that bad visibility. As you'll know yourself, in conditions of that kind and the mild confusion one tends to get when a number of ships are in action here and there, reports have to be,' he shrugged, 'sorted out, interpreted . . . But Crockford was actually talking to me on the radio telephone when *Foremost* was hit by one of those five-point-ones. He turned back into his own smoke – they had his range, and they'd surely have finished him in the next few minutes if he'd held on as he was. They were holding off, for the moment, presumably wanting to eliminate him so they could then move in unopposed to do a thorough job on the convoy. Rather typical of their tactics, actually. But – well, my three ships were under helm, turning south – our little fracas being over, those three Huns high-tailing it into the sleet, and the convoy under close, immediate threat. *Foremost*, too. Which as you can imagine was very much in my mind. I told John Ready in *Legend* to get himself and *Leopard* down there fast – if by this time he wasn't otherwise engaged – and there we were, split-arsing south.'

'This must have been about four o'clock?'

Trench considered it: then nodded. 'Something like that.'

15

⟫⟩•0•⟨⟪

Time: 03.43. The flooded side-cargo still clung to her, and
its fuse was still active. He'd been manoeuvring her for the
past fifteen minutes or so under the oiler's deep belly,
keeping her in its shadow so that if the cargo should
suddenly give up and slip away its later eruption wouldn't
be wasted. He'd considered trying to wipe it off by running
the midget's port side against the anchor cable which she'd
hit during the approach, but there'd be a risk of raising an
alarm – there might also be a limit to the rough treatment
to which you could subject a two-ton charge of high explosive.

He was looking up through the viewing port, seeing the
target's propellers and rudder pass slowly overhead again.
Gimber had been doing a very good job, considering how
clumsy she was to handle with this list on her, and the
close confines of the space in which he was having to turn
her.

You couldn't hang around forever, though. Times, distances, firing-periods – and other side-cargoes that might
already be lying on the bottom of the fjords with their fuses
running – all contributed to a sense of urgency.

'All right. Listen.'

Heads turned. Gimber's face like a death-mask,

Lanchberry's drawn but calm, the Bomber's questioning. He still wanted to go out through the W and D in his diving gear and try to free the side-cargo from the outside, and he didn't understand why Paul had refused the offer.

Paul told them, 'Only one way out of this balls-up. We dump the starboard side-cargo here, with a five-hour delay on it. Then we nip over to Aaroy and bottom ourselves under *Lützow* if by chance she's there, or otherwise under *Scharnhorst*.'

Scharnhorst would be a much more satisfying target, but they'd been detailed for *Lützow* and if she was within reach she was the one to hit.

He finished, 'Then we abandon ship by DSEA, giving ourselves plenty of time to do it in good order, with the Bomber out first to give us a hand out and shut the hatch behind each man as he emerges. The good side of this is that we make the best use of ourselves we can – in the circumstances – with neither side-cargo wasted. The drawback is we become POWs, instead of getting away, which would have been very nice but I personally wouldn't have put any money on it.'

Gimber said, 'Nor would I.' He nodded. 'I'd say you're right, Paul. No option, really.'

Lanchberry nodded. Brazier continued to look puzzled, like a student in class who doesn't want to admit he hasn't understood. Paul was troubled for the moment by a new thought. The hope of taking plenty of time over the DSEA escape – it might not be all that practicable. They'd have to get out not too long in advance of the firing period which began at eight o'clock, because abandoning too soon could give *Tirpitz* time to shift out of her berth and dozens of patrol boats could start dropping depthcharges. One had to think of the other X-craft, not only X-12. He didn't say anything about this, as it wasn't strictly necessary at this stage, but he could foresee that waiting around on the bottom under the target until nearly eight, with their own charge set to explode at 08.25 but on its recent showing hardly the most reliable piece of equipment – well, there'd be more comfortable situations.

Even without that thought in their heads, the others weren't looking too happy. Too many things had been going wrong, and not knowing where their target was didn't help.

'Stop the motor. Starboard twenty.'

New technique for turning her in the restricted area. When the screw stopped and she lost most of her forward impetus so that her 'planes ceased to grip the water, her tendency – since Gimber had her trimmed slightly heavy for'ard – was to sink. There was plenty of water between the oiler's keel and the bottom of the cove, so there was room for this, and there was just enough residual way on her to push her round to the reciprocal of her previous course. You accepted a change of depth and the turn was made in silence – and deeply enough so that any German crewman leaning over the rail up there would be unlikely to spot the whale-like intruder.

Lanchberry said, 'Twenty of starboard wheel on . . . Skipper – question?'

'Go ahead.'

'Why not let the Bomber have a go at shifting the fucking thing?'

He explained. It would take too long and it might not work. It might even explode it. By the time Brazier had gone through the routine of shutting himself in the W and D and then flooding it, equalising internal pressure with that of the sea outside so that he could then open the hatch and climb out, and had then done his stuff with the side-cargo – which might or might not have been effective – and come back inside, drained down the W and D into its operating tank so he could then open up and reappear among them – well, you'd have lost valuable time, possibly achieved nothing at all. He explained also that time was precious because the trip over to Aaroy had to be completed long enough before the start of the firing-period for the job to be done and the DSEA escape completed; it would take between three and four hours at normal dived speed, conserving battery power, or as little as two hours if it didn't matter what happened to the battery.

'If your effort didn't pay off, Bomber, we'd be a lot worse off than we are now. Besides which you might blow us up.'

It was 03.48 now. Twenty-three minutes since he'd activated the firing mechanism on the flooded side-cargo. That fuse now had four hours, thirty-seven minutes to run. If the clock could be relied on . . . It could be given an extra hour, of course, by increasing the delay to its maximum of six hours, but that would trigger an eruption in the middle of Altenfjord in a 'safe' period – just when Don Cameron, Godfrey Place, Henty-Creer and Hudspeth might be withdrawing northward.

'Main motor slow ahead.'

Gimber wound the hand-wheel clockwise. X-12 had drifted down to nearly fifty feet – to very near the bottom – and also outward, away from the target's side. You could see its shape up there still but it was no longer black, vague and shimmery-green against surrounding silver.

'Bring her to two-nine-five, Jazz.'

'Two-nine-five, aye aye . . .'

He wondered if this other side-cargo was going to release, now. When one part of the equipment failed, you tended to distrust the rest of it. He edged over to that side, casting a glance over the releasing wheel and the fuse-clock, then looking up through the viewing port at the hardening underwater outline of the oiler as they rose closer and turned in under it.

'Course two-nine-five.'

And still coming up. Gimber was flooding compensatory ballast into the midships trim-tank as she approached the depth ordered.

'Forty-five feet will do.'

'Forty-five.'

Allowing an extra margin overhead so there'd be less danger of scraping or bumping the hull above them. Gimber eased the pump-lever back. The reason she became lighter as she rose was that in shallower, therefore less dense water, the hull expanded enough to increase the volume and weight of the water she displaced. As had been discovered by Archimedes, a body immersed in water experiences an upthrust equal to the weight displaced; so the increased upthrust now – 'upthrust' meaning buoyancy – had to be countered by taking in more ballast. Conversely, on her way down he'd had to pump a few gallons out, or the dive would have got out of control. Paul had learnt about the Principle of Archimedes originally in a physics class in Connecticut, USA, then had it driven home to him in the first hour of the submarine training course. This, now, was a practical application of the classroom lesson – under an enemy ship in an enemy anchorage while a time-fuse buzzed away the minutes.

'Forty-five feet.'

She was under the oiler and near enough in the middle – or would be, after a slight drift onward as she turned. He told Lanchberry, 'Port ten, and steer two-seven-eight.'

'Port ten . . .'

He set the clock to the five-hour mark. Gripping the releasing wheel then, staring up through the port at the dark swell of the oiler's bilge. It seemed to swivel very slowly as the midget completed her turn. And now was as good a time as any. He had to switch on, to activate the clock, then turn the wheel: and if this one didn't separate either . . .

But the switch surely wouldn't fail as well. Unless the whole lot were defective. The other boats – the *Tirpitz* lot, too? It wasn't impossible: one of the things nobody had been able to rehearse had been live firings. But if this one didn't release it wouldn't make all that much difference, except to the oiler, in which at this moment – 03.51 – a whole crew would be asleep, oblivious of the threat beneath them. They'd be spared and that was the only real difference there'd be; you'd be taking two un-detachable side-cargoes across the fjord instead of only one.

He pressed the switch. The light on the clock came on, and its motor started.

'Now here goes.'

Lanchberry raised his crossed-fingers hand. Gimber murmured, 'God bless.' Bless whom, Paul wondered as he pushed the releasing wheel around. He heard the securing links snap away, then the rip of the copper sealing-strip peeling off; this was a sure indication that the side-cargo was actually separating from the hull, its buoyancy chambers filling to drag it down. He might have imagined it, but it felt as if it gave her a small nudge of encouragement as it went.

Bad luck, for those slumbering tankermen. Really very bad.

'Port fifteen.'

The course to get her to the south coast of Aaroy but clear of a one-fathom hazard on the island's southwest corner would have been 110 degrees. But the tide had turned about an hour ago and would now be ebbing strongly. A course of 115 would offset the tidal drift, and still just clear Langnesholm if he happened to be over-compensating: there were no guaranteed-accurate figures for tidal flows available. He thought he'd bring her up in that area – about 3000 yards out from this cove – for a check, but the periscope might have flooded completely by that time and you had to be prepared to make the whole transit blind. And then – well, play it off the cuff.

'Steer one-one-five, Jazz.'

It would be safer to stay deep the whole way over. If there'd been any alarm raised – one of the X-craft sighted,

or submarines' presence even suspected – there'd be a lot
of sharp eyes busily looking for periscopes. He thought his
estimates were safe enough to rely on.

'Course one-one-five. Sir.'

'What makes you so respectful all of a sudden, Jazz?'

'Thought you'd like it.' Lanchberry glanced to his left,
at Brazier. 'Can't please some people.'

'Eighty feet, Louis.'

'Eighty . . .'

Battery power did not need to be conserved. It went
against one's natural submariner's instincts to be profli-
gate with it, but these were unusual circumstances. For
X-12, they were terminal circumstances. They were going
to abandon her with the side-cargo in place, there was
absolutely no chance of getting her away to sea now, so it
would make sense to get over there fast and have the extra
time in hand.

He explained this to Gimber. 'So we might as well step
on it.'

'Skipper?'

Brazier: his head was lowered, eyes showing their whites
under matted brows – the attitude of a bull about to use
its horns. 'Yes, Bomber?'

'Sorry to harp on about it. But I reckon I could shift it.
I'd guess it's gone like it has because with the weight of
one buoyancy chamber flooded there's been distortion on
one or more of the links. If I just prised it away slightly –
at the heavy end, whichever that may be—'

'Depth eighty feet.'

'Keep her grouped down for the moment, Louis.' Paul
squatted against the slight warmth emanating from the
Brown's gyro. 'Bomber, the snag as I see it is the time factor.
If we dash over there flat-out, giving you the time you'd
need for this, then we'd have a flat battery and we couldn't
get away anyhow. If we crossed at economical speed, I
doubt you'd have nearly enough time.'

'Might split the difference? Say group down full ahead? And I'd be all set and ready to go out the minute you got us under here. I could have the chamber flooded before you bottomed her. Half an hour at most – probably much less – and I'm back inside!'

'Isn't that somewhat optimistic? It might take you up to – well, seven-thirty. And the firing-period begins at eight.'

'But,' Brazier gestured towards the side-cargo, 'it's set for eight twenty-five.'

'Come on . . . It's not only ours, Bomber, is it. Hudspeth could be under *Scharnhorst* this very minute, leaving his two bombs set for eight sharp. We might bottom ourselves right on top of them. How's that for larks?'

Lanchberry chuckled. Brazier glanced at him, then back at Paul. One large hand passed around the wide, ginger-stubbled face. 'Well, that's all true, skipper, but . . .'

'Even if *Lützow*'s there and we go for her, X-10's charges under *Scharnhorst* would still blow us to Kingdom Come.'

'But your time of seven-thirty, skipper – that would be the very latest, absolute limit of it. I'd hope to finish long before that. And once I'm back inside and have the hatch shut, you could be on the move right away. I mean, why should you wait for me to drain down?'

He was talking sense. You wouldn't need to wait. The wet-and-dry was flooded from, and drained down into, number two main ballast, which was right under it. The operation in either direction was an internal one, with no effect on the boat's weight or trim.

Paul reached for the chart, to check how far it was from *Scharnhorst*'s last-observed position to the exit at the island's eastern end. The answer was a mile or a mile and a half, depending on exactly where she was berthed. That glimpse of her floodlit forepart last night, at a distance of three or four miles, hadn't exactly pinpointed her. He doubted whether she could have moved since then, either to sea or back into her netted berth in Kafjord, without sight or sound: and the fact was that Brazier's proposals weren't all that crazy, after all. If the diving sortie went smoothly, a lot of problems might be removed.

'You may be right, Bomber. It could work. After you're back in and the side-cargo's on the bottom – latest seven-thirty, and set to go up at eight twenty-five . . .' he was thinking aloud '. . . but we'd have to be clear away, and really legging it, at that.'

'Group up, full ahead!' Brazier's eyes were gleaming. 'Run like a rigger for that gap!'

He laughed, out of excitement at the prospect of having his own job to do – and more than a routine net-cutting operation, at that. Paul nodded slowly. 'Yes . . . But then we'd have to wait there – in the gap, until 0900. Otherwise – well, if we were out in the middle, the blast even from the one we've just planted . . .'

He was thinking aloud again. Gimber broke in, 'Must say, I don't go much on the prospect of barbed wire for the rest of the duration. I mean, if there is a chance we could skin out of it.'

Paul saw Lanchberry nod. And obviously he felt the same way himself. Glancing round, out of habit checking depth, angle of the 'planes, ship's head . . . He said, 'It all hinges on whether you can get the side-cargo off, Bomber. And how long it takes. If it didn't work we'd be in a hell of a spot – you realise that?'

A nod. But then a grin. 'I could do it with my bare hands, skipper. There's no other way that thing could be stuck to us.'

'Jazz. You know more than the rest of us how the side-cargoes are fixed. D'you agree with him?'

'I'd say I do. I'd say it's a good chance, any road.' He glanced sideways at Brazier. 'I'd be dead sure of it if it was me doing the job. Instead of a cack-handed bloody ape.'

Brazier murmured amiably, 'Remind me to put you on a charge, you sod.'

'Louis.' Paul had made his mind up. 'Put main motor to full ahead grouped down.' He looked back at Brazier. 'Bomber, how d'you like the thought of breakfast?'

'Oh, just the job!'

'Your job, then. Tinned fruit, coffee, biscuits and jam. OK?'

Lanchberry muttered, 'Bugger coffee, I'll have tea.'

'You can bugger the jam too, while you're at it.' Vibration increased as Gimber wound her up to full ahead. He added, 'Marmite, I'll have.'

Spirits shooting up. Having been rather thoroughly depressed, the upturn was all the sharper.

Off Langnesholm he brought her up to nine feet for a look around. The periscope was fogged internally but he could see enough through it to take rough bearings of Korsnes, Klubbeneset and Aaroy's left and right-hand edges. He sent the periscope down again and told Gimber, 'Eighty feet.' There'd been some fishing-boats rounding Klubbeneset, and what looked like a tug chugging north from the lower end of the fjord, but he couldn't see anything of *Scharnhorst*: she'd be hidden, just, by the island's western bulge. The intersection of his position lines from the bearings he'd taken wasn't all that neat – he'd known it wouldn't be, because of the twelve-degree angle on her and also the fogged-up prisms – but he chose the most dangerous position in the spread of the 'cocked hat', one from which the present course would just about have scraped her past the one-fathom patch, and played extra safe by altering two degrees to starboard, to 117.

Time now: 04.39. Estimated time of arrival at Aaroy's southwest corner: about 06.00. But the tidal set out in the middle might be slacker than it had been up here where it channelled into the two sunds. When he was off that corner of the island he'd come up for another check, he decided – navigational, and also because from there he'd have a clear view of *Scharnhorst*, possibly of *Lützow* too.

He'd have steered farther out from the Aaroy coast – particularly because of the danger of showing periscope so close to land in these millpond conditions – if he'd had more time in hand; but as things were, a shortcut was essential.

Gimber reported, 'Eighty feet.' He looked round over his shoulder. 'How long, to get over there?'

'Hour and twenty minutes.'

'And on the fuse-clock?'

'It's set for eight twenty-five. Should make – three hours and forty minutes to go.' He checked it, and found the delay left on it was exactly that. 'Keeping good time. That's something.'

Gimber had another question. 'Supposing we make it – out through that gap – how far to the rendezvous with *Setter*?'

'Well. Eight miles to get into Stjernsund.' He had the distances in his head. 'Then twelve through the sund, and another thirty to get out and across the minefield.'

'Total around fifty. Say forty-eight hours' passage.'

Paul nodded. He'd have to time the exit to coincide with high water, to carry them over the moored mines. He said, 'You'll be stir-crazy by then, Louis. If you aren't already.'

'Pain in the arse is the only problem at the moment. This bloody chair.'

'Well, come out of it. I'll take over for an hour.'

Brazier, aided by advice from Lanchberry, was selecting the tools he'd take out with him, but he took over the steering now so Jazz could ease his chair-cramped muscles too. As well as tools he was going to take a heaving-line, which he'd use for slinging himself down over the midget's side. At a quarter to six they all changed round again; Lanchberry had made more tea. Then at five minutes to the hour Paul told Gimber, 'Twenty feet. Slow ahead.'

It was a relief to see her upward movement on the depth-gauge. For half an hour he'd been visualising her approach to that rocky coast, and particularly the shallow patch.

Having made your calculations you had to trust to them, but flying blind in unfamiliar territory required a certain control of nerves.

'Main motor's slow ahead.'

And still nosing up . . .

'Are you fit, Bomber?'

Brazier lifted one rubber-gloved hand, from his position in the W and D. He'd got into his diving gear – rubber tunic, weighted boots on wader-type leggings, oxygen equipment harnessed to his back with the distributor in front and the face-mask dangling. The tools were on his belt, which also had lead weights in it for ballast. X-12 rising past the thirty-foot mark, leaning clumsily to port.

'Depth twenty feet.'

'Make it fifteen.'

Then ten. And when it was clear he had her in good control, nine and a half. Paul felt for the button in the rubber bag, and pressed it.

Greenish water swirling, with diamonds flashing in it. Then surface flurry and a liquid glare of daylight.

'Depth?'

'Nine feet—'

'Christ's sake!'

'Nine and a half. Sorry . . .'

Aaroy's rocks loomed alarmingly close to port. He could see them as if he was looking through a glass of water, but one small section of the lens was clearer than the rest. Circling slowly to the right . . .

'Wow.'

Scharnhorst. Bow-on, enormous, about a mile away. Maybe more – maybe 3000 yards. She was lying parallel to the shoreline and – as far as he could tell – on a single anchor. If that was the case, one might guess she wasn't planning to stay here very long. A second thought was far from cheering: when the tide turned, she'd swing with it – away from any ground-mines laid under her.

Wait for the turn of tide? But it wouldn't be until – seven, seven-thirty.

Bloody impossible, then . . .

Panic flared. He told himself, Hold on, now. Think it out.

No *Lützow*. Over against the far shore – the other side of Leir Botn – a minesweeper lay at moorings. And *Scharnhorst*, of course, might have her stern secured to a buoy, or a stream anchor out. It was wishful thinking, from here you couldn't see at all, but it was none the less quite possible. Other moorings over on that side were empty. Some small stuff right inshore – motor launches, he thought. There was certainly no target other than *Scharnhorst*, anyway. He wondered where X-10 might be: Hudspeth could be making his approach at any moment, and *Scharnhorst* was his target. X-12 was a poacher in his territory.

But they were all poachers. And so far the gamekeepers seemed to be asleep. *Scharnhorst*'s bearing down here was – 082 degrees.

'Take down some bearings, Jazz.'

Lanchberry had a pad and pencil beside him. Paul gave him bearings of Aaroy's edges, of Langnesholm back on the quarter and the mainland point directly south. Four bearings instead of three, to make up for the fact they'd all be distorted anyway.

'Port ten. Steer oh-nine-oh.' He squeezed the rubber bag to send the periscope down, and told Gimber, 'Sixty feet.'

'Sixty . . .'

'Full ahead group down.' He took a log reading, and told them while he was putting that fix on the chart, '*Scharnhorst*'s at anchor, no nets I can see, about a mile, mile and a half away. We'll call it two thousand five hundred yards.' It wasn't really a fix, in the true sense of the term, more a good indication of their position, and it was as much as he needed, anyway.

'Bomber, you can relax for a while.'

He glanced at the depthgauge: she was passing fifty feet, and Gimber had the trim-pump working on the midship's tank. Reporting now, 'Main motor full ahead, grouped down.' Paul told them, 'I'm going to run in one thousand yards by log, then sneak up for another look from broader on her bow. It's getting towards low water and she may swing with the tide, unless she's moored aft, which I can't tell yet. You'll still have plenty of time, Bomber.'

The last half-mile would have to be covered at slow speed, though, to avoid visible disturbance of the water or sound-levels audible on asdics.

He explained, 'I can't afford to wait for the tide to turn. Earliest she'd start swinging is half-seven. Bomber wouldn't be able to get inboard again by eight, so it's out of the question. If she's only anchored for'ard I'll have to guess at how she'll lie by eight-thirty, and hope for the best.'

Hudspeth would be facing the same problem, of course. He might already have done so. X-10's side-cargoes might already be lying on the bottom. Wiser, perhaps, not to speculate on that, when you were going to have to bottom there yourself by and by.

But almost certainly – he saw this suddenly – *Scharnhorst* did have a stream anchor out, holding her stern. Because she was lying the same way she'd lain last night – and last night when they'd seen her the tide had been flooding, whereas right now it was ebbing!

Except she might not have been at anchor, at that moment. Might have been in the process of anchoring – hence the illuminations?

Brazier asked, 'What's the depth there, skipper?'

'About nine fathoms.'

'*Scharnhorst* draws – what, twenty-five feet?'

'That's her mean draft. Call it twenty-seven, to be safe. And nine fathoms. We'll have a clear twenty-five feet of water under her.'

The tidal problem, the single anchor complication, was

a snag he hadn't foreseen when he'd accepted Brazier's arguments. He studied the chart now, trying to see any others that might arise, now or later. And there was one. The withdrawal – distance, time, air supply – particularly as so much of the bottled oxygen had been used . . . After the explosions there'd be an enormous hue and cry, charges dropped, and so on; the crossing to Stjernsund would have to be made deep and at slow speed, sparing the battery as much as possible, and it wouldn't be dark enough to surface until about 08.00 . . . It would mean a hell of a long time shut down. In fact, impossibly long!

He got the answer. Or an answer. Right in that gap between Aaroy and the mainland – or just close to the north of it, near the island's tapering eastern end – he'd bring her to the surface for a very quick guff-through. Then down again very smartly, with a full load of fresh air. There'd be some cover there, and with luck the Germans would be chasing their tails, at that stage, coping with their destroyed or damaged ships.

But all you could establish in advance was a general intention, a delineation of what was feasible and what wasn't. When the moment came – each moment, one on each other's heels – you'd adapt to circumstances. As he'd been realising during the recent hours, nothing was cut and dried.

'All right.' He'd checked the log. 'Twenty feet. Slow ahead.'

He asked Gimber when she was at ten feet, 'Can you manage a stop-trim, while I take a fast shufti?'

'Well.' Gimber's mud-coloured eyes didn't leave the controls in front of him. A stop-trim was a state of accurately neutral buoyancy, a trim so good that you could stop the motor and just hang there. 'Might manage a few seconds' worth.'

'That's all I'll need. When you're ready, nine and a half feet, and stop.'

She'd have no way on, or almost none, so the periscope would poke up with no feather, no rippling wake to it even. This close to the target, in broad daylight and with barely a wrinkle on the surface, it was about the only way you'd get away with it. Gimber had made his adjustments to the trim: his right hand moved to the control-wheel and wound it anti-clockwise to its stop, then pulled out the field switch. Paul had the periscope sliding up, trained on the bearing where he expected to locate his target. Snatching the handles down, pressing his right eye against the rubber.

'Bearing – oh-six-four. I'm thirty on her port bow, and – she has a wire out to a buoy astern!'

He'd squeezed the bag, and the tube was rushing down. Lanchberry muttered, 'Good oh . . .' Brazier clapped gloved hands together. Gimber said, 'Can't hold her, she's so bloody skew-whiff—'

'Slow ahead. Fifty feet. Come to port to oh-six-four, Jazz.'

Seeing that wire out to the buoy under her counter had felt like one of the best moments of his life. X-12 was already slanting down, trembling very slightly under the slow-speed thrust of her screw. As if she, too, were a little excited now.

Too slow-speed, though. He wanted to be there, now, getting on with it. Then, best of all, getting out.

'We'll hang on until we're really close, Bomber. Five minutes short of bottoming. Otherwise by the time we get there you'd be frozen solid.'

Brazier nodded. It wasn't going to be any fun in the wet-and-dry chamber, and he knew it better than any of them.

'Course – oh-six-four.'

Gimber reported, 'Fifty feet.'

The slow creep of the approach was galling. He was constantly checking the distance by log as the minutes passed, and he could see signs of the tension in the others. The temptation to increase to half ahead was difficult to resist: using up so much time like this, when you knew

that once you'd shed the side-cargo you'd need every
minute of it, was maddening. There was also – when your
head was close to it – the purring fuse-clock on the flooded
side: and your distrust of it.

It was six forty-two when he saw *Scharnhorst*'s huge
shadow through the viewing port. The time, and the log
reading, checked exactly.

'Come to oh-six-oh, Jazz.'

'Oh-six-oh . . .'

'Target's in sight.' He tapped the glass. 'Forty feet, Louis.'
There might be as little as eight fathoms where she was
lying. Gimber took his eyes off the starboard side viewing
port. It wasn't easy to stop looking – *Scharnhorst*, one of
the most powerful ships afloat, about a hundred yards
ahead and at their mercy.

Not that 'mercy' would be quite the word for it.

'All right, Bomber. In you go, and flood up. Don't touch
the hatch until I give two bangs on the bulkhead – then
carry on out, quick as you like. Take care you aren't under
the side-cargo when you free it – all right?'

Brazier nodded.

'Three bangs on the bulkhead would mean emergency
of some kind, stop everything and drain down.' Paul leant
over with his hand out. 'Bomber – good luck, now.'

'Yeah.' Lanchberry also reached to shake his hand. 'Best
of British, Bomber.' Gimber was too far away and too busy
for handshaking; he said, 'Bomber, first night back in
Cairnbawn, I'll buy all your drinks.'

Brazier grinned round at them all. 'Arf, arf.' He backed
into the W and D, and slammed its steel door, and they
saw the clips hinge over. Lanchberry muttered, 'Dunno
what we're fussed about. He'll do it on his ear.'

Brazier would have shut and clipped the other door as
well, the one leading into the fore end. So he was now
enclosed in a space in which he could only crouch with his
elbows in contact with both bulkheads and the closed hatch

above his head. He'd put on his mask, and start breathing oxygen from the counter-lung strapped to his chest and fed, via the distributor valve, from the bottles on his back. Equipped like this, being the size he was, he'd only just pass through the hatch when the time came for his exit. In preparation for that outing he'd now be setting about flooding his steel cell by pumping water up from number two main ballast tank. He had a pump-lever in there, similar in operation to the trimming-pump control; the first part of its movement opened the valve from the W and D to the ballast tank and also the vent they shared, and the next started the pump, which was a powerful one producing up to fifty pounds to the square inch. By now the water would be roaring in, flooding up around him, deafening him with its noise as the level rose and the pressure increased. He'd adjust his flow of oxygen, the pressure of it in the lung, to balance that rising pressure. The flooding process lasted about four minutes, unpleasant minutes – and more so than usual, here in seventy degrees north latitude, by the fact of it being only fractionally above freezing point. The worst moment came when the inrush of water, having already closed over Brazier's head, hit the roof of the chamber – the underside of the hatch. At this point the vent lost the battle and pressure jumped suddenly to equal sea-pressure outside. For the diver it was like being slammed against a wall. Brazier would have softened the blow, and saved the counter-lung and his own lungs from being squeezed flat, by stopping the pump just before the chamber filled.

Those controls inside the W and D were duplicated here in the control room. You could do all of it from here, except of course for opening the hatch. That had to be done by the man in the chamber. When the time came he'd reach up, grab the central handwheel above his head and wrench it round so that the dogs would disengage on the rim and allow him to push it up. Brazier wouldn't be doing that yet: he'd be hunched in there now, enclosed in icy water under pressure, waiting for Paul's signal.

Paul waited too – watching the shadow fill the viewing port and darken, its wavy edges firming as the midget crept in under it. *Scharnhorst* was nearly 750 feet long and 100 in the beam; she carried twelve-inch armour on her sides, but the vast expanse of underwater hull now exposed to X-12 had no such protection.

Fifteen hundred men up there inside her. Probably having breakfast.

Rippling silver ended where her great bulk shaded the water under it. The approach had been at an angle of thirty degrees to the battleship's fore-and-aft line, and the small alteration of course he'd made five minutes ago would have brought them in just about amidships, under that funnel with its rakish cap. It was probably the best place to leave a single charge, he thought. If X-10 had placed – or was placing – her two side-cargoes, she'd drop one at each end, a tactic designed to break the ship's back. Another in the middle, therefore, would make a real job of it.

'Stop main motor.'

'Stop . . . Motor's stopped.'

'Port twenty.'

'Port twenty.' Lanchberry span the wheel. 'Twenty of port wheel on, sir.'

'Take her down slowly, Louis.'

A nod. Gimber's left hand moved the pumplever to port, then centred it again. Forty-two feet. Forty-four . . .

'Give her a touch astern.'

Gimber put the motor to slow astern for just long enough to feel the screw churn, taking the way off her. Looking upwards through the ports it was as if an enormous steel shutter stopped sliding over them. It was lifting now, going out of focus. Gimber had stopped the motor. The gauge showed forty-eight feet – eight fathoms. At fifty-four there was a bump for'ard: she lurched, bumped again.

Hard. Too hard.

'Rock.'

As expected. A crunching sound from under their feet lasted for about ten seconds while she settled. The needle was on fifty-four and a half feet, and there was no movement on it at all now. The fore-and-aft bubble was on the centreline, but she was leaning a few degrees to port, canted by the flooded charge's weight although not as much as she had been when she'd been waterborne. She'd be resting on her heavy, level keel, kept upright by the buoyancy in her compartments and in some tanks.

Paul took a wheelspanner from where it was hanging on the deckhead, rapped twice with it on the door of the W and D. The metallic crashes were startlingly loud. Then he went to the stub periscope, the short bifocal one. He was looking into a dim, shifting haze, water and watermovement distorting the overhead view of *Scharnhorst*'s bilges extending into what looked like miles, wavery like sinews in it flexing themselves. He couldn't see X-12's fore hatch until it opened; it was below the periscope's field of view, set down in a short well inside the casing. But he saw its rim appear now – a curve of black at the very bottom of the glass; the hatch had been flung back, and that was the top edge of the lid standing open. Now Brazier was rising into view, ungainly undersea creature dramatically emerging, rising and inclining forward – this way, leaning towards and over the stub periscope – hooking black rubber-gloved claws into the casing's apertures to hold itself down and drag itself aft. Boots loud on the casing's steel, ringing clangs, and bubbles rising in a thin stream from his breathing exhaust.

Astonishing to think you knew that sinister-looking creature – had talked, eaten and drunk with it.

'He's out, and moving aft.'

They'd have known from the fairy footsteps, but he'd forgotten to tell them, in his own fascination with the sight.

Lanchberry said, 'He'll have it done in five minutes. Anyone want to bet?'

Gimber took him up on it. 'I say ten minutes. Starting now. Five bob.'

'You're on.'

The periscope window went black as Brazier loomed over it. Water displaced by that large body's passage through it danced mirage-like above him. You could hear every shift of the leadweighted boots; other metallic sounds would be from the tools slung on his belt. Paul checked the time: six fifty-four. Leaving one hour and six minutes to have the job done and get her through the gap to the blind side of the island. It would be all right as long as the Bomber did take as little as five or ten minutes. Paul was at the viewing port, and he could see Brazier handling his line, letting himself down over the side; he'd have secured it to the periscope standard, or thereabouts. Gimber and Lanchberry had both swung round on their seats to watch – or rather, to catch glimpses, which was all you'd get – and Paul stood aside to clear their view. Then Brazier's body was covering the outside of the port, so there was nothing to be seen at all. Paul had looked round to make some remark to Gimber, when it happened.

An explosion: like a distant rumble of thunder ampli-fied immediately into a deafening clap of it right overhead. Paul's thought was, Side-cargo . . .

(He was right, although he had no idea at the time whose or where it was. Later reconstruction from sources including German naval logs make it clear that it was the charge left by X-12 herself in Ytre Koven and which should still have had two hours' delay left on its clock.)

In the first impact of the shock-wave, Brazier was wiped off the midget's side. Paul saw him receding into black-ness, cartwheeling head over heels; his mask had been blown off and trailed on its pipe. Brazier's limbs were extended – the legs at any rate in their heavy boots,

whirling by centrifugal force as he turned over and over –
in an attitude of crucifixion, whirling away. It was more
horrible than any of the nightmares, and now X-12 was on
the move too, crabbing side-ways, angled over to starboard,
at first just sliding but then grating, bouncing, crashing
over rock. Paul had been sent flying. Gimber was clinging
to his seat but Lanchberry had been ejected backwards,
torpedoing head-first into machinery behind his chair.
Struggling up, imposed over the sight of Lanchberry's head
gashed and blood streaming in a scarlet curtain over his
face was the image still in Paul's brain of Bomber Brazier
in that maelstrom, drowning if the concussion hadn't
already killed him. Which it would have. The boat was on
her side, grinding over the rocky bed of the fjord, and the
obvious counter-measure – to blow main ballast – wasn't
on the cards, because you'd have been blasting her to the
surface under the eyes and guns of fifteen hundred
Germans – under *Scharnhorst*'s guns. Gimber had the pump
running on the midships trimming tank; Paul had crawled
to the lever to do it himself – acting blindly, on instinct, as
it were buried in the noise – and he'd found the lever
already over to starboard, Gimber holding it there with one
hand and clinging to the hydroplane control with the other.
Lanchberry shouted in Paul's ear, 'Blow one and three?'
Paul yelled back 'No!' He saw astonishment in Lanchberry's
face, and allowed himself second thoughts: you could blow
enough ballast out just to get her off the rocks, before she
smashed up completely. He'd got himself half to his feet:
he shouted 'Jazz!' Lanchberry staring at him with a hand
to his head and blood still pouring, just about all over him
by this time. Paul yelled, 'Blow one and three, but only
one short guff in each!'

The motion was easing: these were only dying residues
of blast now, and noise diminished with it. Lanchberry
opened the two high-pressure blows, paused for a count
of three and then jammed them shut again. X-12's bow

lifting: but not her stern . . . He shouted, 'Another guff in three!'

The angle had increased alarmingly. She was bow-up, with an angle of about twenty degrees on her. Her stern, obviously, was still resting on the bottom – you could hear it, the grinding contact with rock – as if that tank hadn't been blown at all. Lanchberry had opened the blow again: Paul heard the thump and rush of air through the pipe, then the noise of it escaping, whooshing out. Lanchberry heard it too and shut the blow.

'Stern tank's holed.'

So it could not be blown. A minute ago, in that deafening cacophony, they hadn't been able to hear the air escaping.

Gimber had stopped the ballast pump. He saw Paul turn to glance at the position of the lever, and explained, 'Wasn't doing any good.' Pointing at the depthgauge: 'Seen that?'

The needle was static at 238 feet.

So she'd been washed away from the Aaroy coast into much deeper water. And at 238 feet the pressure would be something like – he forced his stunned brain to work it out – 125 pounds to the square inch. It made the prospect of escape by DSEA somewhat unattractive. But X-12 was stuck here, finished; there was nothing to do except abandon her.

That same sensation swept over him: that this couldn't be true, couldn't really be happening – you'd wake up suddenly . . .

But it was happening. Had happened. And now had to be coped with. He heard Lanchberry mutter, 'Poor old Bomber.'

The enemy might or might not know there was a submarine down here. It depended on whether those large escapes of air had been seen when they'd frothed the surface.

Gimber said, 'I suppose the side-cargo's still attached.'

The time was eight minutes past seven.

There was an intermittent scraping from the stern, where she was grinding her tail on rock, but also – he was noticing it now for the first time – an internal trickling. He saw Lanchberry also listening to it while he dabbed with a handful of cotton-waste at his gashed head. X-12 resting on her tail, snout pointing upward at the surface, Lanchberry and Gimber both in their seats while Paul crouched with an arm hooked round the barrel of the periscope. Lanchberry said, 'Leaking in aft.' His thin lips twisted. 'Be bloody amazing if it wasn't.'

It would be through some loosened hull-valve, or possibly more than one. It was hardly worth looking for, though, because sooner or later they were going to have to bale out. Sooner, rather than later. But at least with this stern-down angle on her, the water that got in would take a very long time to reach the battery. There'd be no chlorine gassing to worry about, in the short term.

Small mercies . . . Particularly as there couldn't be a long term.

'DSEA then. This depth's going to create problems, but . . .'

He'd checked. He'd been about to tell them, We'll go out through the W and D, one at a time. The first step would have been to operate its valves – its connections with number two main ballast – from here in the control room, in order to drain it down. Then each man would have gone out – Gimber first, then Lanchberry, and finally himself, and each of the first two would have had to shut the hatch behind him before allowing himself to float up to the surface with the rubber apron of his set extended, like a parachute in reverse, to slow the ascent and reduce the likelihood of 'bends'. But you couldn't do it – couldn't use the W and D at all. Because Brazier had left the hatch standing open. Paul remembered it distinctly. It had been only minutes ago, yet already remote in memory – that dream-quality again – but he could see as if he was looking at it now the rim of the open hatch, and then the Bomber like some weird apparition rising out of it, a spectral being from another planet. There was a side thought at this point, a thought within the other one – that the weighted boots and belt would sink the Bomber's body, hold it down at least for quite a long time . . . But he'd left the hatch open because he'd been set on doing a quick job out there and getting back inside within minutes.

Paul hauled himself up to the stub periscope, to check this, but of course at such a depth as this there wasn't any light to see by. Only the roofing shimmer of the surface.

'What's the drill now, skipper?'

'We can't use the wet-and-dry, unfortunately. Bomber left it open.'

A slow blink, slow enough to be a temporary closing of the eyes. Lanchberry said, 'Ah.'

Gimber whispered, 'Shit . . .'

'So we'll have to flood her through the seacocks, and use this hatch.'

'Christ, how long'll that take?'

The short answer was too long. For a variety of reasons, none of them hard to see. The system he was proposing just happened to be the only way out there was. They'd strap on their DSEA sets, and start breathing from them when the water got to about shoulder height. Or so high you had to anyway. You wouldn't use the sets before you had to, because unlike Brazier's proper diving gear a DSEA set was only meant to support life in a man on his way up to the surface, and the oxygen capacity was quite limited. The flooding process would be complicated, too, by the midget's bow-up position. At this angle – if she stayed like this, when she'd taken in that great weight of water – and she might, because the stern compartment would be the first to fill – the air pocket would be up against the top of the W and D bulkhead, not under the hatch as would be normal. The hatch, in fact, would be drowned long before the pressures equalised. That was another factor – the pressure would be huge, really killing, increasing as the flooding continued and finally balanced sea pressure so the hatch could be opened.

By anyone who was still alive to open it.

Well – you could open the door to the W and D, at that stage, and use the fore hatch. Easier than having to dive down and locate the main hatch and open it. But exactly the same applied, of course, about equalising pressure. In fact you could open that W and D door now – you could knock its clips off and allow it to fly open with sea at more than a hundred pounds to the inch behind it, and in the second that it opened you'd all be killed by that blast of pressure.

Hardly profitable.

Lanchberry answered his own question. His sweater was soaked brownish with his blood. He'd stemmed the flow, with cotton-waste stuck to the gash.

'Take an hour, or more. Much as two hours, even.'

Gimber checked the time. Seven-thirteen.

'Firing-period starts at eight.' He nodded towards the boat's port side. 'And that thing's set for twenty-five past.'

At 08.00, or at any time thereafter, there could be other side-cargoes exploding. Not that you'd need them, from X-12's point of view. If she took an hour or more to flood, the three of them would probably be dead from cold long before they'd be in a position to open up and get out. It would have been bad enough for the Bomber in his rubber suit, but without such gear, standing for an hour in ice-water slowly rising until it covered you . . .

'How long's the oxygen last in these?'

Lanchberry was pulling the DSEA sets out of the storage locker. Paul admitted, 'If she floods that slowly, not long enough.'

Forty-five minutes, he was remembering, on the main

cylinder. Then you could switch to the reserve and get another five.

'Can't do it, can we.'

'What we can do,' he'd just started talking, spouting thought aloud, 'is get her up to the surface, abandon ship – and she'll go down again on her own with the hatch open. As she's going to blow up, there's no problem about secret equipment in enemy hands, so . . .'

'Skipper – how?'

'Just listen to me, Jazz.' He leant with a hand on Louis Gimber's shoulder. 'First we'll lighten her as much as we can.' He pointed at the trimming pump. Gimber interrupted, 'Pump's got a hell of a pressure to work against.' Paul nodded. 'Sure, it'll be on the slow side. But we'll start by emptying the stern trim-tanks and comps, shift that weight to the bow or amidships. It'll at least help to balance her. Then we'll blow one and three.'

'Skipper—'

'Hang on. We'll lose air through three, I know, but the blowing will still have some effect, from the air as it passes through. It did start to – remember? Before we heard it escaping and you shut off? Then as soon as she shows signs of stirring, full ahead group up. Planes hard a-rise. Surface. At this angle, and keeping her at full ahead and blowing like hell – well, she ought to get there, and although she won't stay up for long there'd be time to evacuate . . . Right?'

'Ten to one against.'

'Balls, Jazz. But that's better odds than we've got down here, anyway.'

Gimber agreed, 'It's the only hope we've got, isn't it?'

'Exactly. We can pump out number two main ballast too, Jazz. I was thinking we couldn't – for some reason . . . But we do have a chance, you see.' There was a glint of hope in Lanchberry's eyes, at last. Paul told him, 'I'll take over as helmsman, Jazz.'

'Yeah?'

Gimber looked surprised too.

'Because I want to control the blowing myself.'

It would make enough sense – just enough – for them to accept it. In fact he wanted to change places so the two of them would be under the hatch and first out. If she reached the surface. Lanchberry had been near enough right, he thought, with his estimate of the odds against.

16

————⊱•0•⊰————

Trench said, 'That's the lot. Those top sheds are empty, at the moment. Until we disperse the litters, you see.'

Trying not to show my relief too plainly, I pushed the door shut. When you've seen a few thousand minks, you have a fair idea what a mink looks like. I thanked him for the guided tour. 'Fascinating.'

'Really?' He was genuinely surprised, 'D'you think so?'

Unspoilt Norfolk countryside lay around us. There was a village in a dip, thatched cottages clustered round a church with a square stone tower; in woodland between us and the village the trees were in new leaf. Some fighters had roared over at something like Mach 2 while we'd been in the shed, but all was quiet now and it looked as it might have done fifty years ago.

Trench told me as we strolled towards the farm's office building, '*Foremost* was hit a second time, and stopped, just as we got down to support her. The enemy destroyers, in line ahead, had turned towards her and the convoy – which they couldn't see yet, on account of the smoke she'd been laying, but obviously knew where it was . . . They had *Foremost* pretty well for target practice, steering to pass her at close range and no doubt blow her out of the water on their way to make hay with the convoy. Having had their friends lure me away to the north and northeast, you see.'

'D'you think it was a deliberate plan they'd followed?'

'No, I don't. Visibility was too bad, for one thing. I don't think they had much idea of anything until they actually ran into us. They were scouting in separate divisions, that's all, and it's how things happened to turn out.'

'So you were steering south – with the enemy and *Foremost* in sight.'

'The Germans didn't spot us until it was too late – too late for them – and by that time we'd fired torpedoes. It was too late for poor *Foremost* too, of course. She was quite obviously done for, but they were still bombarding her. At times you couldn't see her for their shell-spouts, and the smoke pouring out of her, and fires – and the vis being what it was anyway . . . I was – well, you can imagine. I'd put him in that ship – then left her, gone swanning off on a wild goose chase, and . . .'

He paused, shaking his head. 'I know. I couldn't have stayed down there, ignored the enemy reports from *Legend*. Still . . . *Foremost* was helpless – stopped, burning, one gun firing at irregular intervals – and those bastards methodically completing her destruction. Their job, of course – but there seemed to be a certain Germanic precision about it that got my goat. In fact they were preoccupied with it to the extent that our fish were on the way to them before they knew we were there. I'd have thrown the galley stove at them, if I'd had it handy. What I mean is – I told you earlier I'd intended saving our torpedoes for *Lützow*, obvious thing to do, of course. But here were these swine in a neat line like fairground ducks just waiting to be knocked over, and the long and short of it is, my three ships each fired four torpedoes – holding another four in reserve – and only then opened up with our guns. Of course the very patchy visibility helped, but they should have seen us long before they did. It cost them two destroyers. I've no idea whose torpedoes did the damage, but out of the twelve we'd fired we got three hits, and sank two of them, second and third ships in the line. It left numbers one and four well separated and no doubt shaken to the core – this being their first awareness of our presence. Extremely lucky, of course – unseen approach, snap attack, two enemies destroyed – that's luck, all right. The two survivors turned and ran, in opposite directions. I went after number one, the leader, and told *Laureate* and *Lyric* to attend to the other; and mine, when after a mile or so he saw he had only me on his tail, decided to have a final crack at *Foremost*. He was between me and her, you see. When he turned to run, he crossed my bows at about seven thousand yards but he was closer than that to her. I couldn't see her all the time, only glimpses of her out beyond this Hun; I was turning to starboard to bring my guns to bear on him. I suppose he reckoned he could polish off *Foremost* with a salvo or two – well worth it, for a Knight's Grand Cross or whatever – and then throw a few at me as he took off. He had the legs of me, he'd know that, and he'd also be well aware he out-gunned me. In fact he'd good reason to expect to get away with it.'

Moloch's four-sevens firing as fast as they could be reloaded: every time the four 'gun-ready' lamps glowed in the director, the director layer, with his crosswires on the target, would press his trigger. He'd got the German's range and straddled: one hit glowed and smoked amidships, shell-spouts lifting all around: the firegongs clanged again and another salvo crashed away. Trench, with his glasses on the enemy, saw his stern guns swinging round, shifting target: he still had his glasses trained there when *Foremost* blew up. A huge streak of flame, then the eruption . . .

'I felt it.' He touched his head. 'Like something in here, exploding.'

The German's guns were all directed at *Moloch* now. Most of the first salvoes went over, but one shell hit aft, smashed the searchlight and killed and wounded some torpedomen.

Moloch scored too, with a hit below his bridge, and he was swinging to port.

'Turning away, sir!'

'Port fifteen! Full ahead both!'

Trench told his engineer over the telephone, 'I want every ounce you can give me, Chief! I don't care if you burst the bloody boilers!' He slammed the 'phone down. 'Midships!' He had to repeat that order – it had coincided with the crash of the four-sevens. He'd displaced his navigator at the binnacle now. 'Steer—' sighting over the gyro repeater, 'Oh-eight-three!'

Moloch at full stretch, hurling herself across the swells, spray sheeting aft as she cut through them. He'd turned her enough to follow on a course roughly parallel to the enemy's but with all his guns still bearing. Shell-spouts lifted: and she was racing into them . . .

Then, the bridge was engulfed in flame, deafeningly concussive noise.

'Where I got this.' He touched the empty sleeve. 'Or rather, lost it. Didn't know it at the time, hardly felt a thing. There was a sort of knock-out effect, I knew we'd been hit, of course, but this arm was like – well, just a blow, no more than that. The amount of bleeding became noticeable soon afterwards – the arm wasn't severed so much as smashed. They put a tourniquet on it, up near the armpit, while I was still too busy to take much notice. I'd got one in the jaw as well. I was still conning the ship, you see; I'd been knocked down but only for a moment, it didn't seem to me I'd been seriously hurt at all. We'd had one shell in the bridge and another in the director tower, all four of them killed up there, and radar gone, and wireless – well, a lot of damage. The bridge was a shambles too. McAllister – my navigator – had had his head blown off, Cummings – sub-lieutenant – was dead too, and my yeoman – excellent man called Halliday – was very badly wounded. He survived, I'm glad to say – thanks to Dicky Rudge, my quack – who undoubtedly saved my life as well, with that tourniquet. He was about to give me an injection of morphine, I'm told, but apparently I knocked the thing out of his hand and used some highly abusive language. I don't remember any of it, myself. But the voicepipe to the wheelhouse was intact, Henderson had got the guns into local control – done it by messengers, since the telephones to the TS and the guns themselves had gone to hell – and we were still intact, mobile and manoeuvrable, a fighting unit.'

He paused. Reaching into memory, or putting memories into order. His recollections – as he explained now – were only patchy, in some areas.

'What follows is less from my own remembering than from what they told me. And it's not always clear to me which is which – if you see what I mean. But some bits – visual flashes – are as clear as anything. Above all else I remember an absolute dread of the possibility that the German might get away from me. It was an entirely personal feeling, like wanting your hands on a man's throat, and obviously it was because of *Foremost*. They told me I was – berserk, was the word Dicky Rudge used, and Henderson was honest enough to agree with him. I certainly wasn't rational. I had a bit of that German shell in my jaw, you know – here. Scar doesn't show much now, but I still feel it. I'd barely noticed it at first, but I knew it by this time, and it was distorting my speech as well as giving me a lot of pain. But – sticking to what matters – the German had turned back towards me, for the simple reason he'd found his retreat cut off by *Legend* and *Leopard* and I suppose he preferred to face one rather than two. My guns were still banging away at him, but in local control the shooting wasn't all that good and we'd just been straddled again. So I—'

He'd checked, turned and thrown me a glance. Then looked away again. 'I steered to ram. Straight into those guns of his, which unlike mine were in director control and shooting accurately. It was a lunatic thing to do, of course. Suicidal, and quite unjustifiable. All those bloody great five-point-ones blazing in my face. I jinked her a bit, dodging, turning towards the fall of shot each time – so I'm told – so I couldn't have been completely off my head, but it was madness all the same. The dog in the fight, you know? The pain inflicted being what matters, not the wounds received? And my aim – contrary to everything that's gone on record – was to ram him.'

I began, 'It's understandable . . .'

'Then you don't understand. I had five destroyers under my command. All of them present, intact and fighting fit. I also had a large convoy to protect. What I was doing was indulging a personal hate – revenge – whatever you like to call it, and it was tantamount to throwing my own ship away. The fact she stayed afloat wasn't my doing. Half the for'ard guns' crews were killed, the foremast went over the side, we had a fire amidships and a shell went clean through the upper seamen's messdecks without exploding – and none of it was necessary. D'you see, now?'

'But you headed him off. He'd have got clean away – as you said yourself, he had the legs of you – but you forced him to turn back into the arms of *Legend* and *Leopard*.'

'You've been reading too many official histories.' Trench smiled briefly. 'That was the fortunate end-result of an act – no, period – of lunacy. Which in the record went down as tactical brilliance, forthright leadership and – well, you've read it all. Coolness and courage in the face of the enemy. Coolness, my God!' He shook his head. 'I don't have to tell you about our casualties. Fortunately, I passed out. Loss of blood, Rudge told me afterwards. I don't know, perhaps he got one of his damn needles into me. Henderson took over, and turned her under the German's stern, and we came off a lot less badly then we would have done if I'd been on my feet to see it through. *Moloch* was in almost as bad a state as *Foremost* had been: except we could still steam. As you say, we'd forced our Hun to alter course again and we'd hit him a good few times, and then John Ready caught him on the rebound and applied the finishing touches. That was how Ready described it. *Laureate* and *Lyric* had meanwhile polished off the other one. I was on my back, being shot full of morphine – came round eventually in my bunk with an arm missing, jaw strapped up, couldn't say a word, only listen to Henderson's report. Which, as you'll have guessed, covered for me. Then, and afterwards. All was well, convoy intact and on course for Iceland – the RAF had photographed *Lützow* at anchor somewhere off Narvik—'

'On her way down to Gdynia, I think. Either to refit or pay off.'

He nodded. 'And there were nine survivors out of *Foremost*. Nick Everard, of course, not one of them. I had that to lie there and think about, too.' He added, after a silence, 'I interviewed every one of those nine, not many weeks later, in the hope of finding out what had happened to him.'

I'd spoken to two of them myself, quite recently. From one, a man who'd been the loader on *Foremost*'s B gun, I'd heard the same story he'd told Trench nearly forty years earlier – the story Trench repeated to me now. How Nick Everard had last been seen leading a blinded signalman aft in order to get him into a Carley float before she sank or blew up. Leading this signalman by the arm, helping him down the ladder from the foc's'l break, telling him he was going to be all right, plenty of room in the floats and other ships at hand who'd pick them up, and how eye surgeons could perform marvels these days – that sort of stuff, shouting in the man's ear because *Foremost* had been under fire at the time, on fire, one gun still sporadically in action.

'Apparently he'd turned out and got dressed when she went to action stations. He was on the bridge with Crockford to start with, then helped organise Cramphorn's first-aid and stretcher parties. He was wearing a tin hat with MID painted on it; *Foremost* had no midshipman serving in her at the time, so that one was spare and he wore it. Cramphorn was among the missing, and I wasn't able to establish to what extent Nick had recovered, whether or not he knew who he was or where, or why.' Trench pushed a gate open. 'All we do know is that the end became the man.'

It was a matter of fitting the pieces together – times, and the events which are explainable now but weren't then, to the participants. Such as *Lützow* being on her way south to Gdynia, and *Scharnhorst* anchored not in her usual berth but off that island – Aaroy. In fact *Scharnhorst* was out there because after the raid on Spitzbergen her captain, Hoffmeier, had decided his ship's gunnery wasn't up to scratch, and arranged for some practice shoots. This was why he'd moved her out of her protected berth, and on the morning of the twenty-second was only waiting for permission to proceed to his exercise area up in the wider reaches of the fjord.

'It's running.'

The trimming pump – sucking on number two main ballast. Gimber kept his hands on the pump's casing – getting some slight warmth from it, or hoping to. The bottom of Altenfjord was freezing cold.

Unlike numbers one and three main ballast, which had open holes in the bottom through which when you blew the tanks with high-pressure air the water was expelled, number two had a Kingston valve at the bottom that could be opened or shut. So you could keep this tank full, for trimmed-down ballast and bodily weight at sea, or empty for buoyancy and safety in harbour. It also made possible its use as a reservoir for the flooding or draining-down of the W and D.

Which was unusable because its hatch was standing open.

You could hear the pump's soft whine. It was having to work hard against outside sea pressure. You could also hear the trickling noise from aft where water was seeping in. Then – something quite new . . .

Lanchberry pointed a long forefinger upwards. His eyes were turned up towards the deckhead. Lips drawn back exposing teeth whiter than the whites of his eyes. Face black with stubble, and dried blood in it, bloodstains all over and the soaked cotton-waste, hardening and black, adhering to his scalp. The overall effect was barely human. He said, 'Weighing anchor.'

'*Scharnhorst?*'

'Wouldn't know what else.'

It was so familiar a sound – that steady, rhythmic clanking – that there was no question of not recognising it. The clanks were made by each link of the anchor-chain as it crashed over the lip of the hawsepipe, with enormous strain on the cable as it hauled the 26,000-ton battleship up to her anchor. They'd have taken the wire off the buoy astern before they'd begun heaving in for'ard.

Gimber said, 'Doesn't make much odds, since we didn't leave a bomb under her.'

'X-10 may have done.'

'Could be just shortening-in. If it's timed for eight she may still be there.'

Paul looked at Lanchberry. Thinking, Let's hope we're not still here.

It was 07.20. In forty minutes' time this end of the fjord might erupt. And in a sense you had to hope it would – if it didn't, the operation would have been a failure. But if it did, and you hadn't been able to lighten her enough to get her to the surface . . . He frowned, not wanting to see so far into the future, not liking as much as he could see.

Gimber suggested, 'We could try it now, I suppose.'

Staring at Paul from about a yard away. Lank beard, dull eyes, grey damp skin. If Jane had seen a photograph of him as he looked now she'd have said, No, that's not Louis . . . Paul began, 'Trouble is, if we give it a go too soon and it doesn't work—'

'We'd have used up all the air.'

'Exactly, Jazz.'

'So we'd've had it, chum.' Lanchberry said, with apparent equanamity and back into pidgin Arabic, 'Malish, Sidi Bish . . .' He nodded to Gimber. 'Gyppo for "best carry on pumping", that is. I'd say pump the bastard right out, then try.'

Paul thought he was right. This was the only hope they had of getting out, and you could only attempt it once. When you started you'd either have her on the surface in a matter of two or three minutes or you'd know you weren't going to make it at all. So the sensible thing to do would be to continue pumping either until the tank was empty or until the time was just about running out. He told Gimber, 'Every pint we get out of her improves the chances. We'll pump it dry, or until ten to eight.'

'Isn't that cutting it a bit fine?'

He shrugged. 'Quarter to, if you like.'

He was remembering Gimber leaning against the jamb of his cabin door, in the depot ship in Loch Cairnbawn, mumbling drunkenly 'If you get back and I don't . . .' He told him, 'I'll be your best man yet, Louis. There's no reason this shouldn't work. I just don't want to go off at halfcock.'

Gimber's eyes showed fear, suddenly. Before, there'd been anxiety, and perhaps a lack of hope, but now suddenly you could see – sharp apprehension, might be the way to describe it. As if, looking into that kind of distant future at Paul's invitation, he'd realised it probably did not exist. He blinked, as he looked away. 'Good. I'll hold you to that.'

'Better clean up a bit, before you pop the question.'

He'd glanced back, frowning. 'You light-headed, or something?'

'Light conversation. To pass the time, old horse.'

Brazier cartwheeling, helpless as a leaf in a high wind, in the vortex of that underwater blast . . .

Gimber, making an effort to play the game, asked Lanchberry, 'Come to my wedding, Jazz?'

'Yeah.' Lanchberry snorted. 'I'll sit in the back row and laugh.'

'I'm serious.'

'So'm I. Laugh me bloody head off.'

Scharnhorst still shortening cable. Clank, clank, clank . . .

'Skipper – if we get her up there—'

'When we get her up.'

'Yeah. When we do, and start piling out, Gerry's going to start shooting – right?'

'From *Scharnhorst*, if she's still there. Yes, I suppose—'

'Depending on how far we got carried, we wouldn't be all that far from her, would we?'

'If she's weighing, not just shortening-in, she might have buggered off by then. But,' he nodded, 'I suppose otherwise they'd get some guns manned pretty quick.'

'So how about the first man takes out a white flag with him?'

Paul nodded. 'That's a good idea.'

It also allowed him to make a point that might otherwise have been difficult.

'In the locker, Jazz – you'll find my spare shirt. Pass it to old Louis there – he'll be first out, and . . .'

'Who says so?'

Gimber looked affronted. Paul said, 'I do, as it happens. That's a good enough reason on its own. But I'll give you two more – one, you're nearest to the hatch; two, as you've just pointed out, you have a fiancée.'

'No, I don't, not . . .'

'A potential fiancée. It's more than I have, or Jazz. Anyway, you're detailed for it now. Just be sure when the time comes you move like a scalded cat.' Lanchberry found the white shirt and tossed it to Gimber. Paul told him, 'Wave it over your head as you climb out, then drop it so the next man,' he looked at Jazz, 'can do the same . . . Pass me the chart, will you?'

To estimate, if he could find clues that helped, which way and how far they'd been washed, in that explosion. Two hundred and thirty-eight feet being about forty fathoms . . . And he saw it at once. They'd been shifted southeastward. Soundings there, perhaps seven or eight hundred yards from where they'd started under *Scharnhorst*,' gave thirty-five fathoms to the west and forty-one about a mile east. They were in just under forty here, so interpolating roughly he was reasonably sure X-12 had to be lying about half a mile south of the island's eastern tip. In fact it was a very small offlying island, so small it wasn't even named, about two hundred yards southeast of the tip of Aaroy and with rock shoals in between. East of this islet was the gap through which he'd been planning to get away northward.

There were twelve fathoms in the channel, but it shelved up to rocks edging the mainland shore. Out here the charted depths varied sharply over quite small distances – eight fathoms, fifty-seven, forty-nine . . . It did seem certain that this was the only place they could be, bottomed in just on forty fathoms.

'Here.' He reversed the chart, for the others to see. 'When we were under *Scharnhorst* we were about here. We travelled about seven-fifty yards. See this sounding?'

After a minute's close inspection, Gimber agreed. 'Not much doubt of it.'

Jazz shrugged. 'Take your word for—'

Open-mouthed, listening . . .

Listening to silence. The clanking had ceased.

'She's finished shortening-in, is all.'

'I guess you're . . .'

It had begun again.

Paul thought, visualising the scene up there, cable was up-and-down so they stopped, reported it to the bridge, and got the order 'Weigh!'

It was wishful thinking, of course. He wanted *Scharnhorst* out of it, before he made this attempt to reach the surface, because with no-one up there with guns trained on them there'd be a better chance of one or perhaps two of them surviving. As POWs, of course. He didn't expect that he himself would survive. He didn't have either time or inclination to analyse his own feelings, but he was aware of a sense of surprise and relief in not caring all that much. It might be accounted for by his being preoccupied with the hope of getting the boat up there and these two out of her. He had no suicidal tendencies at all, but as the boat's CO his primary duty, now that no other useful purpose could be achieved, was to save their lives. He'd been well taught, and he'd had not only the recent months of X-craft training but a long and quite intensive period of submarine patrols before that, and awareness of the always-present chances of disaster had caused him to give a lot of thought to the control and direction of his own impulses and reactions. The worst fear of all, as so many had discovered throughout the history of war, was fear of fear, horror at the thought of personal failure in the final emergency; he'd always known this and vaguely recognised it as the main ingredient of those nightmares. The dreams might have helped, even, in a sense rehearsed him for this. Whatever the basis of it, anyway, he was all right; the urge to survive was intact but not predominant.

The clanking stopped again.

He saw hope in Gimber's half-smile. The grounds for it were confirmed then, as the battleship's screws began to churn. She'd weighed anchor, and was on the move.

'Nice timing.' Lanchberry glanced at his own watch. 'Half past.'

It was 07.31, to be exact. If there'd been a side-cargo under her she'd be moving clear of it now. So that attempt – costing Brazier's life and their own predicament now – had been futile. But you couldn't have known and it would have been inexcusable not to have tried. He began, 'Quarter of an hour, then—'

There was a crack like an outsize Christmas cracker being pulled, a puff of blue smoke and a stench of scorched metal. From the ballast pump.

'Just what we needed.' Gimber muttered it to himself as he pushed the lever to its neutral position and switched off the power connection to the pump. Lanchberry said, 'I'll get a spare.' Spare fuse, he meant. 'Get the bloody cover off, will you?' He tossed a screwdriver to Gimber.

07.32. Twenty-eight minutes left, in which to fix this pump, get some more weight out of her, then try to beat the odds. Paul felt half inclined to accept the chances as they were now, get on with it. But in principle the earlier decision had been the right one: every ounce out of that tank now was a step in the right direction.

The doubt was whether, even if you got it completely pumped out, there'd be enough difference to her buoyancy – or lack of buoyancy – to make it work. Another reason for accepting delay, in fact, might have been reluctance to put it to the test. Knowing that if it failed there'd be nothing left: whereas until you tried it, you did have that small hope.

Lanchberry was back with his tools and spares. Gimber had unscrewed one bolt, but there were four in the plate that had to be removed. Lanchberry took the screwdriver from him and crouched over the job, hissing between his teeth. The sound of *Scharnhorst*'s propellers was receding. It was a confused sound, and Paul guessed she might have a tug with her, perhaps to push that long bow round against the tidal stream. He realised that his impulse to attempt surfacing a minute ago had been an undisciplined one: with those enemies on the move the obvious thing to do was to wait, and use the time for pumping.

Lanchberry dropped the screwdriver. It clanged off the pump's casing and disappeared under a twisted mass of piping underneath. He grabbed another, took out the last bolt, and prised off the rectangle of metal. Removing the burnt-out fuse now, gingerly muttering 'Bloody hot, can't hardly touch the sod . . .' Scraping the contacts clean, then pushing in the spare fuse. Like a wheel-change in a motor race, every second counting. Slamming the cover-plate back on and fumbling a bolt into one of the holes: his hands were shaking. Gimber tried to help by putting another bolt in at the same time, but he was in Lanchberry's way.

'Christ's sake . . .'

'Sorry.'

'Too many fucking cooks . . .' Second bolt: driving it home, teeth bared in a snarl as if he hated it. But glancing up now: 'Two'll hold her. Switch on?'

Seven thirty-seven. *Scharnhorst* must have rounded the western end of Aaroy; there was no propeller noise to be heard. Gimber had closed the switch: he moved the lever to its 'pump from for'ard' position. The pump started to work on the tank again, a throbbing whine.

Paul said, 'Seven minutes more.'

The pump's fuse blew, exactly as before.

The impulse was to scream. He saw Gimber's face clench – eyes screwed shut, mouth compressed within the beard. Lanchberry on his knees at the pump again, swearing viciously; Paul getting a grip on his own reeling mind . . . 'It'll blow again, Jazz. Let's get her up.'

It was sheer luck, *Scharnhorst* departing when she had. Not that her presence would have stopped them surfacing – or trying to . . . His thoughts were on the mechanics of it now – or rather, the hydrostatics. Picturing and dreading

the waste of high-pressure air, his boat's life-blood pouring
out of her as she struggled to get up. Lanchberry suggested,
'Have a decko at the chart, so we know which way to swim?'

'Sure. Here.'

The mainland coast would be as near as the islet, he
thought. Whichever looked to be the closest, he told them,
would be the one to make for. It might be a swim of a thousand yards or it could be as little as three hundred; and
anyone who succeeded in getting out might be fit to make
it, or might not.

'If they see us when she breaks surface, there'll be boats
out to us. Might not need to do much swimming.'

You could spin coins till the cows came home, with so
many 'ifs' around. But the odds were she would be spotted.
He remembered seeing small craft in the destroyer
anchorage off Leir Botn's south shore, which was only two
miles away, and there'd be a huge disturbance of escaping
air to herald the arrival of the boat herself. He was leaning
over to point out charted features that were relevant. Eight
p.m. was the earliest you'd expect side-charges to go off,
and you'd want to be out of the water before it happened,
but if there was even as much as three hundred yards to
swim you'd end up like the Bomber – like a stunned fish.

And even that was looking too far ahead. If any of them
got as far as facing that problem, they'd have had enormous luck first.

Lanchberry still clutched the chart in both hands, as if
it was a talisman with some power of its own to save his
life. Gimber's eyes, the expression in them, were telling
him, We won't make it. Or that might have been his own
thought, Gimber's intent stare only a search for reassurance. It was the loss of high-pressure air through the holed
main ballast tank that worried him most, the probability
that with 238 feet to wipe off that clockface she'd use it all,
empty the groups of storage bottles long before she came
even near it.

You still had to try. The only alternative would be to sit and do nothing – until eight twenty-five at the very latest. X-12 was saddled with her own inevitable destruction.

'Are we all set?'

They both nodded. Lanchberry tossed the chart aside.

'Group up, full ahead.' Paul flopped into the helmsman's seat, put his hands on the blowing valves for the two main ballast tanks and looked back over his shoulder at Louis Gimber; he saw him make the field switch and start winding the hand-wheel clockwise to put full battery-power on the main motor. Paul turned back, and wrenched the blows open. Thumping rush of air and its vibration quivering the pipe, the sound of it like sandpaper on steel but drowned now in the speeding of the main motor, its thrumming getting louder as revs built up. He was scared for the rudder as he felt her move, the first lurch.

'Main motor's full ahead, grouped up!'

'Hydroplanes hard a-dive, Louis!'

'Dive angle' on the 'planes tilted them so as to force the stern up in order to push the bow downward. There was no chance of the bow turning down, with the for'ard tank blown, but he hoped it might lift her stern up off the rock. The propeller was reasonably well protected, the rudder being abaft it and the rudder's supports like horizontal guards above it and below; but a lot of her weight would be on that rudder now, on its lower pivot. Noise was increasing: air bubbling from the after tank, a grinding of steel on rock back aft where the danger was, the boat shuddering and rattling from the full power of her screw . . .

Seven forty-four.

If the rudder support collapsed, the screw would crumple, smash itself against the rock, about one second later.

She'd lifted by a foot or two, then dropped back; there'd been a clanging impact aft. She hadn't been designed or built to stand this kind of treatment. He was waiting for the next ringing crash from that battered stern – and dreading it, knowing each one could be the last . . . It hadn't come, though. Not yet. He was holding his breath, every nerve and muscle taut . . . Gimber's report came instead, in a triumphant yell – 'Two-twenty feet!'

But how much air had just eighteen feet of climb used up, he wondered. Admittedly it was something, to have her stern off the bottom. Twenty-five degree angle on her, and she was shaking like something palsied. Number one main ballast indicator light flashed on, telling him the tank was blown right out, empty; he shut the blow. Wishing to God he could shut the other one as well. Her entire store of HP air was gushing out through the stern tank now – maybe giving her a little buoyancy aft as it ripped through.

'Two hundred feet!'

Slightly better. Thirty-eight feet off the bottom, and the time, seven forty-five.

'One-eighty!'

Rising faster, gaining some upward impetus. He looked back, and saw Gimber had set the 'planes level now, no 'dive' or 'rise' angle on them. It was probably the best bet – minimal resistance to the water. One hundred and fifty feet . . . But the vibration was increasing – she was finding the struggle too much for her. He had his hand on the blow to number three main ballast: the dilemma was whether if he shut it off now he'd slow or even stop the rise, or whether it would make no difference except to save some air. Then his brain cleared: there'd be no use for HP air after this: either this succeeded or it failed, and if it failed that would be the end. He took his hand off the blow. Gimber reported, yelling to beat the noise, 'Hundred and twenty feet!'

She was half-way to the surface. Ship's head on 050. It was surprising the gyro hadn't toppled, with this much angle on her. Not that it mattered. The wheel moved in small jerks this way and that, from the force of the sea against the rudder, and he left it to its own devices. Time now: seven forty-six. Coming close to the hundred foot mark.

'Jazz!'

Lanchberry hauled himself up the incline and put his head near Paul's.

'When we hit the surface, you open the hatch, push Louis out, then follow him, quick as you can. I'll be right behind you but for God's sake don't wait for me. OK?'

'Aye aye, sir!'

Lanchberry was tops, he thought. Just as the Bomber had been.

'Ninety feet!'

But the flow of air was slowing. He put his hand up to the pipe connection to three main ballast. A minute ago he'd have felt it, the tremble imparted by the rush of air. Now, he felt nothing except the ice-cold wetness of condensation on the pipe. The noise from the stern was also lessening. He glanced round at Lanchberry and Gimber. Lanchberry's face was set hard, his eyes glaring at the depthgauge: Gimber's head turned this way.

'Ninety.'

Hanging. Holding that depth but making no upward progress. If there was any air still flowing it could only be a dribble.

Lanchberry grated, 'Ninety-one.' His hand came up, pointing accusingly at the gauge – as if it had let him down, as he'd known it would. 'Bloody hell . . .'

Here it was: the final and – he'd known it, really – inevitable outcome. Ninety-two feet. She'd begun to slip back, stern-first. Slowly, at the moment, but the fact she was sinking instead of rising, despite the motor full ahead grouped up, spelt 'curtains'. He'd foreseen it in his imagination, envisaged it, so the event itself now was a replay, the opening stages of a dream he'd had before – another of those nightmares but this time it was real.

It wasn't easy to accept – despite having recognised the facts and probabilities and having had quite a long time in which to think about them.

'Ninety-five feet.'

A full stop on all hope was as difficult to hoist in as the concept of limitless space. The two were similar – you felt there had to be something beyond the full stop . . . Another peculiar fallibility of the human psyche was that you could see it in black and white and still try to convince yourself it wasn't true.

Ninety-eight feet. Gimber said, in a perfectly normal tone, 'We've had it, haven't we.' X-12 still trembling, straining to fight the downward drag of her own weight. She'd exhausted her reserves of air and now she was using up all her battery-power. At full grouped up it wouldn't take long. Seven fifty now. In ten minutes the world would end: at least, they'd be on the fjord's rock bottom waiting for it to end, with nothing to do but wait. Might say prayers, he thought. Open the last tins of fruit. Pray, or tell dirty jokes, sing hymns . . .

There'd been a few narrow squeaks before this. In the Med in *Ultra*; and in his first ship, the destroyer *Hoste* – he'd come very close to drowning, that time. You couldn't go on throwing sixes forever. As this thought appeared in the back of his mind he recognised it as one he'd entertained before, but not of himself, always in thinking about his father and his narrow squeaks.

'Hundred feet.'

Gimber's report brought him back to earth. Or rather, to this limbo. 'Limbo' was how it felt, how it was and would be – because this was perdition, no one could ever know the details of X-12's loss. In that sense one might be dying – about to die – on another planet.

He'd seen the wheel move.

Light had flashed on its rim as it jerked to port. It struck him that although she was sinking, and at a steeply stern-down angle, she must still have some forward way on – possibly a significant amount, was travelling forwards at fair speed as well as losing buoyancy and sinking: would as likely as not respond to her helm if he applied some.

His brain did a double-take on that . . . and woke up.

Ship's head was 054. Course to the shallows on the far side of the channel would be roughly 030 . . . He grabbed the wheel, flung it round to put on twenty degrees of port rudder. If there were only a few hundred yards to go to get her into those shallows – if you could drive her on to them – up them – and if she'd hold herself together while you did it, while she crashed along the bottom, after first hitting the bottom at some point and surviving that . . .

How many 'ifs' was that? But she was answering her rudder, swinging to port.

'Hundred and five . . .'

Crash!

She'd struck stern-first – in seventeen and a half fathoms. She was ploughing on – lurching, staggering, stern scraping over rock.

'Hundred feet!'

Lanchberry was clawing his way back up the incline of densely-packed machinery. He'd been knocked down again and he was growling obscenities. Paul had her on a heading of 030: he shouted, with one hand extended for it, 'Chart!' A hundred feet was about seventeen fathoms. And the point was, she'd risen, she'd been at a hundred and five, struck rock and bounced, finished at a hundred. Well, not finished, not as long as there was still some juice in the battery: and that might be the next thing, sound of the motor slowing . . . The wheel was jumping in his one hand: the imminent danger now was to the rudder, which at any minute could be smashed in one of those clanging impacts on rock.

'Ninety feet!'

Lanchberry pushed the chart over Paul's shoulder. Paul told him as she struck again, the whole body of the boat jarring from it but still driving on, 'Get Louis here – both of you—'

All along the coast opposite the island the bottom shelved quite steeply. So if she could be kept moving that way – uphill – as long as the rudder and propeller could stand up to it – which was a toss-up, second by second – and as long as the side-cargo could endure this battering – the cargo and its running fuse, which was another thought altogether . . . Gimber was close behind him, Lanchberry at his left shoulder: he shouted, having to scream to be heard over the racket as she ground over rock – bow falling slightly as her tail-end crashed against some outcrop and flung upwards – 'East side of the channel – I'm steering for the shallows. Dotted part on that coastline – see?'

'Got it!'

'When we're there – if we make it that far – not much water over us. Abandon by DSEA – OK?'

Lanchberry shouted, 'Still take a bloody hour! More – she'll flood slower!'

He shook his head. 'Through the wet-and-dry. Get sets on, breathing from them, hold on tight and I'll knock the clips off, let the door blast open . . .'

'Christ Almighty!'

He yelled at Gimber, 'Depth now?'

He'd craned round to see the gauge. Clinging to over-head pipes. Sixty feet . . . Ten fathoms. You could see that patch on the chart. A hundred yards to travel – if she got that far before breaking apart. Steeper incline here. She felt and sounded like a tin can being used as a football, noise and motion both stunning, really frightening: she'd split clean open any moment . . . 'Get the sets out, Jazz!' He heard Gimber's scream of 'Fifty feet!' There was a period of savage, penetrating grinding from the stern, the length of her keel touched again, lifted, bounced in a crash and an upward spasm that felt as if the keel had fallen off, to leave (his imagination saw it) her belly unprotected, to be opened on the next bounce like a can ripped by the knife . . . He told himself, teeth gritted, that she'd make it. Her bow had swung up again as if she was trying to push her snout up out of water. For which he wouldn't have blamed her . . . Another crashing impact aft rang her like a gong: she rose, came down again stern-first and – this time – crumpled.

He heard steel ripping, somewhere underneath. Lanchberry let himself go sliding and bouncing to the engineroom bulkhead, slowing his progress by grabbing at fittings as gravity took him aft. He slammed the hatch on the crawl-hole to the engine space, and forced the clips over. Gimber shouted, 'Thirty-three feet!'

She was still driving on . . .

But the rudder had gone. The wheel was stuck, immoveable. She could be turned, deflected into deeper water. He thought, Stop her, then . . . He was turning his head to pass the order: Gimber shouted, 'Twenty-eight feet!' And simultaneously he heard the screw go. A noise like throwing a lump of metal into a meat-grinder, and a violent trembling right through her frames. It lasted about five seconds, by which time the propeller could have no blades left on it: the main motor raced, its hum rising to a howl which cut off as Gimber broke the field-switch.

X-12 sliding on over rock: slowing, but still sliding, sounding like a heap of scrap-iron under tow.

She'd stopped. Still with bow-up angle on her, and a list to starboard instead of port. Time: seven fifty-six.

'Depth?'

The swirl and lap of sea were the only external sounds. But there was water-noise inside her too, internal flooding. Gimber told him, 'Twenty-one feet.'

'Check the side-cargo's still there.'

Lanchberry did so. Panting . . . He turned back, nodding. 'Bastard . . .'

But Paul wanted it to be still there. He'd only questioned it because of the list being to starboard instead of to port now – but that would be caused by the incline of the rock shelf she was resting on. He wanted it there, and to have it blow at eight twenty-five, so it would destroy the boat and all her contents, including equipment that was on the secret list. The orders had been to abandon in deep water, if at all, or otherwise to smash up that gear before leaving, and there wasn't time for such attention to detail now.

'DSEA sets on, boys. Quick as you can. Chuck mine over, Jazz.'

The crunch would come with the opening of the W and D door. Even at this depth, opening up to outside pressure at one blast would be like getting yourselves run over by a truck. But if you could survive it – by hanging on like grim life itself and – essentially – preventing your oxygen mask from being knocked off – then you'd only have to crawl into the W and D and climb out through its open hatch, float to the surface.

With the mainland shore only yards away. He talked to the others about it while they were strapping-on their DSEA sets.

'When I see we're all ready, I'll knock the clips off. See you lads up top. Good luck.'

'Same to you, skipper.' Lanchberry said, 'Done a bloody good job, I'd say.'

'Seven-pound hammer, Jazz. For the clips.'

Gimber began, 'Paul . . .'

'Talk later, Louis. Let's get cracking.'

Lanchberry produced the hammer. Seven fifty-eight. Twenty-seven minutes left on the clock on the port side-cargo, and possibly as little as two minutes on others.

Lanchberry was the first to be breathing from his mask. He settled himself against the after bulkhead and raised a thumb towards Paul. Gimber joined him at that end. Paul fixed his own mask over his mouth and nose and opened the distributor valve; the bag inflated, and he was breathing oxygen. They'd all been through the drill a dozen times in the practice tank at Blockhouse; that tank was a hundred feet deep, but you started in a chamber at the bottom of it that was flooded gradually – rather like the flooding-up of the W and D – not just suddenly flung open . . . He braced himself with his back against the bulkhead beside the W and D door – on the side away from the hinge, so the door would open away from him. There was a small space here in which it had been suggested a half-size chart-table might be fitted, and it gave him room in which to press himself back into the corner. He put his left hand up to his face, grasping the mask by its snout where the flexible pipe joined it from the bag. He glanced at the others, saw they were doing the same, and they both signalled 'Ready'. He raised the hammer.

One clip off.

They could be put on or taken off from either side of the door. Normally you'd do it by hand, but with such sea-pressure in the chamber, forcing the door against the clips, you needed some power to shift them. Only one clip held the door now. He took another quick look at Gimber and Lanchberry – saw they were ready, watching him, like Micky Mouses in their masks. He aimed the hammer, swung it down.

The blast flattened him against the bulkhead. He couldn't breathe in or out: he was dizzy, reeling – down on his knees in a roaring, leaping torrent. Struggling up . . . Left hand still pressing the mask to his face. Then the noise was stopping, and his main impression was of the incredible viciousness of the cold: it was like ice hardening around him. There was a numbness already growing through his arms and legs, but as the roar of inflooding sea quietened he was thinking, That wasn't so bad . . .

As long as one didn't freeze.

He thought afterwards that he might have been unconscious for a few seconds. But he was breathing normally by this time and searching for the others, in darkness relieved by a diffuse radiance entering the viewing ports. He'd expected the control-room lights to stay on, even under water, but they must have shorted out. He half walked, half swam towards the after end of the compartment where they'd been when he'd last seen them. It would be eight by now, he guessed, and shut his mind to it, to the possibility of a new, huge eruption hitting them at any moment. There was only one that he knew for sure was coming, and he had twenty minutes to get away from it.

A hand closed on his arm.

He moved his other hand to the arm of whichever of them this was. Then felt the face and head. Sharp stubble surrounded the mask, not Gimber's beard which in water would be like seaweed. A stubbly scalp, too. Identification positive – Jazz Lanchberry. He was pulling at Paul's arm, trying to lead him. Paul allowed it, went that way, and had his hand placed on the body of Louis Gimber. It was limp and there was no mask on the face. Paul made himself breathe lightly and regularly – through the mouth: there was a clip on his nose to hold the nostrils shut – as per the Blockhouse drill book. There was no point in putting Gimber's mask on for him: he was unconscious, his mouth and windpipe would already be full of water, the only way to save his life would be to get him out and give him artificial respiration as soon as possible. If he could be got out. Recollections of old nightmares had to be held at bay: the feeling of tight enclosure, the hoarse, frighteningly loud sound of your own breathing rasping in the mask, the sensation of being trapped in the bubbling laughter of drowned men. He had a grasp on Gimber, sharing him with Lanchberry, both of them moving awkwardly for'ard with the burden between them. It was likely to be difficult getting him through the crawl-hole into the W and D: one of them would have to be in there with him, and there wasn't space for two. It had to be done, though. Old Louis, to be returned to Jane, if only so she could cheat him for the rest of their natural lives. The mind wandered, vaguely recognising the miraculous fact of being alive and the distinct possibility of suddenly becoming dead. Lanchberry slid into the crawl-hole like a sea-snake entering its cave, then lugged Gimber in after him, with Paul helping from outside, or trying to. They managed that part of it all right, but now Jazz would have either to push the body up through the hatch above him, or get up through it and reach down to pull it up behind him. Limp bodies were extremely difficult things to handle in such circumstances and in very confined spaces. Limbs tended to catch on hatch-rims and in other places, and there'd be a danger of getting him stuck in it. Such things had been known to happen in DSEA escapes, or attempted DSEA escapes. Very much on their side in this one, of course, was the extremely shallow water.

The cold was painful, like heavy ice squeezing, gripping, and you couldn't afford to be delayed for very long. Paul adjusted his distributor valve to give himself a better supply of oxygen, and after what seemed like about ten minutes but was more likely sixty seconds he put his head through the hole and saw Lanchberry's legs disappearing upwards. He could see it because of the surface light showing through the open hatch, a light that was temporarily eclipsed as Lanchberry's body filled the hatch on its way through. Paul was in the W and D by then, crouching, keeping his mask out of the way of Lanchberry's feet, looking up and waiting for the exit to be clear. Then he climbed up into the hatchway. As Bomber Brazier had done only about an hour ago, an hour like half a lifetime.

Thinking of Brazier: and that if a side-cargo went up now, when all three of them were in the sea . . .

Please God, ten minutes more?

Having got this far, he was sharply conscious of the urge to live. It had never really left him, but he'd had to subdue it when there'd seemed to be no hope. He was out of the hatch, holding to X-12's casing to stop himself floating straight up. Breathing loudly, and bubbles streaming from each exhalation. But Lanchberry had gone on up with Gimber, and there was no reason to make himself wait. He let go, arched his body in the approved DSEA training tank position, but didn't bother with the apron in only about twenty feet of water.

Daylight exploded in his face. And the sight of a mountainside with snow on it. Treading water, he wrenched the mask off and gasped cold air into his lungs. Some salt water came in with it, and he was choking for a while. Lanchberry was supporting Gimber. The sea lapped a fringe of rocks that lined the shore, very much as he'd expected. In not much more than a minute, the two of them sharing Gimber's weight again, they were among the rocks and wading. They were floundering towards the shore itself, with only a few yards to cover – but then an almost vertical rock climb, which wouldn't be too easy, with Gimber – when Lanchberry stopped.

'Bloody hell . . .'

Gimber's head lolled on a broken neck. It must have happened inside the boat when the rush of water hit them. They'd brought a corpse out with them.

'Leave him here.'

The body would be better hidden here than it could be up on the shore. It would be a disadvantage to have it found too soon. He didn't quite know why, but in fact he realised later that his thoughts must already have been turning towards escape as distinct from surrender to the Germans. This was crazy, of course – since they were both frozen, wet, exhausted, half-drowned, and hadn't been able to bring any of the overland-escape gear with them.

Lanchberry let Gimber's body down into the shallow water, where it would be contained by the surrounding rocks until some Norwegian fisherman, or German soldier, came across it. Except that when the side-cargo exploded . . .

'What's the time?'

Lanchberry had an expensive, waterproof wristwatch of which he was extremely proud. He glanced at it now. 'Eight-ten.' He shook his head. 'I don't believe it. I thought—'

'Hey! Hey!'

On the rock edge above them – a boy. Kid of about twelve, in rough, warm-looking clothes and a woollen cap on his head. Blunt, freckled features and an expression of excitement.

'English?'

Paul nodded, shivering. 'Yes.'

Lanchberry muttered, 'Well, fuck me!'

'Kom!' The boy beckoned. Looking around – across the water, and back at the coast road behind him. There were cottages in sight, Paul found when he got up there, and he remembered the chart had shown some settlements along this coast. The boy had a sack with him, in which he stowed their DSEA sets when they shed them. He seemed to be quite sure of what he was doing. Paul hoping it wouldn't turn out to have been all on the kid's own initiative, that there'd be some adults around as well. In any case this was the best bet, the only chance of warmth and perhaps a hideout. The boy slung the sack over his shoulder; he'd beckoned again, and he was leading them towards the road when from somewhere in the south and some miles away the explosion of a side-cargo came like a clap of thunder: then, right on its heels, two more, overlapping – a triple-barrelled eruption that went on echoing for half a minute from snow-clad mountainsides. The boy laughed, and shouted back over his shoulder, '*Tirpitz*! Boom-boom-boom!' he beckoned again and broke into a trot.

Eight twelve.

17

<hr/>

Trench confirmed, 'Wielding Christofferson, the boy's name was. I suppose you know Paul became godfather to his first child?'

I did know. Paul had gone over there quite often, after the war – combining a visit to those people with some salmon fishing. They'd been wonderful, he told me, those Norwegians. They hid him and Lanchberry until most of the fuss was over, then kitted them up and briefed them and sent them up the mountain with a guide to point them in the right direction. They had luck in another aspect too. What remained of Louis Gimber was found somewhere up on the shore where the surge from the explosion had dumped it, and the Germans for some reason assumed he was the only one who'd got out before X-12 blew herself to pieces. So they weren't looking for any other survivors.

Don Cameron and his crew, and Godfrey Place and his diver, Aitken, were prisoners on board *Tirpitz* when the side-cargoes from X-6 and X-7 went up. Place's other two crewmen drowned, and X-5 was lost, probably destroyed by gunfire outside the nets. The battleship had been warped aside on her cables before the charges went off, but they still lifted her six feet out of water and put her out of action for six months. Then a Fleet Air Arm strike crippled her

again, and finally the RAF sank her with new, much bigger
bombs.

Cameron and Place were both awarded the Victoria
Cross.

Trench pulled a pipe out of his pocket, looked at it, put
it away again. We were almost at the house. He said, 'Paul
was as tough as old boots, and I suppose his ERA must've
been too. And they had a lot of help from the Lapps they
met along the way. It was still a hell of a journey to have
survived.'

Paul's war hadn't ended there, either. He commanded
one of the midget submarines – XE-craft, the improved
version – which acted as markers for the Normandy assault
waves. As we all know, D-day was postponed by twenty-
four hours because of bad weather, so the midgets had to
lie in exposed positions off those beaches for an extra day
and night in near-impossible conditions, and still played
their part to perfection when the time came. After that he
came back to ordinary submarining, was selected for
COQC – Commanding Officers' Qualifying Course – and
had been given his first full-sized command shortly before
the war ended in the Far East.

And was killed, with his wife Lucy, in a crash on the
M1 motorway ten years later.

He'd been married less than a year, and they'd had no
child, so the title went to Hugh, Nick's son by Kate. (Who
remarried, in Australia, not long after the end of the war.)
Hugh took over Mullbergh, the Everard estate in Yorkshire,
and farmed the land – as Paul had done – living in the
Dower House because Mullbergh itself, that old monstrosity,
had been sold long before and turned into a country club.
He still lives and farms there. The Dower House had been,
of course, Nick's stepmother Sarah's home for many years.
She died in 1944. She'd been knocked sideways by the
news of her son Jack's death – as prisoner of war on the
run in Germany – but she had her first stroke when she

heard about Nick. Despite the fact she'd hated him – or had seemed to – since about 1920. In the West Riding of Yorkshire there was less surprise at this than an outsider might have expected. It was no secret in certain houses up there that Sarah's son Jack had been Nick's, not his father's. There had always been scandal around the Everards, and the funny thing was they'd never seemed to appreciate that their neighbours had eyes, ears, tongues and brains.

There was never anyone called 'Jane'. There was a girl of another name, widow of a serving officer in another service, whom Louis Gimber had hoped to marry, but that was not her name, and Gimber's was neither Gimber nor Louis. This last piece of disguise is simply a matter of discretion: 'Louis' was killed in X-12, and he was the only child of parents who are now dead too.

When Paul told me about 'Jane' – quite soon after the end of the war, and years before he met the girl whom he eventually married – he also told me that after his return to England he only saw her once. It was at her wedding to a then serving officer who has since become internationally famous as well as extremely rich. The engagement had been announced before Paul's return via Sweden, apparently. Paul said, I remember, 'By God, she was fast on her feet, that girl!' He laughed for about a minute, then sobered and added, 'Would have been tough on old Louis, though, wouldn't it.'

Strange as it may seem, that marriage is still in being and the family quite numerous.

At the house, I thanked Eileen Trench for her hospitality, the meal she'd given me, and so on.

'Won't you stay and have some tea? Or a drink?'

'You're very kind. But I've a long way to go.'

Trench walked out with me to my car. I thanked him, too, for the help he'd given me, filling in the gaps.

'That's all right.' We shook hands. 'I know you'll do them justice.'

By 'them', of course, he meant the Everards. I've tried to – warts and all. And that's about all there is.

Postscript

——◆——

I should like to thank a one-time shipmate and former
X-craft CO, Commander Matthew Todd, Royal Navy, for
his kindness in providing answers to technical questions.

Only six X-craft took part in Operation Source. X-11 and
X-12 are fictional. Nor was there any convoy PQ 19 or QP
16; the last in that series were PQ 18 and QP 15, after which
the prefix letters for Arctic convoys were changed from
PQ/QP to JW/AR.

Adding fiction to fact has not been allowed to alter the
facts as they are recorded. For instance, Karl Rasmussen was
caught by the Gestapo and tortured, and did kill himself
rather than betray his colleagues Torstein Raaby and Harry
Pettersen. And *Lützow* did leave Altenfjord just before the
X-craft arrived, just as *Scharnhorst* was at anchor off Aaroy
– moving on the forenoon of the attack into the net-cage
vacated by *Lützow*. Donald Cameron saw *Scharnhorst* in that
vulnerable position when he was on his way south to the
Brattholm islands in X-6, but his target was *Tirpitz* and he
was not to be deflected. I knew Cameron, and feel sure he
would not have objected to my using his 'magnificent feat
of arms' – Admiral Sir Max Horton's description of the operation – as a background to this last Everard story.

A.F.

NACHTBOOT

MICHAEL ROBOTHAM BIJ DE BEZIGE BIJ

De verdenking
Het verlies

Michael Robotham

Nachtboot

Vertaling Joost Mulder

2007

DE BEZIGE BIJ

AMSTERDAM

Cargo is een imprint van uitgeverij De Bezige Bij, Amsterdam

Copyright © 2007 Michael Robotham
Copyright Nederlandse vertaling © 2007 Joost Mulder
Eerste druk januari 2007
Tweede druk maart 2007
Oorspronkelijke titel *The Night Ferry*
Oorspronkelijke uitgever Time Warner Books
Omslagontwerp Studio Jan de Boer
Foto auteur Mike Newling
Vormgeving binnenwerk Peter Verwey, Heemstede
Druk Bariet, Ruinen
ISBN 978 90 234 1949 5
NUR 305

www.uitgeverijcargo.nl

Deze is voor Alpheus 'Two Dog' Williams,
een mentor en maatje

BOEK EEN

When the first baby laughed for the first time, the laugh broke into a thousand pieces and they all went skipping about, and that was the beginning of fairies.

Peter Pan, Sir James Barrie

1

Graham Greene heeft ooit gezegd dat een verhaal geen begin en geen einde heeft. De schrijver pikt gewoon een moment uit, een willekeurig punt, en kijkt ofwel vooruit, of terug. Dat moment is nu, een oktobermorgen waarop ik de metalen klep van de brievenbus de ochtendpost hoor aankondigen. Er ligt een envelop op de deurmat. Er zit een stug papieren kaartje in dat niets zegt en tegelijkertijd alles.

Lieve Ali,
Ik zit in de problemen. Ik moet je zien. Kom naar de reünie, alsjeblieft.
Liefs, Cate.

Achttien woorden. Lang genoeg voor de aankondiging van een zelfmoord. Kort genoeg om een verhouding te beëindigen. Ik weet niet waarom Cate me nu schrijft. Ze haat me. Dat zei ze de laatste keer dat we elkaar spraken, acht jaar geleden. Het verleden. Als je me de tijd gunde, zou ik je de maand, de dag en het tijdstip kunnen noemen, maar dat zijn onbelangrijke details.

Het enige wat je hoeft te weten is het jaar: 1997. Het had de zomer moeten worden waarin we afstudeerden, de zomer dat we met onze rugzakken Europa doorkruisten, de zomer dat ik ontmaagd werd door Brian Rusconi en niet door Cates vader. In plaats daarvan was het de zomer waarin ze vertrok en de zomer waarin ik het huis uit ging – een zomer die niet lang genoeg was voor alles wat er gebeurde.

En nu wil ze me weer zien. Soms weet je wanneer een verhaal begint…

2

Als ze me ooit vragen de kalender opnieuw in te delen, hak ik van januari en februari een week af en maak ik oktober langer. Oktober verdient het om veertig dagen te duren, misschien nog wel meer.

Ik hou van deze tijd van het jaar. De toeristen zijn allang vertrokken en de kinderen weer naar school. De televisie zendt geen eindeloze herhalingen meer uit en ik kan weer onder een dekbed slapen. Maar vooral hou ik van de tinteling die in de lucht zit, zonder de pollen van de platanen, zodat ik mijn longen kan openzetten en vrijuit kan hardlopen.

Ik loop elke ochtend hard. Drie circuitjes Victoria Park, in Bethnal Green, ruim anderhalve kilometer per stuk. Op dit moment passeer ik Durward Street in Whitechapel – het Jack the Ripper-gebied. Ik heb ooit een Ripperwandeling gedaan, een met griezelverhalen opgetuigde kroegentocht. Het laatste slachtoffer, Mary Kelly, is me het meest bijgebleven. Ze stierf op 9 november, de dag van mijn verjaardag.

We vergeten vaak hoe klein het gebied was dat Jack afschuimde. Spitalfields, Shoreditch en Whitechapel beslaan samen minder dan tweeënhalve vierkante kilometer, maar in 1880 zaten daar meer dan een miljoen mensen opgepropt in achterbuurten, zonder behoorlijke waterleiding en riolering. Het is er nog steeds overbevolkt en armoedig, maar dan alleen vergeleken met plekken als Hampstead of Chiswick of Holland Park. Armoede is relatief in een rijk land vol mensen die roepen dat ze arm zijn.

Het is zeven jaar geleden dat ik voor het laatst een wedstrijd liep, op een septemberavond in Birmingham, op een verlicht parcours. Ik wilde naar de Olympische Spelen van Sydney, waar maar twee van ons heen konden. Er zat vier honderdste van een seconde tussen de nummer één en de nummer vijf – een halve meter, een hartslag, een gebroken hart.

Ik loop niet langer om te winnen. Ik loop omdat ik het kan en omdat ik snel ben. Snel genoeg om mijn contouren te laten vervagen. Daarom ben ik nu hier, flirtend met de grond terwijl het zweet tussen mijn borsten loopt en mijn T-shirt aan mijn buik kleeft.

Als ik loop worden mijn gedachten helderder. Meestal denk ik aan mijn werk en verbeeld ik me dat er vandaag iemand zal bellen en me mijn oude baan zal teruggeven.

Een jaar geleden heb ik geholpen een ontvoeringszaak op te lossen en een meisje terug te vinden. Een van de ontvoerders smakte me dwars over een muur, waarbij ik mijn ruggengraat brak. Zes operaties en negen maanden fysiotherapie later ben ik weer fit, met meer staal in mijn ruggengraat dan de achterhoede van het Engelse nationale elftal. Helaas weet niemand bij de Metropolitan Police wat ze met me aan moeten. Voor hen ben ik het vijfde wiel aan de wagen.

Terwijl ik langs de speelplaats ren, zie ik een man die op een bank de krant leest. Er is geen kind op het klimrek achter hem en de andere banken baden in het zonlicht. Waarom heeft hij de schaduw opgezocht?

Hij is halverwege de dertig, met overhemd en stropdas, en kijkt niet op als ik langsloop. Hij bestudeert een kruiswoordpuzzel. Wie zit er op dit uur van de ochtend in een park een kruiswoord-puzzel op te lossen? Een man die niet kan slapen. Een man die zit te wachten.

Tot een jaar geleden bestudeerde ik mensen voor mijn beroep. Ik bewaakte diplomaten en bezoekende staatshoofden, bracht hun echtgenotes naar Harrods om te winkelen en zette hun kinderen af bij school. Het is waarschijnlijk de saaiste baan bij de Metropolitan Police, maar ik was er goed in. In mijn vijf jaar bij de Diplomatieke Beschermingseenheid heb ik me nooit laten uit-lokken te schieten en heb ik nooit een van hun afspraken bij de kapper gemist. Ik was als een soldaat in een raketsilo, biddend dat de telefoon niet zal overgaan.

Tijdens mijn tweede rondje door het park zit hij er nog. Zijn suède jack ligt over zijn knieën. Hij heeft sproeten en glad bruin haar, symmetrisch geknipt en links een scheiding. Een leren akte-tas staat pal naast hem.

Een windvlaag rukt de krant uit zijn vingers. Drie stappen en ik ben er als eerste bij. De krant slaat zich om mijn benen.

Heel even aarzelt hij, alsof hij te dicht bij de rand komt. Zijn sproeten maken hem jonger. Zijn ogen ontwijken de mijne. Verlegen trekt hij zijn schouders samen en bedankt me. De voorpagina zit nog steeds om mijn dij geslagen. Heel even kom ik in de verleiding een geintje te maken. Ik zou een grapje kunnen maken dat ik me voel als de fish and chips van morgen.

De bries voelt koel aan in mijn hals. 'Sorry, ik ben nogal bezweet.'

Hij raakt zenuwachtig zijn neus aan, knikt en raakt opnieuw zijn neus aan.

'Loopt u elke dag?' vraagt hij plotseling.

'Als het even kan wel.'

'Hoe lang?'

'Een kilometer of zes.'

Hij heeft een Amerikaans accent. Hij weet niet wat hij nog meer moet zeggen.

'Ik moet weer verder. Ik wil niet te veel afkoelen.'

'Oké. Prima. Een hele fijne dag nog.' Uit de mond van een Amerikaan klinkt het niet eens onoprecht.

Als ik mijn derde rondje maak is de bank verlaten. Ik kijk of ik hem in de straat zie lopen, maar er zijn geen silhouetten. Alles is weer bij het oude.

Verderop in de straat, nog net zichtbaar op de hoek, staat een bestelbusje langs de stoeprand geparkeerd. Dichterbij gekomen zie ik een witte plastic tent over ontbrekende straatstenen staan. Een metalen hek staat opengevouwen rond het gat. Ze zijn vroeg begonnen.

Zulke dingen doe ik: mensen en voertuigen opmerken. Ik zoek naar dingen die afwijken van het gewone: mensen op de verkeerde plaats of met de verkeerde kleren aan, fout geparkeerde auto's, hetzelfde gezicht op verschillende plekken. Ik kan het niet helpen.

Ik maak mijn veters los, haal een sleutel onder de binnenzool vandaan en open mijn voordeur. Mijn buurman, meneer Mordacai, wuift van achter zijn raam. Ik heb hem ooit zijn voornaam gevraagd en hij zei dat het Yo'man moest zijn.

'Hoe dat zo?'

'Omdat mijn jongens me zo noemen. "Yo man, kan ik wat geld krijgen?" "Yo man, kan ik de auto lenen?"'

Zijn lach klonk als noten die op een dak ploffen.

In de keuken tap ik een groot glas water en drink het gulzig leeg. Met één been op de rugleuning van een stoel balancerend rek ik mijn bovenbeenspieren.

Voor de muis die onder mijn koelkast huist is dit het moment om tevoorschijn te komen. Het is een heel ambivalente muis, die nauwelijks de moeite neemt zijn kopje op te tillen om te laten zien dat hij me opmerkt. Het lijkt hem ook weinig te doen dat mijn jongste broer Hari muizenvallen zet. Misschien weet hij dat ik ze onschadelijk maak en de kaas eruit haal zodra Hari niet kijkt.

Eindelijk kijkt de muis naar me op, alsof hij wil klagen over een gebrek aan kruimels. Hij snuift en maakt zich uit de voeten.

In de deuropening verschijnt Hari, blootsvoets en met ontbloot bovenlijf. Hij opent de koelkast, neemt een pak sinaasappelsap en draait de plastic dop eraf. Hij kijkt me aan, denkt even na en pakt een glas uit de kast. Soms denk ik dat hij knapper is dan ik. Hij heeft langere wimpers en dikker haar.

'Ga je vanavond naar de reünie?' vraag ik.

'Neu.'

'Waarom niet?'

'Je wilt toch niet zeggen dat jij wel gaat, hè? Je wilde er nog niet dood worden aangetroffen.'

'Ik heb me bedacht.'

'Hé, heb jij mijn slipje gezien?' klinkt van boven een stem.

Hari kijkt me schaapachtig aan.

'Ik weet nog dat ik hem had. Op de grond ligt niks.'

'Ik dacht dat je al weg was,' fluistert Hari.

'Ik ben wezen hardlopen. Wie is dat?'

'Een oude vriendin.'

'Dan weet je ook hoe ze heet.'

'Cheryl.'

'Cheryl Taylor!' (Een geblondeerd typetje dat in de White Horse achter de bar staat.) 'Die is ouder dan ik.'

'Niet waar.'

'Wat zie je in 's hemelsnaam in haar?'

'Wat doet dat ertoe?'

'Ik ben gewoon benieuwd.'

'Nou, ze heeft pluspunten.'

'Pluspunten?'

'Hele grote.'

'Vind je?'

'Absoluut.'

'En Phoebe Griggs dan?'

'Te klein.'

'Emma Shipley?'

'Die hangen.'

'De mijne?'

'Heel grappig.'

Cheryl komt de trap af. Ik hoor haar in de voorkamer rommelen. 'Ik heb hem,' roept ze.

Ze komt de keuken binnen terwijl ze het elastiek onder haar rok goed doet.

'O, hallo,' piept ze.

'Cheryl, dit is mijn zus, Alisha.'

'Leuk je weer te zien,' zegt ze zonder het te menen.

De stilte lijkt zich uit te breiden. Misschien zeg ik wel nooit meer iets. Uiteindelijk excuseer ik me en ga naar boven om te douchen. Met een beetje geluk is Cheryl verdwenen tegen de tijd dat ik weer beneden kom.

Hari woont sinds twee maanden bij me in huis omdat dat dichter bij de universiteit is. Hij wordt geacht mijn zedelijkheid te bewaken en mee te betalen aan de hypotheek, maar loopt vier weken achter met de huur en gebruikt mijn logeerkamer als peeskamertje.

Mijn benen tintelen. Ik hou van het gevoel van wegvloeiend melkzuur. Ik kijk in de spiegel en doe mijn haar naar achteren. In mijn irissen glinsteren gele vlekjes als goudvissen in een vijver. Geen rimpels. Zwart blijft strak.

Mijn 'pluspunten' zijn zo slecht nog niet. Toen ik nog wedstrij-

14

den liep was ik altijd blij dat ze aan de kleine kant waren en strak onder een sportbeha konden worden weggestopt. Maar nu zou ik best een maatje meer willen hebben, voor een beetje decolleté.

Hari roept iets. 'Hé zus, ik pak even een twintigje uit je portemonnee.'

'Hoezo?'

'Omdat vreemden boos worden als ik in hún portemonnee zit.'

Ontzettend grappig. 'Je bent me nog huur schuldig.'

'Morgen.'

'Dat zei je gisteren ook.' *En eergisteren.*

De voordeur valt dicht. Het huis is stil.

Beneden pak ik de ansichtkaart weer op en hou hem tussen mijn vingertoppen vast. Daarna zet ik hem op tafel tegen de zout- en pepervaatjes en staar er een tijdje naar.

Cate Elliot. Haar naam doet me nog steeds glimlachen. Een van de rare dingen van vriendschap is dat je de tijd die je samen doorbrengt niet kunt wegstrepen tegen de tijd zonder elkaar. Het een wist het ander niet uit en de periodes liggen ook niet op de een of andere onzichtbare weegschaal. Je kunt een paar uren met iemand doorbrengen die je leven kunnen veranderen of een leven lang met iemand samen zijn zonder dat er iets verandert.

We zijn in hetzelfde ziekenhuis geboren en groeiden allebei op in Bethnal Green, in het East End van Londen, hoewel we er de eerste dertien jaar in slaagden elkaar min of meer te ontlopen. Het lot bracht ons samen, als je tenminste in dat soort dingen gelooft.

We werden onafscheidelijk. Bijna telepathisch. We waren twee handen op één buik, pikten bier uit haar vaders koelkast, keken etalages op Kings Road, aten patat met moutazijn op de weg van school naar huis, glipten het huis uit om bands te zien in het Hammersmith Odeon en filmsterren op de rode loper op Leicester Square.

In het jaar na ons examen gingen we naar Frankrijk. Ik reed een bromfiets in de prak, kreeg een waarschuwing vanwege mijn nepidentiteitsbewijs en probeerde voor het eerst hasj. Bij een nachtelijke zwempartij verloor Cate de sleutel van ons hotel, zodat we om twee uur 's nachts langs de plantensteunen omhoog moesten klauteren.

Geen enkele breuk is zo erg als die tussen beste vriendinnen. Verbroken liefdesrelaties doen pijn. Echtscheidingen zijn altijd rommelig. Gebroken gezinnen zijn soms een verbetering. Onze breuk was het allerergst.

En nu, acht jaar later, wil ze me ontmoeten. Ik voel een aangename huivering. Zal ik erop ingaan? Dan voel ik een zeurderige, niet af te schudden angst. Ze zit in de problemen.

Mijn autosleutels liggen in de voorkamer. Als ik ze pak, zie ik vlekken op de glasplaat van de salontafel. Als ik beter kijk zie ik twee duidelijke bilafdrukken en iets wat volgens mij elleboogafdrukken zijn. Ik zou mijn broertje wel kunnen wurgen!

3

Iemand heeft Bloody Mary gemorst op mijn schoenen. Op zich geen probleem, maar het zijn niet de mijne. Ik heb ze te leen, net als dit topje, dat te ruim zit. Mijn ondergoed is wel van mezelf. 'Leen nooit geld of ondergoed,' zegt mijn moeder altijd aan het eind van haar schoon-ondergoedpreek, met beeldende beschrijvingen van verkeersongevallen en ambulanceverplegers die mijn slip losknippen. Geen wonder dat ik eng droom.

Cate is er nog niet. Ik heb geprobeerd de deur in de gaten te houden en me niet in gesprekken te storten.

Schoolreünies zouden verboden moeten worden. Op de uitnodigingen zouden waarschuwingsstickers moeten zitten. Ze komen nooit op het goede moment. Je bent ofwel te jong, ofwel te oud of te dik.

Dit is niet eens een echte schoolreünie. Iemand heeft de practicumlokalen van natuur- en scheikunde van Oaklands in de as gelegd. Een vandaal met een jerrycan benzine in plaats van een kapotte bunsenbrander. Vandaag wordt er een gloednieuwe vleugel geopend, met een of andere onderminister die de honneurs waarneemt.

Het nieuwe gebouw is functioneel en solide, en ontbeert alle charme van zijn Victoriaanse voorganger. De gewelfde plafonds en boogramen zijn vervangen door houtwolcementplaten, tl-buizen en aluminium kozijnen.

De school is versierd met slingers en ballonnen die van de dakspanten omlaaghangen. Aan de voorkant van het podium is een schoolvaandel gedrapeerd.

Er staat een rij bij de spiegel in de meisjestoiletten. Lindsay Saunders buigt zich langs me heen over de wasbak en wrijft lippenstift van haar tanden. Tevredengesteld draait ze zich om en kijkt me taxerend aan.

'Hou eens op met dat Punjabi-prinsessengedoe en ontspan je. Maak lol.'

'Is dit lol?'

Ik heb Lindsays topje aan, het bronskleurige met veterdunne bandjes, waar ik eigenlijk de borsten niet voor heb. Er glijdt een bandje van mijn schouder. Ik trek het weer recht.

'Ik weet dat je doet alsof het je niks kan schelen. Je bent gewoon zenuwachtig over Cate. Waar is ze?'

'Weet ik niet.'

Lindsay werkt haar lippenstift bij en trekt haar jurk glad. Ze heeft wekenlang naar de reünie uitgekeken, vanwege Rocco Manspiezer. Op school had ze zes jaar lang een oogje op hem, alleen niet de moed het hem te vertellen.

'Waarom denk je dat je hem dit keer wél krijgt?'

'Ik heb echt geen tweehonderd pond aan deze jurk gespendeerd en me in deze rotschoenen gewurmd om me weer door hem te laten negeren.'

In tegenstelling tot Lindsay heb ik geen zin om op te trekken met mensen die ik twaalf jaar lang heb gemeden. Ik hoef niet te horen hoeveel geld ze verdienen of hoe groot hun huis is, of foto's te bekijken van kinderen met namen als shampoomerken.

Dat heb je met schoolreünies: mensen komen alleen om hun leven te vergelijken met dat van anderen en de mislukkingen te zien. Ze willen weten wie van de schoonheidskoninginnen vijf-endertig kilo is aangekomen en wie haar man er met zijn secretaresse vandoor heeft zien gaan, en horen welke leraar gepakt is toen hij stiekem foto's maakte in de kleedkamers.

'Kom op, hé, ben jij niet nieuwsgierig?' vraagt Lindsay.

'Natuurlijk ben ik nieuwsgierig. Ik heb er de pest over in dat ik nieuwsgierig ben. Ik wou dat ik onzichtbaar was.'

'Wees nou geen spelbreker.' Ze haalt haar vinger langs mijn wenkbrauwen.

'Heb je Annabelle Trunzo gezien? God, wat een jurk! En dan dat haar!'

'Rocco heeft helemáál geen haar.'

'Ah, maar hij ziet er nog strak uit.'

'Is hij getrouwd?'

'Hou je mond.'

'Nou, ik vind dat je dat toch op z'n minst te weten moet komen voordat jullie een wip maken.'

Ze grijnst veelbetekenend. 'Ik vraag het na afloop wel.'

Lindsay doet alsof ze een echte mannenverslindster is, maar ik weet dat ze niet echt zo'n jachtgodin is. Dat hou ik mezelf de hele tijd voor, maar ik zou haar niet met mijn broers laten uitgaan.

Weer terug in de hal zijn de lichten gedimd en staat de muziek harder. Spandau Ballet is vervangen door andere hits uit de jaren tachtig. De vrouwen dragen een mix van cocktailjurkjes en sari's. Anderen, in leren jacks en designerjeans, doen alsof het ze allemaal niks kan schelen.

Op Oaklands had je altijd stammen. De blanken vormden een minderheid. De meeste studenten waren Bangla's, daardoorheen een handjevol Paki's en Indiërs.

Ik was een 'curry', een 'yindoo', een olifantendompteur. Indiaas bruin, als je het wilt weten. Als onderscheidend kenmerk kwam daar op Oaklands niets ook maar bij in de buurt. Mijn zwarte haar niet, mijn beugel of mijn dunne benen niet, het feit dat ik op mijn zevende geen ziekte van Pfeiffer had, of dat ik kon rennen als de wind niet. Al het andere verbleekte bij mijn huidskleur en mijn afkomst als sikh.

Het is niet waar dat alle sikhs Singh heten. En we dragen ook niet allemaal een krom mes op onze borst (hoewel dat imago in het East End wel handig is).

Zelfs nu klitten de Bangla's bij elkaar. Mensen zitten naast dezelfde mensen als destijds op school. Ondanks alles wat er in de tussenliggende jaren is gebeurd zijn de kernpunten van onze persoonlijkheden onaangetast. Al onze zwakke en sterke punten zijn hetzelfde gebleven.

Aan de andere kant van de zaal zie ik Cate binnenkomen. Ze ziet er bleek en opvallend uit; heeft een kort, duur kapsel en draagt goedkope sexy schoenen. Met haar lange, lichte kaki rok en zijden bloes ziet ze er elegant en – inderdaad – zwanger uit. Haar handen strijken over haar keurige, compacte zwelling. Het is meer dan een zwelling. Een strandbal. Ze loopt bijna op het einde.

Ik wil niet dat ze me ziet staren. Ik draai me om.

'Alisha?'

'Natuurlijk. Wie anders?' Ik draai me abrupt om en zet een half-gare glimlach op.

Cate buigt zich voorover en kust mijn wang. Ik hou mijn ogen open. Zij ook. We staren elkaar aan. Verbaasd. Ze ruikt naar kindertijd.

Bij haar ooghoeken heeft ze dunne lijntjes. Ik heb ze niet zien ontstaan. Het kleine litteken op haar linkerslaap, net onder haar haarlijn, dat herinner ik me nog wel.

We zijn even oud, negenentwintig, en hebben hetzelfde figuur, op de zwelling na. Ik heb een donkerder huid en verborgen diepten (zoals alle brunettes), maar ik kan verklaren dat ik er nooit zo goed zal uitzien als Cate. Ze heeft geleerd – nee, dat klinkt te bestudeerd – ze is geboren met het vermogen mannen haar te laten bewonderen. Ik ken het geheim niet. Een oogbeweging, een wending van het hoofd, een stembuiging of een aanraking van de arm zorgt voor een moment, een illusie waar alle mannen, homo of niet, oud of jong, voor vallen.

Ik zie de mensen naar haar kijken. Ik betwijfel of ze het überhaupt beseft.

'Hoe gaat het met je?'

'Prima,' zeg ik iets te snel, en ik begin opnieuw. 'Het gaat goed.'

'Is dat alles?'

Ik probeer te lachen. 'Maar nou jij, jij bent zwanger.'

'Ja.'

'Wanneer ben je uitgerekend?'

'Over vier weken.'

'Gefeliciteerd.'

'Dank je.'

De vragen en antwoorden komen te abrupt en te zakelijk. Praten is nog nooit zo moeizaam geweest als nu, althans niet met Cate. Ze kijkt nerveus over mijn schouder, alsof ze bang is dat we afgeluisterd kunnen worden.

'Was jij niet getrouwd met...?'

'Felix Beaumont. Hij staat daar.'

Ik volg haar blik in de richting van een lange, zwaargebouwde figuur in vrijetijdsbroek en een los wit overhemd. Felix zat niet op Oaklands en zijn echte naam is Buczkowski, niet Beaumont. Zijn vader was een Poolse winkelier die een elektrawinkel dreef op Tottenham Court Road.

En nu is hij diep in gesprek met Annabelle Trunzo, die een niemendalletje aanheeft dat door haar borsten omhoog wordt gehouden. Als ze een keer flink uitademt ligt het om haar enkels.

'Weet je wat ik vroeger het ergste vond van avonden zoals deze?' zegt Cate. 'Dat iemand die er onberispelijk uitziet je dan vertelt hoe ze de hele dag bezig is geweest de kinderen naar ballet of voetbal of cricket te brengen. En dan komt de voor de hand liggende vraag: "Heb jij kinderen?" En dan zeg ik: "Nee, geen kinderen." En dan grapt zij: "Waarom neem je er niet eentje van mij?" God, wat heb ik daar een hekel aan.'

'Nou, daar hoef jij anders niet meer bang voor te zijn.'

'Nee.'

Ze pakt een glas wijn van een voorbijkomend dienblad. Ze kijkt opnieuw om zich heen: er niet helemaal bij, zo te zien.

'Waarom ging het mis tussen ons? Het moet aan mij hebben gelegen.'

'Je weet het vast nog wel,' zeg ik.

'Het doet er niet meer toe. Tussen haakjes, ik wil jou vragen als peettante.'

'Ik ben niet eens christelijk.'

'O, dat maakt niet uit.'

Ze ontwijkt datgene waar ze eigenlijk over wil praten.

'Zeg wat er aan hand is.'

Ze aarzelt. 'Dit keer ben ik te ver gegaan, Ali. Ik heb alles op het spel gezet.'

Terwijl ik haar arm pak, leid ik haar naar een rustiger hoekje. Er wordt gedanst. De muziek staat te hard. Cate brengt haar mond dicht naar mijn oor. 'Je moet me helpen. Zeg dat je me zult helpen...'

'Natuurlijk.'

Ze onderdrukt een snik, alsof ze erop bijt. 'Ze willen mijn baby afpakken. Dat mag niet gebeuren. Jij moet ze tegenhouden...'

Een hand raakt haar schouder en ze veert op, geschrokken.

'Hallo, schitterende zwangere dame, wie mag dit zijn?'

Cate doet een stap achteruit. 'Niemand. Gewoon een oude vriendin.' In haar binnenste gebeurt iets. Ze wil ontsnappen.

Felix Beaumont heeft volmaakte tanden. Mijn moeder heeft iets met gebitten, het valt haar als eerste op bij mensen.

'Jou ken ik,' zegt hij. 'Jij kwam na mij.'

'Op school?'

'Nee, aan de bar.'

Hij lacht en trekt een geamuseerd-nieuwsgierig gezicht.

Cate is nog verder weg gaan staan. Mijn ogen ontmoeten die van haar. Met een nauwelijks waarneembaar hoofdschudden zegt ze me dat ik haar met rust moet laten. Ik voel een golf van tederheid voor haar. Ze gebaart met haar lege glas. 'Ik haal er nog eentje.'

'Kalm aan met dat spul, liefje. Je bent niet alleen.' Hij strijkt over haar zwelling.

'De laatste.'

Felix kijkt haar na met een mengeling van droefheid en verlangen. Na een poos draait hij zich weer naar mij.

'Is het Miss of Mrs.?'

'Pardon?'

'Ben je getrouwd?'

'Ik ben alleen.'

'Dat verklaart het.'

'Wat?'

'Degenen met kinderen hebben foto's bij zich. Degenen zonder dragen leukere kleren en hebben minder rimpels.'

Is dat als compliment bedoeld?

Er staan lachrimpels rond zijn ogen. Hij beweegt zich als een beer, van de ene op de andere voet hobbelend.

'Wat doe je eigenlijk, Alisha?'

'Ik zit de hele dag thuis met mijn pantoffels aan op Channel 4 naar herhalingen van soaps en oude films te kijken.'

Hij begrijpt het niet.

'Ik ben met ziekteverlof van de Metropolitan Police.'

'Wat is er gebeurd?'

'Ik heb mijn rug gebroken. Iemand drapeerde me over een muur.'

Hij krimpt ineen. Mijn ogen dwalen langs hem heen.

'Ze komt zo terug,' zegt hij, mijn gedachten lezend. 'Ze laat me nooit lang alleen met een knappe vrouw.'

'Je zult wel in de wolken zijn, over de baby.'

De gladde holte onder zijn adamsappel golft heen en weer terwijl hij slikt. 'Het is onze wonderbaby. We hebben het zo lang geprobeerd.'

Op de dansvloer gaat iemand voorop in een congadans die zich tussen de tafels door slingert. Gopal Dhir pakt me bij mijn middel en schudt mijn heupen heen en weer. Iemand anders trekt Felix een ander deel van de stoet in en we bewegen van elkaar weg.

Gopal tettert in mijn oor: 'Nee maar, Alisha Barba! Loop je nog steeds hard?'

'Alleen voor de lol.'

'Ik had altijd een oogje op je, maar je was veel te snel voor mij.' Over zijn schouder schreeuwt hij naar iemand anders. 'Hé, Rao. Kijk eens wie we hier hebben! Alisha Barba. Heb ik niet altijd gezegd dat ze knap was?'

Rao kan hem onmogelijk boven de muziek uit horen, maar knikt verwoed en maakt een hupje.

Ik probeer mezelf los te rukken.

'Waarom stop je?'

'Ik weiger de conga te doen als er niet iemand uit Trinidad aanwezig is.'

Teleurgesteld laat hij me los en schudt zijn hoofd. Iemand anders probeert me vast te pakken, maar ik huppel weg.

De menigte bij de bar is uitgedund. Cate zie ik niet. Buiten zitten mensen op de trap, anderen verspreiden zich over de binnenplaats. Aan de andere kant van het schoolplein zie ik de beroemde eikenboom, bijna zilverkleurig in het lamplicht. Iemand heeft kippengaas rond de stam gespannen om klimmende kinderen tegen te houden. In mijn laatste jaar viel een van de Bangla's eruit en brak zijn arm, een jochie dat Paakhi heette, Bengali voor 'vogel'. Wat zeggen namen toch weinig.

Het nieuwe practicumgebouw staat aan de overkant van de binnenplaats. Verlaten. Ik steek het schoolplein over, duw een deur open en stap een lange gang in met aan de linkerkant klaslokalen. Ik doe een paar passen en kijk naar binnen. Chromen kranen en gebogen buizen vangen het zwakke schijnsel op dat door de ramen valt.

Als mijn ogen zich aan het donker hebben aangepast zie ik iemand bewegen. Een vrouw met haar rok tot boven haar middel gestroopt staat over een tafel gebogen met een man tussen haar benen.

Terwijl ik achteruitdeins in de richting van de deur voel ik dat er nog iemand kijkt. Ik hoef mijn blik nauwelijks te verplaatsen of we zien elkaar.

Hij fluistert. 'Jij houdt wel van kijken hè, yindoo?'

Ik hervind mijn adem. Een halve adem. Paul Donavon duwt zijn gezicht haast in het mijne. De jaren hebben zijn haar dunner doen worden en zijn wangen boller, maar hij heeft nog dezelfde ogen. Verbazingwekkend hoe ik hem na al die tijd nog net zo intens kan haten.

Zelfs in het schemerlicht zie ik het getatoeëerde kruis in zijn nek. Hij snuffelt aan mijn haar. 'Waar is Cate?'

'Laat haar met rust,' zeg ik iets te hard. Vanuit het duister klinkt gevloek. Lindsay en haar metgezel maken zich van elkaar los. Rocco danst op één been, in een poging zijn broek op te hijsen. Aan de andere kant van de gang gaat een deur open en valt er licht naar buiten terwijl Donavon verdwijnt.

'Jezus, Ali, ik schrik me het leplazarus,' zegt Lindsay terwijl ze haar jurk omlaagtrekt.

'Sorry.'

'Wie was die ander?'

'Niemand. Het spijt me echt. Ga maar gewoon door.'

'Ik denk dat het moment wel voorbij is.'

Rocco loopt al de gang af.

'De hartelijke groeten aan je vrouw,' roept ze hem na.

Ik moet Cate zien te vinden. Ze moet weten dat Donavon er ook is. En ik wil dat ze uitlegt wat ze bedoelde. Wie wil haar baby afpakken?

Ik kijk in de zaal en op de binnenplaats. Ze is nergens te zien. Misschien is ze al weg. Een gek idee dat ik haar zo kort na haar weer te hebben ontmoet alweer kwijtraak.

Ik loop naar de schoolhekken. Aan beide kanten van de weg staan auto's geparkeerd. Overal op de stoep staan mensen. Aan de overkant vang ik een glimp op van Cate en Felix. Ze staat met iemand te praten. Donavon. Ze houdt een hand op zijn arm.

Cate kijkt op en wuift. Ik loop haar kant op, maar ze gebaart me te wachten. Donavon draait zich om. Felix en Cate lopen tussen de geparkeerde auto's door.

Ergens achter hen hoor ik Donavon roepen. Daarna klinkt het geknepen hoge geluid van rubber en asfalt. De wielen van een auto zijn geblokkeerd en piepen. Hoofden draaien zich om alsof ze van een palletje losschieten.

Felix verdwijnt onder de wielen, die bijna zonder te bonken over zijn hoofd omhoog- en weer omlaaggaan. Op hetzelfde moment buigt Cate dubbel over de motorkap en veert weer terug. Midden in de lucht draait ze haar hoofd, dat ineens door de voorruit wordt gegrepen. Als in een vertraagde film tuimelt ze door de lucht, als een trapezeartiest die klaar is om opgevangen te worden. Maar er staat niemand klaar met witbepoederde handen.

In plaats daarvan slaat ze tegen een andere auto, die van de andere kant komt. De bestuurder remt en zwenkt. Cate rolt naar voren en komt met een gestrekte arm en één been onder zich gedraaid op haar rug neer.

Als in een omgekeerde explosie worden mensen naar de klap gezogen. Ze klauteren uit auto's en komen uit deuropeningen gesneld. Donavon reageert sneller dan de meesten en is als eerste bij Cate. Ik laat me naast hem op mijn knieën vallen.

In een moment van aangehouden stilte komen wij drieën weer tot elkaar. Ze ligt op de weg. Uit haar neus sijpelt bloed van een diepe, zacht satijnen zwartheid. Haar lippen, iets van elkaar, borrelen en schuimen. Ze heeft een prachtige mond.

Ik leg mijn arm om haar hoofd. Wat is er met haar schoen gebeurd? Ze heeft er nog maar één. Ineens ben ik gefixeerd op haar ontbrekende schoen en vraag de mensen om me heen ernaar. Ik moet hem vinden. Zwart, met een halfopen hiel. Haar rok is opgekropen. Ze draagt een zwangerschapsonderbroek om haar zwelling te bedekken.

Een jonge man stapt beleefd naar voren. 'Ik heb het alarmnummer gebeld.'

Zijn vriendin ziet eruit of ze bijna moet overgeven.

Donavon trekt Cates rok goed. 'Niet haar hoofd verplaatsen. Ze moet in een korset.' Hij draait zich naar de omstanders. 'Er moeten dekens komen en een arts.'

'Is ze dood?' vraagt iemand.

'Ken je haar?' vraagt iemand anders.

'Ze is zwanger!' roept iemand anders uit.

Cate heeft haar ogen open. Ik zie mezelf erin weerspiegeld. Een stevig gebouwde man met een grijze paardenstaart buigt zich over ons heen. Hij heeft een Iers accent.

'Ze stapten zomaar de weg op. Ik heb ze niet gezien. Ik zweer het.'

Cates hele lichaam verstijft en haar ogen verwijden zich. Ondanks het bloed in haar mond probeert ze iets te roepen en haar hoofd schudt heen en weer.

25

Donavon springt op en pakt het shirt van de bestuurder beet. 'Je had kunnen stoppen, klootzak!'

'Ik heb ze niet gezien.'

'Leugenaar!' Zijn stem is schor van haat. 'Je hebt ze gewoon aangereden.'

De bestuurder kijkt zenuwachtig langs de menigte. 'Ik weet niet waar hij het over heeft. Het was een ongeluk. Ik zweer het. Hij raaskalt.'

'Je zag ze.'

'Pas toen het al te laat was.'

Hij duwt Donavon opzij. Er springen knopen los en zijn overhemd vliegt open. De tatoeage op zijn borst verbeeldt Christus en de kruisiging.

Mensen zijn uit de reünie weggelopen om te zien wat het tumult te betekenen heeft. Sommigen van hen schreeuwen en proberen de straat vrij te maken. Ik hoor de sirenes.

Een ambulanceverpleegkundige duwt de menigte uiteen. Mijn vingers zijn glibberig en warm. Het voelt alsof ik Cates hoofd bij elkaar hou. Er komen nog twee ploegen. De verpleegkundigen groeperen zich. Ik ken de routine: is er vuur, zijn er brandstoflekken, zijn er gebroken elektriciteitskabels? Ze zorgen eerst voor hun eigen veiligheid.

Ik kijk of ik Felix zie. Onder de achteras van de auto zit een donkere gestalte klem. Bewegingloos.

Een verpleger kruipt onder de wielkast. 'Deze is er geweest,' roept hij.

Een andere steekt zijn handen onder de mijne en neemt Cates hoofd over. Twee van hen zijn met haar bezig.

'Luchtwegen geblokkeerd. Ik ga intuberen.'

Hij stopt een gebogen plastic slang in haar mond en zuigt bloed weg.

'Honderdzeventig over negentig. Rechterpupil is verwijd.'

'Ze heeft lage bloeddruk.'

'Leg een kraag aan.'

Iemand zegt iets in een portofoon. 'We hebben een ernstig hoofdtrauma en inwendige bloedingen.'

'Ze is zwanger,' hoor ik mezelf zeggen. Ik weet niet of ze me horen.

'Bloeddruk loopt op. Lage pols.'

'Ze bloedt intracraniaal.'

'Laten we haar erin leggen.'

'Ze heeft vocht nodig.'

Ze leggen de wervelplank naast haar, rollen Cate behoedzaam op haar zij en tillen haar op een brancard.

'Ze is zwanger,' zeg ik nog eens.

'Bent u een bekende van haar?'

'Ja.'

'Er kan één iemand mee. U kunt voorin zitten.' Hij drukt op een rubberen zak waarmee hij lucht in haar longen perst. 'We moeten haar naam, adres en geboortedatum hebben – is ze allergisch voor bepaalde medicijnen?'

'Weet ik niet.'

'Wanneer is ze uitgerekend?'

'Over vier weken.'

De brancard staat in de ziekenwagen. De verplegers stappen in. Een medisch technicus helpt me in de passagiersstoel. De deur valt dicht. We rijden. Door het raampje zie ik de menigte ons aanstaren. Waar komen die zo gauw vandaan? Donavon zit in de goot, verdwaasd kijkend. Ik wil dat hij me ziet. Ik wil hem bedanken.

De verplegers zijn nog steeds bezig met Cate. Een van hen praat in een portofoon, met woorden als 'bradycardisch' en 'intracraniale druk'. Een hartmonitor piept een hakkelende boodschap.

'Gaat ze het redden?'

Niemand zegt iets.

'En de baby?'

Hij knoopt haar bloes los. 'Ik geef twee eenheden.'

'Nee, wacht. Ik voel geen pols meer.'

De monitor geeft een vlakke lijn te zien.

'Ze is asystolisch.'

'Ik ga over op hartmassage.'

Hij scheurt haar bloes open, zodat haar beha en bovenlijf zichtbaar worden.

De verplegers vallen stil en kijken elkaar aan. Eén enkele blik, woordloos maar alleszeggend. Op Cates buik zit een groot stuk schuimrubber gebonden, bijgesneden zodat het over haar buik past. De verpleger trekt het los. Cate is niet zwanger meer.

Terwijl hij met korte bewegingen hard op haar borst drukt, telt hij de compressies. De hartmonitor neemt het op tegen de sirene.

'Geen respons.'

'Misschien moeten we meer kracht geven.'

'Eén ampul adrenaline.' Hij bijt het kapje eraf en injecteert de inhoud in haar nek.

De minuten daarna gaan in een waas van knipperende lichten en gespreksflarden voorbij. Ik weet dat ze haar aan het kwijtraken zijn. Ik denk dat ik dat al die tijd al wist. De verwijde pupillen, de bloedingen in haar hoofd – de klassieke tekenen van hersentrauma. Cate is op te veel plaatsen beschadigd.

De lijn op de monitor stijgt en daalt, en valt weer terug tot een vlakke lijn. Ze tellen het opzwellen af tegen de borstcompressies. Eén keer knijpen op vijf compressies.

'Tommy.'

'Ja?'

'Ik stop de borstcompressies.'

'Waarom?'

'Omdat haar hersenen uit haar hoofd worden geperst.'

Achter haar rechteroor is haar schedel gebroken.

'Ga door.'

'Maar…'

'Gewoon doorgaan.'

Er verstrijkt een halve minuut. Wat ze ook proberen, het hart reageert niet.

'Wat nu?'

'Ik ga tot brekens toe doordrukken.'

Er spoelt een golf van misselijkheid mijn mond binnen. Van de rest van de rit en de aankomst bij het ziekenhuis weet ik niets meer. Geen deuren die dichtslaan of witte jassen die zich door gangen spoeden. In plaats daarvan lijkt alles te vertragen.

Het gebouw slokt Cate in haar geheel op, niet langer heel, maar beschadigd.

Ziekenhuizen, ik haat ze. De lucht, de sfeer van onzekerheid, de witheid. Witte muren, witte lakens, witte kleding. Het enige wat niet wit is, zijn het bloed en de Afro-Caribische verpleegsters.

Ik sta nog steeds bij de ambulance. De verplegers komen terug en dweilen het bloed op.

'Gaat het?' vraagt een van hen. Hij heeft het stuk schuimrubber nog in zijn hand. De bungelende linten zien eruit als de poten van een vreemd zeedier.

Hij geeft me een natgemaakte papieren handdoek. 'Misschien heb je hier iets aan.'

Ik heb bloed op mijn handen, bloed over mijn hele broek.

'Er zit nog wat.' Hij wijst naar mijn wang. Ik veeg de verkeerde af.

'Kom maar, mag ik even?'

Hij neemt de handdoek, pakt mijn kin en veegt mijn wang af. 'Zo.'

'Dank je.'

Hij wil iets zeggen. 'Is ze een goede vriendin van je?'

'We zaten op dezelfde school.'

Hij knikt. 'Waarom zou ze… ik bedoel, waarom deed ze alsof ze zwanger was?'

Ik kijk langs hem heen, niet in staat te antwoorden. Het waarom ontgaat me, ik begrijp er niets van. Ze wilde me zien. Ze zei dat ze haar baby wilden afpakken. Welke baby?

'Is ze… gaat ze het redden?'

Het is zijn beurt om niets te zeggen. De droefheid in zijn ogen is zorgvuldig gedoseerd, omdat meer mensen er nog een beroep op zullen doen.

Er begint een slang te spuiten. Roze water kringelt de afvoer in. De verpleger geeft me de prothese en ik voel iets in me knappen. Ooit dacht ik Cate voorgoed kwijt te zijn. Misschien is het dit keer werkelijk zover.

4

Wachtkamers in ziekenhuizen zijn nutteloze, hulpeloze plekken, vol gefluister en smeekbeden. Iedereen mijdt mijn blik. Misschien komt het door het bloed op mijn kleren. In de toiletten heb ik geprobeerd Lindsays topje schoon te krijgen door het onder de kraan met handzeep te schrobben. Ik heb de vlek alleen maar groter gemaakt.

Artsen en verpleegsters lopen in en uit, zonder een moment van rust. Een patiënt op een rijdende brancard lijkt net een vlieg in een web van slangen en draden. De huid rond zijn mond is gerimpeld en droog.

Ik heb nooit echt over de dood nagedacht. Zelfs toen ik in het ziekenhuis lag met pennen die mijn ruggengraat bij elkaar hielden kwam het niet in me op. Ik heb oog in oog met verdachten gestaan, auto's achtervolgd, ben door deuren gebeukt en verlaten gebouwen binnengelopen, maar heb nooit gedacht dat ik zou kunnen sterven. Misschien is dat wel een van de voordelen als je niet veel waarde aan jezelf hecht.

Een verpleegster heeft Cates familiegegevens genoteerd. Van Felix heb ik geen gegevens. Misschien leeft zijn moeder nog. Niemand kan me iets vertellen, behalve dat Cate op de operatietafel ligt. De verpleegsters zijn onstuitbaar positief. De artsen zijn voorzichtiger. Zij moeten de waarheid onder ogen zien – de realiteit van wat ze wel en niet kunnen repareren.

Op een doodgewone avond, in een rustige straat, wordt een echtpaar door een auto aangereden. De een is dood, de ander heeft gruwelijke verwondingen. Wat is er met Cates andere schoen gebeurd? Wat is er van haar baby geworden?

Er komt een politieagent die me ondervraagt. Hij is van mijn leeftijd en draagt een uniform waaraan alles gepoetst en geperst is. Ik voel me ongemakkelijk over mijn verschijning.

Hij heeft een lijst met vragen: wat, waar, wanneer en waarom. Ik probeer me alles wat is voorgevallen te herinneren. De auto kwam uit het niets. Donavon schreeuwde.

'Dus u denkt dat het een ongeluk was?'

'Ik weet het niet.'

In gedachten hoor ik Donovan nog tegen de bestuurder zeggen dat hij ze met opzet heeft geraakt. De agent geeft me zijn kaartje. 'Als er nog dingen naar boven komen, bel me dan.'

Door de klapdeuren zie ik Cates familie aankomen. Haar vader, haar moeder in een rolstoel en haar oudere broer Jarrod.

Barnaby Elliot spreekt met stemverheffing. 'Hoe bedoelt u dat er geen baby is? Mijn dochter is zwanger.'

'Wat zeggen ze, Barnaby?' vraagt zijn vrouw terwijl ze hem aan zijn mouw trekt.

'Ze zeggen dat ze niet in verwachting was.'

'Dan kan het onze Cate niet zijn. Ze hebben de verkeerde voor zich.'

De arts valt hen in de rede. 'Als u hier wacht, komt er iemand met u praten.'

Mevrouw Elliot wordt hysterisch. 'Betekent dit dat ze de baby heeft verloren?'

'Ze is nooit zwanger geweest. Er was helemaal geen baby.'

Jarrod probeert ertussen te komen. 'Sorry, maar er moet sprake zijn van een misverstand. Cate was over vier weken uitgerekend.'

'Ik wil mijn dochter zien,' eist Barnaby. 'Ik wil haar nú zien.'

Jarrod is drie jaar ouder dan Cate. Vreemd hoe weinig ik me van hem herinner. Hij hield duiven en droeg tot zijn twintigste een beugel. Ik meen dat hij in Schotland naar de universiteit ging en later een baan vond in de City.

Van Cate daarentegen is niets vervaagd, op afstand geraakt of kleiner geworden. Ik herinner me nog steeds de eerste keer dat ik haar zag. Ze zat op een bank buiten de hekken van Oaklands, droeg witte sokken, een korte grijze plooirok en Doc Martens. Haar ogen, die onwaarschijnlijk groot leken, omringd door dikke mascara. Haar tegengekamde haren hadden alle kleuren van de regenboog.

Hoewel ze nieuw was op school, kende Cate binnen een paar dagen meer kinderen en had ze meer vrienden dan ik. Ze was altijd in beweging, sloeg haar armen om mensen heen, tikte met haar voet of zat met haar been te wippen.

Haar vader was vastgoedontwikkelaar, vertelde ze. Het klonk interessant, zoals een dubbele achternaam status geeft. 'Treinmachinist', wat mijn vader was, klonk in elk geval minder indrukwekkend en verschafte ook niet hetzelfde aanzien.

Barnaby Elliot droeg donkere pakken, gesteven witte overhemden en stropdassen van de een of andere club. Hij stond twee keer kandidaat voor de Tory's in Bethnal Green en slaagde er beide keren in een ogenschijnlijke onbereikbare zetel om te zetten in een gegarandeerde zetel voor de Labourpartij.

Ik vermoed dat de kiezersgunst de enige reden was om Cate naar Oaklands te sturen. Hij deed zich graag voor als iemand die zich een weg omhoog had gevochten, met het zwart nog onder zijn nagels en smeerolie in zijn aderen.

In werkelijkheid hadden de Elliots hun dochter volgens mij liever naar een particuliere school laten gaan, een anglicaanse en alleen voor meisjes, in plaats van naar Oaklands. Vooral mevrouw Elliot beschouwde onze school als een vreemd gebied dat ze liever niet bezocht.

Het duurde bijna een jaar voordat Cate en ik met elkaar spraken. Ze was het coolste, meest begerenswaardige meisje van de hele school en toch had ze een achteloze, bijna ongewilde schoonheid. Andere meisjes hingen om haar heen, kletsend en lachend, hengelend naar haar goedkeuring, wat zij niet scheen op te merken.

Ze sprak als iemand uit een tienerfilm, goed gebekt en vrijpostig. Ik weet dat tieners geacht worden zo te praten, maar Cate was de eerste die ik het ook echt hoorde doen. En ze was de enige die ik kende die haar emoties kon indampen tot druppels pure liefde, woede, angst of blijdschap.

Ik kwam van het Isle of Dogs, iets oostelijker, en ging naar Oaklands omdat mijn ouders me 'buiten het gebied' wilden laten leren. Sikhs vormden er een minderheid, maar dat waren de blanken ook, die het meest geducht waren. Sommigen zagen zichzelf als de echte Eastenders, alsof er een of andere koninklijke cockney-bloedlijn te beschermen viel. Paul Donavon was de ergste, een boef en een pestkop die zichzelf graag als vrouwenversierder en voetbaltalent zag. Zijn boezemvriend, Liam Bradley, was bijna even erg. Bradley, die een kop groter was en een voorhoofd had dat rood zag van de puisten, zag eruit of hij zijn gezicht met een kaasrasp schrobde in plaats van met zeep.

Nieuwkomers werden steevast ingewijd. Jongens kregen uiteraard het meest te verduren, maar meisjes bleven niet buiten schot, zeker niet als ze knap waren. Donavon en Bradley waren zeventien en altijd uit op Cate. Zelfs op haar veertiende had ze 'mogelijkheden', zoals de jongens het formuleerden, met volle lippen en een J-Lo-kont die in alles wat maar strak zat goed uitkwam. Het was het soort kont waar mannenogen instinctief naartoe trekken. Mannen en jongens en grootvaders.

Op een dag aan het eind van het schooljaar kwam Donavon op haar af. Hij stond voor de kamer van de directeur te wachten op straf voor zijn zoveelste vergrijp. Cate was met iets anders bezig: het afleveren van een stapeltje absentiebriefjes bij het secretariaat.

Donavon zag haar de gang bij de administratie in lopen. Ze moest pal langs hem. Hij ging haar achterna de trap op.

'Stel dat je verdwaalt,' zei hij op spottende toon terwijl hij haar de weg versperde. Ze stapte opzij. Hij bewoog met haar mee.

'Lekker kontje heb je. Als een perzik. En een prachtige huid. Laat mij eens zien hoe je de trap op loopt. Doe dan. Ik blijf hier staan en jij loopt door. Je rok een beetje omhoog, als het kan. Ik wil die sappige perzik zien.'

Cate probeerde zich om te draaien, maar Donavon danste om haar heen. Hij was altijd al lichtvoetig geweest. Op het voetbalveld was hij spits, langs verdedigers flitsend en ze alle kanten op sturend.

Het trappenhuis was afgesloten met grote zware branddeuren met horizontale stangen. Geluid kaatste hier terug van het koude harde beton, maar drong niet naar buiten door. Cate kon haar ogen niet op zijn gezicht gericht houden zonder zich om te draaien.

'Er bestaat een woord voor meisjes zoals jij,' zei hij. 'Meisjes die zulke rokjes dragen. Meisjes die hun kont laten schudden als perziken aan een boom.'

Donavon sloeg zijn arm om haar schouders en drukte zijn mond tegen haar oor. Hij hield haar armen boven haar hoofd vast bij haar polsen, die hij met zijn vuist omklemde. Zijn andere hand kroop omhoog langs haar been, onder haar rok, haar slipje opzij duwend. Twee vingers werkten zich naar binnen, schurend langs droge huid.

Cate bleef weg uit de klas. Mevrouw Pulanski stuurde me erop uit om haar te zoeken. Ik vond haar terug in de meisjestoiletten. Zwarte mascaratranen bevlekten haar wangen en het leek of haar ogen aan het smelten waren. Ze wilde eerst niet vertellen wat er was gebeurd. Ze pakte mijn hand en drukte hem in haar schoot. Haar jurkje was zo kort dat mijn vingers langs haar dij streken.

'Heb je je pijn gedaan?'

Ze schokschouderde.

'Wie heeft je pijn gedaan?'

Ze hield haar knieën tegen elkaar geperst. Op slot. Ik keek naar haar gezicht. Langzaam deed ik haar knieën uit elkaar. Het wit van haar katoenen slipje was bevlekt met een veeg bloed.

In mijn binnenste werd iets uitgerekt. Uitgerekt tot het zo dun was dat het mee vibreerde met mijn hart. Mijn moeder zegt dat ik nooit het woord 'haat' moet gebruiken. Dat je nooit iemand moet haten. Ik weet dat ze gelijk heeft, maar zij leeft in haar eigen, van elke controverse ontdane sikh-land.

De bel voor de lunchpauze ging. De speelplaats vulde zich met geschreeuw en gelach, dat tegen de kale bakstenen muren en het pokdalige asfalt terugkaatste. Donavon bevond zich aan de zuidkant in het 'vierkant', in de schaduw van een eikenboom waar zo veel initialen in waren gekerfd dat hij al dood had moeten zijn.

'Nee maar, wie hebben we daar?' zei hij terwijl ik op hem af liep. 'Een kleine yindoo.'

'Moet je haar gezicht zien,' zei Bradley. 'Of ze op ontploffen staat.'

'De vleesthermometer is net uit haar reet gefloept – ze is gaar.'

Er werd gelachen en Donavon genoot van zijn moment. Ik

moet hem nageven dat hij kennelijk iets van gevaar bespeurde, want zijn blik liet me niet los. Tegen die tijd was ik op een meter afstand van hem blijven staan. Mijn hoofd kwam tot halverwege zijn borst. Ik had niet bedacht hoe groot hij was. Ik bedacht niet hoe klein ik was. Ik dacht aan Cate.

'Het is die hardloopster,' zei Bradley.

'Nou, rennen dan maar, yindoo, het begint hier te stinken.'

Ik kon nog steeds niet praten. Donavons ogen werden onrustiger.

'Hoor eens, zieke sikh, rot op.'

Ik hervond mijn stem. 'Wat heb je gedaan?'

'Niets.'

Een menigte kinderen kwam onze kant op. Donavon zag ze aankomen. Hij was niet meer zo zeker.

Ik voelde me niet degene die op de speelplaats stond en hem aanstaarde. In plaats daarvan keek ik vanaf de takken van de boom als een vogel omlaag. Een donkere vogel.

'Sodemieter op, gestoord wijf.'

Donavon was snel, maar ik was degene die hard kon lopen. Mensen zeiden later dat ik vloog. Ik overbrugde de laatste meter in een flits. Mijn vingers vonden zijn oogkassen. Hij brulde en probeerde me van zich af te gooien. Ik hield vast in een doodsgreep, klauwend naar het zachte weefsel.

Met zijn vuisten in mijn haar gedraaid wrong hij mijn hoofd naar achteren in een poging me weg te trekken, maar ik liet niet los. Hij bewerkte mijn hoofd met zijn vuisten, terwijl hij gilde: 'Haal haar van me af! Haal haar van me af!'

Bradley had staan toekijken, te geschrokken om te reageren. Hij wist nooit zeker wat hij moest doen, tenzij Donavon het hem zei. Eerst probeerde hij me in een hoofdklem te nemen, mijn gezicht tegen zijn vochtige oksel geklemd, die naar natte sokken en goedkope deodorant rook.

Ik had mijn benen om Donavons middel geklemd. Mijn vingers priemden in zijn ogen. Bradley gooide het over een andere boeg. Hij greep een van mijn handen en trok mijn vingers los terwijl hij mijn arm naar achteren trok. Ik verloor mijn grip. Ik haalde mijn vingers over Donavons gezicht. Hoewel hij door de stroom die uit zijn ogen liep niets kon zien, haalde hij uit en schopte me in mijn gezicht. Mijn mond vulde zich met bloed.

Bradley had mijn linkerarm vast, maar mijn rechter was nog vrij. In een gezin met alleen jongens leer je wel vechten. Als je het enige meisje bent, leer je zelfs gemeen te vechten.

Terwijl ik mezelf op de been slingerde, sloeg ik mijn hand uit naar Donavons gezicht. Mijn wijsvinger en middelvinger priemden zijn neus in en haakten hem als een vis vast. Mijn vuist sloot zich. Wat er hierna ook zou gebeuren, Donavon zou meekomen. Bradley kon mijn arm breken, me achteruitslepen, me door de doelpalen trappen, en dan nog zou Donavon met me meekomen, als een stier met een ring door zijn neus.

Het enige wat ik uit zijn mond hoorde komen was een kreungeluid. Zijn armen en benen schokten.

'Niet aan haar komen. Niet aan haar komen,' smeekte hij. 'Laat haar gaan.'

Bradley liet zijn greep op mijn arm varen.

Donavons ogen waren gezwollen en zaten bijna dicht. Zijn neusvleugels waren door mijn vingers binnenstebuiten gedraaid. Ik hield hem vast, met zijn hoofd naar achteren gekanteld en met zijn onderkaak naar adem happend.

Juffrouw Flower, de muzieklerares, had die dag schoolpleintoezicht. In werkelijkheid zat ze in de docentenkamer een sigaret te roken toen er iemand de trap op kwam rennen om haar te halen.

Donavon bleef maar snotteren dat het hem speet. Ik zei geen woord. Dit was me allemaal niet echt overkomen. Het leek nog steeds of ik vanaf een boomtak toekeek. Het was een ander meisje dat zijn neus vasthield.

Juffrouw Flower was een fit, jeugdig, 'vooruit maar meisjes'-type met een voorkeur voor Franse sigaretten, en gymlerares. Ze nam het tafereel zonder veel drukte waar en besefte dat niemand me zou kunnen dwingen Donavon los te laten. En dus koos ze voor een verzoenende benadering vol troostende woorden en oproepen tot kalmte. Donavon was stilgevallen. Hoe minder hij bewoog, des te minder pijn het deed. Mak als een lammetje.

36

Ik kende juf Flower niet echt, maar ik denk dat ze me doorhad, weet je. Een mager Indiaas meisje met een beugel en bril gaat niet zomaar de grootste kwelgeest van de school te lijf. Ze zat bij me in de ziekenboeg terwijl ik bloed in een kom spuugde. Twee voortanden waren losgerukt uit mijn beugel, en zaten klem in het verwrongen metaal.

Ik had een handdoek om mijn nek en een andere op mijn schoot. Ik weet niet waar ze Donavon mee naartoe hadden genomen. Juf Flower hield een ijszak tegen mijn mond.

'Wil je me vertellen waarom?'

Ik schudde mijn hoofd.

'Ik twijfel er niet aan dat hij het verdiende, maar je zult een verklaring moeten geven.'

Ik reageerde niet.

Ze zuchtte. 'Nou ja, dat komt later wel. Eerst moet je een schoon uniform hebben. Misschien bij de gevonden voorwerpen. Laten we je fatsoeneren voordat je ouders er zijn.'

'Ik wil naar de les,' sliste ik.

'Je moet eerst iets aan die tanden laten doen, lieverd.'

Normaal gesproken was het praktisch onmogelijk op stel en sprong bij een ziekenfondstandarts terecht te kunnen, maar ik had familieconnecties. Mijn oom Sandhu had een tandartspraktijk in Ealing. (Hij is niet echt mijn oom, maar elke oudere Aziaat die mijn familie kende werd oom of tante genoemd.) Oom Sandhu had mijn beugel 'tegen kostprijs' geplaatst. Bada was zo tevreden dat hij me voor bezoekers liet glimlachen om ze mijn tanden te laten zien.

Mama belde mijn schoonzus Nazeem en getweeën namen ze een taxi naar school. Nazeem was moeder van een tweeling en opnieuw zwanger. Ik werd ijlings naar oom Sandhu gebracht, die mijn beugel demonteerde en foto's nam van mijn tanden. Ik zag er weer uit als een slissende zesjarige.

De volgende ochtend was fris en stralend, en vervuld van een schoonheid die zo zuiver was dat de vorige dag niet leek te hebben plaatsgevonden. Cate was niet naar school gekomen. Ze bleef de twee weken voor de zomervakantie weg. Juf Flower zei dat ze pleuritis had.

Op mijn vastgelijmde tanden zuigend hervatte ik mijn lessen. Mensen behandelden me anders. Er was die dag iets gebeurd. Mij waren de schellen van de ogen gevallen; de aarde was het vereiste aantal keren om zijn as gedraaid en ik had mijn kindertijd vaarwel gezegd.

Donavon was van Oaklands gestuurd. Hij ging het leger in, bij de parachutisten, maar was te laat voor Bosnië. Er zou zich snel genoeg een andere oorlog aandienen. Bradley ging in de vakantie van school en werd leerling-cv-monteur. Ik zie hem nog weleens met zijn kinderen, bij de schommels op Bethnal Green.

Niemand heeft ooit iets gezegd over wat er met Cate was gebeurd. Alleen ik wist het. Ik denk dat ze zelfs haar ouders niets heeft verteld, zeker niet haar vader. Penetratie met de vinger geldt niet als verkrachting, omdat de wet onderscheid maakt tussen een penis en een vinger of vuist of fles. Ik ben het daar niet mee eens, maar het is wel een argument voor dure strafpleiters.

Mensen waren aardiger tegen me na mijn gevecht met Donavon. Ze erkenden mijn bestaan. Ik was niet langer alleen 'de hardloopster', ik had een naam. Een van mijn tanden was weer vastgegroeid. De andere werd geel en moest door oom Sandhu door een stifttand worden vervangen.

In de vakantie werd ik gebeld door Cate. Ik weet niet hoe ze achter mijn nummer was gekomen.

'Ik dacht: misschien vind je het leuk om naar de film te gaan.'

'Bedoel je wij samen?'

'We kunnen naar *Pretty Woman* gaan. Tenzij je hem al gezien hebt. Ik ben al drie keer geweest, maar ik wil best nog een keer.' Ze bleef praten. Ik had haar nooit eerder nerveus horen klinken.

Mijn moeder verbood me *Pretty Woman* te gaan zien. Ze zei dat het over een sloerie ging.

'Julia Roberts speelt een hoer met een hart,' legde ik uit, wat het alleen maar erger maakte. Zij mocht wel de term 'sloerie' gebruiken, maar o jee als ik 'hoer' zei. Uiteindelijk gingen we naar *Ghost*, met Patrick Swayze en Demi Moore.

Cate zei niets over Donavon. Ze was nog steeds mooi, met nog altijd een gave huid, en haar vingers vonden de mijne. Ze kneep in mijn hand en ik in de hare.

En zo begon het. We waren als een Siamese tweeling. Zout en peper, noemde juf Flower ons, maar ik vond 'melk en chocola' leuker, de term die meneer Nelson gebruikte. Hij was een Amerikaan en gaf biologie, en protesteerde als iemand zei dat zijn vak het makkelijkste van de exacte keuzevakken was.

Onze hele schooltijd en daarna op de universiteit waren we boezemvriendinnen. Ik hield van haar. Niet op een seksuele manier, al denk ik niet dat ik dat onderscheid op mijn veertiende kende.

Cate beweerde dat ze de toekomst kon voorspellen. Dan beschreef ze onze levenspaden, inclusief carrières, vriendjes, bruiloften, echtgenoten en kinderen. Ze kon zelfs verdrietig worden door te fantaseren dat onze vriendschap op een dag voorbij zou zijn.

'Ik heb nog nooit zo'n vriendin gehad als jij en dat zal ook nooit meer gebeuren. Nooit niet.'

Ik geneerde me.

Ze zei ook: 'Ik neem een heleboel kinderen, omdat die van me zullen houden en me nooit in de steek zullen laten.'

Ik weet niet waarom ze zo praatte. Met liefde en vriendschap ging ze om als een klein schepsel dat in een sneeuwstorm gevangenzit, vechtend om te overleven. Misschien dat ze toen iets wist wat ik niet wist.

5

Een nieuwe morgen. Ergens schijnt de zon. Ik zie blauwe lucht ingeklemd tussen gebouwen en een bouwkraan als in houtskool getekend in het tegenlicht. Ik kan niet zeggen hoeveel dagen er zijn verstreken sinds het ongeluk; het kunnen er vier zijn of veertien. Kleuren zijn hetzelfde: de lucht, de bomen, de gebouwen – niets is veranderd.

Ik ben elke dag naar het ziekenhuis gegaan, de wachtkamer en

Cates familie ontwijkend. In plaats daarvan ga ik in de cafetaria zitten en wacht tot ze weg zijn.

Cate ligt in coma. Ze wordt beademd. Volgens het ziekenhuisrapport heeft ze een geperforeerde long, een gebroken rug en meervoudige fracturen in beide benen opgelopen. De achterkant van haar schedel was verbrijzeld, maar met twee operaties hebben ze de bloeding kunnen stoppen.

Haar neurochirurg legt me uit dat een coma in haar geval gunstig is. Haar lichaam heeft zichzelf uitgeschakeld en probeert zichzelf te redden.

'En hoe zit het met hersenbeschadiging?'

Hij friemelt aan zijn stethoscoop en ontwijkt mijn blik. 'Het menselijk brein is het volmaaktst ontworpen stuk machinerie in het universum zoals we dat kennen,' legt hij uit. 'Helaas is het niet ontworpen om de krachten van een auto te weerstaan.'

'En dat houdt in?'

'Wij classificeren ernstig hersenletsel als een comascore van 8 of minder. Mevrouw Beaumont heeft een score van 4. Het is een buitengewoon ernstige vorm van hersenletsel.'

Halverwege de ochtend komt er een nieuw rapport. Haar toestand is ongewijzigd. In de cafetaria loop ik Jarrod tegen het lijf. We drinken koffie en praten over koetjes en kalfjes: banen en familie, de prijs van eieren, en dat papieren zakken tegenwoordig zo snel scheuren. Ons gesprek wordt onderbroken door lange pauzes, alsof stilte een deel van de taal is geworden.

'De artsen zeggen dat ze helemaal niet zwanger is geweest,' zegt hij. 'Ze is de baby niet kwijtgeraakt. Er was geen sprake van een miskraam of afbreking. Ma en pa zijn over hun toeren. Ze weten niet wat ze ervan moeten denken.'

'Ze moet een reden hebben gehad.'

'Ja, maar ik kan er geen bedenken.' Een zuchtje wind uit de ventilatiekokers speelt door zijn haar.

'Denk je dat Felix het wist?'

'Dat zal wel. Zoiets kun je toch niet geheimhouden voor je man?' Hij kijkt op zijn horloge. 'Ben je al bij haar geweest?'

'Nee.'

40

'Kom mee.'

Jarrod gaat me voor de trap op naar de intensive care. We lopen door pijnlijk witte gangen die er allemaal hetzelfde uitzien. Op de IC zijn maar twee bezoekers per patiënt toegestaan. Je moet een masker dragen en je handen wassen met een desinfecterend middel.

Jarrod komt niet mee naar binnen. 'Er is al iemand bij haar,' zegt hij. 'Ze zal je heus niet bijten,' voegt hij er nog aan toe.

Mijn maag krimpt ineen. Ik kan niet meer terug.

De gordijnen zijn open en het daglicht verlicht een rechthoekig stuk vloer. In haar rolstoel zit mevrouw Elliot als een hologram gevangen in het licht, haar huid bleek en fijn als wit porselein.

Cate ligt naast haar, gevangene van een wirwar aan slangen, plasmazakken en roestvrij staal. Er zijn naalden in haar aderen gestoken en haar hoofd is in verband gewikkeld. Monitoren en machines knipperen en zoemen, haar bestaan is gereduceerd tot een digitaal computerspel.

Ik wil dat ze wakker wordt, nu. Ik wil dat ze haar ogen opendoet en de beademingsslang wegtrekt als een haar die in haar mondhoek is blijven zitten.

Woordloos wijst mevrouw Elliot naar een stoel naast het bed. 'De laatste keer dat ik heb zitten kijken hoe mijn dochter sliep was ze acht. Ze had longontsteking. Ik denk dat ze die had opgelopen in een van de openbare zwembaden. Elke keer dat ze hoestte klonk net alsof iemand op het droge verdrinkt.'

Ik reik over de marmeren lakens en neem Cates vingers tussen de mijne. Ik voel haar moeder kijken. Een koude, vorsende blik. Ze wil niet dat ik hier ben.

Ik herinner me mevrouw Elliot van toen ze nog kon lopen: een lange, slanke vrouw die Cate bij een zoen altijd haar wang toedraaide om haar lippenstift niet te laten vlekken. Ze was ooit een actrice die hoofdzakelijk televisiereclames deed en altijd onberispelijk was opgemaakt, alsof ze altijd klaarstond voor de volgende close-up. Dat was uiteraard voordat ze een hersenbloeding kreeg en aan de rechterkant verlamd raakte.

En nu hangt een van haar oogleden omlaag en kan geen make-up ter wereld de zenuwverlamming rond haar mond camoufleren.

Fluisterend vraagt ze: 'Waarom zou ze liegen over de baby?'

'Dat weet ik niet. Ze wilde me spreken. Ze zei dat ze iets doms had gedaan en dat iemand haar baby wilde afpakken.'

'Welke baby? Ze is nooit zwanger geweest. Nooit! En nu zeggen ze dat haar bekken zo ernstig is beschadigd dat ze, zelfs als ze blijft leven, nooit meer een kind kan dragen.'

Ik ril vanbinnen. Het is een déjà vu uit een ander ziekenhuis en een andere tijd, toen het míjn botten waren die werden gerepareerd. Voor elke ingreep betaal je een prijs.

Mevrouw Elliot klemt een kussen tegen haar borst. 'Waarom zou ze zoiets doen? Waarom zou ze tegen ons liegen?'

Er schuilt warmte in haar stem. Ze voelt zich verraden. Voor schut gezet. Wat moet ze tegen de buren zeggen? Ik heb zin om uit te vallen en Cate te verdedigen, die beter verdient dan dit. In plaats daarvan doe ik mijn ogen dicht en hoor de wind die langs de daken blaast en het elektronische gepiep van de machines.

Hoe heeft ze het voor elkaar gekregen een dergelijke leugen weken en maanden vol te houden? Het moet haar hebben achtervolgd. Een deel van me is gek genoeg jaloers. Ik geloof niet dat ik ooit iets zo intens heb gewild, zelfs olympische medailles niet. Toen ik buiten het team voor de Spelen van Sydney viel, heb ik op de rand van de baan zitten huilen, maar dat waren eerder tranen van frustratie dan van teleurstelling. Het meisje dat mijn plaats innam wilde het gewoon nog liever.

Ik weet dat ik een olympische selectie niet met het moederschap moet vergelijken. Misschien zijn mijn ideeën vertroebeld door de medische realiteit van een opgelapt bekken en een deels vastgezette ruggengraat die nooit de beproevingen van zwangerschap en bevalling aan zullen kunnen. Voor mij is kinderen willen een gevaarlijke ambitie.

Terwijl ik in Cates hand knijp hoop ik dat ze weet dat ik er ben. Jarenlang heb ik gewild dat ze belde, om weer vriendinnen te worden, me weer nodig te hebben. En uitgerekend toen dat eindelijk gebeurde, werd ze weggegrist als een half afgemaakte vraag. Ik moet erachter komen wat ze wilde. Ik moet begrijpen waarom.

Verkeersgarage Euston zit op Drummond Crescent, ingeklemd tussen Euston Station en de British Library. De torenspits van de St.-Aloysiuskerk steekt erboven uit als een raket op een lanceerplatform.

De afdeling Botsingenonderzoek is een merkwaardige plek, een mengeling van geavanceerde technische apparatuur en een ouderwetse garage met krikken, vetvangers en mechanisch gereedschap. Dit is de plek waar ze voertuigen onderwerpen aan wat bij mensen een autopsie heet, en daar lijkt het ook erg op. Het lijdend voorwerp wordt opengemaakt en er worden dingen uit gehaald, gewogen en gemeten.

De dienstagent, een kleine en dikke brigadier in overall, kijkt op van de verwrongen voorkant van een auto. 'Kan ik iets voor u doen?'

Ik stel mezelf voor en laat hem mijn badge zien. 'Vrijdagavond was er een ongeluk op Old Bethnal Green Road. Een echtpaar dat werd overreden.'

'Ja, die heb ik onder ogen gehad.' Hij veegt zijn handen af aan een lap en stopt hem terug in zijn zak.

'Een van hen is een vriendin van mij.'

'Leeft ze nog?'

'Ja.'

'Mazzel.'

'Hoe ver bent u met uw onderzoek?'

'Klaar, ik moet het alleen nog opschrijven.'

'Wat denkt u dat er gebeurd is?'

'Dat leek me nogal duidelijk. Uw vriendin en haar man probeerden een taxi te tackelen.' Het is geen poging ongevoelig te klinken; het is zijn manier van doen. 'Misschien had de bestuurder zijn remmen iets eerder kunnen intrappen. Soms heb je pech. Kies je het verkeerde moment om in je spiegels te kijken, dan gaat die fractie van een seconde af van je reactietijd. Het had misschien anders kunnen lopen. Misschien ook niet. We zullen het nooit weten.'

'Dus er komt geen aanklacht?'

'Voor wat?'

'Gevaarlijk rijden, nalatigheid – er moet iets zijn.'

'Hij had een vergunning, was verzekerd, geregistreerd en goedgekeurd – ik kan deze figuur niets maken.'

'Hij reed te hard.'

'Hij zegt dat ze ineens de weg op stapten. Hij kon niet stoppen.'

'Hebt u de wagen onderzocht?'

'Ter plaatse.'

'Waar staat hij nu?'

Hij zucht. 'Laat mij u de feiten des levens uitleggen, agent. Ziet u dat terrein daar?' Hij gebaart naar een open roldeur die uitkomt op een ommuurd stuk grond. 'Daar staan achtenzestig voertuigen, allemaal betrokken geweest bij een ernstig ongeluk. Wij moeten nog dertien rapporten leveren voor de lijkschouwer, een dikke twintig beoordelingen voor strafzaken. Zelf breng ik de helft van mijn tijd door in de getuigenbank en de andere helft tot aan mijn ellebogen in de motorolie en het bloed. Zoals ik het zie, zijn er geen goede verkeersongevallen, maar dat van vrijdagavond was beter dan de meeste omdat het een simpel ongeval was – triest, maar simpel. Ze stapten tussen geparkeerde auto's vandaan. De bestuurder kon niet op tijd stoppen. Einde verhaal.'

De gemoedelijke nieuwsgierigheid op zijn gezicht is verdwenen. 'We hebben de remmen bekeken. We hebben zijn vergunning bekeken. We hebben zijn staat van dienst bekeken. We hebben zijn promillage bekeken. We hebben ter plekke een verklaring afgenomen en de arme kerel naar huis laten gaan. Soms is een ongeluk gewoon een ongeluk. Als u bewijs hebt van het tegendeel, kom daar dan mee naar voren. Zo niet, dan zou ik het op prijs stellen als u me verder mijn werk laat doen.'

Een ogenblik kijken we elkaar recht in de ogen. Hij is niet zozeer kwaad als wel teleurgesteld.

'Sorry. Het was niet mijn bedoeling uw expertise in twijfel te trekken.'

'Dat deed u wel.' Zijn gezicht ontspant zich. 'Maar dat geeft niet. Het spijt me van uw vriendin.'

'Zou ik misschien een blik mogen werpen op de verklaring van de bestuurder?'

Daar heeft hij geen bezwaar tegen. Hij brengt me naar een kantoortje en gebaart naar een stoel. Op het bureau zoemt een computer en de planken zijn gevuld met archiefdozen als kartonnen bakstenen. De sergeant overhandigt me een map en een video. Heel even aarzelt hij bij de deur, hij weigert me alleen te laten.

De bestuurder heet Earl Blake en als beroep staat stuwadoor vermeld. Hij kluste bij als taxichauffeur om extra geld te verdienen, zei hij.

De video is tot op de seconde nauwkeurig van een tijdmarkering voorzien en begint met een panoramaopname van de straat, in de schokkerige stijl van een vakantievideo. Buiten de hekken van Oaklands lopen feestgangers rond, sommigen nog met een drankje of behangen met serpentines.

Earl Blake staat in de verte met een politieagent te praten. Hij merkt de camera op en lijkt zich af te draaien. Het zegt misschien niets.

Er zijn getuigenverklaringen van een tiental mensen. De meesten hoorden het gepiep van remmen en zagen de botsing. Verderop, bij de hoek van Mansford Street, hadden twee taxichauffeurs geparkeerd gestaan. De taxi kwam hen langzaam voorbijrijden, alsof hij een adres zocht.

Ik kijk of Donavon wordt genoemd. Zijn naam en adres zijn genoteerd, maar er is geen verklaring afgenomen.

'Ja, hem herinner ik me,' zegt de brigadier. 'Hij had een tatoeage.' Hij maakt een kruis in zijn nek onder zijn adamsappel, waar Donavon een tatoeage heeft. 'Hij zei dat hij niets gezien had.'

'Hij heeft het zien gebeuren.'

De brigadier trekt een wenkbrauw op tot een schuttersboog. 'Dat is niet wat hij tegen mij zei.'

Ik schrijf Donavons adres op een stukje papier.

'U gaat toch niet zelf een onderzoek beginnen, agent?'

'Nee, meneer.'

'Als u belangrijke informatie hebt met betrekking tot dit ongeval, bent u verplicht die aan mij mede te delen.'

'Ja, meneer. Ik heb geen informatie. De heer Donavon heeft geprobeerd mijn vriendin het leven te redden. Ik wil hem alleen maar bedanken. Wel zo netjes, begrijpt u? Zo heeft mijn moeder me opgevoed.'

6

Earl Blakes huis blijkt onderdeel te zijn van een klein huizenblok achter Pentonville Road, aan de vervallen kant van King's Cross. Er is niemand thuis. Ik zit hier al zo lang door de voorruit naar buiten te staren en op het stuur te trommelen dat mijn benen slapen. Voor een pub op de hoek staat een straatdealer tegen een lage muur geleund. Zijn gezicht gaat half schuil onder de klep van een honkbalpet. Hij zegt iets tegen twee langslopende tienermeisjes en glimlacht. Ze gooien hun haar in hun nek en versnellen lichtjes hun parmantige pas.

Voor me draait een vijfdeurs auto een parkeerplek in. Er stapt een vrouw van in de vijftig uit, in verpleegstersuniform. Ze pakt een tas met boodschappen uit de laadruimte, loopt naar een van de huizen en vloekt als ze haar sleutelbos laat vallen.

'Bent u mevrouw Blake?' vraag ik.

'Met wie heb ik het genoegen?' Haar blauwgrijze haar wordt met lak op zijn plaats gehouden.

'Ik ben op zoek naar uw man.'

'Maak je een geintje?'

Ze heeft de deur opengemaakt en stapt naar binnen.

'Uw echtgenoot was afgelopen vrijdagavond betrokken bij een aanrijding.'

'Weinig kans.'

Ze loopt verder de gang in.

'Ik heb het over Earl Blake.'

'Zo heet hij, ja.'

'Ik moet hem spreken.'

Over haar schouder roept ze: 'Nou, meissie, dan ben je zes jaar te laat, want toen heb ik hem begraven.'

46

'Is hij dood?'

'Dat mag ik hopen.' Ze glimlacht wrang.

Het huis ruikt naar natte hond en toiletverfrisser.

'Ik ben van de politie,' roep ik haar achterna. 'Mijn excuses als ik abuis ben. Hebt u dan misschien een zoon die Earl heet?'

'Nee.'

Terwijl ze in de keuken haar boodschappen op tafel zet, draait ze zich om. 'Hoor eens, moppie, binnenkomen of buiten blijven. Ik stook me hier een ongeluk.'

Ik volg haar het huis in en trek de deur dicht. Ze heeft aan de tafel plaatsgenomen, haar schoenen uitgeschopt en wrijft haar kousenvoeten over elkaar.

Ik kijk om me heen. In het raamkozijn staat een rij medicamenten, onder koelkastmagneetjes hangen kortingsbonnen. Op de kalender een baby in een uitgeholde pompoen.

'Zet even water op, wil je?'

De kraan spuugt en borrelt.

'Het spijt me van uw man.'

'Laat maar. Hij viel dood neer, precies daar, met zijn gezicht in zijn patat en gebakken ei. Hij zat te mekkeren dat ik de eieren te lang had gebakken en ineens: baf!' Ze laat haar hand op tafel vallen. 'Ik wilde niet dat hij in zijn ondergoed ontbeet, maar hij luisterde nooit. Alle buren stonden te kijken toen hij in zijn oude onderbroek het huis uit werd gereden.'

Ze gooit haar schoenen in de hoek naast de achterdeur. 'Ik weet dat alle mannen er ooit vantussen gaan, maar niet als je net een ei en patat voor ze hebt gebakken. Earl was altijd al verrekte weinig attent.'

Mevrouw Blake duwt zich omhoog en warmt de theepot voor. 'Je bent niet de eerste, weet je.'

'Hoe bedoelt u?'

'Gisteren kwam er een of andere gozer langs. Hij geloofde me ook niet toen ik zei dat Earl dood was. Hij zei dat Earl hem geld schuldig was. Het idee! Alsof hij van gene zijde nog steeds zou gokken.'

'Hoe zag die man eruit?'

'Hij had een tatoeage in zijn nek. Een kruis.'

47

Donavon is op zoek naar Blake.

'Ik haat tatoeages,' gaat ze verder. 'Earl had ze op zijn onderarmen. Voordat ik hem leerde kennen, had hij gevaren. Hij was overal geweest en had ze als souvenir overgehouden. Ik noemde het zijn huidaandoeningen.'

'Had hij er eentje hier?' vraag ik terwijl ik naar mijn borst wijs.

'Van een kruisiging?'

'Earl was nou niet wat je noemt religieus. Hij zei dat religie iets voor mensen was die in de hel geloofden.'

'Hebt u een foto van hem?'

'Ja, een paar. Hij was ooit een knappe vent.'

Ze neemt me mee naar de zitkamer, waar het wemelt van de meubels uit de jaren zeventig en verschoten kleden. Ze rommelt in een kast naast de gashaard en komt tevoorschijn met een fotoalbum.

Ze overhandigt me een kiekje. Earl heeft een jack met bontkraag en fluorescerende strepen aan. Hij lijkt totaal niet op de bestuurder van de taxi, hoewel ze ongeveer van dezelfde leeftijd zijn.

'Mevrouw Blake, komt er weleens post voor uw overleden man?'

'Jazeker, vooral troep. Banken sturen hem voortdurend formulieren voor creditcards. Wat moet híj nou met een creditcard?'

'Hebt u zijn rijbewijs laten opheffen?'

'Ik heb niet de moeite genomen. Ik heb zijn oude bestelbus verkocht. Daar heb ik die vijfdeurs voor gekocht. Ik ben nog getild ook als je het mij vraagt, die vuile Paki. Je maakt mij niet wijs dat dat ding er maar zesduizend kilometer op had zitten.'

Ze beseft wat ze net zei. 'Ik heb het niet over jou, schat.'

'Ik ben geen Pakistaanse.'

'Oké. Ik ken het verschil niet goed.'

Ze duikelt nog een foto op.

'Hebt u weleens huurders of gasten?'

'Nee.'

'Is er ooit bij u ingebroken?'

'Ja, een paar jaar terug.' Ze kijkt me argwanend aan.

Ik probeer haar uit te leggen dat iemand de identiteit van haar echtgenoot heeft ingepikt, wat minder ingewikkeld is dan het klinkt. Een bankafschrift en een gasrekening en je kunt al een kredietwaardigheidsverklaring opvragen, die je een sofi-nummer en een lijst met eerdere woonadressen oplevert. De rest komt dan vanzelf: geboortebewijzen, creditcards, een paspoort.

'Earl deed nooit iets kwaads,' zegt mevrouw Blake. 'Nooit echt veel goeds ook, trouwens.' Als ze staat wankelt ze even en zwaaien haar onderarmen van onder de korte mouwen van haar uniform heen en weer.

Ik wacht de kop thee niet af, wat haar teleurstelt. Als ik mezelf uitlaat, blijf ik heel even stilstaan op het stoepje en hou mijn gezicht in de motregen. Aan de overkant oefenen drie kinderen op een muur hun schrijfkunsten.

Verderop in de straat is een driehoekig parkje met banken en een speelplaatsje, omringd door een halve cirkel van platanen en een bruine beuk. Onder de onderste takken trekt iets mijn aandacht.

Als soldaten leren hoe ze zich in de jungle moeten schuilhouden, wordt hun verteld dat vier dingen hen kunnen verraden: beweging, vorm, schittering en silhouet. Beweging is nummer één. Dat is wat ik zie. Een gestalte staat op van een bank en loopt weg. Ik herken het loopje.

Vreemd hoe ik reageer. Jarenlang zwol er als ik me Donavons gezicht voorstelde een paniek op in de ruimte tussen mijn hart en longen. Nu ben ik niet bang voor hem. Ik ben op zoek naar antwoorden. Waarom is hij zo geïnteresseerd in Cate Beaumont?

Hij weet dat ik hem in de peiling heb. Zijn handen, uit zijn zakken, zwaaien heen en weer als hij het op een lopen zet. Als ik hem tot de andere kant van het parkje laat komen, raak ik hem in de zijstraten kwijt.

Eenmaal de hoek om versnel ik mijn pas over het pad, met aan beide kanten een traliehek en hoge struiken. Op de tegenoverliggende hoek staat een oud sorteerkantoor van de posterijen, met hoge, door geverfd steen omgeven ramen. Ik sla linksaf en volg de omheining. Voor me ligt de uitgang. Er verschijnt niemand. Hij zou er nu toch moeten zijn.

Ik sta stil bij het hek, mijn oren gespitst op voetstappen. Niets. Aan de andere kant van het park slaat een motorfiets aan. Hij is omgedraaid. Slim.

Ga maar. Ren maar, konijntje, ren. Ik weet waar je woont.

In mijn vestibule ruik ik bleekwater en een muffe stofzuigerlucht. Mijn moeder is komen schoonmaken. Dat is een van de tekenen dat mijn leven niet helemaal op orde is. Hoe vaak ik ook klaag dat ik geen schoonmaakster nodig heb, ze staat erop de bus te nemen vanaf het Isle of Dogs en 'een paar dingen aan kant te maken'.

'Ik ben de vriezer aan het ontdooien,' meldt ze vanuit de keuken.

'Dat hoeft niet, dat gaat automatisch.'

Ze maakt een pff-geluid. Haar blauw met groene sari heeft ze in haar panty-elastiek gestoken, wat haar een enorme derrière geeft. Het is gezichtsbedrog, net als haar ogen achter haar brillenglazen, die nat en bruin zijn als verse koemest.

Ze wacht op een kusje op haar wang. Ik moet me bukken. Ze is amper anderhalve meter hoog en peervormig, met uitstaande oren waarmee ze als een vleermuis hoort en een röntgenblik zoals alleen moeders die hebben. Ze heeft ook een wonderbaarlijk selectief reukvermogen dat op vijftien meter afstand de geur van parfum oppikt, maar haar tegelijkertijd wel in staat stelt om aan de onderbroeken van mijn vier broers te snuffelen om te zien of ze in de was moeten. Ik moet bijna kokhalzen bij de gedachte.

'Waarom zit er een hangslot op Hari's deur?'

'Privacy, wellicht?'

Vreemd. Hari doet zijn deur altijd zorgvuldig op slot.

Mama houdt mijn gezicht in haar handen. Ik heb wat dhal en rijst meegebracht.

Ze spreekt perfect school-Engels, zoals ze dat leerden in de oertijd toen zij naar school ging.

In de hoek staat een koffer. Even ben ik bang dat ze van plan is te blijven, maar één koffer zou daarvoor nooit genoeg zijn.

'Je vader was de zolder aan het opruimen,' legt ze uit.

'Waarom?'

'Omdat hij niets beters te doen heeft.' Ze klinkt geërgerd.

Mijn vader is na vijfendertig jaar als treinmachinist met pensioen gegaan en is er nog altijd niet aan gewend. Vorige week heeft hij mijn voorraadkast doorzocht en alles op uiterste verkoopdatum gerangschikt.

Mama opent de koffer. Keurig bovenop ligt mijn oude schooluniform van Oaklands. Ik voel een steek van herkenning en denk aan Cate. Ik zou het ziekenhuis moeten bellen om te vragen hoe het ervoor staat.

'Ik wilde niets weggooien zonder jouw toestemming,' legt ze uit. Ik zie sjaals, schriften, fotoalbums, dagboeken en hardlooptrofeeën. 'Ik wist niet dat jij verliefd was op meneer Elliot.'

'Wát, hebt u in mijn dagboek zitten lezen?'

Even overweeg ik moedermoord.

Ze verandert van onderwerp. 'Kom zondag vroeg, dan kun je helpen met koken. Zorg dat Hari iets leuks aantrekt. Zijn ivoorkleurige shirt.'

Mijn vader viert zijn vijfenzestigste verjaardag en het feest staat al maanden op stapel. Er zal ongetwijfeld minstens één begerenswaardige vrijgezel zijn. Mijn ouders willen dat ik een goede jonge sikh trouw, met baard uiteraard, niet een van die gladgeschoren Indiërs die denken dat ze een Bollywood-filmster zijn. Ze gaan eraan voorbij dat al mijn broers hun haar knippen, behalve Prakabar, de oudste, die de morele waarden van het gezin hooghoudt.

Ik weet dat alle ouders door hun kinderen excentriek worden gevonden, maar voor die van mij schaam je je helemaal. Mijn vader, bijvoorbeeld, is geobsedeerd door energiebesparing. Elk kwartaal bestudeert hij de elektriciteitsrekening en vergelijkt hem met die van de vorige kwartalen en jaren.

Mama kruist hele weken van tevoren weg op de kalender, zodat ze 'het niet vergeet'.

'Maar hoe weet je dan wat voor dag het is?' vroeg ik haar een keer.

'Iedereen weet wat voor dag het is,' was haar antwoord.

Tegen dat soort logica begin je niets.

'Tussen haakjes, je telefoon doet het weer,' meldt ze. 'Vanmiddag is er een aardige man langs geweest.'

'Daar heb ik niet om gevraagd.'

'Nou ja, hij kwam hem repareren.'

Er gaat een rilling over mijn huid alsof iemand een deur heeft laten openstaan. Ik bestook haar met vragen: hoe zag hij eruit? Wat had hij aan? Kon hij zich legitimeren? Mama kijkt eerst bezorgd en dan angstig.

'Hij had een klembord en een gereedschapskoffer bij zich.'

'Maar geen legitimatiebewijs.'

'Daar heb ik niet om gevraagd.'

'Hij had het je moeten laten zien. Heb je hem alleen gelaten?'

'Ik was aan het schoonmaken.'

Mijn ogen schieten van het ene voorwerp naar het andere en maken een inventaris op. Ik ga de trap op en doorzoek mijn kasten en laden. Al mijn sieraden zijn er nog. Mijn bankafschriften, paspoort en reservesleutels liggen nog in de la. Nauwgezet tel ik de pagina's van mijn chequeboek na.

'Misschien heeft Hari de storing gemeld,' zegt ze.

Ik bel hem op zijn mobiele telefoon. In de pub is het zo rumoerig dat hij me nauwelijks kan verstaan.

'Heb jij een probleem doorgegeven met de telefoon?'

'Wat zeg je?'

'Heb jij British Telecom gebeld?'

'Nee, moest dat dan?'

'Laat maar.'

Mijn moeder wiegt met haar hoofd en maakt bezorgde geluidjes. 'Moeten we de politie bellen?'

Die vraag was al bij me opgekomen. Wat zou ik moeten melden? Er was geen inbraak. Voorzover ik kan zien is er niets verdwenen. Het is ofwel de perfecte misdaad, ofwel helemaal geen misdaad.

'Maak je niet bezorgd, mama.'

'Maar die man…'

'Hij heeft alleen maar de telefoon gerepareerd.'

Ik wil niet dat ze zich zorgen maakt. Ze brengt hier al genoeg tijd door.

Mama kijkt op haar horloge. Als ze nu niet gaat is ze niet op tijd thuis voor het avondeten. Ik bied haar een lift aan en ze glimlacht. Het is de breedste, stralendste glimlach ooit geschapen. Geen wonder dat mensen doen wat ze zegt: ze willen haar glimlach zien.

Op mijn nachtkastje ligt een boek waar ik gisteravond in ben begonnen. De boekenlegger zit op de verkeerde plaats, twintig pagina's te ver. Misschien heb ik hem gedachteloos verplaatst. Paranoia is niet de werkelijkheid op een fijnere schaal; het is een dwaze reactie op onbeantwoorde vragen.

7

Op de allerlaatste dag dat ze nog zestien was trof Cate haar moeder bewusteloos aan op de keukenvloer. Ze had iets gehad wat een cerebrovasculair accident wordt genoemd en wat door Cate omschreven werd als 'een soort ontploffing in je hoofd'.

In het ziekenhuis kreeg Ruth Elliot nog twee attaques, waardoor ze aan de rechterkant verlamd raakte. Cate gaf zichzelf de schuld. Ze had thuis moeten zijn. In plaats daarvan waren we weggeglipt om de Beastie Boys te zien in de Brixton Academy. Cate had zich die avond laten zoenen door een jongen. Hij moet minstens vijfentwintig zijn geweest. Antiek.

'Misschien is dit een straf voor mijn liegen,' zei ze.

'Maar je moeder is degene die echt is gestraft,' merkte ik op.

Hierna begon Cate naar de kerk te gaan, althans voor een tijdje. Op een zondag ging ik mee en knielde ik met gesloten ogen neer.

'Wat ben je aan het doen?' fluisterde ze.

'Bidden voor je moeder.'

'Maar je bent niet anglicaans. Zal jouw god je geen overloper vinden?'

'Ik denk niet dat het uitmaakt welke god haar beter maakt.'

Mevrouw Elliot kwam thuis in een rolstoel, niet in staat goed te praten. In het begin kon ze maar één woord zeggen: 'wanneer', meer als constatering uitgesproken dan als vraag.

Wat je ook tegen haar zei, haar antwoord was hetzelfde.

'Hoe gaat het vandaag met u, mevrouw Elliot?'
'Wanneer, wanneer, wanneer.'
'Hebt u al gegeten?'
'Wanneer, wanneer, wanneer.'
'Cate en ik gaan huiswerk maken.'
'Wanneer, wanneer.'
Ik weet dat het afgrijselijk overkomt, maar we haalden er ook weleens geintjes mee uit.
'We hebben een biologieproefwerk, mevrouw E.'
'Wanneer, wanneer.'
'Aanstaande vrijdag.'
'Wanneer, wanneer, wanneer.'
'In de ochtend.'
Wanneer, wanneer.'
'Rond halftien.'
'Wanneer, wanneer.'
'Vierendertig over negen om precies te zijn, Greenwich Mean Time.'

Ze hadden een verpleegster die haar verzorgde. Een rijzige Jamaicaanse die Yvonne heette, met borsten als kussens, vlezige armen en gevlekte roze handen. Ze droeg altijd felle kleuren en mannenschoenen, en schreef haar slechte huid toe aan het Engelse weer. Yvonne was sterk genoeg om mevrouw Elliot in haar armen op te tillen en haar onder de douche en weer terug in haar rolstoel te zetten. En ze praatte voortdurend tegen haar, lange gesprekken die volstrekt plausibel klonken, totdat je echt goed luisterde.

Yvonnes grootste gave was echter dat ze het huis vulde met gelach en liedjes waarmee ze de zwaarte verdreef. Ze had zelf kinderen, Caspar en Bethany, die haar als staalwol hadden en een glimlach als een neonreclame. Van een echtgenoot is me niets bekend, die kwam nooit ter sprake, maar ik weet wel dat Yvonne elke zondag naar de kerk ging en de dinsdagen vrij had en de beste limoenkwarktaart ter wereld bakte.

In de weekenden bleef ik soms bij Cate slapen. We huurden een video en bleven laat op. Haar vader kwam nooit eerder dan na negenen thuis. Gebruind en onvermoeibaar, met een donkere stem en een eindeloze voorraad flauwe moppen. Ik vond hem ongelooflijk knap.

De tragedie van zijn vrouw bezorgde Barnaby veel sympathie, vooral als hij zich uitsloofde om te zorgen dat ze zich speciaal voelde. Met name vrouwen schenen zijn toewijding te bewonderen.

Ruth Elliot leek die bewondering echter niet te delen. Na maanden therapie herwon ze haar spraak, waarna ze Barnaby bij elke mogelijke gelegenheid aanviel en hem in het bijzijn van Yvonne, zijn kinderen en hun vriendjes kleineerde.

'Hoor je dat?' zei ze als de voordeur openging. 'Hij is thui-huis. Hij komt altijd thuis. Naar wie zal hij deze avond ruiken?'

'Kom nou, Ruth, alsjeblieft,' zei Barnaby dan, maar ze hield niet op.

'Hij ruikt naar zeep en shampoo. Hij ruikt altijd naar zeep en shampoo. Welke man doucht er nou voordat hij thuiskomt?'

'Je weet best waarom. Ik ben wezen tennissen op de club.'

'Hij wast zich voordat hij thuiskomt. Hij wast de geur weg.'

'Ruth, lieverd,' probeerde Barnaby, 'laten we het er boven over hebben.'

Dan weerde ze zijn handen af, om zich daarna over te geven als hij haar moeiteloos uit haar stoel tilde en haar de zestien treden op droeg. Dan hoorden we haar schreeuwen en daarna huilen. Hij legde haar als een kind in bed, om zich daarna in de keuken weer bij ons te voegen voor warme chocolademelk.

Toen ik Cate de eerste keer ontmoette, was Barnaby al veertig, maar hij zag er goed uit voor zijn leeftijd. En hij kon een hoop maken omdat hij zo'n enorm zelfvertrouwen had. Ik zag het hem talloze keren doen in restaurants, op open dagen van school en midden op straat. Hij kon de gekste dingen zeggen, vol dubbelzinnigheden en speelse kneepjes, waarna vrouwen alleen giechelden en slappe knieën kregen.

Hij noemde mij zijn 'Indiase Prinses' en 'Bollywood Beauty' en op een keer, toen hij ons mee uit paardrijden nam, voelde ik me zelfs duizelig toen hij zijn handen om mijn middel legde en me uit het zadel tilde.

55

Ik zou het nooit aan iemand hebben bekend, maar Cate raadde de waarheid. Ik bleef mezelf uitnodigen en excuses bedenken om met haar vader te kunnen praten. Ze wist zelfs niets van de keren dat ik op mijn fiets langs zijn kantoor reed en hoopte dat hij me zou zien en zwaaien. Twee keer reed ik tegen een opengeklapt autoportier op.

Cate vond mijn dweperij natuurlijk mateloos lachwekkend, waarmee ze ervoor zorgde dat ik later nooit meer heb toegegeven dat ik van een man hield.

Zie je nou wat voor dingen ik me herinner? Het komt allemaal terug: het goede, het slechte en het lelijke. Mijn hoofd doet er zeer van.

Dit is het moment dat ik heb gevreesd: Barnaby weer ontmoeten. Sinds het ongeluk heeft hij in Cates huis overnacht, zegt Jarrod. Hij is niet naar zijn werk geweest en heeft geen telefoontjes beantwoord.

De voordeur heeft panelen van glas in lood en een klopper in de vorm van een naakte torso, waarvan ik de heupen omvat. Er komt geen reactie. Ik probeer het nog eens.

Er wordt een slot opengedraaid. De deur gaat op een kier. Hij is ongeschoren en ongewassen, en wil me niet ontvangen. Zelfmedelijden vraagt zijn volledige aandacht.

'Alstublieft, laat me binnen.'

Hij aarzelt, maar de deur gaat open. Ik ga naar binnen, langs hem heen stappend alsof hij door een krachtveld wordt omgeven. Het is bedompt en benauwd in het huis. De ramen moeten nodig open, de planten moeten water hebben.

Ik volg hem naar de open keuken annex eetkamer, die uitkijkt op de tuin. De hand van Cate is overal zichtbaar, van de Franse boereneettafel tot aan de art deco-affiches aan de muren. Op de schoorsteenmantel staan foto's. Op een ervan, een trouwfoto, staat Cate in een twintigerjaren bakvissenjurk, afgezet met parelmoer.

Barnaby vlijt zich neer op een bank en slaat zijn benen over elkaar. Onder een opgekropen broekzoom is een kaal scheenbeen te zien. Mensen zeiden altijd dat hij leeftijdloos was en maakten grappen over dat hij net als Dorian Gray een portret op zolder had hangen. Het klopt niet. Zijn gelaatstrekken zijn te vrouwelijk om mooi oud te worden. In plaats van karaktervolle lijnen te krijgen is hij gerimpeld geraakt en op een dag, over tien jaar, zal hij als een oude man wakker worden.

Ik had nooit gedacht dat ik ooit weer met hem zou praten. Het valt me niet echt zwaar, alsof verdriet alles intiemer maakt.

'Ze zeggen dat een vader altijd degene is die dingen als laatste hoort,' zegt hij. 'Cate lachte me altijd uit. "Arme ouwe pa," zei ze. "Weet nooit ergens van."'

Verwarring verduistert zijn blik. Twijfel.

'Wist Felix het?'

'Ze sliepen niet samen.'

'Heeft hij dat verteld?'

'Cate liet hem niet aan haar zitten. Ze zei dat het slecht kon zijn voor de baby. Ze sliepen in aparte bedden, in aparte kamers.'

'Maar een man zou toch zeker...'

'Het huwelijk en seks zijn niet automatisch met elkaar verbonden,' zegt hij, omdat hij dat misschien zelf al te goed weet. Ik voel me ongemakkelijk. 'Cate zei Felix zelfs dat hij een prostituee mocht bezoeken als hij dat wilde. Dat ze dat niet erg zou vinden. Welke echtgenote zegt zoiets? Hij had door moeten hebben dat er iets fout zat.'

'Waarom kon ze niet zwanger worden?'

'Haar baarmoeder vernietigde zijn sperma. Ik weet de medische term er niet voor. Ze hebben het zeven jaar geprobeerd. ivf, medicijnen, injecties, kruidentherapieën; ze hebben boze geesten uit het huis gebannen en Chinese citroengrasolie in de tuin gesprenkeld. Cate was godverdomme een wandelend handboek onvruchtbaarheid. Daarom was het ook zo'n verrassing. Cate was in de wolken; ik heb haar nog nooit zo blij gezien. Ik weet nog dat ik naar Felix keek en dat hij zijn best deed om enthousiast te zijn, wat hij denk ik ook was, maar het was alsof hij met een vraag zat die maar niet weg wilde gaan.'

'Had hij twijfels?'

'Jarenlang stoot zijn vrouw zijn sperma af en ineens is ze zwanger. Iedere man zou zijn twijfels hebben.'

'Maar als dat zo is...'

'Hij wílde het geloven, begrijp je dat niet? Ze had iedereen beet.'

Hij staat op en gebaart me te volgen. Zijn slippers tikken zachtjes tegen zijn hielen terwijl hij de trap op loopt. De deur van de babykamer staat open. De kamer is opnieuw geschilderd en behangen. De meubels zijn nieuw. Een wieg, een commode, een gemakkelijke stoel met een Winnie de Poeh-kussen.

Hij opent een la en pakt er een map uit. Er zitten kassabonnen van het meubilair in en montagevoorschriften voor de wieg. Hij houdt een envelop op zijn kop en schudt hem voorzichtig. Twee vellen foto's, zwart-wit, vallen in zijn hand. Echo's.

Elke foto is maar een paar vierkante centimeter groot. De achtergrond is zwart, de beelden zelf wit. Een moment lang is het alsof ik door een viewmaster naar van die driedimensionale plaatjes kijk. Maar hier zie ik minuscule armpjes en beentjes. Een gezichtje, ogen, een neus.

'Ze zijn genomen met drieëntwintig weken.'

'Maar hoe?'

'Felix had erbij willen zijn, maar Cate had de datums verwisseld. Ze kwam thuis met de foto's.'

De rest van de map levert het bewijs van het bestaan van een ongeboren baby. Ik zie aanvraagformulieren van het ziekenhuis, afspraakbriefjes, medische rapporten, correspondentie en bonnen voor het babykamermeubilair. Een folder van het consultatiebureau legt uit hoe de geboorteaangifte in zijn werk gaat. Een tweede beschrijft de voordelen van foliumzuur tijdens de eerste maanden.

In de la liggen nog meer documenten, waaronder een in een hoek weggestopt bundeltje privé-correspondentie, bankafschriften, een paspoort en polissen van de ziektekostenverzekering. Een aparte map bevat details van haar IVF-behandeling. Sohan Banerjee, een in fertiliteit gespecialiseerde gynaecoloog in Wimbledon, wordt een aantal keren genoemd.

'Waar was ze van plan te bevallen?'

'In het ziekenhuis van Chelsea en Westminster.'

Ik bekijk een brochure over zwangerschapscursussen. 'Wat ik niet begrijp is hoe ze dacht dat het zou eindigen. Wat zou Cate vier weken later doen?'

Barnaby haalt zijn schouders op. 'Ontmaskerd worden als leugenaarster.'

'Nee, denk eens na. Die prothese was bijna een kunstwerk. Ze moet hem in de loop van die maanden twee of drie keer hebben aangepast. Daarnaast moest ze doktersbrieven en afspraken vervalsen. Hoe kwam ze aan echo's? Al die moeite die ze heeft gedaan. Ze moet een plan hebben gehad.'

'Zoals?'

'Misschien had ze een draagmoeder geregeld, of een privéadoptie.'

'Waarom dan die geheimhouding?'

'Misschien kon ze het niemand vertellen. Commercieel draagmoederschap is verboden. Vrouwen mogen geen geld aannemen om een kind te baren. Ik weet dat het vergezocht klinkt, maar is dat niet het uitzoeken waard?'

Hij maakt een spottend en afwerend gebaar. 'Dus over een maand zou mijn dochter zich even uit de voeten maken, de vulling dumpen en terugkomen met een baby, op maat gemaakt, besteld bij de babyfabriek. Misschien heeft IKEA ze inmiddels wel.'

'Ik probeer te bedenken waarom.'

'Ik weet wel waarom. Ze was geobsedeerd. Wanhopig.'

'Wanhopig genoeg om dat te verklaren?' vraag ik terwijl ik naar de echo's wijs.

Hij reikt omlaag, opent de tweede la en pakt er een andere map uit. Deze bevat rechtbankverslagen, aanklachtformulieren en een vonnis.

'Achttien maanden geleden werd Cate betrapt toen ze bij een winkel babykleertjes stal. Bij de rechtbank waren ze heel vriendelijk. Ze gaven haar een voorwaardelijke straf.

Ze had zo'n zes maanden therapie, die leek te helpen. Ze was weer haar oude zelf. Er waren natuurlijk plekken die ze diende te mijden, zoals parken en speelplaatsen, scholen. Maar ze kon er niet mee ophouden zichzelf te kwellen. Ze gluurde in kinderwagens en knoopte gesprekken aan met moeders. Ze werd kwaad als ze vrouwen met grote gezinnen zag die opnieuw in verwachting waren. Het was oneerlijk, zei ze. Ze waren inhalig.

Felix en zij onderzochten of ze een kind konden adopteren. Ze gingen op gesprek en werden gescreend door maatschappelijk werkers. Helaas achtervolgde de veroordeling voor winkeldiefstal haar. De adoptiecommissie verklaarde haar geestelijk labiel. Dat was de druppel. Ze raakte de draad volledig kwijt. Felix vond haar zittend op de vloer van de babykamer, een teddybeer omklemmend. "Kijk nou eens wat een prachtig jongetje." Ze werd naar het ziekenhuis vervoerd en bracht twee weken door op een psychiatrische afdeling. Ze kreeg antidepressiva.'

'Dat wist ik allemaal niet.'

Hij haalt zijn schouders op. 'Dus, Alisha, bega niet de fout dat je mijn dochter rationele gedachten toeschrijft. Cate had geen plan. Wanhoop is de moeder van slechte ideeën.'

Alles wat hij zegt klinkt me logisch in de oren, en toch kan ik het beeld van Cate op de reünie niet uit mijn gedachten zetten, zoals ze me smeekte haar te helpen. Ze zei dat ze haar baby wilden afpakken. Over wie had ze het?

Er is niets zo ontwapenend als een hartgrondige smeekbede. Barnaby's aangeboren voorzichtigheid wankelt.

'Wat wil je hebben?'

'Ik heb lijsten van telefoongesprekken nodig, creditcardafschriften, strookjes van cheques en agenda's. Zijn er grote geldbedragen opgenomen van Cates of Felix' bankrekeningen? Zijn ze ergens heen gereisd of hebben ze nieuwe mensen ontmoet? Deed ze geheimzinnig over geld of afspraken? Ik moet ook haar computer inzien. Misschien kunnen e-mails me iets vertellen.'

Niet in staat het woord 'nee' over zijn lippen te krijgen probeert hij een slag om de arm te houden. Hij denkt aan iets.

'En als je nou op iets stuit wat dit gezin te schande maakt?'

Zijn zielige gedoe maakt me woest. Wat Cate ook gedaan mag hebben, ze heeft hem nu nodig.

De deurbel gaat. Hij draait zich verbaasd om. Ik volg hem de trap af en wacht in de vestibule terwijl hij de voordeur opendoet.

Van diep uit haar keel laat Yvonne een snik horen; ze slaat haar armen om hem heen en plet zijn hoofd tegen haar borst.

'Wat erg. Wat erg,' huilt ze. Haar ogen openen zich. 'Alisha?'

'Hallo, Yvonne.'

Ze duwt Barnaby opzij en smoort me in haar decolleté. Ik herinner me het gevoel. Het is alsof je in een donzige handdoek gewikkeld zit, zo uit de droger. Ze pakt me bij mijn onderarmen en houdt me van zich af. 'Kijk nou toch eens! Je bent helemaal volwassen.'

'Ja.'

'Je hebt je haar afgeknipt.'

'Eeuwen geleden.'

Yvonne is niet veranderd. Misschien een tikje dikker, en misschien is haar pokdalige gezicht wat vleziger. Op haar kuiten tekenen zich overbelaste aderen af en ze draagt nog altijd mannenschoenen.

Ook nadat Ruth Elliot haar spraak terug had gekregen bleef Yvonne bij het gezin komen; ze maakte eten klaar, waste kleren en streek Barnaby's overhemden. Ze was als een ouderwetse bediende, die samen met hen oud werd.

En nu wil ze dat ik blijf, maar ik zeg dat ik moet gaan. Bij de auto gekomen voel ik Barnaby's stoppelbaard nog op mijn wangen op de plek waar hij me gedag kuste. Terwijl ik achteromkijk naar het huis, herinner ik me een andere tragedie, een ander afscheid. Stemmen uit het verleden verdringen elkaar en versmelten. Het verdriet is verstikkend.

8

Het adres dat Donavon de politie gaf is in Hackney, niet ver van London Fields. Het vervallen huis, dat iets naar achteren ligt ten opzichte van de straat, heeft een voortuin van aangestampte aarde en gebarsten beton. Er staat een door de zon gebleekte Escort-bestelbus in geparkeerd, naast een motorfiets.

Een jonge vrouw doet open. Ze is rond de vijfentwintig, met een kort rokje, een vorderende zwangerschap en acnesporen op haar wangen. Tussen haar tenen zitten watten en ze staat plat op haar hakken met haar voorvoeten omhoog.

'Ik ben op zoek naar Donavon.'

'Hier woont niemand die zo heet.'

'Dat is jammer. Ik ben hem geld schuldig.'

'Ik kan het hem wel geven.'

'Je zei net dat hij hier niet woonde.'

'Ik bedoelde dat hij er op dit moment niet is,' zegt ze afgemeten. 'Later misschien wel.'

'Ik geef het hem liever persoonlijk.'

Hier denkt ze heel even over na, nog altijd op haar hakken balancerend. 'Ben je van de gemeente?'

'Nee.'

'Sociale dienst?'

'Nee.'

Ze verdwijnt en in plaats van haar verschijnt Donavon.

'Nee maar, als dat yindoo niet is.'

'Hou daar nou eens mee op, Donavon.'

Hij gaat met zijn tong langs een hoekje uit zijn voortand en laat zijn blik van top tot teen over me heen glijden. Ik ril.

'Heeft jouw moeder je nooit geleerd dat staren onbeleefd is?'

'Mijn moeder heeft me geleerd op te passen voor vreemden die leugens vertellen over dat ze me geld schuldig zijn.'

'Kan ik binnenkomen?'

'Hangt ervan af.'

'Van wat?'

'Ik zou zweren dat ik een Thais meisje had besteld, maar met jou gaat het denk ik ook wel.'

Hij is niks veranderd. Het zwangere meisje staat achter hem. 'Dit is mijn zus, Carla,' zegt hij.

Ze knikt nors.

'Leuk je te ontmoeten, Carla. Ik zat met je broer op school. Heb jij op Oaklands gezeten?'

Donavon antwoordt voor haar. 'Ik heb het daar geloof ik een beetje verpest.'

'Waarom rende je gisteren weg?'

Hij haalt zijn schouders op. 'Je hebt de verkeerde voor je.'

'Ik weet dat jij het was.'

Hij steekt zijn handen op in spottende overgave. 'Gaat u me arresteren, agent? Ik hoop dat u de handboeien bij u hebt. Dat is altijd leuk.'

Ik volg hem door de hal, langs een kapstok en een bonte verzameling schoenen. Aan de keukentafel gaat Carla verder met het lakken van haar teennagels. Ze is lenig, maar ook kippig en trekt haar voet bijna tegen haar neus terwijl ze de lak met een dun kwastje aanbrengt en haar slipje te zien is.

Onder de tafel bonkt een hond een paar keer met zijn staart, maar hij blijft liggen.

'Wil je iets drinken?'

'Nee, dank je.'

'Ik wel. Hé, Carla, haal verderop even een paar blikjes.'

Haar bovenlip krult op als ze het briefje van twintig pond uit zijn vuist grist.

'En dit keer wil ik mijn wisselgeld terug.'

Donavon geeft een rukje aan de stoel. 'Wil je zitten?'

Ik wacht eerst totdat hij zit. Met hem boven me voel ik me niet op mijn gemak. 'Is dit jouw huis?' vraag ik.

'Van mijn ouders. Mijn pa is dood. Ma woont in Spanje.'

'Je bent bij het leger gegaan.'

'Ja, bij de para's.' Zijn vingers trillen tegen de tafelrand.

'Waarom ben je eruit gestapt?'

Hij wijst naar zijn been. 'Afgekeurd. Ik had mijn been op twaalf plaatsen gebroken. We deden een oefensprong boven Andover. Een van de nieuwelingen draaide zijn parachute rond de mijne en we kwamen aan één scherm omlaag. Te snel. Daarna wilden ze me niet meer laten springen. Ze zeiden dat ik een uitkering zou krijgen, maar de regering heeft de regels gewijzigd. Ik moet werken.'

Ik laat mijn blik door de keuken gaan, die eruitziet als een werkplaats, met dozen met repen leer, kristallen, veren en beschilderde stenen kralen. Op tafel zie ik een rol ijzerdraad en tangetjes.

'Wat maak je?'

'Ik verkoop spullen op markten. Snuisterijen en andere prulletjes. Het brengt niet veel op, weet je…'

Hij maakt zijn zin niet af. Hij praat nog wat over de para's, met hoorbaar heimwee naar het soldatenbestaan, totdat Carla terugkomt met een sixpack bier en een pak chocoladekoekjes. Ze trekt zich met de koekjes terug op de trap en gaat zitten eten en meeluisteren. Door een opening in de balustrade zie ik haar gelakte tenen.

Donavon trekt een blikje open en neemt luidruchtig een slok. Hij veegt zijn mond af.

'Hoe gaat het met haar?'

'Mogelijk blijvende hersenbeschadiging.'

Zijn gezicht verstrakt. 'En de baby?'

'Ze was niet in verwachting.'

'Wat?'

'Ze deed alsof.'

'Hoe bedoel je, ze deed alsof? Waarom zou ze…? Dat wil er bij mij niet in.'

De fantoomzwangerschap lijkt voor hem moeilijker te accepteren dan Cates gezondheidstoestand.

'Waarom ben jij zo geïnteresseerd in Earl Blake?'

'Om dezelfde reden als jij.'

'Ja, dag. Wat kan hem jou schelen?'

'Je zou het niet begrijpen.'

'Probeer het maar.'

'Lik me reet!'

'Dat mocht je willen.'

'Die klootzak had best kunnen stoppen,' zegt hij ineens met een woede die aan gewelddadigheid grenst.

'Heb jij gezien dat de auto versnelde? Zwenkte hij hun kant op?'

Hij schudt zijn hoofd.

'Waarom weet je het dan zo zeker?'

'Hij stond te liegen.'

'Is dat het?'

Hij trekt een schouder op alsof hij ermee aan zijn oor wil krabben. 'Vergeet het maar. Oké?'

'Nee, ik wil het weten. Je zei dat de bestuurder loog. Waarom?'
Hij wordt rustiger. 'Dat weet ik gewoon. Hij loog. Hij is op ze in gereden.'

'Hoe kun je dat zo zeker weten?'

Hij draait zich af en mompelt: 'Soms heb ik dat gewoon.'

Mijn moeder zei me altijd dat mensen met groene ogen familie zijn van elfjes, net als de Ieren, en dat als ik ooit iemand tegenkwam met één groen oog en één bruin oog, die persoon was overgenomen door een elfje, maar niet op een enge manier. Donavon is heel eng. De botten van zijn schouders gaan heen en weer onder zijn shirt.

'Ik ben het nodige aan de weet gekomen over Blake,' zegt hij, rustiger nu. 'Hij heeft zich een week geleden bij het taxibedrijf aangemeld en werkte alleen overdag. Aan het eind van elke dienst overhandigde hij tachtig pond voor de huur, maar de gemaakte kilometers kwamen niet overeen met wat hij binnenkreeg. Hij kan niet meer dan een paar kilometer hebben gereden. Tegen een andere chauffeur zei hij dat hij vaste klanten had die wilden dat hij altijd klaarstond. Een van hen was een filmproducent, maar je denkt toch zeker niet dat een hotshot van een filmproducer in een afgetrapte Vauxhall Cavalier door Londen wil rijden?'

Hij gaat rechtop zitten, helemaal in zijn verhaal nu. 'Dus vroeg ik mezelf af: waarom heeft iemand die nergens naartoe gaat de hele dag een auto nodig? Misschien bespiedt hij iemand of wacht hij die op.'

'Dat is een forse denkstap.'

'Ja, maar ik zag hoe Cate naar hem keek. Ze herkende hem.'

Hij had het dus ook gezien.

Hij schopt zijn stoel achteruit, staat op en trekt een keukenla open.

'Dit vond ik. Cate moet het hebben laten vallen.'

Hij overhandigt me een verfrommelde envelop. Mijn naam staat op de voorkant. De krullen en halen van het handschrift zijn die van Cate. Ik trek de flap open en haal een foto tevoorschijn. Een tienermeisje staart afwezig in de camera. Ze heeft dunne ledematen en rafelig, donker haar dat in de wind omhoogstaat. Haar brede lippen krullen omlaag bij de mondhoeken, wat haar eerder melancholiek dan somber maakt. Ze draagt een spijkerbroek, sandalen en een katoenen shirt. Haar handen hangen langs haar lichaam, de palm naar voren, met een wit bandje om haar pols.

Ik draai de foto om. Er staat een naam op de achterkant: Samira.

'Wie is dit?' vraagt Donavon.

'Weet ik niet.'

'En dat nummer?'

In de rechterbenedenhoek staan tien cijfers. Misschien een telefoonnummer.

Terwijl tientallen vragen elkaar verdringen bestudeer ik het plaatje nog eens. Cate simuleerde haar zwangerschap. Heeft dit meisje er iets mee te maken? Ze lijkt te jong om moeder te zijn.

Ik haal mijn mobiele telefoon tevoorschijn en toets het nummer in. Een mechanische stem meldt dat het niet beschikbaar is. Het kengetal komt binnen het Verenigd Koninkrijk niet voor. Misschien is het internationaal.

Donavon lijkt zijn vechthouding te hebben laten varen. Misschien maakt alcohol hem milder.

'Wat ga je doen?' vraagt hij.

'Dat weet ik nog niet.'

Ik sta op en loop naar de deur. Hij roept me na: 'Ik wil helpen.'

'Waarom?'

Hij wil het me nog steeds niet zeggen.

Carla houdt me staande voordat ik bij de deur ben.

'Hij dreigt de draad kwijt te raken,' fluistert ze. 'Hij had alles op een rij, maar in Afghanistan, of waar ze hem ook heen hebben gestuurd, is er iets gebeurd. Hij is niet meer de oude. Hij slaapt niet. Hij maakt zich druk om dingen. Ik hoor hem 's nachts rondlopen.'

'Denk je dat hij hulp nodig heeft?'

'Er moet iets gebeuren.'

9

Het kantoor van hoofdcommissaris-districtschef Lachlan North is op de elfde verdieping van New Scotland Yard, met uitzicht over Victoria Street en Westminster Abbey. Hij staat bij het raam naast een telescoop en tuurt door het oculair naar het verkeer beneden.

'Als die sukkel daar denkt te kunnen keren…'

Hij pakt een portofoon op en geeft een zendcode door aan de verkeerspolitie.

Een vermoeide stem antwoordt. 'Ja, meneer.'

'Er is hier in Victoria Street zojuist een idioot gedraaid. Hebben jullie dat gezien?'

'Ja, meneer, we zitten erachteraan.'

Al pratend kijkt de hoofdcommissaris nog steeds door de telescoop. 'Ik kan zijn nummerplaat lezen.'

'Alles is geregeld, meneer.'

'Goed werk. Over en sluiten.'

De hoofdcommissaris stapt weg van het raam en gaat zitten. 'Er rijden heel wat gevaarlijke mafkezen rond op onze wegen, agent Barba.'

'Ja, meneer.'

'Volgens mij zijn de gekken gevaarlijker dan de criminelen.'

'Ze zijn in elk geval talrijker, meneer.'

'Ja, absoluut.'

Hij buigt zich naar een la en pakt een donkergroene map. Terwijl hij door de inhoud rommelt, schraapt hij zijn keel en glimlacht in een poging warmer en aaibaarder over te komen. Ik voel een knagende twijfel zich in mijn borst vasthaken.

'De resultaten van je medisch onderzoek zijn geëvalueerd, agent Barba, en ook de psychologische beoordeling. Ik moet zeggen dat je herstel na je ongeval opmerkelijk is. Je verzoek om terugkeer naar de actieve dienst bij de Diplomatieke Beschermingseenheid is ons evenmin ontgaan. Moedig is het woord dat daarbij opkomt.' Hij trekt aan zijn manchetten. Nu komt het. 'Maar gegeven de omstandigheden, en na grondige bestudering van de zaak, is besloten je een andere functie te geven. Aarzeling om een vuurwapen te gebruiken valt niet uit te sluiten, zie je, wat niet echt handig is als je diplomaten en buitenlandse staatshoofden beschermt. Het kan tot gênante situaties leiden.'

'Ik heb geen vuurwapenvrees, meneer. Er is nooit op mij geschoten.'

Hij heft zijn hand. 'Toch hebben wij een verantwoordelijkheid jegens onze buitenlandse gasten, en hoewel ik alle vertrouwen in je heb, is het onmogelijk vast te stellen hoe bekwaam jij nog bent als het menens wordt en Abdul de Terrorist de Israëlische ambassadeur onder vuur neemt.' Hij tikt een paar keer op het dossier om zijn stelling kracht bij te zetten.

'Het belangrijkste onderdeel van mijn werk is met mensen en prioriteiten schuiven. Een ondankbare taak, maar ik vraag niet om medailles of lofprijzingen. Ik ben niet meer dan een nederige publieksdienaar.' Zijn borst zwelt. 'We willen je niet kwijt, agent Barba. We hebben meer mensen zoals jij nodig, en daarom ben ik blij je een positie te kunnen aanbieden als wervingsfunctionaris. We moeten meer jonge vrouwen zien te trekken, met name uit minderheidsgroeperingen. Jij kunt daarin een rolmodel zijn.'

Er hangt een waas voor mijn ogen. Hij staat op, loopt weer naar het raam, buigt zich voorover en tuurt weer door zijn telescoop. 'Ongelooflijke eikel!' roept hij hoofdschuddend.

Hij komt weer naar me toe en gaat half op het bureau zitten. Achter zijn hoofd hangt een sepia foto, een beroemde opname van de Bow Street Runners, Londens eerste politiekorps.

'Van jou worden grootse dingen verwacht, agent Barba.'

'Met alle respect, meneer, ik ben niet bang voor vuurwapens. Ik ben fitter dan ooit. Ik loop in vierenhalve minuut een mijl. Ik ben een betere schutter dan wie dan ook in de DBE. Mijn defensieve rijvaardigheid bij hoge snelheid is uitmuntend. Ik ben dezelfde agent als daarvoor…'

'Ja ja, je bent ongetwijfeld zeer capabel, maar de beslissing is genomen. Ik kan niets meer doen. Je meldt je maandagochtend bij het Politiewervingscentrum in Hendon.'

Hij opent de deur van zijn kantoor en wacht tot ik ga. 'Je bent nog steeds een belangrijk teamlid, Alisha. We zijn blij dat je er weer bent.'

Ik weet niets meer te zeggen. Ik weet dat ik in discussie zou moeten gaan of met mijn vuist op tafel slaan en herziening eisen. In plaats daarvan loop ik gedwee de deur uit, die achter me dichtvalt.

Buiten loop ik over Victoria Street. Ik vraag me af of de hoofdcommissaris me nakijkt. Ik heb de neiging omhoog te kijken en hem mijn middelvinger te laten zien.

Dat doe ik natuurlijk niet. Te beleefd, begrijp je. Dat is mijn probleem: ik intimideer niet. Ik koeioneer niet. Ik gebruik geen afgezaagde sporttermen, sla niet op schouders en heb niets tussen mijn benen bungelen. Helaas kan ik ook niet echt terugvallen op bij uitstek vrouwelijke wapens zoals een dodelijk decolleté of billen als J-Lo. De enige kwaliteiten die ik op tafel kan leggen zijn mijn sekse en mijn etnische geloofwaardigheid. Meer vraagt de Metropolitan Police niet van me.

Ik ben negenentwintig jaar oud en denk nog steeds dat ik iets bijzonders van mijn leven kan maken. Ik ben anders, uniek, onvergelijkbaar. Ik heb niet Cates stralende schoonheid of peilloze droefheid, haar welluidende lach of haar vermogen elke man het gevoel te geven dat hij een krijger is. Wat ik heb zijn wijsheid, vastberadenheid en ruggengraat.

Op mijn zestiende wilde ik olympisch goud winnen. Nu wil ik het verschil maken. Misschien wordt verliefd worden wel mijn opmerkelijke wapenfeit. Ga ik het hart van een ander menselijk wezen verkennen. Dat is toch zeker een voldoende grote uitdaging. Dat vond Cate tenminste altijd.

Als ik moet nadenken, ga ik hardlopen. Als ik wil vergeten, loop ik hard. Ik kan er mijn gedachten volledig mee verzetten of ze juist richten, als een vergrootglas dat de wereld buiten de lens doet krimpen. Als ik hardloop zoals ik weet dat ik het kan, speelt alles zich af in de lucht, de zuivere lucht, zwevend boven de grond; ik verhef mezelf zoals grote hardlopers zich dat in hun dromen voorstellen.

De artsen zeiden dat ik misschien nooit meer zou kunnen lopen. Ik heb hun voorspellingen weerlegd. Dat is een prettige gedachte. Ik hou niet van voorspelbaarheid. Ik wil niet doen wat mensen verwachten.

Ik begon met babypasjes. Eerst kruipen, dan lopen, zei Simon, mijn fysiotherapeut. Eerst lopen, dan rennen. Hij en ik lagen voortdurend overhoop. Hij prikkelde me, ik vervloekte hem. Hij draaide aan mijn lichaam, ik dreigde zijn arm te breken. Hij noemde me een huilebalk, ik hem een beul.

'Op je tenen, strekken.'

'Ik doe mijn best.'

'Hou mijn arm vast. Ogen dicht. Voel je het strekken in je kuit?'

'Ik voel het in mijn oogbol.'

Na maanden in tractie en nog langer in een rolstoel had ik er moeite mee te bepalen waar mijn benen ophielden en de grond begon. Ik botste tegen muren en struikelde over de stoep. Elke trap was een nieuwe Mount Everest. Mijn woonkamer was een hindernisbaan.

Ik legde mezelf kleine uitdagingen op, dwong mezelf elke morgen de straat op. Vijf minuten werden er tien, twintig. Na elke operatie hetzelfde liedje. Ik sleepte mezelf door de winter, de lente en een lange hete zomer, waarin de lucht verstopt zat met uitlaatgassen en elke baksteen en elke tegel warmte afgaf.

Ik heb iedere uithoek van het East End verkend, een wijk als een grote oorverdovende fabriek met een miljoen bewegende onderdelen. Ik heb op andere plekken in Londen gewoond en daar nooit oogcontact gemaakt met mijn buren. Nu heb ik meneer Mordacai naast me wonen, die mijn postzegelgrote grasperkje maait, terwijl mevrouw Goldie van de overkant mijn stomerijgoed ophaalt.

Het leven in het East End is van een schetterende, kibbelende gedrevenheid. Iedereen is op voordeel uit – marchanderend, klagend, gebarend en zich op het voorhoofd slaand. Dit zijn de 'mensen van de afgrond', zoals Jack London schreef. Dat was een eeuw geleden. Er is veel veranderd. De rest blijft hetzelfde.

Ik ren bijna een uur door, langs de Theems voorbij Westminster, Vauxhall en de oude elektriciteitscentrale van Battersea. Ik zie waar ik ben: de achterafstraten van Fulham. Mijn vroegere baas woont vlakbij, op Rainville Road: inspecteur Vincent Ruiz, gepensioneerd rechercheur. We bellen elkaar zo'n beetje elke dag. Hij stelt dan dezelfde twee vragen: gaat het goed, heb je iets nodig? Mijn antwoord is steevast: ja, het gaat goed en nee, ik heb niets nodig.

Zelfs van een afstand herken ik hem. Hij zit op een klapstoel bij de rivier, met in één hand een hengel en een boek op schoot.

'Wat ben je aan het doen, meneer?'

'Ik zit te vissen.'

'Niet echt veel kans om iets te vangen.'

'Nee.'

'Waarom dan toch die moeite?'

Hij zucht en zet zijn 'sprinkhaan-wat-heb-jij-nog-veel-te-leren'-gezicht op.

'Vissen gaat niet altijd over vangen, Alisha. Het gaat zelfs niet om de verwachting iets te vangen. Het gaat om uithoudingsvermogen, geduld en het allerbelangrijkste…' hij houdt een blikje omhoog '…om bier drinken.'

Meneer is aangekomen sinds zijn pensionering, te veel gebakjes bij de koffie en het kruiswoordraadsel in de *Times*, en zijn haar is langer. Het is vreemd te bedenken dat hij geen rechercheur meer is, maar gewoon burgerman.

Hij haalt zijn lijn binnen en klapt zijn stoel op.

'Je ziet eruit alsof je net een marathon hebt gelopen.'

'Niet helemaal.'

Ik help hem zijn spullen naar de overkant te dragen. We gaan zijn ruime huis in, met glas-in-loodramen boven lege plantenbakken. Hij vult de ketel en pakt een stapel getikte vellen papier van de keukentafel.

'Waar heb je je zoal mee beziggehouden, meneer?'

'Ik wou dat je dat "meneer" wegliet.'

'Wat moet ik dan zeggen?'

'Vincent.'

'Wat dacht je van IR?'

71

'Ik ben geen inspecteur-rechercheur meer.'

'Als bijnaam dan.'

Hij haalt zijn schouders op. 'Je koelt af. Ik haal een sweater.'

Ik hoor hem boven rommelen. Hij komt terug met een vest dat naar lavendel en mottenballen ruikt. 'Van mijn moeder,' zegt hij verontschuldigend.

Ik heb mevrouw Ruiz precies één keer ontmoet. Ze was als iemand uit een Europees sprookje: een oude vrouw met ontbrekende tanden, een sjaal, ringen en grote sieraden.

'Hoe gaat het met haar?'

'Zo gek als een deur. Ze beschuldigt de medewerkers van het tehuis er voortdurend van dat ze haar klisma's geven. Je zult er maar werken. Je kunt niet anders dan medelijden hebben met die arme kerel die haar verzorgt.'

Ruiz lacht hard, wat aangenaam klinkt. Normaal gesproken is hij buitengewoon zwijgzaam, met een permanente frons en een lage dunk van het menselijk ras, maar dat heeft me nooit afgeschrikt. Ik weet dat er onder zijn norse buitenkant géén hart van goud schuilgaat. Het zijne is van kostbaarder materiaal.

In een hoek zie ik een ouderwetse schrijfmachine staan.

'Ben je aan het schrijven, IR?'

'Nee.' Het komt iets te abrupt.

'Je bent een boek aan het schrijven.'

'Doe niet zo gek.'

Ik probeer niet te glimlachen, maar weet dat mijn lippen zich krullen. Nu wordt hij boos. Hij haat het als mensen om hem lachen. Hij pakt het manuscript en probeert het in een oude aktetas te proppen. Daarna gaat hij weer aan tafel zitten, zijn handen om zijn kop thee.

Ik laat een passende stilte vallen. 'Waar gaat het over?'

'Wat?'

'Het boek.'

'Het wordt geen boek. Gewoon wat aantekeningen.'

'Een soort dagboek.'

'Nee. Een soort aantekeningen.' Klaar.

Sinds mijn ontbijt heb ik niets meer gegeten. Ruiz biedt aan iets klaar te maken. Pasta putanesca. Volmaakt, verfijnder dan ik kan beschrijven en beter dan alles wat ik zelf had kunnen maken. Hij legt wat krullen Parmezaanse kaas op sneetjes zuurdesembrood en roostert ze onder de gril.

'Dit is erg lekker, IR.'

'Je klinkt verbaasd.'

'Ik ben ook verbaasd.'

'Niet alle mannen zijn hopeloos in de keuken.'

'En niet alle vrouwen zijn godinnen in het huishouden.' Ik spreek mijn plaatselijke Indiër vaker dan mijn moeder. Ze noemen het wel het tandoori-dieet.

Ruiz was erbij toen mijn ruggengraat werd verbrijzeld. We hebben het nooit echt gehad over wat er gebeurd is. Een soort onuitgesproken pact. Ik weet dat hij zich verantwoordelijk voelt, maar het was niet zijn schuld. Hij had me niet gedwongen mee te gaan en hij kan er ook niet voor zorgen dat de Metropolitan Police me mijn baan teruggeeft.

De afwas is gedaan en weggeruimd.

'Ik ga je een verhaal vertellen,' zeg ik. 'Het soort verhaal waar je gek op bent, omdat er een raadsel in verborgen zit. Ik wil niet dat je me onderbreekt en ik zeg niet of het waar is of verzonnen. Gewoon zitten. Ik moet alle details op een rijtje zetten om te kunnen horen hoe het klinkt. Als ik klaar ben, stel ik een vraag waar je ja of nee op mag zeggen. Daarna mag je me één vraag stellen.'

'Eentje maar?'

'Ja. Ik wil niet dat je mijn logica aan flarden scheurt of gaten prikt in mijn verhaal. Nog niet. Misschien morgen. Oké?'

Hij knikt.

Zorgvuldig geef ik hem alle details en vertel ik over Cate, Donavon en Earl Blake. Net als bij een knoop in een vislijn zou het verhaal verder in de war raken als ik er te hard aan sjorde en zouden feiten en veronderstellingen nog moeilijker uit elkaar te houden zijn.

'Wat nou als Cate een draagmoeder heeft geregeld en er iets is misgegaan? Er zou ergens een baby kunnen zijn, Cates baby.'

'Commercieel draagmoederschap is verboden,' zegt hij.

'Maar het gebeurt nog steeds. Vrouwen die het vrijwillig doen. Ze krijgen hun onkosten vergoed, wat is toegestaan, maar mogen niet aan de geboorte verdienen.'

'Vaak zijn ze op een of andere manier familie, een zus of een nicht.'

Ik laat hem de foto van Samira zien. Hij neemt de tijd om haar gezicht te bestuderen, alsof ze hem iets zou kunnen vertellen. Als hij de foto omdraait ziet hij de cijfers.

'De eerste vier cijfers kunnen het kengetal van een mobiel nummer zijn, maar niet van hier,' zegt hij. 'Je moet het precieze landnummer weten om het te kunnen bellen.'

Ik ben opnieuw verbaasd.

'Ik ben niet achterlijk,' protesteert hij.

'Maar je tikt je dágboek nog met een inktlint.'

Hij kijkt even naar de oude schrijfmachine. 'Nou ja, eh, ik ben eraan gehecht.'

De wolken wijken lang genoeg uiteen om ons een zonsondergang te tonen. De laatste gouden stralen strijken over de rivier. Nog even en ze zijn verdwenen en rest alleen nog een gure, vochtige kou.

'Ik mocht een vraag stellen,' zegt hij.

'Eentje.'

'Wil je een lift naar huis?'

'Is dat het?'

'Ik dacht: als we nou langs Oaklands gaan, dan kun jij me de plek laten zien waar het gebeurde.'

De inspecteur heeft een oude Mercedes met leren banken en een losse vering. Hij zuipt waarschijnlijk benzine en geeft hem het aanzien van een volkse bowlingspeler, maar Ruiz heeft zich nooit druk gemaakt over het milieu of wat mensen van hem denken.

Het voelt vreemd aan om op de passagiersstoel te zitten in plaats van achter het stuur. Jarenlang is het andersom geweest. Ik weet niet waarom hij mij als zijn chauffeur koos, maar ik hoorde geruchten dat de inspecteur van knappe gezichtjes hield. Zo is hij echt niet.

Toen ik voor het eerst mijn uniform verruilde voor de Groep Zware Misdaad, gaf de inspecteur me respect en een kans mezelf te bewijzen. Hij behandelde me niet anders vanwege mijn huidskleur of leeftijd of mijn vrouw-zijn.

Ik vertelde hem dat ik rechercheur wilde worden. Hij zei dat ik dan beter, sneller en slimmer moest zijn dan elke man die dezelfde positie ambieerde. Ja, het was oneerlijk. Nee, hij verdedigde het systeem niet, hij leerde me slechts hoe het zat.

Ruiz was al een legende toen ik nog in opleiding was. De docenten op Hendon vertelden verhalen over hem. In 1963, als aankomend agent, wist hij een van de daders van de Grote Britse Treinroof, Roger Cordrey, te arresteren en twee ton van de buit terug te vinden. Later, als rechercheur, hielp hij de Kilburn-verkrachter vangen, die Noord-Londen acht maanden lang had geterroriseerd.

Ik weet dat hij niet het type is dat mijmert of praat over die goeie ouwe tijd, maar ik voel dat hij de tijd mist waarin het gemakkelijker was schurken en agenten uit elkaar te houden en het grote publiek respect had voor de mensen die hen beschermden.

Hij parkeert de auto in Mansford Street en we lopen naar de school. De victoriaanse gebouwen, hoog en donker, tekenen zich scherp af tegen het omgevingslicht. Aan de vensters van de zaal hangen nog steeds gekleurde lichtjes. In mijn verbeelding zie ik de donkere vlek op het asfalt waar Cate neerviel. Aan de dichtstbijzijnde lantaarnpaal heeft iemand een boeketje opgehangen.

'Het is een rechte zichtlijn,' zegt hij. 'Het kan niet dat ze goed gekeken hebben.'

'Cate keek om.'

'Ze kan de taxi niet gezien hebben. Het is of dat, of hij is ineens opgetrokken.'

'Twee taxichauffeurs zeiden dat ze de taxi verderop in de straat hadden gezien, bijna stilstaand. Ze dachten dat hij een adres zocht.'

Ik denk terug, speel de gebeurtenissen af. 'Er is nog iets. Volgens mij herkende Cate de bestuurder.'

'Ze kende hem?'

'Misschien had hij haar daarvoor als klant gehad.'

'Of was hij haar gevolgd.'

'Ze was bang voor hem. Dat zag ik aan haar blik.'

Ik vertel over de tatoeage van de bestuurder. De kruisiging. Hij bedekte zijn hele borst. 'Een dergelijke tatoeage is misschien te achterhalen,' zegt de inspecteur. 'We hebben een vriend nodig uit dat wereldje.'

Ik weet waar hij heen wil.

'Hoe gaat het met Groentje Dave?' vraagt hij. 'Doen jullie het nog weleens?'

'Gaat je niks aan.'

Een sikh-meisje bloost vanbinnen.

Dave King is rechercheur bij de Groep Zware Misdaad (afdeling West), Ruiz' oude ploeg. Hij is begin dertig en heeft warrig, rossig haar dat hij kort houdt zodat het niet rechtop gaat staan. De bijnaam Groentje kreeg hij toen hij bij de GZM kwam, maar dat was vijf jaar geleden. Inmiddels is hij brigadier-rechercheur.

Dave woont in een flat in West Acton, pal achter Uxbridge Road, waar gashouders de horizon domineren en de treinstellen van de Paddington-lijn hem elke ochtend wakker ratelen. Het is een typisch vrijgezellenhonk in wording, met een reusachtig bed, breedbeeldtelevisie, een bank en verder bijna niets. De muren zijn half kaal gemaakt en de vloerbedekking is eruit getrokken, maar niet vervangen.

'Leuk opgeknapt hier,' luidt Ruiz' sardonische commentaar.

'Ja, nou ja, ik heb het nogal druk gehad,' zegt Dave. Hij kijkt vragend naar mij.

Ik geef hem een tikje op zijn wang, steek mijn hand onder zijn T-shirt en laat mijn vingers langs zijn ruggengraat gaan. Hij is wezen rugbyen en zijn haar ruikt naar gemaaid gras.

Dave en ik zijn twee jaar geleden voor het eerst met elkaar naar bed geweest en hebben een soort knipperlichtrelatie. Bij dat laatste zou Ruiz meesmuilend kijken. Het is mijn langste relatie ooit, zelfs als ik mijn tijd in het ziekenhuis niet meereken.

Dave denkt dat hij met me wil trouwen, maar hij heeft mijn familie nog niet ontmoet. Met een sikh-meisje trouw je niet. Je trouwt met haar moeder, haar grootmoeder, haar tantes, haar broers… Ik weet dat alle families bagage hebben, maar de bagage van mijn familie hoort thuis in een van die afgetrapte, met touw bij elkaar gehouden koffers die je eindeloos ziet rondcirkelen op de bagageband.

Dave probeert me te overtroeven met verhalen over zijn familie, met name zijn moeder, die doodgereden dieren opraapt en ze in haar vriezer bewaart. Ze heeft zich ten doel gesteld dassen te redden en bewerkt lokale bestuurders om drukke wegen te ondertunnelen.

'Ik heb niets te drinken in huis,' zegt hij verontschuldigend.

'Schaam je,' zegt Ruiz, die bekken staat te trekken naar de foto's op de koelkast. 'Wie mag dit wel niet zijn?'

'Mijn moeder,' zegt Dave.

'Dan lijk je zeker op je vader.'

Dave ruimt de tafel leeg en schuift een paar stoelen aan. Ik loop het verhaal opnieuw door. Daarna geeft Ruiz zijn commentaar, wat het relaas extra cachet geeft. Ondertussen zit Dave een stuk papier open en dicht te vouwen. Hij zoekt een reden om ons niet te helpen.

'Misschien kunnen jullie beter wachten op het officiële onderzoek,' probeert hij.

'Je weet dat ze dingen over het hoofd zien.'

'Ik wil niemand op de tenen trappen.'

'Daar ben jij een veel te goede danser voor, Groentje,' zegt Ruiz plagerig.

Ik kan schaamteloos zijn. Ik kan mijn grote bruine ogen laten knipperen als de beste. Vergeef mij, zusters. Ik pak Dave het stuk papier af en laat mijn vingers heel even op de zijne rusten. Hij pakt ze, wil de aanraking niet kwijt.

'Hij had een Iers accent, maar het meest interessante is de tatoeage,' vertel ik hem.

In zijn slaapkamer heeft Dave op een uit een wc-deur en twee schragen geïmproviseerd bureau een laptop staan. Terwijl hij het beeld voor mij afschermt, tikt hij een gebruikersnaam en wachtwoord in.

De Nationale Politie Computer is een reusachtige database met namen, bijnamen, schuilnamen, littekens, tatoeages, accenten, schoenmaten, lengtes, leeftijden, haarkleuren, oorkleuren, strafbladen, medeplichtigen en werkwijze van elke bekende wetsovertreder en persoon van belang in het Verenigd Koninkrijk. Zelfs deeldetails zijn soms al voldoende om zaken aan elkaar te koppelen en namen van mogelijke verdachten boven water te brengen.

In de goeie ouwe tijd had bijna elke politieman of -vrouw via internet toegang tot de NPC. Helaas kwamen een of twee van hen op het idee geld te gaan verdienen met het verkopen van de informatie. Tegenwoordig moet elk verzoek, zelfs het natrekken van een rijbewijs, worden onderbouwd.

Dave tikt het leeftijdsbereik, het accent en de kenmerken van de tatoeage in. Het duurt nog geen vijftien seconden of er verschijnen acht mogelijke kandidaten. Hij klikt de eerste naam aan en het beeld verspringt. Er verschijnen twee foto's, een vooraanzicht en een zijaanzicht van hetzelfde gelaat. Geboortedatum, afkomst en laatste bekende adres staan onderaan. Hij is te jong, met een te gladde huid.

'Dat is hem niet.'

Kandidaat nummer twee is ouder, heeft een bril met hoornen montuur en borstelige wenkbrauwen. Hij ziet eruit als een bij een pedofielenklopjacht ingerekende bibliothecaris. Waarom zijn politiefoto's altijd zo weinig flatteus? Het is niet alleen het harde licht van de kale witte achtergrond met verticale meetlat voor de lichaamslengte. Iedereen ziet er naargeestig, depressief en – wat het allerergste is – schuldig uit.

Er verschijnt een nieuwe foto. Een man van eind veertig met geschoren hoofd. Zijn ogen hebben iets wat mijn blik vasthoudt. Hij oogt arrogant, alsof hij weet dat hij slimmer is dan de grote meerderheid van zijn medemensen en dit besef geeft hem een neiging tot wreedheid.

Ik strek een arm uit naar het scherm, krom mijn hand tegen de bovenkant van het beeld en probeer me hem voor te stellen met een lange grijze paardenstaart.

'Dat is hem.'

78

'Weet je het zeker?'

'Honderd procent.'

Zijn naam is Brendan Dominic Pearl, in 1958 geboren in Rathcoole, een door de loyalisten beheerste wijk van Noord-Belfast.

'IRA,' fluistert Dave.

'Hoe weet jij dat?'

'Het is de klassieke achtergrond.' Hij verplaatst het beeld naar de biografie. Pearls vader was ketelbouwer in de dokken van Belfast. Zijn oudere broer, Tony, kwam in 1972 om bij een explosie toen een bom per ongeluk afging in een opslagloods die door de IRA als bommenfabriek werd gebruikt.

Een jaar later, vijftien jaar oud, werd Brendan Pearl veroordeeld wegens mishandeling en overtreding van de wapenwet. Hij kreeg achttien maanden jeugddetentie opgelegd. In 1977 voerde hij een mortieraanval uit op een politiepost in Belfast, waarbij vier gewonden vielen. Hij werd tot twaalf jaar veroordeeld.

In de Maze-gevangenis nam hij in 1981 met een vierentwintigtal republikeinse gevangenen deel aan een hongerstaking. Ze protesteerden tegen het feit dat ze als gewone gevangenen werden behandeld en niet als politieke gevangenen. De bekendste onder hen, Bobby Sands, stierf na zesenzestig dagen. Pearl raakte in de ziekenboeg van de gevangenis in coma, maar overleefde het.

Twee jaar later, in juli 1983, klommen hij en medegevangene Frank Farmer vanuit hun afdeling op het dak van de gevangenis en verschaften zich toegang tot de afdeling van de loyalisten. Ze vermoordden een paramilitaire leider, Patrick McNeill, en verminkten twee anderen. Pearl zag zijn straf omgezet in levenslang.

Ruiz komt bij ons staan. Ik wijs naar het scherm. 'Dat is hem, de bestuurder.'

'Weet je dat zeker?'

'Ja, hoezo? Wat is er dan?'

'Ik ken hem.'

Nu ben ik weer verbaasd.

Ruiz bestudeert de foto opnieuw, alsof de kennis moet worden opgeroepen of geruild tegen informatie die hij niet nodig heeft.

'In elke gevangenis heb je bendes. Pearl was een van de beulen van de IRA. Zijn favoriete wapen was een ijzeren stok met een kromme haak eraan, een soort pikhaak waarmee je bijvoorbeeld een grote vis zou kunnen aanpikken. Daarom noemden ze hem de Vissersman van Shankill. Veel vis komt er in de Maze niet voor, maar hij vond een andere toepassing voor zijn werktuig. Terwijl gevangenen lagen te slapen, schoof hij de stok tussen de tralies door en rukte met één polsbeweging hun keel open, waarbij hij tegelijk hun stembanden uitrukte, zodat ze niet om hulp konden schreeuwen.'

Het is alsof mijn slokdarm vol zit met watten. Ruiz stopt even, met gebogen hoofd, beweginloos.

'Toen de vredesovereenkomst van Goede Vrijdag was getekend, werden meer dan vierhonderd gevangenen uit beide kampen, zowel republikeinen als loyalisten, vrijgelaten. De Britse regering stelde een lijst op van uitzonderingen, mensen die ze vast wilden houden. Daar hoorde Pearl bij. Merkwaardig genoeg stemde de IRA in. Zij wilden Pearl net zomin terug als wij.'

'Waarom zit hij dan niet meer gevangen?' vraagt Dave.

Ruiz glimlacht wrang. 'Dat is een hele goede vraag, Groentje. Veertig jaar lang maakt de Britse regering mensen wijs dat zij geen oorlog voerde in Noord-Ierland, dat het een "politieoperatie" was. En toen ondertekenden ze het Goede Vrijdagakkoord en verklaarden ze: "De oorlog is voorbij."

Pearl bezorgde zichzelf een goede advocaat en haakte precies daarop aan. Hij zei dat hij krijgsgevangene was. Er mochten geen uitzonderingen zijn. Bommenleggers, sluipschutters en moordenaars waren op vrije voeten gesteld. Waarom werd hij anders behandeld dan zij? Een rechter was het met hem eens. Frank Farmer en hij kwamen op dezelfde dag vrij.'

Hij strijkt met een hand langs zijn kin, wat een geluid maakt als van schuurpapier. 'Sommige soldaten redden het niet als het vrede is. Die hebben chaos nodig. Pearl is zo iemand.'

'Hoe komt het dat je zoveel over hem weet?'

Zijn ogen staan droef. 'Ik heb de lijst helpen opstellen.'

Naast me gaat Groentje Dave verliggen. Zijn arm komt over mijn borsten te liggen. Ik til de arm op en stop hem weg onder zijn kussen. Hij slaapt zo diep dat ik hem als een animatiepoppetje in elke houding kan leggen die ik wil.

Op het nachtkastje is het schijnsel van een digitale wekker te zien. Ik til mijn hoofd op. Het is zondagochtend, na tienen. Waar zijn de treinstellen? Ze hebben me niet wakker gemaakt. Ik heb minder dan anderhalf uur om me te douchen, aan te kleden en klaar te maken voor mijn vaders verjaardag.

Terwijl ik uit bed rol, kijk ik waar mijn kleren liggen. Daves kleren. Mijn hardloopspullen zijn nog klam van gisteren.

Hij strekt zich naar me uit, beweegt zijn duimen langs de onderkant van mijn borsten, een patroon volgend dat alleen mannen weten te vinden.

'Probeer je weg te sluipen?'

'Ik ben laat. Ik moet gaan.'

'Ik had ontbijt voor je willen maken.'

'Je kunt me naar mijn huis brengen. Daarna moet je Brendan Pearl zoeken.'

'Maar het is zondag. Je hebt me niet verteld...'

'Dat heb je nou met vrouwen. We zéggen niet precies wat we willen, maar behouden ons wel het recht voor pissig te worden als we het niet krijgen. Griezelig, hè?'

Terwijl ik douche maakt hij koffie. Ik blijf malen over de vraag waar Brendan Pearl en Cate Beaumont elkaar mogelijk van kennen. Hoewel ze uit verschillende werelden komen, herkende Cate hem. Het vóélt niet als een ongeluk. Nooit gedaan ook.

Onderweg naar het East End vertelt Dave over zijn werk en zijn nieuwe baas. Hij zegt iets over dat hij niet blij is, maar ik luister niet echt.

'Je kunt later eventueel naar me toe komen,' zegt hij in een poging niet te gretig te klinken. 'We kunnen een pizza laten bezorgen en een film kijken.'

'Lijkt me geweldig. Ik bel nog wel.'

Arme Dave. Ik weet dat hij iets meer wil dan dit. Een dezer dagen volgt hij mijn advies op en vindt hij een andere vriendin. En dan zal ik iets kwijt zijn wat ik nooit heb geprobeerd te behouden. Dingen die ik leuk vind aan hem: hij is lief. Hij verschoont zijn lakens. Hij verdraagt mij. Ik voel me veilig bij hem. Hij maakt dat ik mezelf mooi voel en laat me winnen met darten. Dingen die ik niet leuk vind aan hem: hij lacht te hard. Hij eet junkfood. Hij luistert naar cd's van Mariah Carey. En er groeit haar op zijn schouders (gorilla's hebben haar op hun schouders). Jezus, wat kan ik pedant zijn!

Zijn rugbymaten hebben bijnamen als Bronco en Sluggo en ze praten in een vreemd jargon dat niemand begrijpt, tenzij ze het rugby volgen en de fijnere kneepjes van mauls, rucks en liften in de line-out kennen. Dave heeft me een keer meegenomen naar een wedstrijd. Na afloop gingen we met z'n allen naar de pub, vrouwen en vriendinnen. Het was best leuk. Ze waren allemaal heel aardig en ik voelde me op mijn gemak. Dave week niet van mijn zijde en wierp me telkens stiekem blikken toe en glimlachte.

Ik dronk alleen mineraalwater, maar gaf wel een rondje. Terwijl ik aan de bar stond te wachten, kon ik in de spiegel de hoektafels zien.

'Wat gaan we hierna doen?' vroeg Bronco. 'Ik heb wel trek in een curry.'

Sluggo grinnikte. 'Dave is al voorzien.'

Ze lachten en een paar van hen knipoogden naar elkaar. 'Ik denk dat ze "very hot" is.'

'Nee, absoluut vindaloo.'

Het maakte me niet uit. Het was grappig. Ik vond het niet eens erg dat Dave ook lachte. Maar op dat moment, zo niet al eerder, wist ik dat mijn eerste gevoel juist was geweest. We zouden met elkaar in bad kunnen, naar bed, een weekend doorbrengen, maar nooit een leven delen.

We houden halt in Hanbury Street en ik zie meteen dat er iets ontbreekt.

'Ik maak hem af!'

'Wat is er?'

'Mijn auto. Mijn broer heeft hem gepakt.'

Ik ben Hari al aan het bellen op zijn mobiel. De wind doet zijn woorden verwaaien. Hij rijdt met het raam open.

'Hallo?'

'Breng mijn auto terug!'

'Zusje?'

'Waar zit je?'

'Brighton.'

'Dat meen je niet! Pa is vandaag jarig.'

'Is dat vandáág?' Hij begint naar excuses te zoeken. 'Zeg hem maar dat ik op excursie ben voor mijn studie.'

'Ik ga niet voor jou staan liegen.'

'Hè, toe nou.'

'Nee.'

'Goed dan. Ik kom eraan.'

Ik kijk op mijn horloge. Ik ben al laat. 'Ik haat je, Hari.'

Hij lacht. 'Gelukkig dan maar dat ik wel van jou hou.'

Boven ruk ik kasten open en gooi schoenen in het rond. Om mijn vader tevreden te stellen moet ik een sari aan. In zijn hoofd zijn sari's en verlossing door elkaar geraakt, alsof het ene me het andere zal brengen, of op z'n minst een echtgenoot.

Groentje Dave is beneden.

'Kun je een taxi voor me bellen?'

'Ik breng je wel.'

'Nee, echt.'

'Het is in een paar minuten gepiept, daarna ga ik naar mijn werk.'

Weer in mijn kamer wikkel ik de stof van de sari rond mijn lichaam, van links naar rechts, met de eerste wikkeling in mijn onderrok gestoken en zo dat de onderrand net mijn enkels raakt. Daarna maak ik zeven verticale plooien in het midden, met de vleug mee. Terwijl ik de plooien vasthoud, pak ik achter mijn rug de rest van de stof, haal hem langs mijn bovenlichaam en drapeer hem over mijn linkerschouder.

Deze is gemaakt van varanasi-zijde, rijk versierd in rood en

83

groen, met delicate met zilverdraad vastgezette dierfiguurtjes langs de rand.

Ik steek mijn haar op met een gouden kam, maak me op en doe mijn sieraden om. Indiase vrouwen worden geacht veel sieraden te dragen. Het is een teken van welvaart en maatschappelijk aanzien. Op de trap zittend gesp ik mijn sandalen dicht. Dave staat naar me te staren.

'Is er iets?'

'Nee.'

'Waarom gaap je me dan zo aan?'

'Je ziet er prachtig uit.'

'Zal wel.' Als de etalage van een kilojuwelier.

Hij probeert me aan te raken en ik geef hem een tik op zijn handen. 'Wilt u de artikelen niet aanraken! En rijd in godsnaam voorzichtig. Ik wil niet in deze kleren overlijden.'

Mijn ouders wonen nog altijd in het huis waar ik ben opgegroeid. Mijn moeder houdt niet van verandering. Haar volmaakte wereld is er een waarin kinderen nooit het huis uit gaan of zelf leren koken en schoonmaken. Aangezien dat er niet in zit, heeft ze zoveel mogelijk van onze kinderspullen bewaard en is ze de fulltime curator geworden van het Barba Gezinsmuseum.

Zodra we de doodlopende straat in draaien voel ik het gebruikelijke gloeien van mijn wangen. 'Zet me hier maar af.'

'Waar moet ik zijn?'

'Doet er niet toe. Het is goed zo.'

We houden stil voor een klein rijtje winkels. Vijftig meter verderop zie ik mijn nichtje en neefje in de voortuin spelen. Ze rennen naar binnen om mijn komst te melden.

'Vooruit, keren!'

'Ik kán hier niet keren.'

Te laat! Mijn moeder komt naar buiten en waggelt op ons af. Mijn ergste nachtmerrie wordt bewaarheid.

Ze kust me drie keer en omhelst me zo stevig dat mijn borsten pijn doen.

'Waar is Hari?'

'Ik heb hem eraan herinnerd. Ik heb zelfs zijn overhemd gestreken.'

'Die jongen wordt nog eens mijn dood.' Ze wijst naar haar slaap. 'Zie je die grijze haren?'

Haar blik valt op Groentje Dave. Ze wacht tot hij aan haar wordt voorgesteld.

'Een vriend van mijn werk. Hij moet meteen weg.'

Mama maakt een blaasgeluid. 'Heeft hij een naam?'

'O ja. Brigadier-rechercheur Dave King. Dit is mijn moeder.'

'Aangenaam, mevrouw Barba. Ali heeft me veel over u verteld.'

Mijn moeder lacht. 'Blijft u lunchen, brigadier?'

'Nee, hij moet ervandoor.'

'Onzin, het is zondag.'

'Bij de politie heb je weekenddiensten.'

'Rechercheurs mogen toch een lunchpauze nemen? Klopt dat?'

Mijn moeder glimlacht en ik weet dat ik verloren heb. Tegen die glimlach kan niemand nee zeggen.

Voor ons uit trippelen voetjes de gang door. Harveen en Daj ruziën over wie het nieuws mag brengen dat tante Ali iemand mee heeft genomen. Harveen komt terug, pakt mijn hand en sleept me de keuken in. Ze is zeven jaar oud en heeft rimpels op haar voorhoofd. Daj is twee jaar ouder en, zoals elk mannelijk lid van mijn familie, onwaarschijnlijk knap (en verwend).

'Hebt u iets voor ons meegenomen?' vraagt hij.

'Alleen een kus.'

'En een cadeautje?'

'Alleen voor Bada.'

Afgeladen tafels met eten, de lucht zwaar van de kookdamp en kruiden. De door elkaar heen pratende stemmen van mijn twee tantes en mijn schoonzussen vermengen zich met hun keukengekletter. Er wordt omarmd en gezoend. Glazen die mijn wangen aaien, vingers die aan mijn sari trekken of mijn haar goed doen, en niemand die Groentje Dave uit het oog verliest.

Mijn tantes Meena en Kala zijn zussen, maar lijken totaal niet op elkaar. Meena is nogal mannelijk en opvallend, met een krachtige kaaklijn en stevige wenkbrauwen. Kala daarentegen is in vrijwel alle opzichten onopvallend, wat mogelijk haar sierlijke bril verklaart, die haar gezicht meer karakter moet geven.

Meena speelt nog steeds met mijn haar. 'Zo knap en mooi gebouwd, en dan niet getrouwd.'

Er wordt een baby in mijn armen gelegd, de jongste aanwinst van de familie. Ravi is zes weken oud, met koffiekleurige ogen en vetplooien op zijn armen waar je een stuiver in kunt laten verdwijnen.

Hindoes mogen dan hun heilige koeien hebben, voor sikhs zijn baby's heilig, jongens meer dan meisjes. Ravi pakt mijn vinger en houdt hem omklemd tot zijn ogen dichtvallen.

'Ze is zo leuk met kinderen,' zegt mama stralend. Dave zou ineen moeten krimpen, maar vindt dit leuk. Sadist!

De mannen zijn buiten in de tuin. Ik zie mijn vaders blauwe tulband boven iedereen uitsteken. Zijn baard is van zijn wangen weggekamd en kruipt langs zijn nek als een zilveren waterspoor.

Ik tel de hoofden. Het zijn er meer dan anders. O, nee hè! Ze hebben iemand uitgenodigd om mij te ontmoeten.

Mijn moeder gaat Dave voor naar buiten. Hij werpt me over zijn schouder een blik toe, aarzelt en volgt haar dan. Over de zijtrap, het beschimmelde pad, langs de deur van het washok, komt hij in de achtertuin. Alle gezichten keren zich naar hem toe en de gesprekken vallen stil.

Het is alsof de Rode Zee splijt als mensen een stap terug doen en Groentje Dave voor mijn vader staat. Oog in oog, maar Dave verblikt niet, wat hem siert.

Ik hoor niet wat ze zeggen. Mijn vader kijkt omhoog naar het keukenraam. Hij ziet me. Dan glimlacht hij en steekt zijn hand uit. Dave neemt de uitnodiging aan en ineens worden de gesprekken hervat.

Mijn moeder staat aan het aanrecht mango's te schillen en te snijden. Soepel glijdt ze met het lemmet door het bleekgele vruchtvlees. 'We wisten niet dat je een vriend zou meebrengen.'

'Ik heb hem ook niet meegebracht.'

'Je vader heeft iemand uitgenodigd. Je moet zijn gast ontmoeten. Dat is beleefd. Hij is arts.'

'En een erg goeie ook,' echoot tante Kala. 'Heel succesvol.'

Ik monster de groep mannen en zie hem. Hij staat met zijn rug naar me toe, in een piekfijn gereinigd en gesteven Punjabipak.

'Hij is dik.'

'Een teken van succes,' zegt Kala.

'Goed gereedschap hangt onder een afdakje,' voegt Meena giechelend als een schoolmeisje toe. Kala kijkt misprijzend.

'Kijk niet zo lelijk, zus. Een vrouw moet leren hoe ze haar echtgenoot tevreden houdt in het boudoir.' Terwijl de twee verder kibbelen loop ik weer naar het raam.

De onbekende in de tuin draait zich om en werpt me een blik toe. Hij houdt zijn glas geheven, alsof hij proost. Met een schommelend gebaar geeft hij aan dat het leeg is.

'Gauw, meisje, schenk hem bij,' zegt Meena terwijl ze me een kan geeft.

Ik haal diep adem en loop de zijtrap af de tuin in. Mijn broers fluiten. Ze weten hoe ik baal als ik een sari aan moet. Alle mannen draaien zich naar me om. Ik hou mijn ogen op mijn sandalen gericht.

Mijn vader staat nog steeds te praten met Dave en mijn oom Rashid, een berucht billenknijper. Mijn moeder beweert dat het een dwangneurose is, maar volgens mij is hij gewoon een geile bok. Ze hebben het over cricket. Voor de mannen in mijn familie is dat een obsessie, zelfs als de zomer voorbij is.

De meeste Indiase mannen zijn klein en elegant, met slanke handen, maar mijn broers zijn stoere, potige kerels, behalve Hari, die een prachtige vrouw had kunnen zijn.

Bada kust mijn wang. Ik buig me licht voorover. Hij wenkt zijn gast en stelt ons aan elkaar voor.

'Alisha, dit is dokter Sohan Banerjee.'

Ik knik, mijn ogen nog neergeslagen.

De naam klinkt bekend. Waar heb ik die eerder gehoord?

Arme Dave snapt niet wat er gaande is. Hij is geen sikh, wat waarschijnlijk maar goed is ook. Als ik een sikh had meegebracht, hadden mijn ouders een geit geslacht.

Dokter Banerjee gaat kaarsrecht staan en buigt zijn hoofd. Mijn vader praat door. 'Sohan heeft mij persoonlijk benaderd en gevraagd jou te mogen ontmoeten, Alisha. Van familie tot familie, zoals het hoort.'

Ik word niet geacht iets te zeggen.

'Hij heeft meerdere medische graden,' gaat hij verder.

En meerdere kinnen.

Ik betwijfel of deze dag nog veel erger kan worden. Mensen kijken naar me. Dave staat aan de andere kant van de tuin te praten met mijn oudste broer, Prabakar, het meest religieuze lid van ons gezin, die het niet zal goedkeuren.

De arts praat tegen me. Ik moet me concentreren. 'Je werkt bij de politie?'

'Ja.'

'En je woont zelfstandig. Er zijn niet veel Indiase meisjes met een eigen huis. Hoe komt het dat je niet getrouwd bent?'

Zijn botheid overvalt me. Hij wacht mijn antwoord niet af. 'Ben je nog maagd?'

'Pardon?'

'Ik neem aan dat je moeder je heeft voorgelicht.'

'Dat gaat u niks aan.'

'Geen commentaar betekent ja.'

'Dat doet het niet.'

'In mijn ervaring wel. Drink je alcohol?'

'Nee.'

'Je hoeft niet zo defensief te doen. Mijn ouders vinden dat ik een meisje uit India moet nemen, omdat dorpsmeisjes hard werken en goede moeders zijn. Dat mag zo zijn, maar ik wil geen boerengriet die niet met mes en vork kan eten.'

In mijn keel welt woede op en ik moet verwoed slikken om die in te houden. Ik schenk hem mijn beleefdste glimlach. 'Vertelt u eens, dokter Banerjee...'

'Zeg maar Sohan.'

'Sohan, masturbeer jij weleens?'

Zijn mond opent en sluit zich als die van een buikspreekpop. 'Ik geloof niet...'

'Geen commentaar is ja.'

De flits van woede in zijn ogen is als een bloedrode sluier. Knarsetandend perst hij er een glimlach uit. 'Touché.'

'Wat voor soort arts ben je?'

'Gynaecoloog.'

Ineens weet ik weer waar ik zijn naam heb gelezen: in de map die Barnaby Elliot me liet zien. Sohan Banerjee is fertiliteitspecialist. Hij heeft Cates IVF-behandelingen uitgevoerd.

Er wonen honderdduizend sikhs in Londen en, pak 'm beet, vierhonderd verloskundige artsen. Hoe groot is de kans dat Cates arts hier opduikt?

'We hebben een gemeenschappelijke kennis,' zeg ik. 'Cate Beaumont. Wist je dat ze een ongeluk heeft gehad?'

Zijn blik glijdt naar het gevlekte groene dak van mijn vaders schuurtje. 'Haar moeder belde me. Verschrikkelijk.'

'Heeft ze je verteld dat Cate haar zwangerschap simuleerde?'

'Ja.'

'Wat zei ze nog meer?'

'Het zou buitengewoon onethisch zijn als ik details van ons gesprek onthulde.' Hij stopt even en vervolgt: 'Zelfs tegenover een politieagente.'

Mijn ogen zoeken die van hem, of misschien wel andersom.

'Wanneer heb je Cate voor het laatst gezien?'

'Een jaar geleden.'

'Waarom kon ze niet zwanger worden?'

'Daar was geen enkele reden voor,' zegt hij opgeruimd. 'Ze heeft een laparoscopie gehad, bloedtests, echo's en een baarmoederonderzoek. Er waren geen afwijkingen, vergroeiingen of fibromen. Ze had zwanger moeten kunnen worden. Ongelukkigerwijs waren zij en haar echtgenoot niet compatibel. Felix had een laag spermagehalte, maar had bij een andere vrouw wellicht zonder veel moeite een kind kunnen verwekken. In dit geval werden zijn zaadcellen echter behandeld alsof het kankercellen waren en door het immuunsysteem van zijn vrouw vernietigd. Zwangerschap was theoretisch mogelijk, maar realistisch gezien onwaarschijnlijk.'

'Heb je ooit draagmoederschap genoemd als mogelijkheid?'

'Ja, maar er zijn niet veel vrouwen die voor een ander stel een kind willen baren. Maar er was nog iets…'

'Wat?'

'Zegt achondrogenese je iets?'

'Nee.'

'Het is een buitengewoon zeldzame genetische afwijking, een dodelijke vorm van dwerggroei.'

'Wat heeft dat met Cate te maken?'

'Haar voorzover bekend enige zwangerschap eindigde na zes maanden in een miskraam. De autopsie bracht ernstige misvormingen naar voren. Door een speling van het lot, een soort omgekeerde loterij, waren zij en Felix beiden drager van een recessief gen. Zelfs als ze, door een wonder, weer zwanger zou raken, was er vijfentwintig procent kans dat het weer zou gebeuren.'

'Maar ze bleven het proberen.'

Hij heft zijn hand. 'Sorry Alisha, maar mag ik uit je vragen opmaken dat jij op de een of andere manier betrokken bent bij een onderzoek naar deze zaak?'

'Ik zoek alleen antwoorden.'

'Oké.' Hij denkt na. 'Als ik jou was, zou ik erg voorzichtig zijn. Goede bedoelingen worden soms misverstaan.'

Ik weet niet of dit een advies is of een waarschuwing, maar hij blijft me aankijken tot ik er ongemakkelijk van word. Hij heeft een soort arrogantie over zich die typisch is voor sikhs van zijn generatie, die gedistingeerder doen dan welke Engelsman ook.

Even later ontspant hij wat. 'Ik zal je dit zeggen, Alisha. Mevrouw Beaumont heeft in twee jaar tijd vijf keer een IVF-behandeling ondergaan.'

'Vijf?'

'Correct.'

'Ik dacht zes?'

'Nee, ik ben redelijk zeker van vijf. Het is een heel complexe wetenschap, niet iets wat je thuis doet met een potje en een injectiespuit. Het is de laatste strohalm, als al het andere faalt.'

'Wat gebeurde er in Cates geval?'

'Elke keer een miskraam. Minder dan eenderde van alle IVF's

leidt tot een geboorte. Mijn succespercentage is relatief hoog, maar ik ben arts, geen wonderdoener.'

Zijn opmerking klinkt nu eens niet verwaand. Hij klinkt echt teleurgesteld.

Tante Meena roept iedereen naar binnen voor de lunch. Mijn vader is aan het hoofd van de tafel gezet. Ik zit tussen de vrouwen. De mannen zitten tegenover ons. Groentje Dave en dokter Banerjee zitten naast elkaar.

Hari komt op tijd voor het toetje en wordt door mijn tantes, die met hun vingers door zijn lange haar gaan, begroet als een verloren zoon. Terwijl hij zich bukt fluistert hij in mijn oor: 'Twee tegelijk maar liefst. En ik maar denken dat je een ouwe vrijster was.'

In mijn familie is eten een luidruchtige affaire. Er worden schalen doorgegeven. Mensen praten door elkaar heen. Lachen is als een specerij. Een ceremonie ontbreekt, maar er zijn wel rituelen (wat iets anders is). Er zijn toespraken, de kokkinnen moeten worden bedankt. Niemand praat door mijn vader heen. Alle onenigheden worden bewaard tot na afloop.

Zo lang laat ik Dave niet blijven. Hij moet aan de slag. Sohan Banerjee maakt zich ook op om te gaan. Ik begrijp nog steeds niet waarom hij er is. Het kan geen toeval zijn.

'Zou ik je nog een keer mogen ontmoeten, Alisha?' vraagt hij.

'Nee, sorry.'

'Je zou je ouders een groot plezier doen.'

'Die redden zich wel.'

Hij schudt zijn hoofd en knikt. 'Oké. Ik weet niet wat ik moet zeggen.'

'Tot ziens, zeggen wij meestal.'

Hij stapt achteruit. 'Ja. Tot ziens. Ik hoop dat je vriendin mevrouw Beaumont snel weer de oude is.'

Terwijl ik de voordeur dichtdoe, voel ik een mengeling van spanning en opluchting. Mijn leven kent al genoeg raadsels.

In de gang wacht Hari me op. Zijn donkere ogen vangen het licht en hij slaat zijn armen om me heen. Hij heeft mijn uitgeklapte mobieltje in zijn hand.

'Je vriendin, Cate, is om één uur vanmiddag overleden.'

Op straat en op de oprit voor het huis van de Elliots staan auto's geparkeerd. Dodenwake. Ik zou hen met rust moeten laten. Terwijl ik nog twijfel wat ik zal doen sta ik ineens al bij de voordeur en bel aan.

Hij gaat open. Barnaby. Hij heeft zich gedoucht, geschoren en opgeknapt, maar zijn ogen staan waterig en wazig.

'Wie is daar, lieverd?' klinkt een stem van binnen.

Hij verstrakt en doet een stap achteruit. Piepende wielen op het parket. Cates moeder, Ruth Elliot, komt aanrijden. Ze is in het zwart, wat haar gezicht nog bleker maakt.

'Kom binnen,' zegt ze, haar tanden ontbloot tot een gepijnigde glimlach.

'Ik vind het heel erg van Cate. Als ik iets kan doen…'

Ze reageert niet. Rollende wielen. Ik volg ze naar de zitkamer, die vol zit met bedroefd kijkende vrienden en familie. Enkelen herken ik. Judy en Richard Sutton, broer en zus. Richard was bij twee verkiezingen Barnaby's campagneleider en Judy werkt bij de Chase Manhattan Bank. Cates tante Paula is in gesprek met Jarrod en in de hoek ontwaar ik dominee Lunn, een anglicaanse priester.

Yvonne hangt op een stoel, pratend en snikkend tegelijk. Haar kleren, doorgaans zo kleurig en levendig, weerspiegelen dit keer haar stemming: zwart. Ze heeft haar twee kinderen bij zich, allebei volwassen en meer Engels dan Jamaicaans. Het meisje is een schoonheid. De jongen zou duizend plekken kunnen opnoemen waar hij liever zou zijn.

Voordat ik iets kan zeggen pakt Barnaby mijn arm en trekt me weg.

'Hoe wist je van het geld?' sist hij. Zijn adem ruikt naar alcohol.

'Waar heb je het over?'

Zijn woorden zijn nauwelijks te verstaan. 'Iemand heeft tachtigduizend pond opgenomen van Cates rekening.'

'Hoe kwam ze aan zo'n bedrag?'

Hij gaat nog zachter praten. 'Van haar overleden grootmoeder. Ik ben haar bankrekening nagegaan. De helft van het geld is afgelopen december opgenomen, de rest in maart.'

'Een bankcheque?'

'Contant. Meer wil de bank me niet vertellen.'

'En je hebt geen idee waarvoor?'

Hij schudt zijn hoofd en zet een struikelende stap. Ik leid hem naar de keuken, waar tussen opengescheurde enveloppen de van-harte-beterschap-kaarten liggen. Ze maken een futiele indruk, ingehaald door een groter leed.

Ik pak een glas water en geef het hem. 'De vorige keer zei je iets over een arts, een fertiliteitsspecialist.'

'Wat is daarmee?'

'Heb je hem ooit ontmoet?'

'Nee.'

'Heeft hij ooit andere mogelijkheden dan IVF genoemd, zoals adoptie of draagmoederschap?'

'Niet dat ik weet. Ik weet wel dat hij Cates kansen niet al te rooskleurig voorspiegelde. En hij weigerde meer dan twee embryo's te implanteren. Hij had nog een stelregel: drie slag is uit. Cate smeekte hem om nog een laatste kans. Het werden er uiteindelijk vijf.'

'Vijf.'

'Ze hadden achttien eitjes weggehaald, waarvan er maar twaalf geschikt waren. Per keer werden er twee embryo's geïmplanteerd.'

'Tien in totaal dus. En de andere twee?'

Hij haalt zijn schouders op. 'Dokter Banerjee wilde niet verdergaan. Hij zag hoe breekbaar Cate was geworden, emotioneel gezien. Ze stond op instorten.'

'Ze had naar een andere kliniek kunnen gaan.'

'Dat wilde Felix niet. Nog meer hormonen, de onderzoeken, de tranen – die wilde hij haar besparen.'

Het geld verklaar je er niet mee. Tachtigduizend pond geef je niet zomaar weg. Cate probeerde een kind te kopen maar er ging iets mis. Daarom zocht ze contact met me.

Ik loop het verhaal opnieuw door en leg de bewijzen naast elkaar. Sommige details en halve waarheden hebben de kracht van feiten gekregen. Ik zie Barnaby denken. Hij is bezorgd over zijn politieke ambities. Een schandaal als dit zou zijn kansen voorgoed om zeep helpen.

'Daarom moet ik Cates computer ook zien,' zeg ik.

'Die heeft ze niet.'

'Heb je gekeken?'

'Nee.'

Het glas tinkelt tegen zijn tanden. Hij liegt.

'De mappen die je me liet zien, en Cates brieven, kan ik die lenen?'

'Nee.'

Mijn teleurstelling begint in boosheid te veranderen. 'Waarom doe je zo? Hoe kan ik het je laten begrijpen?'

Zijn hand raakt mijn knie. 'Je zou lief voor me kunnen zijn.'

Ruth Elliot duikt op in de keuken, met geluidloze wielen ditmaal. Ze kijkt alsof ze een kikker heeft uitgespuugd.

'Er gaan al mensen weg, Barnaby. Je moet gedag komen zeggen.'

Hij volgt haar naar de voordeur. Ik grijp mijn jas en glip langs hen heen.

'Bedankt dat je geweest bent, liefje,' zegt ze mechanisch, en ze rekt zich in haar rolstoel uit. Haar lippen op mijn voorhoofd zijn droog als papier.

Barnaby slaat zijn armen om me heen en zijn lippen raken mijn linkeroorlel. Hij buigt zich naar me toe. Ik ga anders staan om onze dijen elkaar niet te laten raken.

'Waarom doen vrouwen dit altijd bij míj?'

Terwijl ik wegrijd kan ik de warmte van zijn adem nog voelen. Waarom denken mannen altijd dat het om hén gaat?

Ik weet zeker dat ik een excuus of een argument zou kunnen bedenken voor wat ik nu ga doen, maar hoe je het ook inkleedt, het blijft overtreding van de wet. Een halve baksteen. Een overjas. De ruit versplintert en valt naar binnen. Nu is het nog vandalisme of criminele schade. Ik steek mijn hand naar binnen en maak de deur open. Nu is het onrechtmatige toegang. Als ik de laptop vind, wordt het diefstal. Is dit wat ze bedoelen met het hellend vlak van de misdaad?

Het is na middernacht. Ik draag zwarte jeans, leren handschoenen en een koningsblauwe coltrui die tante Meena voor me heeft gebreid. Ik heb een grote rol zwart plastic bij me, afdichtingstape, een staaflantaarn en een USB-stick om computerbestanden op te kunnen zetten.

Ik sluit mijn ogen. Ik zie de indeling van de begane grond voor me. Ik herinner me het van drie dagen terug. Glas knarst onder mijn sportschoenen. Op het antwoordapparaat knippert een rood lampje.

Het had niet zover moeten komen. Barnaby loog. Niet dat ik hem van iets ernstigs verdenk. Goede mensen beschermen degenen die ze liefhebben. Maar soms zien ze niet hoe goede bedoelingen en blinde loyaliteit hun denken kunnen verwringen.

Hij is bang voor wat ik zou kunnen vinden. Ik ook. Hij maakt zich zorgen dat hij zijn dochter niet echt kende. Ik ook.

Ik ga de trap op. In de kinderkamer pak ik de rol plastic en plak met de afdichtingstape het raam af. Nu kan ik de staaflamp aandoen.

Voorzorgsmaatregelen zoals deze zijn misschien overbodig, maar ik kan me niet veroorloven dat er buren komen kijken of dat iemand de politie belt. Mijn carrière (welke?) hangt al aan een zijden draadje. Ik open de la van de commode. De mappen zijn verdwenen, het stapeltje brieven ook.

In de volgende kamers doe ik hetzelfde; ik doorzoek klerenkasten en laden onder bedden.

Naast de grote slaapkamer is een studeerkamertje met een bureau en een archiefkast. Het ene raam staat een stukje open. Als ik naar buiten gluur zie ik een maanverlichte tuin, bedekt met gevallen bladeren en schaduwen.

Ik rol een stuk zwart plastic af en blindeer het raam voordat ik mijn staaflamp aandoe. Onder het bureau, net boven de plint, zie ik een telefooncontactdoos. De bovenste la bevat software en een installatiehandleiding voor adsl. Ik zat goed wat betreft die computer. En wat betreft Barnaby.

In de andere laden liggen de gebruikelijke kantoordingen: markeerstiften, een nietmachine, paperclips, een bol elastiekjes, gele Post-It-briefjes, een aansteker...

Daarna doorzoek ik de archiefkast en blader door de hangmappen. Ze hebben geen etiket of datum. Ik moet ze een voor een doorzoeken. De huishoudelijke rekeningen zitten in plastic. Op elke telefoonrekening staat een lijst met uitgaande gesprekken naar mobiele en interlokale nummers. Ik zou ze kunnen natrekken, maar dat kost dagen.

Tussen de facturen zit er een van een internetprovider. Mensen laten soms kopieën van hun e-mails op de server staan, maar dan heb ik wel Cates gebruikersnaam en wachtwoord nodig.

Als ik de studeerkamer heb gehad, ga ik naar de grote slaapkamer, waar op de boekenplanken na geen papier te vinden is. Felix sliep links. Hij droeg een leesbril en hield van Armistead Maupin. Ik ga aan Cates kant zitten. In de la van het nachtkastje zie ik nachtcrème, vochtinbrengende crème, kartonnen nagelvijltjes en een op zijn kop liggend fotolijstje. Ik draai het om.

Twee tienermeisjes lachen naar de camera, de armen over elkaars schouders, de haren druipend van het zeewater. Ik kan het zout op hun huid haast proeven en de golven op het kiezelstrand horen.

In de maand augustus huurden de Elliots altijd een huisje in Cornwall en brachten ze hun dagen door met zeilen en zwemmen. Een keer had Cate me meegevraagd. Ik was vijftien en het was mijn eerste echte strandvakantie.

We zwommen, fietsten, zochten schelpen en keken naar de surfende jongens in Widemouth Bay. Een paar van hen boden aan Cate en mij te leren surfen, maar Barnaby zei dat surfers nietsnutten en hasjrokers waren. In plaats daarvan leerde hij ons in de haven van Padstow en de monding van de Camel zeilen in een eenmansbootje. Hij kon maar een van ons tegelijk meenemen.

Ik schaamde me voor het mintgroene badpak van katoenen wafeltjesstof dat mijn moeder had uitgekozen. Cate had me een van haar bikini's geleend. Als we naast elkaar zaten, raakte Barnaby's been soms het mijne. En om het bootje in balans te houden moesten we achteroverhangen, waarbij hij zijn arm om mijn middel sloeg. Ik hield van de manier waarop hij naar zout en zonnebrandolie rook.

's Avonds deden we spelletjes, zoals lettergreepraadsels en Triviant. Ik probeerde naast hem te gaan zitten omdat hij me in mijn zij porde als hij een van zijn moppen vertelde of tegen me aan leunde totdat we omvielen.

'Je zat met hem te sjansen,' zei Cate toen we in bed lagen. We deelden de zolder. Meneer en mevrouw Elliot hadden de grootste slaapkamer op de verdieping onder ons, Jarrod een eigen kamer aan de achterkant van het huis.

'Niet waar.'

'Wel waar.'

'Doe niet zo belachelijk.'

'Walgelijk gewoon.'

Ze had natuurlijk gelijk. Ik flirtte met hem en hij flirtte terug omdat hij geen andere manier wist om zich tegenover vrouwen of meisjes te gedragen.

Cate en ik lagen boven op ons beddengoed. We konden niet slapen vanwege de warmte. De zolder was niet geïsoleerd en leek de hitte van overdag vast te houden.

'Weet je wat jouw probleem is?' zei ze. 'Jij hebt nog nooit een jongen gezoend.'

'Welles.'

'Ik bedoel niet je broers, ik bedoel echt tongen.'

Ik begon me ongemakkelijk te voelen.

'Je zou moeten oefenen.'

'Pardon?'

'Hier, zo.' Ze hield haar duim en wijsvinger tegen elkaar. 'Doe alsof dit de lippen van een jongen zijn en kus ze.'

Ze pakte mijn hand en kuste hem, bewoog met haar tong tussen mijn duim en wijsvinger totdat ze nat waren van het speeksel.

'Nou jij.' Ze hield haar hand uitgestoken. Hij smaakte naar tandpasta en zeep. 'Nee, te veel tong. Getver!'

'Jij gebruikte ook veel tong.'

'Minder.' Ze veegde haar hand af aan de lakens en keek me met ongeduldige genegenheid aan. 'En nu moet je leren positie te kiezen.'

'Hoe bedoel je?'

'Je moet je hoofd naar links of naar rechts kantelen, zodat onze neuzen niet botsen. We zijn geen eskimo's.'

Ze zwaaide haar paardenstaart over haar schouder en trok me naar zich toe. Met haar handen rond mijn gezicht drukte ze haar lippen op de mijne. Ik voelde haar hartslag en haar bloed pulseren onder haar huid. Haar tong streek langs mijn lippen en danste over mijn tanden. We ademden dezelfde lucht. Mijn ogen bleven dicht. Het was een ongelooflijk, verbazingwekkend gevoel.

'Wauw, jij bent een snelle leerling,' zei ze.

'En jij een goede leraar.'

Mijn hart ging als een razende tekeer.

'Misschien moeten we het hier maar bij laten.'

'Het voelde wel een beetje raar.'

'Ja. Raar.'

Ik veegde mijn handpalmen af aan het voorpand van mijn nachtpon.

'Nou ja, je weet nu hoe het moet,' zei Cate terwijl ze een tijdschrift pakte.

Zelfs op haar vijftiende had ze al veel jongens gezoend, maar ze schepte er niet over op. Er volgden er nog veel meer, als parels en kiezelstenen die zich rond haar hals aaneenregen. Bij elk vriendje dat kwam en weer ging was er nauwelijks meer dan een schouderophaal van berusting of droefheid.

Ik laat mijn vinger over de foto glijden en vraag me af of ik hem mee zal nemen. Wie zou het merken? Op hetzelfde moment schiet me een antwoord te binnen. Ik loop terug naar de studeerkamer, open de la van het bureau en zie de aansteker. Als ik als kind bij Cate bleef logeren, smokkelde ze sigaretten naar boven en hing ze uit het raam te roken, zodat haar ouders het niet zouden ruiken.

Ik trek het zwarte plastic van het raam, schuif het omhoog en hou me aan de vensterbank vast terwijl ik, vijf meter boven de grond, naar buiten leun.

In het duister laat ik mijn blik langs de regenpijp gaan, die met metalen beugels aan de bakstenen is bevestigd. Ik heb meer licht nodig. Ik waag het erop en richt de bundel van de staaflamp op de pijp. Ik kan net het geknoopte eind van een dun koord ontwaren, dat buiten mijn bereik aan de dichtstbijzijnde beugel vastzit.

Hoe deed ze het?

Ik kijk de kamer rond. Achter het bureau, pal tegen de muur, ligt een kleerhanger van ijzerdraad die is verbogen tot een ruitvorm met een haak aan het uiteinde. Terug bij het raam buig ik me naar buiten en haal met het haakje het koord naar me toe. Als ik eraan trek, komt er uit het gebladerte een verfblik omhoog. Zodra ik erbij kan, grijp ik het beet.

Ik haal het blik binnen en wrik met een munt het deksel open. Er zit een half pakje sigaretten in en een groter pakje, in plastic gewikkeld en met elastiekjes bijeengehouden. Ik haal het eruit, doe het deksel weer op het blik en laat het aan het nylonkoord door mijn vingers vieren tot het weer in de struiken is verdwenen.

Ik loop terug naar de grote slaapkamer en haal het elastiek eraf. Het blijkt een opgerolde plastic tas te zijn, met onderin een paar papieren geprop. Ik spreid de inhoud uit op het dekbed: twee luchthaveninstapkaarten, een toeristenkaart van Amsterdam en een brochure.

De instapkaarten zijn voor een British Midlandsvlucht van London Heathrow naar Schiphol op 9 maart, met de terugvlucht op 11 maart.

Op de voorkant van de toeristenkaart, waarvan de vouwranden beschadigd zijn, staat een foto van het Rijksmuseum. De kaart bestrijkt zo te zien het centrum van Amsterdam, met de grachtengordel en dwarsstraten. Op de achterkant staan bus, tram en metroroutes en een lijst met hotels. Een ervan is omcirkeld, het Red Tulip Hotel.

Ik pak de brochure. Een soort promotie voor een stichting, het New Life Adoption Centre, met een telefoonnummer en een postbusnummer in Hayward's Heath, West Sussex. Foto's van baby's en blijde stellen, met een citaat: *Is het niet prachtig dat, als het moederschap voor jou te vroeg komt, je anderen gelukkig kunt maken?*

Eenmaal opengevouwen zijn in de brochure nog meer foto's en getuigenissen te zien.

Uw hoop gevestigd op adoptie? Als u een veilige, succesvolle adoptie wilt, kunnen wij u helpen. Sinds 1995 hebben wij honderden echtparen geholpen een baby te adopteren. Onze selecte groep betrokken professionals kan uw droom van een gezin helpen waarmaken.

Op de tegenoverliggende pagina staat in hoofdletters: BEN JIJ ZWANGER EN ZOEK JE EEN OPLOSSING?

Wij kunnen je helpen! Wij bieden hulp en steun tijdens en na je zwangerschap en studiebeurzen voor de biologische ouder. Open adoptie betekent dat jij de keuzes maakt.

Eronder staat een foto van een kinderhandje dat de vinger van een volwassene omklemt.

Een zekere Julie schrijft: *Bedankt dat jullie van mijn onverhoopte zwangerschap een godsgeschenk voor alle betrokkenen hebben weten te maken.*

Op de volgende pagina nog meer getuigenissen, ditmaal van stellen: *De keuze voor adoptie heeft ons een prachtige dochter gebracht en ons leven compleet gemaakt.*

Er glipt een losse pagina uit het hart van de brochure.

Dit kind kan het uwe worden, staat er. *Deze maand geboren: een jongen, blank, vader onbekend. Moeder, achttien jaar, is prostituee en drugsverslaafde, maar inmiddels clean. Tegen een bemiddelingsvergoeding en vergoeding van de medische kosten kan dit kind het uwe worden.*

Ik stop de papieren terug in de plastic zak en doe de elastiekjes erom.

Voor het telefoonnummer achter op de foto van Samira was een landnummer nodig. Cate was in maart in Nederland. Dat valt ongeveer samen met het moment waarop ze bekendmaakte dat ze in verwachting was.

Ik pak de telefoon naast het bed en bel Inlichtingen Buitenland. Het voelt verkeerd om vanaf de plaats delict te bellen, alsof ik daarmee beken. Een medewerker geeft me het landnummer voor Nederland. Met de 31 ervoor bel ik het nummer.

De telefoon gaat over. Lang en monotoon.

Er wordt opgenomen. Stilte.

'Hallo?'

Niets.

'Hallo, hoort u mij?'

Ik hoor iemand ademen.

'Ik probeer Samira te bereiken? Is ze daar?'

Een schorre stem, borrelend van het slijm, antwoordt: 'Wie is daar?'

Het zou een Nederlands accent kunnen zijn, maar het klinkt eerder Oost-Europees.

'Een vriendin.'

'Uw naam?'

'Beter gezegd: een vriendin van een vriendin.'

'Hoe heet u? Hoe heet die vriendin?'

Wantrouwen overspoelt me als een kille schaduw. Deze stem bevalt me niet. Ik voel hoe hij me opzoekt en in mijn borst graait, op zoek naar mijn ziel.

'Is Samira daar?'

'Er is niemand aanwezig.'

Ik probeer kalm te klinken. 'Ik bel namens Cate Beaumont. Ik heb de rest van het geld.'

Ik extrapoleer op basis van de bekende feiten. Iets minder deftig gezegd: ik doe maar wat. *Hoeveel verder kan ik gaan?*

De verbinding wordt verbroken.

Niet ver genoeg.

Ik leg de telefoon weer op zijn plek, trek het bed glad en graai mijn spullen bij elkaar. Als ik naar de deur loop hoor ik beneden gerinkel. Ik herken het. Precies zo'n geluid maakte ik toen ik een ruitje van de voordeur insloeg.

Er is iemand binnen. Hoe groot is de kans op twee inbrekers op één avond? Magertjes. Nihil. Terwijl ik het pakketje in mijn broekband prop, gluur ik over de balustrade. In de hal klinken gedempte stemmen. Op z'n minst twee. Een lichtbundel strijkt langs de voet van de trap. Ik doe een stap achteruit.

Wat kan ik doen? Ik hoor hier niet te zijn. Zij ook niet. Voor me ligt de trap naar zolder. Ik loop snel omhoog en open een deur, die hoorbaar stroeve scharnieren blijkt te hebben.

Van beneden: 'Hoorde jij iets?'

'Hè?'

'Ik dacht dat ik iets hoorde.'

'Neu.'

'Ik ga boven kijken.'

Een van hen klinkt Iers. Mogelijk Brendan Pearl.

'Hé!'

'Wat?'

'Heb je dat gezien?'

'Heb ik wát gezien?'

'De ramen zijn met plastic afgedekt. Waarom zouden ze dat doen?'

'Al sla je me dood. Ga nou maar door.'

De zolder lijkt allerlei schuine kanten en uithoekjes te hebben. Mijn ogen beginnen te wennen aan het donker. Ik ontwaar een eenpersoonsbed, een staande ventilator en kartonnen dozen met allerlei rommel en prullaria.

Ik pers me in de ruimte tussen de kast en het schuine dak en schuif er een paar dozen voor. De stijlen van het ijzeren bed zijn voorzien van zware bronzen bollen. Voorzichtig schroef ik er een los, trek een sok uit en laat de bol erin glijden. Hij glijdt door tot aan de teen. Ik voel het gewicht. Genoeg om botten te breken.

Vanuit mijn schuilplek luister ik of ik voetstappen hoor op de trap en hou ik de deur in de gaten. Ik moet de politie bellen. Als ik mijn telefoon openklap zal het schermpje oplichten als een neonreclame met de boodschap 'Hier ben ik! Kom me maar halen!'

Met beide handen eromheen bel ik het alarmnummer. Ik krijg een telefonist.

'Agent in moeilijkheden. Insluipers ter plekke.'

Ik fluister het adres en mijn badgenummer. Ik kan niet aan de lijn blijven. De telefoon sluit zich, het scherm wordt donker. Alleen nog mijn ademhaling en de voetstappen…

De deur gaat open. Een lichtbundel flitst aan en zwaait de kamer door. Ik kan de gestalte erachter niet zien. Hij mij ook niet. Hij struikelt over een doos. Er rollen kerstballen uit. Een ervan rolt, vlak bij mijn voeten, de lichtbundel binnen.

Hij legt de staaflamp op het bed, met de lichtbundel naar zich toe. Hij verlicht het voorhoofd. Brendan Pearl. Mijn hele gewicht rust op de ballen van mijn voeten, klaar om te vechten. Wat doet hij nou?

Hij heeft iets in zijn vuist. Een rechthoekige bus. Hij knijpt erin. In een boog spuit een straal vloeistof weg van de tuit, zilverschijnend in de stralenbundel. Hij spuit opnieuw, doordrenkt de kartonnen dozen, tekent grillige lijnen op de muren. Vloeistof spat op mijn voorhoofd en loopt mijn ogen in.

Pijnscheuten als gloeidraden schieten door mijn hoofd en de geur zet zich achter in mijn keel vast. Wasbenzine. Aanstekerbenzine. Vuur!

De pijn is onvoorstelbaar, maar ik mag me niet bewegen. Hij gaat het huis in brand steken. Ik moet wegkomen. Ik zie niets. Trillingen op de trap. Hij is weg. Ik kruip mijn schuilplaats uit, loop naar de deur en leg mijn oor ertegenaan.

Zo gaat het niet, met mijn ogen. Ik moet ze spoelen. Op de eerste verdieping is een badkamer, en nog eentje, en suite, bij de grote slaapkamer. Ik weet ze te vinden, maar pas als Pearl weg is. Ik kan me geen uitstel veroorloven.

Beneden breekt er iets met een knal en valt om. Mijn blik is troebel, maar ik zie licht. Nee, geen licht – vuur!

De begane grond staat in lichterlaaie, rook stijgt omhoog. Me vastklampend aan de leuning bereik ik de overloop. Langs de muur tastend kom ik bij de tweede badkamer. Ik gooi water in mijn gezicht. Ik zie alleen vage contouren, schimmen in plaats van details.

De rook wordt dikker. Op handen en voeten zoek ik op de tast mijn weg door de slaapkamer. Ik ruik de aanstekerbenzine op het tapijt. Als het vuur deze verdieping bereikt, zal het hard gaan. Het studeerkamerraam staat nog open. Ik kruip over de overloop, stoot mijn hoofd tegen een muur. Mijn vingers vinden de plint. Ik voel de hitte.

Bij het raam aangekomen leun ik naar buiten en haal tussen de proestende hoestbuien door diep adem. Achter me klinkt een suizend geluid. Vlammen schieten langs de deuropening. Uitgehongerd, gevoed door de aanmaakvloeistof.

Ik klim op de vensterbank en kijk omlaag. Ik kan de tuin niet zien. Hij moet een meter of vijf meter onder me zijn. Dat kost me mijn benen. Ik draai mijn hoofd naar de regenpijp tegen de muur. Ik zie nog steeds bijna niets. Hoe ver was het? Ruim een meter, misschien iets meer.

Aan de achterkant van mijn benen voel ik de hitte van het vuur. Beneden me springt een raam kapot. Ik hoor glasscherven neerkomen in het struikgewas.

Ik moet mezelf dwingen dit te doen. Ik moet op mijn geheugen en mijn instinct vertrouwen. Ik laat me zijwaarts vallen en strek mijn armen uit.

Mijn linkerhand schampt langs de pijp, mijn rechterhand klauwt zich eromheen. Door de kracht van de val zal ik of los moeten laten, of mijn arm uit de kom laten rukken. Beide handen hebben nu beet. Mijn heup slaat tegen de bakstenen. Ik hou vast.

Hand voor hand slinger ik me omlaag. Ik hoor sirenes. Mijn voeten raken zachte grond. Ik zwaai rond, doe een paar struikelpassen en val over een ligbed languit op mijn gezicht.

Elk raam aan de achterkant van het huis is verlicht. Met mijn waterige blik oogt en klinkt het als een studentenfeest. De ultieme house-warming party.

12

Er zijn twee rechercheurs gearriveerd. Een van hen ken ik van de opleiding, Eric Softell. Een naam als een merk toiletpapier, wat hem op de academie de bijnaam 'Pleerol' bezorgde. Niet bij mij, natuurlijk. Sikh-meisjes wagen het niet mensen uit te schelden.

'Ik hoorde dat je het korps hebt verlaten.'

'Nee.'

'Loop je nog steeds hard?'

'Ja.'

'Niet hard genoeg, hebben ze me verteld.' Hij grijnst naar zijn maat, Billy Marsh, een beginnend rechercheur.

Verhalen over kameraadschap tussen politiemensen zijn vaak schandelijk overdreven. Er zijn niet veel collega's die ik bijzonder aardig of solidair vind, maar de meesten zijn tenminste wel oprecht en sommigen zijn om te koesteren, zoals inspecteur Ruiz.

Een verpleger heeft mijn ogen uitgespoeld met gedistilleerd water. Ik zit op de achterrand van de ambulance met mijn hoofd achterover, terwijl hij watten over mijn linkeroog vastplakt.

'Je moet naar een oogarts,' zegt hij. 'Het duurt soms wel een week voor de schade zich volledig manifesteert.'

'Blijvende schade?'

'Dat moet je aan je oogarts vragen.'

Achter hem liggen brandslangen over het glinsterende wegdek verspreid. Brandweerlieden in fluorescerende hesjes zijn aan het opruimen. Het huis staat er nog, maar het binnenwerk is uitgebrand en smeult nog na. De zolder is onder het gewicht van het water naar beneden gekomen.

Ik heb Hari gebeld of hij me komt ophalen. Met een mengeling van ontzag en afgunst staat hij de brandweerlieden te bekijken. Welke jongen wil er nou niet met een brandslang spelen?

De animositeit tussen Softell en mij ontgaat hem niet. Hij probeert tussenbeide te komen en de beschermende broer te spelen, wat niet echt bij hem past.

'Hé, waaierjongen, als jij ons nou eens even een kopje thee bezorgde,' zegt Softell.

Hari pikt de belediging niet op, maar herkent de toon.

Ik zou kwaad moeten zijn, maar ik ben gewend aan dit soort opmerkingen uit de mond van mensen als Softell. Tijdens de basisopleiding kreeg een groepje van ons oproerschilden uitgereikt met de opdracht naar het exercitieterrein te gaan. Een andere groep rekruten moest ons verbaal en fysiek aanvallen. Er waren geen regels, maar we waren niet in staat ons te verweren.

Softell spuugde me in mijn gezicht en noemde me 'Paki-hoer'. Het scheelde weinig of ik had hem nog bedankt ook. Mijn linkerdij is enigszins gevoelloos, mijn knokkels zijn geschaafd en rauw. Er komen vragen. Antwoorden. De naam Brendan Pearl zegt hun niets.

'Leg nog eens uit wat je in het huis deed.'

'Ik reed langs en zag dat er werd ingebroken. Ik heb het doorgegeven.'

'Vanuit het huis?'

'Jazeker.'

'Dus je bent hem naar binnen gevolgd?'

'Ja.'

Hij schudt zijn hoofd. 'Dus jij reed toevallig langs het huis van een vriendin en zag daar dezelfde man die achter het stuur zat van de auto die haar aanreed. Wat vind jij ervan, Billy?'

'Lulkoek als je het mij vraagt.' Marsh maakt aantekeningen.

'Hoe heb je die aanstekerbenzine in je ogen gekregen?'

'Die sprenkelde hij in het rond.'

'Ja ja, terwijl jij je in een hoek had verstopt.'

Lul!

Achteloos zet hij zijn voet op het plateau van de ambulance. 'Als je je alleen verstopte, waarom dan al die moeite?'

'Ik dacht dat het er maar één was.'

Ik ben een kuil voor mezelf aan het graven.

'Waarom heb je geen versterking gevraagd voordat je naar binnen ging?'

Dieper en dieper.

'Dat weet ik niet, meneer.'

Waterdruppels liggen als kraaltjes op de glimmende neus van zijn schoen.

'Je voelt zeker wel aan hoe dit overkomt?' zegt hij.

'Hoe dan?'

'Er is een huis afgebrand. Er meldt zich een getuige die onder de aanstekerbenzine zit. De eerste regel bij brand is dat, negen van de tien keer, degene die "brand" roept degene is die de zaak heeft aangestoken.'

'Dat kun je niet menen. Waarom zou ik dat doen?'

Zijn schouders gaan op en neer. 'Wie zal het zeggen? Misschien vind jij het wel leuk dingen te zien branden.'

De hele straat is wakker geworden. Op de stoep staan in kamerjassen en overjassen gehulde omwonenden. Kinderen springen boven op een slang en weer weg van de plek waar hij lekt en een zilveren straal het straatlantaarnlicht in spuit.

Buiten de kring brandweerwagens stopt een auto. Ruiz stapt uit. Zonder acht te slaan op de politieman die hem tegen probeert te houden doorbreekt hij de kring pottenkijkers.

Na stilstaand het huis te hebben bekeken, loopt hij door tot hij bij me is. Met mijn witte oogbedekking zie ik eruit als een omgekeerde zeerover.

'Heb jij ooit weleens een normále dag?' vraagt hij.

'Eén keer gehad, een woensdag.'

Hij bekijkt me van top tot teen. Vanwege mijn dij sta ik grotendeels op één been. Tot mijn verrassing buigt hij zich en kust me op de wang, een absolute primeur.

'Ik dacht dat u met pensioen was,' zegt Billy Marsh.

'Dat klopt, mijn jongen.'

'Wat doet u dan hier?'

'Ik heb hem gevraagd te komen,' leg ik uit.

Ruiz monstert de twee rechercheurs. 'Bezwaar als ik meeluister?'

Het klinkt als een vraag, maar is het niet. Dat kan hij af en toe: van een vraag een vaststelling maken.

'Als je ons godverdomme maar niet voor de voeten loopt,' mompelt Softell.

Marsh is aan de telefoon om een onderzoeksteam plaats delict op te roepen. De brandweer zal een eigen onderzoek instellen. Ik strompel weg van de ambulance, die naar elders wordt ontboden. Ruiz pakt mijn arm.

Ik zie dat Hari er nog is. 'Je kunt nu wel naar huis gaan.'

'En jij dan?'

'Dat kan nog wel even duren.'

'Wil je dat ik blijf?'

'Nee, hoeft niet.'

Hij kijkt steels naar Softell en fluistert: 'Ken jij die eikel?'

'Hij is best geschikt.'

'Geen wonder dat mensen een hekel hebben aan smerissen.'

'Hé!'

Hij grijnst. 'Dat geldt niet voor jou, zus.'

Er zijn meer vragen te beantwoorden. Softells interesse in wat ik in het huis deed verflauwt, zijn interesse in Brendan Pearl neemt toe.

'Dus jij denkt dat de brandstichting verband houdt met de dood van de Beaumonts?'

'Ja.'

'Waarom zou Pearl hun huis in de as leggen?'

'Misschien wilde hij bewijsmateriaal vernietigen: brieven, e-mails, lijsten met telefoongesprekken – alles wat in zijn richting zou kunnen wijzen.'

Ik vertel hem over Cates nepzwangerschap en het verdwenen geld van haar rekening. 'Ik denk dat ze een baby probeerde te kopen, maar dat er iets fout liep.'

Marsh neemt het woord. 'Adoptie van buitenlandse kinderen, Chinees, Roemeens, Koreaans, is aan de orde van de dag; waarom zou je dan een kind kopen?'

'Ze heeft adoptie geprobeerd, maar dat kon niet.'

'Hoe koop je een kind?'

Ik heb geen antwoorden. Softell kijkt naar Billy Marsh. Het is heel even stil en ze wisselen iets onzichtbaars uit.

'Waarom heb je hier niet eerder melding van gemaakt.'

'Ik was niet zeker van mijn zaak.'

'Dus ging je op zoek naar bewijsmateriaal. En brak in het huis in.'

'Niet waar.'

'Vervolgens probeerde jij je sporen uit te wissen met een blik aanstekerbenzine en een lulverhaal.'

'Niet waar.'

Ruiz staat vlakbij, met afwisselend gebalde en ontspannen vuisten. Voor het eerst merk ik op hoe oud hij eruitziet in zijn vormloze overjas met sleetse ellebogen.

'Hé, brigadier, ik weet waar jij aan zit te denken,' zegt hij. 'Jij hebt liever een doodgewoon, alledaags zaakje dat voor negenen is opgelost, zodat je nog op tijd bent voor je balletles. Hier staat een van je collega's, een van jullie. Het is jouw taak haar te geloven.'

Softell zwelt op. Te stom om zijn mond te houden. 'En wie denk jij wel dat je bent?'

'Godzilla.'

'Nog eens?'

Ruiz rolt met zijn ogen. 'Ik ben het monster dat die carrière van jou naar de kloten zal helpen als jij deze dame niet wat meer respect betoont.'

Softell kijkt alsof hij een klap heeft gekregen. Hij pakt zijn telefoontje en toetst een nummer in. Ik hoor hem met zijn hoofdinspecteur praten. Ik weet niet wat die hem vertelt. Ruiz heeft nog steeds een hoop vrienden bij de MET, mensen met respect voor zijn staat van dienst.

Na afloop van het gesprek is Softell een gelouterd man. Er gaat een speciaal onderzoeksteam komen en er is een arrestatiebevel uitgegaan voor Brendan Pearl.

'Kom rond de middag naar het bureau voor een verklaring.'

'Dus ik kan gaan?'

'Ja.'

Ruiz wil niet dat ik rijd. Hij brengt me met mijn auto naar huis. Opgepropt achter het stuur van mijn vijfdeurs ziet hij eruit als een seniele dwaas.

'Was het Pearl?'

'Ja.'

'Heb je hem gezien?'

'Ja.'

Met één hand rijdend krabt hij aan zijn kin. Hij mist de helft van zijn ringvinger, met dank aan een hogesnelheidskogel. Zijn vaste grapje is dat zijn derde echtgenote hem met een hakmes te lijf is gegaan.

Ik vertel Ruiz over de instapkaarten en de brochure van het New Life Adoption Centre. We kennen allebei de verhalen over gestolen en gesmokkelde baby's. De meeste gaan richting broodje aap, over babyfokkerijen in Guatemala en orgaandiefstal van in de straten van São Paulo opgepikte weglopertjes.

'Laten we aannemen dat jij gelijk hebt en Cate Beaumont een of andere privé-adoptie heeft geregeld, of de koop van een kind. Waarom dan die nepzwangerschap?'

'Misschien wilde ze Felix doen geloven dat het zijn kind was.'

'Dat is nogal wat. Wat als het kind totaal niet op hem lijkt?'

'Veel mannen geloven maar al te graag dat zij de verwekker zijn. De geschiedenis wemelt van de vergissingen.'

Ruiz trekt een wenkbrauw op. 'Van de leugens, zul je bedoelen.'

Ik hap. 'Ja, vrouwen kunnen doortrapt zijn. Soms moeten we wel. Wij zijn degenen die achterblijven met de poepluiers als een vent besluit dat hij nog niet klaar is om zich te binden, of zijn Harley of zijn pornoverzameling aan de kant te schuiven.'

Stilte.

'Klonk dat als een tirade?'

'Een beetje.'

'Sorry.'

Ruiz begint hardop denkend zijn geheugen door te spitten. Dat is typisch de inspecteur: hij vergeet nooit iets. Terwijl anderen grommen en fronsen als ze de meest simpele feitjes proberen terug te halen, herinnert Ruiz zich moeiteloos feiten, cijfers, uitspraken en namen.

'Drie jaar geleden pakte de Italiaanse politie een bende Oekraïense mensensmokkelaars op die een ongeboren baby te koop aanbood. Ze hielden een soort veiling om de hoogste bieder te vinden. Iemand bood tweehonderdvijftigduizend pond.'

'Cate vloog in maart naar Amsterdam. Mogelijk om een deal te sluiten.'

'In haar eentje?'

'Dat weet ik niet.'

'Hoe onderhielden ze contact met haar?'

Ik denk terug aan de brand. 'Dat zullen we misschien nooit weten.'

Hij brengt me tot voor de deur en spreekt voor de volgende dag af.

'Zorg dat je naar een oogarts gaat.'

'Eerst moet ik mijn verklaring afleggen.'

Boven trek ik de telefoonstekker eruit en zet mijn mobiele telefoon uit. Ik heb vandaag genoeg mensen gesproken. Ik wil een douche en een warm bed. Ik wil in mijn kussen uithuilen en in slaap vallen. Daar heeft een meisje recht op.

13

Politiebureau Wembley is een gloednieuw, met blauw en wit materiaal bekleed gebouw aan Harrow Road. Het nieuwe nationale stadion, waarvan de enorme lichtmasten boven de daken te zien zijn, ligt bijna anderhalve kilometer verderop.

Softell laat me wachten voordat hij me mijn verklaring afneemt. Zijn houding is anders dan gisteravond. Hij heeft Pearl in de computer opgezocht en de nieuwsgierigheid twinkelt in zijn ogen als een aanfloepended gaspit. Softell is het type rechercheur dat zijn hele carrière doorbrengt met zijn hoofd in zijn oksel, zonder enig benul van wat mensen drijft en zonder arrestaties die de krant halen. Nu ruikt hij een kans.

De dood van Cate en Felix Beaumont is bijzaak. Een zijspoor. Ik voel waar hij heen wil. Hij zal Cate terzijde schuiven als een wanhopige vrouw met een psychiatrisch verleden en een strafblad. Pearl is degene waar het hem om gaat.

'Je hebt geen bewijs voor het bestaan van de baby,' zegt hij.

'En het verdwenen geld dan?'

'Waarschijnlijk heeft iemand haar bezwendeld.'

'En daarna vermoord.'

'Volgens het inspectierapport van het voertuig niet.'

Hij overhandigt me een getypte verklaring. Ik moet elke pagina tekenen en wijzigingen paraferen. Ik kijk naar mijn uitspraken. Ik heb gelogen over waarom ik in het huis was en wat er voorafgaand aan de brand gebeurd is. Maakt mijn handtekening het erger?

Hij neemt de verklaring in, legt de vellen recht en drukt op de nietmachine. 'Verdomd professioneel,' sneert hij. 'Je weet dat het nooit stopt, het liegen. Als je eenmaal begint, gaat het van kwaad tot erger.'

'Ja, jij kunt het weten,' zeg ik. Ik was liever met een iets minder zwakke tegenzet gekomen. Maar nog liever zou ik willen dat ik de verklaring kon verscheuren en opnieuw kon beginnen.

In de hal wacht Ruiz me op.

'Hoe is het met je oog?'

'De specialist zei dat ik een week lang een ooglapje moet dragen.'

'Waar is dat dan?'

'In mijn zak.'

We stappen op een zwarte rubberen rechthoek en de deuren gaan automatisch open.

'Je vriend heeft het afgelopen uur zes keer gebeld. Weleens aan gedacht een hond voor in de plaats te nemen?'

'Wat heb je hem verteld?'

'Niets. Daarom is hij ook hier.'

Ik kijk op en zie Dave, leunend tegen Ruiz' auto. Hij neemt me in een stevige omhelzing, zijn gezicht in mijn haren. Ruiz keert zich af, alsof hij zich geneert.

'Zit jij me te besnuffelen, Dave?'

'Yep.'

'Dat is een beetje griezelig.'

'Vind ik niet. Ik ben gewoon blij dat je nog heel bent.'

'Alleen wat kneuzingen.'

'Die kan ik weg kussen.'

'Later misschien.'

Dave, in donkerblauw pak, wit overhemd en kastanjebruine stropdas, gaat sinds zijn promotie netter gekleed, maar op zijn das zie ik een sausvlek die hij niet heeft weten weg te vegen. Zoiets kleins zou mijn moeder ook opmerken. Eng idee.

Ik heb een lege maag. Ik heb sinds gisteren niet gegeten.

Vlak bij Wembley Central vinden we een koffiehuis met een vlekkerig schoolbord als menukaart en genoeg vet in de lucht om Daves haar plat te slaan. Het is een ouderwetse zaak met formica tafels, papieren servetten en een schrikachtige serveerster met een neusknopje.

Ik bestel thee met toast. Ruiz en Dave kiezen het hele-dag-door-ontbijt, ook wel bekend als 'enkeltje monitor', omdat het een op een bord geserveerde hartaanval is. Niemand zegt iets totdat we uitgegeten zijn en de thee is ingeschonken. De inspecteur gebruikt melk en suiker.

'Er is iemand met wie ik nog heb gerugbyd,' zegt hij. 'Hij heeft nooit iets losgelaten over zijn werk, maar ik weet dat hij bij MI5 zit. Ik heb hem vanochtend gebeld. Hij vertelde me iets interessants over Brendan Pearl.

'Wat precies?'

Ruiz haalt een beduimeld opschrijfboek tevoorschijn dat met een elastiek bij elkaar wordt gehouden. Losse blaadjes tuimelen door zijn vingers. Veel rechercheurs geloven niet in aantekeningen maken. Ze willen dat hun geheugen 'flexibel' blijft voor het geval ze ooit in de getuigenbank terechtkomen. Ruiz heeft een geheugen als de spreekwoordelijke ijzeren pot, en toch schrijft hij alles ook nog eens op.

'Volgens mijn vriend heeft Pearl meest recentelijk als beveiligingsexpert bij een bouwbedrijf in Afghanistan gewerkt. Half september 2004 werden drie buitenlandse aannemers gedood toen er een zelfmoordterrorist op hen inreed terwijl ze in konvooi onderweg waren van de centrale luchthaven naar het centrum van Kabul. Pearl lag drie weken in een Duits ziekenhuis en schreef zich daar toen uit. Sindsdien is er niets meer van hem vernomen.'

'Wat brengt hem hier?' vraagt Dave.

'En hoe heeft Cate hem ontmoet?' vul ik aan.

Ruiz pakt de blaadjes bij elkaar en doet het elastiek eromheen. 'Misschien moeten we dat New Life Adoption Centre maar eens gaan bekijken.'

Dave vindt van niet. 'Het is niet ons onderzoek.'

'Officieel niet, nee,' geeft de inspecteur toe.

'En onofficieel ook niet.'

'Het is een onafhankelijk onderzoek.'

'Ongeautoriseerd.'

'Onbeperkt.'

Ik onderbreek hen en doe een voorstel. 'Je zou mee kunnen gaan, Dave.'

Hij aarzelt.

Ruiz ruikt een opening. 'Dat bevalt me zo aan je, Dave: je bent een vrijdenker. Sommige mensen vinden de hedendaagse Britse rechercheur terughoudend en pietluttig, maar dat ben jij niet. De MET kan trots op je zijn. Jij bent niet bang een mening te hebben of een ingeving te volgen.'

Het is alsof ik een visser een vlieg zie uitgooien. Hij krult door de lucht, komt neer op het water en drijft stroomafwaarts, drijft en drijft...

'Een kijkje nemen kan denk ik geen kwaad,' zegt Dave.

Er zijn geen borden die naar het New Life Adoption Centre verwijzen, noch in het nabijgelegen dorp, noch bij de door zandstenen pilaren geflankeerde poort. Een grindpad slingert zich door velden en over een smalle stenen brug. De Friese koeien in de wei kijken nauwelijks op als we passeren.

Uiteindelijk houden we stil bij een groot, geornamenteerd neoklassiek huis binnen de geluidszone van Gatwick Airport. Ik pak Daves arm.

'Moet je horen. Wij zijn zes jaar getrouwd. Het was een enorme sikh-bruiloft. Uiteraard zag ik er prachtig uit. We proberen al vijf jaar een kind te krijgen, maar jouw spermagehalte is te laag.'

'Moet het per se míjn spermagehalte zijn?'

'Doe niet zo kinderachtig. Geef me je ring.'

Hij laat een witgouden ring van zijn pink glijden. Ik doe hem om mijn ringvinger.

Ruiz is achtergebleven in de dichtstbijzijnde dorpspub, in gesprek met de stamgasten. Tot dusverre hebben we ontdekt dat het adoptiecentrum een particuliere liefdadigheidsinstelling is. De oprichter, Julian Shawcroft, was eerder algemeen directeur van de Kliniek voor Infertiliteit en Gepland Ouderschap in Manchester.

Een jonge vrouw, bijna nog een tiener, doet open. Ze draagt

wollige sokken en een bleekblauwe peignoir die nauwelijks ver-
hult dat ze zwanger is.

'Ik kan u niet echt van dienst zijn,' zegt ze meteen. 'Ik let alleen
op de balie omdat Stella moest plassen.'

'Stella?'

'Zij is de baas. Nou ja, niet echt de baas. Meneer Shawcroft is de
echte baas, maar die is er vaak niet. Vandaag wel, wat niet gebruikelijk is. Hij is de voorzitter, of directeur. Ik weet nooit wat het
verschil is. Ik bedoel, wat doet een directeur en wat doet een voorzitter? Ik praat een beetje te veel, vindt u niet? Ik heet Meredith.
Vindt u Hugh een leuke naam voor een jongen? Hugh Jackman is
echt knap. Ik kan even niet op andere Hughs komen.'

'Hugh Grant,' probeer ik.

'Vet cool.'

'Hugh Heffner,' oppert Dave.

'Wie is dat?' vraagt ze.

'Niet belangrijk.'

Haar haar is net lang genoeg voor een staartje; haar nagellak is
afgeschilferd waar ze eraan heeft zitten pulken.

In de hal van het huis staan twee verschoten chesterfields aan
weerszijden van een open haard. De trap, met rijk versierde balustrade, is afgesloten met een blauw kwastkoord dat tussen koperen paaltjes hangt.

Meredith brengt ons naar een kantoortje in een zijvertrek. Op
verschillende bureaus staan computers. Een kopieerapparaat
spuugt pagina's uit, onder de glasplaat glijdt een lichtbundel heen
en weer.

Aan de muur hangen posters. Op een ervan is een stel te zien met
een kind dat aan hun uitgestrekte handen heen en weer zwaait, alleen is het kind eruit gesneden als een ontbrekend puzzelstuk. *Is
dit wat er ontbreekt in uw leven?* staat eronder.

Door openslaande deuren zie ik een rozentuin en een veldje
waar misschien ooit croquet werd gespeeld.

'Wanneer ben je uitgerekend?'

'Over twee weken.'

'Waarom ben je hier?'

Ze giechelt. 'Dit is een adoptiecentrum, dommie.'

'Ja, maar mensen komen hier om een baby te adopteren, niet om te bevallen.'

'Ik heb nog geen besluit genomen,' zegt ze op luchtig nuchtere toon.

Er komt een vrouw binnen, Stella, die zich verontschuldigt voor het wachten. Ze ziet er heel zakelijk uit in een donkere coltrui, zwarte broek en imitatie-slangenleren schoenen met puntneuzen en halfhoge hakken.

Haar ogen nemen me van top tot teen op, alsof ze een inventaris opmaakt. Ik heb zin om te zeggen: 'Nee, de baarmoeder staat leeg.' Ze werpt een blik op een afsprakenboek.

'We hebben geen afspraak,' leg ik uit. 'Het kwam eigenlijk ineens bij ons op om hierheen te gaan.'

'Adoptie mag nooit iets zijn wat ineens opkomt.'

'Nee, dat bedoel ik ook niet. We hebben het er al maanden over. We waren in de buurt.'

'Ik heb hier vlakbij een tante wonen,' helpt Dave.

'Aha.'

'We willen een baby adopteren,' zeg ik, duidelijk ten overvloede.

Stella noteert onze namen. Ik noem mezelf mevrouw King, wat minder raar klinkt dan eigenlijk zou moeten.

'We zijn zes jaar getrouwd en proberen al vijf jaar een kindje te krijgen.'

'Dus u overweegt adoptie omdat u geen kind van uzelf kunt krijgen?'

Het is een suggestieve vraag. 'Ik kom uit een groot gezin. Dat wilde ik zelf ook. Ook al willen we kinderen van onszelf, we hebben het altijd over adoptie gehad.'

'Zijn jullie bereid een ouder kind te nemen?'

'We willen graag een baby.'

'Oké, dat kan, maar er worden in dit land maar heel weinig pasgeboren baby's ter adoptie aangeboden. De wachtlijst is erg lang.'

'Hoe lang?'

'Vijf jaar of langer.'

Dave blaast lucht uit zijn wangen. Hij is hier beter in dan ik dacht. 'Er is vast een manier om dat proces te versnellen,' zegt hij. 'Ik bedoel, zelfs het langzaamste radertje kun je met een drupje olie op weg helpen.'

Stella lijkt gepikeerd over de suggestie. 'Meneer King, wij zijn een instelling zonder winstoogmerk die onder dezelfde regels en voorschriften valt als de adoptiediensten van lokale overheden. Het begint en eindigt met het belang van het kind. Olie komt daar niet aan te pas.'

'Uiteraard. Ik wilde niet suggereren...'

'Mijn man is manager,' leg ik boetvaardig uit. 'Hij gelooft dat vrijwel elk probleem op te lossen valt door er meer geld of meer mensen tegenaan te gooien.'

Ze knikt begrijpend en lijkt voor het eerst mijn huidskleur op te merken. 'Wij bemiddelen ook bij adopties uit het buitenland, maar vanuit het subcontinent worden geen kinderen beschikbaar gesteld. De meeste mensen kiezen voor adoptie vanuit Oost-Europa.'

'Wij zijn niet pietluttig,' gaat Dave verder. Onder de tafel geef ik hem een schop. 'Wij zijn niet gauw van slag, bedoel ik. Het gaat niet om ras.'

Stella neemt hem argwanend op. 'Er zijn tal van slechte redenen voor adoptie. Sommige mensen proberen hun huwelijk te redden, of een overleden kind te vervangen, of doen het uit modieuze overwegingen, omdat al hun vrienden er eentje hebben.'

'Zo zijn wij niet,' leg ik uit.

'Mooi. Goed, bij adopties uit het buitenland is het beoordelings- en goedkeuringsproces precies hetzelfde als voor een binnenlandse adoptie. Het omvat grondig medisch onderzoek, huisbezoeken, antecedentenonderzoek en gesprekken met maatschappelijk werkers en psychologen.'

Ze staat op en opent een archiefkast. Het formulier telt dertig pagina's.

'Ik vroeg me af of de heer Shawcroft er vandaag misschien is.'

'U kent hem?'

'Alleen van naam. Zo heb ik van het centrum gehoord, van een vriendin.'

'En hoe heet uw vriendin?'

'Cate Beaumont.'

Ik kan niet opmaken of ze die naam eerder heeft gehoord. 'De heer Shawcroft is normaliter druk met fondsenwerving, maar vandaag is hij toevallig aanwezig. Wellicht heeft hij paar minuutjes tijd voor u.'

Ze verontschuldigt zich en ik hoor haar de trap op lopen.

'Wat vind jij ervan?' fluistert Dave.

'Hou de deur in de gaten.' Ik loop langs het bureau en trek de la van de archiefkast open.

'Dat is een onwettige zoekactie.'

'Hou die déur in de gaten!'

Mijn vingers lopen de hangmappen langs. Elk adoptiegezin blijkt een eigen map te hebben, maar er is er geen met Beaumont of Elliot. Sommige mappen zijn gemarkeerd met gekleurde stickers. Er staan namen op de etiketten. Ik denk eerst dat het misschien kinderen zijn, maar dat klopt niet met de leeftijden. Dit zijn jonge vrouwen.

Eén naam springt er uit: Carla Donavon. Donavons jongere zus. Zijn zwángere zus. Toeval? Dat kan haast niet.

'Die mappen zijn vertrouwelijk.' Ik schrik van de onzichtbare stem.

Ik kijk naar Dave. Hij schudt zijn hoofd. Er staat een intercom op het bureau. Ik speur het plafond af en zie in de hoek een kleine beveiligingscamera. Die had ik eerder moeten zien.

'Als u iets wilt weten, mevrouw King, dient u dat te vragen,' zegt de stem. 'Ik neem aan dat het uw echte naam is, maar misschien hebt u daar ook al over gelogen.'

'Doet u dat altijd, mensen afluisteren?'

'Doet u dat altijd, wederrechtelijk iemands kantoor doorzoeken en uiterst vertrouwelijke mappen inzien? Wie bent u eigenlijk?'

Dave geeft antwoord. 'Wij zijn van de politie. Ik ben brigadier Dave King, recherche. Dit is agent Alisha Barba, eveneens recherche. We doen onderzoek naar een vrouw die cliënt bij u is geweest.'

De zachte zoemtoon van de intercom valt stil. Er gaat een zij-deur open. Er komt een man binnen, halverwege de vijftig, stevig postuur en een breed gezicht, dat zich heel even plooit als hij ontwapenend glimlacht. Zijn haar, ooit blond en nu grijs, ligt in dichte krullen, als het afdraaisel van een houtdraaibank, tegen zijn hoofd.

'Ik weet zeker dat er een wet is die politiemensen verbiedt zich voor iemand anders uit te geven om ongeautoriseerde zoekacties te doen.'

'De la stond open. Ik deed hem alleen maar dicht.'

Hier moet hij om glimlachen. Hij heeft alle recht om boos en achterdochtig te zijn. In plaats daarvan vindt hij het amusant. Omstandig sluit hij de archiefkast en richt zich weer tot ons.

'Nu we precies weten wie we zijn, kan ik u misschien een rondleiding geven en kunt u mij vertellen wat u komt doen.'

Hij neemt ons mee door de hal en door de openslaande deuren het terras op. De jonge vrouw die we eerder zagen zit op een schommel in de tuin. Haar peignoir bolt op terwijl ze heen en weer schommelt, steeds hoger.

'Voorzichtig, Meredith,' roept hij. En tegen ons: 'Het is een onhandig jong ding.'

'Waarom is ze hier?'

'Meredith weet nog niet wat ze wil. Een baby afstaan is een moeilijke en moedige beslissing. Wij helpen jonge vrouwen zoals zij die beslissing te nemen.'

'Jullie proberen haar te overtuigen.'

'Integendeel. Wij bieden liefde en steun. Wij leren haar ouderschapsvaardigheden, zodat ze er klaar voor is. En als ze besluit haar baby af te staan, hebben wij studiebeurzen zodat ze een flat kan zoeken en een baan vinden. Wij werken met open adopties.'

'Open?'

'De biologische moeder en de adoptiefouders leren elkaar kennen en houden vaak ook daarna contact.'

Shawcroft neemt een niet-aangeharkt grindpad langs de zuidkant van het huis. Achter grote erkerramen is een zaal te zien. Bij een haardvuur zitten enkele jonge vrouwen te kaarten.

'Wij bieden prenatale lessen en massagetherapie en hebben een behoorlijk goed geoutilleerde sportzaal,' legt hij uit.

'Waarom?'

'Waarom niet?'

'Ik begrijp niet waarom dat nodig is.'

Shawcroft heeft oog voor kansen. Het geeft hem de gelegenheid zijn filosofie uiteen te zetten, wat hij gepassioneerd doet, terwijl hij afgeeft op de traditionele houding van waaruit jonge ongehuwde moeders werden verketterd of uitgestoten.

'Het alleenstaand moederschap is meer geaccepteerd geraakt, maar is nog altijd geen gemakkelijke keuze,' legt hij uit. 'Dat is de reden waarom ik dit centrum heb opgezet. Er zijn veel te veel wezen en ongewenste kinderen in onze samenleving en in het buitenland, en te weinig mogelijkheden om hun levens te verbeteren.

Hebben jullie enig idee hoe traag, bureaucratisch en oneerlijk ons adoptiesysteem is? We laten het over aan mensen die gebrek aan fondsen hebben, te weinig medewerkers en te weinig ervaring, mensen die voor God spelen, met de levens van kinderen.'

Dave is iets achter ons gaan lopen.

'Ik ben begonnen in een kantoortje in Mayfair. In mijn eentje. Ik vroeg vijftig pond voor een gesprekssessie van twee uur. Twee jaar later had ik acht fulltime medewerkers en meer dan honderd adopties tot een goed einde gebracht. En nu zitten we hier.' Hij wijst naar Followdale House.

'Hoe kunt u zich deze plek permitteren?'

'Mensen zijn erg gul geweest. We hebben veertien medewerkers, onder wie maatschappelijk werkers, consulenten, beroepskeuzeadviseurs, wijkverpleegkundigen en een psycholoog.'

In een hoek van de tuin zie ik een golftas staan onder een paraplu, en een emmer ballen, klaar om te worden weggeslagen. Hij heeft eeltplekken op zijn vingers.

'Mijn enige verzetje,' legt hij uit terwijl hij over de omheining het weiland in kijkt. 'De koeien zijn nogal bang voor golfballen. Sinds mijn operatie sla ik vaak met meer effect dan goed voor me is.'

'Uw operatie?'

'Mijn heup. De ouderdom komt met gebreken.'

Hij pakt een golfclub en zwaait hem zachtjes tegen een rozenstruik. Een roos spat uiteen in een wolk bloemblaadjes. Hij doet zijn hand open en dicht, en bekijkt zijn vingers.

'In de winter is het altijd lastiger vasthouden. Sommige mensen dragen handschoenen. Ik wil de grip voelen.'

Hij is even stil en draait zich naar me toe. 'Welnu, agent, laten we er niet langer omheen draaien: waarom bent u hier?'

'Kent u ene Cate Beaumont?'

'Nee.' Het antwoord klinkt abrupt.

'U controleert uw cliëntenbestanden niet?'

'Ik herinner me ze stuk voor stuk.'

'Ook de gevallen die niet slagen?'

'Júíst degenen die niet slagen.'

Dave heeft zich bij ons gevoegd. Hij pakt een metalen driver, tuurt naar een koe in de verte, maar ziet er toch maar van af.

'Mijn vriendin deed alsof ze zwanger was en plunderde haar bankrekening. Ik denk dat ze heeft geprobeerd een baby te kopen.'

'Wat verboden is.'

'Ze had een van jullie brochures in huis.'

'Wat niet verboden is.'

Shawcroft is niet beledigd en schiet niet in de verdediging. 'Waar is uw vriendin nu?'

'Ze is dood. Vermoord.'

Hij herhaalt het woord met hernieuwd respect. Zijn handen trillen ook nu niet.

'In de brochure stond een advertentie voor een jongetje van wie de moeder prostituee en drugsverslaafde was. Er was sprake van een bemiddelingsvergoeding en medische kosten.'

Shawcroft strijkt over zijn wang, neemt de tijd. Heel even worstelt er iets in zijn binnenste. Ik wil een ontkenning. Die blijft uit.

'De bemiddelingsvergoeding is voor papierwerk zoals visa en geboortecertificaten.'

'Kinderen verkopen is verboden.'

'De baby was niet te koop. Elke kandidaat wordt nagetrokken. We vragen om referenties en beoordelingsrapporten. Er zijn groepsworkshops en kennismakingssessies. Als laatste is er een adoptiepanel dat de adoptiefouders moet goedkeuren voordat er een passend kind voor hen wordt gezocht.'

'Als deze adopties bonafide zijn, waarom staan er in de advertenties dan postbusnummers?'

Hij kijkt recht vooruit, alsof hij de afstand voor zijn volgende slag probeert in te schatten.

'Weet u hoeveel kinderen er in de wereld elk jaar sterven, agent Barba? Vijf miljoen. Door oorlogen, armoede, ziekte, honger, verwaarlozing, landmijnen en uitbuiters. Ik heb kinderen gezien die zo ondervoed waren dat ze de energie niet hadden om vliegen weg te slaan, moeders met kinderen aan verlepte borsten. Ik heb kinderen over het hek gegooid zien worden bij rijke mensen, of erger nog in de rivier de Ganges, omdat ze ze niet konden voeden. Ik heb aids-wezen gezien, crackbaby's en kinderen die voor een schamele vijftien pond als slaaf werden verkocht. En wat doen wij hier ondertussen? We maken het moeilijker om een kind te adopteren. We vertellen de mensen dat ze te oud zijn, of de verkeerde huidskleur hebben, of het verkeerde geloof.'

Hij doet geen poging de bitterheid in zijn stem te maskeren. 'Het vereist moed voor een land om toe te geven dat het niet voor zijn jongste en zwakste burgers kan zorgen. Veel landen die minder moedig zijn zouden in de steek gelaten kinderen liever zien sterven dan weggaan, op weg naar een beter leven.

Het systeem is oneerlijk. Dus inderdaad, soms ga ik kort door de bocht. In sommige landen kun je een contract tekenen met de biologische moeder. Filmsterren in Hollywood doen dat. Ministers doen het. Kinderen kunnen gered worden. Onvruchtbare stellen kunnen een gezin stichten.'

'Door baby's te kópen.'

'Door ze te rédden.'

Ondanks zijn vaderlijke charme en vriendelijkheid schuilt er onverzettelijkheid in het karakter van deze man en iets onbenoembaar gevaarlijks. Een mengeling van sentimentaliteit en spirituele gedrevenheid dat het hart van tirannen versterkt.

'U vindt het immoreel wat ik doe. Ik zal u vertellen wat nóg immoreler is: níets doen. In je luie stoel blijven zitten in je fijne huis en denken dat je, omdat je toevallig een kind in Zambia sponsort, al genoeg doet.'

'Maar de wet overtreden gaat wel erg ver.'

'Elk gezin dat hier voor adoptie komt wordt grondig onderzocht en gekeurd door een panel deskundigen.'

Hij begint het aantal buitenlandse adopties op te sommen dat het centrum heeft begeleid en de diplomatieke hindernissen die hij heeft moeten overwinnen. Hij heeft zijn argumenten zo goed op orde dat ik er weinig tegenover weet te stellen. Mijn tegenwerpingen klinken bekrompen en vijandig. Ik zou mijn excuses moeten maken.

Shawcroft praat verder, uitvarend tegen het systeem, maar maakt dan zijn enige fout: emotionele chantage.

'Ik betreur het dat uw vriendin dood is, agent Barba, maar ik zou u willen waarschuwen geen onbekookte of ongegronde beweringen te doen over waar wij hier mee bezig zijn. Agenten die aankloppen, vragen stellen, gezinnen van streek maken – is dat wat u wilt?'

Stella komt het terras op lopen en roept hem, met haar hand een telefoongebaar makend.

'Ik moet gaan,' zegt hij met een vermoeide glimlach. 'De baby waar u het over had is vier weken geleden in Washington geboren. Een jongen. Jonge mensen uit Oxford gaan hem adopteren.'

Ik kijk hoe hij het pad weer op loopt, het grind knarsend onder zijn rubberen zolen. Meredith is nog buiten. Hij gebaart haar binnen te komen. Het begint koud te worden.

Groentje Dave komt naast me lopen en we volgen het pad in tegenovergestelde richting terug naar de parkeerplaats. We passeren een beeld van een jong meisje dat een urn vasthoudt en een ander beeld van een faun met een ontbrekende penis.

'Nou, wat denk jij ervan?'

'Welk adoptiecentrum heeft er nou bewakingscamera's?'

14

Op zoek naar Donavon klinkt als de titel van een artistieke Ierse film van Neil Jordan. *Donavons Deconstructie* is ook een goede titel. Het is precies wat ik met hem van plan ben als ik hem vind. Misschien is het toeval en misschien ook niet, maar het bevalt me niet dat zijn naam telkens opduikt wanneer ik Cates gangen naga. Donavon zegt dat hij weet wanneer iemand liegt. Dat komt doordat hij zelf expert is op dat gebied – een geboren bedrieger.

Op de terugrit naar Londen laten we de details van onze ontmoeting met Shawcroft de revue passeren. Ruiz heeft geen bezwaren tegen financieel getinte adoptie als echtparen grondig worden gescreend. Een overmaat aan controle leidt tot het opbloeien van zwarte markten. Misschien heeft hij gelijk, maar bij een fanatiekeling als Shawcroft kan compassie uitmonden in een gevaarlijke kruistocht.

Groentje Dave heeft nog werk liggen. We zetten hem af bij politiebureau Harrow Road en op mijn aandringen belooft hij Shawcroft na te zullen trekken. Hij kust mijn wang en fluistert: 'Stop ermee.'

Dat kan ik niet. Zal ik niet. Hij zegt nog iets: 'Ik vond het léuk met je getrouwd te zijn.'

Het heeft nog korter geduurd dan Britney Spears' eerste huwelijk, maar ik hou me in.

Bij Donavons huis doet niemand open. De gordijnen zijn dicht en zijn motor staat niet buiten. Een buurvrouw tipt ons dat we de markt op Whitechapel Road kunnen proberen. Donavon heeft daar een weekendkraam.

We parkeren achter het Royal London Hospital en gaan op het lawaai, de kleuren en de bewegingen af. Op de stoep en het wegdek staan tientallen kraampjes. Alles is hier te koop: Belgische bonbons uit Polen, Griekse feta uit Yorkshire, Gucci handtassen uit China en Rolexen uit de voering van regenjassen.

Kooplieden schreeuwen door elkaar heen.

'Verse anjers. Twee vijftig een bos!'

'Levende mosselen!'

'Vuurrode tomaten van de kouwe grond!'

Donavon zie ik niet, maar ik herken zijn kraam. Over de metalen buizen gedrapeerd hangen tientallen kunstige halskettingen, of misschien zijn het wel windorgels. Ze wiegen in de zachte bries en weerkaatsen de restanten zonlicht. In de kraam zelf, schots en scheef uitgestald, staan prulradiootjes, digitale klokjes en krultangen uit Korea.

Carla ziet er verkleumd en verveeld uit. Ze draagt een rode wollen maillot en een kort spijkerrokje dat om haar boller wordende buik spant.

Ik stap naar haar toe en leg mijn hand onder haar trui op haar buik tot ik de warmte van haar huid voel.

'Hé!'

Ik trek mijn hand terug alsof ik me gebrand heb. 'Ik wilde het alleen maar even zeker weten.'

'Wat zeker weten?'

'Laat maar.'

Carla kijkt eerst mij argwanend aan en dan Ruiz. Ze zendt een vage, snelle trilling uit, alsof er in haar binnenste iets gruwelijks en geluidloos rondtolt.

'Heb je hem gezien?' vraagt ze gejaagd.

'Wie?'

'Paul. Hij is al twee dagen niet thuis geweest.'

'Wanneer heb je hem voor het laatst gezien?'

'Zaterdag. Hij belde iemand en ging toen weg.'

'Zei hij waarheen?'

'Nee. Zo lang als nu duurt het nooit. Hij belt altijd.'

Dat er zoiets als vrouwelijke intuïtie zou bestaan is veelal een fabeltje. Sommige vrouwen dénken een betere intuïtie te hebben. Ik weet dat ik de zusters ermee teleurstel, maar sekse speelt geen rol. Bloedverwantschap is bepalend. Je familie weet wanneer er iets mis is. Carla's ogen schieten langs het publiek heen en weer, alsof ze met een menselijke legpuzzel bezig is.

Haar mond lijkt iets te willen zeggen waarvoor ze zich geneert. Ik wacht.

'Ik weet niet wat voor soort moeder ik zal zijn. Paul zegt dat het goed komt. Hij zegt dat ik het heb geleerd van een van de sléchtste en daarom niet dezelfde fouten zal maken als onze ma.' Haar handen trillen. 'Een abortus wilde ik niet. Niet vanwege het geloof of zo. Gewoon om hoe ik erover denk, weet je. Daarom dacht ik aan adoptie.'

'Je bent bij Julian Shawcroft geweest.'

'Hij bood aan me te helpen. Hij zei dat ze studiebeurzen hadden, weet je. Ik heb altijd visagiste of schoonheidsspecialiste willen worden. Hij zei dat hij dat kon regelen.'

'Als jij je baby afstond?'

'Ja. Nou ja, je kunt het niet allebei, toch? Niet én voor een baby zorgen én fulltime werken, tenminste niet zonder hulp.'

'En wat heb je besloten?'

Haar schouders krommen zich. 'Dat gaat steeds op en neer. Paul wil dat ik het kind hou. Hij zegt dat hij voor ons zal zorgen.' Ze kluift op een rood geworden vingernagel.

Een jongen met kortgeknipt haar blijft staan en pakt een radiootje in de vorm van een blikje Pepsi.

'Gooi je geld niet in het water, dit is echt bagger,' zegt Carla. De jongen lijkt eerder beledigd dan dankbaar.

'Waarvan kende je het New Life Adoption Centre?'

'Paul had het van een vriendin.'

'Wie?'

Ze haalt haar schouders op.

Haar lichtpaars getinte oogleden trillen. Ze is niet in staat tegen me te liegen. Waarom zou ze? Ik kijk omhoog. Boven haar hoofd zie ik de veren en kralen.

Een van deze versieringen heb ik eerder gezien – in Cates huis, in de babykamer. Het hing boven de nieuwe wieg.

'Wat zijn dat?' vraag ik.

Carla maakt er een los van de kraam en laat hem aan haar vinger bungelen. Door de met veren en kralen behangen gevlochten houten cirkel kijkt ze me aan.

'Dit is een dromenvanger,' legt ze uit. 'Indianen geloven dat de nachtelijke lucht vol dromen zit, deels mooi, deels naar. Ze hangen een dromenvanger boven het kinderbedje zodat hij de voorbijdrijvende dromen kan opvangen. De mooie dromen weten hoe ze door de gaten moeten glippen, langs de zachte veren glijden en zachtjes op het hoofd van het kind neerdalen. Nare dromen raken verstrikt in het web en sneuvelen zodra de zon opkomt.'

Zacht blazend laat ze de veren op en neer kringelen.

Donavon was niet naar de reünie gekomen om het 'goed te maken' met Cate. Hij had haar al eerder ontmoet. Hij gaf haar een dromenvanger, of zij kocht er eentje van hem.

'Hoe goed kende jouw broer Cate Beaumont?'

Carla haalt haar schouders op. 'Ik zou het vriendschap noemen.'

'Dat kan niet.'

Ze steigert. 'Ik sta niet te liegen. Toen Paul bij de para's zat, schreef ze hem brieven. Die heb ik zelf gezien.'

'Brieven?'

'Hij nam ze mee terug uit Afghanistan. Hij had haar brieven bewaard.'

Ik hoor mezelf haar ondervragen, op zoek naar het waar, wanneer en waarom, maar ze kan niet voor haar broer antwoorden. Als ik probeer haar vast te pinnen op specifieke datums en tijdstippen, brengt dat haar nog verder in de war.

Ruiz komt tussenbeide en ik voel me een tikkeltje schuldig dat ik een zwangere vrouw die bezorgd is over haar broer zo op de huid heb gezeten.

De namiddagzon schuift achter de daken en werpt lange schaduwen. Kraamhouders zijn bezig hun spullen in dozen, zakken en metalen koffers te doen. Emmers ijs worden in de goot omgekeerd. Plastic zeilen worden opgerold en vastgebonden.

Nadat we Carla hebben geholpen haar rode Escort-bus in te laden, rijden we achter haar aan. Het huis is nog steeds verlaten. Er zijn geen berichten voor haar. Ik zou kwaad moeten zijn op Donavon, maar ik voel een knagende leegte. Het klopt niet. Waarom zou Cate iemand die haar heeft aangerand brieven schrijven? Op de avond van de reünie sprak ze met hem. Waar hadden ze het over?

Ruiz zet me thuis af. Met afgezette motor staren we naar het straatbeeld, alsof we verwachten dat het ineens zal veranderen na meer dan een eeuw min of meer gelijk te zijn gebleven.

'Kom je nog binnen?'

'Ik kan beter gaan.'

'Ik kan iets voor je koken.'

Hij kijkt me aan.

'We kunnen ook iets halen.'

'Heb je iets alcoholisch in huis?'

'Op de hoek zit een avondwinkel.'

Terwijl ik de deur openmaak en mijn antwoordapparaat afluister, hoor ik hem fluitend op pad gaan. Alle berichten zijn voor Hari. Zijn vriendinnen. Ik zou zijn huur moeten verdubbelen vanwege de telefoonrekening.

De bel gaat. Dat moet Ruiz zijn, maar hij is het niet. Er staat een jongere man voor de deur, in een pepergrijs pak. Gladgeschoren, breedgeschouderd en met Scandinavische trekken. Zijn rechthoekige bril lijkt te klein voor zijn gezicht. Achter hem, naast auto's die dubbel geparkeerd de weg blokkeren, staan nog twee mannen. Ze zien er officieel uit, maar het zijn geen politiemensen.

'Agent Barba, wilt u meekomen alstublieft?' Met zijn tong maakt hij een klakkend geluid dat een teken zou kunnen zijn, maar ook nervositeit.

'Waarom? Wie bent u?'

Hij haalt een badge tevoorschijn. AGZM, het Agentschap Georganiseerde Zware Misdaad. Het agentschap bestaat nog geen jaar en de media hebben het al het Britse antwoord op de FBI genoemd, met een eigen parlementair bekrachtigd statuut, budget en buitengewone bevoegdheden. Wat moeten ze van me?

'Ik ben politieagente,' stamel ik.

'Ik weet wie u bent.'

'Sta ik onder arrest?'

'Belangrijke personen willen u spreken.'

Ik kijk of ik Ruiz zie. Hij komt over de stoep aanrennen met een halve fles whisky in zijn jaszak. Een van de mannen naast de auto's probeert hem de weg te versperren. De inspecteur maakt een schijnbeweging naar links, duikt ineen en gooit de man over een stenen muurtje in een modderplas. Dit kon weleens uit de hand gaan lopen.

'Alles is in orde, meneer.'

'Wie zijn dit?'

'AGZM.'

Zijn gelaatsuitdrukking zegt alles: angst en walging. 'Misschien wilt u nog wat dingen pakken voor onderweg,' zegt de hogere in rang. Ruiz en hij staan tegenover elkaar als hanen in een kippenhok.

Ik doe een spijkerbroek, onderbroekjes en een dunne trui in een sporttas. Mijn pistool ligt in een doek gewikkeld boven op een keukenkastje. Ik speel met de gedachte het mee te nemen, maar verwerp het idee uiteindelijk. Ik heb geen idee wat deze mensen willen, maar ik wil geen herrie met ze schoppen.

Ruiz volgt me naar de auto. Terwijl ik me op de achterbank laat glijden, wordt er een hand op mijn hoofd gelegd. De rem wordt plotseling losgelaten en ik word achteruit in het nieuw ruikende leer geworpen.

'Ik hoop niet dat we uw plannen voor vanavond in het honderd hebben gestuurd, agent Barba,' zegt de man in het grijze pak.

'U weet hoe ik heet. Hoe heet u?'

'Robert Forbes.'

'U werkt voor het AGZM?'

'Ik werk voor de regering.'

'Welk deel van de regering?'

'Het deel waar men niet vaak over praat.' Hij maakt opnieuw het klakkende geluid.

De auto heeft het eind van Hanover Street bereikt. Onder een lantaarn staat een in zwart leer gehulde eenzame toeschouwer tegen een motorfiets geleund. Aan zijn rechterhand bungelt een helm. In zijn knuist smeult een peuk. Het is Donavon.

Het verkeer slingert zich in een tergend langzaam tempo voort, nu eens kruipend dan weer stilstaand. Van de bestuurder kan ik alleen zijn achterhoofd zien. Hij heeft een militair kapsel en een platliggende zonnebril als die van Bono, die er 's avonds met zonnebril eveneens belachelijk uitziet.

Ik probeer me te herinneren wat ik over het AGZM heb gelezen. Het is een samenraapsel van de voormalige Nationale Misdaadbrigade en de Nationale Criminele Inlichtingendienst, met elementen van de Douane en de Immigratiedienst. Vijfduizend agenten werden geselecteerd met het specifieke doel misdaadbendes, drugssmokkelaars en mensensmokkelaars aan te gaan pakken. Het nieuwe agentschap wordt geleid door een voormalig hoofd van de geheime dienst MI5.

'Waar nemen jullie me mee naartoe?'

'Naar een plaats delict,' zegt Forbes.

'Welk delict? Er moet een vergissing in het spel zijn.'

'U bent Alisha Kaur Barba. U bent negenentwintig jaar oud. U werkt bij de London Metropolitan Police, laatstelijk bij de Diplomatieke Beschermingseenheid. U hebt vier broers. Uw vader is gepensioneerd treinmachinist. Uw moeder verricht aan huis naaiwerk. U hebt op Falcon Street Primary en Oaklands Secondary op school gezeten. U hebt aan London University een graad in de sociologie behaald en was op Hendon Police Training College de beste van uw klas. U bent een uitmuntend schutter en voormalig atletiekkampioene. Een jaar geleden raakte u gewond bij een poging een verdachte te arresteren, die bijna uw ruggengraat brak. U accepteerde een medaille voor betoonde moed, maar weigerde een invaliditeitsuitkering. U lijkt er weer aardig bovenop te zijn.'

'Ik zou met gemak een ijzerwinkeltje kunnen beginnen.'

Ik weet niet of zijn kennis bedoeld is om interessant te doen of om mij te intimideren. Er wordt verder niets gezegd. Forbes zal mijn vragen pas beantwoorden als hij daar klaar voor is. Stilte is onderdeel van het murw maken. Dat heeft Ruiz me verteld.

We nemen de A12 via Brentford Londen uit. Ik hou niet van het platteland bij nacht. Te donker en te leeg. Zelfs bij maanlicht ziet het er geschonden en naargeestig uit, als een blauwe plek van een week oud na een val.

Forbes pleegt meerdere telefoontjes, met afgezien van het klakkende geluid in zijn keel alleen 'ja' en 'nee'. Hij is getrouwd. De gouden ring om zijn ringvinger is dik en zwaar. Thuis strijkt iemand zijn hemden en poetst zijn schoenen. Hij is rechtshandig. Hij draagt geen pistool. Hij weet zoveel van mij dat ik weer op gelijke hoogte probeer te komen.

We rijden door Chelmsford in Essex voordat we Colchester laten liggen en naar het oosten de A120 richting Harwich nemen. Voor ons worden de konvooien trekkers en trucks met oplegger steeds dichter. Ik kan de zilte lucht al ruiken.

Een groot bord boven de weg heet ons welkom in Harwich International Port. Over de New Port Entrance Road en twee rotondes komen we bij de ingang voor vrachtwagens. Bij de hekken staan er tientallen te wachten. Een douanebeambte met een lichtstaaf en een fluorescerende hes wuift dat we mogen doorrijden.

In de verte zie ik de haven van Felixtowe. Boven de schepen torenen enorme portaalkranen uit, die containers ophijsen en weer laten zakken. Het ziet eruit als een scène uit *War of the Worlds*, waarin buitenaardse machines zijn geland en nakomelingen creëren voor de volgende generatie. Rij na rij staan er containers boven op elkaar, tot honderden meters in elke richting.

Forbes besluit iets tegen me te zeggen.

'Bent u hier al eens eerder geweest, agent Barba?'

'Nee.'

Harwich is zowel vracht- als passagiershaven. De haven verwerkt cruiseschepen, veerboten, bulktankers en *roll-on-roll-off*-schepen. Er passeren dagelijks duizenden voertuigen uit Denemarken, Zweden, België, Duitsland en Hoek van Holland.

'Waarom ben ik hier?'

Hij wijst naar voren. De auto mindert vaart. In het midden van het douaneterrein is een tent neergezet voor het Team Plaats Delict. Politieauto's staan eromheen als huifkarren rond het kampvuur.

Booglampen in de tent maken de wanden doorschijnend en doen er het silhouet van een vrachtwagen op uitkomen. Achter het zeildoek zie ik mensen rondlopen, als poppen in een kabukitheater.

Forbes is uitgestapt en loopt over het asfalt. De afkoelende motor maakt een tikkend geluid als een klok. Op dat moment gaat een zijflap van de tent open. Er komt een lid van het Team Plaats Delict naar buiten in een overall en witte rubberen handschoenen, die hij als een tweede huid van zijn handen stroopt.

Ik herken hem: Gerard Noonan, forensisch patholoog. Vanwege zijn bleke huid en sneeuwwitte haar noemen ze hem 'de Albino'. Met zijn witte overall, witte handschoenen en witte hoedje lijkt hij op een als zaadcel uitgedoste feestganger.

Hij praat enkele minuten met Forbes. Ik sta te ver weg om te kunnen verstaan wat ze zeggen.

Forbes draait mijn kant uit en wenkt me. Zijn gezicht is hard als het blad van een bijl.

In de tent is de grond afgedekt met plastic zeilen, op hun plaats gehouden door zilverkleurige kisten met medische apparatuur en camera's. In het midden staat een vrachtwagen waarvan de dubbele achterdeuren openstaan. In de auto staan houten pallets met kistjes sinaasappelen. Een deel ervan is naar één kant geschoven om een smal pad door het midden vrij te maken. Er is net voldoende ruimte voor één persoon om naar het uiteinde van de oplegger te komen.

De flits van een camera onthult een ruimte tussen de pallets. Eerst denk ik dat het om etalagepoppen gaat, gebroken modellen of kleifiguren. Dan dringt de werkelijkheid tot me door: lichamen. Ik tel er vijf, op een hoop onder een ventilatiegat. Het zijn drie mannen, een vrouw en een kind. Hun monden staan open. Ademloos. Levenloos.

Het lijken overwegend Oost-Europeanen, in goedkope, bij elkaar geraapte kleren. Een arm steekt omhoog alsof hij aan een draad hangt. De vrouw heeft haar haar naar achteren. Een schildpadden haarklem is losgeschoten en bungelt aan een streng haar op haar wang. Het kind op haar arm draagt een Mickey Mouse-sweatshirt en omklemt een pop.

De flitslamp flitst opnieuw. Ik zie de gezichten op hun plek bevroren, gevangen in het moment waarop hun zuurstof opraakte en hun dromen op uitgedroogde tongen tot stof vergingen. Het is een tafereel dat me zal achtervolgen, een tafereel dat alles anders maakt. En hoewel ik me hun wereld niet kan voorstellen, die onmogelijk vreemd en ver lijkt, is hun dood ondraaglijk nabij.

'Ze zijn niet langer dan twaalf uur geleden gestorven,' zegt Noonan. Automatisch zet ik dit om in persoonlijke tijd. Wat deed ik in die tussentijd? Ik was op weg naar West Sussex. Ik sprak met Julian Shawcroft in het adoptiecentrum.

Noonan houdt een paar in een plastic zakje verzamelde bloederige vingernagels vast. Ik voel mijn maag protesteren.

'Als u moet kotsen, agent, maak dan dat u wegkomt van mijn plaats delict,' zegt hij.

'Ja, meneer.'

Forbes kijkt Noonan aan. 'Vertel haar hoe ze zijn gestorven.'

'Ze zijn gestikt,' antwoordt hij vermoeid.

'Leg het ons eens uit.'

De vraag is voor mijn bestwil. Forbes wil dat ik dit aanhoor en de zoete stank van sinaasappels en uitwerpselen ruik. Noonan gaat erop in.

'Het begint met een toenemende paniek terwijl je voor elke ademteug vecht, hem inhaalt en meer wilt. Het volgende stadium is dat je stil wordt. Berusting. En daarna bewusteloosheid. De stuiptrekkingen en incontinentie zijn onwillekeurig, onderdeel van de doodsstrijd. Niemand weet wat het eerst komt: zuurstofgebrek of kooldioxidevergiftiging.'

Forbes pakt mijn elleboog en leidt me de vrachtwagen uit. Er is een geïmproviseerd mortuarium gebouwd om de lijken te kunnen herbergen. Een ervan ligt al op een brancard, het gezicht omhoog en bedekt met een wit laken. Forbes strijkt met een vinger langs het laken.

'Iemand in de vrachtwagen had een mobiele telefoon,' legt hij uit. 'Toen ze dreigden te stikken hebben ze geprobeerd te bellen en kwamen ze bij een alarmnummer terecht. De telefonist dacht dat het nep was omdat de beller geen locatie kon geven.'

Ik kijk naar het enorme roll-on-roll-off-schip met zijn open boegdeuren.

'Waarom ben ik hier?'

Met een snelle polsbeweging slaat hij het laken terug. Op de koelplaat ligt een jonge jongen met mollige ledematen en donker haar. Zijn hoofd is bijna volmaakt rond en roze, op het blauw rond zijn lippen en de overlappende huidplooien onder zijn kin na.

Forbes heeft zich niet bewogen. Van achter zijn vierkante brillenglazen, die ineens te klein en armoedig voor zijn gezicht lijken, houdt hij me in de gaten.

Ik ruk mijn blik los. Met de vlugheid van een vogel grijpt hij me bij mijn arm. 'Dit is alles wat hij aanhad. Een goedkope broek en een shirt. Geen labels. Normaliter vertellen zulke kleren ons niets. Het zijn goedkope massaproducten.'

Zijn vingers graven zich dieper in. 'Deze kleren zijn anders. Er zat iets in de zoom genaaid. Een naam en een adres. Weet u wiens naam? Wiens adres?'

Ik schud mijn hoofd.

'Het uwe.'

Ik probeer niet te reageren, maar dat is op zich al een reactie.

'Kunt u dat verklaren?' vraagt hij.

'Nee.'

'Zelfs geen vage notie?'

In mijn hoofd raas ik langs de mogelijkheden. Mijn moeder naaide altijd labels in mijn kleding, omdat ze niet wilde dat ik iets kwijtraakte. Mijn naam, niet mijn adres.

'U voelt zeker wel hoe dit eruitziet,' zegt hij, met zijn tong klakkend. 'U bent mogelijke verdachte in een onderzoek naar mensensmokkel en wellicht zelfs een onderzoek naar moord. We denken dat hij Hasan Khan heet. Zegt dat u iets?'

'Nee.'

'De vrachtwagen heeft een Nederlands kenteken. De chauffeur staat als Arjan van Kleek op de passagierslijst.'

Ik schud andermaal mijn hoofd.

Ik ben eerder gevoelloos dan geschokt. Het is alsof er iemand op me af is komen lopen en me op mijn achterhoofd met een metalen dienblad een klap heeft gegeven die nog hoog naklinkt in mijn oren.

'Waarom zijn ze niet eerder gevonden?'

'Weet u wel hoeveel vrachtwagens er elke dag Harwich passeren? Meer dan tienduizend. Als de douane ze allemaal zou doorzoeken, zou er een rij schepen tot in Rotterdam liggen.'

Noonan komt bij ons staan. Hij buigt zich over het lichaam en praat alsof de tiener een patiënt is in plaats van een lijk.

'Oké, jongen, probeer eerlijk te antwoorden. Als je goed meewerkt kunnen we meer over je te weten komen. Goed, laten we eens kijken.'

Hij kijkt van dichterbij, zijn lippen bijna tegen de wangen van de jongen. 'Sporen van petechiale bloedingen, speldenknopgrootte, minder dan een millimeter, op oogleden, lippen, oren, gezicht en nek, overeenkomend met zuurstoftekort weefsel…'

Hij tilt een arm op en bekijkt de huid.

'Het littekenweefsel duidt vermoedelijk op een oude brandwond op de linkeronderarm en hand. Iets buitengewoon intens, mogelijk een explosie.'

Op zijn borst zitten tientallen kleinere littekens. Noonans nieuwsgierigheid is gewekt. Hij meet ze op.

'Zeer ongebruikelijk.'

'Wat zijn dat?'

'Van een mes.'

'Is hij gestoken?'

'Eerder gesneden.' Hij zigzagt met een denkbeeldig mes door de lucht. 'Geen van de wondjes is erg diep. Het lemmet heeft geen organen of grote bloedvaten bedreigd. Uitmuntende beheersing.'

De patholoog lijkt geïmponeerd, alsof hij het werk van een collega bewondert.

Hij ziet nog iets. Hij trekt de rechterarm van de jongen iets opzij en draait zijn pols. Halverwege de handpalm en de elleboog zweeft een getatoeëerde vlinder. Noonan meet de vlinder op en spreekt de gegevens in in een digitaal recordertje.

Forbes heeft me genoeg laten zien.

'Ik wil graag naar huis nu,' zeg ik.

'Ik heb nog meer vragen.'

'Heb ik een advocaat nodig?'

De vraag stelt hem teleur. 'Ik kan voor iemand zorgen, als u dat wilt.'

Ik weet dat ik ongeruster zou moeten zijn, maar mijn honger naar kennis wint het van mijn aangeboren voorzichtigheid. Niet dat ik me onoverwinnelijk waan of denk dat mijn onschuld me zal beschermen. Daarvoor heb ik al te veel rechterlijke dwalingen meegemaakt.

Bij de terminal is een chauffeurscafé. Forbes kiest een tafel en bestelt koffie en een fles water.

Het uur daarna pluist hij mijn privé-leven, mijn vrienden en bekenden na. Keer op keer herhaal ik dat ik geen idee heb hoe een label met mijn naam en adres op Hasan Khans kleding terecht is gekomen.

'Heeft het met mijn huidskleur te maken?' vraag ik uiteindelijk.

Zijn gezicht betrekt. 'Waarom gooien mensen toch altijd weer die racismekaart op tafel? Als iemand uit een minderheidsgroepering wordt ondervraagd, kun je er vergif op innemen. Dit heeft niets te maken met uw huidskleur of geloofsovertuiging of waar u bent geboren. Het zijn úw naam en adres die in de kleren van een dode jongen zitten ingenaaid. Een illegaal. En daarom hebben we u in de peiling.'

Ik wou dat ik de vraag kon terugnemen.

Hij haalt een half pakje sigaretten tevoorschijn en telt ze, zichzelf een rantsoen toemetend. 'Hebt u enig benul van de omvang van mensensmokkel?' Met zijn tong klakkend alsof hij zichzelf vermaant steekt hij het pakje weer weg.

'Het afgelopen jaar werden meer dan vierhonderdduizend mensen West-Europa binnengesmokkeld. De Italiaanse maffia, de Russen, de Albanezen, de Japanse yakuza, de Chinese slangenkoppen – ze zijn er allemaal bij betrokken. En na de grote syndicaten zijn er duizenden kleinere zelfstandige bendes die niet meer gebruiken dan een paar mobiele telefoons, een speedboot en een transportbusje. Ze kopen grenswachten om, politici, politiemensen en douanebeambten. Het is krengenvretend geteisem dat loert op menselijke ellende. Geloof me, ik haat ze.'

Hij kijkt me strak aan. Weer dat geluid met zijn tong. Ineens besef ik waar hij me aan doet denken: aan Road Runner. Wile E. Coyote was altijd bezig die arrogante, piepende vogel te vangen, met de meest vreemdsoortige boobytraps en valstrikken. Ik hoopte altijd dat de coyote een keertje zou winnen. Dat de zware halter, de dynamietstaaf of de katapult zijn werk zou doen en hij die schriele vogelnek kon omdraaien.

Alsof het zo moet zijn klinkt de dubbele piep van Forbes' semafoon. Hij gaat achter in het café staan bellen. Er moet hem iets zijn verteld, want als hij terugkomt is zijn houding veranderd.

'Sorry dat ik u zo lang hier heb gehouden, agent Barba.'

'Dus ik kan gaan?'

'Uiteraard, maar het is al erg laat. Er is onderdak geregeld in de stad. De pub ziet er niet slecht uit. Ik kan u morgenochtend terug naar Londen laten brengen.'

Hij trekt zenuwachtig aan de mouwen van zijn colbert, alsof hij bang is dat ze te kort zijn geworden. Ik vraag me af wie de beller was. Sikh-meisjes hebben geen vrienden in hoge kringen.

De pub is ouderwets en rustiek, hoewel ik nooit precies heb geweten wat 'rustiek' inhoudt. De restaurantuitbouw heeft een lage zoldering met visnetten aan de balken; boven de bar zit een harpoen vastgeschroefd.

Forbes nodigt me uit voor het diner. 'Ook al ben ik dan inspecteur, u mag weigeren,' zegt hij in een poging charmant te doen.

Ik ruik de keuken. Mijn maag rommelt. Misschien kom ik meer te weten over Hasan Khan.

Hij werkt zich uit zijn grijze colbert, strekt zijn benen onder tafel en maakt een heel vertoon van het bestellen en keuren van de wijn.

'Deze is erg goed,' oordeelt hij terwijl hij het glas tegen het licht houdt. 'Weet u zeker dat u niet neemt?' Zonder mijn antwoord af te wachten schenkt hij zichzelf nog eens in.

Ik heb hem tot nu toe 'meneer Forbes' of gewoon 'meneer' genoemd. Hij wil dat ik hem met Robert aanspreek. Hoewel ik hem geen toestemming geef, noemt hij me toch al Alisha. Hij vraagt of ik getrouwd ben.

'Dat weet je al.'

'Dat is waar ook.'

Hij heeft Scandinavische ogen en zijn ondertanden staan scheef, maar hij heeft een plezierige glimlach en lacht gemakkelijk. Het klakgeluid lijkt achterwege te blijven als hij zich ontspant. Misschien is het een zenuwenkwestie, zoals stotteren.

'Vertel eens iets over je familie,' vraagt hij. 'Wanneer zijn ze hierheen gekomen?'

Ik vertel hem over mijn grootvader, geboren in een dorpje in de Gujarat, die op zijn veertiende als keukenhulp bij het Britse leger ging en later kok werd. Na de oorlog nam een majoor van de Royal Artillery hem mee naar Engeland als huiskok. Mijn opa reisde met een stoomschip dat drie weken nodig had voor de reis van Bombay naar Engeland. Hij reisde alleen. Dat was in 1947.

Hij verdiende drie pond per week, maar spaarde desondanks genoeg om mijn grootmoeder over te laten komen. Ze waren de eerste Indiërs in Hertfordshire, maar verhuisden later naar Londen.

Mijn enige herinnering aan mijn grootouders is de keer dat ze me vertelden over hun eerste Engelse winter. Ze hadden nog nooit sneeuw gezien en zeiden dat het net een scène uit een Russisch sprookje was.

Ironie ontgaat me soms, maar mijn grootvader deed zijn hele leven zijn best een blanke te worden, om uiteindelijk op Richmond Hill doodgedrukt te worden onder een omgevallen kolenauto waar hij roetzwart onder vandaan werd gehaald.

Forbes heeft zijn tweede fles wijn achter de kiezen en kijkt melancholiek.

'Ik moet even naar het toilet,' zegt hij.

Ik zie hem tussen de tafels door laveren, afwisselend met zijn linkerschouder en rechterschouder naar voren. Als hij weer terug is, bestelt hij een cognac. Hij vertelt over zijn jeugd in Milton Keynes, een kunstmatige stad die pas in de jaren zestig ontstond. Nu woont hij in Londen. Over een vrouw zegt hij niets, maar die is er wel, weet ik.

Ik wil het met hem over de illegalen hebben voordat hij te ver heen is. 'Hebben jullie de vrachtwagen getraceerd?' vraag ik.

'Transportcontainers hebben een code. Ze kunnen waar ook ter wereld worden gevolgd.'

'Waar kwam deze vandaan?'

'De vrachtwagen vertrok gisterochtend vroeg bij een fabriek aan de rand van Amsterdam. De sloten zouden bestand moeten zijn tegen gerommel.'

'Hoe kwam je aan de naam Hasan Khan?'

'Hij had papieren bij zich. Hij had een stoffen draagtas rond zijn middel gebonden. Volgens de Nederlandse politie was hij negentien maanden geleden uit Afghanistan aangekomen. Hij woonde met een groep asielzoekers boven een Chinees restaurant in Amsterdam.'

'Wat zat er nog meer in die tas?'

Forbes slaat zijn ogen neer. 'Tekeningen en foto's. Ik zou ze je kunnen laten zien...' Hij stopt even. 'We zouden naar mijn kamer kunnen gaan.'

'Je kunt ook even die tas halen,' opper ik.

Hij schurkt met zijn sok langs mijn kuit en trakteert me op zijn stoute-jongensglimlach.

Ik wil iets lelijks zeggen, maar kan er even niet op komen. Ik ben nooit goed in terechtwijzingen. In plaats daarvan glimlach ik beleefd en zeg hem dat hij moet stoppen nu hij nog voorligt.

Hij fronst. Hij begrijpt het niet.

Mijn god, je bent niet eens aantrekkelijk. Bel je vrouw en wens haar welterusten.

Forbes gaat stommelend de trap op. 'We hebben 'm aardig geraakt, niet?'

'Een van ons wel, ja.'

Het duurt even voor hij zijn sleutel heeft. Een paar maal probeert hij vergeefs het sleutelgat te vinden. Ik neem het van hem over. Hij valt op bed neer, rolt om en blijft wijdbeens liggen, als een zoenoffer aan de duivelse god van de drank.

Ik trek hem zijn schoenen uit en hang zijn colbertje over de stoel. De stoffen tas ligt op het nachtkastje. Bij het naar buiten gaan schuif ik de veiligheidsstang voor de deurpost, zodat de deur niet helemaal dichtvalt.

Weer in mijn kamer bel ik Ruiz en Groentje Dave. Dave wil me komen ophalen. Ik zeg hem thuis te blijven. Ik bel hem morgen. Een kwartier later ga ik terug naar Forbes' kamer. De deur staat nog op een kier en hij snurkt. Ik loop de kamer door en luister of zijn ademhaling verandert. Mijn vingers klemmen zich om de tas. Forbes verroert zich niet.

Plotseling klinkt er een ander geluid. Een zangerige beltoon. Ik laat me vallen en hurk tussen de radiator en het gordijn.

Als Forbes het licht aandoet, zal hij me zien of merken dat de tas weg is.

Hij rolt half uit bed, pakt zijn jasje en rommelt met zijn mobiele telefoon.

'Ja, sorry lief, ik had moeten bellen. Ik was laat terug en wilde jou en de kinderen niet wakker maken. Nee, prima, niet dronken, nee. Een paar glazen maar. Het nieuws niet gezien, nee. O, geweldig, ja, oké. Morgenochtend bel ik. Ga maar gauw slapen. Ik ook van jou.'

Hij legt de telefoon naast zich en staart naar het plafond. Heel even denk ik dat hij in slaap valt, totdat hij kreunt en uit bed rolt. Het badkamerlicht floept aan. Achter zijn rug wordt mijn schuilplaats keurig ingekaderd door het schijnsel. Hij laat zijn boxershort zakken en begint te plassen.

Ik kruip weg van het licht, de vloer over, en doe zachtjes de deur achter me dicht. Ik ben duizelig en tril. Ik heb een van Ruiz' basisregels geschonden: in stressvolle situaties nooit vergeten adem te halen.

In mijn kamer laat ik de inhoud van de gekleurde katoenen tas op bed vallen. Er zit een zakmes bij waarvan één lemmet afgebroken is en het andere intact, een spiegeltje, een met zand gevuld medicijnflesje, een houtskooltekening van twee kinderen en een gedeukte koektrommel.

Elk voorwerp is van belang. Waarom zou hij ze anders bij zich hebben? Dit zijn de aardse bezittingen van een zestienjarige jongen. Lucht in zijn longen blazen of me zijn angsten en verlangens duidelijk maken kunnen ze niet. Ze schieten tekort. Hij verdient meer.

In de koektrommel zitten een vlekkerige militaire onderscheiding en een in tweeën gevouwen zwart-witfoto. De opname lijkt van een groep arbeiders te zijn, opgesteld voor een fabriek met een geroest ijzeren dak en houten luiken voor de ramen. Tegen de muur staan verzendkisten gestapeld en er liggen vaten en pallets. Er zijn twee rijen arbeiders. De voorste rij zit op krukjes. In het midden is een familieoudste of de fabriekseigenaar te zien in een stoel met hoge rugleuning. Hij zit kaarsrecht en heeft een strenge houding en een in de verte gerichte blik. Eén hand ligt op zijn knie. De andere hand ontbreekt; zijn mouw is bij de elleboog dichtgebonden.

Naast hem zie ik een andere man, die uiterlijk op hem lijkt, misschien zijn broer. Hij draagt een kleine fez en heeft een keurig verzorgde baard. Ook hij mist een hand en zijn linkeroog lijkt slechts een lege oogkas. Ik laat mijn blik langs de twee rijen arbeiders gaan, van wie velen verminkt, kreupel of onvolledig zijn. Er zijn mensen op krukken, anderen met een huid als gesmolten plastic. Een jongen op de voorste rij knielt op een skateboard. Nee, niet waar. Wat ik eerst denk dat zijn knieën zijn, van onder een korte broek, zijn beenstompen.

Geen van de arbeiders glimlacht. Ze hebben een olijfkleurige huid, hun trekken zijn onscherp en geen enkele vergroting zal het beeld helderder kunnen maken, of de mannen er minder stram en nors kunnen doen uitzien.

Ik doe de foto terug in de trommel en bekijk de rest van de curiosa. De houtskooltekening is gekreukeld aan de hoeken. De twee kinderen, een jongen en een meisje, zijn rond de zes en acht. Ze heeft haar arm om zijn schouders geslagen. Ze heeft een hoog voorhoofd en een kaarsrechte scheiding. Hij ziet er verveeld en rusteloos uit, met een sprankje licht dat door een raam in zijn ogen weerspiegelt. Hij wil buiten zijn.

Het papier voelt zacht aan. De houtskool is met fixatief bespoten tegen het vlekken. In de linkerbenedenhoek staat een handtekening. Nee, een naam. Twee namen. De tekening laat het jongetje Hasan zien met zijn zusje, Samira.

Achteroverliggend staar ik naar het plafond en luister naar de peilloze nacht. Het is zo stil dat ik mezelf hoor ademhalen. Wat een schitterend geluid.

Dit is een verhaal dat uit stukken bestaat. Een kroniek van verzinsels. Cate simuleerde haar zwangerschap. Brendan Pearl reed haar en Felix aan. Haar arts loog. Donavon loog. Een adoptieagentschap loog. Er worden mensen gesmokkeld. Er worden baby's gekocht en verkocht.

Ik las ergens dat mensen die door een lawine zijn overvallen niet altijd meer weten wat onder is en wat boven, en niet weten in welke richting ze moeten graven. Ervaren skiërs en klimmers hebben een trucje: ze kwijlen. De zwaartekracht wijst hun de weg.

Zo'n truc heb ik nodig. Ik ben ondergedompeld in iets duisters en gevaarlijks, en weet niet of ik op de goede weg ben of juist dieper wegzink. Ik ben een toevallig slachtoffer.

Mijn dromen zijn echt. Zo echt als dromen maar kunnen zijn. Ik hoor baby's huilen en moeders voor hen zingen. Ik word achternagezeten door mensen. Het is dezelfde droom als altijd, maar ik weet nooit wie ze zijn. En ik word altijd op hetzelfde moment wakker, terwijl ik val.

Ik bel Ruiz. Bij de tweede keer overgaan neemt hij op. De man slaapt nooit.

'Kun je me komen halen?'

Hij vraagt niet waarom. Hij legt de telefoon neer. Ik zie voor me hoe hij zich aankleedt, in de auto stapt en door het boerenlandschap rijdt.

Hij is dertig jaar ouder dan ik. Hij is drie keer getrouwd geweest en heeft een privé-leven met meer kruitdamp dan een schietbaan, maar ik ken hem beter en vertrouw hem meer dan wie ook.

Ik weet wat me te doen staat. Tot dusverre heb ik geprobeerd me Cates situatie voor te stellen: de plaatsen die ze heeft bezocht, wat ze probeerde te verbergen. Maar het heeft geen zin dezelfde telefoonnummers na te bellen of te proberen me haar omzwervingen voor te stellen. Ik moet in haar voetsporen treden, haar inhalen.

Ik ga naar Amsterdam, Samira zoeken. Ik kijk op de klok. Niet morgen. Vandaag.

Twee uur later laat ik Ruiz binnen. Ik vraag me soms af of hij mijn gedachten kan lezen of dat hij degene is die ze daar heeft geplant en ze daarna leest als een pokerspeler die zijn kaarten telt.

'We moeten naar Amsterdam,' zegt hij.

'Ja.'

BOEK TWEE

The bitterest tears shed over graves are for words left unsaid and deeds left undone.

Harriet Beecher Stowe

1

In ons tweede jaar op de universiteit in Londen werd Cate een keer niet ongesteld. Ze dacht dat ze zwanger was. Wij liepen gelijk – zelfde tijd, zelfde plaats, zelfde stemmingen. Wie van haar foute vriendjes haar verdediging had doorbroken herinner ik me niet meer, haar reactie wel degelijk. Paniek.

We deden een zwangerschapstest en daarna nog een tweede. Ik ging met haar mee naar de gezinsplanningkliniek, een afschuwelijk groen gebouw in Greenwich, niet ver van het observatorium. Waar de tijd werd geboren eindigde het leven.

De verpleegster stelde Cate een aantal vragen en zei haar naar huis te gaan en nog eens zeven dagen te wachten. Kennelijk is te vroeg testen de meest voorkomende oorzaak van een vals-negatieve uitslag.

Ze werd ongesteld.

'Misschien was ik wel zwanger en is het vanzelf afgebroken,' zei ze na afloop. 'Misschien had ik het sterker moeten willen.'

Later, zonder aanleiding, vroeg ze: 'Wat doen ze er eigenlijk mee?'

'Waarmee?'

'Met geaborteerde baby's.'

'Die noemen ze geen baby's. Ik neem aan dat ze die afvoeren.'

'Afvoeren?'

'Ik weet het niet, nou goed?'

Ik vraag me af of deze angstige episode waarin het bijna misliep, haar heeft achtervolgd toen ze later zwanger probeerde te worden. Wist Felix ervan? Vroeg ze zich af of dit Gods straf was omdat ze niet genoeg van de eerste had gehouden?

Ik weet tóch nog hoe het foute vriendje heette. We noemden hem Knappe Barry. Hij was een Canadese skileraar die het hele

147

jaar gebronsd rondliep en onvoorstelbaar witte tanden had. Wat is dat toch met skileraren? In de bergen krijgen ze die goddelijke aura, alsof de ijle lucht hun schoonheid vergroot of (waarschijnlijker) vrouwen minder kritisch maakt. In de kerstvakantie werkten we in een skihotel in de Franse Alpen, in de schaduw van de Mont Blanc (die vanwege de laaghangende bewolking helemaal geen schaduw wierp).

'Heb jij ooit een sikh zien skiën?' vroeg ik Cate.

'Jij kunt de eerste zijn,' drong ze aan.

We deelden een kamer in cellenblok H, zoals we het medewerkersverblijf noemden. Ik werkte als kamermeisje, vijf dagen in de week van zes uur 's ochtends tot halverwege de middag. Cate, die 's avonds in een bar werkte, zag ik nauwelijks. Ze oefende haar Russische accent door zich uit te geven voor Ntalia Radzinsky, dochter van een gravin.

'Waar ben jij in 's hemelsnaam met Barry naar bed geweest?' vroeg ik.

'Ik had je moedersleutel even gepikt. We hebben een van de gastensuites genomen.'

'Jullie hebben wát?'

'Rustig maar. Ik heb er een handdoek onder gelegd.'

Ze leek meer geïnteresseerd in mijn liefdesleven. 'Wanneer ga jij je laten ontmaagden?'

'Als ik er klaar voor ben.'

'Op wie wacht je?'

'Op meneer Perfect,' zei ik, maar ik dacht eigenlijk aan 'meneer Zorgzaam' of 'meneer Waardig', of eigenlijk elke 'meneer' die mij maar graag genoeg wílde.

Misschien was ik toch mijn moeders dochter. Ze was al bezig me te koppelen, aan mijn neef Anwar, die in Bristol filosofie studeerde. Anwar, lang en dun, met grote bruine ogen en een ziekenfondsbrilletje, had een geweldige smaak op kledinggebied en was gek op platen van Judy Garland. Hij ging ervandoor met een jongen van de universiteitsboekwinkel, hoewel mijn moeder nog altijd weigert te geloven dat hij homo is.

Sinds we van Heathrow zijn opgestegen heeft Ruiz nauwelijks iets gezegd. Hij kan heel welbespraakt zwijgen.

Ik had gezegd dat hij niet mee hoefde. 'Jij bent met pensioen.'

'Klopt, maar ik ben nog niet dood,' zei hij terwijl een flauw glimlachje zijn ooghoeken deed rimpelen.

Na zes jaar weet ik nog altijd verbazingwekkend weinig over hem. Hij heeft kinderen – een tweeling – maar heeft het niet over ze. Zijn moeder zit in een bejaardentehuis. Zijn stiefvader is dood. Over zijn echte vader weet ik niets.

Ik heb nog nooit iemand ontmoet die zo genoeg aan zichzelf heeft. Hij lijkt niet te talen naar menselijk contact, niemand nodig te hebben. Als hij zou meedoen aan zo'n survivalprogramma op tv, waarin deelnemers worden gesplitst in elkaar beconcurrerende stammen, zou Ruiz zijn eigen stam zijn, in zijn eentje. En die norse ouwe kerel zou nog elke keer winnen ook.

Amsterdam. Mij doet het denken aan softdrugs, gedoogde prostitutie en klompen. Dit wordt mijn eerste bezoek. Ruiz is eveneens een 'Nederlandse maagd' (zijn uitdrukking, niet de mijne). Hij heeft me zijn minirapport over de Nederlanders al gegeven: 'Uitstekend bier, een paar redelijke voetballers en die kaas met zo'n rode waslaag eromheen.'

'De Nederlanders zijn erg beleefd,' probeer ik.

'Het zijn waarschijnlijk de aardigste mensen ter wereld,' gaf hij toe. 'Ze zijn zo plooibaar dat ze prostitutie en marihuana liever legaliseren dan tegen iemand nee te moeten zeggen.'

Ondanks zijn zigeunerbloed was Ruiz nooit een zwerver geweest. Zijn enige buitenlandse vakantie bracht hij door in Italië. Hij is een gewoontedier – lauw bier, stevig voedsel en rugby – en zijn xenofobie neemt steevast toe naarmate hij verder van huis is.

We hebben een plaats bij de galley weten te veroveren, zodat ik met mijn schoenen uit mijn voeten tegen de muur kan leggen en mijn roze-en-wit gestreepte sokken kan laten zien. De lege stoel tussen ons in heb ik met mijn boek, waterfles en koptelefoon bezet verklaard. Hebben is hebben, maar krijgen is de kunst.

Vanuit het raampje gezien ligt het Nederlandse landschap erbij als een oud biljartlaken, hier en daar opgelapt met rechthoekjes vilt. Ik zie schattige boerderijen, schattige windmolens en af en toe een dorp. Dat hele onder-de-zeespiegel-gedoe is uiterst merkwaardig. Zelfs de bruggen zouden onder water verdwijnen als de dijken het ooit begaven. Maar de Nederlanders zijn zo goed in landaanwinning dat ze waarschijnlijk op een dag de Noordzee zullen dichtgooien en we de M11 kunnen doortrekken naar Moskou.

Tijdens de rit vanaf het vliegveld lijkt de taxichauffeur te verdwalen en rondjes te rijden. Hij steekt althans telkens dezelfde grachten en dezelfde bruggen over. De enige aanwijzingen voor waar Cate is geweest zijn de centrumkaart van Amsterdam en het feit dat het Red Tulip Hotel omcirkeld was.

De baliemedewerker begroet ons met een brede glimlach. Ze is halverwege de twintig, stevig gebouwd en een pondje of twee van overgewicht verwijderd. Achter haar hangt een prikbord met folders van rondvaarten, fietstochten en dagtochten naar de bollenvelden.

Ik leg een foto van Cate op de balie. 'Herkent u deze vrouw?'

Ze kijkt eens goed. Cate is een lange blik waard. Ze herkent haar niet.

'Misschien zegt het een van de andere medewerkers iets.'

Een portier is bezig onze koffers op een trolley te zetten. Hij is in de vijftig en draagt een rode pandjesjas die aan de knopen te zien strak om zijn witte overhemd en buik zit.

Ik laat hem de foto zien. Zijn ogen vernauwen zich van de concentratie. Ik vraag me af wat hij van gasten onthoudt – hun gezichten, hun koffers, hun fooien?

'Kamer 12,' zegt hij heftig knikkend.

Ruiz draait zich naar de balie. 'U hebt hier ongetwijfeld een gastenboek. Ze zou hier in de tweede week van maart kunnen zijn geweest.'

Ze werpt een blik over haar schouder of de manager haar niet ziet en tikt iets in. Ik bekijk de lijst die op het scherm verschijnt. Cate komt er niet op voor. Wacht! Een andere naam herken ik wel. 'Ntalia Radzinsky.'

'Ja, de gravin,' knikt de portier heftig. 'Ze had één blauwe tas,' voegt hij er bij wijze van verder bewijs aan toe. Hij gebaart hoe groot ongeveer. 'En nog een kleinere. Erg zwaar.' Hij spreekt slecht Engels.

'Had ze iemand bij zich?'

Hij schudt zijn hoofd. 'Erg zwaar. Van metaal.'

'U hebt een uitstekend geheugen.'

Hij straalt.

Ik kijk opnieuw naar het scherm. Het voelt alsof Cate een aanwijzing voor me heeft achtergelaten die niemand anders zou herkennen. Het idee dat de doden berichten achterlaten voor de levenden is natuurlijk dwaasheid. De arrogantie van de archeoloog.

Het Red Tulip Hotel telt zestien kamers, waarvan de helft op de gracht uitkijkt. Die van mij is op de eerste verdieping, Ruiz' kamer recht erboven. Het zonlicht weerkaatst in de ramen van een passerende rondvaartboot met toeristen. Bellende fietsers slingeren zich tussen de voetgangers door.

Ruiz klopt aan en we stellen een plan op. Hij gaat langs bij de Immigratie en Naturalisatie Dienst (IND), die in Nederland de aanvragen van asielzoekers behandelt. Ik ga naar het laatst bekende adres van Hasan Khan.

Ik neem een taxi naar de Gerard Doustraat, in de Pijp, of *the pipe*, zoals mijn chauffeur in zijn beste Engels uitlegt. Het echte Amsterdam, meent hij. Lange tijd had het een louche reputatie, maar nu wemelt het er van de restaurants, cafés en bakkerijen.

De Vlammende Wok is een Chinees restaurant met bamboe rolgordijnen en namaak bonsaiboompjes. Er zijn geen gasten. Bij de keukendeur hangen twee obers rond. Aziaten. Keurig verzorgd, in zwarte broeken en witte overhemden.

Van de voordeur kijk ik door tot aan de keuken, waar aan het plafond pannen en stoommandjes hangen. Een oudere man, in het wit, is bezig gerechten voor te bereiden. In zijn hand stuitert een mes.

De obers spreken menu-Engels. Ze blijven me een tafel opdringen. Ik vraag naar de eigenaar.

Terwijl hij zijn handen aan een theedoek afveegt komt meneer Weng zijn keuken uit. Hij buigt.

'Ik wil iets weten over de mensen die hierboven hebben gewoond.'

'Zij weg.'

'Ja.'

'U wil flat?'

'Nee.'

Hij haalt onverschillig zijn schouders op, wijst naar een tafel, gebaart me te gaan zitten en roept om thee. De obers, zijn zoons, verdringen zich om die te mogen brengen.

'Over die huurders...' zeg ik.

'Zij komen, zij gaan,' antwoordt hij. 'Soms vol, soms leeg.' Zijn handen fladderen terwijl hij praat. Af en toe pakt hij ze vast, alsof ze weg zouden kunnen vliegen.

'Uw laatste huurders, waar kwamen die vandaan?'

'Overal vandaan. Estland, Polen, Oezbekistan...'

'En deze jongen?' Ik laat hem het houtskoolportret van Hasan zien. 'Hij is ouder nu – zestien.'

Hij knikt beslist. 'Deze goed. Hij doen afwas voor eten. Anderen uit vuilnisbak eten.'

De groene thee is gearriveerd. Meneer Weng schenkt in. Theeblaadjes wervelen rond in de kleine witte kopjes.

'Wie betaalde de huur?'

'Geld vooruitbetalen. Zes maanden.'

'Maar u moet een huurovereenkomst hebben gehad?'

Meneer Weng begrijpt het niet.

'Was er een contract?'

'Niet contract.'

'En de elektriciteit, de telefoon?'

Hij knikt en glimlacht. Hij is te beleefd om te zeggen dat hij geen antwoord paraat heeft.

Ik wijs naar het meisje op de tekening en haal de foto van Samira tevoorschijn. 'En dit meisje?'

'Veel meisjes komen.' Hij kromt zijn linkerwijsvinger en duim en steekt zijn andere wijsvinger door het gat. 'Plostituee,' zegt hij verontschuldigend, alsof de toestand van de wereld hem bedrukt.

Ik vraag of ik de flat mag zien. Een van zijn zoons biedt zich aan. Hij gaat me voor door een nooddeur die uitkomt in een steeg. We gaan een achtertrap op. Boven doet hij een deur van het slot. Ik ben vaker in deprimerende appartementen geweest, maar hier is het zeldzaam bedrukkend. De woning bestaat uit één slaapkamer, een zitkamer, een keuken en een badkamer. Het enige meubilair is een lage ladekast met spiegel en een bank met brandgaten.

'De matrassen zijn weggegooid,' legt hij uit.

'Hoeveel mensen woonden hier?'

'Tien.'

Ik heb de indruk dat hij de huurders beter kende dan zijn vader.

'Herinner jij je dit meisje?' Ik laat hem de foto zien.

'Zou kunnen.'

'Woonde ze hier?'

'Ze kwam weleens op bezoek.'

'Weet je waar ze woont?'

'Nee.'

De huurders hebben niets achtergelaten, behalve een paar blikjes voedsel, oude kussens en gebruikte internationale telefoonkaarten. Dit levert niets op.

Ik neem een taxi en tref Ruiz voor een bar op de Nieuwmarkt, een bestraat vierkant plein vlak bij de Oude Kerk. Hier buiten zijn de meeste tafels leeg. Voor rugzakkers en Amerikaanse toeristen begint het te laat in het jaar te worden.

'Ik had niet gedacht dat je er een zou kopen,' zeg ik terwijl ik naar zijn gidsje wijs.

'Nou ja, eh… ik heb een hekel aan de weg vragen,' bromt hij. 'Ik weet zeker dat ik te horen krijg: "U wilt wáárheen?" En dat ik dan ontdek dat ik in het verkeerde kloteland ben.'

Het stel aan de tafel naast ons is van hier. Ik kan niet uitmaken of ze ruzie hebben of het juist roerend met elkaar eens zijn.

'Nederlanders weten meer lettergrepen in een zin te persen dan wie ook,' zegt Ruiz, iets te hard. 'En die raspende Nederlandse *gggg* is helemaal een vuile provocatie.'

153

Hij kijkt weer in zijn gidsje. We bevinden ons aan de westkant van de hoerenbuurt, de Wallen.

'Dat gebouw met al die kantelen is de Waag,' legt hij uit. 'Het was ooit een stadspoort.'

Een jonge serveerster komt onze bestelling opnemen. Ruiz wil nog een bier, 'met minder schuim en meer Heineken'. Ze glimlacht begripvol mijn kant op.

Met zijn gemarmerde opschrijfboek opengeslagen vertelt Ruiz hoe Hasan en Samira Khan in juni 2004 in het bagageruim van een toeristenbus over de Duitse grens Nederland werden binnengesmokkeld. Ze werden naar een aanmeldcentrum in Ter Apel gebracht en door de IND ondervraagd. Hasan beweerde vijftien jaar oud te zijn en Samira zeventien. Ze vertelden de autoriteiten dat ze in Kabul geboren waren en drie jaar in een vluchtelingenkamp in Pakistan hadden gewoond. Nadat hun moeder was gestorven aan dysenterie nam hun vader, Hamid Khan, de kinderen mee terug naar Kabul, waar hij in 1999 werd doodgeschoten. Hasan en Samira werden naar een weeshuis gestuurd.

'Dat is het verhaal dat ze, zowel samen als onafhankelijk van elkaar, in elk verhoor en gesprek vertelden. Zonder haperen.'

'Hoe kwamen ze hier terecht?'

'Via smokkelaars, maar allebei weigerden ze namen te noemen.' Ruiz kijkt opnieuw in zijn opschrijfboek. 'Na gescreend te zijn werden ze ondergebracht in een centrum voor minderjarige asielzoekers van de Valentijnstichting. Drie maanden later werden ze overgeplaatst naar een centrum in Deelen, dat aan honderdtachtig kinderen onderdak biedt. In december vorig jaar werd hun visum ingetrokken.'

'Waarom?'

'Dat weet ik niet. Ze kregen achtentwintig dagen de tijd om Nederland te verlaten. Er werd beroep aangetekend, maar ze verdwenen.'

'Verdwenen?'

'Dit soort mensen blijft meestal niet rondhangen tot ze worden uitgezet.'

'Wat bedoel je met "dit soort mensen"?'

Hij kijkt me ongemakkelijk aan. 'Foutje.' Hij nipt aan zijn bier. 'Ik heb de naam van een advocaat die hen vertegenwoordigde, Lena Caspar. Ze heeft een kantoor hier in Amsterdam.' Er zit wit schuim op zijn bovenlip. 'En nog iets. De jongen is al eerder het Kanaal overgestoken. Hij werd gesnapt en binnen vierentwintig uur weer uitgezet naar Nederland.'

'Hij heeft kennelijk een nieuwe poging gedaan.'

'En had opnieuw pech.'

2

Het advocatenkantoor aan de Prinsengracht is gehuisvest in een vier verdiepingen tellend pand dat een graad of twee lijkt over te hellen boven de straatklinkers. Via een hoge gewelfde doorgang komen we op een klein plaatsje waar een oude vrouw met emmer en dweil het natuursteen aan het dweilen is. Ze wijst naar de trap.

Op de eerste verdieping stappen we een wachtkamer vol Noord-Afrikanen binnen, voor een groot deel met kinderen. Een jongeman kijkt op van zijn bureau en duwt zijn Harry Potter-brilletje recht. We hebben geen afspraak. Hij bladert door het afsprakenboek.

Op dat moment gaat er achter hem een deur open en verschijnt er een Nigeriaanse, gekleed in een volumineuze jurk. Een klein meisje houdt haar hand vast, op haar schouder slaapt een baby.

Heel even zie ik niemand anders. Dan duikt er een kleine vrouw op, als uit de plooien van de jurk van de Nigeriaanse.

'Zodra ik het bezwaar heb ingediend stuur ik je een afschrift,' zegt ze. 'Als je intussen verhuist, moet je het me laten weten.'

Met haar katoenen blouse met lange mouwen, zwarte vest en grijze broek ziet ze er zeer advocaatachtig en zakelijk uit. Ze glimlacht afwezig mijn kant uit, alsof we elkaar kennen, kijkt naar Ruiz en rilt.

'Mevrouw Caspar, sorry dat we storen, maar een woordje apart, zou dat kunnen?'

Ze lacht. 'Wat een typisch Engelse beleefdheid. Eén woordje maar? Ik zou bijna ja zeggen, alleen om te horen wat dat woord dan wel mag zijn.' De huid rond haar ogen is gerimpeld als een perzikpit. 'Vandaag zit ik vol. U zult geduld moeten hebben tot...'

Halverwege de zin zwijgt ze opeens. Ik hou een foto van Samira op. 'Haar broer is dood. We moeten haar zien te vinden.'

Mevrouw Caspar houdt de deur van haar kantoor voor ons open. De kamer is bijna vierkant, de houten vloer is glimmend gepoetst. Ze vertelt dat het pand al generaties lang familiebezit is. Ook haar grootvader en vader hadden hier hun advocatenpraktijk.

Ook al vertelt ze dit uit zichzelf, mevrouw Caspar is op haar hoede, zoals elke advocaat.

'U ziet er niet uit als een politieagent,' zegt ze tegen me. 'Ik dacht dat u een beroep op mijn diensten kwam doen.' Ze draait zich naar Ruiz. 'U daarentegen ziet er echt uit als een politieman.'

'Niet meer.'

'Over Hasan,' zegt ze, nu weer tegen mij. 'Wat is er met hem gebeurd?'

'Wanneer hebt u hem voor het laatst gezien?'

'Elf maanden geleden.'

Ik vertel hoe ze in de vrachtwagen zijn lichaam ontdekten en dat mijn naam en adres in zijn kleding zaten genaaid. Mevrouw Caspar staat met haar gezicht naar het raam. Misschien wel met opkomende tranen, al betwijfel ik of een vrouw als zij tegenover vreemden haar emoties toont.

'Wat moest hij met uw naam?'

'Dat weet ik niet. Ik hoopte dat u het wist.'

Ze schudt haar hoofd.

'Ik probeer Samira te vinden.'

'Waarom?'

Hoe ga ik dit aanpakken? Recht vooruit maar. 'Ik verdenk een vriendin van me, die geen kinderen kon krijgen, ervan dat ze geprobeerd heeft in Amsterdam een baby te kopen. Ik vermoed dat ze Samira heeft ontmoet.'

'Samira heeft geen kind.'

'Nee, maar wel een baarmoeder.'

Mevrouw Caspar kijkt me ongelovig aan. 'Een moslimmeisje leent haar baarmoeder niet uit voor geld. U vergist zich.'

Haar opmerking klinkt bot, als een feit of dogma. Ze loopt naar de andere kant van de kamer, opent een archiefkast en pakt er een map uit. Aan haar bureau gezeten loopt ze de inhoud door.

'De regering hier moedigt asielzoekers niet aan. Het wordt hun steeds moeilijker gemaakt. We hebben zelfs een minister voor Vreemdelingenzaken die beweert dat maar twintig procent van de aanvragers uit "echte vluchtelingen" bestaat, en dat de rest leugenaars en bedriegers zijn.

Helaas worden ook legitieme asielzoekers verketterd. Ze worden behandeld als economische vluchtelingen die van land naar land trekken tot ze ergens definitief worden toegelaten.'

Haar bittere stem doet haar kleine lijf trillen.

'Samira en Hasan hadden geen papieren bij zich toen ze hier arriveerden. De IND beweerde dat ze die opzettelijk hadden vernietigd. Ze geloofden niet dat Samira minderjarig was. Ze zag er eerder uit als twaalf dan als twintig, maar toch lieten ze haar tests ondergaan.'

'Tests?'

'Een leeftijdstest. Een röntgenfoto van het sleutelbeen, waarmee je geacht wordt te kunnen bepalen of iemand jonger of ouder dan twintig is. Van Hasan werd zijn pols gefotografeerd. Er werd een rapport opgemaakt door Harry van der Pas, fysisch antropoloog aan de Universiteit van Tilburg.

Het keerde zich tegen hen. Zij leek zelfs nog jonger dan de leeftijd die ze opgegeven had. Eenzijdige voeding en ondervoeding hadden haar groei geremd. Ze kregen allebei een tijdelijk visum. Ze mochten blijven, maar slechts totdat er aanvullend onderzoek was gedaan.'

Ze slaat een bladzijde om.

'Tegenwoordig is het beleid om minderjarige asielzoekers terug te sturen naar het land van herkomst. Hasan en Samira hádden geen familie meer. Afghanistan is nauwelijks in staat zijn mensen te voeden. Kabul is een stad van weduwen en wezen.'

Ze schuift een vel aantekeningen mijn kant op, een familiege-schiedenis. 'Ze waren wees. Beiden spraken Engels. Hun moeder was opgeleid aan de Universiteit van Delhi. Tot de taliban de macht greep werkte ze als vertaalster voor een uitgeverij.'

Ik bekijk de aantekeningen. Samira werd in 1987 geboren, tijdens de Russische bezetting van Afghanistan. Ze was twee jaar toen de Sovjets vertrokken en tien toen de taliban kwam.

'En hun vader?'

'Die had een fabriek.'

Ik herinner me de foto die Hasan bij zich droeg.

'Ze maakten vuurwerk,' legt mevrouw Caspar uit. 'De taliban sloot de fabriek. Vuurwerk was verboden. Het gezin vluchtte naar Pakistan en leefde daar in een kamp. Hun moeder stierf aan dysenterie. Hamid Khan had het er moeilijk mee om als alleenstaande vader zijn kinderen op te voeden. Toen hij het zat was om als bedelaar in een vreemd land te leven, nam hij zijn gezin mee terug naar Kabul. Nog geen zes maanden later was hij dood.'

'Hoe?'

'Samira en Hasan waren getuige van zijn executie. In hun appartement dwong een tiener met een kalasjnikov hem te knielen en schoot hem daarna door het achterhoofd. Ze gooiden zijn lichaam uit een raam op straat en dwongen zijn kinderen het acht dagen lang met rust te laten. Tegen die tijd hadden de honden zich er al aan tegoed gedaan.'

Ze heeft een brok in haar keel. 'Ik heb Samira een Afghaans gezegde horen gebruiken: *Voor een mierenkolonie is de dauw een vloed.*'

Verdere uitleg is overbodig.

'Wanneer hebt u haar voor het laatst gezien?'

'Half januari. Ze had een verrassing voor mijn verjaardag. Zelf-gemaakt vuurwerk. Ik weet niet hoe ze aan de chemicaliën en het kruit kwam. Ik had nog nooit zoiets moois gezien.'

'En hun asielaanvraag?'

De advocate haalt nog een brief tevoorschijn. 'Voor een asiel-zoeker in dit land is achttien een sleutelleeftijd. Vanaf die leeftijd

word je behandeld als een volwassene. Samira's tijdelijke verblijfs-
vergunning werd herzien. Ze werd oud genoeg geacht om voor
Hasan te zorgen, dus zijn visum werd ook ingetrokken. Hun beiden werd asiel geweigerd en ze moesten vertrekken.

Uiteraard tekende ik beroep aan, maar ik kon niet voorkomen
dat ze op straat terechtkwamen. Ze moesten de campus in Deelen
af. Zoals zo veel afgewezen jonge asielzoekers kozen ze ervoor te
vluchten in plaats van op uitzetting te wachten.'

'Waarheen?'

Ze heft haar handen.

'Hoe kunnen we Samira op het spoor komen?'

'Dat gaat niet.'

'Ik moet het proberen. Had ze vrienden in het asielzoekerscentrum?'

'Ze had het weleens over een Servisch meisje. Haar naam weet
ik niet.'

'Is die nog daar?'

'Nee. Ze is of uitgezet, of weggelopen.'

Mevrouw Caspar kijkt Ruiz aan en dan mij weer. De toekomst
staat in de lijnen op haar gezicht geschreven. Het is een moeilijke
reis.

'Een vriend van mij, een gepensioneerd politieman, net als u,
meneer Ruiz, heeft zijn halve leven in het gebied rond de Wallen
gewerkt. Hij kent iedereen: de prostituees, de pooiers, de dealers
en hun klanten. Langs de muren kruipen muizen, muizen hebben
oren en hij kan ze verstaan.'

Ze noteert de naam van ons hotel en belooft een bericht achter
te zullen laten.

'Als jullie Samira vinden, doe dan rustig aan. Als ze hoort wat er
met haar broer gebeurd is, zal dat hard aankomen.'

'Denkt u dat we haar zullen vinden?'

Ze kust me op beide wangen. 'Als je je gevoel volgt, wie weet.'

Terug in het hotel bel ik inspecteur Forbes. Het eerste wat hij
vraagt is waar ik zit. Een stemmetje in mijn binnenste zegt me te
liegen. Een stemmetje dat ik de laatste tijd vaker heb gehoord.

'Is de vrachtwagenchauffeur al verhoord?'

'Zit jij in Amsterdam?' kaatst hij terug.

'Wat heeft hij gezegd?'

'Jij kunt niet zomaar het land uit gaan, godverdomme. Je bent verdachte.'

'Van enige beperking is me niets verteld.'

'Gelul. Als jij op eigen houtje op onderzoek uit bent, laat ik disciplinaire maatregelen treffen. Je carrière kun je dan wel vergeten. En thuiskomen ook.'

Ik hoor het irritante klakgeluid weer. Zijn vrouw zal er wel gek van worden, alsof ze met een levende metronoom samenleeft.

Als ik hem over Hasan vertel, komt hij eindelijk tot bedaren. We wisselen informatie uit. De vrachtwagenchauffeur is aangeklaagd voor doodslag, maar er is een complicerende factor. Voordat het roll-on-roll-off-schip in Harwich afmeerde waren Britse immigratieofficieren getipt over een verdacht voertuig. Ze wisten het kenteken en hadden gehoord dat ze moesten uitkijken naar een groep illegale immigranten.

'Van wie kwam die tip?'

'Bij de havenautoriteiten in Rotterdam kwam twee uur na vertrek een anoniem telefoontje binnen. Wij vermoeden van de smokkelaars.'

'Hoe dat zo?'

'Als afleidingsmanoeuvre.'

'Dat begrijp ik niet.'

'Door een klein groepje illegalen op te offeren, zouden ze vele handen kunnen binden. De douane en immigratiedienst zouden het zo druk hebben dat ze een veel groter transport over het hoofd zouden zien.'

'Aan boord van hetzelfde schip?'

'Met twee trucks met oplegger is iets aan de hand. De op de vrachtbrief genoemde bedrijven bestaan niet. In hun laadruim zouden zo'n honderd mensen kunnen zijn binnengesmokkeld.'

'Zouden de luchtgaten opzettelijk dicht kunnen zijn gestopt, om de valstrik nog effectiever te maken?'

'Dat zullen we mogelijk nooit te weten komen.'

'Ik zoek geen fitnesscentrum, maar een sportschool,' zeg ik tegen de receptioniste, die het verschil niet snapt. Ze duikt weg voor mijn boksbeweging. Nu snapt ze het.

Ik weet wel iets van sportscholen. In ons laatste jaar op Oaklands wist ik Cate over te halen mee naar karateles te gaan. De lessen werden gegeven in een achterafzaaltje in Penwick Street, dat vooral bezocht werd door boksers en in hemdjes geklede oude mannen wier aderen op hun hoofd opzwollen als ze op de halterbank lagen.

De karateleraar was een Chinees met een cockney-accent die door iedereen 'Peking' werd genoemd, wat tot PK werd afgekort, waar hij geen bezwaar tegen leek te hebben.

Je had daar een boksring en een gewichtenzaal met spiegels en voor karate een apart uitbouwtje met matten op de vloer. De eerste lessen besteedde PK aan de principes waarop karate is gebaseerd, wat Cate niet bovenmatig interesseerde. 'De mentale discipline, fysieke training en beoefening zelf dragen bij aan het respect voor de medemens,' zei hij.

'Ik wil ze gewoon een trap voor hun kloten kunnen geven,' zei Cate.

'De twee Japanse karakters waaruit het woord "karate" bestaat, betekenen letterlijk "lege handen",' legde PK uit. 'Het is een systeem voor zelfverdediging dat zich in de loop der eeuwen heeft ontwikkeld. Elke beweging is gebaseerd op kennis van de spieren en gewrichten, en de relatie tussen beweging en balans.'

Cate stak haar hand op. 'Wanneer leer ik nou klappen uit te delen?'

'Je gaat hier de technieken van de tegenaanval leren.'

Daarna legde hij uit dat het woord 'karate' afstamde van Mandarijnse en Kantonese uitdrukkingen als *Chan Fa* en *Ken Fat*, wat Cate een giechelaanval bezorgde. De letterlijke betekenis is 'de wet van de vuist'. Aanvallen naar het kruis van de tegenstander worden in de meeste vechtsporten niet getolereerd. In karate zijn daarnaast de heupgewrichten, knieën, wreef, schenen, bovenbenen en het gezicht geen legitiem doelwit.

'Wat heb je er dan aan?'

'Ik denk dat hij het over wedstrijdkarate heeft.'

'Wedstrijden interesseren me niet. Ik wil hun ballen laten schrijnen.'

Ze bleef de theorie volgen, maar viel hem elke week weer lastig met dezelfde vraag: 'Wanneer leren we nou de kruistrap?'

Uiteindelijk ging PK overstag. Hij gaf Cate na sluitingstijd een privé-les. De gordijnen gingen dicht en hij deed alle lampen uit, op de ringverlichting na.

Ze kwam met een blos en een glimlach op haar gezicht naar buiten, met een vlek in haar nek die verdacht veel op een zuigzoen leek. Het was haar laatste les in zelfverdediging.

Ik bleef gaan en werkte verschillende banden af. PK wilde dat ik voor de zwarte band opging, maar ik zat inmiddels al op de politieacademie.

Als ik het restaurant binnenkom, zit Ruiz aan zijn tweede biertje. Hij kijkt hoe de pizzabakker een schijf deeg de lucht in gooit, op zijn knokkels opvangt en weer opgooit.

De bediening is jong. Twee van hen staan naar me te kijken en zeggen iets tegen elkaar. Ze gissen wat voor relatie ik heb met Ruiz. Wat doet een jonge Aziatische vrouw met een twee keer zo oude man? Voor hen ben ik ofwel een importbruidje, ofwel zijn minnares.

Het restaurant is bijna leeg. In Amsterdam eet niemand zo vroeg. Bij de ingang zit een oude man met een hond. Onder tafel voert hij hem stukjes eten.

'Ze kan overal en nergens zijn,' zegt Ruiz.

'Ze zou niet zijn weggegaan uit Amsterdam.'

'Waarom denk je dat?'

'Hasan was pas zestien. Ze zou hem niet alleen hebben gelaten.'

'Hij is twee keer zonder haar het Kanaal overgestoken.'

Daar weet ik niets op te zeggen.

Tot dusverre hebben we onze speurtocht kunnen doen zonder de aandacht te trekken. Waarom zouden we niet van tactiek veranderen? Posters laten maken of een advertentie zetten.

Ruiz is het niet met me eens. 'Cate Beaumont probeerde dit in de openbaarheid te brengen, en zie wat er van haar is geworden. Dit is geen spontane operatie waarbij iemand in paniek is geraakt en de Beaumonts heeft vermoord. We hebben te maken met een georganiseerde bende, met figuren als Brendan Pearl.'

'Ze zullen het niet verwachten.'

'Maar wel te weten komen dat we op zoek zijn.'

'We jagen ze uit hun schuilplaats.'

Ruiz blijft tegenwerpingen maken, maar begrijpt wat ik bedoel. Wat er nu gaat gebeuren zal niet door het toeval of het lot worden bepaald. Wij kunnen ervoor zorgen dat er dingen gaan gebeuren.

Eenpersoons hotelkamers in onbekende steden zijn eenzame plekken waar de menselijke geest haar dieptepunt kan bereiken. Ik lig op bed, maar kan de slaap niet vatten. Mijn hoofd weigert het beeld los te laten van een kind in een Mickey Mouse-T-shirt dat naast zijn moeder ligt, onder een dichtgestopt ventilatiegat.

Ik wil de klok terugdraaien naar de avond van de reünie en verder. Ik wil tegenover Cate zitten en om beurten praten en huilen en zeggen dat het ons spijt. Ik wil de afgelopen acht jaar goedmaken. Maar bovenal wil ik vergiffenis.

3

Onder mijn kussen trilt zachtjes een telefoon.

Ik hoor de stem van Ruiz. 'Hup, eruit jij.'

'Hoe laat is het?'

'Even over zevenen. Er staat iemand beneden. Gestuurd door Lena Caspar.'

Ik trek mijn spijkerbroek aan, gooi water over mijn gezicht en doe mijn haar naar achteren.

Nicolaas Hokke is halverwege de zestig en heeft springerig, kort grijs haar en een baard. Zijn ruim een meter tachtig lange gestalte helpt het beginnende buikje te verbloemen dat onder zijn versleten leren jasje zichtbaar is.

'Ik heb begrepen dat u een gids nodig hebt,' zegt hij terwijl hij met beide handen mijn hand pakt. Hij ruikt naar tabak en talkpoeder.

'Ik ben op zoek naar een meisje.'

'Een meisje.'

'Een asielzoekster.'

'Hmm. Laten we aan het ontbijt verder praten.'

Hij weet een gelegenheid. Op loopafstand. De kruispunten zijn een wirwar van trams, auto's en fietsen. Hokke laveert ertussendoor met de zelfverzekerdheid van een god die over een meer loopt.

Ik begin nu al van Amsterdam te houden. Met zijn bestrate pleinen, grachten en gevels als bruidstaarten is de stad lieflijker en schoner dan Londen. Ik voel me hier veiliger: de anonieme buitenlander.

'Veel mensen vragen om een rondleiding door de rosse buurt,' vertelt Hokke. 'Schrijvers, sociologen, buitenlandse politici. Ik neem ze twee keer mee: één keer overdag en nog een keer 's avonds. Zo zien ze als het ware twee kanten van de medaille: licht en donker.'

Hokke loopt slenterend, zijn in elkaar gestrengelde handen op zijn rug. Af en toe blijft hij staan om iets markants aan te wijzen of een straatnaam uit te leggen.

'Was dit jouw wijk?' vraagt Ruiz.

'Uiteraard.'

'Wanneer ben je gestopt?'

'Twee jaar terug. En jij?'

'Een jaar geleden.'

Ze knikken elkaar toe alsof ze elkaar niets hoeven te vertellen.

We slaan een hoek om en voor het eerst zie ik de beroemde 'ramen' van Amsterdam. Op het eerste gezicht zijn het simpele glazen deuren met houten kozijnen en koperen huisnummers. Van sommige zijn de gordijnen gesloten. Andere zijn open voor klandizie.

Pas als ik dichterbij ben, zie ik wat dat inhoudt. Op een krukje zit een magere, donkere vrouw in een glitterbeha en string met haar benen over elkaar en laarzen dichtgeritst tot op haar dijen. In het ultraviolette licht zien de kneuzingen op haar dijen eruit als grauwe vlekken.

De schaamteloosheid van haar pose en haar bedoelingen doet me heel even ineenkrimpen. Ze werpt me een agressieve blik toe. Ze wil niet dat ik hier met deze mannen ben. Met mij erbij zullen ze niet bij haar naar binnen gaan.

We gaan nog meer steegjes door. We passeren ramen die zo dicht tegenover elkaar liggen dat mijn blik naar links en naar rechts wordt getrokken, alsof ik bij een tenniswedstrijd de heen en weer gaande bal volg. Ruiz kijkt recht voor zich uit.

Een grote Dominicaanse vrouw roept iets naar Hokke en zwaait. Haar enorme borsten worden door een rode met kwastjes versierde push-upbeha op hun plaats gehouden. Ze zit ineengezakt op een kruk. Haar uitpuilende buik bedekt haar kruis.

Hokke blijft staan, praat even met haar in het Nederlands en komt weer terug.

'Ze heeft vier kinderen,' legt hij uit. 'Eentje zit op de universiteit. Al twintig jaar prostituee, maar nog altijd vrouw.'

'Hoe bedoelt u, vrouw?'

'Sommigen veranderen in hoeren.'

Hij zwaait naar verschillende andere prostituees, die hem kusjes toewerpen of hem jennen door op hun pols te slaan. Even verderop komt een oudere vrouw een winkel uit lopen en ze omhelst hem als een lang verloren zoon. Ze geeft hem een zak met kersen.

'Dit is Gusta,' stelt hij haar voor. 'Ze zit nog altijd achter de ramen.'

'Parttime,' verbetert ze hem.

'Maar u bent toch al...'

'Vijfenzestig,' zegt ze trots. 'Ik heb vijf kleinkinderen.'

Hokke moet lachen om onze verbazing. 'Jullie vragen je natuurlijk af hoeveel klanten er naar bed zouden willen met een grootmoeder.'

Gusta legt haar handen op haar heupen en beweegt ze verleidelijk heen en weer. Hokke zoekt naar een beleefde manier om onze vraag te beantwoorden.

'Bij sommige jongere, knappere meisjes staan de mannen buiten in de rij. Zij maken zich niet druk of klanten terugkomen of niet.

Er staan er altijd genoeg te wachten. Maar een vrouw als Gusta moet het niet van een lieve glimlach of een stevig lichaam hebben. En dus moet ze kwaliteit leveren en een bepaalde expertise die met de jaren komt.'

Gusta knikt instemmend.

Hokke lijkt de prostituees en hun werk niet af te keuren. De drugsverslaafden en dealers zijn een ander verhaal. Een Noord-Afrikaanse man hangt tegen een brugleuning. Hij herkent Hokke en danst zijn richting uit. Hokke blijft niet staan. De Afrikaan heeft betelvlekken op zijn tanden en verwijde pupillen. Hokkes gezicht is leeg, neutraal. De Afrikaan kakelt in het Nederlands, woest grinnikend. Hokke loopt door.

'Een oude vriend?' vraag ik.

'Ik ken hem al dertig jaar. Zo lang is hij ook al aan de heroïne.'

'Dat hij dan nog leeft.'

'Verslaafden gaan niet dood aan de drugs, maar aan hun levensstijl,' zegt hij stellig. 'Als drugs minder duur waren, zou hij niet hoeven te stelen om ze te kunnen betalen.'

Aan de andere kant van de brug komen we nog een junkie tegen, jonger en met een nog minder appetijtelijk uiterlijk. Met de punt van zijn brandende sigaret wijst hij mijn kant op en zegt op vleierige toon iets tegen Hokke. Er ontstaat ruzie. Ik weet niet wat ze zeggen.

'Ik vroeg hem of hij clean was,' legt Hokke uit.

'En?'

'Hij zei: "Ik ben altijd clean." '

'Jullie maakten ruzie.'

'Hij wilde weten of jij te koop was.'

'Is hij een pooier?'

'Als het hem uitkomt wel.'

We komen bij het café aan en nemen buiten een tafel onder de kale takken van een grote, met feestverlichting versierde boom. Hokke drinkt zijn koffie zwart en bestelt geroosterd zuurdesembrood met jam. Na afloop stopt hij een pijp die zo klein is dat hij voor leerling-pijprokers gemaakt lijkt.

'Mijn enige zonde,' zegt hij.

166

Ruiz lacht. 'Dus in al die jaren ben je nooit in de verleiding gekomen?'

'Welke verleiding?'

'Om met sommigen van die vrouwen achter de ramen naar bed te gaan. Er moeten zich ongetwijfeld kansen hebben voorgedaan.'

'Kansen wel, ja. Ik ben al veertig jaar getrouwd, Vincent. Als je ik je Vincent mag noemen. Ik heb alleen met mijn eigen vrouw geslapen. Aan haar heb ik genoeg. Deze vrouwen doen het voor geld. Dan moet je niet verwachten dat ze hun lichaam gratis weggeven. Welke zakenvrouw zou dat doen?'

Zijn gezicht verdwijnt bijna in een wolk pijprook.

'Dat meisje dat jullie zoeken, denken jullie dat ze mogelijk prostituee is?'

'Ze is uit Afghanistan gesmokkeld.'

'Afghaanse prostituees zijn een zeldzaamheid. De moslimmeisjes zijn meestal Turks of Tunesisch. Als ze hier illegaal is, zal ze pas achter de ramen gaan werken als ze valse papieren heeft.'

'Kost dat veel moeite?'

'Nigeriaanse en Somalische vrouwen ruilen hun papieren onderling omdat ze op elkaar lijken, maar normaliter zijn de ramen het gemakkelijkst te controleren. Op straat en in privé-clubs is dat lastiger. Het is als met een ijsberg: wij zien alleen het topje. Onder water zijn er honderden prostituees, van wie sommigen minderjarig, die op parkeerterreinen, in toiletten of in clubs hun werk doen. Hun klanten krijgen ze via mond-tot-mondreclame en de mobiele telefoon.'

Ik vertel hem over Samira's verdwijning uit het opvangcentrum.

'Wie heeft haar naar Nederland gebracht?'

'Smokkelaars.'

'Hoe heeft ze hen betaald?'

'Hoe bedoel je?'

'Ze willen natuurlijk iets terugzien in ruil voor het smokkelen.'

'Zij en haar broer zijn wees.'

Hij klopt zijn pijp uit op de rand van de asbak.

'Misschien hebben ze nog niet betaald.' Terwijl hij zijn pijp weer stopt, legt hij uit hoe bendes binnen asielzoekerscentra opereren. Ze pikken meisjes op en maken ze tot prostituee, terwijl de jongens als drugskoerier of bedelaar worden ingezet.

'Soms nemen ze niet eens de moeite om de kinderen te kidnappen. Ze halen ze op voor het weekend en brengen ze weer terug. Dat is veiliger voor de pooiers, omdat de meisjes niet compleet verdwijnen en men geen aanleiding ziet tot een zoekactie. Ondertussen worden ze gevoed en gehuisvest en leren ze een beetje Nederlands, op kosten van de Nederlandse regering.'

'Denk je dat dat Samira is overkomen?'

'Ik weet het niet.'

'Als ze jong is zal ze van stad naar stad worden verhuisd of verkocht aan handelaren in andere landen. Het is net een carrousel. Jonge en nieuwe meisjes worden aangeprezen als vers vlees. Ze leveren meer geld op. Door ze steeds te verhuizen zijn ze voor de politie of hun familie lastiger op te sporen.'

Hokke staat op en rekt zich uit. Hij gebaart ons mee te komen. Over de keien gaan we links- en rechtsom, dieper de rosse buurt in. Er zijn nu meer ramen open. Vrouwen tikken op de ruit om Hokkes aandacht te trekken. Een Marokkaanse schudt naar hem met haar borsten. Een ander slaat zich op haar achterwerk, wiegend op een liedje dat alleen zij kan horen.

'Kent u ze allemaal?' vraag ik.

Hij lacht. 'Ooit misschien wel, ja. Ik hoorde al hun verhalen. Tegenwoordig is er een soort muur tussen de politie en de prostituees. Vroeger was het merendeel Nederlands. Daarna kwamen de Dominicaanse en de Colombiaanse vrouwen. Daarna de Surinaamse. En nu komen ze uit Nigeria en Oost-Europa.'

Elke straat is weer anders, legt hij uit. De Oudekerksteeg is Afrikaans gebied. De Boomsteeg is van de Zuid-Amerikanen, de Aziaten domineren de Oudekennissteeg en Barndesteeg, terwijl de Bloedstraat de transseksuelen herbergt. De Oost-Europese meisjes zitten in de Molensteeg en op de Achterburgwal.

'Het wordt steeds moeilijker om geld te verdienen. Een prostituee moet minstens twee klanten hebben om de huur van haar raam te kunnen betalen. Daarna nog eens vier klanten voor het aandeel dat haar pooier pakt. Dan is ze door zes mannen gebruikt en heeft ze voor zichzelf nog geen cent verdiend.

In vroeger tijden spaarden prostituees om een raam te kunnen kopen en zelf verhuurster te worden aan andere meisjes. Nu behoren de ramen toe aan ondernemingen, die ze soms gebruiken om geld wit te wassen door de verdiensten van de meisjes kunstmatig te verhogen.'

In weerwil van zichzelf klinkt hij melancholiek. Hij heeft heimwee naar vroeger.

'Het gebied is tegenwoordig schoner. Minder gevaarlijk. De problemen hebben zich naar verderop verplaatst.'

We lopen langs een gracht, langs striptenten en bioscopen. Op afstand zien de seksshops eruit als souvenirwinkels. Pas als je dichterbij komt blijken de snuisterijen dildo's en kunstvagina's te zijn. Het fascineert en verwart me. Ik wil naar binnen gluren en uitzoeken wat waarvoor bedoeld is.

Hokke is een steeg ingeslagen en klopt ergens aan. Een grote man met uitpuilende buik en bakkebaarden doet open. Achter hem zie ik een kamertje waarin hij maar net zijn kont kan keren. Langs de wanden staan rijen pornovideo's en filmspoelen.

'Dit is Nico, de hardst werkende filmoperateur van Amsterdam.'

Nico grijnst ons aan terwijl hij zijn handen afveegt aan zijn shirt.

'Sommigen van de actrices zijn inmiddels oma,' zegt Nico.

'Zoals Gusta,' valt Hokke hem bij. 'Dat was me toch ooit een schoonheid.'

Nico knikt instemmend.

Hokke vraagt hem of hij Afghaanse meisjes kent die achter de ramen werken of in clubs.

'Afghaans? Nee. Ik herinner me wel een Irakese. Weet je nog, Hokke? Basinah. Jij had een oogje op haar.'

'Ik? Welnee,' lacht de ex-politieman. 'Ze had problemen met haar huisbaas en vroeg of ik kon helpen.'

'Heb je hem opgepakt?'

'Nee.'

'Hem neergeknald?'

'Nee.'

'Jij was niet echt geslaagd als politieman, of wel soms, Hokke? Altijd maar fluiten. De drugsdealers hoorden je van mijlenver aankomen.'

Hokke schudt zijn hoofd. 'Als ik ze wilde pakken, werd er niet gefloten.'

Ik laat Nico de foto van Samira zien. Hij herkent haar niet.

'De meeste handelaars houden het dicht bij huis. Meisjes uit China worden gesmokkeld door Chinezen, Russische door Russen.' Hij spreidt zijn handen. 'Afghanen blijven thuis en geven hun papavers water.'

Nico zegt in het Nederlands iets tegen Hokke.

'Dat meisje. Waarom zijn jullie naar haar op zoek?'

'Omdat ze waarschijnlijk iets af weet van een baby.'

'Een baby?'

'Ik heb een vriendin.' Ik verbeter mezelf. 'Ik hád een vriendin die deed alsof ze zwanger was. Ik vermoed dat ze met iemand in Amsterdam had geregeld dat die haar een baby zou leveren. Mijn vriendin werd vermoord. Ze liet deze foto na.'

Hokke stopt andermaal zijn pijp. 'Denk je dat ze bezig waren die baby te smokkelen?'

'Ja.'

Hij stopt halverwege, de lucifer nog brandend tussen zijn vingers. Ik heb hem verrast – de man die dacht dat hij na dertig jaar hier alles al gezien en gehoord had.

Ruiz wacht buiten en neemt het carnaval van geiligheid en gulzigheid in zich op. Er zijn nu meer mensen op straat. Gekomen om de beroemde rosse buurt te zien, maar niet aan te raken. Een groep Japanners wordt voortgestuwd door een vrouw die een felgele paraplu boven haar hoofd houdt.

'Samira had een broer,' leg ik aan Hokke en Nico uit. 'Hij verdween tegelijk met haar uit het opvangcentrum. Waar zou hij in dat geval heen gaan?'

'Ook jongens kunnen de prostitutie in gaan,' zegt Hokke zakelijk. 'Ze kunnen ook drugskoerier worden, of zakkenroller of bedelaar.

Ga maar eens naar het Centraal Station. Het wemelt ervan.'

Ik laat hem het houtskoolportret van Hasan zien. 'Hij heeft een tatoeage aan de binnenkant van zijn pols.'

'Wat voor tatoeage?'

'Een vlinder.'

Hokke en de filmoperateur kijken elkaar aan.

'Dat is een eigendomstatoeage,' zegt Nico terwijl hij zich onder zijn oksel krabt. 'Hij is iemands bezit.'

Hokke kijkt strak naar de geblakerde binnenkant van zijn pijpje. Het is duidelijk geen goed nieuws.

Ik wacht op zijn uitleg. Terwijl hij met zorg zijn woorden kiest, vertelt hij dat bepaalde criminele bendes delen van de stad beheersen en vaak het eigendom over asielzoekers en illegalen opeisen.

'Ze moet uit de buurt blijven van De Souza,' zegt Nico.

Hokke houdt een vinger tegen zijn lippen. Ik zie een blik van verstandhouding.

'Wie is De Souza?' vraag ik.

'Niemand. Vergeet die naam maar.'

Nico knikt. 'Dat is beter voor iedereen.'

Er zijn inmiddels nog meer ramen open. Meer klanten. Mannen die elkaar passeren houden hun ogen omlaag gericht.

Ik heb prostitutie altijd verwarrend gevonden. In mijn jeugd gaven films als *Pretty Woman* en *American Gigolo* er een geïdealiseerd en gesteriliseerd beeld van. De eerste keer dat ik echte prostituees zag was met Cate. We waren in Leeds voor een atletiekevenement. Vlak bij het station, waar de meeste goedkopere hotels zaten, zagen we vrouwen op straathoeken staan. Sommigen zagen er uitgeput en onfris uit, heel anders dan Julia Roberts. Anderen zagen er zo verscheurend uit dat ze meer weg hadden van zeeduivels dan van lustobjecten.

Misschien is mijn idee van seks als iets moois of magisch of bovenaards wel naïef. Dat kan het zijn. Ik heb nooit van schuine moppen of seksueel geladen gedrag gehouden. Cate noemde me preuts. Prima, houden zo.

'Waar denk je aan, meneer?'

'Ik vraag me af waarom ze het doen.'

'De vrouwen?'

'De mannen. Ik vind het niet erg als iemand de toiletbril voor me voorverwarmt, maar er zijn plekken waar ik liever niet als tweede kom, of derde…'

'Vind je dat prostitutie verboden moet worden?'

'Ik constateer slechts.'

Ik vertel hem over een artikel dat ik op de universiteit las, van Camille Paglia. Zij stelde dat prostituees niet het slachtoffer waren van mannen, maar juist hun overwinnaars.

'De feministen op hun achterste benen zeker?'

'Dat kun je wel zeggen, ja.'

In stilte lopen we verder. Na een tijdje gaan we ergens zitten. Een veeg zonneschijn strijkt over het plein. Op een onder een boom neergezette zeepkist staat iemand in het Nederlands te preken of voor te dragen. In mijn oren zou het *Hamlet* kunnen zijn, maar voor hetzelfde geld is het het telefoonboek.

Terug in het hotel plegen we een reeks telefoontjes. We werken Hokkes lijst met namen van stichtingen, asieladvocaten en steungroepen af. Hoewel we het grootste deel van de dag aan het bellen zijn, weet niemand iets over Samira. Misschien moeten we dit op de ouderwetse manier aanpakken: langs de deuren gaan.

Op het Damrak vind ik een kopieerwinkel. Een medewerker maakt een vergroting van Samira's portret en draait er een stapeltje kleurenkopieën van. De geur van papier en inkt nestelt zich in mijn hoofd.

Ruiz gaat met de foto naar het Centraal Station om hem aan mensen te laten zien. Ik ga de vrouwen achter de ramen langs, die tegenover mij waarschijnlijk spraakzamer zullen zijn. Ruiz is het helemaal eens met de taakverdeling.

Voor ik op pad ga bel ik Barnaby Elliot over de komende begrafenissen. Hij heeft mijn stem nog niet gehoord of hij begint me ervan te beschuldigen dat ik het huis van Cate en Felix in de as heb gelegd.

'De politie zegt dat jij daar bent geweest, dat jij de brand hebt gemeld.'

'Ik heb een inbraak gemeld, geen vuur aangestoken.'

'Wat deed je daar? Je vroeg om haar computer en haar brieven. Die kwam je nu zeker stelen, hè?'

Ik reageer niet, wat hem nog woester maakt.

'We hebben hier rechercheurs over de vloer gehad met vragen. Ik heb hun verteld dat jij allerlei wilde beweringen hebt gedaan over Cate. Door jouw toedoen willen ze de lichamen niet vrijgeven. We kunnen de begrafenis niet regelen – de kerk, de toespraken, de rouwadvertentie, niks. We kunnen geen afscheid nemen.'

'Dat spijt me, Barnaby, maar daar kan ik niks aan doen. Cate en Felix zijn vermoord.'

'EN NU HOU JE OP! OPHOUDEN!'

'Luister nou...'

'Nee! Ik hoef die verhalen van jou niet. Ik wil dat je mijn gezin met rust laat. Blijf uit onze buurt.'

Zodra hij heeft opgehangen tjilpt mijn mobiele telefoon als een jong vogeltje.

'Hallo? Alisha? Hallo.'

'Ik hoor u, mama.'

'Alles goed?'

'Ja, prima.'

'Heeft Hari je nog gebeld?'

'Nee.'

'Er heeft ene commissaris North geprobeerd je te bereiken. Je was niet op je werk verschenen, zei hij.'

Hendon! Mijn nieuwe baan bij Werving en Selectie. Volkomen vergeten.

'Hij wil dat je terugbelt.'

'Oké.'

'Weet je zeker dat alles goed is?'

'Ja, mama.'

Ze begint een verhaal over mijn neefjes en nichtjes – wie er aan het wisselen is, hun eerste glimlachje, stapjes of woordjes. Daarna de balletvoorstellingen, voetbalwedstrijden en schoolconcerten.

Kleinkinderen vormen het middelpunt van haar leven. In plaats van overweldigd voel ik me eerder leeg.

'Kom zondag lunchen. Iedereen is er. Behalve Hari. Hij heeft een studieafspraak.'

Aha, de nieuwe benaming.

'Vraag die aardige sergeant ook.' Ze bedoelt Groentje Dave.

'Ik had hem laatst niet uitgenodigd, hoor.'

'Hij was heel aardig.'

'Mama, hij is geen sikh.'

'Trek je maar niets van vader aan. Die blaft harder dan hij bijt. Ik vond je vriend heel beleefd.'

'Beleefd.'

'Ja. Je moet er niet op rekenen dat je een prins trouwt. Maar met een beetje geduld en hard werken kun je er wel een máken. Kijk maar naar mij en je vader.'

Ik kan het niet helpen, ik hou van haar. Ze drukt een kusje op de hoorn. Dat zie je niet vaak meer. Ik stuur een kusje terug.

Als op commando belt Groentje Dave. Misschien spelen ze wel onder één hoedje.

'Hallo, lief meisje.'

'Dag, lieve jongen.' Ik hoor duidelijk zijn ademhaling, alsof hij naast me staat.

'Ik mis je.'

'Iéts in je mist me.'

'Nee, alles.'

Gek genoeg mis ik hem ook. Een nieuw gevoel.

'Hebben jullie haar gevonden?'

'Nee.'

'Ik wil dat je naar huis komt. We moeten praten.'

'Ga je gang.'

Hij wil me iets meedelen. Ik hoor hem bijna oefenen hoe hij het zal brengen. 'Ik neem ontslag.'

'Mijn god!'

'Aan de zuidkust staat een kleine zeilschool te koop.'

'Een zeilschool.'

'Het is een goede broodwinning. 's Zomers komt er geld binnen en 's winters kan ik op een vissersboot werken of in de beveiliging.'

'Waar denk je het geld vandaan te halen?'

'Ik koop het samen met Simon.'

'Die werkt toch in San Diego?'

'Ja, maar Jacquie en hij komen terug.'

Simon is Daves broer. Hij is zeilmaker of bootontwerper; ik kan nooit onthouden welke van de twee.

'Maar ik dacht dat je het naar je zin had als rechercheur.'

'Het is geen baan voor iemand met een gezin, als dat ervan komt.'

Daar heeft hij gelijk in. 'En je bent dichter bij je pa en ma.' (Die wonen in Poole.)

'Dat ook, ja.'

'Zeilen kan leuk zijn.' Meer weet ik niet te zeggen.

'En nu komt het, Ali. Ik wil dat je met me meekomt. Als zakenpartner.'

'Partner?'

'Je weet dat ik verliefd op je ben. Ik wil met je trouwen. Samen met je zijn.' Hij spreekt snel nu. 'Je hoeft nog geen antwoord te geven. Denk er maar over na. Ik neem je mee naar het zuiden. Ik heb een huisje gevonden in Milford-on-Sea. Het is schitterend. Zeg geen nee. "Misschien" is genoeg. We gaan eerst kijken.'

Ik voel iets in me verspringen. Ik wil zijn grote hand in mijn kleine handen nemen en zijn oogleden kussen. Wat hij ook zegt, ik weet dat hij een antwoord verwacht. Dat kan ik hem niet geven. Vandaag niet, morgen niet. De toekomst is een panorama dat elk uur verspringt.

4

Ik kom andermaal langs de Oude Kerk en de Trompettersteeg. Hokke had gelijk: bij avond is de rosse buurt anders. Ik kan de testosteron en de gebruikte condooms bijna ruiken.

Bij elk raam dat ik passeer houd ik een foto tegen de ruit. Sommige prostituees schreeuwen tegen me of schudden boos met een vinger. Anderen glimlachen verleidelijk. Ik wil hen niet in de ogen kijken, maak ik moet er zeker van zijn dat ze naar Samira kijken.

Ik loop door de Goldbergersteeg en Bethlehemsteeg en prent mezelf in van welke ramen de gordijnen dicht zijn, zodat ik later terug kan komen. Er is maar één vrouw die probeert me over te halen binnen te komen. Ze legt twee vingers tegen haar lippen en steekt haar tong ertussendoor. Ze zegt iets in het Nederlands. Ik schud mijn hoofd.

In het Engels nu. 'You want a woman.' Ze schudt haar in paarsrood gehulde borsten.

'Ik doe het niet met vrouwen.'

'Maar je hebt er weleens aan gedacht.'

'Nee.'

'Ik kan een man zijn. Ik heb het gereedschap.' Nu lacht ze naar me.

Ik loop verder, de hoek om, langs de gracht, door de Boomsteeg naar de Molensteeg. Er zijn drie ramen naast elkaar, bijna beneden straatniveau. Van het middelste raam is het gordijn geopend. Een jonge vrouw slaat haar ogen op. In het ultraviolette licht lichten haar blonde haar en witte slipje op als neon. Een minuscuul driehoekje bedekt haar kruis, twee driehoekjes iets hoger op haar borst zijn samengetrokken om een decolleté te creëren. De enige andere schaduwen verduisteren de uitholling aan weerszijden van haar schaambeen, waar de bikini strak om haar heupen gespannen zit.

Aan de ruit hangt een ballon. Serpentines. Verjaardagsversiering? Ik hou de foto tegen het glas. Een flits van herkenning. Iets in haar ogen.

'Ken je haar?'

Ze schudt haar hoofd. Ze liegt.

'Help me.'

In haar jukbeenderen en kaaklijn gaan nog sporen van schoonheid schuil. Ze heeft haar haar in een scheiding. De dunne haargrens is donker in plaats van wit. Ze slaat haar ogen neer. Ze is nieuwsgierig.

De deur gaat open. Ik stap naar binnen. De kamer is net breed genoeg voor een tweepersoonsbed, een stoel en een kleine wastafel aan de muur. Alles is roze: de kussens, de lakens en de schone handdoek daarbovenop. Een spiegel die ditzelfde tafereel laat zien beslaat een complete wand, zodat het lijkt of we de kamer delen met een ander 'raam'.

Ze nipt van een blikje frisdrank. 'Ik heet Eva, net als de eerste vrouw op aarde.' Ze lacht sarcastisch. 'Welkom in mijn Hof van Eden.'

Ze buigt zich voorover en pakt van onder haar kruk een pakje sigaretten. Haar borsten deinen. Ze heeft niet de moeite genomen het gordijn te sluiten. In plaats daarvan blijft ze bij het raam. Ik kijk naar het bed en de stoel en vraag me af waar ik zal gaan zitten.

Eva wijst naar het bed. 'Twintig euro, vijf minuten.'

Haar accent is een mengsel van Nederlands en Amerikaans. Het is het zoveelste bewijs van de macht van Hollywood, dat generaties mensen in uithoeken van de wereld Engels heeft leren spreken.

Ik overhandig het geld. Ze grist het weg als een goochelaar die een speelkaart laat verdwijnen.

Ik hou opnieuw de foto op. 'Ze heet Samira.'

'Ze is een van de zwangeren.'

Ik ga rechtop zitten. Onzichtbaar pantser. Kennis.

Eva haalt haar schouders op. 'Maar goed, ik kan het ook mis hebben.'

De duimafdruk op haar arm is een bloeduitstorting. Die in haar nek is nog donkerder.

'Waar heb je haar gezien? Wanneer?'

'Soms word ik gevraagd te helpen met de nieuwe meisjes. Ze dingen te laten zien.'

'Wat voor dingen?'

Ze lacht en steekt een sigaret op. 'Wat dacht je? Soms kijken ze toe vanuit de stoel of vanaf het bed, afhankelijk van waar de klant voor heeft betaald. Sommigen vinden het leuk te worden bekeken. Dan gaat het sneller.'

Ik sta op het punt te vragen waar ze een stoel voor nodig heeft als ik de reep vloerbedekking zie om haar knieën te beschermen.

'Maar je zei dat ze zwanger was? Waarom zou je haar dit dan laten zien?'

Ze rolt met haar ogen. 'Ik geef je de vijf-minutenversie. Dat is waar je voor hebt betaald.'

Ik knik.

'In januari zag ik haar voor het eerst. Ik weet het nog omdat het die dag zo koud was.' Ze wijst naar de wastafel. 'Alleen koud water. Als ijs. Ze brachten haar hier om toe te kijken. Haar ogen waren groter dan zo.' De prostituee balt haar handen tot vuisten. 'Ik dacht dat ze zou gaan overgeven. Ik zei dat ze de wastafel moest gebruiken. Ik wist dat ze het nooit zou gaan redden. Het is maar seks. Een fysieke daad. Ze kunnen me hier raken of hier,' zegt ze terwijl ze naar haar hart en hoofd wijst. 'Dit meisje gedroeg zich alsof ze zichzelf spaarde. Nog zo'n rotmaagd!' Ze tikt de as van haar sigaret.

'En toen?'

'De tijd is om.' Ze houdt haar hand op voor meer geld.

'Dat was geen vijf minuten.'

Ze wijst naar de wand achter me. 'Zie je die klok? Op mijn rug liggen en ernaar kijken is mijn beroep. Niemand die zo precies vijf minuten aftelt als ik.'

Ik geef haar nog eens twintig euro. 'Je zei dat ze zwanger was.'

'Dat was de volgende keer dat ik haar zag.' Eva duidt de zwelling aan. 'Het was in een kliniek in Amersfoort. Ze zat daar in de wachtkamer met een Servisch meisje. Ze waren allebei zwanger. Ik ging ervan uit dat het was om een uitkering te krijgen, of dat ze probeerde in het land te blijven door hier een kind te baren.'

'Heb je met haar gesproken?'

'Nee. Ik weet nog dat ik verbaasd was omdat ik dacht dat zij de laatste maagd op aarde zou zijn.' De sigaret brandt tot vlak bij haar knokkels.

'Ik heb de naam en het adres van de kliniek nodig.'

'Dokter Beyer. Hij staat in het telefoonboek.'

Ze vermorzelt de sigaret onder haar open schoentje. Een klop op het raam trekt haar aandacht. Buiten staat een man, die eerst naar mij en dan naar Eva wijst.

'Hoe heet je?' fluistert ze samenzweerderig.

'Alisha.'

Ze buigt zich naar de deur. 'Hij wil ons allebei, Alisha.'

'Niet opendoen!'

'Doe niet zo bleu. Hij ziet er schoon uit. Ik heb condooms.'

'Ik ben geen...'

'Geen hoer. Maar ook geen maagd. Je kunt wat verdienen. Knappe kleren kopen.'

Buiten is een oploop ontstaan. Er gluren meer mannen naar binnen. Ik ben gaan staan. Ik wil weg. Ze probeert me nog steeds over te halen.

'Wat heb je te verliezen?'

Ik wil zeggen: mijn zelfrespect.

Ze doet de deur open. Ik moet me langs haar wringen. Haar vingernagel strijkt langs mijn wang en haar tongpunt bevochtigt haar onderlip. Mannen verdringen zich in het steegje met zijn gladde en harde klinkers. Ik moet me een weg langs hen heen banen. Ik ruik hun lichamen terwijl ik langs ze schamp. Mijn voet raakt een stoepje en ik struikel. Een hand strekt zich uit om me te helpen. Het is niet echt logisch, maar ik sla hem weg en wil de man keihard uitschelden. Ik zat goed wat betreft Samira. Goed wat betreft de baby. Dáárom simuleerde Cate haar zwangerschap en had ze Samira's foto bij zich. Ik wou dat ik fout zat.

Boven de menigte doemt een klein stukje grijze lucht op. Plotseling ben ik ervan verlost en sta ik in een bredere straat, diep ademhalend. Het donkere water van de gracht is met rode en paarse strepen doorsneden. Ik hang over een leuning en kots mijn eigen bijdrage aan de kleurenpracht uit.

Mijn mobiele telefoon trilt. Ruiz is op de been.

'Misschien heb ik iemand gevonden.' Hij hijgt een beetje. 'Bij het Centraal Station heb ik Samira's foto laten zien. De meeste mensen wilden nergens van weten, maar deze jongen deed heel raar toen hij de foto zag.'

'Denk je dat hij haar kende?'

'Misschien. Hij zou de waarheid nog niet zeggen als God de Almachtige het hem vroeg.'

'Waar is hij nu?'

'Hij liep weg. Ik loop vijftig meter achter hem.'

De inspecteur raffelt een beschrijving af van een tiener in een kaki camouflagejack, spijkerbroek en sportschoenen.

'Verdomme!'

'Wat is er?'

'Mijn batterij is bijna leeg. Ik had hem vannacht moeten opladen. Er belt verdomme nooit iemand.'

'Ik wel.'

'Ja, nou, dat laat ook meteen zien wat voor een armzalig bestaan jij leidt. Even kijken of ik je de naam van een zijstraat kan geven. Verderop is een gracht.'

'Welke?'

'Ze zien er allemaal hetzelfde uit.'

Op de achtergrond hoor ik muziek en meisjes die van achter de ramen roepen.

'Wacht even. Barndesteeg,' zegt hij.

In het schijnsel van een straatlantaarn vouw ik een toeristenkaart open en laat mijn vinger langs de namen gaan tot ik de coördinaten van de straten heb. Ze liggen niet ver uit elkaar.

Films en tv-series doen het voorkomen alsof het heel simpel is iemand te achtervolgen zonder zelf gezien te worden, maar de werkelijkheid is anders. Als dit een echte schaduwactie van de politie was, zouden we twee auto's hebben, een motorrijder en twee of zelfs drie agenten te voet. Elke keer dat het doelwit afsloeg, zou hij een nieuw iemand achter zich hebben lopen. Die luxe hebben wij niet.

Ik steek de Sint-Jansbrug over en loop snel langs de gracht. Ruiz is twee straten oostelijker en komt me door de Stoofsteeg tegemoet. De jongen zal me dichtbij passeren.

Het is druk op straat. Ik moet naar links en naar rechts stappen, strijk hier en daar langs schouders. De lucht is zwaar van de hasj en frituurgeuren.

Ik zie hem pas op het allerlaatste moment. Hij is al bijna voorbij. Hij heeft holle wangen, met behulp van gel en zijn vingers opgezette haren, en springt van de stoep in de goot en weer terug om mensen te ontwijken. Hij kijkt over zijn schouder. Hij weet dat hij wordt gevolgd, maar hij is niet bang.

Ruiz heeft zich laten terugzakken. Ik neem het over. We komen bij de gracht en steken de brug over. Ik loop bijna dezelfde weg van daarnet terug. Hij loopt dichter bij het water dan bij de gevels. Als hij een achtervolger wil afschudden, waarom dan de open kant genomen?

Dan begint het me te dagen: hij lokt Ruiz weg. Iemand op het station moet Samira hebben gekend. Hij wil niet dat Ruiz hem of haar vindt.

Hij houdt in en wacht. Ik loop langs hem. De inspecteur duikt niet op. Ineens draait de jongen om, om zeker te zijn. Nu waant hij de kust veilig.

Hij kijkt niet om als hij weer doorloopt. Ik volg hem door de smalle stegen tot hij de Warmoesstraat bereikt en daarna de Dam. Bij een beeld blijft hij wachten tot er een slank meisje opduikt in een spijkerboek en een roze corduroy jasje. Haar steile korte haar heeft de kleur van sterke thee.

Hij praat druk gesticulerend tegen haar, zijn betoog illustrerend met handgebaren. Ik bel Ruiz op zijn mobiel. 'Waar ben je?'

'Achter je.'

'Heb je bij het station een meisje gezien in een spijkerbroek en een roze jasje? Donker haar. Achttien, negentien jaar. Nu nog knap.'

'Samira?'

'Nee. Een ander meisje. Ik vermoed dat hij je probeerde weg te lokken. Hij wilde niet dat je haar zou vinden.'

Ze maken nog steeds ruzie. Het meisje schudt haar hoofd, de jongen trekt aan haar mouw. Ze rukt zich los. Hij roept iets. Ze kijkt niet om.

'Ze gaan verschillende kanten op,' fluister ik in mijn mobiele telefoon. 'Ik ga achter het meisje aan.'

Ze heeft een merkwaardig lichaam, een lange romp en korte benen, met licht gespreide voeten als ze loopt. Ze haalt een blauwe sjaal uit haar zak en wikkelt hem om haar hoofd, met een knoop onder haar kin. Het is een hidjab, een hoofdbedekking. Ze zou moslima kunnen zijn.

Ik blijf dicht achter haar, me bewust van de menigte en het verkeer. In het midden van de weg voeren de trams op de rails met hun beugels een soort steekspel uit. Auto's en fietsen slingeren zich erlangs. Wat is ze klein. Ik verlies haar telkens uit het oog.

Het ene moment loopt ze nog voor me en het volgende... Waar is ze gebleven? Ik sprint vooruit en kijk vergeefs in portieken en etalages. Ik zoek de zijstraten af in de hoop een glimp op te vangen van haar roze jasje of het blauw van haar hidjab. Op een vluchtheuvel draai ik me om en doe een stap naar voren. Er klinkt een doordringend gebel. Ik draai mijn hoofd om. Een onzichtbare hand rukt me terug op het moment dat er in een wirwar van geluid en luchtdruk een tram langs me heen schiet.

Het meisje in het roze jasje staart me aan; haar hart klopt sneller dan het mijne. De vlekken onder haar ogen zijn tekenen van vroege rijpheid of verval. Ze wist dat ik haar volgde. Zij was degene die me redde.

'Hoe heet je?'

Haar lippen verroeren zich niet. Ze draait zich om en loopt weg. Ik moet een paar sprintpassen doen om vóór haar te komen.

'Wacht! Niet weglopen. Kunnen we even praten?'

Ze antwoordt niet. Misschien begrijpt ze me niet.

'Spreek je Engels?' Ik wijs op mezelf. 'Ik heet Alisha.'

Ze stapt langs me heen.

'Stop. Alsjeblieft.'

Ze stapt opnieuw langs me heen. Ik moet mensen ontwijken terwijl ik tegelijkertijd achteruit probeer te lopen en tegen haar praat. Ik hou mijn handen samen als in gebed. 'Ik ben op zoek naar Samira.'

Ze stopt niet. Ik kan haar niet dwingen met me te praten.

Ineens slaat ze af, een gebouw binnen, een zware deur openduwend. Ik zie haar geen sleutel gebruiken of een zoemer indrukken. Binnen ruikt het naar soep en elektrische kachels. Achter een tweede deur duikt een grote, kale zaal vol tafels en stoelen met schrapende poten op. Er zitten mensen te eten. Een non in zwarte tuniek schept vanaf een rolwagen soep in kommen. Een motortype met een lange baard deelt borden en lepels uit. Iemand anders deelt broodjes rond.

Aan de dichtstbijzijnde tafel zit een oude man over zijn eten gebogen. Hij doopt stukken brood in het dampende mengsel. Hij heeft zijn rechterarm om de kom gelegd, alsof hij hem beschermt. Naast hem doet een lange figuur met een wollen muts op met zijn hoofd op tafel een poging om te slapen. Ik schat dat er zo'n dertig mensen in de zaal zijn, het merendeel met grauwe kleren, zenuwtrekken en een lege maag.

'Wou je iets eten?'

Ik keer me naar de stem.

'*Would you like something to eat?*' klinkt het nu in het Engels.

De vraag komt van een oudere non met een smal gezicht en een speelse blik. Haar zwarte tuniek is groen afgebiesd en haar witte achteroverliggende haar verdwijnt onder een kapje.

'Nee, dank u.'

'Er is genoeg. Het is goede soep. Ik heb hem zelf gemaakt.'

Een werkschort ter breedte van haar schouders reikt tot aan haar enkels. Ze haalt borden van de tafels, die ze op één arm opstapelt. Ondertussen heeft het meisje een rij metalen blikken bij de soepketel neergezet.

'Wat is dit hier?'

'Wij zijn zusters augustinessen. Ik ben zuster Vogel.'

Ze moet in de tachtig zijn. De andere nonnen zijn van een vergelijkbaar bouwjaar, maar minder ineengekrompen. Ze is klein, krap anderhalve meter, met een stem als grind dat ronddraait in een trommel.

'Weet je zeker dat je niets wilt eten?'

'Nee, dank u.' Mijn blik blijft op het meisje gericht.

De non gaat voor me staan. 'Wat wil je van haar?'

'Alleen even praten.'

'Dat zal niet gaan.'

'Waarom niet?'

'Ze zal je niet horen.'

'Nee, u begrijpt me niet. Als ik alleen even met haar kan praten...'

'Ze kán je niet horen.' Haar stem wordt zachter. 'Ze is een van Gods speciale kinderen.'

Eindelijk begrijp ik het. Het gaat niet om taal of om willen. Het meisje is doof.

De soepblikken zijn gevuld. Het meisje schroeft op elk blik een deksel en doet ze in een schoudertas. Ze steekt haar hoofd door het hengsel en legt hem over haar borst. Ze vouwt een papieren servet open en pakt twee stukken brood in. Een derde stuk neemt ze mee, knabbelend aan de randen.

'Weet u hoe ze heet?'

'Nee. Ze komt drie keer per week eten halen.'

'Waar woont ze?'

Zuster Vogel is niet van plan dat uit zichzelf te zeggen. Er is maar één stem die ze gehoorzaamt: die van een superieur.

'Ze heeft niets misdaan,' stel ik haar gerust.

'Waarom wil je met haar praten?'

'Ik ben naar iemand op zoek. Het is heel belangrijk.'

Zuster Vogel zet de soepborden neer en veegt haar handen af aan haar schort. In plaats van door de zaal te lopen, lijkt ze in haar lange tuniek een fractie boven de vloerplanken te zweven. Naast haar voel ik me een lomperik.

Ze gaat voor het meisje staan en tikt haar handpalm aan voordat ze er met haar vingers figuren in begint te tekenen.

'Spreekt u gebarentaal?'

'Ik ken sommige letters. Wat wil je vragen?'

'Haar naam.'

Ze wisselen tekens uit.

'Zala.'

'Waar komt ze vandaan?'

'Afghanistan.'

Ik haal de foto uit mijn jaszak. Zuster Vogel pakt hem aan. De reactie komt onmiddellijk. Zala schudt heftig haar hoofd. Angstig. Ze wil het beeld niet nog een keer zien.

Zuster Vogel probeert haar te kalmeren. Haar stem is zacht. Haar handen zijn nog zachter. Zala blijft haar hoofd schudden, zonder met haar ogen ook maar een moment de grond los te laten.

'Kunt u vragen of ze Samira kent?'

Zuster Vogel probeert de tekens te maken, maar Zala deinst terug.

'Ik moet weten waar Samira is.'

De non schudt haar hoofd en wijst me terecht. 'Mensen bang maken doen wij hier niet.'

Zala is al bij de deur. Door het gewicht van de soep kan ze niet rennen. Als ik aanstalten maak haar te volgen grijpt zuster Vogel me bij de arm. 'Laat haar alsjeblieft met rust.'

Ik kijk haar smekend aan. 'Dat kan ik niet.'

Zala is buiten. Over haar schouder kijkt ze om. Haar wangen glimmen onder de straatlantaarns. Ze huilt. Haar haren zijn deels losgeraakt van onder haar hidjab. Ze heeft geen hand meer vrij om het uit haar gezicht te strijken.

De inspecteur neemt zijn mobiele telefoon niet op. Waarschijnlijk een lege accu. Ik laat me terugvallen en blijf achter Zala terwijl ze me wegleidt van het klooster. De straten en grachten komen me niet langer bekend voor. Ze worden geflankeerd door oude, afbladderende panden, die opgedeeld zijn in eenkamerappartementen, flats en maisonnettes. Deurbellen vormen keurige rijen.

We komen langs een rijtje winkels waarvan de luiken dicht en op slot zijn. Op de volgende hoek steekt ze de straat over en gaat een hek binnen. Het hoort bij een groot, vervallen blok appartementen dat midden op een T-splitsing staat. De struiken buiten steken als wolkjes groen af tegen de donkere bakstenen. De ramen op de begane grond zijn van stangen voorzien, de hogere verdiepingen hebben luiken. Achter de luiken brandt licht.

Ik loop langs het hek en kijk of er nog andere ingangen zijn. Ik wou dat Ruiz hier was. Wat zou hij doen? Op de deur kloppen? Zich voorstellen? Nee, hij zou wachten en kijken. Hij zou kijken wie er binnenging en wie er naar buiten kwam. Het ritme van de plek bestuderen.

Ik kijk op mijn horloge. Het is even over achten. Waar zit hij? Hopelijk leest hij mijn sms'je met het adres.

De wind is aangewakkerd. Rond mijn voeten dwarrelen bladeren en papiertjes. Weggedoken in een portiek ben ik beschermd, verborgen.

Ik heb het geduld niet om te gaan staan posten. Ruiz is daar goed in. Hij kan alles buitensluiten en geconcentreerd blijven zonder te dagdromen of te worden afgeleid. Als ik te lang naar hetzelfde schouwspel kijk, brandt het zich in mijn onderbewuste in en draait het zichzelf keer op keer in een lus af, tot ik de veranderingen niet meer waarneem. Dat is waarom surveillanceteams bij de politie elke paar uur worden afgelost. Verse paren ogen.

Er stopt een auto. Dubbel geparkeerd. Er gaat een man het gebouw binnen. Vijf minuten later komt hij naar buiten met drie vrouwen. Keurig opgemaakt. Piekfijn gekleed. Ruiz zou zeggen dat het naar seks ruikt.

Twee andere mannen stappen naar buiten om te roken. Ze zitten op de trap met hun benen uit elkaar, op hun gemak. Achter een van hen duikt een jongetje op dat speels zijn ogen dichthoudt. Vader en zoon stoeien vrolijk, totdat het jongetje weer naar binnen wordt gestuurd. Het lijken me immigranten. Het is het soort plek waar Samira naartoe zou gaan, om de bescherming van de grotere getallen te zoeken.

Ik kan hier niet de hele avond blijven. En ik kan het me ook niet permitteren weg te gaan en het risico te lopen de verbinding met haar kwijt te raken. Waar zit Ruiz nou toch, verdomme?

De mannen op de trap kijken op als ik dichterbij kom.

'Samira Khan?'

Een van de twee gooit zijn hoofd in zijn nek: boven. Ik stap langs hen heen. De deur is open. De hal ruikt naar specerijen en duizend uitgemaakte sigaretten.

Aan de voet van de trap spelen drie kinderen. Een van hen pakt mijn been en probeert zich achter me te verstoppen, en rent vervolgens weer weg. Ik klim naar de eerste overloop. Tegen de muren staan lege gasflessen naast zakken afval. Er huilt een baby. Kinderen maken ruzie. Ingeblikt gelach dringt door dunne muren naar buiten.

Voor de deur van een flat zitten twee tienermeisjes met de hoofden bij elkaar gestoken geheimen uit te wisselen.

'Ik zoek Samira.'

Een van hen wijst omhoog.

Ik klim verder naar boven, van verdieping naar verdieping, me bewust van het afbrokkelend stucwerk en opkrullend linoleum. Er hangt wasgoed over trapleuningen en ergens is een toilet overgelopen.

Ik bereik de bovenste verdieping. Aan het eind van de gang staat een badkamerdeur open. In de deuropening verschijnt Zala, haar schouders gekromd onder een emmer water. In het halfduister van de gang zie ik nog een deur openstaan. Ze wil hem bereiken voordat ik erbij ben. De emmer valt. Er gutst water langs haar voeten.

In strijd met alles wat ik heb geleerd ren ik een onbekende kamer binnen. Op een zitbank met hoge rug zit een meisje. Ze is jong. Zelfs in haar te ruime trui en boerenrok is ze overduidelijk in verwachting. Haar schouders krommen zich, alsof ze zich schaamt voor haar borsten.

Zala wringt zich langs me en gaat tussen ons in staan. Samira is gaan staan, met een hand op de schouder van het dove meisje. Haar ogen nemen me op alsof ze me probeert thuis te brengen.

'Ik wil je geen pijn doen.'

Haar Engels is schools. 'U moet weg hier. Het is hier niet veilig.'

'Ik ben Alisha Barba.'

Haar ogen lichten op. Ze kent mijn naam.

'Gaat u alstublieft weg. Nu.'

'Vertel me hoe je weet wie ik ben.'

Ze geeft geen antwoord. Haar rechterhand glijdt naar haar bolle buik. Ze streelt hem zachtjes en schommelt lichtjes heen en weer, alsof ze haar passagier in slaap wiegt. De beweging lijkt haar vechtlust te temperen.

Ze gebaart naar Zala dat ze de deur op slot moet doen en duwt haar naar de keuken, waar glad gesleten spikkeltjeslinoleum op de vloer ligt en een plank hangt met potjes kruiden en een zak rijst. De soepblikken zijn afgewassen en staan naast de spoelbak te drogen.

Ik laat mijn blik door de rest van het appartement gaan. De

kamer is groot en vierkant. Langs de randen van het hoge plafond lopen scheuren en er zijn bladderende sporen van een lekkage. Tegen de muren staan matrassen geleund, met keurig gevouwen dekens erbovenop. Er staat een klerenkast waarvan de deuren met een metalen hangertje dicht worden gehouden.

Ik zie een koffer, een houten kist met daarop een ingelijste foto. Hij is van een gezin in een formele pose. De moeder zit met een baby in haar armen. De vader staat achter hen, een hand op de schouder van zijn vrouw. Aan haar voeten zit een klein meisje – Samira – dat de zoom van haar rok vasthoudt.

Ik draai me naar haar om. 'Ik heb je gezocht.'

'Alstublieft, gaat u weg.'

Ik kijk heel even naar haar zwangere buik. 'Wanneer moet het komen?'

'Binnenkort.'

'Wat ga je met de baby doen?'

Ze steekt twee vingers op. Heel even denk ik dat ze iets tegen Zala zegt, maar dit gebaar heeft niets met doofheid te maken. De boodschap is voor mij. Twee baby's! Een tweeling.

'Een jongen en een meisje,' zegt ze terwijl ze haar handen samenvouwt, smekend. 'Alstublieft, gaat u nu. U mag hier niet zijn.'

Mijn nekharen kriebelen. Waarom is ze zo bang?

'Wat betreft de baby's, Samira, ga je ze houden?'

Ze schudt haar hoofd.

'Wie is de vader?'

'Allah de Barmhartige.'

'Ik begrijp je niet.'

'Ik ben nog maagd.'

'Je bent zwanger, Samira. Je weet best hoe dat komt.'

Ze reageert opstandig op mijn sceptische toon. 'Ik heb nog nooit met een man geslapen. Ik ben maagd.'

Wat voor fantasieën zijn dit? Het is belachelijk. En toch heeft haar stelligheid de overtuiging van een bekeerling.

'Wie heeft de baby's in jou gestopt, Samira?'

'Allah.'

'Heb je hem gezien?'

'Nee.'

'Hoe heeft hij het gedaan?'

'De dokters hebben hem geholpen. Zij hebben de eitjes in me gestopt.'

Ze heeft het over IVF. De embryo's zijn ingeplant. Daarom draagt ze een tweeling.

'Van wie zijn de eitjes in je buik?'

Bij deze vraag kijkt Samira omhoog. Ik weet het antwoord al. Cate had twaalf geschikte embryo's. Barnaby zei dat ze zes IVF-behandelingen had ondergaan, maar dokter Banerjee was er zeker van dat het er maar vijf waren. Daarmee zijn twee eitjes nog niet verklaard. Cate moet ze mee naar Amsterdam hebben genomen. Ze had een draagmoederschap geregeld.

Daarom moest ze ook doen alsof ze zwanger was. Ze ging Felix zijn eigen kind geven, dat genetisch volmaakt overeenkwam, zodat niemand zou kunnen bewijzen dat het niet van hen was.

'Ga nu weg, alstublieft,' zegt Samira. Ze huilt bijna.

'Waarom ben je zo bang?'

'U begrijpt het niet.'

'Vertel me alleen waarom je dit doet.'

Met haar duim en wijsvinger strijkt ze haar haar naar achteren. Haar ogen houden de mijne gevangen tot precies het moment waarop het ongemakkelijk wordt. Ze heeft een sterke wil. Opstandig.

'Heeft iemand je geld betaald? Hoeveel? Was het Cate?'

Ze geeft geen antwoord. In plaats daarvan wendt ze haar gezicht af en staart naar het raam, een donkere rechthoek tegen een donkere muur.

'Ken je daardoor mijn naam? Cate heeft hem je gegeven. Ze zei dat als er iets zou gebeuren, als er iets misging, dat je contact met mij moest zoeken. Klopt dat?'

Ze knikt.

'Ik moet weten waarom je dit doet. Wat hebben ze je geboden?'

'Vrijheid.'

'Van wat?'

Ze kijkt me aan alsof ik het nooit zal begrijpen. 'Slavernij.'

Ik kniel neer en pak haar hand, die verrassend koel is. In een van haar ooghoeken zit een beetje slaap. 'Ik wil dat je me precies vertelt wat er gebeurd is. Wat hebben ze je verteld? Wat hebben ze je beloofd?'

Op de gang klinkt een geluid. Zala stapt bij de deur weg. Op haar gezicht staat angst geschreven. Haar hoofd schiet heen en weer, zoekend naar een plek om zich te verstoppen.

Samira gebaart haar naar de keuken te gaan en draait zich om naar de deur. Wachten. Een brokkelig schraapgeluid. Mijn zenuwuiteinden trillen.

De deur gaat open. Een magere man met roze omrande ogen en een slecht gebit lijkt een rolling te krijgen als hij me ziet. Zijn rechterhand doet een greep in zijn dichtgeritste nylonjack.

'Wie bent u?' blaft hij in het Nederlands

Ik geloof dat hij vraagt wie ik ben.

'Ik ben de verpleegster,' zeg ik.

Hij kijkt naar Samira. Ze knikt.

'Dokter Beyer heeft me gevraagd op weg naar huis hierlangs te gaan en Samira te onderzoeken. Ik woon hier niet ver vandaan.'

Hij maakt een zuigend geluid met zijn tong en zijn ogen schieten door de kamer alsof hij de muren ervan beschuldigt dat ze deel uitmaken van het bedrog. Hij gelooft me niet, maar is er niet zeker van.

Samira wendt zich tot mij. 'Ik heb krampen gehad. Ik kan er 's nachts niet van slapen.'

'U bent geen verpleegster,' zegt hij beschuldigend. 'U spreekt geen Nederlands!'

'Ik ben bang dat u zich vergist. Engels is de officiële taal van de Europese Gemeenschap.' Ik zet mijn beste Mary Poppins-stem op. Autoritair. Zakelijk. Ik weet niet hoe ver ik bij hem kan gaan.

'Waar woont u?'

'Zoals ik al zei: hier vlak om de hoek.'

'Het adres?'

Ik herinner me een zijstraat. 'Als u het niet erg vindt, ik heb hier nog een onderzoek te doen.'

Hij vertrekt zijn mond tot een spotlach en iets in zijn ongenaakbare houding doet diepere gronden van wreedheid vermoeden. Wat zijn relatie met Samira of Zala ook is, hij boezemt hun angst in. Ze had het over slavernij. Hasan had een eigendomstatoeage op zijn pols. Ik heb niet alle antwoorden, maar ik moet hier weg zien te komen.

Hij blaft opnieuw een vraag in het Nederlands.

Samira knikt terwijl ze haar ogen neerslaat.

'Lieg niet tegen me, kutwijf. Ik vermoord je!'

Hij heeft zijn rechterhand nog steeds in zijn zak. Hij is lenig en pezig als een marathonloper en zal iets boven de tachtig kilo wegen. Het verrassingselement meegerekend zou ik hem misschien aankunnen.

'Wilt u even de kamer uit gaan?' vraag ik.

'Nee, ik blijf hier.'

Zala kijkt toe vanuit de keuken. Ik wenk haar en vouw een deken uit, die ik haar als een gordijn laat ophouden zodat Samira wat privacy heeft.

Samira ligt achterover op de bank en doet haar trui omhoog tot aan haar borsten. Mijn handen zijn klam. Haar dijen zijn glad. Bovenin bevindt zich een strakke driehoek van witte katoen. De huid van haar gezwollen buik is als overtrekpapier, zo strakgetrokken dat ik de vage blauwe bloedvaten onder het oppervlak kan zien.

De baby's bewegen. Haar hele romp lijkt te rimpelen. Een elleboog of een knie maakt een uitstulpinkje en schiet weer weg. Onder haar huid voel ik de contouren van kleine lichaampjes, harde kleine schedeltjes en gewrichtjes.

Ze tilt haar knieën op en kantelt haar heupen, als teken dat ik haar ondergoed moet uittrekken. Ze heeft net zomin als ik een idee wat we moeten doen. Haar oppasser staat nog steeds bij de deur. Samira kijkt hem strijdlustig aan, alsof ze wil zeggen: 'Wil jij dit echt zien?'

Hij slaagt er niet in haar blik te blijven beantwoorden. In plaats daarvan draait hij zich om en loopt de keuken in terwijl hij een sigaret opsteekt.

'Wat kunt u goed liegen,' fluistert Samira.

'Anders jij wel. Wie is hij?'

'Yanus. Hij zorgt voor ons.'

Ik kijk de kamer rond. 'Niet al te best, als je het mij vraagt.'

'Hij brengt ons eten.'

Yanus staat weer in de deuropening.

'Nou, de baby's liggen in elk geval goed,' zeg ik hardop. 'Ze zijn op weg omlaag. De krampen zouden Braxton Hicks-contracties kunnen zijn, een soort oefenweeën. Je bloeddruk is iets hoger dan voorheen.'

Ik heb geen idee waar ik deze informatie vandaan haal; een deel via verbale osmose, van mijn moeders plastische beschrijvingen van de manier waarop mijn neefjes en nichtjes ter wereld kwamen. Ik weet veel meer dan me lief is over slijmproppen, ontsluiting en fundusmetingen. Daarnaast ben ik ook nog eens een kenner op het gebied van pijnbestrijding: ruggenprikken, pethidine, Entonox, elektrostimulatieapparaten en elk homeopathisch, de geest beïnvloedend huismiddeltje dat er bestaat.

Yanus loopt weer weg. Ik hoor hem de toetsen van zijn mobiele telefoon indrukken. Hij belt iemand. Voor advies. Ik heb niet veel tijd meer.

'Je hebt een vriendin van mij ontmoet. Cate Beaumont. Herinner je je haar nog?'

Ze knikt.

'Zijn jouw baby's van haar?'

Hetzelfde knikje.

'Cate is afgelopen zondag gestorven. Ze werd aangereden en vermoord. Haar echtgenoot is ook dood.'

Samira klapt dubbel alsof haar ongeborenen het nieuws hebben begrepen en nu al rouwen. Haar ogen schieten vol met een mengeling van ongeloof en waarheidsbesef.

'Ik kan je helpen,' zeg ik smekend.

'Niemand kan me helpen.'

Yanus staat in de deuropening. Hij grijpt opnieuw in zijn jaszak. Ik zie zijn langer wordende schaduw op de grond. Ik draai me naar hem om. Hij heeft zijn hand om een blik bonen geklemd. Hij haalt uit met een korte zwaai vanaf de heup. Ik voel het aankomen, maar kan niet op tijd reageren. De klap doet me door de kamer tollen. Het is alsof één kant van mijn hoofd in brand staat.

Samira slaakt een kreet. Het is meer een gesmoord huilen dan een schreeuw.

Yanus komt opnieuw op me af. Ik proef bloed. Eén kant van mijn gezicht zwelt al op. Hij geeft me een klap, waarbij hij het blik als een hamer hanteert. In zijn rechterhand blikkert een mes.

Hij houdt zijn ogen met extatische intensiteit op de mijne gericht. Dit is zijn roeping: pijn doen. Voor mijn ogen danst het lemmet heen en weer, telkens een acht beschrijvend. Het had een verrassingsaanval moeten zijn. Het tegenovergestelde is gebeurd. Ik heb hem onderschat.

Nog een voltreffer. Metaal op bot. De kamer wordt een waas.

Sommige dingen, echte dingen, lijken half in de geest en half in de buitenwereld te gebeuren, terwijl ze ergens halverwege gevangenzitten. De geest ziet ze eerst, zoals nu, een laars die mijn kant op zwaait. Ik vang een glimp op van Zala, die zich afzijdig houdt. Ze wil wegkijken, maar kan haar ogen niet van me afhouden. De laars maakt contact en ik zie een felle kleurengloed.

Yanus graait hardhandig in mijn zakken en haalt er mijn mobiele telefoon, paspoort en een paar honderd euro uit.

'Wie ben jij?'

'Een verpleegster.'

'Leugenaar!'

Hij houdt het mes tegen mijn hals. De punt prikt in mijn huid. Op het uiteinde van het lemmet blijft een bloedrode traan achter.

Zala loopt op hem af. Ik gil dat ze moet blijven staan. Ze kan me niet horen. Yanus slaat haar opzij met het blik bonen. Zala valt en grijpt naar haar gezicht. Hij vloekt. Ik hoop dat hij zijn vingers heeft gebroken.

Mijn gezwollen linkeroog zit nu dicht en uit mijn oor druppelt bloed, dat warm aanvoelt in mijn nek. Hij dwingt me rechtop te gaan staan, trekt mijn armen naar achteren en doet een plastic bandje om mijn polsen. De nokjes trekken het zo strak dat het in mijn huid snijdt.

Hij slaat mijn paspoort open. Leest de naam.

'Politieagent! Hoe ben je hier terechtgekomen?' Hij spuugt naar Zala. 'Zíj heeft je de weg gewezen.'

'Als je ons verder met rust laat, zal ik mijn mond houden. Je kunt weggaan.'

Yanus vindt dit grappig. De punt van zijn mes glijdt langs mijn wenkbrauw.

'Mijn maat weet dat ik hier ben. Hij is onderweg. Hij brengt nog meer mensen mee. Als je nu vertrekt, kun je nog wegkomen. Wat zoek je hier?'

'Ik zocht Samira.'

In het Nederlands zegt hij iets tegen Samira. Ze begint haar spullen te pakken.

Een paar kledingstukken, de familiefoto.

'Wacht buiten op me,' zegt hij tegen haar.

'Zala.'

'Buiten.'

'Zala,' zegt ze opnieuw, vastberadener.

Hij zwaai het mes voor haar gezicht. Ze vertrekt geen spier. Ze is als een standbeeld. Onbeweeglijk. Ze gaat hier niet weg zonder haar vriendin.

Plotseling klapt de deur naar binnen, alsof hij uit zijn scharnieren wordt geblazen. Ruiz vult de deuropening. Ik vergeet weleens hoe groot hij zichzelf kan maken.

Yanus deinst nauwelijks terug. Hij draait zich om, zijn mes vooruit. Dit is een nieuwe uitdaging. De avond is voor hem nog vol beloften. Ruiz neemt de situatie in zich op en laat zijn blik op Yanus rusten, met dezelfde intensiteit.

Maar ik weet wat er staat te gebeuren. Yanus gaat hem mollen. Hem langzaam doodmaken. Het mes is als een verlengstuk van hemzelf, een dirigeerstokje dat een onzichtbaar orkest leidt. Naar stemmen luistert.

De inspecteur houdt iets in zijn hand. Een halve baksteen. Het is niet genoeg. Yanus gaat in spreidstand staan, heft een hand en kromt een uitnodigende vinger.

Ruiz laat zijn vuist door de lucht zwaaien. Ik kan de turbulentie voelen. Yanus maakt een schijnbeweging naar links. De baksteen daalt neer en mist. Yanus grijnst. 'Je bent te langzaam, ouwe.'

Het lemmet leeft. Ik kan de beweging bijna niet volgen. Er welt een donkere vlek op op Ruiz' hemdsmouw, maar hij blijft naar voren stappen en dwingt Yanus achteruit.

'Kun je lopen, Alisha?'

'Ja, meneer.'

'Sta dan op en smeer 'm.'

'Niet zonder jou, meneer.'

'Alsjeblieft, wees nou eens voor één keer…'

'Ik maak jullie allebei kapot,' zegt Yanus.

Mijn handen zitten op mijn rug. Ik kan niets doen. In mijn keel komt de zure prikkeling van misselijkheid op. Samira gaat voor me uit en stapt de gang op. Zala, die nog altijd haar wang vasthoudt, volgt haar. Yanus schreeuwt tegen haar in het Nederlands, dreigend. Hij haalt uit naar Ruiz, die het lemmet ontwijkt. Ik keer me naar de deur en ren naar de trap, wachtend op het geluid van een vallend lichaam.

Op elke verdieping gooi ik mijn schouder tegen de gesloten deuren, bonk er met mijn hoofd tegenaan en schreeuw om hulp. Ik wil dat iemand mijn handen losmaakt, de politie belt, me een wapen geeft. Niemand reageert. Niemand wil het weten.

We bereiken de begane grond en de straat, slaan rechts af en rennen richting gracht. Samira en Zala liggen op me voor. Wat een merkwaardig trio vormen we terwijl we ons door de nacht haasten. We komen bij de hoek. Ik draai me naar Samira. 'Ik moet hem gaan helpen.' Ze begrijpt het. 'Ik wil dat je rechtstreeks naar de politie gaat.'

Ze schudt haar hoofd. 'Dan sturen ze me terug.'

Ik heb geen tijd voor tegenargumenten. 'Ga dan naar de nonnen. Snel. Zala weet de weg.'

Ik voel nog steeds de adrenaline door mijn lichaam pompen. Hardlopend nu, me bewust van de leegte in mijn maag, sprint ik naar het huis. Buiten lopen mensen rond. Ze drommen samen rond een gestalte die ineengedoken op de trap zit. Ruiz. Iemand heeft hem een sigaret gegeven. Hij trekt er gretig aan, zuigt zijn wangen naar binnen en ontspant ze langzaam weer.

Opluchting stroomt als vloeistof onder mijn huid door me heen. Ik weet niet of ik moet huilen of lachen, of allebei. Zijn overhemd is doorweekt met een donkere vlek. Hij houdt een vuist tegen zijn borst gedrukt.

'Ik denk dat je me misschien maar naar een ziekenhuis moet brengen,' zegt hij, moeizaam ademend.

Als een gek geworden vrouw begin ik tegen mensen te gillen dat ze een ziekenwagen moeten bellen. Een tiener verzamelt genoeg moed om me te zeggen dat er een onderweg is.

'Ik moest dichtbij komen,' legt Ruiz met hese fluisterstem uit. Zijn voorhoofd en bovenlip zijn bezaaid met zweetdruppeltjes. 'Ik moest hem me laten steken. Als hij mij kon raken, kon ik hém raken.'

'Niet praten. Gewoon stil zijn.'

'Ik hoop dat die klootzak er geweest is.'

Er komen meer mensen uit de flats naar buiten. Ze willen de bloedende man bekijken. Iemand snijdt mijn boeien door en het plastic krult zich als sinaasappelschillen aan mijn voeten.

Ruiz staart naar de nachtelijke hemel boven de daken.

'Een paar van mijn exen hebben me dit al tijden toegewenst,' zegt hij.

'Dat is niet waar. Miranda is nog steeds gek op je.'

'Hoe weet jij dat?'

'Dat zie ik. Ze flirt de hele tijd met je.'

'Daar kan ze niets aan doen. Ze flirt met iedereen. Dat doet ze om aardig te zijn.'

Zijn ademhaling gaat moeizaam. Er gorgelt bloed in zijn longen.

'Wil je een mop horen?'

'Niet praten, rustig blijven zitten.'

'Het is een hele ouwe. Ik hou van ouwe moppen. Hij gaat over een beer. Ik hou van beren. Beren kunnen grappig zijn.'

Dit houdt niet op.

'In het Noordpoolgebied woont een familie ijsberen. Het is midden in de winter. Op een dag gaat baby ijsbeer naar zijn moeder en zegt: "Mam, ben ik echt een ijsbeer?"

"Natuurlijk ben jij een ijsbeer, zoon," zegt ze.

Waarop het beertje antwoordt: "Weet u zeker dat ik geen pandabeer ben, of een zwarte beer?"

"Ja, honderd procent zeker. Ga nu maar buiten in de sneeuw spelen."

Maar hij is nog steeds verward en dus gaat baby ijsbeer op zoek naar zijn vader en treft hem vissend aan bij een gat in het ijs. "Hé, pa, ben ik een ijsbeer?"

"Maar natuurlijk, zoon," antwoordt hij knorrig.

"Weet u zeker dat ik geen grizzlybeer ben, of misschien wel een koala?"

"Nee, zoon, ik kan je vertellen dat je een honderd procent zuivere ijsbeer bent, net als ik en je moeder. Waarom vraag je dat in 's hemelsnaam?"

"Omdat mijn ballen eraf vriezen hier buiten."'

De inspecteur lacht en kreunt tegelijk. Ik sla mijn armen om zijn borstkas heen om hem warm te houden. In mijn hoofd, onuitgesproken, klinkt luider en luider een mantra: 'Alsjeblieft, ga niet dood. Alsjeblieft, ga niet dood. Alsjeblieft, ga niet dood.'

Dit is mijn schuld. Hij had hier niet moeten zijn. Er is zo veel bloed.

5

Spijt is zo'n rare emotie omdat het altijd net te laat komt, op een moment waarop je het gebeurde alleen in je verbeelding nog zou kunnen herschrijven. De dingen waarvan ik spijt heb zijn als bloemen die tussen de pagina's van een dagboek geperst zitten. Broze herinneringen aan voorbije zomers, zoals de laatste zomer voor ons eindexamen, de zomer die niet groot genoeg was om zijn eigen geschiedenis te kunnen bevatten.

Het zou het laatste feest moeten zijn geweest voordat ik de 'echte wereld' zou betreden. De London Metropolitan Police had me een toelatingsbrief gestuurd. Ik behoorde tot de volgende groep die de opleiding in Hendon zou gaan doen. Lichting 1998.

Toen ik naar de lagere school ging, kon ik me niet voorstellen dat ik ooit naar de middelbare school zou gaan. En op Oaklands dacht ik nooit na over de vrijheid van de universiteit. En toch stond ik daar, op het punt mijn diploma te krijgen en uit te groeien tot een heuse, gesalarieerde volwassene met een sofi-nummer en een studieschuld. 'Godzijdank halen wij de veertig niet,' grapte Cate.

Ik had twee baantjes: de telefoon aannemen in de garage van mijn broers en een weekendbaantje achter een marktkraam. De Elliots hadden me weer uitgenodigd voor Cornwall. Cates moeder had toen al haar attaque gehad en was tot een rolstoel veroordeeld.

Barnaby Elliot had nog altijd politieke ambities, maar er was geen veilige zetel vrijgekomen. Hij was niet uit het juiste hout gesneden: niet traditioneel genoeg om de fanatieke Conservatieven te behagen en niet vrouwelijk, beroemd of etnisch genoeg om de nieuwlichters binnen de partij tevreden te stellen.

Ik vond hem nog steeds knap. En hij bleef met me flirten en vond altijd een aanleiding om tegen me aan te hangen of een stomp tegen mijn arm te geven of me zijn 'Bollywood Beauty' of 'Indiase Prinses' te noemen.

Zondagochtend gingen de Elliots steevast in het dorp naar de kerk, ongeveer tien minuten lopen. Ik bleef in bed liggen tot ik ze had horen weggaan.

Ik weet niet waarom Barnaby terugkwam, welk excuus hij voor de anderen had bedacht. Ik stond onder de douche. De tv stond hard, op een videoclipzender. De klok tikte alsof er niets was gebeurd.

Ik hoorde hem niet de trap op komen. Hij was er ineens. Ik trok de handdoek tegen me aan, maar gilde niet. Hij liet zijn vingers zachtjes over mijn schouder en langs mijn armen gaan. Volmaakte vingernagels. Ik keek omlaag. Ik kon zijn grijze broek zien en de neuzen van zijn schoenen die daar onderuit groeiden.

Hij kuste me in mijn hals. Ik moest mijn hoofd achteroverbuigen om plaats voor hem te maken. Ik keek naar het plafond en hij bewoog zijn lippen omlaag naar de ruimte tussen mijn borsten. Ik hield zijn hoofd vast en drukte me tegen hem aan.

Mijn haar was lang in die tijd, samengebonden in een Franse vlecht die tot op mijn lendenen hing. Hij hield hem in zijn vuisten en draaide hem als een touw om zijn knokkels. Terwijl hij nietszeggende woordjes in mijn oor fluisterde die meer betekenden dan dat, duwde hij op mijn schouders om aan te geven dat ik moest knielen. Ondertussen blèrde de tv en tikte de klok en kookte het water in de fluitketel.

Ik had de deur beneden niet horen opengaan en ook geen voetstappen gehoord op de trap. Ik weet niet waarom Cate was teruggekomen. Sommige details doen er niet toe. Ze moet onze stemmen en de andere geluiden hebben gehoord. Ze moet het geweten hebben, maar kwam, aangetrokken door de geluiden, steeds dichterbij, tot ze bij de deur was.

In de vastgoedwereld is locatie alles. Barnaby stond naakt achter me. Ik stond op handen en voeten met mijn knieën uit elkaar. Cate zei geen woord. Ze had genoeg gezien, maar bleef staan kijken voor meer. Ze zag me niet vechten of worstelen. Ik vocht of worstelde ook niet.

Zo herinner ik het me. Hoe het gebeurde. Het enige wat er nog restte was dat Cate me zei dat ik moest gaan en dat ze me nooit meer wilde zien. Er was genoeg tijd voor haar om op bed te gaan liggen snikken. Een bed verder pakte ik mijn tas in. Ik ademde haar verdriet in en deed mijn best om iets door te slikken wat ik niet kon uitspugen.

Barnaby bracht me zwijgend naar het station. De meeuwen krijsten, beschuldigden mij van verraad. De regen was gekomen en verdronk de zomer.

Het was een lange reis terug naar Londen. Ik trof mama aan achter haar naaimachine, bezig aan een jurk voor de bruiloft van mijn nicht. Voor het eerst sinds jaren wilde ik bij haar op schoot kruipen. In plaats daarvan ging ik naast haar zitten en legde mijn hoofd op haar schouder. Toen huilde ik.

Later die avond stond ik met mama's grote kleermakersschaar voor de badkamerspiegel en knipte voor het eerst mijn haar af. De bladen van de schaar sneden door de strengen en ze dwarrelden op de grond. Ik knipte mijn haar zo kort als de schaar toeliet en nam huid mee. Bloed bevlekte de schaarbladen en pieken stonden als ontkiemende tarwe rechtop op mijn schedeldak.

Het waarom kan ik niet uitleggen. Op de een of andere manier werkte het verzachtend. Mama was ontzet. (Ze zou minder geschokt zijn geweest als ik mijn polsen had doorgesneden.)

Ik liet berichten achter voor Cate en schreef haar briefjes. Ik kon haar niet thuis opzoeken zonder een ontmoeting te riskeren met haar vader of, nog erger, haar moeder. Wat als ze ervan wist? Ik nam dezelfde bussen en treinen als Cate. Ik orkestreerde toevallige ontmoetingen en volgde haar soms gewoon, maar het had geen effect. Spijt was niet genoeg. Ze wilde me niet meer zien of met me praten.

Uiteindelijk staakte ik mijn pogingen. Ik sloot mezelf uren achtereen op, kwam alleen naar buiten om hard te lopen en te eten. Een maand later liep ik een persoonlijk record. Ik wilde niet langer de toekomst inhalen, ik was bezig weg te rennen van het verleden. Ik stortte me op mijn politieopleiding en studeerde fanatiek. Schreef kladblokken vol. Flitste door examens.

Mijn haar groeide weer aan. Mama kwam tot rust. In de jaren daarop dagdroomde ik vaak dat Cate en ik elkaar weer zouden ontmoeten en op de een of andere manier de verloren jaren zouden inhalen. Maar één beeld bleef me achtervolgen: dat van Cate die zwijgend in de deuropening stond te kijken hoe haar vader haar beste vriendin neukte op het ritme van een tikkende klok en een afkoelende elektrische waterkoker.

In alle jaren nadien is er geen dag voorbijgegaan dat ik niet wilde veranderen wat er was gebeurd. Cate vergaf me niet. Ze haatte me met een haat die fataler was dan onverschilligheid, omdat hij het tegenovergestelde was van liefde.

Nadat er geruime tijd was verstreken dacht ik niet meer elk uur of elke dag aan haar. Ik stuurde haar kaarten op haar verjaardag en met kerst. Ik hoorde van haar verloving en zag de trouwfoto's in de etalage van een fotograaf in Bethnal Green. Ze zag er gelukkig uit, Barnaby trots. Haar bruidsmeisjes (ik kende al hun namen) droegen het soort jurkjes waarvan ze altijd had gezegd dat ze die wilde. Felix kende ik niet. Ik wist niet waar ze elkaar hadden leren kennen of hoe hij haar had gevraagd. Wat zag ze in hem? Was het liefde? Ik zou het haar nooit kunnen vragen.

Ze zeggen dat de tijd alle wonden heelt, maar met make-up niet overweg kan. Mijn wonden werden er echter niet door geheeld. De tijd bedekte ze met lagen berouw en ongemakkelijkheid als lagen pancake. Wonden zoals die van mij genezen niet. De littekens worden alleen dikker en blijvender.

De gordijnen zwaaien heen en weer; ze ademen in en uit als longen die rusteloze lucht binnenhalen. Langs de randen valt licht binnen. Een nieuwe dag.

Ik moet in slaap zijn gedommeld. Ik slaap nog maar zelden echt vast. Niet zoals toen ik een kind was en de wereld nog een mysterie. Tegenwoordig schiet ik bij het minste geluidje of beweginkje wakker. De littekens op mijn rug kloppen en zeggen me te gaan staan en strekoefeningen te doen.

Ruiz ligt op een bed in het halfduister. Hij zit gevangen in draden, vloeistoffen en machines. Een kapje levert zuurstof. Drie uur geleden hebben chirurgen een buisje ingebracht in zijn borstkas en zijn rechterlong weer opgepompt. Ze hebben zijn arm gehecht, waarbij ze opmerkingen maakten over zijn talrijke littekens.

Mijn oor is ingezwachteld met kleefpleister. Het ijskompres op mijn wang is inmiddels gesmolten, de zwelling is minder geworden. De beurse plekken zullen er straks lelijk uitzien, maar ik kan mijn haar losmaken en de ergste erachter verbergen.

De arts en het verplegend personeel zijn erg aardig geweest. Gisteravond wilden ze dat ik de kamer van de inspecteur zou verlaten. Ik argumenteerde. Ik smeekte. Daarna meen ik me te herinneren dat ik op de linoleumvloer lag en zei dat ze me dan maar moesten wegslepen. Ze lieten me blijven.

Ik voel me verdoofd. In loopgraafshock. Dit is mijn schuld. Ik sluit mijn ogen voor het duister en luister hoe hij ademt. Iemand heeft een dienblad neergezet met een glas jus d'orange waarop een gekarteld papieren dekseltje zit. Er liggen koekjes. Ik heb geen trek.

Dit gaat dus allemaal om een baby. Twee baby's. Cate Beaumont probeerde vergeefs zwanger te worden via IVF. Daarna ontmoette ze iemand die haar ervan wist te overtuigen dat voor tachtigduizend pond een andere vrouw haar baby voor haar zou baren. Niet zomaar een baby, maar haar eigen genetische nakomeling.

Ze reisde naar Amsterdam, waar twee van haar bevruchte eicellen werden teruggeplaatst in de baarmoeder van een Afghaans tienermeisje dat geld schuldig was aan mensensmokkelaars. Beide embryo's begonnen te groeien.

Ondertussen liet Cate in Londen mensen weten dat ze 'zwanger' was. Vrienden en familie vierden het nieuws. Ze begon aan een ingewikkelde misleiding die ze negen maanden moest zien vol te houden. Wat was er misgegaan? Op Cates echo's, die nep waren, was maar één baby te zien. Zelf hield ze geen rekening met een tweeling.

Iemand moet de IVF-procedure hebben geregeld. Er waren artsen bij nodig. Fertiliteitsspecialisten. Vroedvrouwen. Oppassers.

In de deuropening verschijnt een verpleegster. Een engel in gebroken wit. Ze loopt om het bed heen en fluistert iets in mijn oor. Er is een rechercheur die me wil spreken.

'Hij slaapt nog wel even,' fluistert ze met een blik op Ruiz. 'Ik hou de wacht.'

Een plaatselijke politieman heeft op de gang de hele nacht op wacht gezeten. Hij ziet er heel verzorgd uit in een donkerblauwe broek, een lichtblauw overhemd, een stropdas en een jasje. Hij praat tegen een superieur. Ik wacht tot ze klaar zijn.

De hogere in rang stelt zichzelf voor als Spijker, wat uit zijn mond als een soort straf klinkt. Een voornaam geeft hij me niet. Misschien heeft hij maar één naam. Hij is lang en dun, met een smal gezicht en dunner wordend haar. Hij kijkt me met waterige ogen aan alsof hij nu al allergisch reageert op wat ik zou kunnen gaan zeggen.

Een kleine moedervlek op zijn bovenlip danst op en neer als hij spreekt. 'Uw vriend gaat het wel redden, denk ik.'

'Ja, meneer.'

'Ik zal met hem moeten praten zodra hij wakker is.'

Ik knik.

We lopen naar de conversatiezaal, die veel verzorgder is dan alles wat ik ooit in een Brits ziekenhuis heb gezien. Er zijn eieren en vleeswaren en plakken kaas op een schaal, met daarnaast een mand broodjes. De rechercheur wacht tot ik zit en pakt een vulpen, die hij op een groot schrijfblok legt. Zelfs zijn kleinste handelingen hebben een functie.

Spijker legt uit dat hij voor de jeugd- en zedenpolitie werkt. Onder normale omstandigheden zou dit me misschien als een vreemde combinatie in de oren hebben geklonken, maar niet als ik denk aan Samira's leeftijd en wat ze heeft doorgemaakt.

Terwijl ik hem het verhaal vertel, gebeurtenissen verklaar, valt me op hoe onwaarschijnlijk het allemaal klinkt. Een Engelse vrouw neemt in een kleine koelbox bevruchte eicellen mee naar Amsterdam. De eitjes worden in de baarmoeder van een onvrijwillige draagmoeder geplaatst. Een maagd.

Met zijn handen op de zijkanten van zijn stoel leunt Spijker iets voorover. Heel even denk ik dat hij misschien aambeien heeft en even de druk wil verlichten.

'Wat geeft jou het idee dat dit meisje gedwongen werd zwanger te worden?'

'Dat heeft ze me verteld.'

'En jij gelooft haar?'

'Ja, meneer.'

'Misschien stemde ze toe.'

'Nee. Ze was smokkelaars geld schuldig. Ofwel ze werd prostituee, ofwel ze zou een baby baren.'

'Mensensmokkel is een ernstig vergrijp. Commercieel draagmoederschap is eveneens verboden.'

Ik vertel hem over de prostituee in de Molensteeg, die zei dat ze nóg een zwanger meisje had gezien, een Servische. Volgens Lena Caspar had Samira in het asielzoekerscentrum een Servische vriendin.

Er zouden er meer kunnen zijn. Baby's geboren voor geld, onder bedreigingen en afpersing de wereld in gestuurd. Ik heb geen idee hoe groot deze zaak is en hoeveel mensen erbij betrokken zijn.

Spijkers gezicht verraadt niets. Hij praat langzaam, alsof hij zijn Engels oefent. 'En dit is dus de reden van uw bezoek aan Amsterdam?'

Aan de vraag zit een weerhaakje. Hier heb ik op zitten wachten: de kwestie van bevoegdheid. Mag een Britse politieagent achter mogelijk in Nederland gepleegde misdaden aan? Er moeten protocollen worden gevolgd, er zijn regels waaraan moet worden voldaan.

'Ik was als privé-persoon informatie aan het verzamelen. Het is geen officieel onderzoek.'

Spijker lijkt tevredengesteld. Hij heeft duidelijk gemaakt wat hij wilde zeggen: ik ben binnen Nederland niet bevoegd.

'Waar is de vrouw die zwanger is?'

'Veilig.'

Hij wacht, tot ik hem een adres geef. Ik vertel hem over haar asielaanvraag en het uitzettingsbevel. Ze is bang dat ze terug naar Afghanistan wordt gestuurd.

'Als dit meisje de waarheid spreekt en getuige wordt, zijn er wetten die haar beschermen.'

'Zou ze dan kunnen blijven?'

'Tot aan het proces.'

Ik wil hem vertrouwen, ik wil dat Samira hem vertrouwt, en toch heeft zijn houding iets wat richting scepsis gaat. Het kladblok en de vulpen heeft hij niet aangeraakt. Het zijn slechts rekwisieten.

'Een interessant verhaal dat u daar vertelt, agent. Werkelijk heel interessant.' (Hij lijkt te genieten van zijn kennis van het Engels.) De moedervlek op zijn bovenlip trilt. 'Ik heb echter een andere versie te horen gekregen. De man die we ter plaatse bewusteloos aantroffen zegt dat hij jou bij thuiskomst in zijn appartement aantrof. Jij beweerde dat je verpleegster was en bezig was zijn verloofde te onderzoeken.'

'Zijn verloofde?'

'Inderdaad, zijn verloofde. Hij zegt dat hij u om een identiteitsbewijs vroeg. U weigerde. Hebt u juffrouw Khan lichamelijk onderzocht?'

'Zij wist dat ik geen verpleegster was. Ik probeerde haar te helpen.'

'De heer Yanus beweert daarnaast dat hij door uw collega werd aangevallen toen hij probeerde zijn verloofde te beschermen.'

'Yanus had een mes. Kijk wat hij gedaan heeft!'

'Uit zelfverdediging.'

'Hij liegt.'

Spijker knikt, maar niet uit instemming. 'U begrijpt mijn dilemma, agent Barba. Ik heb twee verschillende versies van dezelfde gebeurtenis. De heer Yanus wil jullie beiden aanklagen voor geweldpleging en het ontvoeren van zijn verloofde. Hij heeft een goede advocaat. Een érg goede advocaat zelfs.'

'Dit is belachelijk. U gelooft hem toch zeker niet?'

De rechercheur onderbreekt me met een handgebaar. 'Wij Nederlanders staan bekend om onze ruimdenkendheid, maar dat is niet hetzelfde als onwetendheid of naïviteit. Ik heb bewijzen nodig. Waar is het zwangere meisje?'

'Ik kan u naar haar toe brengen, maar dan moet ik eerst met haar praten.'

'Om jullie verhalen kloppend te maken, zeker?'

'Nee!' Ik klink te schel. 'Haar broer is drie dagen geleden gestorven. Ze weet het nog niet.'

In stilte rijden we terug naar mijn hotel. Ik krijg de tijd om me te douchen en om te kleden. Spijker wacht in de lobby.

Ik trek mijn kleren uit, trek een hotelkamerjas aan en ga in kleermakerszit op het bed zitten. Ik blader door de berichten die bij de receptie lagen te wachten. Groentje Dave heeft vier keer gebeld, mijn moeder twee keer en commissaris North heeft een kort leg-dat-maar-eens-uit-bericht achtergelaten. Ik maak er een prop van en spoel hem door. Misschien is dit wat hij bedoelde met mensen en prioriteiten herschikken.

Ik zou Ruiz' familie moeten bellen. Wie eigenlijk? Ik heb de nummers van zijn kinderen en zijn ex-vrouwen niet, zelfs niet dat van de laatste in de rij, Miranda.

Ik pak de telefoon en toets een nummer. Dave is op het bureau. Op de achtergrond hoor ik stemmen.

'Hallo lieve meid, waar heb jij gezeten?'

'Mijn mobiele telefoon is gestolen.'

'Hoe?'

'Bij een ongeluk.'

Zijn stemming verandert. 'Een ongeluk?'

'Niet echt een ongeluk.' *Dit pak ik niet echt goed aan.*

'Wacht even.' Ik hoor dat hij zich tegenover iemand verontschuldigt. Hij schakelt me over naar een toestel waar we alleen zijn met elkaar.

'Wat is er? Gaat het goed?'

'De inspecteur ligt in het ziekenhuis. Iemand heeft hem neergestoken.'

'Shit!'

'Je moet iets voor me doen. Het nummer van zijn ex-vrouw.'

'Welke?'

'Miranda. Zeg haar dat hij in het Academisch Medisch Centrum ligt. Een ziekenhuis in Amsterdam.'

'Komt hij er weer bovenop?'

'Ik denk het wel. Ze hebben hem geopereerd.'

Dave wil alle details weten. Ik probeer er zo'n draai aan te geven dat het klinkt als een scenario van op het verkeerde moment op de verkeerde plaats. Helaas. Hij is niet overtuigd. Ik weet wat er nu gaat komen. Hij gaat vast heel aanhankelijk en pathetisch doen en vragen of ik naar huis kom, en alle redenen waarom ik niet getrouwd ben zullen me weer helder voor de geest staan.

Maar dat gebeurt niet. Hij is zakelijk en direct, noteert het nummer van het ziekenhuis en Spijkers naam. Hij gaat uitzoeken waar de Nederlandse politie mee bezig is.

'Ik heb Samira gevonden. Ze is zwanger.'

Ik kan horen dat Dave in zijn hoofd de implicaties daarvan de revue laat passeren. Hij is zorgvuldig en methodisch, als een timmerman die twee keer meet en één keer zaagt.

'Cate heeft voor een baby betaald. Een draagmoeder.'

'Jezus, Ali.'

'Het wordt nog erger. Ze heeft zelf de embryo's gedoneerd. Het is een tweeling.'

'Aan wie behoren de baby's toe?'

'Dat weet ik niet.'

Hij wil het hele verhaal horen, maar ik heb geen tijd. Ik sta op het punt op te hangen als hij zich iets herinnert.

'Het is waarschijnlijk niet het goede moment,' zegt hij, 'maar ik ben gebeld door je moeder.'

'Wanneer?'

'Gisteren. Ze heeft me uitgenodigd om zondag te komen lunchen.'

Dat dreigde ze al te doen, en ze heeft het nog gedaan ook!

Dave wacht op een reactie.

'Ik weet niet of ik dan al terug ben,' zeg ik.

'Maar je wist ervan?'

'Natuurlijk,' lieg ik. 'Ik heb haar gevraagd je uit te nodigen.'

Hij lijkt gerustgesteld. 'Ik dacht heel even dat ze het misschien wel achter jouw rug om deed. Dat zou pas een blamage zijn: de moeder van mijn vriendin die afspraakjes voor me regelt. Het verhaal van mijn leven: moeders die mij mogen en hun dochters die het op een lopen zetten.'

Nu zit hij te wauwelen.

'Het is goed, Dave.'

'Geweldig.'

Hij wil niet ophangen. In plaats daarvan doe ik het voor hem. De douche loopt. Ik stap onder de straal en schrik als het hete water mijn wang en de snee in mijn oor raakt. Schoon en droog open ik mijn tas en pak mijn Dolce & Gabbana-broek en een donkere bloes. In de spiegel zie ik minder van mezelf terug dan ik me kan herinneren. Toen ik nog wedstrijden liep was zesenvijftig kilo mijn ideale gewicht. Ik kwam aan toen ik bij de MET ging werken. Zo gaat dat als je nachtdiensten draait en kantinevoer eet.

Ik ben altijd nogal weinig meisjesachtig geweest. Ik ga niet naar een manicure of pedicure en lak mijn nagels alleen bij speciale gelegenheden (zodat ik de lak er weer af kan pulken als ik me verveel).

De dag waarop ik mijn haar afknipte was bijna een overgangs-rite. Nadat het weer aangroeide hield ik een praktisch laagjeskapsel. Mijn moeder huilde. Bij haar zijn tranen nooit op rantsoen geweest.

Sinds mijn tienerjaren ben ik voortdurend doodsbang geweest voor sari's en rokken. Ik droeg pas op mijn veertiende een beha en werd later ongesteld dan wie ook. Ik stelde het me voor als iets wat zich achter een damwand ophoopte en, als de deuren werden opengezet, het op een scène uit een Tarantino-film zou lijken, maar dan zonder Harvey Keitel om de boel op te ruimen.

In die tijd dacht ik dat ik me nooit vrouw zou voelen, maar langzaam gebeurde dat toch. Nu ben ik bijna dertig en zelfbewust genoeg om make-up te dragen – een beetje lipgloss en mascara. Ik epileer mijn wenkbrauwen en hars mijn benen. Ik heb nog altijd geen enkele rok, en elk voorwerp in mijn kledingkast, op mijn spijkerbroeken en sari's na, is een variatie op de kleur zwart. Dat geeft niet. Kleine stapjes.

Ik pleeg nog één telefoontje. Ik word doorgeschakeld en Lena Caspar neemt op. Op de achtergrond galmt een omroepsysteem. Ze staat op een perron. Ze heeft een hoorzitting in Rotterdam, legt ze uit. Een asielzoeker wordt beschuldigd van het stelen van levensmiddelen.

'Ik heb Samira gevonden.'

'Hoe is het met haar?'

'Ze heeft uw hulp nodig.'

De details komen later wel. Ik geef haar Spijkers naam en telefoonnummer.

Als ze willen dat ze getuigt, zal Samira bescherming nodig hebben en garanties ten aanzien van haar status.

'Ze weet het niet van Hasan.'

'Jij moet het haar vertellen.'

'Weet ik.'

De advocate begint hardop te denken. Ze gaat iemand zoeken die de rechtszaak in Rotterdam van haar kan overnemen. Dat kan een paar uur duren.

'Ik heb een vraag.'

Mijn woorden gaan verloren in een spoorwijziging die wordt omgeroepen. Ze wacht even. 'Sorry. Wat zei je?'

'Ik heb een hypothetische vraag voor u.'

'Ja?'

'Als een getrouwd stel een embryo levert aan een draagmoeder die later het kind baart, aan wie zou de baby dan toebehoren?'

'De draagmoeder.'

'Zelfs als het kind het DNA van het echtpaar heeft?'

'Dat maakt niet uit. De Nederlandse wet zegt hetzelfde als de Britse: de moeder die het kind baart is de wettige moeder. Niemand anders kan die status opeisen.'

'En de vader dan?'

'Die kan om omgangsrecht vragen, maar de rechtbank zal ten gunste van de moeder oordelen. Waarom wil je dat weten?'

'Dat zal Spijker u uitleggen.'

Ik hang op en kijk opnieuw in de spiegel. Mijn haar is nog nat. Als ik het los laat hangen zal het de zwelling op mijn wang verbergen. Ik zal mijn natuurlijke neiging om het achter mijn oren te strijken moeten onderdrukken.

Beneden tref ik de rechercheur en de receptionist in gesprek aan. Er staat een opengeklapte laptop. Zodra ze me zien stoppen ze met praten. Spijker is mijn gegevens aan het natrekken. Dat zou ik bij hem ook doen.

Het is maar een kort ritje naar het augustinessenklooster. We draaien de Warmoesstraat in en zetten de auto in een parkeergarage. Een Afrikaanse parkeerwacht komt aanrennen. Spijker laat hem een badge zien en verscheurt het parkeerkaartje.

Tegen beter weten in heeft hij erin toegestemd dat ik eerst met Samira praat. Ik heb twintig minuten. Ik ga de betonnen trappen af en open een zware branddeur. Aan de overkant van de straat staat het klooster. Uit de voordeur komt een bekende. Gekleed in haar roze jasje en enkellange rok, met haar gezicht omlaag, haast ze zich over de stoep. Haar blauwe hijab verbergt de kneuzing op haar gezicht. Ze zou niet buiten moeten zijn. Ik bedwing de aanvechting haar te volgen.

Een rijzige non met een blozend gezicht doet open. Net als de anderen is ze gerimpeld en aan het verschrompelen, terwijl ze probeert het gebouw te overleven. Door een gang word ik naar zuster Vogels kantoor geleid, dat een curieuze mix van oude en nieuwe dingen bevat. Een kast met glazen deuren is in dezelfde donkere kleur geschilderd als het mahoniehouten bureau. In de hoek staan een fax en een kopieerapparaat. Op de schoorsteenmantel staat een hartvormige doos met kaarsen, met daarnaast foto's die van haar neefjes en nichtjes zouden kunnen zijn. Ik vraag me af of zuster Vogel weleens spijt heeft van haar roeping. God kan een barre echtgenoot zijn.

Ze duikt naast me op. 'Je hebt me niet verteld dat je politieagente was.'

'Zou dat iets hebben uitgemaakt?'

Ze reageert niet. 'Je hebt nog meer mensen gestuurd om te voeden.'

'Ze eten maar weinig.'

Ze slaat haar armen over elkaar. 'Zit dat meisje in de problemen?'

'Ja.'

'Is ze in de steek gelaten?'

'Misbruikt.'

Verdriet vult elke groef en rimpel van haar gezicht. Ze ziet de kneuzing op mijn wang en maakt een meelevend gebaar. 'Wie heeft je dit aangedaan?'

'Maakt niet uit. Ik moet Samira spreken.'

Ze neemt me mee naar een kamer op de tweede verdieping, die met dezelfde donkere panelen is gedecoreerd. Samira staat bij het raam als de deur opengaat. Ze draagt een lange knoopjesjurk met een plat, rond kraagje. Onder de stof tekent in het vensterlicht de omtrek van haar lichaam zich af. Terwijl ze me aandachtig aankijkt neemt ze plaats op de bank. Haar zwangere buik rust op haar dijen.

Zuster Vogel blijft niet. Als de deur zich sluit, kijk ik de kamer rond. Aan de muur hangt een schilderij van de Maagd Maria, Johannes de Doper en het Kindeke Jezus. Ze staan afgebeeld naast een riviertje waarlangs vruchten aan de bomen hangen en dikke, naakte nimfen boven het water dansen.

Samira ziet me kijken. 'Ben jij christen?'

'Sikh.'

Ze knikt, tevredengesteld.

'Heb je een hekel aan christenen?'

'Nee. Mijn vader heeft me verteld dat christenen minder geloven dan wij. Ik weet niet of dat waar is. Ik ben geen erg goede moslim. Ik vergeet soms te bidden.'

'Hoe vaak word je geacht te bidden?'

'Vijf keer per dag, maar mijn vader zei altijd dat drie keer genoeg was.'

'Mis je hem, je vader?'

'Bij elke ademteug.'

Haar koperkleurige ogen zijn doorschoten met goud en onzekerheid. Ik kan me geen voorstelling maken van wat ze in haar korte leven al hebben gezien. Als ik me Afghanistan voorstel, zie ik in zwart gehulde vrouwen als afgedekte standbeelden, met sneeuw gekroonde bergen, oude karavaansporen, niet-geëxplodeerde mijnen, verschroeiende woestijnen, huizen van klei, antieke monumenten en eenogige woestelingen.

Dit keer stel ik mezelf netjes voor en vertel Samira hoe ik haar heb gevonden. Ze kijkt beschaamd weg als ik de prostituee in de Molensteeg ter sprake breng. Op hetzelfde moment houdt ze haar hand tegen haar borstkas en drukt erop. Op haar voorhoofd zie ik pijn.

'Gaat het?'

'Maagzuur. Zala is een middeltje aan het halen.' Ze werpt een blik op de deur, mist haar vriendin nu al.

'Waar heb je haar leren kennen?'

'In het weeshuis.'

'Zijn jullie niet samen uit Afghanistan weggegaan?'

'Nee. We moesten haar achterlaten.'

'Hoe is ze hier gekomen?'

'Achter in een vrachtwagen en daarna per trein.'

'In haar eentje?'

Samira's gezicht verzacht zich. 'Zala slaagt er altijd in duidelijk te maken wat ze bedoelt.'

'Is ze al haar hele leven doof?'

'Nee.'

'Hoe komt het dan?'

'Haar vader vocht met de moedjahedien tegen de taliban. Toen de talibs de macht overnamen, hebben ze hun vijanden gestraft. Zala en haar moeder werden gevangengezet en gemarteld met zuur en smeltend plastic. Het duurde acht dagen voordat haar moeder stierf. Tegen die tijd kon Zala haar al niet meer horen schreeuwen.'

Het verhaal zuigt de zuursof uit de kamer en ik voel mezelf naar adem happen. Samira kijkt weer naar de deur, wachtend op Zala. Haar vingers liggen gespreid op haar buik, alsof ze de bobbels en de schopjes leest. Hoe zou dat aanvoelen, als er in je binnenste iets groeit? Een leven, een organisme dat zonder te vragen neemt wat het nodig heeft, slaap rooft, hormonen verandert, uit elkaar duwt en op organen drukt. Ik heb mijn vriendinnen en schoonzusters horen klagen over broze nagels, haaruitval, pijnlijke borsten en striae. Het is een offer dat mannen niet zouden kunnen brengen.

Samira zit naar me te kijken. Ze wil iets vragen.

'U zei dat mevrouw Beaumont dood is.'

'Ja.'

'Wat gaat er nu met haar baby's gebeuren?'

'Dat is aan jou.'

'Waarom?'

'Ze zijn van jou.'

'Nee!'

'Het zijn jouw baby's.'

Haar hoofd draait van links naar rechts. Ze is heel stellig.

Ineens staat ze op, schommelt lichtjes en strekt haar hand uit, leunend op de rug van de bank. Ze loopt de kamer door en staart uit het raam, in de hoop Zala te zien.

Ik denk nog steeds na over haar ontkenning. Houdt ze van haar ongeboren tweeling? Stelt ze zich voor hoe hun toekomst eruit zal zien? Of draagt ze de kinderen alleen maar en telt ze de dagen af tot de bevalling, als haar taak erop zal zitten?

'Wanneer heb je mevrouw Beaumont ontmoet?'

'Ze kwam naar Amsterdam. Ze kocht kleren voor me. Yanus was erbij. Ik moest net doen of ik geen Engels sprak, maar mevrouw Beaumont praatte toch tegen me. Ze gaf me een papiertje met uw naam. Ze zei dat ik, als ik ooit in de problemen kwam, u zou moeten zien te vinden.'

'Wanneer was dat?'

'In maart zag ik haar voor het eerst. In september kwam ze me opnieuw opzoeken.'

'Wist ze dat je een tweeling ging krijgen?'

Ze haalt haar schouders op.

'Had ze enig idee waarom?'

'Hoe bedoelt u?'

'Wist ze van de schuld? Wist ze dat jij was gedwongen zwanger te worden?'

Haar stem wordt milder. 'Ze bedankte me. Ze zei dat ik met iets goeds bezig was.'

'Iemand dwingen een kind te baren is een misdaad. Ze deed iets heel doms.'

Samira haalt opnieuw haar schouders op; ze weigert zo hard te oordelen. 'Soms doen vrienden dwaze dingen,' zegt ze. 'Mijn vader zei me dat vrienden als gouden munten zijn. Schepen worden stukgebeukt door stormen en liggen honderden jaren op de zeebodem. Wormen vernietigen het hout. IJzer corrodeert. Zilver wordt zwart, maar goud verandert niet in zeewater. Het verliest niets van zijn glans of kleur. Het komt net zo boven water als toen het zonk. Dat is ook met vriendschap zo. Ook die overleeft schipbreuken en de tijd.'

De zwelling in mijn borst doet ineens pijn. Hoe kan iemand die zo jong is zo wijs zijn?

'Je moet de politie vertellen wat er is gebeurd.'

'Dan sturen ze me terug.'

'Deze mensen hebben hele slechte dingen gedaan. Je bent hun niets verschuldigd.'

'Yanus zal me weten te vinden. Hij zal me nooit laten gaan.'

'De politie kan je beschermen.'

'Ik vertrouw ze niet.'

'Vertrouw mij dan.'

Ze schudt haar hoofd. Ze heeft geen reden mij te geloven. Praatjes vullen geen gaatjes en wekken ook geen dode broers tot leven. Ze weet het nog steeds niet van Hasan. Ik kan me er niet toe zetten het haar te vertellen.

'Waarom zijn jullie uit Kabul weggegaan?'

'*Brother.*'

'Je broer?'

'Nee. Een Engelsman. We noemden hem Brother.'

'Wie is hij?'

'Een heilige.'

Met haar wijsvinger tekent ze de omtrek van een kruis in haar hals. Ik moet denken aan Donavons tatoeage. Zou het kunnen?

'Die Engelsman, was hij soldaat?'

'Hij zei dat hij door God gestuurd was.'

Ze vertelt dat hij het weeshuis bezocht en voedsel en dekens meebracht. Er zaten zestig kinderen tussen de twee en zestien jaar oud, die in slaapzalen sliepen, 's winters dicht tegen elkaar aan gekropen, levend van liefdadigheid en wat ze bij elkaar konden scharrelen.

Toen de taliban de macht had gegrepen, nam ze jongens uit het weeshuis mee om hun geweren te helpen laden, en de meisjes als echtgenotes. De wezen juichten toen de Noordelijke Alliantie en de Amerikanen Kabul bevrijdden, maar het nieuwe regime bleek nauwelijks anders. Soldaten kwamen naar het weeshuis, op zoek naar meisjes. De eerste keer verborg Samira zich onder een stapel dekens. De tweede keer kroop ze de latrine in. Een ander meisje wierp zich van het dak, liever dan te worden meegenomen.

Ik ben verbaasd hoe ambivalent ze klinkt. Doorslaggevende beslissingen, zaken van leven en dood, verteld met de nuchterheid van een boodschappenlijstje. Ik kan niet zeggen of ze gewend is geraakt aan schokkende dingen of er juist door is verpletterd.

Brother kocht de soldaten af met geld en medicijnen. Hij zei Samira dat ze weg moest uit Afghanistan omdat het niet veilig was. Hij zei dat hij werk voor haar zou vinden in Londen.

'En Hasan?'

'Brother zei dat hij moest achterblijven. Ik zei dat ik niet zonder hem zou vertrekken.'

Ze werden voorgesteld aan een smokkelaar die Mahmoud heette, en die hun reis regelde. Zala moest achterblijven omdat geen enkel land een doof meisje zou toelaten, vertelde Mahmoud hun. Hasan en Samira werden per bus over land naar Pakistan gebracht en via Quetta naar het zuiden gesmokkeld en daarna in westelijke richting Iran binnen, totdat ze Tabriz bereikten, bij de grens met Turkije. In de eerste week van de lente liepen ze door het Araratgebergte en werden ze bijna het slachtoffer van de vriesnachten en de wolven.

Aan de Turkse kant van de bergrug smokkelden schaapherders hen van dorp naar dorp en zorgden ervoor dat ze achter in een vrachtwagen naar Istanbul werden gebracht. Twee maanden lang werkten broer en zus in een duister atelier in de textielwijken van Zeytinburno, waar ze schapenleren jasjes in elkaar zetten.

Het smokkelsyndicaat eiste meer geld voor de tocht naar Engeland. De prijs was gestegen tot tienduizend Amerikaanse dollars. Samira schreef een aan Brother gerichte brief, maar wist niet waar ze hem heen moest sturen. Eindelijk gingen ze op weg. Een vissersboot bracht hen de Egeïsche Zee over naar Italië, waar ze met vier andere illegalen een trein naar Rome namen. Ze werden opgewacht op het station en meegenomen naar een huis.

Twee dagen later ontmoetten ze Yanus. Hij nam hen mee naar een busstation en verstopte hen in het bagageruim van een toeristenbus die via Duitsland naar Nederland ging. 'Niet bewegen en niet praten, anders vinden ze jullie,' zei hij tegen hen. Zodra de bus de Nederlandse grens had bereikt moesten ze asiel aanvragen. Hij zou hen weten te vinden.

'Maar we moeten naar Engeland,' zei Samira.

'Engeland komt later,' antwoordde hij.

De rest van het verhaal komt overeen met wat ik van Lena Caspar heb gehoord.

Zuster Vogel klopt zachtjes op de deur. In haar handen heeft ze een dienblad met thee en koekjes. De oortjes van de verfijnde kopjes zijn beschadigd. Door een kapot zeefje schenk ik de thee in. Samira pakt een koekje en wikkelt het in een papieren servetje om het voor Zala te bewaren.

'Zegt de naam Paul Donavon je iets?'

Ze schudt haar hoofd.

'Van wie hoorde je over de IVF-kliniek?'

'Yanus. Hij zei dat we hem moesten betalen voor onze reis vanuit Kabul. Hij dreigde me te zullen verkrachten. Hasan probeerde hem tegen te houden, maar Yanus bewerkte hem met een mes. Wel honderd sneden.' Ze wijst op haar borst. Wat Noonan had gezien waren de sporen van de verwondingen op Hasans bovenlichaam.

'Wat wilde Yanus dat je deed?'

'Hoer worden. Hij liet me zien wat ik zou moeten doen. Daarna stelde hij me voor de keus. Hij zei dat ik met een baby mijn schuld kon afbetalen. Zonder mijn maagdelijkheid te verliezen.'

Het laatste zegt ze bijna strijdlustig. Dit is een waarheid die Samira overeind houdt. Ik vraag me af of ze juist daarom een moslimmeisje hebben genomen. Ze zou bijna alles hebben gedaan om haar maagdelijkheid te beschermen.

Ik weet nog altijd niet hoe Cate erbij betrokken is geraakt. Was het haar idee of dat van Donavon?

Buiten wacht Spijker. Ik kan dit niet langer uitstellen. Ik open mijn tas, haal de houtskooltekening eruit en strijk de hoeken glad.

De opwinding doet haar ogen van binnenuit stralen. 'Hasan! U hebt hem gezien!'

Ze wacht. Ik schud mijn hoofd. 'Hasan is dood.'

Haar hoofd schiet omhoog alsof het aan een touw vastzit. Het licht in haar ogen maakt plaats voor woede. Ongeloof. Ik doe snel mijn verhaal, in de hoop haar te sparen, maar er is geen pijnloze manier om dit te vertellen. Zijn reis. Zijn overtocht. Zijn gevecht om in leven te blijven.

Ze slaat haar handen over haar oren.

'Het spijt me, Samira. Hij heeft het niet gehaald.'

'U liegt! Hasan is in Londen.'

'Ik spreek de waarheid.'

Ze wiegt heen en weer, met haar ogen dicht; haar mond gaat geluidloos open en weer dicht. Het woord dat ze wil zeggen is nee.

'Je moet je toch hebben afgevraagd waarom je niets van hem hoorde?' zeg ik. 'Hij zou nu toch moeten hebben gebeld of geschreven? Jij naaide mijn naam in zijn kleding. Op die manier heb ik je weten te vinden.' Ik ga dichter bij haar zitten. 'Ik heb geen reden om tegen je te liegen.'

Ze verstijft en deinst terug terwijl ze me met een angstwekkend intense blik aankijkt.

Van beneden galmt de stem van Spijker. Hij is het wachten beu.

'Je moet de politie alles vertellen wat je mij hebt verteld.'

Ze antwoordt niet. Ik weet niet of ze het begrijpt.

Terwijl ze zich naar het raam keert noemt ze Zala's naam.

'Zuster Vogel zorgt wel voor haar.'

Ze schudt koppig haar hoofd, haar ogen vol stompzinnige hoop.

'Ik zal haar vinden en voor haar zorgen.'

Heel even verzet iets in haar binnenste zich nog. Dan laat ze het los en geeft zich over. Het noodlot zelf bevechten is te zwaar. Ze moet zichzelf sparen om datgene te bevechten waar het noodlot mee voor de dag komt.

Midden op de Wallen is een apotheek, legt zuster Vogel uit. De apotheker is een vriend van haar. Ze heeft Zala naar hem toe gestuurd. Ze had een briefje bij zich.

Achter elke hoek die ik omsla verwacht ik een roze flits te zien of haar blauwe hijab op me af te zien komen. Ik passeer een groentewinkel en vang de geur van sinaasappels op, waardoor ik aan Hasan denk. Wat gaat er nu met Samira gebeuren? Wie zal er voor haar zorgen?

Ik sla de Oudekerksteeg in. Nog altijd geen teken van Zala. Ik voel een tikje op mijn arm en draai me om. Eerst herken ik Hokke niet, die een wollen muts draagt. In combinatie met zijn lichte baard ziet hij eruit als een Noordzeevisser.

'Hallo vriendin.' Hij bekijkt me van dichtbij. 'Wat heb je ge-daan?' Zijn vinger strijkt langs de kneuzing op mijn wang.

'Geknokt, misschien?'

'En, gewonnen?'

'Nee.'

Over zijn schouder heen speur ik het plein af naar Zala. Mijn gespannen blik doet ook hem omkijken.

'Ben je nog steeds op zoek naar dat Afghaanse meisje?'

'Nee, nu gaat het om een ander meisje.'

Het klinkt achteloos, alsof ik de hele tijd mensen kwijtraak. Hokke heeft in een café op het plein gezeten. Zala moet hem ge-passeerd zijn, maar hij kan zich niet herinneren dat hij haar heeft gezien.

'Misschien kan ik je helpen zoeken.'

Terwijl ik de mensen om ons heen bekijk, loop ik achter hem aan tot we bij de apotheek komen. De kleine zaak heeft smalle looppaden en keurig ingerichte schappen. Achter een toonbank staat een man in een gestreept overhemd en witte jas klanten te helpen. Als hij Hokke ziet, spreidt hij zijn armen en omhelzen ze elkaar. Oude vrienden.

'Een doof meisje zou ik me moeten herinneren,' zegt hij in het Engels.

'Ze had een briefje bij zich van zuster Vogel.'

Hij roept iets naar een assistent. Van achter een rek ansichtkaar-ten komt een hoofd tevoorschijn. Opnieuw gepraat in het Neder-lands. Schouderophalen. Niemand heeft haar gezien.

Hokke loopt met me mee naar buiten. Ik doe een paar passen en blijf tegen een muur geleund staan. Er komt een vage trilling in me opzetten, een dreigende gedachte die zich niet laat bedwin-gen. Zala is niet weggelopen. Ze zou Samira niet moedwillig in de steek laten. Nooit.

Het hoofdbureau van politie is gelegen aan een meer naar buiten gelegen gracht, ten westen van het centrum. Het product van de verbeelding van een architect ziet er schoongeboend uit en werpt een lange schaduw over het water. De glazen deuren openen zich automatisch. Beveiligingscamera's zoeken de entree af. Er gaat een melding naar Spijker, die ergens boven zit. Hij antwoordt dat ik bij de receptie moet wachten. Mijn haast heeft geen enkel effect op de receptioniste, die net zo'n uitgestreken gezicht heeft als de boerendochter op het schilderij *American Gothic*.

Hier heb ik geen bevoegdheden. Ik heb geen macht om eisen te stellen of op mensen te leunen.

Hokke biedt aan me gezelschap te houden. Hij heeft niet één keer gevraagd hoe ik Samira heb gevonden of wat er met Ruiz is gebeurd. Hij stelt zich tevreden met de informatie die hem wordt geboden, in plaats van ernaar op zoek te gaan.

Er is veel gebeurd de afgelopen week en toch voelt het alsof ik geen stap vooruitgekomen ben. Het is net als met de klok aan de muur boven de receptiebalie, met zijn witte wijzerplaat en dikke zwarte wijzers die het vertikken sneller te gaan.

Samira is ergens boven mij. Er zullen wel niet veel kelders zijn in Amsterdam, een stad die lijkt te drijven op vaste pontons die door de bruggen bijeen worden gehouden. Misschien zakt hij wel langzaam weg in de prut, als een Venetië van het Noorden.

Ik kan niet stilzitten. Ik zou bij Ruiz in het ziekenhuis moeten zijn. Ik zou in Londen aan mijn nieuwe baan moeten beginnen of ervoor moeten bedanken.

Aan de overkant van de hal glijden de dubbele deuren van een lift open. Er klinken stemmen en diep, sonoor gelach. Een van de stemmen is die van Yanus. Zijn linkeroog is gezwollen en zit gedeeltelijk dicht. Verwondingen aan het hoofd beginnen in te raken. Hij is niet geboeid en heeft geen politiebegeleiding.

De man naast hem moet zijn advocaat zijn. Hij is groot en ziet er afgetobd uit, met een breed voorhoofd en een nog breder achterwerk. Zijn gekreukte pak heeft een driedubbele split en permanente vouwen.

Yanus kijkt me aan en vertrekt zijn dunne lippen tot een glimlach.

'Dit misverstand spijt me heel erg,' zegt hij. 'Vergeten en vergeven?'

Hij biedt me zijn hand. Ik kijk uitdrukkingsloos. Links van hem, iets achter hem, verschijnt Spijker.

Yanus is nog altijd aan het woord. 'Ik hoop dat ze goed voor meneer Ruiz zorgen. Het spijt me heel erg dat ik hem heb gestoken.'

Ik heb mijn blik nog steeds op Spijker gericht. 'Wat gaan jullie doen?'

'De heer Yanus wordt op vrije voeten gesteld. Het kan zijn dat we hem later nog verhoren.'

De dikke advocaat tikt ongeduldig met zijn voet. Zijn gezicht schudt ervan. 'Samira Khan heeft bevestigd dat de heer Yanus haar verloofde is. Ze is van hem in verwachting.' Zijn Engels is overdreven gewichtig, met een vleugje neerbuigendheid. 'Ze heeft ook een verklaring afgelegd die zijn versie van het gebeurde van gisteravond bevestigt.'

'Nee!'

'Gelukkig voor u heeft de heer Yanus ermee ingestemd geen officiële aanklacht wegens mishandeling, opzettelijke verwonding en het ontvoeren van zijn verloofde te zullen indienen tegen u of uw collega. In ruil daarvoor heeft de politie besloten hem niet in staat van beschuldiging te stellen.'

'Ons onderzoek zal worden voortgezet,' werpt Spijker tegen.

'De heer Yanus heeft zijn volledige medewerking verleend,' reageert de dikke advocaat laatdunkend.

Lena Caspar is zo klein dat ik bijna niet zie dat ze achter hem staat. Ik voel hoe ik iedereen beurtelings aankijk, als een kind dat wacht op de uitleg van een volwassene. Yanus heeft zijn hand teruggetrokken. Bijna instinctief steekt hij hem in zijn jaszak, waar normaal gesproken zijn mes zou zitten.

Terwijl ik denk dat ik er wel versuft en als met stomheid geslagen uit zal zien, is het tegenovergestelde het geval. Ik zie mezelf weerspiegeld in de tientallen glaspanelen rondom me en zie dat het nieuws de manier waarop ik kijk helemaal niet heeft beïnvloed. In mijn binnenste is het een heel ander verhaal. Van alle mogelijke uitkomsten was deze niet te voorspellen.

'Laat me met Samira praten.'

'Dat gaat niet.'

Lena Caspar legt haar hand op de mijne. 'Ze wil met niemand praten.'

'Waar is ze?'

'Onder de hoede van de Immigratie en Naturalisatie Dienst.'

'Wordt ze het land uit gezet?'

De dikke advocaat is haar voor. 'Mijn cliënt is bezig met de aanvraag van een visum waarmee zijn verloofde in Nederland kan blijven.'

'Ze is zijn verloofde helemaal niet,' kaats ik terug.

De advocaat zwelt nog verder op (wat nauwelijks mogelijk lijkt). 'U hebt echt geluk, juffrouw Barba, dat mijn cliënt zo vergevingsgezind is. Als dat niet zo was, dan zouden u ernstige zaken ten laste worden gelegd. De heer Yanus eist dat u hem nu met rust laat, en zijn verloofde eveneens. Elke poging van uw kant om een van hen te benaderen zal zeer hoog worden opgenomen.'

Yanus lijkt zich bijna te generen voor zijn eigen grootmoedigheid. Zijn hele persoonlijkheid is milder geworden. De kille, onverhulde, onwankelbare haat van gisteravond is verdwenen. Het is alsof ik naar een gladde zee kijk nadat de storm is geluwd. Hij steekt opnieuw zijn hand uit. Dit keer ligt er iets in: mijn mobiele telefoon en mijn paspoort. Hij geeft ze me en draait zich om. Hij en de dikke advocaat gaan weg.

Ik kijk Spijker aan. 'U weet dat hij liegt.'

'Dat maakt niets uit,' antwoordt hij.

Mevrouw Caspar vraagt me te gaan zitten.

'Er moet toch iets zijn,' zeg ik op smekende toon.

'Je zult het moeten begrijpen. Zonder Samira's getuigenverklaring is er helemaal geen zaak, geen bewijs van gedwongen zwangerschappen of een zwarte markt voor embryo's en ongeboren baby's. Een DNA-test of vaderschapstest zou het bewijs kunnen leveren, maar die kunnen niet plaatsvinden zonder Samira's toestemming en een chirurgische ingreep die de tweeling in gevaar kan brengen.'

'Zala zal mijn verhaal bevestigen.'

'Waar is ze?'

De toegangsdeuren glijden open. De dikke advocaat gaat als

221

eerste. Yanus haalt een lichtblauwe zakdoek uit zijn zak en veegt zijn voorhoofd af. Ik herken het weefsel. Hij laat het achter elkaar door zijn vingers gaan. Het is geen zakdoek. Het is een hoofddoek. Zala's hijab.

Spijker ziet me bewegen en houdt me tegen. Ik verzet me tegen zijn greep en roep beschuldigingen door de deuropening. Yanus draait zich om en glimlacht, waarbij hij een paar tanden ontbloot. De glimlach van een haai.

'Kijk, in zijn hand, de sjaal,' schreeuw ik. 'Dat is de reden waarom ze loog.'

Mevrouw Caspar gaat voor me staan. 'Het is te laat, Alisha.'

Spijker laat langzaam mijn armen los en ik ruk me los uit zijn vingers. Hij geneert zich dat hij me heeft aangeraakt. Er is nog iets anders in zijn houding: begrip. Hij gelóóft me! Hij had geen andere keus dan Yanus op vrije voeten stellen.

Frustratie, teleurstelling en woede wellen in me op, totdat ik het wil uitschreeuwen. Ze hebben Zala. Samira zal de volgende zijn. Met alle kneuzingen en bloedvergieten heb ik ze niet eens kunnen afremmen. Ik ben als Wile E. Coyote, platgedrukt onder een steen, die het satanische, triomfantelijke, gekmakende 'miep, miep!' van de Road Runner hoort.

6

Ruiz' huid is vaalgrijs en zijn ogen zijn bloeddoorlopen van de morfine. De jaren hebben hem in zijn slaap overvallen en al zijn zestig verjaardagen zijn hem aan te zien.

'Ik wist dat je het zou redden,' zeg ik. 'Jouw huid is taaier dan die van een neushoorn.'

'Wil je zeggen dat ik een dikke kont heb in deze pyjama?'

'Nee, in déze niet.'

De gordijnen zijn open en wat er nog over is van de dag verzamelt zich aan de einder.

Het kan aan de morfine liggen of aan zijn belachelijke mannelijke trots, maar de inspecteur blijft opscheppen over het aantal hechtingen dat hij in zijn borst en arm nodig had. Straks gaan we nog littekens zitten vergelijken. Ik heb dat niet nodig – de mijne zijn groter dan die van hem.

Waarom wordt het bij mannen altijd een wedstrijd? Is hun ego zo broos of zijn hun hormonen zo krachtig dat ze zichzelf moeten bewijzen? Wat een armoedzaaiers!

Ik geef hem een dikke, natte kus op zijn wang. Hij is sprakeloos.

'Ik heb iets voor u meegebracht, meneer.'

Hij zendt me een snelle blik toe, niet zeker of hij me kan vertrouwen. Ik haal een fles whisky uit een papieren zak. Het is een heimelijk grapje. Toen ik in het ziekenhuis lag met een kapotte ruggengraat nam Ruiz een fles voor me mee. Het is nog altijd de enige keer dat ik alcohol heb gedronken. Een eenmalig drankje, naar binnen geslurpt door een maf rietje, dat mijn ogen deed tranen en mijn keel branden. Wat zien mensen toch in alcohol?

Ik verbreek de sluiting en schenk hem in, met een beetje water erbij.

'Neem jij niet?'

'Nee, niet nu. Je mag de mijne opdrinken.'

'Dat is heel genereus van je.'

Er komt een verpleegster binnen. Hij stopt het glas weg. Ik verstop de fles. Ze geeft hem een plastic bekertje met twee pillen. Omdat we gestopt zijn met praten en schuldig kijken blijft ze bij de deur stilstaan. Ze zegt iets in het Nederlands. Een heilwens misschien, maar ik heb mijn twijfels.

'Ik denk dat ik hier maar blijf,' zegt Ruiz. 'Het eten is hier een stuk beter dan wat je in Engeland krijgt en de verpleegsters zijn best charmant. Ze doen me denken aan de vrouwelijke huismeesters op kostschool.'

'Dat lijkt verontrustend veel op een seksuele fantasie.'

Hij grijnst half. 'Niet helemaal.'

Hij neemt nog een nipje. 'Heb jij weleens gedacht over wat je zou willen dat er gebeurt als je doodgaat? De afspraken.'

'Ik heb een testament.'

'Oké, maar heb je iets op schrift staan voor de begrafenis? Cremeren of begraven of je as uit laten strooien vanaf het eind van de pier in Margate?'

'Niet specifiek, nee.' Dit begint nogal morbide te worden.

'Ik wil dat ze mijn as in een raket stoppen.'

'Maar natuurlijk, ik bel wel even met de NASA.'

'In een vuurpijl, bedoel ik. Ik wil uiteengeblazen worden in duizend vallende sterren. Dat kan tegenwoordig, as in vuurwerk stoppen. Dat heb ik ergens gelezen.'

'Weggaan met een knal.'

'In een glorieuze gloed.'

Hij glimlacht en houdt zijn glas op voor meer. 'Nog niet, uiteraard.'

'Uiteraard.'

De waarheid is dat ik er wel aan heb gedacht, aan doodgaan. Gedurende mijn zwarte herfst en winter, de maanden van operaties en fysiotherapie, waarin ik mezelf niet kon wassen, voeden of verzorgen, was een klein, geheim, kinderlijk deel van me bang dat ik nooit meer zou kunnen lopen. En een stilzwijgend, schuldbeladen, volwassen deel van me besloot dat ik dan liever zou sterven.

Iedereen vindt me zo sterk. Ze verwachten dat ik herfsten en winters zoals die van toen in de ogen kijk en vervolgens neersla, ze op de vlucht jaag. Maar zo sterk ben ik niet. Ik doe maar alsof.

'Ik ben gisteren gebeld door Miranda,' zegt hij. 'Ik weet nog steeds niet hoe ze aan het nummer was gekomen of wist dat ik in het ziekenhuis lag. Voorzover ik weet was ik gisteren het grootste deel van de dag buiten bewustzijn.' Zijn ogen vernauwen zich.

'Probeer wat minder schaapachtig te kijken, lammetje-lief.'

'Ik zei je toch dat ze nog steeds om je geeft.'

'Maar liever niet met me lééft.'

'Dat is omdat je een brompot bent.'

'En jij bent expert in dit soort zaken, zeker?'

'Nou, Groentje Dave heeft me anders wel ten huwelijk gevraagd.' Het floept eruit, niet gepland, spontaan.

Ruiz denkt even na. 'Ik had niet gedacht dat hij dat zou durven.'

'Denk je dat hij bang voor me is?'

'Elke man met enig benul zou een beetje bang voor jou moeten zijn.'

'Hoezo?'

'Ik bedoel dat op de aardigst mogelijke manier.' Zijn ogen dansen.

'Je hebt gezegd dat ik te scherp voor hem was.'

'En jij zei dat een man die jouw broek past niet in je broek mocht zitten.'

'Hij houdt van me.'

'Dat is een goed begin. En jij?'

Ik kan geen antwoord geven. Ik weet het niet.

Het is raar over liefde te praten. Ik had altijd een hekel aan het woord. Haat is te sterk. Ik was het zat er in boeken over te lezen, het in liedjes te horen, het in films te zien. Het leek me dat je een enorme last op iemand anders legt door hem lief te hebben, hem zoiets ontzettend breekbaars te schenken en te verwachten dat hij het niet stukmaakt, kwijtraakt of in bus 96 laat liggen.

Ik dacht dat ik een keuze had: verliefd worden, niet verliefd worden. Hij houdt van me, hij houdt niet van me. Zie je wel? Ik ben echt niet zo slim!

Mijn gedachten dwalen af naar Samira. Ik weet niet wat ik moet doen. Mijn ideeën zijn uitgeput. Tot nu toe ben ik ervan overtuigd geweest dat ik Cates baby's zou vinden, en dan – ja, wat dan? Wat stelde ik me voor dat er zou gebeuren? Cate overtrad de wet. Ze huurde een baarmoeder. Misschien realiseerde ze zich niet dat Samira gedwongen zou worden mee te werken. Van díe twijfel gun ik haar het voordeel.

Cate liep altijd vlak langs de rand. Dichter bij de dood, dichter bij het leven. Ze was een beetje gek. Niet voortdurend, maar af en toe. Zoals wanneer de wind vlak voor een storm plotseling anders wordt en kinderen op hol slaan en in kringetjes rond gaan lopen als opdwarrelende snippers papier. Cate kreeg dan zo'n zelfde gloed in haar ogen en dreef af naar de verkeerde kant van de scheidslijn.

Ze is meer herinnering dan realiteit. Ze hoort bij een tijd van tienerverliefdheden, eerste zoenen, volle collegezalen en rokerige pubs. Zelfs als ze nog had geleefd hadden we misschien niets anders gemeen gehad dan het verleden.

Ik zou het los moeten laten. Als Ruiz voldoende hersteld is, gaan we terug. Dan slik ik mijn trots in en neem ik elk baantje aan dat me wordt aangeboden, of ik trouw met Dave en ga met hem in Milford-on-Sea wonen. Ik had niet naar Amsterdam moeten komen. Hoe heb ik ooit kunnen denken dat ik iets kon uitrichten? Ik kan Cate niet terughalen. En toch, ondanks dit alles, laat één fundamentele vraag me maar niet los: wat gaat er met de baby's gebeuren?

Yanus en zijn trawanten zullen ze aan de hoogste bieder verkopen. Of dat, of ze zullen in Nederland ter wereld komen en ter adoptie worden aangeboden. Of, nog erger: teruggestuurd worden naar Afghanistan met Samira, die zal worden uitgestoten en als paria behandeld. In sommige delen van Afghanistan worden vrouwen die buitenechtelijke kinderen hebben gestenigd.

Cate loog en bedroog. Ze overtrad de wet. Ik weet nog altijd niet waarom Brendan Pearl haar heeft vermoord, al vermoed ik dat het was om haar het zwijgen op te leggen. Ze wendde zich tot mij. Dat zal me wel medeverantwoordelijk maken.

Ben ik aan nog iets schuldig? Is er iets anders dat ik had moeten doen? Moet ik Felix' familie vertellen dat hun zoon over een paar weken vader zou zijn geworden? Barnaby en mevrouw Elliot zijn de pseudo-grootouders van een surrogaattweeling.

Ik had nooit gedacht dat ik nog eens medelijden zou hebben met Barnaby – niet na wat er gebeurd was. Op de dag dat hij mij bij het station in Cornwall afzette dacht ik zijn ware aard te zien. Hij kon me niet eens aankijken of gedag zeggen.

Ik weet nog steeds niet of hij het zijn vrouw heeft verteld. Ik betwijfel het. Barnaby is het type dat ontkent, ontkent en ontkent, totdat hij met onweerlegbaar bewijs wordt geconfronteerd. Dan zal hij zijn schouders ophalen, zijn excuses aanbieden en de tragische held uithangen, onderuitgegaan door een overmaat aan liefde in plaats van een tekort.

Toen ik hem de eerste keer zag in het ziekenhuis, toen Cate in coma lag, viel me op dat hij nog altijd campagne voerde, nog steeds stemmen probeerde te winnen. Hij probeerde de hele tijd in de glazen deuren een glimp van zijn spiegelbeeld op te vangen, om zeker te kunnen zijn dat hij het goed deed, het rouwen. Misschien is dat niet eerlijk: een man schoppen die onderuit is gegaan.

Ruiz slaapt. Ik pak het glas van hem af, spoel het om in de wasbak en stop de fles in mijn tas.

Ik ben nog steeds niet dichter bij een besluit. Het is alsof ik een wedstrijd loop waarin ik niet weet hoeveel ronden er nog te gaan zijn of wie voorop ligt en wie gedubbeld is. Hoe weet ik wanneer ik moet aanzetten voor de laatste bocht en aan mijn eindsprint moet beginnen?

Een taxi zet me af bij mijn hotel. De bestuurder luistert naar een voetbalwedstrijd die op de radio wordt uitgezonden. De commentator heeft een tenorstem die meegolft met het eb en vloed van de actie op het veld. Ik heb geen idee wie er speelt, maar het donderende geluid van het publiek bevalt me. Het maakt dat ik me minder somber voel.

Er steekt een witte envelop uit mijn postvakje bij de receptie. Ik maak hem direct open.

Drie woorden: 'Hallo lief meisje.'

De receptioniste maakt een oogbeweging. Ik draai me om. Groentje Dave staat achter me.

Hij slaat zijn armen om me heen en ik begraaf mijn gezicht in zijn shirt. Ik blijf zo staan. Ik hou hem stijf vast, want ik wil niet dat hij mijn tranen ziet.

7

Het ene moment slaap ik, het volgende ben ik wakker. Ik kijk op de wekker. Vier uur 's nachts. Dave ligt naast me op zijn zij met zijn wang plat tegen het laken gedrukt. Zijn lippen trillen zachtjes.

Gisteravond hebben we niet gepraat. Uitputting en een warme

douche en de aanraking van zijn handen deden me in slaap vallen. Als hij wakker is, zal ik het goedmaken. Ik weet dat het niet best is voor het ego van een man als een vrouw zomaar naast hem in slaap valt.

Op één elleboog liggend bekijk ik hem. Zijn haar is zacht en gekreukeld als dat van een rode cyperse kater, met kleine plukjes blond erdoorheen. Hij heeft een groot hoofd. Wil dat zeggen dat hij grote baby's zou verwekken, met een groot hoofd? Onwillekeurig knijp ik mijn dijen samen.

Dave krabt aan zijn oor. Hij heeft leuke oren. Op het oor dat ik kan zien is iets zichtbaar dat erop zou kunnen wijzen dat er ooit een gaatje in heeft gezeten. Zijn hand ligt naar mij toe uitgestrekt op het laken. De nagels zijn breed en plat, recht afgeknipt. Ik laat mijn vingers langs de zijne gaan, ongemakkelijk dat ik me zo gelukkig voel.

Gisteren was misschien wel de rotste dag van mijn leven. En toen ik hem gisteravond vasthield voelde het alsof ik me aan drijfhout vastklampte. Hij maakte dat ik me veilig voelde. Hij sloeg zijn armen om me heen en de pijn sijpelde weg.

Misschien voel ik me daarom zoals nu, lig ik zo stil: omdat ik niet wil dat dit moment voorbijgaat.

Ik heb geen ervaring met de liefde. Sinds mijn puberteit heb ik de liefde gemeden, afgewezen, ernaar verlangd. (Die tegenstrijdigheid is een van de symptomen.) Ik ben de wijze vrouw geweest voor al mijn vriendinnen, luisterend naar hun huilverhalen over gearrangeerde huwelijken, ontrouwe echtgenoten, mannen die niet bellen of zich niet willen binden, over tijd zijn, seksuele neuroses, trouwplannen, postnatale depressie en mislukte afslankpogingen. Ik weet alles over de liefdesaffaires van anderen, maar ben een volslagen nieuweling als het om mezelf gaat. Daarom ben ik bang. Ik ga het vast verpesten.

Dave raakt de bloeduitstorting op mijn wang aan. Ik schrik. 'Wie heeft dat gedaan?'

'Hij heet Yanus.'

Ik kan bijna zien hoe hij deze informatie opslaat voor later gebruik. Ruiz en hij lijken wat dat betreft op elkaar. Bij hen gebeurt niets halfslachtig of onbekookt. Zij zijn in staat hun kans op wraak af te wachten.

'Je hebt geluk dat hij je jukbeen niet heeft verbrijzeld.'

'Hij had nog veel meer schade kunnen aanrichten.'

Ik doe een stapje naar voren en kus hem op zijn lippen, snel, impulsief. Dan draai ik me om en ga douchen. Als ik me weer omdraai om iets te zeggen, zie ik hem een triomfantelijk vuistgebaar maken in de lucht.

Hij bloost.

'Zo'n bijzondere kus was het nou ook weer niet.'

'Voor mij wel.'

Even later zit hij op bed te kijken hoe ik me aankleed, wat me een ongemakkelijk gevoel geeft. Ik hou mijn rug naar hem toe gekeerd. Hij buigt zich opzij en omvat mijn borsten voordat mijn beha ze omsluit.

'Ik bied me aan als vrijwilliger,' zegt hij.

'Dat is heel edelmoedig van je, maar jij gaat echt niet de hele dag mijn borsten vasthouden.'

Ik duw zachtjes zijn handen opzij en ga verder.

'Je vindt mij echt aardig, hè?' zegt hij. Zijn brede, gekke grijns weerspiegelt zich in de kleerkastspiegel.

'Niet te ver gaan, jij,' waarschuw ik hem.

'Maar het is zo. Je vindt me écht aardig.'

'Dat zou kunnen veranderen.'

Zijn lach is niet geheel overtuigend.

We ontbijten in een café in de Paleisstraat, vlak bij de Dam. Blauwwitte trams ratelen en sissen onder zoemende bovenleidingen langs het raam. Een mager zonnetje weet amper door de wolken heen te breken en een bries rukt aan de kleding van voetgangers en fietsers.

Het café heeft een met zink beklede toog die één hele kant van de zaak bestrijkt. Boven de toog hangt een schoolbord met het menu en liggen vaten wijn of port. De zaak ruikt naar koffie en gebakken kaas. Mijn smaak komt weer terug. We bestellen vleeswaren, brood en kaas en koffie met geklopte melk.

Ik praat Dave bij over de gebeurtenissen. Af en toe onderbreekt hij me met een vraag, maar voor het merendeel eet en luistert hij. De hele zaak is doorregen met halve waarheden en in elkaar gedraaide verzinsels. De onzekerheden en dubbelzinnigheden lijken talrijker dan de feiten, en ze knagen aan me, maken me onrustig en onbehaaglijk.

Ik leen zijn schrijfblok en begin namen te noteren:

Brendan Pearl
Yanus
Paul Donavon
Julian Shawcroft

Daarnaast schrijf ik een tweede rij namen; de slachtoffers:

Cate en Felix Beaumont
Hasan Khan
Samira Khan

Er zijn er waarschijnlijk meer. Waar zet ik de mensen die ertussenin vallen, zoals Barnaby Elliot? Ik denk nog steeds dat hij tegen me gelogen heeft over Cates computer. En dokter Banerjee, haar fertiliteitsspecialist. Het was wel erg toevallig dat hij opdook op mijn vaders verjaardagsfeestje.

Ik ben er niet zeker van wat ik wil bereiken door dingen op te schrijven. Misschien geeft het me een frisse blik op de zaak of brengt het een nieuw verband naar boven. Ik ben op zoek naar een centrale figuur achter de gebeurtenissen, maar misschien is dat iets te simpel gedacht. Mensen zouden ook stuk voor stuk verbonden kunnen zijn als de spaken van een wiel, die alleen in het midden samenkomen.

Er is nog iets: waar moest de overdracht van de baby plaatsvinden? Misschien was Cate van plan een vakantie of een lang weekend in Nederland door te brengen. Ze zou 'weeën' krijgen, iedereen vertellen dat ze was bevallen en de baby mee naar huis nemen en daar nog lang en gelukkig leven.

Maar ook een pasgeboren baby heeft reisdocumenten nodig. Een paspoort. Dat betekent een geboorteakte, officiële verklaringen en van een handtekening voorziene foto's. Ik zou het Britse consulaat in Den Haag moeten bellen en vragen hoe Britse staatsburgers in het buitenland geboorteaangifte doen.

In een geval als dit zou het veel makkelijker zijn als de baby in hetzelfde land werd geboren als de aanstaande ouders. Het zou een thuisbevalling kunnen zijn, of een in een andere privé-woning, zonder dat er een kliniek of zelfs maar een vroedvrouw bij betrokken is.

Als de genetische ouders het pasgeboren kind eenmaal in handen hadden, zou niemand ooit kunnen bewijzen dat het hun niet toebehoorde. Bloedmonsters, DNA- en vaderschapstests zouden stuk voor stuk hun rechten onderschrijven.

Samira zei dat Hasan haar vooruit zou gaan naar het Verenigd Koninkrijk. Ze ging ervan uit dat ze hem zou volgen. Wat als ze van plan zijn haar daarheen te brengen? Het zou ook verklaren waarom Cate Samira mijn naam gaf voor het geval er iets mis zou gaan.

'Gisteravond zei je dat je het opgaf en naar huis ging,' zegt Dave.

'Ik weet het. Ik dacht alleen…'

'Je zei zelf dat de baby's aan Samira toebehoren. Dat is nooit anders geweest.'

'Iemand heeft mijn vriendin vermoord.'

'Dat kun jij niet ongedaan maken.'

'Ze hebben haar huis in de fik gestoken.'

'Het is jouw zaak niet.'

Ik voel een golf van boosheid. Verwacht hij echt van me dat ik dit aan Softell en zijn debiele kompanen overlaat? En Spijker boezemt me niet echt veel vertrouwen meer in nu hij Yanus heeft laten lopen.

'Gisteravond huilde je tranen met tuiten. Je zei dat het voorbij was.'

'Gisteravond, ja.' Ik kan de woede in mijn stem niet verbergen.

'Wat is er nu anders?'

'Mijn gedachten. Dat is een vrouwelijk voorrecht.' Ik wil zeggen: 'Wees toch niet zo'n enorme eikel, Dave, en hou op me na te bouwen.' Wat is dat toch met mannen? Net als je denkt dat het rationele vertegenwoordigers van het menselijk ras zijn, worden ze enorme neanderthalers en gaan ze je beschermen. Straks vraagt hij me nog hoeveel partners ik heb gehad en hoe de seks was.

Andere gasten beginnen onze kant op te kijken. 'Ik geloof niet dat we dit hier moeten bespreken,' fluistert hij.

'We gaan dit helemáál niet bespreken.' Ik maak aanstalten om te gaan.

'Waar ga je heen?'

Ik wil hem zeggen dat het hem geen moer aangaat. In plaats daarvan zeg ik dat ik een afspraak heb met Samira's advocaat, wat niet helemaal waar is.

'Ik ga met je mee.'

'Nee. Jij gaat bij Ruiz langs. Dat zal hij op prijs stellen.' Mijn stem wordt zachter. 'We zien elkaar later.'

Hij kijkt bedrukt, maar protesteert niet. Dat moet je hem nageven: hij leert snel.

De wachtkamer van Lena Caspar wordt gestofzuigd en aan kant gemaakt. Op een tafel liggen keurige stapels tijdschriften en het speelgoed is in een glimmende houten kist gestopt. Haar bureau is al net zo opgeruimd en leeg, op een doos tissues en een dienblad met een karaf water na. Zelfs de prullenbak is schoon.

De advocate draagt een knielange rok en een bijpassend jasje. Zoals veel vrouwen van haar leeftijd is ze perfect opgemaakt.

'Ik kan je niet vertellen waar ze is,' begint ze.

'Dat weet ik. Maar u kunt me wel vertellen wat er gisteren gebeurd is.'

Ze wijst naar een stoel. 'Wat wil je weten?'

'Alles.'

Ze legt haar handpalmen plat op het bureau. 'Ik wist dat er iets scheef zat toen ik de tolk zag. Samira's Engels is voortreffelijk, en toch deed ze alsof ze niet begreep wat ik tegen haar zei. Alles moest heen en weer worden vertaald. Samira liet niets los waar niet om werd gevraagd.'

'Is Yanus alleen met haar geweest.'

'Natuurlijk niet.'

'Heeft ze hem gezien?'

'Yanus nam deel aan een keuzeconfrontatie. Ze heeft hem van achter een confrontatiespiegel aangewezen.'

'Hij kon Samira niet zien?'

'Nee.'

'Had Yanus iets in zijn handen?'

Ze zucht, geïrriteerd door mijn wijsneuzigheid.

Ik dring aan: 'Had hij iets in zijn handen?'

Ze staat op het punt nee te zeggen, maar herinnert zich iets. 'Hij had een blauwe zakdoek en liet hem als een goochelaar in zijn vuist verdwijnen.'

Hoe had hij Zala weten te vinden? Behalve de nonnen wist niemand dat ze in het klooster was. Zuster Vogel zou haar niet hebben verraden. De Wallen vormen een klein gebied. Hoe had de advocate het ook alweer gezegd? 'Langs de muren zitten muizen en die muizen hebben oren.'

Mevrouw Caspar luistert geduldig terwijl ik uitleg wat er volgens mij is gebeurd. Zala is haar zorg niet. Ze heeft vierhonderd asielzoekers onder haar hoede.

'Wat gaat er nu met Samira gebeuren?' vraag ik.

'Ze zal worden teruggestuurd naar Afghanistan, wat denk ik een betere optie is dan een huwelijk met Yanus.'

'Hij zal niet met haar trouwen.'

'Nee.'

'Hij zal haar opsporen en haar baby's afpakken.'

Ze haalt haar schouders op. Hoe kan ze een dergelijke afloop zo monter accepteren? Op de vensterbank leunend kijkt ze omlaag naar de binnenplaats, waar aan de voet van een eenzame boom duiven zitten te pikken.

'Sommige mensen zijn geboren om te lijden,' zegt ze peinzend. 'Voor hen houdt het nooit op, geen seconde. Kijk maar naar de Palestijnen. Hetzelfde geldt voor Afghanen, Sudanezen, Ethiopiërs en Bangladeshi's. Oorlog, hongersnood, droogte, overstromingen – het lijden stopt nooit. Ze zijn ervoor gemaakt, ontlenen er hun bestaansrecht aan.

Wij in het Westen denken graag dat het anders kan, dat we die landen en die mensen kunnen veranderen, alleen omdat we ons dan beter voelen als we onze kinderen met gevulde magen in hun warme bedjes instoppen en onszelf vervolgens een glas wijn inschenken en toezien hoe op CNN andermans tragedie zich ontrolt.' Ze kijkt naar haar handen alsof ze er een afkeer van heeft. 'Tenzij we echt begrijpen hoe het is om in hun schoenen te staan, zouden we niet over mensen als Samira moeten oordelen. Zij doet haar best datgene te redden wat ze nog heeft.'

Er trilt nog iets door in haar stem: berusting. Acceptatie. Waarom is ze zo bereid het op te geven? In die fractie van een seconde besef ik dat ze iets voor me verzwijgt. Of ze kan zich er niet toe zetten het te zeggen, of Spijker heeft haar gewaarschuwd. Haar aangeboren gevoel voor eerlijkheid en rechtvaardigheid staat haar niet toe rechtstreeks tegen me te liegen.

'Wat is er met Samira gebeurd?'

'Ze is vannacht verdwenen uit het asielzoekerscentrum op de luchthaven Schiphol.'

8

Er is een wetenschappelijke theorie die bekendstaat als het 'onzekerheidsprincipe' en die stelt dat het onmogelijk is om iets echt te observeren zonder het te veranderen. Ik heb meer gedaan dan observeren. Door Samira op te sporen heb ik de loop der dingen veranderd.

Tijdens de taxirit naar het hoofdbureau van politie zijn mijn vuisten gebald en drukken mijn vingernagels zich in het zachte vlees. Ik wil het uitschreeuwen. Ik heb Spijker gewaarschuwd dat dit zou gebeuren. Ik zei dat Samira zou weglopen of dat Yanus haar zou vinden.

Ik ga ervan uit dat hij me niet zal willen ontvangen. Hij zal zich verschuilen achter werkdruk of de smoes dat ik al genoeg van zijn tijd heb verspild. Andermaal zit ik in de hal te wachten. Dit keer word ik direct ontboden. Misschien heeft hij dan toch een geweten.

De gangen zijn gestoffeerd met lichtgrijze vloerbedekking en staan vol met palmen. Het doet eerder aan een handelsbank denken dan aan een politiebureau.

Spijker heeft geen jasje aan. Zijn mouwen zijn opgerold. Het haar op zijn onderarmen heeft dezelfde kleur als zijn sproeten. De deur gaat dicht. Zijn jasje bungelt aan een hangertje aan de achterkant.

'Hoe lang ben je van plan in Amsterdam te blijven?' vraagt hij.

'Hoezo, meneer?'

'Je bent al langer gebleven dan gebruikelijk. De meeste bezoekers blijven maar een dag of twee.'

'Wilt u zeggen dat ik moet gaan?'

'Daar heb ik de bevoegdheid niet toe.' Hij draait rond op zijn stoel en staart uit het raam. Zijn werkkamer kijkt uit op het oosten, over het uitgaanscentrum tot aan de neogotische torens van het Rijksmuseum. Op de vensterbank staan rijtjes kleine cactussen in beschilderde aardewerken potjes. Dit is zijn tuin: vlezig, bolvormig en stekelig. Hij is op zijn planten gaan lijken.

Tijdens mijn taxirit had ik mijn verhaal voorbereid, waarin ik mijn gal spuwde en waarmee ik de taxichauffeur, die me in zijn achteruitkijkspiegel bekeek, een paar angstige momenten bezorgde. Nu lijken al mijn beste formuleringen zinloos en verspilde moeite. Ik wacht tot de rechercheur het woord neemt.

'Ik weet wat jij denkt, agent Barba. Jij denkt dat ik in deze zaak de bal heb laten vallen. Dat is een rugbyterm, toch? Een Brits spelletje, geen Nederlands. In Nederland pakken we de bal niet op. Alleen een doelman mag dat.'

'Had u haar niet moeten beschermen?'

'Ze heeft er zelf voor gekozen weg te lopen.'

'Ze is acht maanden zwanger en achttien jaar oud. U was niet in staat haar vierentwintig uur vast te houden.'

'Had ik haar handboeien om moeten doen soms?'

235

'U had haar tegen kunnen houden.'

'Ik probeer dit onderzoek buiten de schijnwerpers te houden. Ik wil niet dat de media er lucht van krijgen. Op de zwarte markt aangeboden baby's zorgen voor dramatische koppen.'

'Het was dus een politieke beslissing?'

'Binnen de Nederlandse politie speelt politiek geen rol.'

'Nee?'

'Niemand heeft het over politiek gehad.'

Ondanks zijn omlaagwijzende mondhoeken en droeve ogen komt Spijker over als een optimist, als een man die vertrouwen heeft in de mensheid.

'Ik heb er twintig dienstjaren op zitten. Ik weet hoe ik een zaak hard moet maken. Ik ben als het varkentje dat zijn huis van bakstenen bouwt. Jij bent het varkentje dat haar huis van stro bouwt. Weet je nog wat er met zo'n huis gebeurt?' Hij bolt zijn wangen en blaast. Er dwarrelt sigarettenas van zijn bureau in mijn schoot.

Sportmetaforen en sprookjesmetaforen – wat komt er nog meer? Hij doet de bovenste la van zijn bureau open en pakt er een map uit.

'Er is een fertiliteitskliniek in Amersfoort. Ze hebben een zeer goede reputatie en hebben duizenden echtparen geholpen een gezin te starten. Incidenteel, in gevallen waarin IVF geen resultaat had, is de kliniek ermee akkoord gegaan embryo's te plaatsen in de baarmoeder van een surrogaatmoeder. Dit wordt hoogtechnologisch draagmoederschap genoemd. In 2002 vonden slechts vier van dergelijke procedures plaats, op vijftienhonderd reguliere IVF-terugplaatsingen. In 2003 en 2004 waren het er in totaal twee.' Hij kijkt even naar de map. 'Het afgelopen jaar waren het er tweeëntwintig.'

'Tweeëntwintig! Dat is een toename van meer dan duizend procent.'

'Hoogtechnologisch draagmoederschap is in Nederland wettelijk toegestaan. Commercieel draagmoederschap niet. Evenmin als afpersing en slavernij.

Directie en staf van de kliniek houden vol dat ze zich er niet van bewust waren dat ze iets verkeerds deden. Volgens hen waren de surrogaatmoeders op de juiste wijze gescreend. Ze waren lichamelijk, financieel en psychologisch onderzocht.

Op 26 januari van dit jaar onderging Samira Khan een dergelijke reeks onderzoeken. Haar werden vragen gesteld over haar menstruatiecyclus en ze kreeg pillen en injecties – oestrogeen en progesteron – om haar baarmoeder gereed te maken voor de inplanting.

Op 10 maart kwam ze opnieuw naar de kliniek. Het terugplaatsen van de embryo's nam minder dan een kwartier in beslag. Via haar vagina werd een zacht buisje ingebracht op een vooraf bepaalde plek. Vervolgens werd een dunne binnenkatheter gevuld met twee embryo's, die in de uterus werden geïnjecteerd. Men vertelde Samira Khan dat ze een halfuur stil moest liggen, waarna ze kon gaan. Ze werd in een rolstoel naar de parkeerplaats gebracht en reed in de auto van Yanus weg. Twee weken later kwam de bevestiging dat ze zwanger was. Een tweeling.'

Uiteindelijk kijkt hij me weer aan. 'Maar dit weet je allemaal al.'

Er zitten nog meer documenten in de map.

'Hebt u de namen van de beoogde ouders?'

'Er is een juridische overeenkomst vereist tussen de echtparen en de surrogaatmoeders. De kliniek stelt die contracten niet zelf op, maar vraagt wel een schriftelijke verklaring van een jurist dat een dergelijk contract er is.'

'Hebt u de contracten gezien?'

'Ja.'

Een moment lang denk ik dat hij gaat zitten wachten tot ik het vraag, maar hij is geen wrede man.

'Het contract is getekend door Samira Khan en mede ondertekend door Cate Beaumont. Is dat wat je wilde weten?'

'Ja.'

Hij legt de map weer in de la en staat op uit zijn stoel, terwijl hij het uitzicht met een mengeling van trots en beschermingsdrang in zich opneemt.

'Van de tweeëntwintig procedures mondden er achttien uit in een zwangerschap. Een van de mislukkingen betrof een vrouw die

237

Zala Haseeb heette. Artsen stelden vast dat ze niet in staat was zwanger te worden als gevolg van een eerdere beschadiging aan haar voortplantingsorganen ten gevolge van met een stomp voorwerp toegebracht trauma.'

'Ze is gemarteld door de taliban.'

Hij reageert niet, maar ik weet dat hij me gehoord heeft. Lange tijd staart hij uit het raam, luisterend naar hoe de herfstwind tegen het glas drukt. Met een bedroefd gezicht draait hij zich om en kijkt me aan.

'Twaalf van de surrogaatmoeders zijn voorbij het einde van hun zwangerschap, maar we hebben nog geen bevestiging van de geboorten. Normaliter volgt de kliniek elk stadium van de zwangerschap en houdt men voor statistische doeleinden alle resultaten bij. In dit geval is men de vrouwen echter uit het oog verloren.'

'Uit het oog verloren?'

'We zijn bezig ze op te sporen. De kliniek heeft ons hun namen gegeven, maar de opgegeven adressen lijken niet te kloppen.'

'Ik denk dat u in Nederland geen spoor van de geboorten zult vinden,' zeg ik. 'Ik denk dat de moeders over de grens, of zelfs over zee, zijn gesmokkeld naar de plek waar de wensouders wonen. Op die manier kunnen de baby's direct na hun geboorte worden overhandigd en zonder verdere vragen worden aangegeven.'

Spijker ziet de logica hiervan in. 'Wij sporen de wensouders op via financiële transacties. Er zijn betalingsafschriften en onder ede afgelegde verklaringen.'

'Wie stelde de contracten op?'

'Een advocatenkantoor hier in Amsterdam.'

'Staan ze onder verdenking?'

Spijker blijft even zwijgen. 'Je hebt de seniorpartner gisteren ontmoet. Hij treedt op namens de heer Yanus.'

Zijn starende blik verstrakt. Voor het eerst besef ik wat voor een last hij torst. Ik was op jacht naar de waarheid omtrent één enkele vrouw. Hij heeft nu een zaak die tientallen, misschien wel honderden levens raakt.

Spijker stapt weg van het raam. Na een lange stilte zegt hij: 'Heb jij kinderen?'

'Nee, meneer.'

'Ik heb er vier.'

'Zo!'

'Te veel, niet genoeg – ik kom er niet uit.' Er speelt een lachje om zijn lippen. 'Ik begrijp wat het voor mensen betekent, dat ze zo erg naar een kind kunnen verlangen dat ze er bijna alles voor over-hebben.' Hij buigt zich iets naar voren en houdt zijn hoofd scheef. 'Ken je de legende van de doos van Pandora, agent Barba?'

'Ik ken de uitdrukking.'

'De doos was niet van Pandora. Hij was gemaakt door de Griek-se god Jupiter en was volgestopt met alle ziekten, rampen, zon-den en misdaden die de mens maar zouden kunnen treffen. Een boosaardiger brouwsel dan ik me kan voorstellen. De god Jupiter schiep ook Pandora, een schitterende vrouw, onderzoekend van aard. Hij wist dat ze de verleiding van een blik in de mysterieuze doos niet zou kunnen weerstaan. Ze hoorde een deerniswekkend fluisteren van uit de doos en tilde het deksel een klein stukje op. Al het kwaad in de wereld vloog naar buiten en streek neer op de zorgelozen en onschuldigen, en veranderde hun vreugde in kre-ten van wanhoop.'

Hij strekt zijn vingers en laat zijn handpalmen zien: leeg. Dit is waar hij bang voor is. Met een onderzoek als dit loop je het risico hele families uit elkaar te rukken. Hoeveel van die baby's hebben nu een liefdevol thuis? Bedenk wat een geluk zij hebben in een wereld waarin zo veel kinderen worden misbruikt en ongewenst zijn. Het argument roept een gevoel van déjà vu op. Julian Shaw-croft hield een soortgelijk betoog toen ik hem bij het adoptiecen-trum opzocht.

Ik begrijp de bezorgdheid, maar mijn beste vriendin is ver-moord. Niets wat iemand me zal zeggen zal haar dood kunnen rechtvaardigen en hun onheilspellende waarschuwingen klinken hol als ik me Cate voor de geest haal die geknakt op het wegdek ligt.

De les is voorbij. Spijker staat nogal formeel op en begeleidt me naar beneden.

'Gisteravond heb ik contact gehad met ene hoofdinspecteur

North van Scotland Yard. Hij vertelde me dat u zonder toestemming weg bent gebleven van de London Metropolitan Police. U staan disciplinaire maatregelen te wachten wegens plichtsverzuim.'

Daar kan ik niets op zeggen.

'Ik heb ook ene inspecteur Forbes gesproken, die de dood van een aantal illegalen op een veerboot in Harwich onderzoekt. U helpt hem bij het onderzoek. En er was, meen ik, ook een brigadier Softell die u wil spreken over een verdachte brand.'

Spijker had ook 'als verdachte van' kunnen zeggen, maar is daar veel te beleefd voor.

'Deze mannen hebben me gevraagd u op de eerstvolgende vlucht naar Londen te zetten maar, zoals ik hun heb uitgelegd, daar heb ik geen bevoegdheid toe.' Met zijn duim en wijsvinger knijpt hij in de brug van zijn neus. 'Daarnaast neem ik aan dat je Amsterdam niet zult willen verlaten zonder je vriend, meneer Ruiz. Ik heb hem vanochtend gesproken. Hij is aardig aan de beterende hand.'

'Ja, meneer.'

'Hij is dol op je.'

'We kennen elkaar al heel lang.'

'Hij denkt dat je een uitstekende speurder zult worden. Hij gebruikte een uitdrukking die ik niet kende. Hij zei dat je "scherper dan een gepunte stok" was.'

Dat klinkt als de inspecteur.

'Ik begrijp waarom je hier bent en waarom je wat langer zult willen blijven, maar het is nu tijd om dit onderzoek aan mij over te laten.'

'En Samira dan?'

'Ik zal haar vinden.'

9

Meestal vallen mensen me niet op als ik hardloop. Ik sluit me van de wereld af en zweef boven de grond als een vage schim. Vandaag is het anders. Ik hoor mensen praten, ruziën en lachen. Er zijn gedempte voetstappen en dichtslaande autoportieren, het geroeze-moes van verkeer en machines. Het onbekende van de stad maakt het lastig me te oriënteren. Voor me zie ik twee identieke kerktorens. Ik sla opnieuw af en ren langs winkels met rechte puien en tralies voor de ramen of metalen rolluiken. Sommige dwarsstraten en stegen zijn alleen voor fietsers of voetgangers breed genoeg.

Als ik eenmaal het Vondelpark bereik, kan ik flink doorrennen zonder me zorgen te maken over autodeuren die opengaan of mensen die plotseling voor me staan. Het doet me denken aan rennen in Victoria Park, tussen de bomen, langs meren, over bruggen.

Regen dreigt al de hele middag, maar het lukt me om net voor de eerste druppels bij het Red Tulip Hotel terug te zijn. Ik neem een douche en trek andere kleren aan voordat ik een taxi pak naar het ziekenhuis waar Groentje Dave op me wacht.

De gangen zijn stil, regendruppels maken strepen op de ramen. Ruiz slaapt.

'Hoe gaat het met hem?'

'Hij verveelt zich kapot. Vandaag heeft hij geprobeerd een massale uitbraak uit het ziekenhuis naar het dichtstbijzijnde café te organiseren. Hij wist twee gasten over te halen om mee te doen, allebei met een beenamputatie. Hij zei dat ze toch al niet op hun benen konden staan en dat het dus niet uitmaakte.'

'Hoe ver zijn ze gekomen?'

'Tot de cadeauwinkel van het ziekenhuis. Een verpleegster kwam achter het ontsnappingsplan en waarschuwde de beveiliging.'

'Hoe reageerde de inspecteur?'

'Hij zei dat de ondergrondse hem morgen komt bevrijden.'

Dave heeft met de artsen gesproken. 'Ruiz zou binnen een paar dagen in staat moeten zijn het ziekenhuis te verlaten, maar mag een maand lang niet vliegen.'

'We kunnen de veerboot nemen,' opper ik.

Dave speelt met mijn vingers en aait met zijn duim over mijn handpalm. 'Eigenlijk hoopte ik dat je morgen met mij terug zou vliegen. Ik heb maandag een rechtszaak in de Old Bailey.'

'Ik kan de inspecteur niet achterlaten. We zijn hier samen aan begonnen.'

Hij begrijpt het. 'Hoe ga je dat doen met die baan?'

'Weet ik nog niet.'

'Je had al begonnen moeten zijn.'

'Weet ik.'

Er is nog iets wat hij wil vragen. Zijn gezichtsspieren worstelen ermee.

'Heb je al over dat andere nagedacht?' Hij bedoelt de zeilschool en het huisje aan zee. Het gevoel van verwachting en vrees vreet aan hem. Ik ben nog altijd verbaasd dat hij de moed heeft weten te verzamelen om het me te vragen. Soms is het leven net een film, met publiek dat joelt: 'Vraag het haar gewoon. Vraag het haar gewoon.'

'Ik dacht dat je altijd rechercheur had willen worden,' zeg ik.

'Toen ik zes was wilde ik brandweerman worden. Daar ben ik overheen gegroeid.'

'Ik werd verliefd op meneer Sayer, mijn pianoleraar, en wilde concertpianist worden.'

'Ik wist niet dat je pianospeelde.'

'Daar is men het ook nog steeds niet over eens.'

Hij wacht nog altijd op mijn antwoord.

'Wat is er dan gebeurd, Dave? Waarom heb je besloten te stoppen?'

Hij haalt zijn schouders op.

'Er moet iets zijn geweest.'

'Herinner jij je Jack Lonsdale nog?'

'Ik heb gehoord dat hij gewond is geraakt.'

Dave brengt zijn handen tot zwijgen door ze in zijn zakken te steken. 'We gingen achter een tip aan over iemand in de wijk White City die op borgtocht vrij was maar niet op de rechtszitting was verschenen. Een drugsdealer. Op de beste momenten is het daar al een godvergeten treurige plek, maar dit keer was het een zaterdagavond, halverwege juli. Heet. We vonden zonder moeite het huis en klopten aan. Het zou een simpele ophaalactie worden. Ik was bezig de dealer de handboeien om te doen toen zijn zoontje van vijftien de keuken uit kwam en een mes in Jonny's borst stak. Precies hier.' Hij wijst de plek aan. 'Het knaapje ging aan het mes hangen in een poging zijn ingewanden aan gort te trekken, maar ik wist hem los te wringen. Hij had ogen als schotels. Hij was verder heen dan een 747 in volle vlucht. Ik probeerde Jonny naar de auto te slepen, maar er stonden tweehonderd mensen buiten de flat, de meesten van West-Indische afkomst, die scheldwoorden riepen en met rotzooi gooiden. Ik dacht dat ons laatste uur geslagen had.'

'Waarom heb je me dit niet verteld?'

'Jij had je eigen sores.'

'Hoe is het nu met Jonny?'

'Ze hebben een stuk van zijn darm moeten weghalen en hij is met vervroegd pensioen. De dealer zit in de gevangenis in Brixton, zijn zoontje in een kindertehuis. De moeder leefde niet meer, geloof ik.'

Dave slaat zijn ogen neer, hij wil me niet aankijken. 'Ik weet dat het laf klinkt, maar ik moet er steeds aan denken dat ik daar zelf had kunnen liggen, bloedend op die smerige vloer – of erger nog: dat jij het had kunnen zijn.'

'Daarmee ben je nog geen lafaard. Het maakt je menselijk.'

'Nou ja, dat was in elk geval het moment waarop het idee opkwam om iets anders te gaan doen.'

'Misschien heb je gewoon behoefte de bakens te verzetten.'

'Misschien wel, ja.'

'Misschien wil je niet echt met me trouwen.'

'Ja, dat wil ik wel.'

'Als er geen kinderen kwamen, zou je het dan nog steeds willen?'

'Hoe bedoel je?'

'Ik vraag het je.'

'Maar jij wilt ze toch, kinderen?'

'En als ik nou geen kinderen kan krijgen?'

Hij schiet omhoog. Hij begrijpt het niet.

Ik probeer het uit te leggen. 'Soms komen er gewoon geen kinderen. Neem nou Cate. Ze kon niet zwanger worden, en daardoor raakte ze zo in de knoop dat ze een dwaasheid beging. Vind jij ook niet dat, als twee mensen van elkaar houden, dat genoeg zou moeten zijn?'

'Misschien wel, ja.'

Hij voelt nog steeds niet waar ik heen wil. Ik kan nergens anders heen dan naar de waarheid. Woorden tuimelen naar buiten en ik ben verrast hoe goed geordend ze klinken. Bijna volmaakte zinnen. Het bekken van een vrouw wordt geacht op te rekken en te kantelen als er in haar binnenste een baby groeit. Mijn bekken kan dat niet. Mijn ruggengraat wordt bijeengehouden door metalen platen en pennen. Mijn bekken kan niet buigen of draaien. Een zwangerschap zou een enorme belasting betekenen voor de tussenwervelschijven en gewrichten in mijn onderrug. Met als risico dat ik verlamd raak en mijn baby zal moeten verzorgen terwijl ik in een rolstoel zit.

Hij ziet er verslagen uit. Desolaat. Het maakt niet uit wat hij nu gaat zeggen, ik heb een glimp van zijn ziel opgevangen. Hij wil een kind grootbrengen. En voor de eerste keer in mijn leven besef ik dat ik dat ook wil. Ik wíl moeder worden.

De uren daarna passeren alle mogelijkheden de revue. Tijdens de taxirit naar het hotel, aan tafel en daarna in bed. Dave heeft het over second opinions, alternatieven en operaties. We verbruiken zo veel lucht in de kamer dat ik nauwelijks kan ademhalen. Hij heeft mijn oorspronkelijke vraag niet beantwoord. De belangrijkste vraag. Hij heeft niet gezegd of het hem uitmaakt.

Nu ik toch aan het opbiechten ben, vertel ik hem over de keer dat ik met Barnaby Elliot heb geneukt en over de breuk met Cate. Er zijn momenten dat ik hem ineen zie krimpen, maar hij moet dit horen. Ik ben niet degene die hij denkt voor zich te hebben.

Mijn moeder zegt dat de waarheid er niet toe doet als het om de liefde gaat. Een gearrangeerd huwelijk heeft alles te maken met de verzinsels die men elkaar binnen een familie vertelt. Misschien heeft ze gelijk. Misschien betekent verliefd worden wel dat je een verhaal verzint en de waarheid ervan accepteert.

10

Tegen het ochtendgloren word ik wakker met zijn hart tegen mijn rug en zijn arm om me heen. Een deel van me wil zo blijven liggen, zonder te bewegen, bijna zonder adem te halen. Een ander deel wil de hotelgang en de trap af rennen, de straat op, de stad uit, weg!

Als ik me eenmaal uit bed heb laten glijden, loop ik de badkamer in. Ik trek een spijkerbroek en bloes aan, en steek geld en mijn mobiele telefoon bij me in mijn jasje. Ik buk me om mijn veters vast te maken en neem de pijn in mijn ruggengraat, die zo langzamerhand deel van me uitmaakt, voor wat hij is.

Daglicht sijpelt over de daken en de straten beginnen tot leven te komen. Een machine met draaiende borstels lijkt de keitjes te poetsen met de regen van de afgelopen nacht. Op de Wallen zijn de meeste ramen dicht, met toegetrokken gordijnen. Alleen de wanhopigen en eenzamen zijn op dit uur op straat.

Ik vraag me af of het zo voelt om vluchteling te zijn, om ergens vreemdeling te zijn, wanhopig en hoopvol tegelijk. Wachtend op wat komen gaat. Zo heb ik nog nooit geleefd.

Hokke staat voor het koffiehuis op me te wachten. Hij heeft het gehoord van Samira. 'Van een vogel,' verklaart hij terwijl hij zijn ogen opslaat. Alsof dit een teken was fladdert er een duif neer op een tak boven ons hoofd.

Binnen in het café is de lucht rumoerig van sissend stoom en kletterende pannen. De mensen achter de toog en de serveersters begroeten Hokke met gezwaai, geroep en handen schudden. Hij laat me heel even alleen en baant zich een weg tussen de tafels door. De keukendeur staat open. Drie jonge mannen staan over aanrechten gebogen pannen te schrobben. Ze begroeten Hokke met respect. Hij woelt door hun haar en ze lachen om een grap.

Ik kijk het koffiehuis rond, dat bijna leeg is, op een tafel met hippies na, die in een geheimtaal van onder hun haar komende klik- en klakgeluiden lijken te communiceren. Een jong meisje zit in haar uppie achter een warm drankje. Ze ziet er verwaarloosd en hologig uit: het ideale type om door pooiers met warme maaltijden en beloften te worden ingepalmd.

Hokke is weer terug. Ook hij merkt het meisje op. Hij wenkt een serveerster en bestelt op rustige toon een ontbijt voor het meisje: dikke sneden toast, jam, kaas en ham. Ze neemt het argwanend aan, overtuigd dat er iets aan vast zal zitten, en begint gulzig te eten.

Hij richt zijn aandacht weer op mij.

'Ik moet Samira vinden.'

'Alweer.'

'Er moet een manier zijn. Vluchtelingen hebben hun netwerken. Dat zei u zelf. U noemde een naam: De Souza. Zou hij me kunnen helpen?'

Hokke brengt een vinger naar zijn lippen. Hij buigt zich voorover en praat uit zijn ene mondhoek als een gevangene onder het oog van een bewaker. 'Alsjeblieft, kijk goed uit wanneer je een dergelijke naam in de mond neemt.'

'Wie is hij?'

Hokke antwoordt niet direct. Hij schenkt koffie uit een pot, waarbij het metaal het glas raakt. 'In tegenstelling tot wat jij hebt gelezen wordt Nederland eerder gekenmerkt door wat verboden is dan door wat we door de vingers zien. We hebben geen sloppenwijken. Graffiti wordt onmiddellijk verwijderd. Kapotte ruiten worden gerepareerd, autowrakken weggesleept. We verwachten dat treinen en trams op tijd rijden. We staan in de rij. De mensen worden er natuurlijk niet anders van, alleen de buitenkant.'

Hij knikt in de richting van de keuken. 'Nederland telt een half miljoen illegale arbeidskrachten – Iraniërs, Sudanezen, Afghanen, Bosniërs, Kosovaren, Irakezen. Ze werken in restaurants, hotels, wasserijen en fabrieken. Zonder hen zouden er geen kranten worden bezorgd, zouden hotellakens ongewassen blijven en huizen niet worden schoongemaakt. Mensen klagen, maar we kunnen niet zonder hen.'

In zijn hand duikt een pijp op. Hij stopt hem langzaam, met zijn duim tabak in de opening duwend. Een lucifer ontbrandt en flakkert op terwijl hij inhaleert.

'Stel je voor dat er iemand was die al die arbeidskrachten in zijn macht had. Hij zou machtiger zijn dan welke vakbondsleider of politicus ook.'

'Bestaat er zo iemand?'

Nu zet hij een fluisterstem op. 'Hij heet Eduardo de Souza. In deze stad is er niemand die meer werkelijke macht heeft dan hij.

Hij beschikt over een leger aan koeriers, opruimers, chauffeurs en spionnen. Hij kan je alles bezorgen: een pistool, een vals paspoort, een kilo van de beste Afghaanse heroïne. Drugs en prostitutie maken er maar een klein deel van uit. Hij weet welke politici met welke meisjes naar bed gaan, welke illegalen op hun kinderen passen of hun huizen schoonmaken of hun tuinen doen. Dat is échte macht. Lotsbestemming.'

Hij gaat weer achteroverzitten en knippert met zijn zachtblauwe ogen door de rook heen.

'U bewondert hem.'

'Het is een heel interessante man.'

Zijn antwoord komt merkwaardig over. Het doet vermoeden dat er dingen zijn die hij me niet heeft verteld.

'Hoe lang kent u hem al?'

'Al vele jaren.'

'Is hij een vriend?'

Hokke knippert opnieuw tegen de rook. 'Vriendschap is iets wat ik naarmate ik ouder word een steeds groter raadsel vind.'

'Zal hij me helpen Samira te vinden?'

'Hij zou achter de hele zaak kunnen zitten.'

'Waarom zegt u dat?'

'Yanus heeft ooit voor hem gewerkt.'

Hij legt zijn handen op tafel en drukt zichzelf op om te gaan staan, vermoeid.

'Ik zorg dat hij bericht krijgt.'

Zijn pijp glijdt in zijn jaszak. Hij wil me niet laten betalen voor het ontbijt. De rekening is al geregeld, zegt hij met een knik naar de eigenaar.

Buiten regent het weer. De glanzende plassen zijn zwart als olie. Hokke biedt me een paraplu aan. 'Ik bel je over een uur of wat. Doe inspecteur Ruiz de groeten van me, als je wilt. Zeg hem dat oude politiemannen nooit sterven. Ze krijgen alleen een nieuwe wijk.'

Barnaby neemt snel op, alsof hij een telefoontje verwacht. En het regent waarschijnlijk ook in Londen. Ik hoor autobanden over

247

een nat wegdek slissen en regendruppels tikken op zijn paraplu. Ik vraag hem naar de begrafenissen. Er volgt een lange stilte. Ik neem de telefoon in mijn andere hand.

'Vrijdag op het West London Crematorium. Ze geven de lichamen niet eerder dan woensdag vrij.'

Er valt opnieuw een stilte. De gedachte aan Samira en de tweeling zwelt op in mijn borstkas. Juristen en medisch ethici kunnen debatteren wat ze willen over wie 'eigenaar' is van de tweeling, het feit blijft dat Cate de embryo's heeft geleverd. Barnaby zou het moeten weten.

'Ik moet je iets vertellen.'

Hij bromt een antwoord.

'Ik weet waarom Cate deed alsof ze zwanger was. Ze had een draagmoeder geregeld. Haar embryo's zijn in de baarmoeder van iemand anders geplaatst.'

Diep in zijn borstkas lijkt iets te bewegen. Een grom. 'Ik heb je gezegd dat je je buiten de zaken van mijn dochter moet houden.'

Deze reactie had ik niet verwacht. Hij zou toch nieuwsgierig moeten zijn? Wil hij niet weten wat ervan geworden is? Dan dringt tot me door dat dit alles geen nieuws voor hem is. Hij weet het al.

Hij loog over Cates computer, wat inhoudt dat hij al haar e-mails heeft gelezen. Als hij het inderdaad weet, waarom is hij dan niet naar de politie gestapt?

'Waar ben je mee bezig, Barnaby?'

'Mijn kleinkinderen te krijgen.'

Hij heeft geen idee waar hij tegenover staat. 'Luister naar me, Barnaby. Dit is niet wat jij denkt. Cate heeft de wet overtreden.'

'Gedane zaken nemen geen keer.'

'Deze mensen zijn moordenaars. Je kunt niet met hen onderhandelen. Kijk wat er met Cate is gebeurd.'

Hij luistert niet. In plaats daarvan barst hij los in een poging om dat wat volgens hem als volgende zou moeten gebeuren van logica en eerlijkheid te voorzien.

'Stop, Barnaby. Dat is gekkenwerk.'

'Cate zou het zo hebben gewild.'

'Niet waar. Het wordt je dood. Zeg me alleen waar je bent. Laten we er rustig over praten.'

'Hou jij je erbuiten. Bemoei je er niet mee.'

De verbinding valt weg. Hij zal niet nog een keer opnemen.

Voor ik Spijker kan bellen komt er een ander telefoontje binnen. De stem van inspecteur Forbes is hees van verkoudheid en het klakkende geluid in zijn keel wordt gedempt door slijm. Ik stel me voor dat een van zijn kinderen het van school heeft meegebracht en het als een plaag door het huis heeft verspreid.

'Heb je een leuke vakantie?'

'Het is geen vakantie.'

'Je weet het verschil tussen jou en mij: ik loop niet weg als het moeilijk wordt. Ik ben een professional. Ik blijf op mijn post. Ik heb vrouw en kinderen, verantwoordelijkheden...' *En losse handjes.*

Hij niest en snuit zijn neus. 'Ik wacht verdomme nog steeds op die verklaring van je.'

'Ik kom terug.'

'Wanneer?'

'Vrijdag of daaromtrent.'

'Nou, reken maar op een warm onthaal. Er heeft ene commissaris North gebeld. Hij zei dat je niet op je werk bent verschenen. Hij klonk niet vrolijk.'

'Niet belangrijk,' zeg ik in een poging van onderwerp te veranderen. Ik vraag hem naar de twee niet-ingeschreven vrachtwagens op de veerboot die Hasan en de anderen vervoerde. Hij zegt dat de ene drie maanden geleden is gestolen van een Duits goederenemplacement en daarna overgespoten en in Nederland geregistreerd. Volgens de vrachtbrief had hij installatiemateriaal geladen bij een magazijn in Amsterdam, maar het adres daarvan bleek vals. De tweede vrachtwagen werd vijf weken geleden gehuurd van een zelfstandig chauffeur. Die dacht dat hij een rit deed van Spanje naar Nederland. De namen op de huurdocumenten en bankafschriften zijn vals.

Deze zaak wemelt van de mensen die op geesten lijken die met valse papieren grenzen over zweven. Mensen als Brendan Pearl.

'Ik moet u om een gunst vragen.'

Dit lijkt hem te amuseren. 'Ik zou niet eens met je moeten práten.'

'We zitten in hetzelfde team.'

'Hekkensluiters.'

'Maar steeds beter in vorm.'

'Waar gaat het om?'

'Dat u voor mij de douane- en immigratiebestanden van de afgelopen twee jaar nagaat. Waren er onder de verstekelingen en illegalen ook zwangere vrouwen?'

'Uit mijn hoofd twee gevallen in de afgelopen drie maanden. Ze zaten achter in een container verborgen.'

'Wat is er met hen gebeurd?'

'Dat weet ik niet.'

'Kunt u daarachter komen?'

'Ja, hoor. Naast de duizend andere rotklussen die ik op mijn bordje heb liggen.'

Ik voel mijn wangen gloeien.

'Er is nog iets. Hasan Khan heeft een zus, Samira. Ze is zwanger. Ik denk dat smokkelaars gaan proberen haar het Verenigd Koninkrijk binnen te krijgen.'

'Wanneer?'

'Dat weet ik niet. Misschien kunt u de douane tippen?'

'Ik ben in dit soort zaken niet vrij om te handelen.'

'Eén telefoontje maar. Als u het niet wilt, zeg het dan gewoon.'

'Niet zo snel aangebrand jij. Hoe gaan ze haar vervoeren?'

'Waarschijnlijk houden ze zich aan de bekende weg.'

'We kunnen niet elke vrachtwagen en container doorzoeken.'

Ik hoor hem een aantekening krassen op een schrijfblok. Hij vraagt hoe het bij Spijker ging en ik vertel hem de details van de draagmoederaffaire.

'Ik heb nog nooit iemand ontmoet die problemen aantrekt zoals jij.'

'Nu bent u net mijn moeder.'

'Hou je met haar wél rekening?'

'Niet echt.'

Het gesprek is ten einde en ik doe heel even mijn ogen dicht. Als ik ze weer opendoe, zie ik een klas schoolkinderen met hun juf. De jongens en meisjes houden elkaars handen vast terwijl ze wachten tot de stoplichten verspringen. Op onverklaarbare wijze voel ik een brok in mijn keel opkomen. Ik zal er nooit zo een hebben.

Voor het hotel staat een politiewagen geparkeerd. Bij de receptie wacht een agent in uniform, bijna in de houding.

Groentje Dave drentelt heen en weer als een jaloerse vrijer.

'Waar was je?'

'Ik moest iemand spreken.'

Hij pakt mijn hand stevig vast.

De agent stelt zichzelf voor en overhandigt me een portofoon. Van ver weg klinkt Spijkers stem. Ik hoor water. Meeuwen. 'We hebben iemand gevonden.'

'Wie?'

'Ik hoop dat jij me dat kunt vertellen.'

In mijn maag draait iets zachts en nats zich om.

De agent neemt de radio weer over om te horen wat de verdere instructies zijn.

'Ik ga met je mee,' zegt Dave.

'En je vliegtuig dan?'

'We hebben nog tijd.'

Tijdens de rit zwijgen we. Frustratie staat op zijn voorhoofd gegrift. Hij wil iets zeggen over gisteravond dat hij heeft voorbereid, gepland, maar het is nu niet het moment.

Ik heb een merkwaardig dubbel gevoel. Misschien is dat een teken dat ik niet klaar ben voor het huwelijk en niet echt verliefd. Het hele idee was een van die wat-als-momenten die de kater of het genadeloze ochtendlicht niet overleven.

De Nederlandse agent put uit een Engelse woordenschat van vier woorden en is niet bereid of niet in staat uit te leggen waar we naartoe gaan. Ondertussen voert hij ons langs smalle straten en bruggen en door een industriegebied met havenbekkens en opslagloodsen. Het lijkt alsof we dezelfde grauwe rechthoeken water meerdere malen passeren voordat we halt houden bij een verweerde houten pier. Politieauto's staan met de neuzen bij elkaar alsof ze uit dezelfde trog drinken.

Spijker is een kop groter dan de andere rechercheurs. Hij draagt een donker pak en gepoetste schoenen maar lijkt nog steeds niet geschikt voor zijn rol in het leven, alsof hij zich verkleed heeft in zijn vaders kleren.

Er is een houten helling die vanaf de kade afloopt in het water. Halverwege ligt een Zodiac, gemaakt van zwaar canvasrubber en met een houten bodem. Een tweede rubberboot ligt op het water te wachten met vier mannen aan boord.

Spijker overhandigt me een paar rubberlaarzen en een oliejack voor over mijn trui. Nadat hij voor Dave soortgelijke kleren heeft gevonden trekt ook hij zijn laarzen aan.

De Zodiac glijdt met een vloeiende beweging te water. Spijker houdt een hand uitgestoken en helpt me aan boord stappen. De koppeling pakt en we varen weg. De lucht is als een ononderbroken grijs laken zonder enige diepte. Zo'n vierhonderd meter verderop zie ik het vlak van een peddel opkomen en weer neerduiken: een kanoër die langs de oever vaart. Verder weg zie ik een veerpont, met stompe boeg en slierten zwarte rook uitstotend.

Ik probeer me te oriënteren. Meer dan tien kilometer naar het westen ligt de Noordzee. We lijken in een westelijke haven te varen. De lucht ruikt zoetig, naar chocola. Misschien is er in de buurt een fabriek. Dave zit naast me. Ik voel hem als ik opzij wieg en zijn linkerarm heel even mijn borst raakt.

Spijker is op zijn gemak als hij een boot bestuurt. Misschien krijg je dat erbij als je beneden de zeespiegel leeft, beschermd door dijken en vloedkeringen.

'Wat weet jij van de zee, agent Barba?'

Wat valt er te weten? Hij is koud, nat, ziltig...

'Mijn vader zat bij de koopvaardij,' vertelt hij zonder mijn antwoord af te wachten. 'Toen ik zeven was scheidde hij van mijn moeder, maar ik bracht wel de vakanties met hem door. Hij voer niet meer, maar aan wal was hij een andere man. Hij leek kleiner.'

Dave heeft niet veel gezegd sinds ik de twee aan elkaar heb voorgesteld, maar begint nu over de zeilschool die hij wil kopen. Algauw zijn ze druk in gesprek over zeilbootjes en zeiloppervlakten. Ik kan me Dave echt voorstellen in een kabeltrui, gebukt onder een giek. Hij lijkt geschikt voor het buitenleven, voor weidse ruimten vol wind, lucht en water.

Zo'n honderdvijftig meter voor ons uit vaart een containerschip. De haven van Amsterdam heeft honderden miljoenen uitgegeven in de waan dat ze Rotterdam zouden kunnen evenaren als spil in de internationale handel, legt Spijker uit. Het was weggegooid geld.

Langs het schip varend komen we aan bij een houten pier die steunend op palen en balken zeven meter boven het wateroppervlak uitsteekt. Aan onze kant ligt een drijvend platform afgemeerd.

Spijker zet de motor in z'n vrij en laat hem stationair draaien. Hij legt de Zodiac stil, gooit een touw om een roestige klamp op het platform en trekt ons dichterbij. Op hetzelfde moment floept er een lichtbundel aan die naar de donkere schaduwen onder de pier draait en het verweerde grijze hout afzoekt. Iets wits licht op. Een boven het water hangende gestalte, die op mij neerkijkt. Er is een lus om haar nek geslagen. Een tweede eind touw om haar middel hangt in het water, verzwaard.

Het lichaam wiegt zachtjes heen en weer, als door een onzichtbare hand bewogen, en haar gestrekte tenen lijken pirouetten te draaien op het wateroppervlak.

'Is dat het dove meisje?' vraagt Spijker.

Zala heeft haar ogen open. Twee karmozijnrode bollen. In het oogwit zijn bloedvaten gesprongen en de pupillen lijken te zijn verdwenen. Ze heeft hetzelfde roze jasje en dezelfde rok aan die ik haar de laatste keer zag dragen. Zout in de lucht heeft het weefsel stug gemaakt.

De Zodiac gaat op en neer op de lichte deining. Spijker houdt hem stil en ik stap het platform op. Een metalen ladder, die met bouten aan een steunpijler vastzit, loopt omhoog naar de pier. Vanaf de boeien en een nabijgelegen schuit kijken meeuwen toe. De andere Zodiac is gearriveerd, met aan boord touwen en een kooibrancard.

Spijker klimt de ladder op en ik volg hem. Dave komt achter mij aan. De planken van de pier zijn oud en diep gegroefd, met spleten ertussen die zo breed zijn dat ik de bovenkant van Zala's hoofd en haar schouders kan zien.

Het touw rond haar nek is vastgemaakt aan een bolder waaraan normaal gesproken schepen worden vastgelegd.

Een politieagent in klimuitrusting laat zich over de rand omlaagzakken. Hij bungelt in een gordel naast Zala's lichaam en we kijken zwijgend toe hoe ze in de gesloten brancard wordt vastgesnoerd. Het touw om haar middel zit vast aan een gasbetonblok. Ik kan het betonstof op haar handen en het voorpand van haar jasje zien zitten.

Ze hebben haar gedwongen te springen. De onweerlegbaarheid ervan is als een visioen. Ze hield het blok in haar armen en ze hebben haar het laatste duwtje gegeven. Ze viel vijf meter omlaag voordat het touw haar val brak. Het gasbetonblok werd uit haar handen gerukt en viel verder tot het tweede touw, om haar middel gebonden, zich straktrok. Mijn maag maakt de val opnieuw mee.

'Ze is even voor halftien door een visser gevonden,' zegt Spijker. 'Hij meldde zijn vondst aan de waterpolitie.' Ter bevestiging draait hij zich om naar een lagergeplaatste collega.

'Wat bracht u op het…?' Hij laat me mijn vraag niet afmaken.

'Ze voldeed aan de beschrijving.'

'Hoe is ze hier terechtgekomen?'

Spijker gebaart langs de pier. 'Alles is omheind. Er hangen waarschuwingsborden. Uiteraard moedigt dat mensen alleen maar aan.'

'U denkt niet aan zelfmoord?'

'Jouw dove meisje heeft dat brok beton echt niet zelf hierheen gezeuld.'

In de verte, waar het water minder beschut is, zijn schuimkoppen te zien van de wind. Er komt een vissersboot binnen, de ra-

254

men blikkerend in een karig straaltje zonlicht.

Ondanks zijn cynisme van de oudgediende voelt Spijker de behoefte medeleven te tonen en me te condoleren. Op de een of andere manier ben ik zijn enige schakel met dit meisje geworden.

'Ze kwam uit Kabul. Ze was wees,' leg ik uit.

'De zoveelste.'

'Hoe bedoelt u?'

'De lijst met draagmoeders van de IVF-kliniek. Zeker tien van hen waren wees. Dat maakt het moeilijk ze op te sporen.'

Wezen. Illegale immigranten. Wat een volmaakte combinatie van ongewensten en wanhopigen.

'Samira had het over een bezoek aan het weeshuis. Een westerling die zei dat hij een baan voor haar kon regelen. Hij had een kruis in zijn nek getatoeëerd. Ik weet mogelijk wie het is.' Ik geef hem Donavons naam en hij belooft hem na te zullen trekken in zijn bestanden.

Aan het andere uiteinde van de pier zijn de kadehekken van het slot gehaald. Er komt een busje met een forensisch team aanrijden. Een tweede auto krijgt opdracht ons naar ons hotel terug te brengen.

Terwijl ik de pier af loop, heb ik het gevoel dat Amsterdam is veranderd en donkerder en gevaarlijker is geworden. Ik snak naar het vertrouwde. Naar huis.

Dave komt naast me lopen.

'Gaat het?'

'Ja, prima.'

'Het is niet jouw schuld.'

'Wat weet jij daar nou van?' bits ik. Meteen ben ik kwaad op mezelf. Hij heeft niets misdaan. Na een paar minuten probeer ik mijn schuldgevoel te verlichten. 'Bedankt dat je erbij was. Sorry van gisteravond. Vergeet alles wat ik heb gezegd.'

'Ik denk dat we er nog eens over moeten praten.'

'Er valt niets te bepraten.'

'Ik hou van je.'

'Maar het is anders nu, toch?'

Dave legt zijn hand op mijn onderarm om me te laten stoppen.

'Het maakt me niet uit. Ik wil bij je zijn.'

'Dat zeg je nu, maar stel je het eens over vijf jaar of tien jaar voor. Dat zou ik je toch niet aan kunnen doen?'

Aan de oever staat een verlaten hijskraan te roesten. Hij ziet eruit als een wrak uit een langvervlogen oorlog. In gedachten zie ik Zala's lichaam nog ronddraaien, met haar tenen pirouetten draaiend in de golven.

Ik ben een dwaas geweest. Mijn goede bedoelingen hebben een keten van gebeurtenissen in gang gezet met dit als resultaat. Ik weet niet waar het eindigt of wie er nog meer slachtoffer zal worden. Ik ben van maar één ding zeker: ik wil elk wakend moment besteden aan de jacht op de mensen die Cate van me hebben weggenomen en Zala dit hebben aangedaan. Het gaat hier niet om oog om oog; het is groter dan dat. Ik wil hun ellende schrijnender en verschrikkelijker maken dan alles wat zij anderen hebben aangedaan. Nog nooit in mijn leven heb ik me zo in staat gevoeld iemand te doden.

Zijn haren zijn gekamd. Zijn tas is gepakt. Er is een taxi besteld naar de luchthaven. De klok is niet vooruitgekomen. Nog geen seconde. Ik zweer het. Ik haat het laatste uur voordat iemand vertrekt. Alles is gezegd en gedaan. Minuten slepen zich voort. Opmerkingen worden herhaald. Tickets worden nagekeken.

'Volgens mij is het tijd om dit te laten rusten,' zegt Dave terwijl hij zijn tandenborstel schoonspoelt. 'Het is over.'

'Hoe zijn we bij "over" gekomen?'

'Misschien denk jij,' zegt hij, zorgvuldig zijn woorden kiezend, 'dat ik dit zeg vanwege jou en mij. Dat is niet zo. Ik zou hetzelfde zeggen als ik niet van je hield.'

'Maar daarom zou jíj het ook moeten begrijpen.'

Hij pakt zijn tas op en zet hem weer neer.

'Je zou met me mee kunnen komen.'

'Ik laat Ruiz niet achter.'

Hij trekt zijn jasje aan.

'Jij zou kunnen blijven,' probeer ik.

'Ik moet getuigen voor de rechtbank.'

'Ik heb je nodig.'

'Jij hebt helemaal niemand nodig.'

Het is niet kwetsend bedoeld, maar ik krimp ineen alsof ik een klap krijg.

Hij opent langzaam de deur. Al die tijd blijf ik hopen dat hij zich zal omdraaien, me in zijn armen zal nemen, me zal dwingen in zijn ogen te kijken, me zal zeggen dat hij om niets anders geeft dan om mij – hopen dat hij het begrijpt.

De deur valt achter hem dicht. Mijn borstkas is leeg. Hij heeft mijn hart met zich meegenomen.

11

Twintig minuten lang staar ik naar de deur, wens ik dat hij open zal gaan, hoop ik dat hij terugkomt.

Toen ik met mijn beschadigde wervelkolom in het ziekenhuis lag, bang dat ik nooit meer zou kunnen lopen, begon ik gemene opmerkingen te maken tegen mensen. Ik bekritiseerde de verpleegsters en klaagde over het eten. Een mannelijke hulpverpleger noemde ik Dikke Albert, naar de figuur uit de *Cosby Show*.

Dave kwam me elke dag opzoeken. Ik weet nog dat ik tegen hem tekeerging en hem een imbeciel noemde. Dat verdiende hij niet. Ik had medelijden met mezelf omdat iedereen medelijden met me had. En gemeen doen tegen mensen leidde mijn gedachten een tijdlang af van mezelf.

Dave kwam daarna niet meer op bezoek. Ik wilde hem bellen. Ik wilde zeggen dat het me speet dat ik kwaad was geworden en of hij alsjeblieft terug wilde komen. Ik deed het niet. In plaats daarvan schreef ik hem een brief. Flink hoor. Ik verdien hem niet.

Op tafel rinkelt mijn mobiele telefoon.

'Je bent niet komen lunchen vandaag.'

'Ik zit nog op het vasteland, mama.'

'Je tante Meena had kulfi-ijs gemaakt. Je favoriet.'

Toen ik zes was, ja.

'Alle jongens waren er. Zelfs Hari.'

Typisch: hij komt pas opdagen als hij me daarmee voor schut kan zetten.

'Je vriend, inspecteur King, belde dat hij het niet ging redden.'

'Dat weet ik, mama.'

'Maar een andere buitengewoon begerenswaardige heer was er wel. Hij was teleurgesteld dat hij jou niet trof.'

'Wie hebt u nu weer de arm op zijn rug gedraaid?'

'Dokter Banerjee lijkt erg dol op je te zijn.'

Het kan geen toeval zijn. 'Wat moest hij?'

'Hij kwam bloemen brengen voor jou. Een heel attente man. En zijn tafelmanieren zijn onberispelijk.'

Als we trouwen zal ik schone tafelkleden hebben.

'Waar heb je hem gezegd dat ik zat?'

'Ik heb gezegd dat je in Amsterdam was. Je doet hier wel heel geheimzinnig over. Je weet dat ik niet van geheimen hou.'

Ze gaat door met een beschrijving van de brave arts en een grappig verhaal dat hij haar vertelde over zijn pasgeboren neefje. Ik hoor de clou niet. Ik ben te druk bezig hem in verband te brengen met Samira.

Banerjee had in totaal twaalf embryo's van Cate. In plaats van zes IVF-cycli waren er maar vijf, wat inhield dat er twee embryo's overbleven, bevroren en bewaard in vloeibare stikstof. Hij gaf ze aan Cate, wat betekent dat hij van haar draagmoederplan wist. Daarom regelde hij een uitnodiging voor mijn vaders verjaardagsfeestje: hij wilde me waarschuwen hiervan af te zien.

'Ik moet gaan, mama.'

'Wanneer ben je weer thuis?'

'Gauw.'

Ik hang op en bel Groentje Dave, die net in het vliegtuig stapt.

'Betekent dit dat je me mist?'

'Dat is een gegeven. Ik wil je om een gunst vragen.'

'Eentje maar?'

'Als je terug bent in Londen, buig je dan over dokter Sohan Banerjee.'

'Hij was op het feestje van je vader.'

'Die ja.'

'Wat wil je weten?'

'Of hij connecties heeft met fertiliteitsklinieken buiten het Verenigd Koninkrijk. Ga ook na of hij connecties heeft met adoptie-organisaties of liefdadigheidsfondsen voor kinderen.'

'Ik zal kijken wat ik kan doen.'

Een stewardess komt zeggen dat hij zijn telefoon moet uitschakelen.

'Behouden vlucht.'

'Jij ook.'

Forbes' verkoudheid is erger aan het worden en hij heeft een zeehondenhoest ontwikkeld die wordt afgewisseld met het klakkende geluid in zijn keel. Hij klinkt als een menselijke beatbox.

'Je had thuis moeten blijven,' opper ik.

'Mijn huis zit vol met zieken.'

'En dus besloot je de rest van de bevolking te gaan besmetten.'

'Inderdaad, ik ben Patiënt Nul.'

'Heb je ze gevonden, de zwangere asielzoeksters?'

'Ik had je moeten opsluiten toen ik de kans had.' Hij snuit zijn neus. 'Ze zijn begin juli in een vrachtcontainer het land binnengekomen. Een Russische, achttien jaar oud, en een Albanese, eenentwintig jaar. Ze zagen er allebei uit alsof ze elk moment konden bevallen. Hun vingerafdrukken werden afgenomen, ze kregen identiteitspapieren en werden naar een opvangcentrum in Oxfordshire gebracht. Drie dagen later werden ze naar een pension in Liverpool overgebracht. Ze hadden twee weken om een bewijsverklaring in te vullen en naar een advocaat te gaan, maar ze kwamen geen van beiden opdagen. Sinds die tijd zijn ze niet meer gezien.'

'En de baby's?'

'Bij geen enkel NHS-ziekenhuis is een melding van de geboorten terug te vinden, maar dat zegt nog niets. Veel mensen bevallen tegenwoordig thuis, tot in het bad aan toe. Godzijdank was ons bad niet groot genoeg.'

Ik heb plotseling het beeld voor ogen van zijn vrouw, als een walvis in de badkuip van het gezin.

'Veel logica zit er nog altijd niet in,' zegt hij. 'Een van de dingen waar asielzoekers op afkomen is gratis gezondheidszorg. Deze vrouwen hadden hun kinderen in een NHS-ziekenhuis ter wereld kunnen brengen. De regering verstrekt daarnaast een eenmalige toelage van driehonderd pond per pasgeboren baby en extra geld voor melk en luiers. Dat komt boven op de gewone voedselcoupons en de uitkering. Deze vrouwen beweerden dat ze geen familie of vrienden binnen het Verenigd Koninkrijk hadden die hen konden onderhouden, en toch maakten ze geen gebruik van de beschikbare voorzieningen. Dan komt toch de vraag op hoe ze zich in leven hebben gehouden.'

'En óf ze in leven zijn gebleven.'

Daar wil hij niet op ingaan.

In het Academisch Medisch Centrum zit Ruiz beneden op me te wachten. Hij ziet eruit als een jongetje dat van zomerkamp wordt opgehaald, maar dan zonder de vervelde neus of opengehaalde knieën.

'De staf wenste me een lang en gezond leven,' vertelt hij. 'Ze zeiden ook dat ik maar nooit meer in Nederland ziek moest worden.'

'Ontroerend.'

'Dat vond ik ook. Ik ben godverdomme een medisch wonder.' Hij houdt zijn ontbrekende vinger omhoog en begint te tellen. 'Ik ben neergeschoten, bijna verdronken en nu ook nog neergestoken. Wat heb je nog meer?'

'Ze zouden je kunnen opblazen, meneer.'

'Is al geprobeerd. Brendan Pearl en zijn IRA-vriendjes vuurden een mortiergranaat af die een politiebureau in Belfast binnenvloog. Hij miste me op een haar na.' Hij doet zijn Agent 86-imitatie.

Bij de draaideur staat hij even stil. 'Heb je gehuild, sprinkhaan?'

'Nee, meneer.'

'Ik dacht dat je misschien had zitten treuren.'

'Treuren niet, meneer.'

'Vrouwen mogen best warm en wollig zijn.'

'Dat klinkt alsof ik een speelgoedbeest ben.'

'Met heel scherpe tanden.'

Hij is in een goede stemming. Misschien van de morfine. Die houdt niet lang stand. Ik vertel hem over Zala en ik kan de pijn zien optrekken tot in zijn schouders en doorschieten naar zijn nek. Zijn ogen zijn gesloten. Ademend. Wachtend.

'Ze gaan Samira Engeland binnensmokkelen,' zeg ik.

'Dat kun je niet met zekerheid zeggen.'

'Zo is het met de anderen ook gegaan. Op die manier komen de baby's in het land van de ouders ter wereld.'

'De Beaumonts zijn dood.'

'Ze zullen andere kopers weten te vinden.'

'Wie zijn die "ze"?'

'Yanus. Pearl. Anderen.'

'Wat zegt Spijker?'

'Dat ik naar huis moet gaan.'

'Een wijs man.'

'Hokke zegt dat er iemand is die ons zou kunnen helpen Samira te vinden.'

'Wie dan?'

'Eduardo de Souza. Yanus heeft voor hem gewerkt.'

'Dit begint beter en beter te worden.'

Mijn mobiele telefoon gaat. Hokke is ergens waar het rumoerig is. De rosse buurt. Hij brengt daar tegenwoordig meer tijd door dan toen hij daar nog gewoon zijn ronde liep.

'Ik pik je om zeven uur op bij het hotel.'

'Waar gaan we heen?'

'Antwoorden om zeven uur.'

12

In het oosten is een enorme vaalbleke maan opgekomen die langs de hemel lijkt te bewegen, achter onze taxi aan. Zelfs in het donker herken ik sommige wegen. Schiphol is niet ver hiervandaan.

Dit is een ander gedeelte van Amsterdam. De schilderachtige gevels en historische bruggen hebben plaatsgemaakt voor het functionele en strenge: betongrijze flatgebouwen en winkels die beschermd worden door metalen rolluiken. Er is maar één winkel open. Voor de deur staat een tiental zwarte jongeren.

De Souza heeft geen vast adres, legt Hokke uit. Hij verplaatst zich van plek naar plek en slaapt nooit langer dan één nacht in hetzelfde bed. Hij woont bij de mensen die voor hem werken. Zij beschermen hem.

'Wees heel voorzichtig met wat je tegen hem zegt. En onderbreek hem niet als hij aan het woord is. Hou je ogen neergeslagen en je handen langs je lichaam.'

We zijn gestopt voor een flatgebouw. Hokke houdt het portier voor me open.

'Komt u met me mee?'

'Je moet alleen gaan. Wij zullen hier wachten.'

'Nee,' zegt Ruiz stellig. 'Ik ga met haar mee.'

Hokke antwoordt al even beslist: 'Ze gaat alleen, of er zal niemand op haar staan te wachten.'

Ruiz blijft protesteren, maar ik duw hem terug de auto in, waar hij zijn gezicht vertrekt en zijn armen voor zijn ingezwachtelde borstkas houdt.

'Onthoud wat ik je heb gezegd,' zegt de Nederlander terwijl hij naar een gebouw wijst dat identiek is aan het gebouw ernaast en dat daar weer naast. Tegen een muur staat een jongen geleund. Een tweede jongen bekijkt ons vanuit een raam op een verdieping. Uitkijkposten. 'Je moet nu gaan. Bel me als er een probleem is.'

Ik laat me uit de taxi glijden. De tegen de muur geleunde jongen is verdwenen. De tweede tiener staat nog steeds bij het raam. Ik loop over een betonnen galerij een rechthoekige binnenplaats op. Lichten weerspiegeld op water. Aan bladloze, tussen het onkruid opschietende bomen hangen Chinese lantaarns.

Ik duw een branddeur open en loop de trappen op, onderweg de verdiepingen tellend. Links afslaand op de verdieping vind ik de tweede deur. Er zit een klein wit knopje op bij wijze van deurbel.

Voor me verschijnt een andere tiener. Zijn glimmend zwarte ogen monsteren me, maar wenden zich af als ik zijn blik beantwoord. In de smalle gang staan schoenen en sandalen in een rij. De tiener wijst naar mijn laarzen. Ik trek ze uit.

De vloer kraakt heel even terwijl ik hem achternaloop naar het woongedeelte. Een groepje van vijf mannen van in de veertig en vijftig zit op kussens langs de randen van een geweven kleed. Eduardo de Souza is onmiddellijk herkenbaar aan zijn positie in het midden. Gekleed in een wijdvallende witte lange broek en een donker shirt, ziet hij er Turks of zelfs Koerdisch uit, met een hoog voorhoofd, gebeeldhouwde kaken en een minzame glimlach. Hij staat op uit zijn kleermakerszit en raakt kort mijn hand aan.

'Welkom, juffrouw Barba, ik ben Eduardo de Souza.'

Zijn keurig getrimde baard is zwart met grijs – het grijs als van in een donkere vacht hangende ijssplinters. Niemand praat of beweegt, en toch hangt er een voelbare energie in de lucht, van een zich verscherpende concentratie. Ik hou mijn blik omlaaggericht terwijl ogen over me heen dwalen.

Door de deuropening naar de keuken zie ik een jonge Nigeriaanse vrouw in een golvende jurk met felle kleuren. Drie kinderen, twee jongetjes en een meisje, verdringen zich in de opening en kijken gefascineerd mijn kant uit.

Hij neemt opnieuw het woord. 'Dit zijn vrienden van me. Dit is Sunday. Hij is vanavond onze gastheer.'

Sunday glimlacht. Hij is een Nigeriaan, zijn tanden zijn blinkend wit. De man naast hem is een Iraniër met een Zwitser-Duits accent. Hij heet Farhad en zijn ogen liggen zo diep in hun kassen dat ik ze nauwelijks kan zien. Naast hem zit Oscar, die me Marokkaans lijkt en met een Frans accent spreekt.

Als laatste is er nog Dayel, een gladgeschoren Indiër met een litteken van een brandwond in zijn nek.

'Een van uw landgenoten, al is hij geen sikh,' zegt De Souza. Dayel glimlacht om de introductie.

Hoe weet hij dat ik een sikh ben?

Naast hem is een brokaatkussen onbezet. Ik word geacht te

gaan zitten. Sundays vrouw komt de kamer binnen met een dienblad met een bonte verzameling glazen en begint zoete thee in te schenken. Haar haren zijn in een gordijn van lange kralenstrengen gevlochten. Ze glimlacht verlegen naar me. Haar gebit is volmaakt en haar brede neusvleugels gaan zachtjes op en neer met haar ademhaling.

Er worden schotels binnengedragen. Een maaltijd. Met zijn handen tegen elkaar zit De Souza me over zijn vingertoppen heen te bestuderen, afwegend of hij me zal helpen of niet. Zijn Engels is onberispelijk, overgoten met een Brits accent dat vooral in de lange klinkers te horen is.

'Dit gedeelte van Amsterdam wordt de Bijlmermeer genoemd,' zegt hij met een blik uit het raam. 'In oktober 1992 steeg er een vrachtvliegtuig op van Schiphol en verloor twee motoren. Het boorde zich in een flatgebouw als dit, vol immigrantenfamilies die aan hun avondeten zaten. Bij de eerste klap werden vijftig appartementen verwoest. Nog eens honderd brandden later uit toen er vliegtuigbrandstof als rivieren van vuur door de galerijen stroomde. Mensen wierpen zich van balkons en daken om aan de vlammen te ontkomen.

Eerst zeiden ze dat het dodental tweehonderdvijftig bedroeg. Later werd de schatting verlaagd tot vijfenzeventig en officieel zijn slechts drieënveertig mensen omgekomen. De waarheid is dat niemand het echte aantal kent. Illegale immigranten hebben geen papieren en houden zich verborgen voor de politie. Het zijn geesten.'

Hij heeft het eten niet aangeraakt, maar lijkt buitengewoon voldaan de anderen te zien eten.

'Neem me niet kwalijk, juffrouw Barba, ik praat te veel. Mijn vrienden hier zijn te beleefd om me tot kalmte te manen. Het is gebruikelijk dat een gast iets meebrengt naar het feest of een of andere vorm van vermaak aanbiedt. Zingt of danst u misschien?'

'Nee.'

'Misschien bent u een verhalenverteller?'

'Ik begrijp echt niet wat u bedoelt.'

'U gaat ons een verhaal vertellen. De beste verhalen, heb ik het idee, gaan over leven en dood, liefde en haat, trouw en verraad.'

Hij wuift met zijn hand alsof hij door de lucht roert. Zijn amber-kleurige ogen zijn op de mijne gefixeerd.

'Ik ben geen erg goede verhalenverteller.'

'Laat dat oordeel maar aan ons over.'

Ik vertel hem het verhaal van twee tienermeisjes, die elkaar op school hebben leren kennen en boezemvriendinnen zijn gewor-den. Zielsverwanten. Later, op de universiteit, ging een van hen met de vader van de ander naar bed. Hij had haar verleid. Zij liet toe dat ze werd verleid. De vriendschap was voorbij.

Ik noem geen namen, maar waarom zou ik hun een dergelijk persoonlijk verhaal vertellen?

Naadloos schakel ik over op een tweede stel tienermeisjes, die elkaar hebben leren kennen in een stad van weduwen en wezen. Mensensmokkelaars hebben hen Afghanistan uit gesmokkeld en tot aan Amsterdam gebracht. Ze kregen te horen dat ze hun nog een bedrag verschuldigd waren voor hun ontsnapping. Ze kregen de keuze om de prostitutie in te gaan of een baby te dragen voor een kinderloos stel. Maagden kregen embryo's ingeplant in wat een geritualiseerde vorm van medische verkrachting was. Ze wa-ren de perfecte broedmachines. Fabrieken. Koeriers.

Nog terwijl ik dit verhaal aan het vertellen ben, krijg ik een dro-ge keel doordat er alarmbellen bij me gaan rinkelen. Waarom heb ik hem zulke persoonlijke verhalen verteld? Het kan net zo goed zijn dat De Souza erbij betrokken is. Hij zou de aanstichter kun-nen zijn. Ik heb geen tijd om over de implicaties na te denken. Ik weet niet of ze me kunnen schelen. Ik ben al te ver op weg om me nog terug te kunnen trekken.

Als ik klaar ben, is het even stil. De Souza buigt zich naar voren naar een schaaltje en pakt een chocolaatje, dat hij op zijn tong laat rollen terwijl hij er langzaam op kauwt.

'Het is een goed verhaal. Vriendschap is iets wat lastig te om-schrijven valt. Oscar hier is mijn oudste vriend. Hoe zou jij vriendschap omschrijven, Oscar?'

Hij gromt zachtjes, alsof het antwoord zonneklaar is. 'Vriend-schap gaat over keuze en chemie. Het laat zich niet definiëren.'

'Maar dat is toch zeker niet het enige?'

'Het is een bereidheid fouten door de vingers te zien en te accepteren. Ik zou een vriend toestaan mij pijn te doen zonder terug te slaan,' zegt hij glimlachend, 'maar niet meer dan één keer.'

De Souza lacht. 'Bravo, Oscar, bij jou kan ik er altijd op vertrouwen dat je een argument weet terug te brengen tot zijn zuiverste vorm. Wat denk jij, Dayel?'

De Indiër rolt met zijn hoofd, trots dat hij is gevraagd als volgende te spreken.

'Vriendschap is voor iedereen anders en verandert in de loop van onze levens. Als je zes bent, gaat het over de hand vasthouden van je beste vriend. Op je zestiende gaat het om het avontuur dat voor je ligt. Op je zestigste gaat het over herinneren.' Hij steekt een vinger op. 'Je kunt het niet met één woord omschrijven, hoewel eerlijkheid er misschien het dichtstbij komt...'

'Nee, geen eerlijkheid,' onderbreekt Farhad hem. 'Integendeel, vaak moeten we onze vrienden afschermen van wat we werkelijk denken. Het is als een onuitgesproken overeenkomst. We negeren elkaars fouten en houden vertrouwelijkheden voor ons. Vriendschap gaat niet over eerlijk zijn. Liefde gaat over jezelf kennen. Wij zien onszelf door de ogen van onze vrienden. Die zijn als een spiegel die ons in staat stelt te beoordelen hoe het er met ons voor staat.'

Nu schraapt De Souza zijn keel. Ik vraag me af of hij zich bewust is van het ontzag dat hij de anderen inboezemt. Ik vermoed dat hij te intelligent en te menselijk is om dat niet te beseffen.

'Vriendschap kan niet worden gedefinieerd,' zegt hij streng. 'Zodra we redenen gaan noemen voor het feit dat we iemands vriend zijn, ondermijnen we de magie van de relatie. Niemand wil weten dat anderen van hem houden vanwege zijn geld of zijn gulheid of zijn schoonheid of zijn spitsvondigheid. Kies een motief uit en je geeft die persoon de gelegenheid te zeggen: "Is dat de enige reden?"'

De anderen lachen. De Souza valt in. Dit is een voorstelling.

Hij gaat verder. 'Proberen uit te leggen waarom we bepaalde vriendschappen aangaan is als proberen te vertellen waarom we van een bepaald soort muziek houden of van een bepaald gerecht. Je houdt er gewoon van, klaar.'

Hij richt zich nu op mij. 'Uw vriendin heet Cate Beaumont.'

Hoe weet hij dat?

'Bent u ooit jaloers op haar geweest?'

'Ik begrijp niet wat u bedoelt.'

'Vriendinnen kunnen jaloers op elkaar zijn. Oscar hier is afgunstig op mijn positie en mijn rijkdom.'

'Echt niet, mijn vriend,' protesteert de aangesprokene smekend.

De Souza glimlacht veelbetekenend. 'Was u jaloers op Cate Beaumonts schoonheid, of op haar succes?'

'Soms.'

'U wilde dat zij er minder van had en u meer.'

'Ja.'

'Dat is heel natuurlijk. Vriendschappen kunnen dubbelzinnig en tegenstrijdig zijn.'

'Ze is dood,' ga ik verder, hoewel ik voel dat hij dat al weet.

'Ze heeft geld betaald voor een baby. Een misdrijf,' stelt hij vroom vast.

'Ja.'

'Probeert u haar te beschermen?'

'Ik probeer de draagmoeder en de baby's te redden.'

'Misschien wilt u wel een baby voor uzelf?'

Mijn ontkenning is te heftig. Ik maak het erger. 'Ik heb nooit... Ik zou...'

Hij tast in een kleine buidel die aan de ceintuur van zijn lange hemd vastzit. 'Vindt u mij een crimineel, juffrouw Barba?'

'Ik weet niet genoeg...'

'Uw mening graag.'

Ik wacht. De gezichten in de kring bekijken me met een mengeling van geamuseerdheid en fascinatie.

'Dat is niet aan mij,' stamel ik.

Stilte. Er loopt zweet mijn rugholte in, kringelend langs de bobbels van mijn wervels.

De Souza wacht. Hij buigt zich dicht naar me toe, zijn gezicht op enkele centimeters van het mijne. Zijn ondertanden zijn brokkelig en gekarteld, vergeeld als een oude krant. Hij heeft eigenlijk helemaal niet zo'n volmaakt gezicht.

'U hebt mij niets te bieden,' zegt hij laatdunkend.

Ik voel dat de situatie me ontglipt. Hij is niet van plan me te helpen.

De woede die plotseling in me opborrelt, aangewakkerd door vijandige gedachten en beelden van Zala, vindt ineens een uitlaatklep. Woorden tuimelen naar buiten. 'Voor mij bent u een crimineel en een vrouwenhater, maar u bent geen boosaardig mens. U buit geen kinderen uit en verkoopt geen baby's aan de hoogstbiedende.' Ik wijs naar Sundays echtgenote, die onze borden is komen ophalen. 'U zou deze vrouw, de vrouw van een vriend, niet vragen een van haar kinderen op te geven of haar dwingen het kind van een andere vrouw te baren. U steunt asielzoekers en illegale immigranten, u geeft hun banen en zorgt voor onderdak. Ze respecteren en bewonderen u. Wij kunnen deze handel stoppen. Ik kan hem stoppen. Help me.'

De vrouw van Sunday geneert zich dat de aandacht op haar valt. Ze gaat verder met het ophalen van de borden en maakt zich zo snel mogelijk uit de voeten. De spanning in de kamer wordt versterkt door de stilte. Elk van de mannen heeft zijn ogen op mij gericht. Oscar maakt een stikgeluid achter in zijn keel. Hij zou aan één hartslag genoeg hebben om mij de keel door te snijden.

Ineens staat De Souza op. De bijeenkomst is voorbij. Oscar doet een stap in mijn richting. De Souza gebaart hem te stoppen. In zijn eentje begeleidt hij me naar de voordeur en pakt mijn hand. In zijn vingers zit een klein stukje papier gedrukt.

De deur sluit zich. Ik bekijk het briefje niet. Het is te donker om het te lezen. De taxi staat te wachten. Ik laat me op de achterbank glijden en leun tegen Ruiz aan terwijl ik het portier dichttrek. Hokke geeft de bestuurder opdracht te gaan rijden.

Het kattebelletje is opgerold, tussen mijn duim en wijsvinger geklemd. Mijn handen trillen als ik het afrol en bij het binnenlampje hou.

Vijf woorden. Handgeschreven: *Ze vertrekt vanavond uit Rotterdam.*

268

Onze taxichauffeur rijdt de oprit naar een snelweg op.

'Hoe ver is het?'

'Vijfenzeventig kilometer.'

'En de haven?'

'Nog verder.'

Ik kijk op mijn horloge. Het is acht uur 's avonds. 'De haven van Rotterdam is veertig kilometer lang,' zegt Hokke. 'Er zijn tienduizenden containers, honderden schepen. Hoe denk je haar te vinden?'

'Via een scheepsnaam?' oppert Ruiz.

'Of een vertrektijd,' reageert Hokke.

Ik staar naar het velletje papier. Het is niet voldoende. We kunnen niet alvast bellen en de douane of politie waarschuwen. Wat zouden we moeten zeggen?

'Het meest waarschijnlijke is dat ze haar het Verenigd Koninkrijk willen binnensmokkelen,' zeg ik. 'Ze hebben Harwich al eerder gebruikt.'

'Ze zouden dit keer een andere haven kunnen kiezen.'

'Of zich houden aan wat ze kennen.'

Hokke schudt zijn hoofd. Het is een lukrake, onmogelijke jacht. Rotterdam is de grootste containerhaven van Europa. Hij heeft een idee. Een vriend, een voormalig politieagent, werkt voor een particulier beveiligingsbedrijf dat een aantal terminals bewaakt.

Hokke belt hem. Ze praten kortaf met elkaar, in zinnen vol Nederlandse medeklinkers. Ondertussen hou ik de helverlichte verkeersborden in de gaten en tel de kilometeraanduidingen en de minuten af. In het maanlicht ontwaar ik windmolens, als spookachtige reuzen over de velden verspreid.

Op de rechterbaan rijden vrachtwagens en trucks bumper aan bumper. Ik vraag me af of Samira zich in een van die voertuigen zou kunnen bevinden. Hoe zou dat zijn? Oorverdovend. Zwart. Eenzaam.

Hokke beëindigt het telefoongesprek en schetst de mogelijkheden. Rond de terminals en de havens is de bewaking streng, met camera's op de hekken, infraroodscanners en nog meer honden. Meer dan zesenhalf miljoen vrachtcontainers passeren jaarlijks de haven. Ze moeten op een speciale manier zijn verzegeld. Lege containers die wachten op een nieuwe bestemming zijn een ander verhaal, maar zelfs als iemand door de beveiliging heen zou breken en bij de containers zou kunnen komen, zou hij niet weten aan boord van welk schip ze gebracht zullen worden, tenzij hij over informatie van ingewijden beschikt.

'Wat inhoudt dat de kans groot is dat ze zich op een vrachtwagen zullen storten voordat die de haven bereikt,' zegt Ruiz. 'Een wagen waarvan ze weten dat hij op weg is naar het Verenigd Koninkrijk.'

Hokke knikt. 'Dan hebben we het waarschijnlijk over roll-on-roll-off-veerboten. Er zijn twee grote rederijen met veerdiensten van en naar Rotterdam. Stena Line heeft een terminal in Hoek van Holland. P&O opereert vanuit een haven vijftien kilometer landinwaarts, dicht bij het centrum.'

We zijn nog zo'n dertig kilometer van onze bestemming en het is bijna halfnegen.

Hokke pleegt nog een telefoontje en krijgt een lijst met namen en vertrektijden te horen, die hij hardop aan ons doorgeeft. Om negen uur vertrekt er een veerboot van P&O naar Hull. De nachtboot van Stena Line naar Harwich vertrekt om elf uur. Ze komen allebei in de vroege ochtend in Groot-Brittanië aan.

'Heb je een paspoort bij je, sprinkhaan?'

'Ja, meneer.'

'Wil je die eerste boot nemen of de tweede?'

'Ik neem de tweede.'

Hij knikt instemmend. 'Weet iemand iets van de weersvoorspelling?'

Hokke belt met P&O om te vragen of ze de passagiershekken open willen houden. Ze worden geacht een kwartier voor vertrek dicht te gaan, wat inhoudt dat we het niet gaan redden.

Onze aannames zijn gebaseerd op een verhouding van zo'n twee procent feiten en achtennegentig procent wensdenken. Zelfs als Samira zich aan boord van een van de veerboten bevindt, zal ze zich niet onder de andere passagiers mengen. Ze zullen haar verborgen houden. Hoe moeten we haar vinden?

Mijn hoofd doet zeer als ik aan haar denk. Ik heb beloftes gedaan. Ik zei dat ik Zala zou vinden en zou zorgen dat ze veilig was. Wat ga ik haar vertellen?

De Souza vroeg of ik de baby's voor mezelf wilde houden. Het was een idiote suggestie. Waarom zou hij dat zeggen? Ik doe dit voor Cate en voor Samira. Voor de tweeling.

De havens zijn kilometerslang verlicht. Hijskranen en loopkranen werken als enorme lichttorens die de rompen van schepen en rijen opgestapelde containers in het licht zetten. Het tussenliggende water is donker en ondoorgrondelijk. De golven zijn hun naam nauwelijks waard, eerder rimpels op een trage rivier.

De taxi stopt buiten de P&O-terminal. Ruiz staat al buiten voordat we helemaal stilstaan. Een week van gekmakende pijn en morfine zal hem niet afremmen.

'Succes!' roept hij zonder om te kijken. 'Ik ga haar als eerste vinden.'

'Tuurlijk. Jij gaat de hele reis lopen overgeven.'

Zijn hand komt omhoog, één vinger gestrekt.

De Stena Line-terminal bevindt zich aan de westkant van het havengebied, op de plek waar Hoek van Holland de Noordzee in steekt. De taxi zet me af en ik neem afscheid van Hokke.

'Ik zal je nooit kunnen terugbetalen.'

'Ik dacht het wel,' lacht hij terwijl hij naar de meter wijst.

Ik geef hem mijn laatste euro's. Hij moet nog thuis zien te komen.

Hij kust me drie keer – linkerwang, rechterwang en nog een keer mijn linkerwang.

'Wees voorzichtig.'

'Doe ik.'

Ik heb nog een uur voordat de Stena Britannica vertrekt. Het schip beheerst het uitzicht en torent boven de omliggende bouwsels uit. Het is zo lang als twee voetbalvelden en zo hoog als een gebouw van vijftien verdiepingen, met twee identieke schoorstenen die achteroverhellen en, zij het niet geheel overtuigend, de indruk van snelheid geven.

In de bundel van de schijnwerpers happen meeuwen naar insecten. In volle vlucht zien ze er elegant uit, maar eenmaal op de grond gaan ze als viswijven tegen elkaar tekeer. Ze klinken ook altijd zo wanhopig triest, miserabel uithalend als schepselen die bij leven al tot de hel veroordeeld zijn.

Veel vrachtwagens en aanhangers zijn al aan boord. Ik zie ze in rijen op de open dekken staan, dicht bij elkaar en vlak tegen de reling van het achterschip.

Er staan nog meer vrachtwagens in de rij om aan boord te mogen. Personenauto's en bestelwagens staan binnen een ander omheind gedeelte te wachten. De jonge vrouw in het kaartverkoopkantoor draagt een lichtblauwe rok en bijpassend jasje, als een soort zeestewardess.

'U dient de gegevens van uw voertuig in te vullen,' zegt ze.

'Ik heb geen voertuig.'

'Het spijt me, maar op deze dienst is geen loopbrug voor voetgangers. We kunnen geen voetpassagiers meenemen.'

'Maar ik móet deze boot halen.'

'Dat zal niet gaan.' Ze werpt een blik over haar schouder. 'Misschien, eh…?'

Er is zojuist een ouder echtpaar gestopt in een bejaarde Range Rover die een ouderwetse caravan trekt die eruitziet als een pompoenkoets uit Assepoester. De man is kaal en heeft een klein sikje dat hij net zo goed bij het scheren over het hoofd zou kunnen hebben gezien. Zijn vrouw is twee keer zijn omvang, met meters ribfluweel rond haar heupen. Ze komen uit Wales.

'Wat is er aan de hand, meid?' vraagt ze als ik haar kop thermosthee onderbreek.

'Ze willen me niet als voetpassagier aan boord laten gaan. Ik moet absoluut terug naar Engeland. Ik vroeg me af of ik met u mee kon rijden.'

De man en de vrouw kijken elkaar aan.

'Ben je een terrorist?'

'Nee.'

'Heb je drugs bij je?'
'Nee.
'Stem je conservatief?'
'Nee.'
'Ben je katholiek?'
'Nee.'
Hij knipoogt naar zijn vrouw. 'Niets op aan te merken.'
'Welkom aan boord,' zegt ze terwijl ze haar hand uitsteekt. 'Ik ben Bridget Jones. Niet het dikkerdje uit de films, maar uit Cardiff. Dit is Bryce, mijn echtgenoot.'
De Range Rover is afgeladen met koffers, boodschappentassen en taxfree aankopen. Hollandse kazen, Franse worst, twee dozen Stella Artois, een fles Bailey's Irish Cream en een verzameling souvenirs.
Ze zijn heel schattig. Een popperig stel met bijpassende afgedankte kussens en reismokken. Meneer Jones draagt vingerloze rallyhandschoenen en zij heeft wegenkaarten die met kleuren zijn gemerkt in een houder op het dashboard staan.
'We zijn in Polen geweest,' zegt ze ongevraagd.
'Zo.'
'Niemand die we kennen is ooit in Polen geweest. Zelfs onze vrienden Hettie en Jack van de caravanclub niet, die denken dat ze overal geweest zijn.'
'En naar Estland,' vult haar echtenoot aan. 'We hebben 5252 kilometer afgelegd sinds we op 28 augustus van huis zijn gegaan.' Hij streelt het stuurwiel. 'Ze heeft één op zes gereden, wat verdomd goed is voor een oud beestje, zeker na die tank slechte diesel in Gdansk.'
'Gdansk was kantje-boord,' valt zijn vrouw hem bij.
'Het zal wel koud zijn met zo'n caravan.'
'Daar hebben wij geen last van,' giechelt ze. 'Een wederhelft verwarmt beter dan een warme kruik.'
Meneer Jones knikt. 'Ja, het oudje rijdt nog lekker.'
Ik weet niet of hij het over zijn vrouw heeft of nog steeds over de auto.
Vóór ons is het verkeer gaan rijden. Voertuigen rijden de hel-

lingbaan op en verdwijnen naar binnen, waar ze in smalle rijen worden gemanoeuvreerd die nauwelijks breed genoeg zijn voor hun asbreedte.

'Niet lummelen, lieverd,' zegt mevrouw Jones. 'Het buffet is bij de prijs inbegrepen. We willen de rij vóór zijn, nietwaar?'

Meneer Jones knikt. 'Hun appelkruimeltaart met custard is echt heel lekker.'

Bij mijn ticket zit een kaartsleutel. Hij hoort bij een hut op een van de hoteldekken. Op dek 8 hangen bordjes met het verzoek de rust te bewaren omdat er vrachtwagenchauffeurs slapen. Sommigen van hen zijn waarschijnlijk al uren geleden aan boord gegaan. Hoe moet ik Samira vinden?

Ik doe geen moeite naar mijn hut te gaan. Ik heb geen bagage om weg te stouwen. In plaats daarvan bestudeer ik een plattegrond van het schip, die bij een nooduitgang aan de wand geschroefd zit. Er zijn vier autodekken, waar gedurende de reis alleen bevoegd personeel mag komen. Op dek 10 hebben alleen bemanningsleden toegang. Waarschijnlijk de brug.

De gangen tussen de hutten zijn net breed genoeg om twee mensen elkaar te kunnen laten passeren. Ik loop ze af, op zoek naar het bekende en het onbekende. Dat was mijn taak in de tijd dat ik voor de Diplomatieke Beschermingseenheid werkte: letten op kleine veranderingen, proberen in een menigte de aanwezigheid van iemand te voelen of met één blik vast te stellen dat die persoon er niet meer is. Het kan iemand zijn die daar niet op zijn plaats is of die juist te hard zijn best doet daar op zijn plaats te zijn, of iemand op wie je oog om een andere reden valt.

De motoren van het schip zijn gestart. Ik voel de vage trillingen door mijn voeten gaan; ze lijken te worden doorgegeven aan mijn zenuwuiteinden.

Het buffet staat uitgestald in het Globetrotter Restaurant. De meeste passagiers lijken vrachtwagenchauffeur te zijn, gekleed in spijkerbroek en T-shirt. Het voedsel ligt hoog opgetast op hun borden: gestolde curry's, lamsvleespasteitjes, vegetarische lasagne. Dikke motoren moeten bijtanken.

De Nederlandse chauffeurs kaarten, terwijl de Britse chauffeurs roken en tabloids lezen. De veerboot is losgegooid en de rivier op gevaren. Terwijl de lichtjes op het land langs het raam glijden, voelt het alsof het land beweegt in plaats van de veerboot. Engeland is vijf uur varen.

Hokke had gelijk: de hooiberg is te groot. Ik zou de veerboot weken kunnen doorzoeken zonder haar te vinden. Ze zou opgesloten kunnen zitten in een vrachtwagen of in een van de hutten. Ze zou zelfs helemaal niet aan boord kunnen zijn. Misschien was het De Souza's bedoeling niet om mij haar te laten vinden, maar simpelweg om mij Nederland uit te krijgen.

Onder me bevinden zich de holle en donkere autodekken. Sommige zijn blootgesteld aan de elementen, terwijl andere afgesloten zijn. Ik zal ze moeten doorzoeken. Hoe? Moet ik op de zijkant van elke vrachtwagen bonken en haar naam roepen? Zal ze antwoorden?

Als er ook maar de kleinste kans is dat ze aan boord is, moet ik haar zien te vinden. Door gangen en langs trappen rennend hou ik mensen staande en laat hun Samira's foto zien. Ik loop mezelf achterna, verdwaald in een doolhof. Ben ik deze gang al door geweest? Is dat dezelfde passagier aan wie ik het daarnet al heb gevraagd? De meesten van hen zijn nu in hun hutten en leggen zich te ruste voor de nacht.

Ik sla de zoveelste hoek om en ineens weet ik het. Een siddering in de lucht. Het is een griezelig gevoel, alsof ik dingen kan voorvoelen. Verderop in een lange gang staat een gestalte met zijn rug naar me toe stil om een hutdeur open te maken. Ik zie iemands profiel en druk mezelf plotseling plat tegen een wand. Mijn schimmen zitten me op de hielen.

14

Het schip verandert van ligging en ik zet me schrap tegen een wand. Het metalen frame voelt koud aan tegen mijn handpalm. Ik weet zeker dat hij het is. Brendan Pearl. Hij is hier omdat zij hier is.

Mijn eerste reactie is de aftocht te blazen. Ik loop terug en haal op de trap een paar keer diep adem, ondertussen overdenkend wat ik zal doen. Ik haal mijn mobiele telefoon tevoorschijn en kijk of ik bereik heb. Niets. De veerboot is al te ver de zee op. Ik zou met de kapitein moeten praten. Hij kan per radio Forbes op de hoogte laten brengen.

Een bemanningslid komt de trap op lopen. Ondanks zijn donkere broek en witte overhemd met epauletten ziet hij er te jong uit voor een zeeman. Hij heeft een naamplaatje op zijn borst. Raoul Jackson.

'Hebt u de sleutels van alle hutten?'

'Is er een probleem?'

'Er is een man aan boord die gezocht wordt door de Britse politie. Hij verblijft in hut 8021.' Ik wijs langs het gangpad. Zijn ogen volgen mijn uitgestoken hand. 'Ik ben Brits politieagent, recherche. Is er een passagierslijst?' Ik toon hem mijn badge.

'Ja, uiteraard.'

Hij doet een deur open waarop *Authorised Personnel Only* staat, pakt een klembord en gaat met zijn vinger de pagina af tot hij het hutnummer heeft.

'Die hut wordt gebruikt door een zekere Patrick Norris. Een Britse chauffeur.'

Pearl heeft een nieuwe identiteit.

'Is het mogelijk na te gaan welk voertuig hij aan boord heeft gereden?'

Hij raadpleegt opnieuw de lijst. 'v743 LFB. Op dek 5.'

'Ik moet dat voertuig inspecteren.'

'Passagiers zijn niet gerechtigd zich op dat dek te bevinden.'

'Ik ben op zoek naar een illegale passagier. Ze zou in de vrachtwagen opgesloten kunnen zitten.'

'Misschien kunt u het best met de kapitein praten.'

'Dat begrijp ik, maar daar is nu geen tijd voor. Als u nou voor me naar de kapitein gaat. Ik wil dat hij deze man een bericht stuurt.' Ik krabbel Forbes' nummer op het klembord. 'Zijn naam is inspecteur Robert Forbes, recherche. Noem mijn naam. Zeg hem dat Brendan Pearl zich aan boord van deze veerboot bevindt.'

'Is dat het?'

'Hij begrijpt het wel.'

Raoul kijkt naar het telefoonnummer en werpt een blik de gang in naar Pearls hut.

'Is deze persoon gevaarlijk?'

'Ja, maar is geen reden tot paniek. Laat hem slapen.' Ik kijk op mijn horloge. 'Over vier uur zijn we in Harwich.' Ik kijk naar de trap. 'Zeg het tegen de kapitein. Ik moet gaan.'

Met twee treden tegelijk de trap af rennend zwaai ik de verdiepingen langs en kom op dek 5. Als ik op de rode knop sla, hoor ik sissend de lucht ontsnappen door de verbroken verzegeling. De metalen deur schuift open. Het lawaai van de scheepsmotoren wordt versterkt door de holle ruimte en zet zich met pulserende trillingen door in de vloer.

Ik stap de drempel over en loop langs de eerste rij voertuigen. Er staan telkens zeven rijen vrachtwagens bumper aan bumper, zo dicht bij elkaar dat er net genoeg ruime is om je ertussendoor te wurmen. Ik wou dat ik een zaklantaarn had. De tl-verlichting dringt nauwelijks door het duister heen en ik heb er moeite mee de nummerplaten te lezen.

In de lengterichting loop ik het hele dek af en weer terug, de looppaden volgend. Op momenten dat het schip beweegt en op de deining rolt, zet ik me met mijn hand schrap tegen een wielkast of een aanhanger. Mijn verbeelding trekt me de voertuigen binnen. Ik kan Hasan en de anderen zien zitten, gevangen, stikkend. Ik wil op de metalen zijkanten timmeren en de deuren opengooien, lucht binnenlaten.

Ik ben in de tweede doorgang aan stuurboord als ik beetheb. Het gevaarte bestaat uit een roodbruine Mercedes-truck en een witte oplegger. Ik stap op de treeplank, grijp de spiegel vast en trek mezelf op om in de cabine te kunnen kijken. De vloer ligt bezaaid met koffiebekertjes en etensverpakkingen.

Ik stap weer omlaag en loop langzaam om de trailer heen. Met mijn oor tegen de stalen huid gedrukt luister ik of ik hoor niezen of hoesten of fluisteren, welk geluid dan ook. Niets. De achterdeuren zijn verzegeld met een metalen grendel en een sluitnok. De trommel is gesloten en van een hangslot voorzien.

Er komt iemand mijn kant op lopen die een staaflantaarn vasthoudt. De lichtbundel zwaait van links naar rechts en verblindt me heel even. Ik schuif zijwaarts weg van de trailer. De duisternis dwarrelt om me heen.

'Jij hoort hier beneden niet te zijn,' zegt een stem.

Op datzelfde moment slaat een hand zich rond mijn gezicht en bedekt mijn mond. Alle geluid wordt gesmoord.

Ik krijg geen adem. Mijn voeten zijn van de grond. Zijn vingers graven in mijn wangen, rukken aan mijn kaken. Zijn andere onderarm slingert zich rond mijn nek, op zoek naar mijn luchtpijp. Ik zet mijn handen ertegenaan en schop naar achteren, in een poging zijn wreef of zijn knie te raken. Ik raak hem amper.

Hij tilt me nog hoger. Mijn tenen krabbelen over de grond, zonder grip te krijgen. Ik kan het bloed in mijn oren horen kloppen. Ik snak naar lucht.

Mijn karatetraining heeft me iets geleerd over drukpunten. Er is er een in het zachte vlees tussen de duim en de wijsvinger, boven de huidplooi. Ik vind de plek. Hij gromt van de pijn en laat zijn greep op mijn mond en neus los. Ik kan nog altijd niet ademen. Mijn luchtpijp wordt dichtgedrukt. Ik blijf mijn duim in zijn vlees jagen.

Een knie boort zich in mijn nieren. Een golf van pijn schoot door mijn lichaam. Ik laat zijn rechterhand niet los, maar zie op dat moment niet dat zijn linkervuist zich klaarmaakt. De klap komt aan alsof er met geweld een punt wordt gezet. Duisternis wast de pijn en de herinneringen weg. Ik ben bevrijd van Cate en Samira. Vrij van de ongeboren tweeling. Eindelijk vrij. Bevrijd van de veerboot en het niet-aflatende lawaai van de motoren.

Langzaam wordt de wereld breder. Lichter. Een moment lang zweef ik een paar centimeter boven mijn lichaam, neerkijkend op een merkwaardig tafereel. Mijn handen zijn met isolatietape achter mijn rug gebonden. Een ander stuk tape bedekt mijn mond, rond mijn hoofd gewikkeld als een masker, trekkend aan mijn gebarsten lip.

Er is een zwak schijnsel van een zaklantaarn die bij mijn voeten op de grond ligt. Mijn hoofd ligt op Samira's schoot. Ze buigt zich voorover en fluistert iets in mijn oor. Ze wil dat ik stillig. Er valt licht in haar pupillen. Haar vingers zijn als ijs.

Mijn hoofd ligt tegen haar baarmoeder gedrukt. Ik voel haar baby's bewegen. Ik kan het zuigen en gorgelen van het vruchtwater horen, de melodie van hun hartslag. Bloed glijdt heen en weer onder haar huid, zich in allengs nauwere kanaaltjes persend, zuurstof brengend.

Ik vraag me af of tweelingen zich bewust zijn van elkaars bestaan. Horen ze elkaars hartslag? Houden ze elkaar vast of communiceren ze via aanraking?

Beetje bij beetje veranderen verwarring en duisternis in iets wat in de buurt komt van ordening. Als ik me ontspannen hou, kan ik door de tape heen ademhalen.

Samira's lichaam vertrekt opeens en slaat vanaf haar middel dubbel, waardoor mijn hoofd tegen haar dijen wordt geperst. Ze hervindt zich, leunt achterover en haalt diep adem. Ik probeer mijn hoofd op te tillen. Ze wil dat ik stillig.

Door de knevel kan ik niet praten. Ze haakt haar vingers onder de plastic tape en trekt hem net ver genoeg van mijn lippen om me iets te kunnen laten zeggen.

'Waar zijn we?'

'In een vrachtwagen.'

Ons gefluister wordt uitvergroot door de holheid.

'Gaat het?'

Ze schudt haar hoofd. In haar ooghoeken wellen tranen op. Haar lichaam trekt zich weer samen. Ze heeft weeën.

'Wie heeft me hier gebracht?'

'Yanus.'

Pearl en hij werken waarschijnlijk samen.

'Je moet me losmaken.'

Haar ogen schieten in de richting van de gesloten achterdeuren en ze schudt haar hoofd.

'Alsjeblieft.'

'Ze vermoorden je.'

Ze vermoorden me hoe dan ook.

'Help me rechtop te zitten.'

Ze tilt mijn hoofd en schouders op tot ik met mijn rug tegen een wand geleund zit. Mijn inwendige gyroscoop is volkomen van slag. Misschien is er een trommelvlies gescheurd.

Zo te zien staat de trailer vol met pallets en kisten. Door een vierkante smalle opening zie ik een kruipruimte met een matras en drie plastic flessen. Iemand heeft een valse wand opgetrokken om in de trailer een geheim compartiment te maken. Douanebeambten zouden het verschil niet opmerken, tenzij ze de binnen- en buitenkant van de vrachtwagen zouden opmeten.

'Wanneer zijn de weeën begonnen?'

Ze kijkt me hulpeloos aan. Hier binnen kan ze niet beoordelen hoe laat het is.

'Hoeveel tijd zit ertussen?'

'Een minuut.'

Hoe lang ben ik buiten bewustzijn geweest? Raoul zal inmiddels wel naar de kapitein zijn gegaan. Ze zullen Forbes bellen en naar me op zoek gaan. Forbes zal hun zeggen dat ze voorzichtig moeten zijn.

'Maak mijn handen los.'

Samira schudt haar hoofd.

Ze laat de tape los en trekt een deken om mijn schouders. Ze maakt zich meer zorgen om mij dan over zichzelf.

'Je had niet moeten komen.'

Ik kan geen antwoord geven. Een nieuwe wee doet haar gezicht vertrekken. Haar hele lichaam lijkt op slot te slaan.

De achterdeuren zwaaien open. Ik voel de tocht en hoor Samira ademhalen.

'Ik zei dat je van haar af moest blijven,' zegt Yanus, die de trailer in springt. Hij pakt haar vast en wrijft zijn handen over haar gezicht, alsof hij haar met vuil besmeurt. Dan trekt hij haar lippen vaneen, wringt haar kaken open en spuugt in haar mond. Ze kokhalst en probeert zich weg te draaien.

Dan keert hij zich naar mij en rukt de knevel los. Het voelt alsof mijn halve gezicht mee getrokken wordt.

'Wie weten er dat je hier bent?'

'De kapitein. De bemanning… Ze sturen per radio een bericht vooruit,' zeg ik met dikke tong.

'Je liegt!'

In de achteropening van de trailer staat een tweede gestalte. Brendan Pearl. Hoewel hij daar niet langer dan een paar tellen kan hebben gestaan, heb ik het gevoel dat hij me al langere tijd aan het bekijken is.

Het licht achter hem doet zijn gelaatstrekken vervagen, maar ik kan zien hoe hij zijn uiterlijk heeft veranderd sinds de laatste keer dat ik hem zag. Hij laat zijn haar groeien en draagt een bril. De wandelstok is een aardige toevoeging. Hij houdt hem ondersteboven. Waarom? Het is geen wandelstok. Hij heeft een kromme haak, als een soort bootshaak. Ik herinner me hoe Ruiz hem noemde: de Vissersman van Shankill.

Yanus schopt me in mijn buik. Ik rol om en hij zet een schoen in mijn nek en duwt hem omlaag. Hij staat op mijn nek, met zijn volle gewicht op het punt waar mijn wervelkolom overgaat in mijn schedel. Hij zal ongetwijfeld breken.

Samira schreeuwt het uit, haar lichaam ten prooi aan een nieuwe contractie. Pearl zegt iets en Yanus tilt zijn voet op. Ik kan ademen. Hij loopt de lege trailer rond, komt terug en plant zijn hak opnieuw in mijn nek.

Ik dwing mezelf mijn arm uit te strekken en wijs naar Samira. Ze kijkt vol afgrijzen naar haar handen. Vocht bevlekt haar rok en verzamelt zich onder haar knieën.

Pearl duwt Yanus opzij.

'Haar vliezen zijn gebroken,' mompel ik.

'Ze heeft zichzelf bepist,' sneert Yanus.

'Nee. Ze is aan het bevallen. Ze heeft een arts nodig.'

'Zorg dat het stopt,' zegt Pearl.

'Dat kan ik niet.'

Een nieuwe wee dient zich aan, krachtiger dan tevoren. Haar schreeuw kaatst terug van de metalen wanden. Pearl legt de getande haak in haar nek. 'Nog één zo'n geluid en ik ruk haar strot eruit.'

Samira schudt haar hoofd en slaat haar handen voor haar mond.

Pearl trekt me in een zithouding en snijdt de tape rond mijn handen los. Hij stopt heel even terwijl hij op zijn wang kauwt als op een tabakspruim. 'Ze ziet er niet erg gezond uit, wel?' zegt hij in zangerig Iers.

'Ze heeft een arts nodig.'

'Er komt geen arts hier.'

'Maar ze krijgt een tweeling!'

'Al kreeg ze puppy's. Jij zult ze ter wereld moeten helpen.'

'Ik weet niet hoe dat moet!'

'Dan zou ik dat maar snel leren.'

'Doe niet zo stom!'

De stok van de pikhaak slaat tegen mijn kaak. Als de pijn verdwenen is, tel ik met mijn tong mijn tanden en kiezen na. 'Waarom zou ik jullie helpen?'

'Omdat ik je vermoord als je dat niet doet.'

'Vermoorden ga je me toch.'

'Ah, dat weet je.'

Samira's hand schiet uit en grijpt mijn pols. Haar knokkels zijn wit en de pijn staat op haar gezicht gegrift. Ze wil geholpen worden. Ze wil dat de pijn weggaat. Ik kijk naar Pearl en knik.

'Dat is buitengewoon grootmoedig.' Hij staat op en rekt zich uit terwijl hij de pikhaak in zijn vuist laat draaien.

'Hier kan het niet,' zeg ik. 'We moeten haar naar een hut zien te krijgen. Ik heb licht nodig. Schone lakens. Water.'

'Nee.'

'Kijk nou eens om je heen!'

'Ze blijft hier.'

'Dan gaat ze dood. En haar baby's ook! En degene die jullie betaalt, wie het ook is, krijgt niets.'

Ik heb het idee dat hij me weer gaat slaan. In plaats daarvan weegt hij de stok in beide handen, waarna hij hem omlaagzwaait tot de haak op de vloer rust en hij er weer op leunt als op een wandelstok. Yanus en Pearl overleggen fluisterend. Er moeten beslissingen worden genomen. Hun plan dreigt in duigen te vallen.

'Probeer het nog even vol te houden,' zeg ik tegen Samira. 'Het komt goed.'

Ze knikt, veel rustiger dan ik zelf ben.

Waarom is niemand me komen zoeken? Ze zullen Forbes nu toch wel hebben gebeld? Hij zal hun vertellen wat ze moeten doen.

Pearl komt terug.

'Oké, we gaan haar verplaatsen.' Hij tilt zijn overhemd op en laat zijn in de broekband gestoken pistool zien. 'Geen gekloot. Als jij ervandoor gaat, zal Yanus de baby's uit haar snijden. Hij is een gemankeerde kutchirurg.'

De Ier pakt Samira's spullen bij elkaar: een kleine katoenen tas en een reservedeken. Dan helpt hij haar overeind. Ze houdt haar handen beschermend onder haar buik, alsof ze het gewicht overneemt. Ik wikkel de deken om haar schouders. Haar klamme grijze rok kleeft aan haar dijen.

Yanus is vooruitgegaan om te kijken of het trappenhuis vrij is. Ik stel me voor dat bemanningsleden hem opwachten. Hij zal worden overmeesterd. Pearl zal geen andere keuze hebben dan zich over te geven.

Hij tilt Samira uit de laadruimte. Ik kom erachteraan en struikel lichtjes als ik neerkom. Pearl duwt me opzij, sluit de achterdeuren door de trommelsluiting op zijn plaats te schuiven. Er is iets veranderd aan de truck. De kleur. Die is niet hetzelfde.

Mijn maag draait om. Er zijn twee vrachtwagens. Yanus en Pearl moeten elk een vrachtwagen aan boord hebben gereden. Als ik naar het dichtstbijzijnde trappenhuis kijk, zie ik het oplichtende bordje EXIT. We bevinden ons op een ander dek. Ze weten niet waar ze me moeten zoeken.

Samira gaat als eerste. Ze heeft haar kin tegen haar sleutelbeen getrokken en lijkt een gebed te prevelen. Een wee doet haar plotseling stilstaan, haar knieën knikken. Pearl slaat een arm om haar middel. Hoewel hij halverwege de vijftig is, heeft hij in zijn bovenlichaam de kracht van iemand die zichzelf in de halterkamer van de gevangenis heeft opgepompt.

We gaan snel de trap op en lege gangen door. Yanus heeft een hut gevonden op dek 8, waar minder passagiers zijn. Hij neemt Samira over van Pearl en ik bekijk ze, vluchtig, van opzij. Het lijkt me sterk dat ze denken hiermee weg te kunnen komen. De tweepersoonshut is akelig netjes. Er is een smalle eenpersoonskooi op zo'n dertig centimeter boven de grond en een tweede direct daarboven, scharnierend en plat tegen de wand gedraaid. Er is een vierkante patrijspoort met ronde hoeken. Het raam is donker. Land is opgehouden te bestaan en ik kan me alleen de leegte van de Noordzee voorstellen. Ik kijk op mijn horloge. Het is halfeen. Harwich is nog drie uur varen. Als Samira erin slaagt kalm te blijven en de weeën zich stabiliseren, zijn we misschien op tijd in Harwich. Op tijd voor wat?

Haar ogen staan wijd open en op haar voorhoofd parelt zweet. Tegelijkertijd bibbert ze. Ik zit op het bed met mijn rug tegen het schot, haar met mijn armen om haar heen tegen me aan trekkend, in een poging haar warm te houden. Haar buik bolt op tussen haar knieën en haar hele lichaam springt bij elke wee op.

Ik ga op mijn intuïtie af. Doe mijn best niet in paniek te raken of angst te tonen. De cursus EHBO die ik kreeg toen ik bij de MET ging was uitgebreid, maar bevallen zat er niet bij. Ik herinner me iets wat mijn moeder tegen mijn schoonzussen zei: 'Het zijn niet de artsen die kinderen ter wereld helpen, maar de vrouwen.'

Yanus en Pearl bewaken om beurten de deur. Er is niet genoeg ruimte in de hut voor hen allebei. Eentje houdt de gang in de gaten.

Yanus leunt tegen het smalle tafelblad en kijkt met lusteloze belangstelling toe. Hij haalt een sinaasappel uit zijn zak, pelt hem behendig en verdeelt hem in partjes, die hij op een rijtje op de bank legt. Uiteindelijk wordt elk partje tussen zijn tanden fijngedrukt en zuigt hij het sap zijn keel in, om daarna het wit en de pitten op de grond te spugen.

Ik heb nooit geloofd dat mensen echt verdorven konden zijn. Psychopaten worden gemaakt, niet geboren. Yanus zou de uitzondering kunnen zijn. Ik probeer me hem voor te stellen als jongen en me vast te klampen aan een sprankje hoop dat er ergens in hem warmte schuilt. Hij moet van iemand hebben gehouden, van iets – een huisdier, een ouder, een vriend. Ik kan geen spoor ervan ontwaren.

Een of twee keer kan Samira haar schreeuwen niet onderdrukken. Hij gooit een rol afplakband in mijn schoot. 'Zorg dat ze haar bek houdt.'

'Nee! Ze moet me kunnen zeggen wanneer de weeën komen.'

'Zorg dan dat ze zich koest houdt.'

Waar heeft hij zijn mes? Aan zijn borst gegespt aan de linkerkant, pal naast zijn hart. Hij lijkt mijn gedachten te raden en tikt op zijn jasje.

'Ik kan ze uit haar snijden, weet je. Dat heb ik al eerder gedaan, bij dieren. Ik begin gewoon hier te snijden.' Hij houdt zijn vinger net boven de gesp van zijn riem en trekt hem over zijn navel en verder omhoog. 'Dan sla ik haar huid terug.'

Samira huivert.

'Hou toch je mond, man.'

Hij schenkt me zijn haaienglimlach.

De nacht drukt zich tegen de patrijspoort. Er mogen dan vijfhonderd passagiers aan boord van de veerboot zijn, op dit moment voelt het alsof het licht van de hut in een koude, vijandige woestenij schijnt.

Samira buigt haar hoofd naar achteren tot ze me in de ogen kan kijken.

'Zala?' vraagt ze.

Ik wou dat ik tegen haar kan liegen, maar ze leest de waarheid op mijn gezicht. Ik kan haar bijna achteruit de duisternis in zien glijden en verdwijnen. Het is de blik van iemand die weet dat het lot haar in de steek heeft gelaten, met een triestheid zo diep dat niets haar nog kan raken.

'Ik had haar nooit moeten laten gaan,' fluistert ze.

'Het is niet jouw schuld.'

Haar borst gaat op en neer in een gesmoorde snik. Haar ogen hebben zich afgewend. Het is een gebaar dat alles zegt. Ik had gezworen Zala te vinden en haar te beschermen. Ik heb mijn belofte gebroken.

De weeën lijken minder heftig te zijn geworden. Haar ademhaling wordt rustiger en ze slaapt.

Yanus is afgelost door Pearl.

'Hoe is het met haar?'

'Uitgeput.'

Hij zet zich met zijn rug schrap tegen de deur en laat zich omlaagglijden tot hij gehurkt zit, zijn armen op zijn knieën. In een kleine ruimte als deze lijkt hij groter, uit proporties, met grote handen. Yanus heeft vrouwelijke handen, welgevormd en delicaat, snel met een mes. Die van Pearl zijn als botte werktuigen.

'Hier komen jullie nooit mee weg, dat weet je.'

Hij glimlacht. 'Er zijn veel dingen die ik weet en nog veel meer dingen die ik niet weet.'

'Luister. Jullie maken het alleen maar erger. Als zij sterft of de baby's sterven, worden jullie aangeklaagd wegens moord.'

'Ze gaat niet dood.'

'Ze heeft een arts nodig.'

'Genoeg gepraat.'

'De politie weet dat ik hier ben. Ik had je al gezien. Ik heb de kapitein gevraagd een radiobericht vooruit te sturen. In Harwich zullen honderd agenten staan te wachten. Je komt niet weg. Laat mij Samira meenemen. Misschien is er een arts aan boord, of een verpleegkundige. Ze hebben ongetwijfeld medicamenten en verbandmiddelen.'

Het lijkt hem niets te kunnen schelen. Is dat wat er gebeurt als je het grootste deel van je leven in de gevangenis doorbrengt of besteedt aan het plegen van de daden waardoor je daar terechtkomt?

Mijn hoofdhuid tintelt. 'Waarom heb je mijn vriendin Cate en haar man vermoord?'

'Wie?'

'De Beaumonts.'

Zijn ogen, die niet helemaal recht in zijn hoofd staan, maken een asymmetrische indruk, totdat hij praat en zijn gelaatstrekken ineens in lijn liggen. 'Ze was hebberig.'

'Op welke manier?'

'Ze had maar geld voor één baby, maar wilde ze allebei.'

'Heb je haar gevraagd te kiezen?'

'Ik niet. Iemand anders.'

'Walgelijk.'

Hij schokschoudert. 'Dat lijkt me niet al te moeilijk. Het leven draait om keuzes.'

Daar doelde Cate tijdens de reünie dus op toen ze zei dat ze probeerden haar baby af te pakken: ze wilden haar dubbel laten betalen. Haar bankrekening was leeg. Moest ze kiezen? De jongen of het meisje. Hoe kan een moeder een dergelijke beslissing nemen en de rest van haar leven in de ogen van het ene kind staren en daarin een ander kind weerspiegeld zien dat ze nooit heeft gekend?

Pearl is nog steeds aan het woord. 'Ze dreigde naar de politie te stappen. We waarschuwden haar. Ze negeerde het. Dat is het probleem met die lui van tegenwoordig: niemand neemt de verantwoordelijkheid voor zijn handelingen. Bega een vergissing en je betaalt de rekening. Zo is het leven.'

'Heb jij voor jouw vergissingen de rekening betaald?'

'Mijn hele leven lang.' Zijn ogen zijn gesloten. Hij wil me liever weer negeren.

Er wordt geklopt. Pearl haalt het pistool uit zijn riem en richt het op mij, met een vinger tegen zijn lippen. Hij opent de deur op een kier. Ik kan geen gezicht zien. Iemand vraagt iets over een passagier die zoek is. Ze zijn naar mij op zoek.

Pearl gaapt. 'Moet u me daarvoor wakker maken?'

Een tweede stem. 'Neem ons niet kwalijk, meneer.'

'Hoe ziet ze eruit?'

Ik kan het signalement niet verstaan.

'Nou, die heb ik niet gezien. Misschien is ze gaan zwemmen.'

'Dat hoop ik niet, meneer.'

'Oké, en nou moet ik gaan slapen.'

'Sorry, meneer, we zullen u niet meer storen.'

De deur sluit zich. Pearl wacht een moment, zijn oren tegen de deur gedrukt. Gerustgesteld steekt hij het pistool terug in zijn broekriem.

Er wordt opnieuw geklopt. Yanus.

'Waar zat je nou, godverdomme?' vraagt Pearl op hoge toon.

'Ik stond op de uitkijk,' antwoordt Yanus.

'Je had me moeten waarschuwen, eikel.'

'Dat had niet uitgemaakt. Ze kloppen op alle deuren. Ze komen nu niet meer terug.'

Samira schiet met een schreeuw omhoog. De wee is extreem heftig en ik schaar mijn benen om haar heen om haar op haar plaats te houden. Een onzichtbare kracht heeft haar in de greep en bestookt haar lichaam met stuiptrekkingen. Ik voel hoe ik naar haar pijn toe word getrokken. Erin gevangen raak. Ik adem als zij ademt.

Vrijwel meteen komt er een volgende wee. Haar rug kromt zich en haar knieën schieten omhoog.

'Ik moet nu persen.'

'Nee!'

'Het moet.'

Het is zover. Ik kan haar niet tegenhouden. Ik laat me achter haar vandaan glijden, leg haar neer, doe haar benen uit elkaar en trek haar ondergoed uit.

Pearl weet niet goed wat te doen. 'Diep ademhalen, goed zo meisje. Mooie, diepe halen. Heb je dorst? Ik haal een slokje water voor je.'

In de kleine badkamer vult hij een glas water en verschijnt weer.

'Moet je de baarmoederhals niet bekijken?'

'Jij zult er wel alles van weten.'

'Ik heb films gezien.'

'Als je het wilt overnemen, geef je maar een seintje.'

Hij bindt in. 'Wat kan ik doen?'

'Laat wat warm water in de wasbak lopen. Ik moet mijn handen kunnen wassen.'

Samira ontspant haar kaken als de pijn wat afneemt. Haar korte, hortende ademhaling wordt langer. Ze richt zich op Pearl en begint aanwijzingen te geven. Ze heeft dingen nodig: een schaar en draad, klemmen en handdoeken. Even denk ik dat ze ijlt, maar ik besef al snel dat zij meer van het baringsproces weet dan wie van ons ook.

Hij doet de deur open en geeft de aanwijzingen door aan Yanus. Ze maken ruzie.

Pearl bedreigt hem

Samira heeft nog een aanwijzing: er mogen geen mannen aanwezig zijn bij de bevalling. Ik verwacht dat Pearl nee zal zeggen, maar zie hem aarzelen.

Ik richt me tot hem. 'Kijk eens om je heen. We kunnen geen kant op. Eén deur en een patrijspoort vijftien meter boven het wateroppervlak.'

Hij stemt toe en kijkt even op zijn horloge. Het is over tweeën. 'Over een uur moet ze weer in de vrachtwagen zijn.' Zijn hand rust op de deurkruk. Hij draait zich om en richt zich tot mij.

'Mijn moeder is een goede katholiek. Anti-abortus, begrijp je? Zij zou zeggen dat er al vijf mensen in deze ruimte zijn, inclusief de baby's. Als ik terugkom, verwacht ik datzelfde aantal te zien. Zorg dat ze blijven leven.'

Hij sluit de deur en Samira ontspant zich iets. Ze vraagt me een flanellen waslap uit de badkamer te halen. Ze vouwt hem een paar keer dubbel en klemt hem tussen haar tanden zodra ze een wee voelt opkomen.

'Waar heb je al die kennis vandaan?'

'Ik heb baby's geboren zien worden,' legt ze uit. 'Soms kwamen er vrouwen naar het weeshuis om te bevallen. Ze lieten de baby's bij ons achter omdat ze ze niet mee naar huis konden nemen.'

Haar weeën komen nu om de veertig seconden. Haar ogen puilen uit en ze bijt hard in het flanel. De pijn ebt weg.

'Jij moet voor me kijken of ik klaar ben,' fluistert ze.

'Hoe?'

'Steek twee vingers in me om te meten.'

'Hoe kan ik het zien?'

'Kijk naar je vingers,' zegt ze. 'Kijk hoe lang ze zijn. Meet daarmee.'

Ik doe wat ze vraagt. Ik heb nog nooit een vrouw zo intiem aangeraakt, ben ook nog nooit zo bang geweest.

'Ik denk dat je klaar bent.'

Ze knikt, klemt haar tanden op het flanel tijdens het eerste deel van de wee en ademt daarna met korte stoten om de pijn te verlichten.

'Ik moet op de grond zien te komen.'

'Ga je bidden?'

'Nee, ik ga een baby krijgen.'

Ze hurkt met haar benen wijd en zet zich met haar armen schrap tussen de bank en de klaptafel. De zwaartekracht zal haar bijstaan.

'Je moet voelen waar het hoofdje zit,' zegt ze.

Mijn hand zit in haar, draaiend en tastend. Ik voel een babyhoofdje. De bovenkant is nu zichtbaar. Zou er nu bloed moeten zijn?

'Als de baby's er eenmaal zijn, zullen ze je vermoorden,' fluistert Samira. 'Je moet weg zien te komen.'

'Later.'

'Nee, je moet gaan.'

'Maak je over mij geen zorgen.'

Er wordt geklopt. Ik doe de grendel los en Pearl overhandigt me een schaar, een bolletje draad en een roestige klem. Achter hem roept Yanus iets. 'Laat dat wijf haar kop houden!'

'Hou je bek. Ze is aan het bevallen!'

Hij valt naar me uit. Pearl duwt hem terug en sluit de deur. Samira is nu aan het persen, drie keer per wee. Ze heeft lange, slanke, maki-achtige voeten, met ruw eelt langs de buitenranden. Haar kin ligt tegen haar hals en vettige haarkrullen vallen over haar ogen.

'Als ik flauwval, moet je zorgen dat de baby's eruit komen. Laat ze niet in me zitten.' Tanden trekken aan haar onderlip. 'Doe wat je moet doen.'

'Ssst.'

'Beloof het.'

'Ik beloof het.'

'Bloed ik erg?'

'Je bloedt. Of het te erg is, weet ik niet. Ik kan het hoofdje van de baby zien.'

'Het doet pijn.'
'Ja.'

Het bestaan vernauwt zich tot ademen, pijn en persen. Ik strijk haar uit haar ogen en hurk tussen haar benen. Haar gezicht verkrampt. Ze schreeuwt in het flanel. Het hoofdje van de baby is eruit. Ik houd het in mijn gebogen hand, voel de kuiltjes en holtes van de schedel. De schouders zitten klem. Voorzichtig steek ik mijn vinger onder het kinnetje en het lichaampje draait zich binnen in haar. Bij de volgende wee verschijnt de rechterschouder, dan de linker, en de baby glijdt mijn handen in.

Een jongen.

'Wrijf met je vinger langs zijn neus,' zegt Samira.

Een vingertopje is hiervoor genoeg. Er klinkt een zacht, hikkend snikje, gereutel en dan ademhaling.

Samira geeft instructies. Ik moet het draad gebruiken om de navelstreng op twee plaatsen af te binden, en daarna tussen de twee knopen knippen. Mijn handen trillen.

Ze huilt. Uitgeput. Ik help haar op bed en ze leunt tegen het tussenschot. Ik wikkel het jongetje in een handdoek, houd hem dicht tegen me aan, ruik zijn warme adem, laat zijn neus langs mijn wang strijken. Wie ben jij eigenlijk, vraag ik me af?

Ik kijk op mijn horloge en prent me de tijd in: 2 uur 55 's nachts. Welke datum is het? 30 oktober. Waar zullen ze zeggen dat hij geboren is? In Nederland of Groot-Brittannië? En wie zal zijn echte moeder zijn? Wat een verwarde manier om een leven te beginnen.

De weeën zijn weer begonnen. Samira kneedt haar buik, zoekend naar de nog niet geboren tweeling.

'Wat is er?'

'Ze ligt de verkeerde kant op. Je moet haar draaien.'

'Ik weet niet hoe dat moet.'

Elke nieuwe wee brengt een kreun van berusting. Ze is bijna te uitgeput om nog te schreeuwen, te moe om te persen. Dit keer moet ik haar rechtop houden. Ze hurkt. Haar dijen spreiden zich.

Ik voel opnieuw in haar, probeer de baby terug te duwen, haar lichaampje te draaien, tegen de zwaartekracht en de weeën in. Mijn handen zijn glibberig. Ik ben bang haar pijn te doen.

'Het komt.'

'Persen nu.'

Het hoofdje verschijnt in een golf van bloed. In een flits zie ik iets wits met blauwe strepen om het nekje gewikkeld.

'Stop! Niet persen!'

Mijn handen glijden langs het gezichtje van de baby tot mijn vingers onder het kinnetje zijn en ik maak de navelstreng los.

'Samira, de volgende keer moet je écht persen. Dat is heel belangrijk.'

De wee begint. Ze perst één keer, twee keer... Niets.

'Persen.'

'Kan ik niet.'

'Dat kun je wel. Nog een laatste keer. Ik beloof het je.'

Ze gooit haar hoofd achterover en onderdrukt een schreeuw. Haar lichaam verstijft en schokt. Er komt een meisjesbaby tevoorschijn, blauw, glibberig, gerimpeld, in mijn twee tot een kom gevouwen handen. Ik wrijf haar neusje. Niets. Ik hou haar op haar zij, met mijn wijsvinger over haar mond en keel wrijvend in een poging het druipende slijm weg te vegen.

Ik leg haar over mijn hand, met haar armpjes en beentjes bungelend, en geef haar een harde tik op de billen. Waarom ademt ze niet?

Ik leg haar op een handdoek en begin met de punten van mijn wijsvingers en middelvingers ritmisch te drukken. Tegelijkertijd buig ik me voorover en blaas lucht in haar mond en neus.

Ik weet iets van reanimatie. Ik heb de cursus gevolgd en verpleegkundigen het tientallen keren zien doen. En nu sta ik in een lichaam te ademen dat nog nooit heeft ademgehaald. Kom op, kleine. Kom op.

Samira hangt half op het bed en half op de grond. Haar ogen zijn gesloten. De eerste van de tweeling is ingebakerd en ligt tussen haar arm en haar zij.

Ik blijf drukken en adem inblazen. Het is als een mantra, een lichamelijke bede. Bijna onopgemerkt komt het nietige borstkasje omhoog en knipperen er oogleden. Blauw is veranderd in roze. Ze leeft. Prachtig.

15

Een jongen en een meisje elk met tien vingers en tien tenen, wipneusjes, kleine oortjes. Heen en weer wiebelend op mijn hakken heb ik zin om te lachen van opluchting, totdat ik mezelf in de spiegel zie. Ik zit onder het bloed en de tranen, maar heb een blik van totale verwondering op mijn gezicht.

Samira kreunt zachtjes.

'Je bloedt.'

'Dat stopt wel zodra ik ze voed.'

Hoe komt het dat ze zoveel weet? Ze is haar buik aan het masseren, die rimpelt en zwabbert van leegte. Ik wikkel het meisje in en leg haar naast Samira.

'Ga nou!'

'Ik kan je niet alleen laten.'

'Alsjeblieft!'

Een gevoel van uitzonderlijke kalmte en zelfvertrouwen vloeit door me heen. Ik heb maar twee mogelijkheden: vechten of ten onder gaan. Ik neem de schaar, weeg hem in mijn hand. Misschien is er een uitweg.

Ik open de deur. Pearl staat op de gang.

'Snel! Ik heb een rietje nodig. Het meisje. Haar longen zitten vol vocht.'

'En als ik dat nou niet heb?'

'Een balpen, een buisje, iets wat erop lijkt. Schiet op!'

Ik sluit de deur. Hij zal de gang aan Yanus overlaten.

Ik neem de baby's over van Samira en leg ze zij aan zij op de badkamervloer, tussen het wasbakje en het toilet. Ik hou mijn handen onder de kraan, spoel het bloed af en was mijn gezicht.

Ik ben getraind in het gebruik van een vuurwapen. Met een pistool kan ik op de overdekte schietbaan vanaf dertig meter de perfecte score halen. Wat heb ik daar nu aan? Mijn vaardigheden met de blote hand zijn defensief gericht, maar ik weet waar de vitale organen zitten. Ik werp opnieuw een blik op de schaar.

Het is een plan dat ik maar één keer kan proberen. Liggend op de badkamervloer kijk ik richting slaapruimte, met de schaar als een ijspriem in een omgekeerde greep. Mijn duim zit door het oog van de schaar gehaakt. Als ik langs mijn tenen kijk zie ik de baby's.

Met een diepe ademteug open ik mijn longen en schreeuw om hulp. Hoe lang zal het duren?

Yanus beukt de deur open, het slot breekt. Hij stormt naar binnen met het mes voor zich uit. Halverwege kijkt hij omlaag. Onder zijn geheven voet ligt de nageboorte, paars glibberend en glinsterend. Ik weet niet wat hij denkt dat het is, maar de mogelijkheden gaan zijn begripsvermogen te boven. Hij deinst terug en ik drijf de schaar in het zachte vlees van zijn knieholte, mikkend op de slagader en de pezen die zijn been bedienen. De knie knikt en hij zwaait zijn arm met een boog omlaag in een poging mij te steken, maar ik lig te laag en het lemmet suist langs mijn oor.

Ik grijp zijn arm en zet hem op slot, priem de schaar in zijn elleboogholte, waarmee ik nog een slagader raak. Het mes glipt uit zijn vingers.

Hij probeert zich te draaien en me vast te grijpen, maar ik ben al buiten zijn bereik. Ik sta op, spring op zijn rug en werk hem naar de grond. Ik zou hem kunnen doden als ik wil. Ik zou het lemmet in zijn nieren kunnen planten.

In plaats daarvan voel ik in zijn zak en haal het afplakband tevoorschijn. Zijn rechterbeen gaat op en neer als de houten ledematen van een marionet. Ik trek zijn goede arm op zijn rug en tape hem in een soort omgekeerde mitella vast. Een ander stuk tape gaat over zijn mond.

Yanus kreunt. Ik grijp hem bij zijn gezicht. 'Luister. Ik heb de slagader in je been doorgesneden en de slagader in je arm. Jou als messenman vertel ik daarmee niets nieuws. Je weet ook dat je doodbloedt als je geen druk houdt op de wonden. Je zult op je hurken moeten gaan zitten en deze arm gebogen moeten houden.

Ik zorg dat iemand je komt helpen. Als je doet wat ik zeg, leef je misschien nog als we aankomen.'

Samira heeft met een merkwaardige afstandelijkheid zitten kijken. Ze kruipt het bed af en doet een paar pijnlijke stappen zijn kant op, om vervolgens voorover te bukken en hem in zijn gezicht te spugen.

'We moeten gaan.'

'Nee, jíj moet gaan. Neem de baby's mee.'

'Niet zonder jou.

Ik pak de kleinste van de tweeling, het meisje, dat me met open ogen ligt aan te kijken. Samira neemt het slapende jongetje. Voorzichtig speur ik de gang af. Pearl zal spoedig terugkomen.

Samira houdt een handdoek tussen haar dijen geklemd. Zo snel als haar toestand toelaat lopen we naar het trappenhuis. De gang is zo smal dat ik tegen de wand bots als ik Samira's arm probeer vast te houden. De mensen slapen. Ik weet niet welke hutten bezet zijn.

Er is een dienstlift. Ik kan de deur niet openen. Samira's benen wankelen. Ik hou haar overeind. Dit is dek 8. De brug is op dek 10. Ze is niet sterk genoeg om de trappen te kunnen nemen. Ik moet haar van de hut weg zien te krijgen en haar ergens verbergen.

Er is een linnenkamer met aan weerszijden planken vol gevouwen lakens en handdoeken. Ik zou haar hier kunnen achterlaten en op hulp uitgaan. Nee, ze mag niet alleen gelaten worden.

Ik hoor iets bewegen. Er is iemand wakker. Ik klop op de deur van de hut, die gehaast opengaat. Een man van middelbare leeftijd in pyjama en grijze sokken. Hij kijkt geërgerd. Uit de V-hals van zijn shirt piept een toef rood haar, waardoor het lijkt of zijn vulling naar buiten komt.

Ik duw Samira voor me uit. 'Help haar! Ik moet een arts zien te vinden!'

Hij zegt iets in het Duits. Dan ziet hij de bebloede handdoek tussen haar benen. Ik druk hem het meisje in zijn armen.

'Wie bent u?'

'Politie. Er is geen tijd om het uit te leggen. Help haar.'

Samira gaat op het bed liggen, haar armen om het andere kindje.

'Niet opendoen. Niemand mag weten dat ze hier is.'

Voordat hij kan protesteren stap ik weer de gang op en ren naar de trap. De passagierslounge is verlaten, op twee ruw uitziende mannen die over hun pints gebogen zitten na. Achter een kassa zit een vrouw haar nagels te vijlen.

Ik roep om de kapitein. Het is niet de wanhoop in mijn stem die de meeste indruk maakt; het is het bloed op mijn kleding. Ik kom van een nachtmerrieachtige plek, uit een andere dimensie.

Rennende mensen. Leden van de bemanning duiken op; ze roepen bevelen en leiden me verder omhoog. Tussen snuivende snikken door stromen de zinnen uit me. Ze luisteren niet naar me. Ze moeten Samira en de tweeling vinden.

De kapitein is een grote man met borstelige wenkbrauwen en een halve cirkel haar die zich over zijn oren en nek aan zijn schedel vastklampt. Zijn wit-blauwe uniform past bij de kleur van zijn ogen.

Hij staat in het midden van de brug, zijn hoofd naar voren gestoken, en hoort me aan zonder enig spoor van scepsis. De toestand van mijn kleren is voldoende bewijs. Er wordt een verpleger geroepen en ook de hoofdwerktuigkundige. Ondertussen heeft de kapitein via de noodfrequenties radioverbinding gemaakt en praat hij met de Britse kustwacht, de douane en de politie op het vasteland. Vanuit Felixtowe is een motorbarkas gestuurd om langszij te komen en vanuit Prestwick in Schotland wordt in allerijl een helikopter geregeld.

Pearl bevindt zich ergens aan boord. Yanus is dood aan het bloeden. Dit duurt te lang.

'U moet naar Samira,' hoor ik mezelf zeggen. Mijn stem klinkt schel en angstig. 'Ze heeft medische verzorging nodig.'

De kapitein laat zich niet opjagen. Hij volgt de protocollen en procedures die zijn vastgelegd voor gevallen van piraterij of noodsituaties op zee. Hij wil weten met z'n hoevelen ze zijn. Zijn ze gewapend? Zullen ze mensen in gijzeling nemen?

De informatie wordt doorgegeven aan de kustwacht en de politie. Het is nog twintig minuten naar de haven. Door enorme glazen ruiten is de naderende kustlijn te zien, die nog steeds in duisternis is gehuld. De brug is hoog geplaatst en kijkt uit over de boeg. Er is niets wat ook maar op een stuurwiel lijkt. In plaats daarvan zijn er computerschermen, knoppen en toetsenborden. De hoofdwerktuigkundige wil me onderzoeken. Ik schud hem af, stap op de kapitein af en zeg dat hij naar me moet luisteren.

'Ik begrijp dat u een Brits politiefunctionaris bent,' zegt hij kortaf. 'Maar dit is een Nederlands vaartuig en u bent hier niet bevoegd. Mijn verantwoordelijkheid geldt de passagiers en de bemanning. Ik ga hun veiligheid niet in gevaar brengen.'

'Er is zojuist een vrouw bevallen. Ze bloedt. Ze heeft medische verzorging nodig.'

'Over twintig minuten meren we af.'

'Dus u doet niets?'

'Ik wacht mijn instructies af.'

'En de passagiers hier beneden? Ze zijn wakker aan het worden.'

'Ik denk niet dat die in paniek gebracht moeten worden. Onze noodplannen schrijven voor dat passagiers in de Globetrotter Lounge bijeen worden gebracht, waar de meesten zo meteen zullen ontbijten.'

De hoofdwerktuigkundige is een keurige, kleine man met een kostschoolkapsel.

'Gaat u met me mee?'

Hij aarzelt. Ik pak de EHBO-doos van tafel en draai me om om te gaan. De machinist kijkt naar de kapitein, om toestemming vragend. Ik weet niet wat zich tussen hen afspeelt, maar hij blijkt bereid me te volgen.

'Zijn er wapens aan boord?'

'Nee.'

God, wat maken ze het moeilijk! Dit keer gebruiken we een dienstlift om op dek 8 te komen. De deuren gaan open. Het gangpad is verlaten. Op het bovenliggende dek zitten de vrachtwagenchauffeurs, die als eersten van boord zullen gaan.

Op elke hoek verwacht ik Pearl te zien. Dit is voor hem gesneden koek. Zelfs mijn aanwezigheid op de veerboot bracht hem niet van de wijs. Hij stelde gewoon zijn verwachtingen bij en maakte een nieuw plan. Yanus is de meest onvoorspelbare van de twee, maar Pearl is de gevaarlijkste omdat hij in staat is zich aan te passen. Ik kan hem voor me zien, even van zijn à propos doordat hij Samira en de tweeling kwijt is, maar nog altijd zijn kansen op ontsnapping wegend.

Al voordat ik bij de hut ben, kan ik zien dat er iets niet in orde is. Een handvol passagiers verdringt zich op de gang, reikhalzend om over elkaars hoofd heen te kunnen kijken. Tussen hen in staat het echtpaar uit Wales. Mevrouw Jones ziet er zonder lippenstift naakt uit en heeft zich in een grijs trainingspak gehuld dat met moeite haar billen omsluit.

'Ze zitten overal,' zegt ze tegen de anderen. 'Schurken en misdadigers. En wat doet de politie? Niets. Te druk met bonnen uitdelen voor te hard rijden. En als ze al terechtstaan, dan komt er een of andere rechter of magistraat die hen vrijlaat vanwege hun drugsverslaving of moeilijke jeugd. En de slachtoffers dan? Daar hoor je niemand over.'

De deur van de hut staat open, het slot is opengebroken. Op zijn bed zit de Duitse vrachtwagenchauffeur met zijn hoofd naar achteren om zijn bloedneus te stoppen. Van Samira en de tweeling is geen spoor te bekennen.

'Waar zijn ze?' Ik grijp hem bij zijn schouder. 'Waar?'

De woede is niet het ergste. Het moordzuchtige verlangen achter die woede wel.

Mijn mobiele telefoon gaat. We hebben kennelijk bereik. Ik herken het nummer niet.

'Hallo?'

'Hallo,' zegt Pearl. 'Ken je die tv-reclame met dat Duracell-konijntje dat maar blijft gaan en gaan en gaan? Jij hebt wel iets van dat kolerekonijn weg. Jij stopt gewoon niet.'

Er zit een echo in zijn stem. Hij staat op het autodek.

'Waar is ze?'

'Ik heb haar gevonden, kleintje.'

'Ja.'

'En weet je hoe? Het bloed. Jullie hadden een heel spoor achtergelaten.' Op de achtergrond huilt een baby. 'Yanus heb ik ook gevonden. Je had hem aardig toegetakeld, maar ik heb hem opge-lapt.'

'Hij zal doodbloeden.'

'Maak jij je daar maar geen zorgen over, kleintje. Ik laat mijn vrienden tenminste niet achter.'

Ik ben al op weg en ren door de gang naar de eerste hut. De hoofdwerktuigkundige heeft moeite me bij te benen. Yanus is weg. De vloer is glimmend rood en er staan bloederige voetafdrukken in het gangpad, tientallen.

Mensen zijn ongelooflijk. Ze lopen een schouwspel als dit straal voorbij en negeren het omdat het hun gewone, banale, alledaagse begrip te boven gaat.

Hij is nog steeds aan de lijn. 'Jij komt nooit van de boot af,' gil ik. 'Laat ze gaan. Alsjeblieft.'

'Ik moet de kapitein spreken.'

'Hij zal niet willen onderhandelen.'

'Ik wil godverdomme ook niet onderhandelen! Wij hebben een gemeenschappelijk belang.'

'Wat dan?'

'Wij willen allebei dat ik dit schip verlaat.'

Mijn hoofd is helderder nu. Anderen nemen beslissingen voor me. Het is drie uur voor zonsopgang en de kust van Essex ligt er-gens voor ons in het duister. Vanaf de brug kan ik de motoren niet horen en zonder aanknopingspunten lijkt het of de veerboot niet beweegt. Twee kustwachtschepen varen naast de Stena Brittanica om ons naar de haven te escorteren. De kapitein communiceert rechtstreeks met zijn superieuren in Rotterdam.

Ik word erbuiten gehouden, op armlengte afstand, alsof ik een sta-in-de-weg ben, of erger nog: een hysterische vrouw. Wat had ik anders kunnen doen? Wijsheid achteraf is een onbarmhartige leermeester. Ik had Samira en de tweeling nooit alleen moeten laten. Ik had bij hen moeten blijven. Misschien had ik Pearl wel de baas gekund.

Mijn gedachten gaan verder terug. Ik had nooit naar Amster-dam moeten gaan om haar te zoeken. Ik heb dingen erger gemaakt in plaats van beter. Ziedaar mijn levensverhaal: goede bedoelingen. En een honderdste van een seconde te traag zijn voor de overwinning in een wedstrijd waarin de eerste en de laatste een borstkasdikte uit elkaar lagen.

Hoe zouden ze met Pearl kunnen onderhandelen? Hij is niet te vertrouwen. De hoofdwerktuigkundige geeft me iets warms te drinken.

'Het duurt nu niet lang meer,' zegt hij terwijl hij naar de ramen wijst. De lichten van Harwich duiken op en verdwijnen weer terwijl we op de deining meebewegen. Reusachtige kranen met vier poten en langwerpige bovenkanten lijken wachters bij de toegangspoorten van de stad. Ik blijf bij het raam staan kijken hoe ze dichterbij komen.

De kapitein en de stuurman turen naar schermen terwijl buitencamera's hen helpen het schip te manoeuvreren en het voorzichtig tegen de kade te leggen. We staan zo hoog dat de havenwerkers eruitzien als lilliputters die een reus proberen vast te binden.

Inspecteur Forbes is als eerste aan boord en houdt net lang genoeg stil om mijn kleren met een mengeling van ontzag en walging te bekijken. Hij neemt de telefoon over van de kapitein.

'Vertrouw hem niet!' roep ik door de stuurruimte. Het is het enige wat ik nog kan uitbrengen voordat hij zich aan Pearl voorstelt. Ik kan maar één kant van het gesprek horen, maar Forbes herhaalt hardop de gestelde eisen. Na elke eis klinkt zijn klakkende keelgeluid als een soort leesteken.

Pearl wil dat de hoofddeuren van de veerboot worden geopend en voertuigen worden verplaatst om een doorgang voor zijn vrachtwagen te maken. Niemand mag naderbij komen. Als hij een politieagent ziet op het dek, of als hij een brandalarm hoort afgaan of er zich iets afwijkends of ongewensts voordoet, zal hij Samira en de tweeling doden.

'U moet me meer tijd gunnen,' zegt Forbes. 'Ik heb minstens een uur nodig. Dat is niet lang genoeg. Ik kan het niet in vijftien minuten. Geef me Samira. Ja, daarom wil ik ook met haar praten. Nee, dat wil ik niet. Er mogen geen gewonden vallen.'

Op de achtergrond huilt een van de baby's, of misschien wel allebei. Klinken tweelingen hetzelfde? Harmoniseren ze als ze huilen?

Op de autodekken zijn beveiligingscamera's. Een ervan is op de truck gericht. Yanus is duidelijk te zien achter het stuur. Samira zit op de bijrijdersstoel.

De overige passagiers worden over de loopbruggen geëvacueerd naar het hoofdgebouw van de terminal. Het havengebied is gesloten en afgegrendeld door speciale eenheden in zwarte kogelvrije vesten. Op omringende daken bevinden zich scherpschutters.

In mijn binnenste is het leed van de afgelopen uren verder aangezwollen, wat ademen moeilijk maakt. Ik voel mezelf in de achtergrond wegzinken.

Forbes heeft ermee ingestemd een beperkt aantal voertuigen van het schip te halen om zo een doorgang voor de truck te maken. Terwijl hij aanwijzingen geeft voor de ontruiming loop ik achter de rechercheur de loopplank af naar de kade. Mannen in gele reflecterende vesten gebaren de eerste opleggers de afrit af.

Forbes heeft Pearl op de luidspreker gezet. Hij knikt kalm. Zelfverzekerd. Misschien is het stoerdoenerij. Hij praat boven het geluid van motoren uit en zegt Forbes haast te maken. Langzaam ontstaat er op het autodek een duidelijke doorgang. De Mercedes-truck staat achterin, met felle koplampen en draaiende motor.

Ik begrijp nog steeds niet hoe hij denkt weg te komen. Buiten staan burgerwagens van de politie, in de lucht hangen helikopters. Hij kan ze niet ontlopen.

Yanus is dood aan het bloeden. Zelfs met een verbonden been en onderarm zal zijn bloeddruk blijven teruglopen. Hoe lang duurt het voordat hij het bewustzijn verliest?

'Je weet zeker dat je een pistool hebt gezien?' zegt Forbes, voor het eerst direct tegen mij.

'Ja.'

'Zou hij nog andere vuurwapens kunnen hebben?'

'Ja.'

'Wat voor lading heeft de truck?'

'Deze is leeg. Er staat er nog een op dek 3. Die heb ik niet van-binnen gezien.' Ik geef hem het kenteken.

'Het zou dus een smokkelrit kunnen zijn. Er zijn mogelijk illegalen aan boord.'

'Dat zou kunnen, ja.'

De laatste opleggers zijn weggehaald. Yanus heeft vrij baan. Pearl is nog steeds bezig instructies te geven. De tweeling is stil.

In een moment van koortsige stilte realiseer ik me dat er iets niet klopt. Pearl is te rustig, te zelfverzekerd. Zijn plan snijdt geen hout. Op het moment dat dit tot me doordringt ben ik al op weg, duw me langs Forbes en sprint de hellingbaan op. De honderd meter is niet mijn favoriete afstand, maar ik loop hem in minder tijd dan de meeste mensen nodig hebben om hun veters vast te maken.

Forbes schreeuwt dat ik moet stoppen. Hij is te laat. Als reactie op de nieuwe gang van zaken geeft hij de teams specialisten opdracht op te rukken. Zware laarzen stampen achter me aan de hellingbaan op en verspreiden zich langs de buitenste rijen vrachtwagens.

Yanus zit nog altijd achter het stuur, starend door de voorruit, niet onder de indruk van mijn nadering. Zijn ogen lijken me te volgen terwijl ik me naar de portiergreep draai en hem open-wring. Zijn handen zijn met tape aan het stuurwiel vastgemaakt. Op de vloer en rond zijn voeten is bloed gestroomd. Ik druk mijn hand tegen zijn nek. Hij is dood.

Samira's handen zijn eveneens vastgebonden. Ik buig me over Yanus heen en raak haar schouders aan. Haar ogen openen zich.

'Waar zijn ze?'

Ze schudt haar hoofd.

Ik zwaai omlaag en ren naar de achterkant van de truck. Het team specialisten heeft de deuren al opengemaakt, karabijnen zwaaien van links naar rechts. De trailer is leeg.

Forbes heeft ons ingehaald, met gepuf en gepiep waarin zijn verkoudheid nog doorklinkt. Ik grijp zijn telefoon. De verbinding is weggevallen.

In de commotie van de daaropvolgende minuten zie ik dingen op halve snelheid en kost het me moeite speeksel te vinden om mijn mond te bevochtigen. Forbes loopt bevelen te blaffen en schopt kwaad tegen de banden van de truck. Als hij niet kalmeert moet iemand hem straks nog neerleggen met een verdovingsgeweer.

De veerboot is afgezet door groepen politieagenten. Niemand mag erop of eraf. In de terminalhal worden passagiers gescreend en ondervraagd. De schijnwerpers rond het havenbassin doen het geheel eruitzien als een reusachtig toneel of filmset, klaar om de camera's te laten lopen.

Yanus kijkt en zit stil, alsof hij op zijn claus wacht. Mijn hart slaat over als ik besef dat ik hem heb gedood. Goed, hij verdiende het, maar ik was degene die het deed. Ik heb hem om het leven gebracht. Mijn kleren zijn nog steeds bevlekt met zijn bloed, naast dat van Samira.

Verplegers tillen haar op een brancard. De handdoek zit nog steeds tussen haar dijen geklemd. Als ik kom aanlopen, leiden de helpers me zorgzaam naar één kant. Ze kan nu niet met me praten. Ik wil zeggen dat het me spijt, dat het mijn schuld is. Dat ik haar nooit alleen had mogen laten. Dat ik bij hen had moeten blijven. Misschien had ik hem kunnen tegenhouden.

Een tijdje later komt Forbes me zoeken.

'Laten we een eindje lopen.'

Instinctief pak ik zijn arm vast. Ik ben bang dat mijn benen me in de steek laten.

'Hoe laat is het?'

'Vijf uur dertig.'

'Volgens mijn horloge vijf uur vijftien.'

'Dat loopt achter.'

'Hoe weet jij dat het jouwe niet voorloopt?'

'Omdat de rederij van die grote joekels van klokken aan de muur heeft hangen die zeggen dat jouw horloge het in vier verschillende tijdzones bij het verkeerde eind heeft.'

We lopen de hellingbaan af, over de kade, weg van de veerboot. Tanks van raffinaderijen en scheepscontainers werpen schaduwen tegen de helder wordende lucht. Wind, rook en voortjagende wolken bewegen boven ons langs.

'Je gelooft niet dat hij nog op de boot zit, hè?' vraagt Forbes.

'Inderdaad.'

Opnieuw een lange stilte. 'We hebben ontdekt dat er aan stuurboordzijde een reddingsboei ontbreekt. Hij kan overboord zijn gesprongen.'

'Dan had iemand hem gezien.'

'We werden afgeleid.'

'Dan nog.'

Ik kan nog altijd de tweeling ruiken en de zachtheid van hun huid voelen. We denken beiden aan hetzelfde: wat is er van hen geworden?

'Je had nooit aan boord van die veerboot moeten gaan,' zegt hij.

'Ik kon niet zeker weten of ze aan boord was of niet.'

Hij haalt een pakje sigaretten uit zijn zak en telt de inhoud.

'Je zou niet moeten roken met een verkoudheid.'

'Ik zou helemaal niet moeten roken. Volgens mijn vrouw kunnen mannen en vrouwen precies dezelfde kwaal hebben, met dezelfde symptomen, maar is het dan altijd de man die er slechter aan toe is.'

'Dat komt doordat mannen hypochonders zijn.'

'Ik heb een andere theorie. Ik denk dat het komt doordat, hoe ziek een vrouw ook is, er altijd een klein deel van haar brein is dat aan schoenen denkt.'

'Ik wed dat je dat niet tegen haar hebt gezegd.'

'Ik ben wel ziek, maar niet achterlijk.'

Zijn houding is veranderd. In plaats van sarcasme en cynisme proef ik bezorgdheid en toenemende vastberadenheid.

'Wie zit hierachter?'

'Samira had het over een Engelsman die zichzelf Brother noemt. Ze zei dat hij een kruis in zijn nek had. Er is iemand die je zou moeten natrekken. Hij heet Paul Donavon. Hij zat bij Cate Beaumont en mij op school. Hij was er die avond bij toen ze werd aangereden.'

'Denk je dat hij hierachter zit?'

'Samira ontmoette Brother in een weeshuis in Kabul. Donavon was met het Britse leger in Afghanistan. Ze richtten zich op wezen omdat dat minder complicaties gaf. Geen families die naar hen op zoek zouden gaan of vragen zouden stellen. Sommigen werden gesmokkeld voor de seksindustrie. Anderen kregen de keuze om draagmoeder te worden.'

'De zwangere illegalen waar jij naar vroeg. Die beweerden allebei wees te zijn.'

Forbes heeft nog altijd zijn sigaret niet aangestoken. Hij hangt tussen zijn lippen en wipt op en neer als hij praat. Over zijn schouder werpt hij een blik op de veerboot.

'Wat betreft die avond.'

'Welke avond.'

'Toen we dat etentje hadden.'

'O ja.'

'Heb ik toen mijn fatsoen weten te houden? Ik bedoel, heb ik me gedragen?'

'Je was een absolute heer.'

'Gelukkig,' mompelt hij. 'Ik bedoel, dat dacht ik ook.' Stilte. 'Je hebt toen iets meegenomen wat niet van jou is.'

'Ik beschouw het liever als gedeelde informatie.'

Hij knikt. 'Misschien zou je eens na moeten denken over je loopbaankeuze, agent Barba. Ik weet niet of jij wel een, zoals ik het noem, teamspeler bent.'

Hij kan niet blijven. Er is een debriefing waar hij bij moet zijn en die pittig wordt. Zijn superieuren zullen willen weten hoe hij Pearl heeft kunnen laten ontkomen. En als de media hier eenmaal lucht van krijgen, zal het voorlopig nog niet uit de aandacht zijn verdwenen.

Forbes kijkt naar mijn kleren. 'Als hij niet meer op de veerboot zit, hoe is hij er dan af gekomen?'

'Hij zou nog steeds aan boord kunnen zijn.'

'Dat geloof je zelf niet.'

'Nee. Wat dacht je van de bemanning?'

'Denk je dat hij een uniform heeft gepikt?'

'Dat is een mogelijkheid.'

Hij draait zich abrupt om en beent weg in de richting van de wachtende politiewagens. De beelden van de bewakingscamera's zullen hoogstwaarschijnlijk het antwoord gaan leveren. Op elke uithoek van de kade en op elk dek van het schip hangen camera's. Een ervan moet Pearl toch hebben vastgelegd.

'Bananen,' roep ik hem na.

'Pardon?'

'Mijn moeders middeltje tegen verkoudheid.'

'Je zei dat je nooit naar haar luisterde.'

'Bijna nooit.'

De afgelopen tijd zijn er te veel ziekenhuizen geweest. Te veel lange zitten op ongemakkelijke stoelen, te veel snacks uit automaten en bekers met instantkoffie en poedermelk. Dit ziekenhuis ruikt naar gekookt eten en uitwerpselen, en er liggen macabere geblokte tegels op de gangen, gladgesleten door de rolwagens.

Ruiz belde me vanuit Hull, waar zijn veerboot afmeerde. Hij wilde me komen ophalen, maar ik heb hem gezegd naar huis te gaan en te rusten. Hij heeft genoeg gedaan.

'Wordt er voor je gezorgd?'

'Het gaat prima.'

'Samira?'

'Die herstelt wel.'

Ik hoop dat ik gelijk heb. Ze slaapt al tien uur en werd zelfs niet wakker toen ze haar uit de ambulance tilden en naar een eigen kamer reden. Daar heb ik zitten wachten, wegdoezelend in mijn plastic stoel, met mijn hoofd naast haar schouder op het bed.

Het is halverwege de middag als ze uiteindelijk wakker wordt. Ik voel het matras bewegen, sla mijn ogen op en kijk in de hare.

'Ik moet naar de wc,' fluistert ze.

Ik pak haar bij haar elleboog en help haar naar het zijkamertje.

'Waar ben ik?'

'In een ziekenhuis.'

'Welk land?'

'Engeland.'

Een instemmend knikje, maar geen teken van een reis die is volbracht of een doel dat is bereikt.

Ze wast haar gezicht, oren, handen en voeten, intussen zachtjes in zichzelf pratend. Ik pak haar weer bij de arm en begeleid haar terug naar het bed.

Ze gebaart naar het raam, ze wil naar buiten kijken. Boven de daken en tussen de gebouwen door is nog net de Noordzee te zien. Hij heeft de kleur van mat staal.

'Als kind vroeg ik me altijd af hoe de zee eruit zou zien,' zegt ze. 'Ik had er alleen foto's van gezien in boeken en op tv.' Ze staart naar de horizon.

'En hoe vind je hem nu?'

'Hij lijkt wel hoger dan het land. Waarom kan het water niet binnenrollen en ons wegspoelen?'

'Dat gebeurt ook weleens.'

Ik zie dat ze een handdoek in haar hand heeft. Ze wil hem als gebedskleed gebruiken, maar weet niet welke kant Mekka op ligt. Ze draait langzaam rond als een kat die zich aan het nestelen is.

Er staan tranen in haar ogen en haar lippen trillen terwijl ze worstelt met de woorden.

'Ze zullen straks honger hebben. Wie zal ze voeden?'

BOEK DRIE

Love and pain are not the same. Love is put to the test – pain is not. You do not say of pain, as you do of love: 'That was not true pain or it would not have disappeared so quickly.'

'The Blue Afternoon', William Boyd

1

Sinds de geboorte van de tweeling ben ik 's nachts talloze malen verdronken, trappelend en rukkend aan het beddengoed. Ik zie kleine lichamen in velden zeewier drijven of aanspoelen op stranden. Mijn longen geven het op voordat ik bij ze kan komen en laten me naar adem snakkend en verdoofd door een duistere angst achter. Ik vraag me af of er zoiets bestaat als een gezwollen hart.

Ook Samira is wakker. Om drie uur 's ochtends loopt ze door het huis alsof haar voeten met de grond hebben afgesproken dat zij altijd lichtvoetig zal lopen en in ruil daarvoor nooit meer een pad zal tegenkomen dat te steil is. Er zijn vijf dagen verstreken sinds de verdwijning van de tweeling. Pearl is door de kieren gezakt en verdwenen. We weten hoe hij van het schip af is gekomen. Een bewakingscamera op dek 3 pikte een man op met een veiligheidshelm en reflecterend jack, die niet als een van de bemanningsleden kon worden geïdentificeerd. Op het materiaal kwam zijn gezicht niet duidelijk in beeld, maar wel was te zien dat hij een reiskooi voor huisdieren droeg. In de vierkante doos van grijs plastic hadden twee Siamese katten moeten zitten, die echter ronddolend in een trappenhuis werden aangetroffen.

Een andere camera op het douaneterrein gaf de helderste beelden van de onbekende man. Op de voorgrond worden trucks gescand met infraroodapparatuur voor het opsporen van illegalen. Op de achtergrond echter, aan de rand van het beeld, is een pompoenvormige caravan zichtbaar die achter een oud model Range Rover hangt. Te zien is hoe de heer en mevrouw Jones uit Cardiff na doorzocht te zijn hun belastingvrije aankopen en souvenirs opnieuw inpakken. Als de auto en caravan wegrijden is op het asfalt naast de plek waar zij geparkeerd stonden een vierkante grijze reiskooi te zien.

Het echtpaar uit Wales werd zondag kort na de middag op de M4 even ten oosten van Reading aangehouden. De caravan was leeg, maar op de tafel en de aluminium deur werden Pearls vingerafdrukken aangetroffen. Het echtpaar was bij een benzinepomp aan de M25 gestopt om te tanken. Een kassamedewerker kon zich herinneren dat Pearl zuigflessen en babymelkpoeder kocht. Kort daarna, om 10.42 uur, werd gemeld dat er van een aanpalend parkeerterrein een auto was gestolen. Het voertuig is nog niet teruggevonden.

Forbes leidt het onderzoek, in nauw contact met Spijker in Amsterdam. Ze hebben hun krachten gebundeld en laten hun gezamenlijke wilskracht op het probleem los. Ze zijn de namen van de IVF-kliniek aan het vergelijken met de gegevens van de Britse Immigratiedienst.

Tegenover de pers zijn geen mededelingen gedaan over de vermiste tweeling. Inspecteur Forbes heeft die beslissing genomen. Gestolen kinderen zorgen voor dramatische krantenkoppen en hij wil paniek voorkomen. Een jaar geleden werd een pasgeborene weggegrist uit een ziekenhuis in Harrogate en werden er de eerste twee dagen twaalfhonderd vermeende waarnemingen gemeld. Moeders werden lastiggevallen op straat en als kidnappers behandeld. Huizen werden onnodig bestormd. Onschuldige gezinnen hadden te lijden.

De enige openbare mededeling had betrekking op Pearl, voor wie een arrestatiebevel is uitgevaardigd. Het zoveelste. Ik zal mijn pistool weer moeten gaan dragen. Zolang hij op vrije voeten is, zal ik het bij me houden. Ik wil Samira niet nog een keer kwijtraken.

Ze logeert bij me sinds ze woensdag het ziekenhuis heeft verlaten. Hari heeft de logeerkamer afgestaan en slaapt beneden op een bedbank. Hij lijkt nogal gecharmeerd van onze logee. Sinds kort draagt hij overal in huis een shirt, omdat hij voelt dat ze zijn andere dracht afkeurt.

Ik moet voor een tuchtcommissie van de politie verschijnen. Plichtsverzuim, liegen en misbruik van gezag zijn nog maar drie van de aanklachten. Het feit dat ik niet op Hendon ben verschenen is nog de minste zorg. Barnaby Elliot heeft me beschuldigd van intimidatie en brandstichting. Het onderzoek staat onder supervisie van de klachtencommissie van de politie. Ik ben schuldig tot het tegendeel bewezen is.

Op de gang spoelt een toilet door. Een lichtschakelaar klikt uit. Een paar minuten later klink het zoemgeluid van een machine en het ritmische zuigen van een elektrisch kolfapparaat. Samira's melkproductie is op gang gekomen en ze moet elke zes uur afkolven. Het geluid van de pomp is merkwaardig slaapverwekkend. Ik doe mijn ogen weer dicht.

Ze heeft niets gezegd over de tweeling. Ik vraag me telkens af wanneer ze zal instorten, in stukken gebroken door het verlies. Zelfs toen ze in het mortuarium van Westminster Hasans lichaam identificeerde hield ze alles binnen.

'Het is niet erg om te huilen,' zei ik tegen haar.

'Daarom heeft Allah ons tranen geschonken,' antwoordde ze.

'Denk je dat God hier een rol in speelt?'

'Hij zou mij dit lijden niet schenken als Hij niet dacht dat ik het kan verdragen.'

Hoe kan ze zo wijs zijn en tegelijkertijd zo aanvaardend? Gelooft zij echt dat dit onderdeel is van een of ander groots overkoepelend plan, of dat Allah haar zo wreed op de proef zou stellen?

Een dergelijk geloof lijkt volkomen middeleeuws, en toch is ze leergierig. Dingen die ik vanzelfsprekend vind, vindt zij fascinerend, zoals de centrale verwarming, toiletten met twee spoelstanden en mijn wasmachine-drogercombinatie. In Kabul moest ze water de trap op dragen naar hun flat en viel de stroom bijna dagelijks uit. In Londen heeft elke straat verlichting die de hele nacht brandt. Samira vroeg of wij Britten misschien bang zijn voor het donker. Ze begreep niet waarom ik moest lachen.

Gisteren nam ik haar mee uit winkelen in Canary Warf, voor kleding. 'In heel Afghanistan is niet zo veel glas als hier,' zei ze, wijzend naar de kantoortorens die in de ochtendzon schitterden. Ik kon zien hoe ze de kantoorwerkers observeerde die in de rij stonden voor koffie en 'light' muffins, de vrouwen in nauwsluitende rokken, strakke topjes en jasjes, terwijl ze vluchtig een hand door hun korte haar haalden en in hun mobiele telefoons babbelden. De kledingboetieks waren te veel voor haar. De winkelmeisjes gingen gekleed als begrafenisgangers en de winkels voelden aan als uitvaartcentra. Ik zei Samira dat er een betere plek was om kleren op te duiken. We gingen op pad naar Commercial Road, waar kledingstukken opeengepakt aan rekken hingen en uit bakken puilden. Ze koos twee rokken uit: een bloes met lange mouwen en een vest. Bij elkaar was het minder dan zestig pond.

Ze bestudeerde de biljetten van twintig pond.

'Is dat jullie koningin?'

'Ja.'

'Ze ziet eruit alsof ze haar in gips hebben gedoopt.'

Ik moest lachen. 'Ja, nou je het zegt.'

Overal hingen kerstversieringen. Zelfs de bagelbakkerij en de halalslager hadden kerstlampjes en nepsneeuw. Samira stopte even om in de etalage van een restaurant het kreeftenaquarium te bekijken.

'Ik ga nooit in zee zwemmen.'

'Waarom niet?'

'Ik wil niet een van die beesten tegenkomen.'

Volgens mij had ze visioenen van kreeften die krioelend over elkaar heen kropen, net als in het aquarium.

'Voor jou moet zoiets als dit sciencefiction zijn.'

'Science? Fiction?'

'Dat betekent "als in een fantasie". Onwerkelijk.'

'Ja, onwerkelijk.'

Door Londen door haar ogen te zien heb ik een nieuwe kijk op de stad gekregen. Zelfs het meest alledaagse tafereel wordt nieuw leven ingeblazen. Toen ik haar meenam de trap af om de ondergrondse te nemen hield ze mijn hand vast terwijl een naderende trein door de tunnel raasde en, zoals zij het noemde, klonk als een 'monster in een grot'.

De achteloze weelde die uitgestald ligt is gênant. In het East End zijn meer dierenartsen dan er artsen waren in Kabul. En de dieren zijn beter gevoed.

Het kolven is gestopt. Ze heeft Hari's tv aangezet en zapt van zender naar zender. Ik laat me uit bed glijden, loop op mijn tenen de gang over en klop op haar deur. Ze heeft mijn oude peignoir aan, die met een geborduurde uil op een van de zakken.

'Kun je niet slapen?'

'Nee.'

'Ik maak een slaapdrankje voor ons klaar.'

Haar ogen worden groot.

Ze volgt me de trap af, door de hal de keuken in. Ik doe de deur dicht, pak een fles melk uit de koelkast en schenk twee mokken vol. Twee minuten in de magnetron en ze staan te dampen. Ik breek stukken donkere chocola af, laat ze in de melk vallen en kijk hoe ze smelten. Samira vist de smeltende brokken eruit met haar lepeltje en likt het schoon.

'Vertel me eens over je familie.'

'De meesten van hen zijn dood.'

Ze likt nog eens aan het lepeltje. Ik breek meer stukken chocola af en doe ze in haar mok.

'Had je een grote familie?'

'Niet echt. In Afghanistan overdrijven mensen wat hun familie allemaal heeft gedaan. Die van mij niet uitgezonderd. Een van mijn voorouders zou met Marco Polo naar China zijn gereisd, beweren ze, maar ik geloof dat niet. Ik denk dat hij een smokkelaar was die buskruit van India naar Afghanistan bracht. De koning hoorde hoe betoverend het was en vroeg om een demonstratie. Volgens mijn vader vlogen er wel duizend vuurpijlen langs de hemel. Bamboe kastelen dropen van het vuur. Vuurwerk werd het familiebedrijf. De recepten werden van vader op zoon doorgegeven, en aan mij.'

Ik herinner me de uit Hasans spullen afkomstige foto van een fabriek met in rijen opgestelde arbeiders ervoor, de meesten met ontbrekende ledematen of ogen, of op een andere manier incompleet. Hasan had littekens van brandwonden op zijn armen.

'Het moet gevaarlijk werk zijn geweest.'

Samira steekt haar handen omhoog en laat haar vingers zien.

'Ik ben een van degenen die geluk hebben gehad.' Ze klinkt bijna

315

teleurgesteld. 'Mijn vader raakte allebei zijn duimen kwijt toen er een voetzoeker ontplofte. Oom Rashid verloor zijn rechterarm en zijn vrouw haar linker. Ze hielpen elkaar bij het koken, het naaiwerk en autorijden. Mijn tante schakelde en mijn oom stuurde. Mijn vaders andere broer, Farhad, raakte zijn vingers kwijt bij een groot vuurwerk. Hij was een bedreven gokker, maar begon te verliezen toen hij niet meer zelf de kaarten kon schudden. Mijn grootvader heb ik nooit gezien. Hij kwam vóór mijn geboorte om bij een fabrieksontploffing. Bij dezelfde brand kwamen nog twaalf mensen om, onder wie twee van zijn broers. Mijn vader zei dat het een offer was dat alleen onze familie in staat was te brengen. Eén hand is genoeg om te zondigen, zei hij. Eén hand is genoeg om te redden.'

Ze kijkt naar de donkere rechthoek die het raam is. 'Het was onze roeping om de hemel te beschilderen. Mijn vader geloofde dat onze familie op een dag een vuurpijl zou maken die de weg naar de hemel zou verlichten. In de tussentijd zouden we vuurpijlen maken die de blik van Allah zouden trekken, in de hoop dat Hij onze familie zou zegenen en ons geluk en goede gezondheid zou schenken…' Ze zwijgt even en denkt na over de ironie van haar uitspraak. Roerloos zit ze schuin over de tafel gebogen, sterk en toch breekbaar. Haar starende blik lijkt van diep achter in haar ogen te komen.

'Wat is er van de fabriek geworden?'

'De talibs hebben hem dichtgegooid. Vuurwerk was zondig, zeiden ze. Mensen vierden feest toen ze verschenen. Ze zouden de krijgsheren een halt toeroepen en een eind maken aan de corruptie. Dingen veranderden, maar niet ten goede. Meisjes mochten niet naar school. Ramen werden dichtgeschilderd, zodat vrouwen niet meer konden worden gezien. Er was geen muziek of tv of video's, geen kaartspelen, geen vliegers. Ik was acht en ze dwongen me een boerka te dragen. Ik mocht geen dingen kopen bij mannelijke winkeliers. Ik mocht niet met mannen praten. Ik mocht niet lachen in het openbaar. Vrouwen moesten er onopvallend uitzien. Onzichtbaar zijn, onwetend. Mijn moeder gaf ons in het geheim les. De boeken werden elke avond verstopt, ons huiswerk moesten we vernietigen.

Mannen met baarden en tulbanden patrouilleerden over straat, de oren gespitst of ze muziek of video's hoorden spelen. Ze sloegen mensen met in water geweekte zwepen en met kettingen. Sommigen werden afgevoerd en kwamen niet meer terug. Mijn vader nam ons mee naar Pakistan. We leefden in een kamp. Daar stierf mijn moeder en mijn vader gaf zichzelf de schuld. Op een dag kondigde hij aan dat we naar huis teruggingen. Hij zei dat hij liever verhongerde in Kabul dan te moeten leven als een bedelaar.'

Ze valt stil en schuift heen en weer op haar stoel. De motor van de koelkast komt rammelend tot leven en ik voel eenzelfde soort siddering door me heen gaan.

'De Amerikanen wierpen vanuit de lucht strooibiljetten waarin stond dat ze ons kwamen bevrijden, maar er was niets meer om ons van te bevrijden. Desondanks juichten we omdat de talibs waren vertrokken, als bange honden. Maar de Noordelijke Alliantie was niet veel anders. We hadden geleerd niet te veel te verwachten. In Afghanistan slapen we met de doornen en niet met de bloemen.'

De inspanning die het haar heeft gekost om herinneringen op te halen heeft haar slaperig gemaakt. Ik spoel de mokken om en volg haar naar boven. Bij mijn deur blijft ze staan. Ze wil iets vragen.

'Ik ben niet gewend aan de rust.'

'Vind jij Londen rustig?'

Ze aarzelt. 'Zou ik misschien bij jou op de kamer mogen slapen?'

'Is er iets niet goed? Het bed?'

'Nee.'

'Ben je bang?'

'Nee.'

'Wat is er dan?'

'In het weeshuis sliepen we op de grond, in dezelfde kamer. Ik ben het niet gewend om alleen te zijn.'

Mijn hart krimpt samen. 'Waarom heb je niet eerder wat gezegd? Natuurlijk kun je bij mij slapen.'

Ze haalt een deken en spreidt hem uit op de grond naast mijn klerenkast.

'Mijn bed is groot genoeg voor ons allebei.'

'Nee, dit is beter.'

Ze rolt zich op op de grond en ademt zo zachtjes dat ik de neiging heb te kijken of ze er nog is.

'Welterusten,' fluister ik. 'Dat je maar tussen de bloemen mag slapen, in plaats van tussen de doornen.'

De volgende ochtend verschijnt inspecteur Forbes vroeg als altijd. Gekleed in een antracietkleurig pak en gele das is hij klaar om de pers te woord te staan. De radiostilte naar de media is opgeheven. Hij heeft hulp nodig bij zijn zoektocht naar de tweeling.

Ik ga hem voor naar de keuken. 'Je verkoudheid klinkt al beter.'

'Ik kan geen banaan meer zien.'

Hari zit met Samira in de voorkamer. Hij laat haar zijn oude X-Box zien en probeert uit te leggen wat er allemaal mee kan.

'Je kunt mensen neerschieten.'

'Waarom?'

'Voor de lol.'

'Waarom zou je voor de lol mensen neerschieten?'

Ik kan Hari's teleurstelling bijna horen. Arme jongen. De twee hebben iets gemeen. Hari studeert chemische techniek en Samira weet meer van chemische reacties dan wie van zijn docenten ook, zegt hij.

'Het is een apart grietje,' zegt Forbes fluisterend.

'Hoe bedoel je?'

'Ze zegt niet veel.'

'De meeste mensen praten te veel en hebben niets te melden.'

'Wat is ze van plan te gaan doen?'

'Weet ik niet.'

Wat zou ik doen als ik in haar schoenen stond? Ik ben nog nooit van vrienden of familie afgesneden geweest of gestrand in een vreemd land (tenzij je Wolverhampton meerekent, dat echt al behoorlijk vreemd is).

Hari komt de keuken binnenlopen en kijkt nogal zelfvoldaan.

'Samira gaat me leren hoe ik vuurwerk moet maken,' meldt hij terwijl hij een koekje pakt van het schoteltje van Forbes.

'Zodat je jezelf kunt opblazen.'

'Ik ben heel voorzichtig.'

'O ja. Zoals die keer dat je die koperen buis met buskruit vulde en een gat in de gevelbetimmering blies.'

'Toen was ik vijftien.'

'Oud genoeg om beter te weten.'

'Zondag is het Guy Fawkes' Night. We gaan een donderster maken.'

'En dat is?'

'Een vuurpijl die fluit en witte en rode sterren spuugt, met een saluut aan het eind.'

'Aha, een saluut.'

'Een grote knal.'

Hij heeft al een lijst met ingrediënten opgesteld: kaliumnitraat, zwavel, bariumchloraat en koperpoeder. Ik heb geen idee wat dit spul doet, maar ik zie bijna voor me hoe het vuurwerk in zijn ogen ontploft.

Forbes bekijkt het lijstje. 'Is dit spul toegestaan?'

'We gaan niet verder dan tot acht centimeter dik.'

Het is geen antwoord op de vraag, maar de inspecteur laat het erbij.

Hoewel ze niets zegt over de tweeling twijfel ik er niet aan dat ze aan hen denkt, net als ik. Er gaat vrijwel geen minuut voorbij of mijn gedachten dwalen weer naar hen af. Ik kan hun huid tegen mijn lippen voelen en hun smalle ribbenkastjes zien bewegen bij elke ademhaling. Het meisje had moeite met ademhalen. Misschien waren haar longetjes niet volgroeid. We moeten haar vinden.

Forbes heeft het portier opengedaan en wacht tot Samira achterin plaatsneemt. Ze heeft haar nieuwe kleren aan: een lange wollen rok en witte bloes. Ze lijkt heel beheerst. Kalm. Ze draagt een landschap in zich waar ik nooit bij zal kunnen komen.

'Je hoeft straks geen vragen te beantwoorden,' legt hij uit. 'Ik zal je helpen een verklaring op te stellen.'

Hij rijdt voorovergebogen over het stuur en kijkt met een frons naar de weg alsof hij het stadsverkeer haat. Ondertussen praat hij. Spijker en hij hebben vijf asielzoeksters achterhaald die in de fertiliteitskliniek zwanger zijn gemaakt en die daarna in het Verenigd Koninkrijk zijn opgedoken.

'Ze geven alle vijf toe een kind gebaard te hebben en beweren dat de baby's hun zijn afgenomen. Ze hebben elk vijfhonderd pond gekregen en te horen gekregen dat hun schuld was ingelost.'

'Waar zijn ze bevallen?'

'Een privé-adres. Ze konden geen precieze locatie geven. Ze waren daar in het laadruim van een bestelbusje met afgeplakte ramen heen gebracht. Twee van hen hadden het over vliegtuigen die binnenkwamen om te landen.'

'Ligt het onder een aanvliegroute?'

'Dat denk ik, ja.'

'Geboorten moeten worden aangegeven. Op die manier kunnen we de baby's ongetwijfeld vinden.'

'Het is niet zo simpel als jij denkt. Normaliter brengt het ziekenhuis of de zorginstelling de burgerlijke stand op de hoogte van een geboorte, maar niet als die in een privé-woning of buiten de nationale gezondheidszorg om plaatsvindt. In dat geval is het aan de ouders. En hoe gaat dat dan? Ma en pa hoeven niet eens bij de burgerlijke stand te verschijnen. Ze kunnen iemand anders sturen die bij de bevalling aanwezig was, of de eigenaar van het huis.'

'Is dat alles? En hoe zit het dan met doktersattesten en medische rapporten?'

'Niet nodig. Het kost meer papierwerk om een auto te laten registreren dan een baby.'

We passeren het Royal Chelsea Hospital op de Embankment, gaan linksaf over Albert Bridge en rijden om Battersea Park heen.

'Hoe zit het met dokter Banerjee?'

'Hij geeft toe dat hij Cate Beaumont haar overtollige embryo's heeft overhandigd, maar zegt niets te weten van het plan voor draagmoederschap. Ze zei hem dat ze naar een andere fertiliteitskliniek zou gaan die een hoger slagingspercentage had.'

'En u gelooft hem?'

Forbes haalt zijn schouders op. 'De embryo's behoorden haar toe. Ze had alle recht ze mee te nemen.'

Dit verklaart nog altijd niet waarom Banerjee tegen mij loog. Of waarom hij opdook op mijn vaders verjaardagsfeestje.

'En Paul Donavon?'

'Hij maakte twee missies naar Afghanistan mee en zat zes maanden in Irak. Kreeg de Queen's Gallantry Medal. Die vent is verdomme een roodkoperen held.'

Samira heeft geen woord gezegd. Soms heb ik het idee dat ze is afgehaakt of zich heeft afgewend, of andere stemmen volgt.

'We zijn bezig contact op te nemen met het weeshuis in Kabul en twee andere in Albanië en Rusland,' zegt Forbes. 'Hopelijk kunnen die ons meer vertellen dan alleen een bijnaam.'

De vergaderzaal is een kale, raamloze ruimte met plastic stoelen en lichtbollen vol verbrande vliegjes. Dit was ooit het gebouw van de Nationale Criminele Inlichtingen Dienst, dat inmiddels is verbouwd en omgedoopt tot onderkomen voor het nieuwe misdaadbestrijdingsagentschap, inclusief nieuwe initialen. Ondanks alle persaandacht en geavanceerde apparatuur doet het AGZM mij eerder denken aan Loch Ness dan aan Elliot Ness, jagend op schimmige monsters die zich op donkere plekken schuilhouden.

De voorste rij is in beslag genomen door radioverslaggevers die bezig zijn het logo van hun zender op de microfoons te plakken. In de middelste rijen zitten dagbladjournalisten onderuitgezakt, terwijl hun collega's van de televisie, met wittere tanden en beter gekleed, achterin staan.

Tijdens mijn inspecteursopleiding op Bramshill moesten we in groepjes een lijkschouwing bijwonen. Ik zag de patholoog sectie verrichten op het lijk van een kampeerder die na twee weken was gevonden.

Terwijl hij een glazen potje omhooghield, zei hij: 'Dit knaapje hier is een Sarcophaga-vlieg, maar ik noem hem altijd onze misdaadrapporteur. Let op de rode dronkemansoogjes en zijn grijze geblokte buik, waar bloedvlekken zo lekker op blijven zitten. Belangrijker is echter dat hij een lijk altijd als eerste opmerkt…'

Forbes kijkt op zijn horloge. Het is elf uur precies. Hij doet zijn das recht en trekt even aan de mouwen van zijn pak.

'Ben je er klaar voor?'

Samira knikt.

Flitslampen gaan af en verblinden me terwijl ik achter Samira aan naar de vergadertafel loop. Fotografen vechten om een plekje, hun camera's boven hun hoofd als in een merkwaardige schommeldans.

Forbes biedt Samira een stoel aan, reikt over tafel naar een kan water en schenkt voor haar een glas vol. Zijn ietwat pokdalige gezicht is bleek in het felle licht van de tv-ploegen.

Hij schraapt zijn keel en begint. 'We zijn bezig met een onderzoek naar de ontvoering van twee pasgeboren baby's, een tweeling van een jongen en een meisje, geboren zondag, vroeg in de ochtend, aan boord van een veerboot die onderweg was van Hoek van Holland naar Harwich. De Stena Brittanica meerde om 3 uur 36 in de ochtend aan en de baby's zijn dertig minuten eerder voor het laatst gezien.'

Flitslampen flitsen in zijn ogen.

Forbes maakt geen melding van babyhandel of illegaal draagmoederschap. In plaats daarvan beperkt hij zich tot de details van de reis en de ontvoering. Op het scherm achter hem wordt een afbeelding van Brendan Pearl geprojecteerd, met een gedetailleerde beschrijving.

'Agent Barba was op de terugreis van een kort verblijf in Amsterdam toen ze op een mensensmokkeloperatie stuitte. Ze hielp de tweeling ter wereld brengen, maar kon niet voorkomen dat de baby's werden weggenomen.

Ik wil met nadruk verklaren dat het hier niet om een ruzie in de huiselijke sfeer gaat en dat Brendan Pearl geen familiebanden heeft met de tweeling. Pearl is voorwaardelijk vrijgelaten in het kader van het Goede Vrijdag-akkoord. Hij wordt als gevaarlijk beschouwd. We raden mensen aan hem onder geen beding aan te spreken, en de politie te bellen als ze zijn verblijfplaats kennen. Juffrouw Khan zal nu een korte verklaring afleggen.'

Hij schuift de microfoon naar Samira. Ze bekijkt hem argwanend en vouwt een vel papier open. De flitslampen zorgen voor een muur van licht en ze struikelt over de eerste woorden. Iemand roept dat ze harder moet praten. Ze begint opnieuw: 'Ik wil iedereen bedanken die de afgelopen dagen voor me heeft gezorgd, met name juffrouw Barba voor haar hulp toen ik op de veerboot van de tweeling beviel. Ik ben ook de politie dankbaar voor alles wat die heeft gedaan. Ik roep de man die de tweeling heeft ontvoerd op ze terug te brengen. Ze zijn heel klein en hebben medische verzorging nodig. Breng ze alstublieft naar een ziekenhuis of laat ze op een veilige plek achter.'

Samira kijkt op van het papier. Ze gaat van haar script afwijken. 'Dit vergeef ik je, maar Zala vergeef ik je niet. Daarvoor hoop ik dat je eeuwig zult lijden, elke seconde van elke dag van de rest van je leven.'

Forbes houdt zijn hand over de microfoon in een poging haar te stoppen. Samira staat op om te gaan. Vanuit de zaal worden vragen geroepen.

'Wie is Zala?'

'Kende u Brendan Pearl?'

'Waarom heeft hij uw baby's ontvoerd?'

In het verhaal zitten meer gaten dan in de stemkaarten in Florida. De journalisten ruiken dat hier een groter verhaal in zit. Het decorum sneuvelt.

'Is er losgeld geëist?'

'Hoe kon Pearl met de tweeling van de veerboot af komen?'

'Denkt u dat ze nog in leven zijn?'

Samira krimpt ineen onder de vragen.

'Hebben ze al namen?'

Ze draait zich om naar de vragensteller en knippert met haar ogen in het flitslicht. 'Een maagd kan dingen naamloos laten, een moeder moet haar kinderen een naam geven.'

Het antwoord brengt de zaal tot zwijgen. Mensen kijken elkaar aan, zich afvragend wat ze bedoelt. Moeders? Maagden? Wat heeft dat er nou mee te maken?

Forbes' schouders staan strak van woede.

'Godverdomme, wat een ramp,' moppert hij als ik hem op de gang achterhaal.

'Zo erg was het nou ook weer niet.'

'God weet wat ze morgen zullen schrijven.'

'Ze zullen schrijven over de tweeling. Dat is waar het ons om gaat. We gaan ze vinden.'

Hij houdt ineens stil en draait zich om. 'Dat is nog maar het begin.'

'Wat bedoel je?'

'Ik wil je iemand laten zien.'

'Wanneer?'

'Nu.'

'Vandaag zijn de begrafenisplechtigheden.'

'Het duurt niet lang.' Hij kijkt voor ons uit. Samira staat te wachten bij de lift. 'Ik zorg dat ze wordt thuisgebracht.'

Twintig minuten later houden we stil voor een blok victoriaanse herenhuizen in Battersea, met uitzicht op het park. Krullende takken van een blauweregen, naakt en grijs, omlijsten de beneden-ramen. De hoofdingang is open. Er staat een lege kinderwagen, klaar voor een uitstapje. Ik hoor de moeder de trap af komen. Ze is aantrekkelijk, ergens in de dertig. Op haar arm heeft ze een baby, te oud om een van de tweeling te zijn.

'Mevrouw Piper?'

'Ja.'

'Ik ben inspecteur Forbes van de recherche. Dit is agent Barba.'

Haar glimlach verflauwt. Nauwelijks waarneembaar verstevigt ze haar greep op het kind. Een jongetje.

'Hoe oud is hij?' vraag ik.

'Acht maanden.'

'Wat een knappe jongen ben jij.' Ik buig me voorover. De moeder buigt zich achterover.

'Hoe heet hij?'

324

'Jack.'

'Hij lijkt op u.'

'Hij heeft meer weg van zijn vader.'

Forbes onderbreekt ons. 'We hoopten dat we heel even met u konden praten.'

'Ik sta op het punt om weg te gaan. Ik heb een afspraak met iemand.'

'Het hoeft niet lang te duren.'

Haar ogen schieten van zijn gezicht naar het mijne. 'Ik denk dat ik beter mijn man kan bellen,' zegt ze. En met nadruk voegt ze eraan toe: 'Hij werkt bij Binnenlandse Zaken.'

'Waar hebt u uw kind ter wereld gebracht?' vraagt Forbes.

Ze stottert nerveus. 'Het was een thuisbevalling. Ik ga naar boven om mijn man te bellen.'

'Waarom?' vraagt Forbes. 'We hebben u nog niet eens verteld waarvoor we hier zijn, en u maakt zich nu al druk over iets. Waarom hebt u toestemming van uw man nodig om met ons te praten?'

Het moment vertoont een breuk, een rimpeling van onrust.

Forbes gaat verder: 'Bent u ooit in Amsterdam geweest, mevrouw Piper? Hebt u daar een fertiliteitskliniek bezocht?'

Achteruitlopend naar de trap schudt ze haar hoofd, minder als ontkenning dan uit ijdele hoop dat hij zal stoppen met vragen stellen. Ze staat op de trap. Forbes loopt naar haar toe. Hij houdt een visitekaartje in zijn hand. Ze wil het niet aannemen. In plaats daarvan legt hij het op de kinderwagen.

'Wilt u uw man vragen mij te bellen?'

Ik hoor mezelf excuses maken dat we haar hebben lastiggevallen. Tegelijkertijd wil ik van haar weten of ze heeft betaald voor een baby. Aan wie? Wie regelde het? Forbes heeft mijn arm vast en dirigeert me de trap af. Ik stel me mevrouw Piper voor, boven, aan de telefoon. De tranen en de verwarring.

'Hun namen doken op in de bestanden die Spijker me heeft gestuurd,' legt Forbes uit. 'Ze hebben een draagmoeder gebruikt. Een meisje uit Bosnië.'

'Dan is het dus niet hun baby.'

'Hoe bewijzen we dat? Je hebt het kind gezien. Vaderschapstests, DNA-tests, bloedmonsters – ze zullen stuk voor stuk laten zien dat de kleine Jack bij de Pipers hoort. En er is hoe dan ook geen rechter in dit land die ons toestemming zou geven om monsters af te nemen.'

'We kunnen bewijzen dat ze in Nederland een IVF-kliniek hebben bezocht. We kunnen bewijzen dat hun embryo's bij een surrogaatmoeder zijn ingeplant. We kunnen bewijzen dat dit resulteerde in een zwangerschap en een geslaagde bevalling. Dat is toch zeker genoeg?'

'Het bewijst nog niet dat er geld van eigenaar is gewisseld. We hebben een van deze stellen nodig als getuige.'

Hij overhandigt me een lijst met namen en adressen:

Robert & Helena Piper
Alan & Jessica Case
Trevor & Toni Jury
Anaan & Lola Singh
Nicholas & Karin Pederson

'Ik heb alle vijf de stellen ondervraagd. Ze hebben stuk voor stuk een advocaat gebeld en hun verhaal volgehouden. Geen van hen zal meewerken, niet als dat betekent dat ze hun kind kwijtraken.'

'Ze hebben de wet overtreden!'

'Misschien heb je gelijk, maar hoeveel rechtbankjury's zullen een veroordeling uitspreken? Als dat jouw vriendin was daarnet, met haar kindje op haar arm, zou jij het dan van haar afnemen?'

2

De begrafenissen zijn om twee uur. Ik heb een zwart gilet, een zwart jasje, een zwarte broek en zwarte schoenen aangetrokken. Het enige kleuraccent is mijn lippenstift.

Samira gebruikt na mij de badkamer. Het is moeilijk te geloven dat ze net een stel kinderen heeft gebaard. Over haar buik lopen striae, maar voor de rest is haar huid smetteloos. Af en toe merk ik een tic of een trilling van pijn op als ze zich beweegt, maar verder wijst niets op eventueel ongemak.

Ze legt haar kleren uit op het bed en vermijdt zorgvuldig dat haar bloes kreukt.

'Je hoeft niet mee te komen,' zeg ik tegen haar, maar haar besluit staat al vast. Ze heeft Cate maar twee keer ontmoet. Ze spraken via Yanus in vormelijke zinnen in plaats van een echt gesprek te voeren. En toch deelden ze een band als geen andere: een ongeboren tweeling.

We zitten naast elkaar in de taxi. Ze is gespannen, rusteloos. In de verte braakt een schoorsteen een kolom witte rook uit, als een stoomtrein die nergens heen gaat.

'De politie zal de tweeling vinden,' meld ik, alsof we diep in gesprek zijn.

Ze geeft geen antwoord.

Ik probeer het nog eens. 'Wil jij dat ze gevonden worden?'

'Mijn schuld is voldaan,' fluistert ze terwijl ze op haar onderlip bijt.

'Je bent deze mensen niets verschuldigd.'

Ze antwoordt niet. Hoe kan ik het haar laten begrijpen? Onaangekondigd komt ze zelf met een antwoord, haar woorden in zorgvuldige zinnen gegoten.

'Ik heb geprobeerd niet van ze te houden. Ik dacht dat het makkelijker zou zijn ze af te staan als ik niet van ze hield. Ik heb zelfs geprobeerd ze de schuld te geven van wat er met Hasan en Zala is gebeurd. Dat is niet eerlijk, toch? Ik kan niet anders. Mijn borsten lopen over, voor hen. In mijn dromen hoor ik ze huilen. Ik wil dat dat geluid ophoudt.'

Voor de kapel van het West London Crematorium staat een dubbele baar. Een tapijt van kunstgras voert naar een oprit waar op een klein zwart bord met verwisselbare letters de namen van Felix en Cate staan.

Samira loopt met verbazingwekkende elegantie over het grindpad, wat niet gemakkelijk is. Ze blijft staan om de marmeren en stenen graftomben te bekijken. Tuinlieden leunen op hun spade en bekijken haar. Ze lijkt haast buitenaards, uit een andere wereld.

Barnaby Elliot begroet mensen en neemt condoleances in ontvangst. Ruth Elliot zit naast hem in haar rolstoel, gestoken in rouwkleding die haar huid er bloedeloos en broos doet uitzien. Zij ziet mij als eerste. Haar mond vouwt zich om mijn naam. Barnaby draait zich om en komt naar me toe lopen. Hij kust me op beide wangen en ik ruik de scherpe alcoholgeur van zijn aftershave.

'Wie heb jij in Amsterdam opgezocht?' vraagt hij.

'Een rechercheur. Waarom heb je gelogen over Cates computer?'

Hij geeft geen antwoord. In plaats daarvan slaat hij zijn ogen op naar de bomen, waarvan er enkele zich nog vastklampen aan de geelgouden overblijfselen van de herfst.

'Ik vind dat je moet weten dat ik een advocaat opdracht heb gegeven de voogdij over de tweeling te verkrijgen. Ik wil ze allebei.'

Ik kijk hem ongelovig aan.

'En Samira dan?'

'Het zijn ónze kleinkinderen. Ze horen bij ons.'

'Niet volgens de wet.'

'De wet weet niets.'

Ik kijk opzij naar Samira, die is achtergebleven, misschien omdat ze voelt dat er een probleem is. Aan Barnaby is die discretie niet besteed. 'Wíl ze ze eigenlijk wel?' zegt hij op iets te luide toon.

Ik moet mijn kaken uit elkaar wringen om iets te kunnen uitbrengen. 'Jij blijft uit haar buurt.'

'Hoor eens…'

'Nee! Jíj moet luisteren. Ze heeft al genoeg meegemaakt. Zij is álles kwijt.'

Terwijl hij me plotseling verdwaasd intens aanstaart, haalt hij met zijn vuist uit naar een heg. De mouw van zijn jas blijft hangen en hij rukt er zo wild aan dat de stof scheurt en op en neer flappert. Met dezelfde snelheid hervindt hij zijn beheersing. Het is alsof ik naar een diepe ademhalingsoefening uit een cursus zelf-beheersing kijk. Hij grijpt in zijn zak en haalt een visitekaartje tevoorschijn.

'De executeur-testamentair van Felix en Cate heeft morgenmiddag om drie uur een raadkamerzitting in Grey's Inn. Hij wil dat jij daarbij aanwezig bent.'

'Waarom?'

'Dat heeft hij niet gezegd. Dit is het adres.'

Ik pak het kaartje aan en kijk hoe Barnaby terugloopt naar zijn vrouw. Ze pakt zijn arm, draait haar hoofd in zijn handpalm en houdt de hand tegen haar wang. Ik heb hen nog nooit innig zien doen, niet zoals nu. Misschien heb je wel de ene tragedie nodig om de andere te herstellen.

De kapel is zacht verlicht door achter glas flikkerende rode lampjes. De kisten zijn bedekt met een tapijt van bloemen dat doorloopt tot op het middenpad en bijna tot aan mevrouw Elliots rolstoel. Barnaby zit naast haar, met Jarrod aan zijn andere kant. Ze houden alle drie elkaars handen vast, alsof ze elkaar steun geven.

Ik herken andere familieleden en vrienden. De enige die ontbreekt is Yvonne. Misschien had ze het gevoel dat ze een dag als deze niet zou aankunnen. Het moet zijn alsof je een dochter verliest.

Aan de andere kant van de kerk zit de familie van Felix, die er veel Poolser uitzien dan Felix ooit heeft gedaan. De vrouwen zijn klein en hoekig, met sluiers op hun hoofd en rozenkranskralen tussen hun vingers.

De begrafenisondernemer draagt zijn hoge hoed op zijn gebogen arm. Zijn zoon, identiek gekleed, heeft zijn houding overgenomen, al zie ik achter zijn oor een propje kauwgum zitten.

Er wordt een psalm ingezet, 'Komt laat ons onze vrienden volgen naar omhoog', die niet helemaal in Cates straatje past. Maar het moet ook moeilijk zijn om iets passends te vinden voor iemand die ooit haar eeuwige liefde betuigde aan een foto van Kurt Cobain.

In zijn lezing uit de bijbel zegt dominee Lund iets over de wederopstanding en dat we allemaal op dezelfde dag zullen opstaan en als Gods kinderen verder zullen leven. Terwijl hij dit doet, strijkt hij met een vinger langs de rand van Cates kist, alsof hij het vakmanschap ervan bewondert.

'Liefde en pijn zijn niet hetzelfde,' zegt hij, 'maar soms voelt het of dat wel zo zou moeten zijn. Liefde wordt elke dag op de proef gesteld. Pijn niet. En toch zijn de twee onlosmakelijk met elkaar verbonden, omdat echte liefde geen gescheiden-zijn kan verdragen.'

Zijn stem klinkt ver weg. Ik heb de afgelopen acht jaar in een toestand van uitgestelde rouw om Cate geleefd. Triviale, alledaagse geluiden en geuren roepen herinneringen op: hopeloze zaken, jazzschoenen, cola met smeltend schaafijs, liedjes van Simply Red, een tiener met een haarborstel als microfoon, paarse oogschaduw... Dit soort dingen doet me of bijna glimlachen, of zwelt pijnlijk op in mijn borst. Daar heb je het weer: liefde en pijn.

Ik zie niet meer hoe de kisten uit het zicht verdwijnen. Tijdens de laatste psalm glip ik naar buiten, op zoek naar frisse lucht. Aan de overkant van de parkeerplaats, in de schaduw van een boog, zie ik een lange, bekende gestalte rustig staan wachten. Hij draagt een overjas en een rode das. Donavon.

Samira wandelt door de rozentuin aan de kant waar de kapel staat. Ze zal hem zien zodra ze de hoek omgaat.

Zonder me een moment te bedenken overbrug ik de afstand. Als iemand me zag, zou hij verklaren dat wat ik doe aan geweld grenst. Ik grijp Donavons arm beet, draai die op zijn rug en duw hem tegen een muur, met zijn gezicht tegen de bakstenen.

'Waar zijn ze? Wat heb je met ze gedaan?'

'Ik weet niet waar je het over hebt.'

Ik wil dat hij verzet biedt. Ik wil hem pijn doen. Samira bevindt zich achter me, aarzelend omdat ze misschien voelt dat er problemen dreigen.

'Ken jij deze man?'

'Nee.'

'De Engelsman die je in het weeshuis hebt ontmoet. Je zei dat hij een kruis in zijn nek had.' Ik trek Donavons sjaal opzij en ontbloot zijn tatoeage.

Ze schudt haar hoofd. 'Een góuden kruis. Hier.' Ze tekent de omtrek in haar hals.

Donavon lacht. 'Schitterend speurwerk, yindoo.'

Ik heb zin om hem te slaan.

'Jij was in Afghanistan.'

'Als dienaar van koningin en vaderland.'

'Laat dat vaderlandslievende gelul maar achterwege. Je hebt tegen me gelogen. Je hebt Cate al vóór de reünie ontmoet.'

'Inderdaad.'

'Waarom?'

'Dat zou jij niet begrijpen.'

'Probeer het maar.'

Ik laat hem los en hij draait zich om, langzaam knipperend. Zijn bleke ogen zijn iets meer bloeddoorlopen dan ik me herinner. Begrafenisgangers verlaten de kapel. Hij kijkt naar de menigte met een mengeling van gêne en bezorgdheid. 'Niet hier. Laten we ergens anders praten.'

Ik laat hem voorgaan. We verlaten het kerkhof en lopen in oostelijke richting langs Harrow Road, die verstopt zit met verkeer en een polonaise van bussen. Terwijl ik af en toe een tersluikse blik op Donavon werp, kijk ik hoe hij naar Samira kijkt. Hij lijkt haar niet te herkennen. In plaats daarvan houdt hij zijn ogen neergeslagen in een houding van berouw en bedenkt antwoorden op de vragen waarvan hij weet dat ze gaan komen. Meer leugens.

We kiezen een café met krukken voor het raam en daarachter tafels. Donavon bekijkt het menu, om tijd te winnen. Samira laat zich van haar stoel glijden en knielt bij het tijdschriftenrek. Ze bladert ze door in een tempo alsof ze verwacht dat iemand haar elk moment kan tegenhouden.

'De tijdschriften zijn gratis,' leg ik uit. 'Je kunt ze rustig inkijken.'

Donavon draait aan zijn pols, wat een witte striem op zijn huid achterlaat. Bloed stroomt terug in de uitgerekte huid.

'Ik kwam Cate drie jaar geleden tegen,' vertelt hij. 'Het was net voordat ik de eerste keer naar Afghanistan ging. Het duurde even voordat ik haar had gevonden. Ik wist niet hoe ze heette sinds ze was getrouwd.'

'Waarom?'

'Ik wilde haar ontmoeten.'

Ik wacht tot er nog iets volgt. Hij verandert van onderwerp. 'Heb je weleens parachute gesprongen?'

'Nee.'

'Dat is echt kicken. Geen enkel ander gevoel haalt het daarbij. Op drieduizend meter hoogte in de deuropening van een vliegtuig staan, met bonzend hart, helemaal opgeladen. Dan neem je die laatste stap en de schroefwind zuigt je naar buiten. En dan vallen, alleen voelt het niet als vallen. Het is vliegen. De lucht drukt je wangen naar binnen en giert langs je oren. Ik ben op grote hoogte uitgesprongen, met zuurstof, van ruim achtduizend meter. Ik zweer je dat ik mijn armen had kunnen spreiden en de hele planeet had kunnen omarmen.'

Zijn ogen glanzen. Ik weet niet waarom hij me dit vertelt, maar ik laat hem praten.

'Het beste wat me ooit is overkomen is dat ik van school getrapt werd en bij de para's ben gegaan. Tot die tijd deed ik maar wat. Kwaad. Ik had geen enkele ambitie. Het heeft mijn leven veranderd.

Ik heb inmiddels een dochtertje. Ze is drie. Haar moeder woont niet meer bij me. Ze zitten in Schotland, maar ik stuur ze elke maand geld, en cadeautjes met haar verjaardag en met kerst. Ik bedoel geloof ik te zeggen dat ik veranderd ben.'

'Waarom vertel je me dit?'

'Omdat ik wil dat je het begrijpt. Jij denkt dat ik een schurk en een bullebak ben, maar ik ben veranderd. Wat ik Cate heb aangedaan was onvergeeflijk, maar ze heeft het me vergeven. Daarom zocht ik haar. Ik wilde te weten komen hoe het met haar gegaan was. Ik wilde niet blijven denken dat ik haar leven had verpest met wat ik haar had aangedaan.'

Ik wil hem niet geloven. Ik wil hem blijven haten, omdat de

332

wereld er volgens mij zo uitziet. De geschiedenis zoals vastgelegd door mij.

'Waarom wilde Cate jou ontmoeten?'

'Ik denk dat ze nieuwsgierig was.'

'Waar zagen jullie elkaar?'

'We hebben koffiegedronken in Soho.'

'En?'

'We hebben gepraat. Ik zei dat het me speet. Ze zei dat het goed was. Vanuit Afghanistan heb ik haar een paar brieven geschreven. Als ik met verlof thuis was gingen we meestal een keer lunchen of koffiedrinken.'

'Waarom heb je me dit niet eerder verteld?'

'Zoals ik al zei: je zou het niet begrijpen.'

Het is niet goed genoeg als reden. Hoe kon Cate hém vergeven voordat ze míj vergaf?

'Wat weet jij van het New Life Adoption Centre?'

'Cate heeft me een keer meegenomen. Ze wist dat Carla maar niet kon besluiten wat ze met de baby aan moest.'

'Hoe wist Cate van het adoptiecentrum?'

Hij haalt zijn schouders op. 'Haar fertiliteitsspecialist zit in de adoptiecommissie.'

'Dokter Banerjee. Weet je dat zeker?'

'Ja.'

Julian Shawcroft en dokter Banerjee kennen elkaar. Nog meer leugens.

'Heeft Cate je verteld waarom ze naar Amsterdam ging?'

'Ze zei dat ze nog een keer IVF zou ondergaan.'

Ik kijk even naar Samira. 'Ze heeft betaald voor een draagmoeder.'

'Dat begrijp ik niet.'

'Er is een tweeling.'

Hij lijkt met stomheid geslagen. Sprakeloos.

'Waar?'

'Ze worden vermist.'

Ik kan zien hoe de informatie doordringt in zijn hoofd en blijkt te kloppen met andere details. Het nieuws over de tweeling heeft de radio en de vroege edities van de *Evening Standard* al gehaald. Ik heb hem heviger geraakt dan ik voor mogelijk hield.

'Wat Cate deed, was in strijd met de wet,' breng ik uit. 'Ze was van plan de zaak openbaar te maken. Klokkenluider te zijn. Daarom wilde ze met me praten.'

Donavon heeft iets terug van wat op kalmte lijkt. 'Is dat de reden dat ze haar hebben vermoord?'

'Ja. Cate heeft Samira niet toevallig gevonden. Iemand heeft hen bij elkaar gebracht. Ik ben op zoek naar een man die "Brother" wordt genoemd, een Engelsman die naar Samira's weeshuis in Kabul kwam.'

'Julian Shawcroft is in Afghanistan geweest.'

'Hoe weet jij dat?'

'Het kwam zo ter sprake. Hij vroeg me waar ik had gediend.'

Ik klap mijn mobiele telefoon open en druk een snelkiesnummer in. Groentje Dave neemt bij de tweede keer overgaan op. Sinds Amsterdam heb ik hem niet meer gesproken. Ik heb niet gebeld. Uit sloomheid. Uit angst.

'Hallo, lieve jongen.'

Hij klinkt aarzelend. Ik heb geen tijd om te informeren waarom.

'Toen je Julian Shawcroft natrok, wat heb je toen gevonden?'

'Hij is eerder directeur geweest van een kliniek voor gezinsplanning in Manchester.'

'En daarvoor?'

'Hij heeft theologie gestudeerd in Oxford en is daarna bij een of andere religieuze orde gegaan.'

'Een religieuze orde?'

'Hij trad in als broeder.'

Daar heb je het verband! Cate, Banerjee, Shawcroft en Samira – ik kan ze koppelen.

Dave is niet meer aan de lijn. Ik weet niet meer of ik gedag heb gezegd.

Donavon heeft tegen me gepraat, vragen gesteld. Ik heb niet geluisterd.

'Leken ze op Cate?' vraagt hij.

'Wie?'

'De tweeling.'

Ik weet niet goed wat ik moet antwoorden. Ik ben niet goed in het beschrijven van pasgeboren baby's. Ze lijken allemaal op Winston Churchill. Waarom zou het hem interesseren?

3

Een zilverkleurige Lexus rijdt de oprit op van een vrijstaand huis in Wimbledon, Zuid-Londen. Hij heeft een persoonlijke kentekenplaat waarop BABYDOC staat. Sohan Banerjee pakt zijn spullen van de achterbank en schakelt de centrale vergrendeling in. Er flitsen lampjes. Kon alles in het leven maar met één druk op de knop worden geregeld.

'Op mensensmokkel staat een straf van veertien jaar,' zeg ik.

Hij draait zich om, zijn aktetas als een schild tegen zijn borst geklemd. 'Ik weet niet waar je het over hebt.'

'Ik weet niet wat er staat op commercieel draagmoederschap, maar als je medische verkrachting en ontvoering erbij optelt, weet ik zeker dat je lang genoeg in de gevangenis zult zitten om nieuwe vrienden te maken.'

'Ik heb niets misdaan.'

'En dan vergeet ik bijna nog moord. Automatisch levenslang.'

'Je pleegt huisvredebreuk,' schreeuwt hij.

'Bel de politie maar.'

Hij kijkt naar zijn huis en vervolgens naar de aanpalende huizen, wellicht bezorgd over wat ze wel zullen denken.

'Jij wíst dat Cate Beaumont naar Amsterdam zou gaan. Jij gaf haar een vaatje vloeibare stikstof met daarin haar overgebleven embryo's. Je vertelde haar over de Nederlandse kliniek.'

'Nee, nee.' Zijn onderkinnen trillen.

'Zou jij de bevalling doen?'

'Ik weet niet waar je het over hebt.'

'Hoe goed ken jij Julian Shawcroft?'

'We hebben een werkrelatie.'

'Jullie waren tegelijkertijd in Oxford. Hij studeerde theologie. Jij studeerde medicijnen. Zie je wat ik allemaal weet? Niet slecht, hè, voor een stijfkoppig sikh-meisje dat maar niet aan de man kan komen.'

Zijn aktetas rust nog steeds op de richel van zijn maag. Mijn huid prikt van iets wat lichamelijker is dan walging.

'Jij zit in zijn adoptiecommissie.'

'Een onafhankelijk orgaan.'

'Jij hebt Cate over het New Life Adoption Centre verteld. Jij hebt haar bij Shawcroft geïntroduceerd. Wat dacht je dat je aan het doen was? Dit was niet de een of andere menslievende kruistocht om de kinderlozen te helpen. Jij hebt je met vrouwensmokkelaars en moordenaars ingelaten. Jonge vrouwen zijn verkracht en uitgebuit. Er zijn mensen gestorven.'

'Je hebt het helemaal mis. Ik heb met dat soort dingen niets van doen gehad. Welk motief zou ik gehad kunnen hebben?'

Motief? Ik begrijp het waarom nog steeds niet. Geld kan het niet zijn. Misschien was hij klemgezet of er ingeluisd om iemand een dienst te bewijzen. Eén uitglijder is genoeg om de haak te laten aanslaan.

Hij kijkt opnieuw naar het huis. Binnen is geen vrouw die op hem wacht. Geen kinderen in de deuropening.

'Het is iets persoonlijks, hè?'

Hij geeft geen antwoord.

Forbes heeft me een lijst met namen laten zien. Er stonden echtparen op die embryo's hadden geleverd aan de IVF-kliniek in Amsterdam. Ineens dringt zich een naam op: Anaan en Lola Singh uit Birmingham.

'Heb jij familie in het Verenigd Koninkrijk, dokter Banerjee? Een zus wellicht? Nichten of neven?'

Hij wil het ontkennen, maar de waarheid staat in zijn gelaatstrekken gedrukt als vingerafdrukken in klei. Mama zei dat hij een neef had. De brave arts was zo trots dat hij tijdens de zondagse lunch verhalen over hem opdiste. Ik doe een gooi naar de rest van het verhaal. Zijn zus kon niet zwanger raken. En zelfs haar zo slimme broertje, een fertiliteitsspecialist, kon haar niet helpen.

Julian Shawcroft opperde dat er mogelijk een uitweg was. Hij regelde een surrogaatmoeder in Nederland en Banerjee bracht het kind ter wereld. Hij dacht dat het een eenmalig iets was, maar Shawcroft wilde dat hij nog meer baby's ter wereld zou helpen brengen. Nee zeggen kon niet.

'Wat wil je van me?'

'Dat je me Julian Shawcroft bezorgt.'

'Dat kan ik niet doen.'

'Maak je je zorgen over je carrière, je reputatie?'

Hij glimlacht wrang, een gebaar van verslagenheid. 'Ik woon al tweederde van mijn leven in dit land, Alisha. Ik heb masters en doctoraten behaald in Oxford en Harvard. Ik heb artikelen gepubliceerd, lezingen gegeven en ben gastonderzoeker geweest aan de Universiteit van Toronto.' Hij werpt opnieuw een steelse blik op de dichte gordijnen en lege kamers verderop. 'Mijn reputatie is het enige wat ik heb.'

'Je hebt de wet overtreden.'

'Is het zo erg? Ik dacht dat wij de kinderlozen hielpen en asielzoekers een nieuw leven boden.'

'Jullie hebben ze uitgebuit.'

'We hebben ze uit het weeshuis gered.'

'En sommigen van hen het bordeel in gedwongen.'

Zijn dichte wenkbrauwen fronsen zich.

'Geef me Shawcroft. Leg een verklaring af.'

'Ik moet mijn zuster en haar kind beschermen.'

'Door hém te beschermen.'

'We beschermen elkaar.'

'Ik zou je kunnen laten arresteren.'

'Ik zal alles ontkennen.'

'Vertel me dan in elk geval waar de tweeling is.'

'Ik zie de gezinnen nooit. Die kant van de zaak regelt Julian.' Zijn stem wordt anders. 'Ik smeek je: laat dit rusten. Er kan niets goeds uit voortkomen.'

'Voor wie?'

'Voor wie dan ook. Mijn neefje is een prachtig jongetje. Hij is bijna een jaar.'

'Als hij groter is, ga je hem dan vertellen over de medische ver-
krachting die tot zijn geboorte heeft geleid?'
'Het spijt me.'
Iedereen heeft maar spijt. Het zal de tijdgeest wel zijn.

4

Forbes schudt een stapeltje foto's en legt ze in drie rijen uit op
een bureau, alsof hij gaat patiencen. Julian Shawcrofts foto ligt
helemaal rechts. Hij ziet eruit als de zo uit de kaartenbak van het
castingbureau geplukte baas van een liefdadigheidsinstelling: har-
telijk, glimlachend, joviaal...
'Ik wil dat je als je iemand herkent diens foto aanwijst,' zegt de
rechercheur.
Samira aarzelt.
'Maak je geen zorgen dat je iemand in de problemen brengt, zeg
me alleen of hier iemand tussen zit die je al eens hebt gezien.'
Haar ogen gaan de foto's langs en houden plotseling stil. Ze
wijst naar Shawcroft.
'Deze.'
'Wie is hij?'
'Brother.'
'Weet je zijn echte naam?'
Ze schudt haar hoofd.
'Waarvan ken je hem?'
'Hij bezocht het weeshuis.'
'In Kabul?'
Ze knikt.
'Wat kwam hij daar doen?'
'Hij bracht dekens en eten.'
'Heb je met hem gesproken?'
'Hij sprak geen Afghaans. Ik vertaalde voor hem.'
'Wat voor dingen vertaalde je?'
'Hij had besprekingen met meneer Jamal, de directeur. Hij zei dat
hij voor een deel van de wezen een baan kon regelen. Hij wilde al-

leen meisjes. Ik zei hem dat ik zonder Hasan niet weg kon. Hij zei dat het dan meer geld ging kosten, maar dat ik hem kon terugbetalen.'

'Hoeveel geld?'

'Tienduizend Amerikaanse dollars per persoon.'

'En hoe werd je geacht dat geld terug te betalen?'

'Hij zei dat God voor mij een manier zou vinden om te betalen.'

'Zei hij iets over een kind baren?'

'Nee.'

Forbes haalt een vel papier uit een map. 'Dit is een lijst met namen. Ik wil dat je me zegt of sommige je bekend voorkomen.'

Haar vinger glijdt over de pagina en stopt. 'Dit meisje, Allegra. Zij zat in het weeshuis.'

'Waar ging ze heen?'

'Ze vertrok eerder dan ik. Brother had een baan voor haar.'

De rechercheur glimlacht strak. 'Zeg dat wel, ja.'

Forbes' kantoor bevindt zich op de tweede verdieping, tegenover de ruime kantoortuin die de meldkamer vormt. Op een archiefkast staat een foto van zijn vrouw. Ze ziet eruit als een nuchtere plattelandsmeid die er nooit helemaal in is geslaagd haar babyvet kwijt te raken.

Hij vraagt Samira buiten te wachten. Er staat een drankautomaat bij de lift. Hij geeft haar wat kleingeld. We kijken hoe ze wegloopt, een vrouw in wording.

'We hebben voldoende voor een aanhoudingsbevel,' zeg ik.

'Nee.'

'Ze heeft Shawcroft aangewezen.'

'Jawel, maar dat brengt hem nog niet in verband met het draagmoedercomplot. Het is haar woord tegen het zijne.'

'Maar de andere wezen…'

'Die hebben het over een vroom man die aanbood ze te helpen. We kunnen niet bewijzen dat hij hun smokkel geregeld heeft. We kunnen ook niet bewijzen dat hij hen met chantage onder druk heeft gezet om zwanger te worden. We moeten een van de kopers als getuige laten optreden, wat wel inhoudt dat ze zichzelf tot verdachte maken.'

'We zouden ze tegen vervolging kunnen laten vrijwaren.'

'Als ze eenmaal toegeven dat ze voor een draagmoeder hebben betaald, kan de draagmoeder haar kind opeisen. We kunnen ze niet vrijwaren tegen een civielrechtelijke aanklacht.'

Ik hoor het in zijn stem: berusting. Het blijkt een te zware taak. Hij zal niet opgeven, maar ook niet dat stapje extra zetten, het extra telefoontje plegen, nog één deur verder aankloppen. Hij vindt dat ik me aan strohalmen vastklamp, dat ik dit niet goed heb doordacht. Ik ben nog nooit zekerder geweest.

'Samira moet naar hem toe gaan.'

'Wat?'

'Ze zou een zendertje kunnen dragen.'

Forbes zuigt lucht tussen zijn tanden. 'Ben je gek geworden? Shawcroft zou het onmiddellijk doorzien. Hij wéét dat ze aan onze kant staat.'

'Dat klopt, maar onderzoek doen is druk opbouwen. Op dit moment denkt hij dat we hem niks kunnen maken. Hij is op zijn gemak. We moeten hem even door elkaar schudden, hem van zijn gerieflijke plekje duwen.'

Er bestaan strikte regels voor het afluisteren van telefoons en gesprekken in huizen van mensen. Er moet toestemming zijn van de rechter-commissaris. Een zendertje is iets anders, zolang het maar binnen de openbare ruimte blijft.

'Wat moet ze tegen hem zeggen?'

'Dat hij haar een baan heeft beloofd.'

'Is dat alles?'

'Ze hoeft niet eens wat te zeggen. Laten we zien wat hij zegt.'

Forbes vermorzelt een keelpastille tussen zijn tanden. Zijn adem ruikt naar citroen.

'Kan ze het aan?'

'Dat denk ik wel.'

5

Je kunt elke sport belachelijk laten klinken als je hem in zijn bouwstenen ontleedt – stok, bal, gat – maar de aantrekkingskracht van golf heb ik nooit goed begrepen. De banen zijn op een kunstmatige manier mooi, als Japanse tuinen die tot op het laatste steentje en struikje gepland zijn.

Julian Shawcroft speelt elke zondagochtend met hetzelfde viertal, met naast hemzelf een stedebouwkundige, een autodealer en een plaatselijke zakenman. Ze slaan even na tienen af.

De club ligt op de grens van Sussex en Surrey, in de groene zoom annex het rijkeluisgebied. Bruin is een kleur die je hier zelden ziet, tenzij je de bal mist en een pol gras wegmept.

Samira heeft een batterij ter grootte van een luciferdoosje onder op haar rug zitten en een dunne rode draad loopt onder haar oksel door naar een knopgroot microfoontje dat tussen haar borsten zit vastgeplakt.

Terwijl ik haar bloes goed doe sla ik mijn ogen naar haar op en glimlach bemoedigend. 'Je kunt nog terug als je wilt.'

Ze knikt.

'Weet je al wat je gaat zeggen?'

Opnieuw een knikje.

'Als je bang wordt, loop je gewoon weg. Als je je bedreigd voelt, weglopen. Bij alles wat naar onraad ruikt, oké?'

'Ja.'

Groepjes golfspelers staan buiten de kleedkamer en op het oefenveldje, wachtend tot de starter hun namen afroept. Shawcroft heeft de hardste lach, maar niet de schreeuwerigste broek, die omhult de benen van een van zijn medespelers. Naast de eerste tee maakt hij een oefenswing en hij ziet Samira boven aan de stenen trap staan, met de zon in haar rug. Hij schermt zijn ogen af.

Zonder te aarzelen loopt ze op hem af en blijft op een meter of twee staan.

'Kan ik iets voor u doen?' vraagt een van de andere spelers.

'Ik kom voor Brother.'

Shawcroft aarzelt en kijkt langs haar heen. Zijn ogen zoeken ons.

'Er is hier niemand die Brother heet, meisje,' zegt de autodealer.

Samira wijst. Ze draaien zich om naar Shawcroft, die een ontkenning stottert. 'Ik ken haar niet.'

Forbes past het volume van de digitale opnameapparatuur aan. We staan op iets minder dan tachtig meter afstand geparkeerd onder de takken van een plataan, tegenover de golfwinkel.

Samira is een kop kleiner dan de mannen. Haar lange rok waaiert uit in de wind.

'Waarom maak je haar geen caddie, Julian?' grapt een van hen.

'Je kent me nog wel, Brother,' zegt Samira. 'Jij hebt me gevraagd hiernaartoe te komen. Je zei dat je een baan voor me had.'

Shawcroft kijkt verontschuldigend naar zijn medespelers. Achterdocht begint in woede te veranderen. 'Gewoon negeren. Laten we beginnen.'

Hij draait zich om, maakt een gehaaste oefenzwaai en produceert als openingsslag een afzwaaier die naar rechts vliegt en tussen de bomen neerkomt. Vol weerzin smijt hij zijn club op de grond.

De anderen slaan af. Shawcroft zit al achter het stuur van een golfkarretje. Het schiet vooruit en hij snelt weg.

'Ik zei al dat hij hier niet in zou trappen.'

'Wacht. Kijk.'

Samira loopt hen achterna de fairway af, de zoom van haar rok steeds donkerder van de dauw. De karretjes hebben nu elk een andere richting genomen. Shawcroft is in de struiken op zoek naar zijn wilde slag. Hij kijkt op en ziet haar naderen. Ik hoor hem naar zijn partner roepen: 'Verloren bal, ik sla opnieuw af.'

'Je hebt nog niet eens naar deze gezocht.'

'Doet er niet toe.'

Hij laat een nieuw balletje vallen en geeft het een zwiep, meer als een houthakker dan als een golfer. Het wagentje begint weer te rijden. Samira vertraagt haar pas niet.

Ik voel een brok in mijn keel. Dit meisje blijft me verbazen. Ze volgt ze helemaal tot aan de green, omzeilt de bunkers en neemt een smal houten bruggetje over een beek. Shawcroft, die voortdurend over zijn schouder kijkt, haalt uit naar de bal en haast zich verder.

'Ze dreigt buiten ons bereik te komen,' zegt Forbes. 'We moeten haar tegenhouden.'

'Wacht. Nog heel even.'

Het viertal is meer dan driehonderd meter van ons vandaan, maar ik kan ze door de verrekijker nog behoorlijk goed zien. Samira staat aan de rand van de green toe te kijken en te wachten.

Eindelijk verliest Shawcroft zijn geduld. 'Van de golfbaan af jij, of ik laat je oppakken.'

Zwaaiend met zijn club stormt hij op haar af. Ze vertrekt geen spier.

'Rustig aan, ouwe jongen,' probeert iemand.

'Wie is dat, Julian?' vraagt een ander.

'Niemand.'

'Het is een lekker ding. Heb je niemand nodig om je ballen te wassen?'

'Hou je bek! Hou jij gewoon je bek!'

Samira is onbeweeglijk blijven staan. 'Ik heb mijn schuld voldaan, Brother.'

'Ik weet niet waar je het over hebt.'

'Je zei dat God een manier voor me zou vinden om te betalen. Ik heb dubbel betaald. Een tweeling. Ik heb voor Hasan en mij betaald, maar hij is dood. Zala heeft het evenmin gehaald.'

Shawcroft grijpt haar ruw bij haar arm en sist: 'Ik weet niet wie je gestuurd heeft. Ik weet niet wat je wilt, maar ik kan je niet helpen.'

'En die baan dan?'

Hij leidt haar weg van het groepje. Een van zijn medespelers roept: 'Waar ga je heen, Julian?'

'Ik ga haar van de baan laten gooien.'

'En ons rondje dan?'

'Ik haal jullie wel in.'

De autodealer moppert: 'Toch niet weer, hè?'

Een ander viertal is al tot halverwege de fairway gevorderd. Shawcroft loopt langs hen terwijl hij Samira nog altijd bij haar arm heeft. Ze moet rennen om niet te vallen.

'U doet me pijn.'

'Hou je bek, stomme slet. Ik weet niet wat voor kunstje je aan het uithalen bent, maar het zal je niet lukken. Wie heeft je gestuurd?'

'Ik heb mijn schuld afgelost.'

'Die schuld zal me aan mijn reet roesten. Ik heb geen baan voor je! Je valt me lastig. Als je in mijn buurt komt, laat ik je arresteren.'

Samira geeft niet op. God, wat is ze goed.

'Waarom is Hasan gestorven?'

'Dat heet leven. Dingen gebeuren.'

Ik geloof mijn oren niet. Hij citeert Donald Rumsfeld. Waarom gebeuren die dingen niet bij mensen als Shawcroft?

'Het heeft me lang gekost u te vinden, Brother. We hebben in Amsterdam gewacht tot u zou komen of iets van u zou laten horen. Op het laatst konden we niet langer wachten. Ze maakten aanstalten ons terug te sturen naar Kabul. Hasan ging alleen op weg. Ik wilde met hem mee, maar hij zei dat ik moest wachten.' Haar stem staat op breken. 'Hij zou u gaan opzoeken. Hij zei dat u uw belofte was vergeten. Ik zei hem dat u een eerbaar en vriendelijk mens was. In het weeshuis bracht u ons eten en dekens. U had het kruis om...'

Shawcroft draait haar pols om, in een poging haar tot zwijgen te brengen.

'En nou hou je je mond!'

'Iemand heeft Zala vermoord.'

'Ik weet niet waar je het over hebt.'

Ze naderen het clubhuis. Forbes is uit de auto gestapt en loopt op hen toe. Ik blijf achter. Shawcroft gooit Samira in een bloembed. Ze stoot haar knie en schreeuwt het uit.

'Dat geldt als geweldpleging.'

Shawcroft kijkt op en ziet de rechercheur. Dan kijkt hij langs hem heen en ziet mij.

'U hebt het recht niet! Mijn advocaat zal hiervan horen.'
Forbes overhandigt hem een aanhoudingsbevel. 'Prima. Ik hoop
voor u dat hij vandaag geen golfafspraken heeft.'

6

Shawcroft beschouwt zichzelf als een intellectueel en halve advocaat, maar lijkt het wetboek van strafrecht en de Geneefse Con-
ventie door elkaar te halen als hij er vanuit zijn arrestantencel allerlei beschuldigingen over inhumane behandeling uitgooit.
Intellectuelen lopen er te veel mee te koop en wijze mensen zijn
gewoon saai. (Mijn moeder zegt me de hele tijd dat ik geld opzij
moet leggen, vroeg naar bed moet gaan en geen dingen moet uit-
lenen.) Ik geef de voorkeur aan slimme mensen die hun talenten
verborgen houden en zichzelf niet al te serieus nemen.

Een tiental agenten is bezig archiefmappen en computerbestanden van het New Life Adoption Centre door te spitten. Anderen
zijn bezig in Shawcrofts huis in Hayward's Heath. Ik verwacht niet
dat ze een papieren spoor zullen vinden dat naar de tweeling leidt.
Daar is hij te zorgvuldig voor.

Er is echter wel een kans dat kandidaat-kopers in eerste instantie
voor een legale adoptie naar het centrum zijn gekomen. Tijdens
onze eerste ontmoeting vroeg ik hem naar de brochure die ik in
Cates huis had aangetroffen en waarin het verhaal van een jongetje
stond dat door een prostituee ter wereld was gebracht. Shawcroft
hield stug vol dat alle adoptiefouders grondig werden gescreend.
Dat kon gesprekken omvatten, rapporten van psychologen en het
nagaan van een mogelijk strafblad. Als hij me destijds de waarheid
heeft verteld, zou degene bij wie de tweeling nu is in het verleden op
een wachtlijst van het adoptiecentrum kunnen hebben gestaan.

Sinds zijn arrestatie zijn er vier uur verstreken. Forbes had geregeld dat we hem door de voordeur binnen konden leiden, langs
de openbare wachtruimte. Hij wilde een maximum aan ongemak
en schaamte teweegbrengen. Hoewel hij ervaren is, voel ik dat hij
niet van het niveau is van Ruiz, die precies weet wanneer hij on-

vermurwbaar moet zijn en wanneer hij iemand nog een uurtje extra moet laten zweten in een arrestantencel, in gezelschap van zijn demonen.

Shawcroft wacht op zijn advocaat, Eddie Barrett. Ik had kunnen raden dat hij om de 'Bulldog' zou vragen, een ouderwetse letselschadejager met een zekere faam voor hofmakerij richting de media en het tegen de haren in strijken van politiefunctionarissen. Ruiz en hij zijn oude tegenstanders met een wederzijdse afkeer en een niet van harte beleden wederzijds respect.

Op de gang klinkt bewonderend gefluit en gelach. Barrett is gearriveerd, gekleed in spijkerbroek, cowboylaarzen, ruitjeshemd en een enorme hoed.

'Hé, daar heb je Willie Nelson!' roept iemand.

'Is dat een proppenschieter in je zak, Eddie, of ben je gewoon allejezus blij me te zien?'

Iemand barst los in een vrolijk dansje. Eddie haakt zijn duimen achter zijn broekriem en maakt een paar lijndanspasjes. Het lijkt hem niet te deren dat ze de draak met hem steken. Meestal is het andersom en laat hij tijdens ondervragingen of voor de rechtbank de politie een modderfiguur slaan.

Barrett is een vreemd uitziende man met een ondersteboven gekeerd lichaam (korte benen en een lang bovenlichaam) en hij loopt net als George W. Bush, dus met zijn armen van het lichaam af, een onnatuurlijk rechte rug en zijn kin te ver omhoog. Misschien iets wat cowboys doen.

Een van de mannen in uniform gaat hem voor naar een verhoorkamer. Shawcroft wordt naar boven gehaald. Forbes doet een plastic dopje in zijn oor, een ontvanger die ons in staat stelt tijdens de ondervraging met elkaar te praten. Hij pakt een stapel mappen en een lijst met vragen. Dit heeft net zoveel te maken met voorbereid líjken als met voorbereid zíjn.

Ik weet niet of Forbes zenuwachtig is, maar ik kan de spanning voelen. Het gaat over de tweeling. We zullen ze nooit vinden als Shawcroft niet breekt of samenwerkt.

De liefdadigheidsman heeft nog steeds z'n golfkleren aan. Barrett zit naast hem en legt zijn cowboyhoed op tafel. De formaliteiten worden afgewerkt: namen, locatie en tijdstip van het verhoor. Vervolgens legt Forbes vijf foto's op tafel. Shawcroft neemt niet de moeite ernaar te kijken.

'Deze vijf asielzoeksters beweren dat u hen hebt overgehaald hun vaderland te verlaten en illegaal het Verenigd Koninkrijk binnen te komen.'

'Nee.'

'U beweert dat u ze niet kent?'

'Misschien heb ik ze ooit ontmoet. Ik kan het me niet herinneren.'

'Misschien helpt het als u hun gezichten bekijkt.'

Barrett komt tussenbeide. 'Mijn cliënt heeft uw vraag beantwoord.'

'Waar zou u hen kunnen hebben ontmoet?'

'Mijn stichtingen hebben vorig jaar meer dan een half miljoen pond binnengehaald. Ik heb weeshuizen bezocht in Afghanistan, Irak, Albanië en Kosovo.'

'Hoe weet u dat deze vrouwen wees zijn? Dat heb ik niet gezegd.'

Shawcroft verstrakt. Ik kan bijna zien hoe hij zichzelf in stilte uitfoetert vanwege de uitglijder.

'Dus uként deze vrouwen?'

'Zou kunnen.'

'En Samira Khan kent u ook.'

'Ja.'

'Waar hebt u haar ontmoet?'

'In een weeshuis in Kabul.'

'Hebt u het toen gehad over haar overkomst naar het Verenigd Koninkrijk?'

'Nee.'

'Hebt u haar een baan aangeboden hier?'

'Nee.' Hij glimlacht zijn onschuldige glimlach.

'U hebt haar in contact gebracht met een man die haar naar Nederland heeft gesmokkeld en daarna naar Groot-Brittannië.'

'Nee.'

'De prijs was tienduizend Amerikaanse dollars. U zei haar dat

347

God voor haar een manier zou vinden om dat bedrag terug te betalen.'

'Tijdens mijn reizen heb ik tal van weeskinderen ontmoet, inspecteur, en ik geloof niet dat er ook maar één was die niet weg wilde. Daar droomden ze van. Voor het slapengaan vertelden ze elkaar verhalen over ontkomen naar het Westen, waar zelfs bedelaars autoreden en honden op dieet moesten, zo veel voedsel was er.'

Forbes legt een foto van Brendan Pearl op tafel. 'Kent u deze man?'

'Dat kan ik me niet herinneren.'

'Hij is veroordeeld wegens moord.'

'Ik zal voor hem bidden.'

'En zijn slachtoffers, gaat u daar ook voor bidden?' Forbes houdt een foto van Cate op. 'Kent u deze vrouw?'

'Ze zou het adoptiecentrum kunnen hebben bezocht. Dat kan ik niet met zekerheid zeggen.'

'Wilde ze een adoptie?'

Shawcroft haalt zijn schouders op.

'U zult een antwoord moeten geven voor de bandopname.'

'Ik kan het me niet herinneren.'

'Kijk nog eens goed.'

'Er mankeert niets aan mijn ogen, inspecteur.'

'En aan uw geheugen?'

Barrett onderbreekt ons. 'Hoor eens, dokter Phil, het is vandaag zondag. Ik heb wel wat beters te doen dan te gaan zitten luisteren hoe u uw paal zit op te wrijven. Waarom vertelt u niet gewoon wat mijn cliënt geacht wordt te hebben gedaan?'

Forbes legt een bewonderenswaardige zelfbeheersing aan de dag. Hij legt nog een foto op tafel, ditmaal van Yanus. Het vragen gaat verder. De antwoorden zijn steeds hetzelfde: 'Dat weet ik niet meer. Kan ik me niet herinneren.'

Julian Shawcroft is geen pathologische leugenaar (waarom zou je liegen als je meer hebt aan de waarheid?), maar hij is een geboren misleider, en misleiden gaat hem net zo makkelijk af als ademhalen. Telkens als Forbes hem onder druk heeft staan, ontrolt hij met zorg een lappendeken van leugens, flinterdun en toch

348

zorgvuldig in elkaar gezet en hij repareert elk foutje in het weefsel voordat het een grote scheur kan worden. Hij verliest zijn geduld niet en is niet zichtbaar angstig. In plaats daarvan straalt hij een grote kalmte uit en is zijn blik krachtig en vast.

In de in het adoptiecentrum aangetroffen mappen komen de namen voor van minstens twaalf stellen die ook voorkomen in de papieren van de IVF-kliniek in Amsterdam. Ik geef de informatie via een zendertje door aan Forbes. Ter bevestiging tikt hij tegen zijn oor.

'Bent u weleens in Amsterdam geweest, meneer Shawcroft?' vraagt hij.

Ik spreek het hier in en het komt er daar uit – net tovenarij.

'Meerdere malen.'

'Hebt u ooit een fertiliteitskliniek in Amersfoort bezocht?'

'Kan ik me niet herinneren.'

'U zou zich die kliniek toch zeker nog wel herinneren.' Forbes noemt de naam en het adres. 'Zoveel zult u er toch niet bezoeken.'

'Ik ben een drukbezet man.'

'Dat is precies waarom ik ervan uitga dat u agenda's en afsprakenlijstjes bijhoudt.'

'Klopt.'

'Waarom hebben we dan niets van dat alles aangetroffen?'

'Ik bewaar mijn programma nooit langer dan een paar weken voordat ik het weggooi. Ik haat rommel.'

'Kunt u verklaren hoe het komt dat echtparen die door uw adoptiecentrum zijn gescreend ook voorkomen in de bestanden van een IVF-kliniek in Amsterdam?'

'Misschien kwamen ze daar voor een IVF-behandeling. Mensen die aan adoptie denken proberen vaak eerst IVF.'

Barrett staart naar het plafond. Bij hem dreigt de verveling toe te slaan.

'Deze stellen hebben geen IVF-behandeling gekregen,' zegt Forbes. 'Ze leverden embryo's aan die werden ingeplant in de baarmoeders van asielzoeksters die gedwongen werden de vrucht te voldragen, waarna de baby's van hen werden afgenomen.'

Forbes wijst naar de vijf foto's op tafel. 'Deze vrouwen, meneer Shawcroft, dezelfde vrouwen die u in verschillende weeshuizen hebt ontmoet, dezelfde vrouwen die u aanmoedigde te vertrekken, deze vrouwen hebben u herkend. Ze hebben verklaringen afgelegd bij de politie. En elk van hen herinnert zich dat u hetzelfde zei: "God zal een manier voor je vinden om je schuld terug te betalen."'

Barrett pakt Shawcrofts arm. 'Mijn cliënt doet een beroep op het zwijgrecht.'

Forbes' antwoord komt rechtstreeks uit het boekje: 'Ik hoop dat uw cliënt zich realiseert dat, als hij nalaat feiten te melden waarvan hij later bij zijn verdediging gebruikmaakt, dit door de hoven negatief kan worden geïnterpreteerd.'

'Daar is mijn cliënt zich van bewust.'

Barretts kleine donkere ogen schitteren. 'Doe wat u moet doen, inspecteur. Wat we tot dusverre hebben gehoord is een reeks verzonnen verhalen die voor feiten moeten doorgaan. Wat zegt het als mijn cliënt met deze vrouwen heeft gesproken? U hebt geen bewijs dat hij hun illegale binnenkomst in dit land heeft georganiseerd. En ook geen bewijs dat hij betrokken was bij dit Goebbelsiaanse sprookje over gedwongen zwangerschappen en gestolen baby's.'

Hij zit volmaakt bewegingloos, in evenwicht. 'Mijn indruk, inspecteur, is dat uw hele zaak berust op de getuigenis van vijf illegale immigranten die alles zullen doen om maar in dit land te mogen blijven. Als u daar een zaak op wilt baseren, ga uw gang.'

Barrett staat op, strijkt zijn smal toelopende spijkerbroek glad en doet zijn riemgesp met buffelschedel goed. Hij kijkt even naar Shawcroft. 'Ik adviseer u te zwijgen.' Hij opent de deur en loopt met verende tred de gang af, zijn hoed in de hand. Opnieuw dat loopje.

7

'Stuivertje voor Guy Fawkes.'

Een groep jongens met piekhaar hangt rond op de straathoek. De kleinste is uitgedost als zwerver, in kleren die hem te groot

zijn. Hij ziet eruit alsof hij getroffen is door een krimpstraal.
Een van de jongens geeft hem een zetje. 'Laat se je tanden eens
sien, Lachie.'

Lachie doet traag zijn mond open. Twee tanden zijn zwartge-
maakt.

'Stuivertje voor Guy Fawkes,' zeggen ze opnieuw in koor.

'Jullie gaan hem toch niet op een vreugdevuurtje gooien, hè?'

'Nee, mevrouw.'

'Gelukkig.' Ik geef ze een pond.

Samira heeft staan toekijken. 'Wat zijn ze aan het doen?'

'Geld aan het ophalen voor vuurwerk.'

'Door te bedelen.'

'Niet helemaal.'

Hari heeft haar uitgelegd wat Guy Fawkes Night is. Het resultaat
is dat ze de afgelopen drie dagen met z'n tweeën in mijn tuinschuurtje hebben doorgebracht, als manische wetenschappers in
katoenen kleren gestoken en ontdaan van alles wat statische elektriciteit zou kunnen opwekken of een vonk veroorzaken.

'Die Guy Fawkes, hè, was dat een terrorist?'

'Ja, in zekere zin wel. Hij probeerde het House of Lords op te
blazen met vaten buskruit.'

'Om de koning te vermoorden?'

'Ja.'

'Waarom?'

'Zijn medesamenzweerders en hij waren ontevreden over de
manier waarop de koning de katholieken achterstelde.'

'Het ging dus om het geloof?'

'Eigenlijk wel, ja.'

Ze kijkt naar de jongens. 'En zij vieren dat?'

'Toen het complot mislukte, staken mensen vreugdevuurwerk
af en verbrandden ze poppen die Guy Fawkes moesten voorstellen. Dat doet men nog steeds.' *Laat niemand je ooit wijsmaken dat
protestanten geen wrok koesteren.*

Terwijl we richting Bethnal Green lopen, denkt ze hier in stilte
over na. Het is bijna zes uur en de lucht is al zwaar van de geur van
zwavel en rook. Overal op het gras zijn vreugdevuurtjes te zien

met gezinnen eromheen, met dekens om zich heen geslagen tegen de kou.

Mijn hele familie is gekomen om naar het vuurwerk te kijken. Hari, die uit het schuurtje is opgedoken met een oude munitiekist in zijn armen waarin de vruchten van zijn inspanningen en Samira's kennis zitten, is in zijn element. Ik weet niet waar hij de benodigdheden vandaan heeft gehaald: de chemicaliën, speciale zouten en metaalpoeders. Het belangrijkste ingrediënt, buskruit, kwam van een hobbywinkel in Notting Hill, of liever gezegd: uit zorgvuldig uit elkaar gehaalde schaalmodellen, waarna het werd fijngewreven.

Overal op het gras dansen fakkels en wordt klein vuurwerk ontstoken. Kleine vuurpijlen, Romeinse kaarsen, vliegende slangen, rotjes en Bengaalse vuurpotjes. Kinderen tekenen met sterretjes in de lucht en elke hond in Londen blaft, zodat elke baby wakker is. Ik vraag me af of de tweeling zich onder hen bevindt. Misschien zijn ze nog te klein om bang te zijn voor het lawaai.

Met mijn arm door die van Bada gehaakt kijken we hoe Samira en Hari een zware plastic pijp in de grond planten. Samira heeft haar rok tussen haar benen gestoken en strak rond haar dijen geslagen. Haar hoofddoek zit ingestopt onder de kraag van haar jas.

'Wie is er zo gek geweest hem dat bij te brengen?' zegt Bada. 'Straks blaast hij zichzelf nog op.'

'Hij redt zich wel.'

Hari is altijd de favoriet onder zijn gelijken geweest. Als jongste heeft hij mijn ouders de afgelopen zes jaar voor zichzelf gehad. Ik denk soms dat hij het enige is wat hen nog verbindt met de middelbare leeftijd.

Met haar handpalm een bleke, taps toelopende kaars afschermend hurkt Samira laag bij de grond. Er gaan een of twee seconden voorbij. Een vuurpijl zoeft de lucht in en verdwijnt uit het zicht. Een, twee, drie seconden gaan voorbij, totdat hij plotseling hoog boven ons in neerdruppelende sterren uiteenspat die in het duister wegsmelten. Vergeleken met het eerdere vuurwerk is dit hoger, feller en harder. Mensen onderbreken hun eigen vuurwerk om te kunnen kijken.

Hari roept zingzeggend de namen af – Drakenadem, Gouden Feniks, Glitterpalm, Ontploffende Appels – terwijl Samira rustig tussen de buizen heen en weer loopt. Grondvuurwerk sproeit bundels vonken om Samira heen en haar ogen weerspiegelen de lichtjes.

Hari's Luchthuiler vormt de finale. Samira laat hem de lont aansteken. Het projectiel schiet gillend omhoog tot het niet meer dan een vlekje licht is, om even later als een madeliefje uiteen te spatten in een cirkel van wit. Net als het geheel lijkt te stoppen, ontploft er een rode bal binnen de eerste kring. Het eindsaluut is een harde knal die de ramen in de buurt doet rammelen en hier en daar een autoalarm doet afgaan. De menigte applaudisseert. Hari maakt een buiging. Samira is al bezig de geschroeide papieren kokers en flarden papier op te ruimen, die ze in de oude munitiekist stopt.

Hari is in de wolken. 'We moeten het vieren,' zegt hij tegen Samira. 'Ik neem je mee uit.'

'Uit?'

'Ja.'

'Waar is uit?'

'Kan me niet schelen. We kunnen iets gaan drinken of naar een bandje gaan luisteren.'

'Ik drink niet.'

'Je kunt een sapje nemen, of frisdrank.'

'Ik kan niet met jou uitgaan. Het is niet goed als een meisje met een jongen alleen is.'

'We zijn vast niet alleen. De pub zit altijd stampvol.'

'Ze bedoelt zonder chaperonne,' zeg ik tegen hem.

'O, oké.'

Ik vraag me soms af waarom ze Hari als mijn slimste broertje beschouwen. Hij kijkt beteuterd.

'Het heeft iets met het geloof te maken, Hari.'

'Maar ik ben helemaal niet gelovig.'

Ik geef hem een draai om zijn oren.

Ik heb Samira nog altijd niet verteld wat er tijdens Shawcrofts ondervraging is gebeurd of – nog belangrijker – wat er níet is gebeurd. De liefdadigheidsbaas liet niets los. Forbes moest hem laten gaan.

Hoe kan ik de regels van bewijs en bewijslast uitleggen aan iemand die nooit de luxe van rechtvaardigheid of eerlijkheid heeft gekend?

Ik laat de anderen voorgaan, geef Samira een arm en probeer het haar duidelijk te maken.

'Maar hij is degene die al die dingen heeft gedaan,' zegt ze terwijl ze zich naar me toe draait. 'Dit zou allemaal niet gebeurd zijn als hij er niet was geweest. Hasan en Zala zouden er nog zijn. Er zijn zo veel mensen dood.' Ze slaat haar ogen neer. 'Misschien zijn zij wel de geluksvogels.'

'Dat mag je niet zeggen.'

'Waarom niet?'

'Omdat de tweeling een moeder nodig zal hebben.'

Ze onderbreekt me met een vinnig handgebaar. 'Ik zal nóóit hun moeder zijn!'

Haar gezicht staat anders. Verwrongen. Ik zie een ander gezicht onder het eerste, een gevaarlijk gezicht. Het duurt maar een fractie van een seconde, maar lang genoeg om me van slag te brengen. Ze knippert en het is weg. Ik heb haar weer terug.

We zijn bijna thuis. Zo'n vijftien meter achter ons is een auto langzamer gaan rijden, traag voortrollend zonder ons in te halen. Angst kruipt mijn keel in. Ik reik naar achteren en trek mijn hemd losser. De Glock zit in een holster onder op mijn rug.

Hari is al de hoek om, Hanbury Street in. Mama en Bada zijn naar huis gegaan. Tegenover het volgende verkeerslicht loopt een voetpad tussen de huizen door. Samira heeft de auto opgemerkt.

'Niet omkijken,' zeg ik tegen haar.

Als we onder de straatlantaarn zijn, duw ik haar in de richting van het voetpad en roep dat ze het op een lopen moet zetten. Ze gehoorzaamt zonder iets te vragen. Ik kan de bestuurder niet goed zien. Ik richt mijn pistool op zijn hoofd en zijn handen gaan omhoog, de handpalmen naar voren, als een mimespeler tegen een denkbeeldige wand.

Een van de achterramen gaat open. Het binnenlampje springt

aan. Ik zwenk mijn wapen naar de opening. Julian Shawcroft heeft één hand op het portier en in de andere iets wat een gebedenboek zou kunnen zijn.

'Ik wil je iets laten zien,' zegt hij.

'Gaat u mij ook laten verdwijnen?'

Hij kijkt teleurgesteld. 'Vertrouw op God als je beschermer.'

'Brengt u me naar de tweeling?'

'Ik zal je helpen het te begrijpen.'

Een windvlaag, gespetter van regendruppels: de avond is stormachtig aan het worden en slechtgeluimd. Mensen zijn op weg naar huis, vreugdevuren doven langzaam uit. We steken de rivier over en rijden door Bermondsey zuidwaarts. Tussen gebouwen door en boven de boomtoppen is de uivormige koepel van St. Paul's te zien.

Shawcroft zwijgt. In de bundel van passerende koplampen kan ik zijn gezicht zien – ik met mijn pistool op schoot, hij met zijn boek. Ik zou bang moeten zijn. In plaats daarvan voel ik een merkwaardige kalmte. Ik heb alleen mijn huis gebeld, om te controleren of Samira veilig was thuisgekomen.

De auto draait de weg af een oprit op en houdt stil op een achterplaats. Tegen de achtergrond van het glimmende dak zie ik voor het eerst het gezicht van de bestuurder. Het is niet Brendan Pearl. Dat had ik ook niet verwacht. Shawcroft is ook weer niet zo gek dat hij zich met een moordenaar laat zien.

Aan Shawcrofts kant duikt een vrouw op in een Franse boerinnenrok en een ruimvallende trui. Haar haar is zo strak achterovergespeld dat haar wenkbrauwen omhoog worden getrokken.

'Dit is Delia,' zegt hij. 'Ze runt een van mijn stichtingen.'

Ik schud een gladde, droge hand.

Door dubbele deuren gaat ze ons voor, een smalle trap op. Aan de muur hangen affiches met confronterende beelden van honger en verwaarlozing. Op een ervan is een Afrikaans kindje afgebeeld met een opgezwollen buik en smekende bolle ogen. In de benedenhoek staat een logo van een tikkende klok met in plaats van cijfers de letters O R P H A N W A T C H, en het gezichtje van een kind op 12.

Achter op mijn rug laat ik mijn wapen in de holster glijden. Er is een kantoor met bureaus en archiefkasten en een beeldscherm, donker en in slaapstand. Shawcroft keert zich naar Delia.

'Is hij open?'

Ze knikt.

Ik loop achter hem aan een tweede kamer binnen, die is ingericht als een kleine huisbioscoop met een scherm en een projector. Er hangen nog meer posters en ook krantenknipsels, waarvan sommige aan de randen omgevouwen, gescheurd of gerafeld. Een klein meisje in een vieze witte jurk kijkt de camera in, een jongetje met zijn armen over elkaar kijkt me uitdagend aan. Er zijn meer beelden, tientallen, die de muur bedekken. De spotjes waaronder ze hangen maken ze tot tragische kunstwerken.

'Dit zijn kinderen die we hebben kunnen redden,' zegt hij met zijn bleke priesterhanden gevouwen voor zich.

De wandpanelen zijn als een harmonica samengevouwen. Hij trekt ze uit om nog meer foto's te laten zien.

'Herinner je je de weeskinderen van de tsunami in Azië nog? Niemand weet precies hoeveel het er zijn, maar sommige schattingen hielden het op twintigduizend. Dakloos. Verstoken van alles. Getraumatiseerd. Gezinnen stonden in de rij om ze te adopteren, regeringen werden bestormd met aanbiedingen, maar vrijwel alle verzoeken werden afgewezen.'

Zijn blik glijdt over me heen. 'Zal ik je vertellen wat er met de tsunamiwezen is gebeurd? In Sri Lanka lijfden de Tamil Tijgers ze in om te vechten, sommigen pas zeven jaar oud. In India ruzieden hebzuchtige verwanten om de kinderen vanwege de door de overheid geboden hulpgelden, om ze vervolgens in de steek te laten zodra het geld binnen was.

In Indonesië weigerden de autoriteiten adoptie aan ieder echtpaar dat geen moslim was. Soldaten haalden driehonderd wezen van een reddingsvlucht, omdat die georganiseerd was door een christelijke liefdadigheidsinstelling. Ze werden zonder voedsel aan hun lot overgelaten. Zelfs landen die adoptie door buitenlanders toestaan, zoals Thailand en India, sloten plotseling hun grenzen, schichtig geworden door onbevestigde verhalen over weeskinderen die het land uit werden gesmokkeld door bendes pedofielen. Het was te gek voor woorden. Als iemand een bank berooft, ga je niet het internationale bancaire systeem platleggen. Je grijpt de bankrovers. Je vervolgt ze. Helaas wil men, telkens als er sprake is van kindersmokkel, het internationale adoptiesysteem stilleggen en maakt men de zaken voor miljoenen weeskinderen nog erger. Mensen hebben geen idee van de enorme schaal van dit probleem. Jaarlijks worden twee miljoen kinderen gedwongen de prostitutie in te gaan. En in Afrika worden wekelijks meer kinderen wees dan het totale aantal weeskinderen als gevolg van de tsunami in Azië. In het gebied beneden de Sahara zijn het er alleen al dertien miljoen.

De zogenaamde deskundigen zeggen dat kinderen niet als handelswaar mogen dienen. Waarom niet? Is het niet beter als handelswaar te worden behandeld dan als een hond? Hongerig. Koud. In vuiligheid levend. Als slaaf verkocht worden. Verkracht. Ze zeggen dat het niet om geld mag gaan. Om wat dan wel? Hoe gaan we die kinderen anders redden?'

'U vindt dat het doel de middelen heiligt.'

'Ik vind dat het in ieder geval een rol moet spelen.'

'U kunt mensen niet als een soort grondstof behandelen.'

'Natuurlijk kan ik dat. Economen doen niet anders. Ik ben een pragmaticus.'

'U bent een monster.'

'Ik bekommer me er tenminste om. De wereld heeft mensen zoals ik nodig. Realisten. Mannen die van wanten weten. Wat doen jullie? Een kind sponsoren in Burundi of donateur worden van de Cliniclowns. Jullie proberen één kind te redden terwijl tienduizend anderen verhongeren.'

'En wat is het alternatief?'

'Er eentje opofferen en tienduizenden redden.'

'Wie bepaalt dat?'

'Pardon?'

'Wie kiest het ene kind dat je opoffert?'

'Dat doe ik. Ik vraag niet van anderen om dat voor me te doen.'

Dit is het moment waarop ik hem haat. Met al zijn donkere charme en verfijnde intensiteit is hij een beul en een fanaticus. Dan heb ik nog liever Brendan Pearls motieven. Hij probeert zijn moorden tenminste niet te rechtvaardigen.

'En als de cijfers nou anders liggen? Zou u vijf levens opofferen om er vijfhonderd te redden? En tien om er elf te redden?'

'Zullen we dat maar aan de mensen zelf vragen?' antwoordt hij sarcastisch. 'Elf stemmen voor mij, jij maar tien. Ik heb gewonnen.'

Heel even, tot mijn schrik, begrijp ik wat hij zegt, maar ik kan een wereld die zo meedogenloos zwart-wit is niet accepteren. Moord, verkrachting en marteling zijn het gereedschap van terroristen en niet van beschaafde samenlevingen. Als we zoals zij worden, welke hoop rest ons dan nog?

Shawcroft beschouwt zichzelf als een rechtschapen mens, een barmhartig mens, een vroom mens, maar dat is hij niet. Hij is deel geworden van het probleem in plaats van de oplossing – door vrouwen te smokkelen, baby's te verhandelen, de kwetsbaren uit te buiten.

'Niets geeft u het recht die keuzes te maken,' zeg ik hem.

'Ik heb die rol aanvaard.'

'U denkt dat u God bent.'

'Inderdaad. En weet je waarom? Omdat iemand dat moet doen. Weekhartige types zoals jij bewijzen de armen en hulpbehoevenden alleen lippendienst. Jullie dragen een gekleurd armbandje en beweren dat jullie de armoede tot het verleden zullen laten behoren. Hoe dan?'

'Dit gaat niet over mij.'

'O, jawel.'

'Waar is de tweeling?'

'Er wordt van ze gehouden.'

'Waar?'

'Waar ze thuishoren.'

Het pistool ligt tegen mijn onderrug, warm als bloed. Mijn vingers sluiten zich eromheen. In één beweging zwaait het wapen naar hem toe, tot tegen zijn voorhoofd.

Ik verwacht angst te zien. In plaats daarvan knipoogt hij mismoedig naar me. 'Dit is als een oorlog, Alisha. Ik weet dat we die term al te gemakkelijk hanteren, maar soms is hij gerechtvaardigd. Sommige oorlogen zijn gerechtvaardigd. De oorlog tegen de armoede. De oorlog tegen honger. Zelfs pacifisten kunnen niet tegen dat soort oorlogen zijn. Bij conflicten raken onschuldige mensen gewond. Jouw vriendin was een slachtoffer.'

'U hebt haar opgeofferd.'

'Om anderen te beschermen.'

'Om uzelf te beschermen.'

Mijn vinger spant zich om de trekker. Twee ons druk erbij en het is over. Langs de loop kijkt hij me aan, nog altijd niet bang. Een kort moment denk ik dat hij bereid is te sterven nu hij zijn zegje heeft gedaan en vrede met zichzelf heeft gesloten.

Hij doet zijn ogen niet dicht. Hij wéét dat ik het niet kan doen. Zonder hem vind ik de tweeling misschien wel nooit terug.

8

Op een groot portret boven de schouw is een aristocratisch uitziende man te zien in rechterstoga, met op zijn onderarm een paardenharen pruik die verrassend veel weg heeft van een Shi-Tzu. Hij kijkt ernstig neer op een glimmend gepoetste tafel die omgeven is door stoelen met hoge rugleuning.

Felix' moeder is gekleed in een tweedjasje en zwarte vrijetijdsbroek en houdt haar handtas vast alsof ze bang is dat iemand hem pikt. Naast haar zit een andere zoon met zijn vingers op tafel te trommelen, nu al verveeld.

Barnaby staat door het raam de kleine binnenplaats te bestuderen. Ik zie Jarrod niet als hij komt aanlopen. Hij raakt mijn schouder aan.

'Is het waar? Ben ik oom?'

Zijn haar is bij zijn slapen naar achteren geborsteld en blijkt al dunner te worden.

'Ik weet niet precies wat jij bent, technisch gesproken.'

'Mijn vader zegt dat het een tweeling is.'

'Ze behoren niet toe aan Cate. Een meisje werd gedwongen ze te dragen.'

Zijn ogen stralen onbegrip uit. 'Biologisch gezien behoren ze bij Cate. Dat maakt mij tot hun oom.'

'Misschien wel, ik weet het niet.'

De juridisch adviseur komt de spreekkamer binnen en neemt een stoel. Hij is midden vijftig, gekleed in een driedelig krijtstreeppak, stelt zich voor als William Grove en vertrekt zijn gezicht tot een strak glimlachje. Zijn hele houding is er een van ingehouden vaart. Tijd is geld. Elk kwartier is factureerbaar. Stoelen gaan schrapend naar achteren. Mensen gaan zitten. Meneer Grove werpt een blik op zijn instructies.

'Dames en heren, aan dit testament werd zes weken geleden een codicil toegevoegd met als ontstaansgrond de gerede kans dat de Beaumonts ouders van een kind zouden worden.'

Een huivering verstoort de lucht als een plotselinge verandering van luchtdruk. De jurist kijkt op en geeft een rukje aan de manchetten van zijn overhemd. 'Mag ik hieruit concluderen dat dit huwelijk kinderen heeft voortgebracht?'

Stilte.

Uiteindelijk schraapt Barnaby zijn keel. 'Daar lijkt het wel op.'

'Hoe bedoelt u? Verklaar u nader.'

'Wij hebben reden om aan te nemen dat Cate en Felix een draagmoederschap hadden geregeld. Acht dagen geleden is er een tweeling geboren.'

De volgende minuut is er een van uitroepen en ongeloof. Felix' moeder maakt achter in haar keel een snikgeluid. Barnaby kijkt naar zijn handen en wrijft met zijn vingertoppen. Jarrod heeft zijn ogen niet van me afgewend.

Meneer Grove, die niet goed weet wat hij nu moet, neemt even de tijd om tot rust te komen. Hij besluit verder te gaan. De nalatenschap bestaat uit een zwaar verhypotheekeerde eengezinswoning in Willesden Green, Noord-Londen, die recentelijk beschadigd is door brand. De verzekering zal de kosten van herbouw vergoeden. Felix had daarnaast een door zijn werkgever verstrekte levensverzekering.

'Als niemand bezwaar maakt, zal ik de laatste wilsbeschikkingen voorlezen, die ogenschijnlijk gelijkluidend zijn.' Hij neemt een slokje water.

'"Dit is de uiterste wilsbeschikking en testament van mij, Cate Elisabeth Beaumont (geboren Elliot), opgesteld op de veertiende dag van september 2006. Ik herroep hierbij alle wilsbeschikkingen eerder door mij opgesteld en verklaar dat dit mijn laatste wilsbeschikking en testament is. Ik benoem William Grove van Sadler, Grove & Buffett tot executeur en bewindvoerder van onderhavige wilsbeschikking. Ik geef, vermaak en testeer aan mijn echtgenoot Felix Beaumont (eerder bekend als Felix Buczkowski) mijn gehele nalatenschap, op voorwaarde dat hij mij dertig dagen overleeft. Indien dit laatste niet het geval is gaat mijn volledige nalatenschap over op mijn kind of kinderen, door hen gelijkelijk te verdelen als gemeenschappelijke eigenaren.

Ik benoem Alisha Gaur Barba tot voogd over mijn pasgeboren kinderen en draag haar op hen lief te hebben en te verzorgen en zoveel als nodig van de nalatenschap aan te wenden voor hun opvoeding, opleiding en vooruitgang in het leven."'

Barnaby is opgestaan, zijn kaak gaat in protest op en neer. Heel even denk ik dat er misschien wel sprake is van een hartaanval.

'Dit is belachelijk! Ik laat mijn kleinkinderen godverdomme niet door een vreemde opvoeden.' Hij priemt met een vinger in mijn richting. 'Jij wist hiervan!'

'Nee.'

'Jij hebt het al die tijd geweten.'

'Nee, dat heb ik niet.'

Meneer Grove probeert hem tot bedaren te brengen. 'Meneer, ik kan u verzekeren dat alles correct is ondertekend in het bijzijn van getuigen.'

'Denkt u dat ik gek ben? Dit is gelul. Ik laat me door niemand mijn kleinkinderen afpakken.'

Na de uitbarsting is het doodstil in de kamer. Het enige geluid is dat van de airconditioning en waterleidingen die zich in de verte vullen en weer leeglopen. Een moment lang denk ik dat Barnaby me weleens zou kunnen gaan slaan. In plaats daarvan schopt hij zijn stoel naar achteren en stormt naar buiten met Jarrod achter hem aan. Mensen draaien zich naar me om. Mijn nek wordt warm.

Meneer Grove heeft een brief voor me. Als ik hem aanpak, moet ik mijn hand dwingen niet te trillen. Waarom zou Cate dit doen? Waarom kiest ze mij? Ik voel de verantwoordelijkheid al tegen mijn longen drukken.

Terwijl ik de spreekkamer verlaat, door de hal loop en zware glazen deuren openduw, zit de envelop gekreukt in mijn hand. Ik heb geen idee waar ik heen loop. Is dit het? Eén lullig briefje dat alles moet verklaren? Zal het opwegen tegen acht jaar stilte?

Ineens krijgt mijn verwarring gezelschap van nog een gedachte: misschien wordt mij hier wel de kans geboden het goed te maken, mezelf te bevrijden van schuld. Om rekenschap af te leggen voor mijn nalatigheid, mijn fouten, de onuitgesproken dingen, alles wat me ontgaan is en wat ik begaan heb. Mij wordt gevraagd haar kostbaarste erfenis te beschermen en daar beter mee om te gaan dan met onze vriendschap.

In de portiek van een drankwinkel blijf ik staan en haal mijn vinger onder de flap van de envelop door.

Lieve Ali,
Het is maf om een brief te schrijven die pas zal worden geopend en gelezen als je dood bent. Het lukt me echter niet er al te bedroefd over te worden. En als ik dood ben is het aan de late kant om me nog druk te maken, want dan nemen gedane zaken pas echt geen keer meer.
Het enige waar ik me druk om maak ben jij. Jij bent het enige wat me spijt. Vanaf dat we elkaar op Oaklands leerden kennen en jij met Paul Donavon vocht om mijn eer te verdedigen en je je voortanden verloor, heb ik bevriend met je willen zijn. Jij was écht, Ali, en geen nepper.
Ik weet dat je spijt hebt van wat er is voorgevallen met mijn

vader. Ik weet dat het eerder zijn fout was dan de jouwe. Jou heb ik het al lang geleden vergeven. Hem heb ik het vergeven omdat – nou ja, je weet wel hoe dat gaat met vaders. Jij was, tussen haakjes, niet de eerste met wie hij een scheve schaats reed, maar dat had je denk ik al in de smiezen.

De reden dat ik je dit nooit heb kunnen vertellen is een belofte die ik mijn moeder heb gedaan. Ze was erachter gekomen van jou en mijn vader. Hij had het haar verteld omdat hij dacht dat ik het haar zou vertellen.

Mijn moeder liet me beloven dat ik jou nooit meer zou zien, nooit meer met je zou praten, je nooit meer bij ons uit zou nodigen en nooit meer jouw naam in de mond zou nemen.

Ik weet dat ik haar had moeten negeren. Ik had moeten bellen. Dat is vele malen bijna gebeurd. Dan had ik de telefoon al beet. Soms had ik het nummer van je ouders al ingetoetst, maar dan wist ik niet wat ik tegen je moest zeggen. We hadden er te veel tijd overheen laten gaan. Hoe zouden we ooit om een stilte die zo groot was als een olifant die in de kamer zit heen kunnen komen?

Ik ben altijd aan je blijven denken. Ik volgde zo goed als ik kon je carrière, pikte verhalen op van andere mensen. Die arme Felix werd gek van mijn verhalen over jouw wapenfeiten en avonturen – als we in een brandend vliegtuigwrak omkomen of zelfmoordterroristen hun oog hebben laten vallen op de supermarkt op Willesden Green, willen we dat jij voogd wordt over onze kinderen.

Mijn moeder krijgt een rolberoerte als ze dit te weten komt, maar ik heb me aan mijn belofte gehouden, waarin niets stond over postuum contact met jou. Er zijn geen kleine lettertjes. Ik ga geen beperkende bepalingen of instructies geven. Als jij de taak op je wilt nemen, is hij van jou. Ik weet dat je net zoveel van mijn kinderen zult houden als ik. En ik weet dat je hun zult leren voor elkaar te zorgen. Je zult de dingen tegen ze zeggen die ik zou hebben gezegd en hun vertellen over mij en over Felix. De goede dingen, uiteraard.

Ik weet niet wat ik nog meer moet zeggen. Ik denk vaak hoe an-

ders mijn leven zou zijn geweest – hoeveel gelukkiger – als jij er deel van had uitgemaakt. Ooit.
Liefs, Cate

Het is even over vijven. Door mijn tranen heen zijn de straatlantaarns vlekkerig. Gezichten glijden voorbij. Hoofden keren zich af. Tegenwoordig vraagt niemand een huilende vrouw nog wat er is, niet in Londen. Ik ben gewoon een van de mafkezen die je ontwijkt. Tijdens de taxirit naar West Acton zie ik mezelf weerspiegeld in het raam. Donderdag word ik dertig – dichter bij de zestig dan bij mijn geboorte. Ik zie er nog steeds jong uit, maar wel uitgeput en koortsig, als een kind dat op een volwassenenfeestje te lang is opgebleven.

Voor de flat van Groentje Dave staat een bord met TE KOOP. Het is hem ernst, hij gaat de kit verlaten om zeilles te gaan geven aan kinderen.

Ik overleg bij mezelf of ik naar boven zal gaan. Ik loop naar de voordeur, staar naar de bel en loop terug naar de weg. Ik wil geen dingen uitleggen. Ik wil gewoon een fles wijn opentrekken, een pizza bestellen en me op de bank neervlijen met zijn benen tussen de mijne en zijn handen die mijn tenen warm wrijven, die ijskoud aanvoelen.

Sinds Amsterdam heb ik hem niet meer gezien. Voor die tijd belde hij me elke dag, soms twee keer. Toen ik hem na de begrafenissen belde, klonk hij aarzelend, bijna nerveus.

Het is de olifant in de kamer. Je kunt er niet over praten, maar je kunt hem ook niet negeren. Mijn opgelapte bekken is ook zoiets. Mensen willen me ineens kinderen geven. Is dat ironisch? Ik weet het nooit met ironie; die term wordt zo vaak misbruikt.

Ik loop opnieuw naar de deur. Het duurt een tijd voor er iemand reageert. Door de intercom klinkt een vrouwenstem. Verontschuldigend. Ze stond onder de douche.

'Dave is er niet.'

'Mijn schuld. Ik had moeten bellen.'

'Hij is onderweg naar huis. Wil je binnenkomen en wachten?'

'Nee, dat hoeft niet.'

Wie is zij? Wat doet zij hier?

'Ik zal zeggen dat je bent geweest.'

'Oké.'

Een stilte.

'Je moet nog zeggen wie je bent.'

'O ja. Sorry. Laat maar. Ik bel hem wel.'

Ik loop terug naar de weg terwijl ik mezelf wijsmaak dat het me niets kan schelen.

Kut! Kut! Kut!

Het huis is merkwaardig stil. In de voorkamer staat de tv zachtjes aan en boven brandt licht. Ik glip het zijpad over en de achterdeur door. Hari is in de keuken.

'Je moet haar tegenhouden.'

'Wie?'

'Samira. Ze gaat weg. Ze is boven aan het pakken.'

'Waarom? Wat heb je met haar gedaan?'

'Niets.'

'Heb je haar alleen gelaten?'

'Twintig minuutjes maar, ik zweer het. Dat is alles. Ik moest de auto van een vriend wegbrengen.'

Samira is in mijn slaapkamer. Haar kleren liggen gevouwen op bed: een paar simpele rokken, bloes, een versleten trui... Hasans koektrommel staat boven op de stapel.

'Waar ga je heen?'

Ze lijkt haar adem in te houden. 'Ik ga. Jullie willen me niet.'

'Waarom zeg je dat? Heeft Hari iets gedaan? Heeft hij iets gezegd dat hij niet had moeten zeggen?'

Ze wil me niet aankijken, maar ik zie de bloeduitstorting die op haar wang opkomt, een ruwe cirkel onder haar rechteroog.

'Wie heeft dat gedaan?'

Ze fluistert: 'Er kwam een man langs.'

'Wat voor man?'

'De man die met jou praatte, bij de kerk.'

'Donavon?'

'Nee, die andere man.'

Ze bedoelt Barnaby. Hij is langs geweest om ruzie te zoeken.

'Hij stond op de deur te slaan, hij maakte een hele hoop herrie. Hij zei dat je tegen mij had gelogen en tegen hem had gelogen.'

'Ik heb nog nooit tegen jou gelogen.'

'Hij zei dat je de baby's voor jezelf wilde en dat jij en ik nog niet van hem af waren.'

'Je moet niet naar hem luisteren.'

'Hij zei dat ik niet welkom was in dit land, dat ik terug moest gaan naar waar ik vandaan kwam, tussen de terroristen.'

'Nee.'

Ik steek mijn arm naar haar uit. Ze deinst terug.

'Heeft hij je geslagen?'

'Ik probeerde de deur dicht te doen. Hij duwde.' Ze voelt aan haar wang.

'Hij had het recht niet om zulke dingen te zeggen.'

'Is het waar? Wil jíj de baby's hebben?'

'Cate heeft een testament geschreven, een juridisch document. Ze heeft mij benoemd tot voogd voor als ze kinderen zou krijgen.'

'Wat betekent voogd? Is de tweeling dan van jou?'

'Nee. Jij hebt ze gebaard. Ze mogen dan Cates ogen hebben en Felix' neus, ze zijn in jouw lichaam gegroeid. En wat mensen ook zullen zeggen, ze behoren jou toe.'

'En als ik ze nou niet wil?'

Mijn mond opent zich, maar ik antwoord niet. Iets heeft zich in mijn keel vastgezet: verlangen en twijfel. Wat Cate ook wilde, het zijn niet mijn baby's. Mijn motieven zijn zuiver.

Ik sla mijn arm om Samira's schouders en trek haar dicht tegen me aan. Haar adem voelt warm in mijn nek en haar eerste snik ploft neer als een schep die in de natte klei neerkomt. Er breekt iets in haar binnenste. Ze heeft haar tranen gevonden.

9

De digitale cijfers van mijn wekker gloeien op in het donker. Het is net vier uur. Slapen zal ik niet meer. Samira ligt opgerold naast me, zachtjes ademend. Ik spaar olifanten. Sommige zijn pluchen speelgoedfiguren, andere beeldjes van geslepen glas, porselein, jade of kristal. Mijn favoriet is vijftien centimeter hoog en gemaakt van zwaar glas, ingelegd met spiegeltjes. Normaal gesproken staat hij onder mijn leeslampje en strooit kleurige sterren uit over de muren. Nu staat hij er niet. Ik vraag me af wat ermee gebeurd kan zijn.

Ik laat me zachtjes uit bed glijden, trek mijn loopspullen aan en stap naar buiten de duisternis van Hanbury Street in. Er zit een scherp kantje aan de wind. Wisseling der seizoenen.

Vroeger hielp Cate me na school bij mijn trainingen. Dan reed ze op haar fiets naast me en zette aan als we de heuvels naderden, omdat ze wist dat ik haar er in de klim uit kon lopen. Toen ik meeliep met de nationale leeftijdskampioenschappen in Cardiff, smeekte ze haar ouders haar mee te laten gaan. Ze was de enige leerling van Oaklands die me daar zag winnen. Die dag vloog ik als de wind. Snel genoeg om onscherp op de foto te komen.

Ik kon haar niet zien zitten op de tribunes, maar kon wel mijn moeder eruit pikken, die een fel karmozijnrode sari droeg die als een lik verf afstak tegen de blauwe zitjes en grauwe toeschouwers.

Mijn vader heeft me nooit een wedstrijd zien lopen. Hij keurde het niet goed.

'Hardlopen is niet iets wat een dame betaamt. Een vrouw gaat ervan zweten,' zei hij tegen me.

'Mama zweet de hele tijd als ze in de keuken is.'

'Dat is een ander soort zweet.'

'Ik wist niet dat er verschillende soorten zweet waren.'

'Ja hoor, dat is een bekend wetenschappelijk feit. Het zweet van hard werken en het bereiden van eten is zoeter dan het zweet van heftige lichaamsoefening.'

Ik lachte niet. Een brave dochter respecteert haar vader.

Later hoorde ik mijn ouders ruziemaken.

'Hoe kan een jongen haar nou te pakken krijgen als ze zo hard loopt?'

'Ik wil niet dat jongens haar te pakken krijgen.'

'Heb je haar kamer gezien? Ze heeft gewichten. Mijn dochter tilt halters.'

'Ze is in training.'

'Gewichten zijn niet vrouwelijk. En heb je gezien wat ze aanheeft? Die korte broeken zijn net ondergoed. Ze rent in haar ondergoed.'

In het donker loop ik twee rondjes Victoria Park; ik hou me aan de asfaltpaden en gebruik de straatlantaarns als kompas.

Mijn moeder vertelde me vaak een volksverhaaltje over een dorpsezel die altijd werd bespot omdat hij dom en lelijk was. Op een dag kreeg een goeroe medelijden met het dier. 'Als je kon brullen als een tijger zouden ze niet lachen,' meende hij. Dus nam hij een tijgervel en legde het over de rug van de ezel. De ezel ging terug naar het dorp en ineens werd alles anders. Vrouwen en kinderen renden gillend weg. Mannen verscholen zich in hoeken. Al snel was de ezel alleen op de markt en deed zich tegoed aan de heerlijke appels en wortelen.

De dorpelingen waren doodsbang en moesten de 'tijger' kwijt zien te raken. Er werd een vergadering bijeengeroepen en ze besloten de tijger terug te jagen naar het woud. Trommelslagen weerklonken over de markt en de arme, van zijn stuk gebrachte ezel ging nu eens die kant op en dan weer die. Hij rende het woud in, maar de jagers kwamen hem op het spoor.

'Dat is geen tijger,' riep een van hen. 'Het is die ezel van de markt maar.'

De goeroe verscheen en lichtte kalm het tijgervel op van het doodsbange beest. 'Onthoud dit,' zei hij tegen de mensen. 'Dit beest heeft de huid van een tijger, maar de ziel van een ezel.'

Zo voel ik me nu: een ezel in plaats van een tijger.

Op het moment dat ik Smithfield Market passeer, daalt er een besef op me neer. Het begint als niet meer dan een vaag vermoeden. Ik vraag me af waardoor zo'n reactie wordt opgewekt. Misschien is het een patroon van voetstappen of een geluid dat daar niet hoort of een beweging die een gedachte op gang brengt. Een gedachte die nu in me opkomt. Ik weet hoe ik de tweeling kan vinden!

Tot nu toe heeft Forbes zich geconcentreerd op echtparen die erin zijn geslaagd een kind te krijgen met behulp van een genetisch surrogaat. Die kunnen geen belastende verklaring tegen Shawcroft afleggen zonder een verdenking op henzelf te laden. Waarom zouden ze dat ook doen? Ze hebben de wetenschap aan hun kant. Niemand kan bewijzen dat zij de ouders niet zijn. Maar degenen die de tweeling hebben, moeten het doen zonder een genetisch vangnet. DNA-tests zullen hen ontmaskeren in plaats van steunen. Zij hebben geen tijd gehad om een zwangerschap te simuleren of een ingewikkelde kunstgreep toe te passen. Ze moeten zich op dit moment kwetsbaar voelen.

Op dit uur van de ochtend valt het niet mee om in Kennington, vlak bij Forbes' kantoor, een parkeerplaats te vinden. De meeste rechercheurs beginnen om negen uur, wat betekent dat de meldkamer verlaten is, op een agentrechercheur na die nachtdienst heeft gehad. Hij is ongeveer van mijn leeftijd en op een norse manier behoorlijk knap. Misschien heb ik hem wakker gemaakt.

'Forbes heeft me gevraagd hierheen te komen,' lieg ik.

Hij kijkt me bedenkelijk aan. 'De baas heeft vanochtend een bespreking op Binnenlandse Zaken. Hij is pas later weer op kantoor.'

'Hij wil dat ik een mogelijke aanwijzing natrek.'

'Wat voor aanwijzing?'

'Gewoon een idee, meer niet.'

Hij gelooft me niet. Ik bel Forbes om zijn goedkeuring te vragen.

'Als dit godverdomme maar wel belangrijk is,' hoor ik hem brommen.

'Goedemorgen, meneer.'

'Met wie spreek ik?'

'Agent Barba.'

'Laat dat goedemorgen maar achterwege.'

'Sorry, meneer.'

Ik hoor de gedempte stem van mevrouw Forbes zeggen dat hij stil moet zijn. Beddenpraat.

'Ik wil Shawcrofts telefoongegevens inzien.'

'Het is zes uur in de ochtend.'

'Ja, meneer.'

Hij staat op het punt nee te zeggen. Hij vertrouwt me niet. Ik breng narigheid of onheil. Alles wat ik heb aangeraakt is in stront veranderd. Ik voel dat er nog een reden is: een bepaalde nervositeit. Sinds hij Shawcroft heeft laten gaan is hij aan het terugkrabbelen en verontschuldigingen aan het maken. Hij zal hier en daar wel een douw hebben gekregen, maar dat hoort bij de risico's van het vak.

'Ik wil dat je weer naar huis gaat, agent Barba.'

'Ik heb een aanknopingspunt.'

'Geef maar door aan de rechercheur van dienst. Jij maakt geen deel uit van dit onderzoek.' Zijn stem wordt milder. 'Zorg voor Samira.'

Waarom is hij zo negatief? En vanwaar de briefing bij Binnenlandse Zaken? Die gaat vast over Shawcroft.

'Hoe maakt uw vrouw het, meneer?'

Forbes aarzelt. Ze ligt naast hem. Wat kan hij zeggen?

Er volgt een lange stilte. 'We staan aan dezelfde kant, meneer,' fluister ik. 'U hebt me die avond niet guh-neukt, dit keer wil ik niet worden vur-neukt.'

'Prima. Ja, dat lijkt me geen probleem,' antwoordt hij. Ik geef de telefoon aan de nachtrechercheur en luister naar hun 'ja meneer, nee meneer'-gesprek. Ik krijg de telefoon terug. Forbes wil nog een laatste woord.

'Alles wat je vanaf nu tegenkomt, draag je aan mij over.'

'Ja, meneer.'

Het gesprek is ten einde. De nachtrechercheur kijkt me aan en we glimlachen allebei. Het wakker bellen van een meerdere is een van de kleine genoegens des levens.

Hij heet Rod Beckley, maar iedereen noemt hem Becks. 'Omdat ik voetbal als een krant,' grapt hij.

Nadat hij een bureau voor me heeft vrijgemaakt en een stoel gepakt, komt hij met een stuk of tien ringbanden aanzetten. Elk binnenkomend en uitgaand gesprek van het New Life Adoption Centre staat vermeld, inclusief de nummers, de duur van elk gesprek, het tijdstip en de datum. Ze hebben zes gesprekslijnen en twee faxlijnen, plus een rechtstreeks nummer naar Shawcrofts kantoor.

Andere mappen betreffen zijn mobiele telefoon en telefoon thuis. Sms'jes en e-mails zijn afgedrukt en in chronologische volgorde aan elkaar geniet.

Ik pak een markeerstift en begin de gesprekken te groeperen. In plaats van me op de telefoonnummers te richten, kijk ik naar de tijdstippen. De veerboot kwam om 3 uur 26 op zondagochtend in Harwich aan. We weten dat Pearl even na vieren van de boot liep. Om 10 uur 25 kocht hij luiers en babymelkpoeder bij een benzinestation aan de M25, om daarna een auto te stelen.

Ik bekijk de lijst met telefoontjes naar Shawcrofts mobiele nummer. Er was een binnenkomend gesprek om 10 uur 18 dat minder dan dertig seconden duurde. Ik kijk het nummer na. Het komt maar één keer voor. Het zou een verkeerd verbonden kunnen zijn.

Aan de andere kant van het kantoor zit Becks op een toetsenbord te rammelen. Ik ga op de rand van zijn bureau zitten tot hij opkijkt.

'Kunnen we uitzoeken van wie dit nummer is?'

Hij maakt verbinding met de landelijke politiecomputer en tikt de cijfers in. Er verschijnt een kaart van Hertfordshire. De gegevens worden in een apart venster getoond. Het telefoonnummer is van een openbare telefooncel bij Potter's Bar, een pompstation aan de M25 vlak bij afslag 24. Het is hetzelfde pompstation waar Brendan Pearl voor het laatst is gezien. Hij moet Shawcroft hebben gebeld voor instructies over waar hij de tweeling moest afleveren. Dichter bij een verband tussen de twee mannen ben ik nog niet eerder geweest, maar sluitend is het niet.

Als ik me weer over de mappen buig, loopt mijn spoor dood. De drie uren daarna heeft Shawcroft zijn mobiele telefoon niet gebruikt. Als zijn plan mis dreigde te lopen, zou hij zeker iemand hebben gebeld.

Ik probeer me afgelopen zondagochtend voor de geest te halen. Shawcroft was op de golfbaan. Zijn viertal sloeg af om 10 uur 05. Een van zijn medespelers zei iets toen Samira hun potje onderbrak en Shawcroft haar van de baan probeerde te slepen: 'Nee hè, niet weer.'

Het was kennelijk al een keer gebeurd, een week eerder. Na het telefoontje van Pearl moet Shawcroft zijn ronde eraan hebben gegeven. Waar ging hij heen? Hij moest de koper of kopers laten weten dat de tweeling was gearriveerd. Hij moest de overdracht naar voren schuiven. Het was riskant om zijn eigen mobiele telefoon te gebruiken, dus zocht hij een andere telefoon, een die niet te traceren viel.

Ik loop weer naar Becks. 'Is het mogelijk erachter te komen of er een openbare telefooncel is op een golfclub in Surrey?'

'Misschien wel. Heb je een naam?'

'Ja. Twin Bridges Country Club. Hij zou zich buiten een kleedkamer kunnen bevinden of in een lounge. Ergens waar het rustig is. Ik ben geïnteresseerd in de uitgaande gesprekken die er op zondag 20 oktober tussen 9 uur 20 en 10 uur 30 zijn geweest.'

'Is dat alles?' vraagt hij schertsend.

'Nee. Daarna moeten we ze naast de wachtlijst voor adoptie van het New Life Adoption Centre leggen.'

Hij begrijpt het niet, maar begint desondanks aan zijn zoektocht. 'Jij denkt dat we een overeenkomst zullen vinden.'

'Als we geluk hebben.'

10

Groentje Dave hoort mijn stem door de intercom en wacht heel even voordat hij op de zoemer drukt om de voordeur te ontgrendelen.

Als ik bij zijn flat aankom, staat de deur op een kier. Hij is in de keuken, verf aan het roeren.

'Je gaat het huis dus echt verkopen.'

'Ja.'

'Heb je al bieders?'

'Nog niet.'

In het afdruiprek staan twee kopjes en in de gootsteen liggen naast een verfroller en kwasten twee koude theezakjes uit te lekken. De plafonds moeten een sneeuwwitte tint krijgen. Ik heb hem de kleuren helpen uitzoeken. De muren zijn vaag groen, half gemengd met wit; de drempels en deurposten zijn onverdund gedaan.

Ik loop achter hem aan naar de eetkamer. De paar meubelstukken die hij heeft zijn naar het midden geschoven en met oude lakens afgedekt.

'Hoe gaat het met Samira?' vraagt hij.

Die vraag had ik niet verwacht. Dave heeft haar nooit ontmoet, maar zal de tv-verslagen en de kranten wel hebben gezien.

'Ik maak me zorgen over haar. Ik maak me zorgen over de tweeling.'

Hij doopt zijn roller in het verfbakje.

'Wil je me helpen?'

'Het is onze zaak niet.'

'Ik heb ze mogelijk gevonden. Help me, alsjeblieft.'

Hij klimt de trapleer op en haalt de roller met lange strepen verf over het plafond.

'Wat maakt het uit, Dave? Je hebt ontslag genomen. Je vertrekt. Mijn carrière is voorbij. Het maakt niet uit op welke tenen we gaan staan of wie we tegen de haren in strijken. Er is iets mis met deze zaak. Mensen lopen er behoedzaam omheen, supervoorzichtig, terwijl de echte boosdoeners bezig zijn documenten te verscheuren en hun sporen uit te wissen.'

'Je doet alsof die kinderen van jou zijn.'

Ik moet mezelf dwingen om niet boos omhoog te kijken. Van boven aan het trapje kijkt hij op me neer. Waarom zetten mensen telkens vraagtekens bij mijn drijfveren? Eduardo de Souza, Barnaby, en nu Dave. Ben ik degene die de waarheid niet kan zien? Nee, ze hebben het mis. Ik wil de tweeling niet voor mezelf.

'Ik doe dit omdat een vriendin van me, mijn beste vriendin,

mij datgene heeft toevertrouwd waarvan ze het meeste hield, haar kostbaarste bezit. Cate heb ik niet kunnen redden en Zala ook niet, maar de tweeling kan ik wel redden.'

Er volgt een lange stilte. Maar slechts een van ons tweeën voelt zich ongemakkelijk. Groentje is altijd makkelijker te typeren geweest door wat hij niet leuk vindt dan door wat hij wel leuk vindt. Hij heeft een hekel aan katten, bijvoorbeeld, en aan hypocrieten. Hij walgt daarnaast van reality-tv, rugbyfans uit Wales en getatoeëerde vrouwen die in de supermarkt tegen hun kinderen tekeergaan. Met zo'n man kan ik leven. Zijn stiltes zijn een ander verhaal. Hij schijnt er geen problemen mee te hebben. Ik wil weten wat hij denkt. Is hij kwaad dat ik niet samen met hem uit Amsterdam ben vertrokken? Stoort het hem hoe we de dingen hebben laten rusten? We hebben allebei zo onze vragen. Ik wil weten wie gisteravond de intercom opnam en zo uit zijn douche kwam.

Ik draai me om naar zijn slaapkamer. De deur staat open. Ik zie een koffer tegen de muur staan en een bloes die aan de binnenkant van de deur hangt. Ik realiseer me niet dat ik sta te staren en merk niet dat Dave het trapje af is gekomen en met zijn roller naar de keuken is gelopen. Hij wikkelt hem zorgvuldig in vershoudfolie en legt hem op het aanrecht. Hij trekt zijn shirt uit en gooit het in een hoek.

'Geef me vijf minuten. Ik moet even douchen.' Hij krabt aan zijn ongeschoren kin. 'Of nee, maak er maar tien van.'

Twee adressen: eentje net over de rivier in Barnes en het andere in Finsbury Park, Noord-Londen. Het eerste adres is van een stel waarvan de namen ook op een wachtlijst van het New Life Adoption Centre voorkomen. Het adres in Finsbury Park komt niet in de bestanden voor.

Zondag een week geleden, even na tienen, kwam op beide adressen een telefoontje binnen afkomstig van een openbare telefoon bij de kleedkamers van de Twin Bridges Country Club in Surrey. Op het moment dat de telefoontjes werden gepleegd was Shawcroft daar.

Het is een vermoeden. Te veel dingen die samenvallen om nog

toeval te kunnen zijn. Het is een bezoekje waard.

Dave is gekleed in een lichte ribbroek, een overhemd en een leren jasje.

'Wat ben je van plan?'

'Een kijkje nemen.'

'Hoe zit het met Forbes?'

'Dat soort sprongen maakt hij niet. Uiteindelijk zal hij er misschien wel op uitkomen, door de vakjes af te vinken, zonder na te denken, maar stel nou dat daar geen tijd voor is?'

Ik zie de kleinste van de tweeling voor me, worstelend om adem te halen. Mijn eigen keel wordt dichtgeknepen. Ze zou in het ziekenhuis moeten liggen. We hadden haar nu eigenlijk al gevonden moeten hebben.

'We hebben twee adressen. Ik weet nog steeds niet wat je van plan bent.'

'Misschien klop ik wel gewoon op de voordeur en vraag ik: "Hebt u een tweeling die niet van u is?" Ik kan je wel vertellen wat ik níet ga doen. Ik ga niet achteroverleunen en wachten tot ze verdwenen zijn.'

Bruine bladeren dwarrelen vanuit een parkje op straat en weer terug het gras op, alsof ze de straat niet over willen. De temperatuur is niet uit de enkele cijfers gekomen en de wind drukt hem verder omlaag.

We staan geparkeerd in een typische straat in Barnes, met huizen met hoge gevels en platanen langs de stoep die zo woest zijn gesnoeid dat ze bijna misvormd lijken.

Dit is een voorstad van effectenmakelaars, vol welvarende middenklassegezinnen die hierheen zijn verhuisd vanwege de scholen en parken en de nabijheid van de City. Ondanks de kou zijn er een stuk of zes moeders of au pairs op de speelplaats; ze houden kleuters in de gaten die eruitzien als michelinmannetjes, zo veel kleren hebben ze aan.

Terwijl Dave de appetijtelijke mammies bestudeert, richt ik mijn blik op het huis, nummer 85.

Robert en Noelene Gallagher rijden in een Volvo-stationcar, be-

talen hun kijkgeld op tijd en stemmen op de liberaal-democra-
ten. Ik raad natuurlijk maar wat, maar zo'n soort wijk is het, zo'n
soort huis.

Dave harkt met zijn vingers door zijn scheve haarbos.

'Mag ik iets vragen?'

'Tuurlijk.'

'Heb je ooit van me gehouden?'

Dit had ik niet zien aankomen.

'Wat geeft jou het idee dat ik nu niet van je hou?'

'Je hebt het nooit gezegd.'

'Hoe bedoel je?'

'Misschien heb je het woord weleens gebruikt, maar niet in een
zin waar mijn naam in voorkwam. Je hebt nooit gezegd: "Ik hou
van je, Dave."'

Ik laat mijn gedachten teruggaan, wil het ontkennen, maar hij
lijkt heel zeker. De nachten dat we naast elkaar lagen, zijn armen
om me heen, voelde ik me zo veilig, zo gelukkig. Heb ik het nooit
tegen hem gezegd? Ik herinner me mijn filosofische discussies en
argumenten over het wezen van de liefde en hoe ondermijnend
die kan zijn. Speelden die zich allemaal in mezelf af? Ik probeerde
mezelf wijs te maken dat ik níet van hem hield. Vergeefs, maar dat
kon hij onmogelijk weten.

Ik zou het nu tegen hem moeten zeggen. Maar hoe? Het zal ge-
kunsteld of geforceerd klinken. Het is te laat. Ik kan proberen excuses te vinden. Ik kan het op het feit gooien dat ik geen kinderen
kan krijgen, maar de waarheid is dat ik hem van me af stoot. Er
woont een andere vrouw in zijn flat.

Hij doet het weer: niets zeggen. Wachten.

'Je hebt iets met iemand,' gooi ik eruit, wat klinkt als een beschuldiging.

'Hoe kom je daarbij?'

'Ik heb haar ontmoet.'

Hij draait zich met zijn hele lichaam om in de chauffeursstoel
en kijkt eerder verbaasd dan schuldbewust.

'Ik was gisteren bij je aan de deur. Je was niet thuis. Ze beant-
woordde de intercom.'

'Jacquie?'

'Ik heb haar naam niet genoteerd.' *Ik klink godvergeten jaloers.*

'Mijn zus.'

'Je hebt geen zus.'

'Mijn schoonzus. De vrouw van mijn broer. Jacquie.'

'Die zitten in San Diego.'

'Ze logeren bij mij. Simon is mijn nieuwe zakenpartner. Dat heb ik je gezegd.'

Kan dit nog erger worden? 'Je zult me wel een enorme oen vinden,' zeg ik. 'Sorry. Ik bedoel, ik ben niet van het jaloerse type, meestal. Alleen dacht ik, na wat er in Amsterdam was gebeurd, toen je mij niet belde en ik jou niet... het is echt stom hoor... dat je iemand anders had gevonden die niet zo onhandig, moeilijk of lastig was. Lach me niet uit, alsjeblieft.'

'Ik lach niet.'

'Wat doe je dan?'

'Ik kijk naar die auto.'

Ik volg zijn blik. Tegenover het voorhek van nummer 85 staat een Volvo-stationcar geparkeerd. Door het naar ons toe gekeerde achterraampje zie ik een zonneschermpje en iets wat eruitziet als een babyzitje.

Dave biedt me een uitweg. Hij is als een galante heer die zijn jas uitspreidt over een modderplas.

'Ik moet even gaan kijken,' zeg ik terwijl ik het autoportier open. 'Wie weet is er een babyzitje.'

Dave kijkt me na. Hij weet dat ik andermaal de kwestie ontwijk. Ik heb hem onderschat. Hij is slimmer dan ik. Aardiger.

Ik steek over, loop de stoep af en stop even bij de Volvo om mijn veters vast te maken. De ramen zijn getint, maar aan de binnenkant kan ik afdrukken van kinderhandjes onderscheiden en een Garfield-sticker op het achterraam.

Ik kijk Daves kant uit en maak een klopbeweging met mijn knuist. Hij schudt zijn hoofd. Het teken negerend doe ik het voorhek open en loop de treden op.

De deurbel klinkt. De deur gaat op een kier. Een meisje van ongeveer vijf kijkt me heel serieus aan. Op haar handen zitten verf-spatten en boven haar wenkbrauwen zit een opgedroogde roze verfvlek als een uit koers geraakte bindi.

'Hallo, hoe heet jij?'

'Molly.'

'Wat een mooie naam.'

'Weet ik.'

'Is je mammie thuis?'

'Die is boven.'

Ik hoor een schreeuw uit die richting: 'Als dat de man van de cv-ketel is, die hangt recht de hal door in de keuken.'

'Het is niet de man van de ketel,' roep ik terug.

'Het is een Indiase mevrouw,' zegt Molly.

Mevrouw Gallagher verschijnt boven aan de trap. Ze is midden veertig en draagt een corduroy rok met een brede riem die laag op haar heupen hangt.

'Sorry dat ik u lastigval. Mijn man en ik komen hier in de straat wonen, en ik hoopte dat ik u iets mag vragen over de scholen hier en huisartsen, dat soort dingen.'

Ik zie haar nadenken wat ze zal doen. Het is meer dan gewone voorzichtigheid.

'Wat een prachtige krullen,' zeg ik terwijl ik Molly's haar streel.

'Dat zegt iedereen,' antwoordt het grietje.

Waarom zou iemand met een kind een baby kopen?

'Ik heb het momenteel nogal druk,' zegt mevrouw Gallagher terwijl ze haar pony naar achteren strijkt.

'Ik begrijp het volkomen. Neem me niet kwalijk.' Ik draai me om en wil weer gaan.

'Welk huis hebt u gekocht?'

'Nee, niet gekocht. Nog niet. Een huurhuis, nummer 68.' Ik wijs langs de straat in de richting van het Te Huur-bordje.

'We komen uit Noord-Londen. Mijn man heeft een nieuwe baan. We werken allebei. Maar we willen snel een gezin stichten.'

Mevrouw Gallagher is nu beneden aan de trap. Het is te koud om de deur open te laten. Of ze vraagt me binnen, of ze vraagt me te gaan.

'Het is nu niet echt een goed moment,' zegt ze. 'Misschien zou ik u, als ik een telefoonnummer had, later kunnen bellen.'

'Heel erg bedankt.' Ik zoek naar een pen. 'Hebt u misschien een velletje papier?'

Ze zoekt op de plank op de verwarming. 'Ik pak er eentje voor u.'

Molly wacht in de vestibule, nog altijd de deur vasthoudend.

'Wilt u een van mijn schilderijen zien?'

'Graag.'

'Ik ga er een halen.' Ze vliegt naar boven. Mevrouw Gallagher is in de keuken. Ze vindt een gebruikte envelop en komt weer terug, rondkijkend waar Molly is.

'Ze is naar boven gegaan om een van haar schilderijen te halen,' leg ik uit. 'Een kunstenaar in de dop.'

'Ze smeert meer verf op haar kleren dan op het papier.'

'Zo is mijn vriend ook.'

'Ik dacht dat u zei dat u getrouwd was.' Ze fixeert me met een strakke blik. Er gaat onverzettelijkheid achter schuil.

'We zijn verloofd. We zijn al zo lang bij elkaar dat het voelt alsof we getrouwd zijn.'

Ze gelooft me niet. Molly gilt van boven aan de trap: 'Mammie, Jasper huilt.'

'O, u hebt er nog een?'

Mevrouw Gallagher maakt een beweging naar de deur. Mijn voet is sneller. Mijn schouder komt direct daarna. Ik heb geen recht om naar binnen te gaan. Ik heb een huiszoekingsbevel nodig of een gerede grond.

Ik sta onder aan de trap. Mevrouw Gallagher schreeuwt tegen me dat ik weg moet gaan. Ze grijpt mijn arm. Ik schud hem af. Boven het lawaai uit hoor ik een baby huilen.

Ik ren met twee stappen tegelijk de trap op en ga op het geluid af. De eerste deur is de echtelijke slaapkamer. De tweede die van Molly. Ze heeft een schildersezel neergezet op een oud laken. Ik probeer een derde deur. Felgekleurde vissen draaien langzaam in het rond boven een wieg. In de wieg, strak ingewikkeld, ligt een baby tegen de schepping te protesteren.

Mevrouw Gallagher wringt zich langs me heen en pakt het jongetje op. 'Ga mijn huis uit!'

'Is hij van u, mevrouw Gallagher?'

'Ja.'

'Hebt u hem ter wereld gebracht?'

'Eruit! Eruit! Ik bel de politie.'

'Ik bén de politie.'

Zonder dat ze iets zegt schudt ze haar hoofd heen en weer. De baby is stil geworden. Molly trekt aan haar rok.

Ineens zakken haar schouders omlaag en lijkt ze in mijn bijzijn leeg te lopen. Nog altijd met de baby in haar armen, weigerend los te laten, valt ze in mijn armen. Ik weet haar naar een stoel toe te manoeuvreren.

'We hebben hem geadopteerd,' fluistert ze. 'Hij is van ons.'

Ze schudt haar hoofd. Ik kijk de kamer rond. Waar is ze? Het meisje. Mijn hart springt over tussen de slagen door. Langzaam, dan snel.

'Er was ook een meisje. Zijn tweelingzusje.'

Ze kijkt in de richting van de wieg. 'Hij is alleen.'

Nu gaan de ergst denkbare scenario's door mijn hoofd. Ze was zo klein. Ze vocht om adem te halen. God, alstublieft, laat haar veilig zijn!

Mevrouw Gallagher heeft een papieren zakdoekje opgedoken in de mouw van haar vest. Ze snuit haar neus en snottert. 'Ons werd verteld dat hij ongewenst was. Ik zweer dat ik het niet wist, niet van de vermiste tweeling. Pas toen ik het op tv zag. Toen begon ik me af te vragen...'

'Wie heeft hem u gegeven?'

'Een man heeft hem gebracht.'

'Hoe zag hij eruit?'

'Halverwege de vijftig, kort haar – hij had een Iers accent.'

'Wanneer was dat?'

'Vorige week zondag.' Ze veegt haar ogen af. 'Het was een volslagen verrassing. We verwachtten hem pas twee weken later.'

'Wie had de adoptie geregeld?'

'Meneer Shawcroft zei dat er een jong meisje was dat een tweeling verwachtte, maar niet voor allebei kon zorgen. Ze wilde een van de twee ter adoptie aanbieden. Voor vijftigduizend pond zouden wij de eersten zijn.'

'U wist dat het in strijd met de wet was.'

'Meneer Shawcroft zei dat het wettelijk onmogelijk was om tweelingen uit elkaar te halen. We moesten alles in het geheim doen.'

'U deed alsof u zwanger was.'

'Daar was geen tijd voor.'

Ik kijk naar Molly, die met een doos schelpen zit te spelen en ze in patronen neerlegt.

'Is Molly...?' Ik maak de vraag niet af.

'Ze is van mij,' zegt ze afgemeten. 'Ik kon geen kinderen meer krijgen. Er waren complicaties. Medische problemen. Ze vertelden ons dat we te oud waren om te adopteren. Mijn man is zesenvijftig, weet u.' Ze veegt in haar ogen. 'Ik zou hem moeten bellen.'

Van beneden hoor ik mijn naam roepen. Groentje Dave moet de aanvaring in de deuropening hebben gezien. Hij hield het niet meer.

'Hier, boven.'

'Alles in orde?'

'Ja ja.'

Hij duikt op bij de deur en neemt het tafereel in zich op. Mevrouw Gallagher. Molly. De baby.

'Het is een van de tweeling,' zeg ik.

'Eén?'

'Het jongetje.'

Hij gluurt in de wieg. 'Weet je het zeker?'

Ik volg zijn blik. Het is verbazingwekkend hoe een pasgeborene in nog geen tien dagen van uiterlijk kan veranderen, maar ik weet het zeker.

'En het meisje?'

'Dat is niet hier.'

Shawcroft pleegde twee telefoontjes vanaf de golfclub. Het tweede was naar het adres in Finsbury Park, naar een zekere mevrouw Y. Moncrieffe, een naam die niet overeenkomt met enige naam in de bestanden van het New Life Adoption Centre.

Ik kan niet weg. Ik moet blijven en met Forbes praten (en hem daarna ongetwijfeld van het plafond lospeuteren).

'Kun jij op het andere adres gaan kijken?'

Dave legt de implicaties en verwikkelingen naast elkaar. Hij maakt zich geen zorgen over zichzelf. Ik ben degene die voor een tuchtcommissie moet verschijnen. Hij kust me op de wang.

'Soms maak je het wel moeilijk, dat weet je.'

'Ja, weet ik.'

11

Inspecteur Forbes dendert het huis door, zijn gezicht verstrakt tot een masker van razernij en kille haat. Hij gebiedt me mee te komen naar de achtertuin, waar hij het modderige gras negeert en heen en weer begint te benen.

'Je had geen enkele bevoegdheid!' roept hij uit. 'Het was een onwettige huiszoeking.'

'Ik had reden om aan te nemen…'

'Wat voor reden?'

'Ik was een mogelijk aanknopingspunt aan het natrekken.'

'Dat je aan míj had moeten vertellen. Dit is godverdomme míjn onderzoek!'

Zijn rechthoekige bril wiebelt op zijn neus. Ik vraag me af of het hem stoort.

'Mijn oordeel als professional zegt dat ik een noodzakelijke keuze maakte, meneer.'

'Je weet niet eens of het een van de tweeling is. Er zijn geen geboorteakten of adoptiepapieren.'

'Mevrouw Gallagher heeft mij bevestigd dat zij niet de biologische moeder is. De baby werd bij haar afgeleverd door een man die voldoet aan Brendan Pearls signalement.'

'Je had moeten wachten.'

'Met alle respect, meneer, u deed er te lang over. Shawcroft is vrij. Hij is bezig bestanden te vernietigen, zijn sporen uit te wissen. U wílt hem niet vervolgen.'

Ik heb het idee dat hij op ontploffen staat. Zijn stem draagt tot in de omliggende tuinen en modder zuigt aan zijn schoenen.

'Ik had je bij de tuchtcommissie moeten aangeven toen je naar Amsterdam ging. Je hebt getuigen gekweld, je bevoegdheden misbruikt en de orders van een hoger geplaatste genegeerd. Je bent er bij vrijwel elke gelegenheid in geslaagd je onprofessioneel te gedragen.'

Zijn voet gaat omhoog en zijn schoen blijft staan. Een sok zakt zuigend tot aan zijn enkel in de modder. We doen allebei of het niet gebeurd is.

'Je bent voorlopig van je functie ontheven. Begrijp je me? Ik ga er persoonlijk voor zorgen dat jouw carrière voorbij is.'

Het maatschappelijk werk is erbij geroepen, in de persoon van een grote vrouw met een enorm achterwerk, waardoor het lijkt of ze een tournure draagt. Meneer en mevrouw Gallagher praten in de zitkamer met haar. Ze lijken bijna opgelucht dat het voorbij is. De afgelopen paar dagen moeten ondraaglijk zijn geweest, vol vragen en wachtend op de klop op de deur. Bang om verliefd te raken op een kind dat misschien wel nooit echt het hunne zou zijn.

In haar slaapkamer laat Molly een politieagente zien hoe ze bloemen schildert en het papier op de verwarming te drogen legt. De baby slaapt. Ze hebben hem Jasper genoemd. Hij heeft nu een naam.

Forbes heeft zijn sok afgestroopt en hem in de vuilnisbak gegooid. Op de achtertrap zittend schraapt hij met een schroevendraaier de modder van zijn schoenen.

'Hoe wist je het?' vraagt hij, gekalmeerd.

Ik vertel hem over de telefoontjes vanaf de golfclub en het vergelijken van de nummers met de adoptiebestanden, op zoek naar een overeenkomst.

'Zo heb ik de Gallaghers opgespoord.'

'Pleegde hij nog meer telefoontjes?'

'Eentje.'

Forbes wacht even. 'Moet ik je soms laten arresteren om je eindelijk echt te laten meewerken?'

Elk restje kameraadschap is verdwenen. We zitten niet langer in hetzelfde team.

'Ik had vanochtend een interessant gesprek met een jurist,' zegt hij. 'Hij vertegenwoordigde Barnaby Elliot en beweerde dat jij in deze zaak een belangenconflict hebt.'

'Er is geen conflict, meneer.'

'De heer Elliot vecht de laatste wilsbeschikking van zijn overleden dochter aan.'

'Hij kan geen wettelijke aanspraak maken op de tweeling.'

'En jij ook niet!'

'Dat weet ik, meneer,' fluister ik.

'Als Samira Khan besluit dat ze de kinderen niet neemt, zullen ze in een kindertehuis worden geplaatst en uiteindelijk bij pleegouders.'

'Dat weet ik. Ik doe dit niet voor mezelf.'

'En dat weet je zeker.'

Het is een beschuldiging, geen vraag. Mijn motieven liggen weer onder vuur. Misschien hou ik mezelf voor de gek. Ik kan het me niet permitteren dat te geloven. Dat zal ik ook niet.

Mijn mobiele telefoon trilt in mijn zak. Ik klap hem open.

'Ik heb haar mogelijk gevonden,' zegt Dave. 'Maar er is een probleem.'

12

De Neonatale Intensive Care Unit (NICU) van het Queen Charlotte's Hospital bevindt zich op de derde verdieping, boven de kraamkamers en kraamafdeling. Tussen gedimde lampen, behoedzaam lopende mensen en het gezoem van apparaten staan vijftien van een hoog koepeldeksel voorziene couveuses.

Het afdelingshoofd loopt twee passen voor me uit, Dave twee passen achter me. Onze handen zijn gewassen met een desinfecterend middel en onze mobiele telefoons zijn uitgeschakeld.

Bij het eerste wiegje kijk ik omlaag. Het lijkt leeg, op een roze dekentje en een teddybeer, na die in een hoek zit. Dan zie ik een armpje, niet dikker dan een vulpen, onder het dekentje uitsteken. Vingertjes krommen en strekken zich. Oogjes blijven gesloten. Slangetjes worden in een piepklein neusje gestoken en persen snelle ademstoten lucht in onvolgroeide longen. Het hoofd staat stil en wacht. Misschien doen mensen dat hier vaak: stilstaan, staren en bidden. Pas op dat moment merk ik de gezichten aan de andere kant van het wiegje op, vervormd door het glas.

Ik kijk om me heen. In het halfduister zitten meer ouders, kijken en wachten, praten op fluistertoon. Ik vraag me af wat ze tegen elkaar zeggen. Kijken ze naar andere wiegjes en vragen ze zich af of die baby sterker of zieker of nog vroeger geboren is? Het is onmogelijk dat ze het allemaal zullen halen. Bidden ze stiekem: 'Red die van mij! Red die van mij!?'

We zijn aan de andere kant van de NICU aangekomen. De stoelen naast het wiegje zijn leeg. Op een hoge kruk zit een verpleegster bij een beeldscherm; ze houdt de machines in de gaten die een kind in de gaten houden.

In het midden van een effen wit laken ligt een meisjesbaby, met alleen een luier aan. Ze is kleiner dan ik me herinner, maar wel twee keer zo groot als sommige andere te vroeg geborenen op de NICU. Op haar borstkas zijn kleine kussentjes bevestigd die haar hartslag en haar ademhaling registreren.

'Claudia is gisteravond binnengebracht,' legt het hoofd uit. 'Ze heeft een ernstige longinfectie. We geven haar antibiotica en voeden haar intraveneus. Het apparaatje aan haar been is een bloedgasmonitor. Hij zendt licht door haar huid zodat we kunnen zien hoeveel zuurstof haar bloed bevat.'

'Gaat ze het redden?'

Ze neemt heel even de tijd om haar woorden te kiezen. De vertraging duurt lang genoeg om me de stuipen op het lijf te jagen. 'Ze is stabiel. De volgende vierentwintig uur zijn erg belangrijk.'

'U noemde haar Claudia.'

'Dat is de naam die we hebben doorgekregen.'

'Van wie?'

'De vrouw die met haar mee was gekomen in de ziekenauto.'

'Ik wil graag het opnameformulier zien.'

'Natuurlijk. Als u meeloopt naar kantoor, print ik een exemplaar voor u uit.'

Dave tuurt door het glas. Ik kan zijn lippen bijna zien bewegen, meeademend met de baby. Claudia heeft zijn aandacht gevangen, ook al zijn haar slaapoogjes dichtgekleefd.

'Is het goed als ik nog even blijf?' vraagt hij, evenzeer aan mij als aan het hoofd. Elke andere patiënt op de afdeling heeft iemand naast zich zitten. Claudia is alleen. Hij vindt het niet eerlijk.

We draaien ons om en ik volg het hoofd naar haar kantoor.

'Ik heb vanochtend maatschappelijk werk gebeld,' zegt ze. 'Politie had ik niet verwacht.'

'Wat bracht u ertoe te bellen?'

'Sommige antwoorden die ik kreeg bevielen me niet helemaal. Claudia kwam even na middernacht binnen. Eerst zei de vrouw dat ze het kindermeisje van de baby was. Als naam van de moeder gaf ze Cate Beaumont op. Daarna begon ze een ander verhaal en zei ze dat Claudia was geadopteerd, maar dat ze me geen nadere gegevens over het adoptiebureau kon verstrekken.'

Ze overhandigt me het opnameformulier. Claudia's geboortedatum staat vermeld als zondag 29 oktober. De naam van de moeder als Cate Elisabeth Beaumont. Het adres is Cates door brand beschadigde huis.

Waarom Cates naam? Hoe zou ze die zelfs maar kunnen weten?

'Waar is die vrouw nu?'

'Een van onze consulterend specialisten wilde met haar praten. Ik denk dat ze in paniek is geraakt.'

'Is ze weggelopen?'

'Ze pleegde een telefoontje. Daarna is ze naar buiten gegaan.'

'Hoe laat was dat?'

'Rond zes uur 's ochtends.'

'Weet u met wie ze belde?'

'Nee, maar ze heeft wel mijn telefoon gebruikt.'

Ze wijst naar haar bureau. Het telefoontoestel is een moedertoestel, met een geheugen voor de laatst gekozen nummers. Op een LCD-schermpje is de gesprekslijst te zien. Het afdelingshoofd herkent het nummer en ik druk op de nummerherhaling.

Er neemt een vrouw op.

'Hallo?'

'Met het Queen Charlotte's Hospital,' zeg ik. 'Iemand heeft vanochtend vanaf dit nummer naar uw huis gebeld.'

Ze geeft geen antwoord, maar in de stilte herken ik een geluid. Ik heb het eerder gehoord: het piepen van wielen op een parketvloer.

Ik beschik niet over Ruiz' fotografische geheugen of zijn moeders gaven om de toekomst te voorspellen. Ik weet niet eens of ik wel een bepaalde werkwijze heb. Ik voeg feiten op goed geluk bij elkaar. Soms door een sprong vooruit te maken of te kijken of dingen passen. Het is niet erg efficiënt. Het valt niet aan te leren, maar voor mij werkt het.

De vrouw zegt weer iets. Zenuwachtig. 'U hebt waarschijnlijk het verkeerde nummer.'

Het is een doordringende stem, net geen kostschooltimbre. Het is de stem waarmee ik haar, ook al is het tien jaar geleden, vaak genoeg haar man een uitbrander heb horen geven omdat hij te laat thuis was en naar shampoo en doucheschuim rook.

De verbinding is verbroken. Ruth Elliot heeft opgehangen. Op hetzelfde moment wordt er op de deur geklopt. Een verpleegster glimlacht verontschuldigend en fluistert iets tegen het afdelingshoofd, dat me vervolgens aankijkt.

'U vroeg naar de vrouw die Claudia heeft binnengebracht. Ze is niet weggelopen. Ze zit beneden in de kantine.'

Een drukplaat in de vloer opent automatisch de deuren. De kantine is klein en licht, met gespikkelde tafels om de kruimels te verbergen. Bij de deuren staan dienbladen opgestapeld. Uit warmhoudbakken stijgt damp op.

Een handjevol verpleegsters is bezig sandwiches en een kop thee te pakken. Gezonde keuzes uit een menu waarvan al het overige met patat wordt geserveerd.

Yvonne zit op een afgeschutte bank, met haar hoofd op haar onderarmen. Heel even denk ik dat ze misschien slaapt, maar haar hoofd komt omhoog en ze knippert naar me met vochtige ogen. Er ontsnapt haar een diepe kreun en ze laat haar hoofd zakken. Waar haar grijze haar dunner is geworden is de bleekheid van haar hoofdhuid te zien.

'Wat is er gebeurd?'

'Ik heb iets echt doms gedaan, meissie,' zegt ze, in haar elleboogholte pratend. 'Ik dacht dat ik haar beter kon maken, maar ze werd almaar zieker en zieker.'

Een schuddende ademhaling doet haar lichaam trillen. 'Ik had haar mee moeten nemen naar een arts, maar meneer en mevrouw Elliot zeiden dat niemand ooit van Cates baby mocht weten. Zij zei dat mensen Claudia wilden weghalen en haar aan iemand wilden geven bij wie ze niet hoort. Ik weet niet waarom mensen zoiets zouden doen. Mevrouw Elliot legde het niet echt goed uit, niet goed genoeg voor mij, begrijp je?'

Ze gaat rechtop zitten, hopend dat ik het misschien begrijp. Haar ogen zijn vochtig en er kleven kruimels aan haar wang.

'Ik wist dat Cate helemaal geen baby ging krijgen,' legt ze uit. 'Ze had helemaal geen baby in haar buik. Ik weet het wanneer een vrouw zwanger is. Ik kan het aan haar ogen zien, en aan haar huid. Ik kan het ruiken. Soms kan ik het zelfs zien als een vrouw het kind van een andere man draagt, door de huid rond haar ogen, die donkerder is omdat ze bang is dat haar man erachter zal komen.

Ik heb geprobeerd iets tegen mevrouw Elliot te zeggen, maar ze zei dat ik gek was en lachte. Ze heeft het waarschijnlijk aan kleine Cate verteld, want die ontweek me daarna. Als ik aan het werk was, kwam ze niet langs.'

Details beginnen te bewegen en te verschuiven, zoekend naar hun juiste plek. Gebeurtenissen zijn niet langer hersenspinsels of raadsels, niet langer onderdeel van mijn fantasie. Barnaby wíst dat ik in Amsterdam was. En al voordat ik Samira ter sprake bracht wíst hij dat ze in verwachting was van een tweeling. Hij had Cates e-mails gelezen en begon haar sporen uit te wissen.

In het begin was het waarschijnlijk om zijn kostbare reputatie te beschermen. Later bedachten zijn vrouw en hij een ander plan. Ze

388

zouden afmaken waar zij aan begonnen was. Barnaby benaderde Shawcroft met een boodschap: 'Aan het leven van Cate en Felix is een eind gekomen, aan onze afspraak niet.'

Waarom zou Shawcroft ermee instemmen? Hij moest wel. Barnaby had de e-mails. Hij zou naar de politie kunnen stappen en de illegale adopties en babyhandel onthullen. Chantage is een akelig woord. Kidnapping ook.

Bij de begrafenis zei hij tegen me dat hij voor de tweeling zou vechten. 'Ik wil ze allebei,' zei hij. Ik realiseerde me toen niet wat hij bedoelde. Hij had al een van de twee, Claudia. Hij wilde ook het jongetje. En zijn tirade op kantoor bij zijn advocaat en de scène voor de deur van mijn huis waren slechts voor de show. Hij was bang dat hij zou worden geweigerd, zo niet door Samira dan wel door mij.

De Elliots lieten Yvonne zweren dat ze haar mond zou houden. Ze droegen haar op voor Claudia te zorgen en hopelijk voor haar broertje als ze de tweeling wisten te herenigen. Als het schandaal openbaar zou worden en Shawcroft werd ontmaskerd, zouden ze de bedroefde ouders kunnen spelen die hun best hadden gedaan hun dochters kostbare erfenis, hun kleinkinderen, te beschermen.

Yvonne aanvaardde de loodzware last. Ze kon het niet riskeren met Claudia naar een arts te gaan. Ze probeerde haar eigen middeltjes: de warme kraan laten lopen en de badkamer met stoom vullen, in een poging haar beter te laten ademen. Ze gaf haar druppeltjes paracetamol, wreef haar met warme flanellen doeken, lag de hele nacht naast haar wakker, horend hoe haar longetjes zich met vocht vulden.

Barnaby kwam de baby opzoeken, zijn duimen achter zijn broekriem gehaakt en de voeten uit elkaar. Hij keek in het wiegje met een bevroren glimlach, enigszins teleurgesteld. Misschien wilde hij het jongetje, de gezonde van de twee.

Ondertussen werd Claudia steeds zieker en Yvonne steeds wanhopiger.

'Ik kon het niet meer aan,' fluistert ze terwijl ze haar ogen opslaat naar het plafond. 'Ze was stervende. Elke keer dat ze hoestte schokte haar lichaampje, tot ze niet meer de kracht had om te hoesten. Op dat moment heb ik de ambulance gebeld.'

Ze knippert met haar ogen. 'Ze gaat dood, hè?'

'Dat weten we niet.'

'Dan is het mijn fout. Arresteer me maar. Sluit me op. Ik verdien het.'

Ik wil dat ze ophoudt met over de dood te praten. 'Wie heeft de naam gekozen?'

'Mevrouw Elliot heet zo.'

'Haar voornaam is Ruth.'

'Haar middelste naam. Ik weet dat je mevrouw Elliot niet echt mag, maar ze is strenger voor zichzelf dan voor wie ook.'

Wat ik vooral voel is wrok. Misschien hoort dat wel bij rouwen. Het voelt niet alsof Cate weg is. Ik denk telkens dat ze gewoon weggelopen is en zo meteen terug zal komen en deze warboel in orde zal maken.

Ik heb wekenlang in haar leven lopen graven, haar gangen en motieven nagetrokken, en ik begrijp nog steeds niet hoe ze zo veel risico's heeft kunnen nemen en zovelen in gevaar heeft kunnen brengen. Ik blijf de hoop koesteren dat ik ergens in een stapeltje papieren of een stoffig bundeltje brieven op het antwoord zal stuiten. Ik weet dat het zo niet zal gaan. De ene helft van de waarheid ligt boven, vastgemaakt als een insect dat opgeprikt zit in een glazen vitrine. De andere helft is onder de hoede van het maatschappelijk werk.

Het klinkt belachelijk, maar ik ben nog altijd bezig haar handelwijze te rechtvaardigen, in een poging een vriendschap uit het hiernamaals tevoorschijn te toveren. Ze was een onhandige dief, een kinderloze echtgenote en een dwaze dromer. Ik wil niet meer over haar nadenken. Ze heeft haar eigen herinnering bedorven.

'De politie zal willen dat je een verklaring aflegt,' zeg ik.

Yvonne knikt en veegt haar wangen af.

Ze staat niet op als ik wegloop. En hoewel ze haar gezicht naar het raam gedraaid heeft, weet ik dat ze me nakijkt.

Op de NICU zit Groentje Dave nog altijd naast Claudia, voorovergebogen op een stoel door het glas te turen. Hij pakt mijn hand. We zitten bij elkaar. Ik weet niet hoe lang. De klok aan de wand verspringt niet. Nog geen seconde, ik zweer het. Misschien gaat dat zo op een plek als deze: dat de tijd trager wordt. Iedere seconde gaat tellen.

'Je bent een klein meisje met heel veel geluk, Claudia. Weet je waarom? Je hebt twee moeders. Eentje die je nooit zult ontmoeten, maar dat geeft niet, ik zal je over haar vertellen. Ze heeft een paar vergissingen begaan, maar ik weet zeker dat je niet te hard over haar zult oordelen. Je andere moeder is ook heel bijzonder. Jong. Mooi. Bedroefd. Soms kan het leven in een oogwenk veranderen, zelfs in een wenk van zulke kleine oogjes als die van jou.'

Het afdelingshoofd tikt me op mijn schouder. Een politiefunctionaris wil me spreken.

Forbes klinkt ver weg. 'De Gallaghers hebben een verklaring afgelegd. Ik ben onderweg naar de arrestatie van Julian Shawcroft.'

'Dat is mooi. Ik heb het meisje gevonden. Ze is heel ziek.'

Dit keer volgt er geen tirade. 'Wie moeten we hebben?'

'Barnaby Elliot en zijn vrouw, en hun huishoudster, Yvonne Montcrieffe.'

Achter me gaat een deur open en klinkt een elektronisch alarm. Door een kijkraam zie ik dat de gordijnen rond Claudia's bedje worden dichtgetrokken.

De telefoon ligt niet meer in mijn hand. Net als iedereen lijk ik te bewegen. Ik duw me door de gordijnen heen. Iemand duwt me terug en ik struikel.

'Wat is er aan de hand? Wat zijn ze aan het doen?'

Een arts staat aanwijzingen te geven. Een hand met daarin een masker bedekt Claudia's gezichtje. Een zak wordt samengeknepen en opnieuw samengeknepen. Het masker gaat omhoog en er wordt een slangetje in haar neus gestoken en langzaam tot in haar longen gevoerd. Witte pleisters zitten in een kruis op haar wangen.

Dave heeft mijn arm vast en probeert me weg te trekken.

'Wat zijn ze aan het doen?'

'We moeten buiten wachten.'

'Ze doen haar pijn.'

'Laat ze hun werk doen.'

Dit is mijn fout. Mijn vergissing. Als ik sterker, fitter en sneller was geweest, had ik Claudia uit Pearls handen kunnen redden. Ze zou rechtstreeks naar het ziekenhuis zijn gegaan in plaats van de veerboot af te zijn gesmokkeld. Ze zou nooit bij Yvonne terecht zijn gekomen of een longinfectie hebben opgelopen.

Dit soort gedachten kwellen me terwijl ik de minuten aftel, vijftien om precies te zijn, uitgerekt en vervormd door mijn verbeelding. De deur zwaait open. En verschijnt een jonge arts.

'Wat is er gebeurd?'

'De bloedgasmonitor sloeg alarm. Haar zuurstofspiegels waren te laag geworden. Ze is te zwak om zelf te ademen en daarom hebben we haar aan de beademing gelegd. We gaan haar een tijdje helpen met ademen en kijken hoe sterk ze morgen is.'

Het gevoel van opluchting zuigt het laatste restje energie uit me weg en ik voel me plotseling duizelig. Mijn ogen plakken en ik kan de kopersmaak in mijn mond niet wegkrijgen. Ik heb het Samira nog niet verteld en nu al is mijn hart aan flarden.

13

Soms is Londen een parodie op zichzelf. Zoals vandaag. De hemel is dik en zwaar en de wind koud, zij het niet koud genoeg voor sneeuw. De wedkantoren van Ladbrokes wedden 3 tegen 1 dat Londen een witte kerst krijgt. Eén enkele sneeuwvlok op het dak van het Meteorologisch Instituut is voldoende.

De borgtochthoorzitting is vandaag. Ik heb mijn rechtbankkleren aan: een rode kokerrok, een crèmekleurige bloes en een kort jasje dat fraai genoeg gesneden is om een duur merkje te hebben, maar helemaal geen merkje heeft.

Shawcroft heeft mensensmokkel, gedwongen zwangerschap en vergrijpen conform de wet op de kinderbescherming ten laste gelegd gekregen. Alleen al voor smokkel geldt een maximumstraf van dertig jaar. Er hangen hem nog meer zaken boven het hoofd, waaronder mogelijke uitlevering aan Nederland.

Samira zit op het bed toe te kijken hoe ik me opmaak. Op haar schoot ligt een overjas. Ze is al uren aangekleed, na vroeg te zijn ontwaakt en te hebben gebeden. Ze hoeft niet eerder te getuigen dan tijdens de rechtszaak, wat nog wel een jaar kan duren, maar ze wil toch mee naar de hoorzitting van vandaag.

'Shawcroft is nog slechts verdachte,' zeg ik. 'In ons rechtssysteem is een verdachte onschuldig tot het tegendeel bewezen is.'

'Maar wij weten dat hij schuldig is.'

'Ja, maar dat moet een jury uitmaken, na alle bewijs te hebben aangehoord.'

'Wat is borgtocht?'

'Een rechter zal in sommige gevallen een beklaagde tot aan het proces op vrije voeten laten als hij belooft niet te zullen vluchten en geen contact te zoeken met eventuele getuigen. Om te garanderen dat dit ook echt niet gebeurt zal de rechter een hoog geldbedrag opleggen dat de beklaagde niet terugkrijgt als hij de wet overtreedt of niet komt opdagen.'

Ze kijkt stomverbaasd. 'Gaat hij de rechter geld geven?'

'Dat geld is in feite een borgsom.'

'Een omkoopsom.'

'Nee, geen omkoopsom.'

'Dus jij wilt zeggen dat Brother geld kan betalen en dan de gevangenis uit mag?'

'Ja, maar het is niet wat jij denkt.'

Het gesprek blijft in kringetjes ronddraaien. Ik leg het niet al te best uit.

'Ik weet zeker dat het niet zal gebeuren,' stel ik haar gerust. 'Hij zal niet nog eens iemand kwaad kunnen doen.'

Er zijn drie weken verstreken sinds Claudia uit het ziekenhuis is gekomen. Ik maak me nog steeds zorgen over haar – ze lijkt zo klein in vergelijking met haar broertje – maar de infectie is over en ze begint aan te komen.

De tabloids hebben de tweeling tot beroemdheden gemaakt: Baby X en Baby Y, zonder voornamen of achternamen. De rechter die over de voogdij beslist heeft om DNA-tests verzocht en om medische rapporten uit Amsterdam. Samira zal moeten aantonen dat zij hun moeder is en dan beslissen wat ze wil.

Ondanks het gerechtelijk onderzoek dat naar hem gaande is, heeft Barnaby zijn campagne voor het voogdijschap voortgezet door links en rechts advocaten in te huren en weer weg te sturen. Vanwege zijn voortdurende onderbrekingen en beschuldigingen van partijdigheid heeft rechter Freyne gedreigd hem wegens minachting van het hof te laten opsluiten.

Ik had ondertussen mijn eigen hoorzitting te doorstaan: een tuchttribunaal ten overstaan van drie hoge politiefunctionarissen. Op de eerste dag diende ik mijn ontslag in. De voorzitter weigerde het te aanvaarden.

'Ik dacht dat ik het makkelijker voor ze maakte,' zei ik tegen Ruiz.

'Ze kunnen je niet ontslaan en ze willen je niet laten gaan,' legde hij uit. 'Denk je de krantenkoppen eens in.'

'Wat willen ze dan?'

'Je ergens veilig wegstoppen in een kantoor, waar je geen problemen kunt veroorzaken.'

Samira doet haar borstkompressen goed en knoopt haar bloes dicht. Ze kolft vier keer per dag melk af voor de tweeling, die per koerier naar het pleeggezin wordt gebracht. Ze mag ze elke middag drie uur lang onder begeleiding zien. Ik heb haar nauwlettend geobserveerd, op zoek naar een signaal dat ze naar hen toe trekt. Ze voedt, baadt en zorgt en maakt de indruk dat ze veel bedrevener en beter thuis is in het moederschap dan ik ooit had kunnen denken. Tegelijkertijd zijn haar bewegingen bijna mechanisch, alsof ze doet wat van haar verwacht wordt in plaats van wat ze zelf wil.

Ze heeft een merkwaardige tic ontwikkeld als ze met de tweeling bezig is. Of ze nu aan het kolven is, luiers verwisselt of ze aankleedt, ze gebruikt alleen haar rechterhand. Als ze een van de twee oppakt, steekt ze haar arm tussen hun beentjes langs hun ruggengraat en pakt ze in één beweging op, het hoofdje met haar handpalm ondersteunend. En als ze hen voedt, klemt ze een fles onder haar kin of legt ze de baby op haar dijen.

Een tijdlang dacht ik dat het een moslimgewoonte was, zoals dat je alleen met je rechterhand eet. Toen ik haar ernaar vroeg, sloeg ze smalend haar ogen op. 'Eén hand is genoeg om te zondigen. Eén hand is genoeg om te redden.'

'Wat betekent dat?'

'Precies wat het zegt.'

Hari is beneden. 'Weet je zeker dat je niet wilt dat ik met je meega?'

'Heel zeker.'

'Ik zou een paraplu omhoog kunnen houden.'

'Het regent niet.'

'Dat doen ze voor filmsterren die niet gefotografeerd willen worden, een paraplu omhooghouden. Hun lijfwachten doen dat.'

'Jij bent geen lijfwacht.'

Hij is als een smachtende puppy. De universiteit is dicht vanwege kerst en hij wordt geacht zijn broers te helpen in de garage, maar hij vindt telkens weer excuses om tijd door te brengen met Samira. Ze vindt het zelfs goed om alleen met hem te zijn, maar dan alleen in het tuinschuurtje om aan een pyrotechnisch project te werken. Het vuurwerk had iets eenmaligs zullen zijn, maar Hari heeft een bepaald lontje brandend gehouden, om voor de hand liggende redenen.

Groentje Dave staat ons buiten op te wachten.

'Draag je geen zwart?'

'Gek, hè, vind je niet?'

'Rood staat je goed.'

'Dan moet je mijn ondergoed eens zien,' fluister ik.

Samira trekt haar overjas aan, met houtjes in plaats van knopen. Hij is van Hari geweest en de mouwen zijn zo lang dat de manchetten twee keer moeten worden teruggeslagen.

De dag begint lichter te worden, op weg naar de middag. Dave laveert door het verkeer en parkeert één straat bij de rechtbank in Southwark vandaan, klaar voor het spervuur. Voor ons uit, op de stoep, staan televisiecamera's en fotografen te wachten.

De aanklachten tegen Julian Shawcroft zijn niet meer dan een extra attractie bij het hoofdprogramma – het voogdijgevecht om de tweeling – dat alles in zich heeft waar de tabloids van smullen: seks, een knappe 'maagd' en gestolen baby's.

Om ons heen gaan flitslampen af. Samira buigt het hoofd en houdt haar handen in haar zakken. Dave forceert een pad door de menigte, niet bang om zijn schouder in iemand te boren die niet opzij wil gaan. Het zijn manoeuvres die op het rugbyveld thuishoren, niet op een zeilschool.

De rechtbank van Southwark is een zielloos modern bouwwerk met minder charme dan de Old Bailey. We lopen de detectiepoortjes door en gaan de trap op. Ik herken sommige mensen die in de gangen staan te overleggen en met hun raadslieden de laatste tactische manoeuvres doornemen. In de verwachting dat hij zal worden aangeklaagd heeft dokter Sohan Banerjee zijn eigen raadsman ingehuurd. Shawcroft en hij hebben zich nog altijd niet op elkaar gestort, maar volgens Forbes zijn beschuldigende vingers nog slechts een kwestie van tijd.

Shawcrofts advocaat is een vrouw, een meter vijfenzeventig op vijf centimeter lange naaldhakken, met witblond haar en pareloorhangers die heen en weer zwaaien als ze praat.

De aanklager, Francis Hague, *Queen's Counsel*, is ouder en grijzer, met zijn bril boven op zijn hoofd. Hij praat met Forbes en maakt aantekeningen op een smal schrijfblok. Ook brigadier Softell is gekomen, misschien in de hoop op een aanknopingspunt in de zoektocht naar Brendan Pearl, die van de aardbodem verdwenen lijkt. Ik vraag me af hoeveel verschillende identiteiten hij inmiddels heeft gestolen.

Samira is nerveus. Ze beseft dat mensen naar haar kijken, rechtbankmedewerkers en verslaggevers. Ik heb geprobeerd haar gerust te stellen dat de publiciteit zal stoppen zodra de tweeling thuis is. Niemand zal hun identiteit te weten mogen komen.

We nemen plaats op de publieke tribune achter in de rechtszaal, Dave aan de ene kant en ik aan de andere. Samira duikt in haar jas ineen. Ik zie Donavon de rij achter ons in glippen. Zijn ogen zoeken de rechtszaal af en rusten even op mij voordat hij verder loopt. De perstribune is al snel gevuld en er zijn geen zitplaatsen meer op de publieke tribune. De griffier, een Aziatische vrouw van onbestemde leeftijd, komt binnen, gaat zitten en begint op een toetsenbord te tikken.

Geschuifel van voeten en iedereen staat op voor de rechter, die verrassend jong is en op een saaie manier best aantrekkelijk. Enkele minuten later verschijnt Shawcroft via een trap die rechtstreeks naar de beklaagdenbank voert. Gekleed in een net pak, een gespikkelde das en gepoetste schoenen draait hij zich om en glimlacht naar de tribune, de atmosfeer in zich opzuigend alsof dit een voorstelling is die te zijner bate is georganiseerd.

'U wilt een aanvraag indienen voor borgtocht?' vraagt de rechter.

Shawcrofts raadsvrouw, Margaret Curillo, is al opgestaan en stelt zich op geaffecteerde en onderdanig-kruiperige toon voor. Francis Hague plant zijn handen op tafel, komt met zijn billen een paar centimeter van zijn stoel en stelt zich mompelend voor. Misschien heeft hij het idee dat iedereen hem al kent of op z'n minst zou moeten kennen.

De deur van de rechtszaal gaat zachtjes open en er komt een man binnen. Hij is lang en dun en heeft iets verwijfds over zich. Hij knikt afwezig naar de rechter en tilt zijn gepoetste schoenen nauwelijks van het tapijt als hij naar de advocatentafel schrijdt. Vooroverbuigend zegt hij iets tegen Hague, die zijn hoofd scheef houdt.

Mevrouw Curillo is begonnen aan haar openingspleidooi en schetst de talrijke 'uitnemende verrichtingen' van haar cliënt gedurende een 'leven van dienstbaarheid aan de gemeenschap'.

Dit keer staat de aanklager wel helemaal op.

'Edelachtbare, ik moet me verontschuldigen dat ik mijn waarde collega onderbreek, maar ik wil u om een korte schorsing verzoeken.'

'We zijn net begonnen.'

'Ik moet nader advies inwinnen, edelachtbare. Klaarblijkelijk is de directeur van het Openbaar Ministerie bezig een aantal details van deze zaak opnieuw te bekijken.'

'Met welk oogmerk?'

'Daar kan ik op dit moment geen antwoord op geven.'

'Hoe lang hebt u nodig?'

'Als ik zo vrij mag zijn, edelachtbare, wil ik voorstellen deze zaak voor drie uur vanmiddag opnieuw op de rol te zetten.'

De rechter staat abrupt op en veroorzaakt een kettingreactie in de rechtszaal. Shawcroft wordt al de trap af geleid. Ik kijk naar Dave, die zijn schouders ophaalt. Samira kijkt naar ons, wachtend op een verklaring. Buiten, op de gang, zoek ik Forbes, die lijkt te zijn verdwenen, evenals Softell. Wat is er in 's hemelsnaam gaande?

De twee daaropvolgende uren wachten we. Er worden zaken afgeroepen voor verschillende rechtbanken. Advocaten houden besprekingen. Mensen komen en gaan. Samira zit met haar schouders gekromd, nog altijd in haar overjas.

'Geloof jij in de hemel?' vraagt ze.

De vraag is zo onverwacht dat ik mijn mond iets voel openzakken. Ik doe hem bewust weer dicht. 'Waarom vraag je dat?'

'Denk je dat Hasan en Zala in de hemel zijn?'

'Dat weet ik niet.'

'Mijn vader geloofde dat wij onze levens vele malen moeten leven, dat het elke keer beter wordt en we pas naar de hemel gaan als we volkomen gelukkig zijn.'

'Ik weet niet of ik het leuk zou vinden keer op keer hetzelfde leven te leiden.'

'Waarom niet?'

'Het zou afbreuk doen aan de gevolgen. Ik stel dingen nu al uit tot een andere dag. Stel je voor dat ik ze uitstel tot een volgend leven.'

Ze slaat haar armen om zich heen. 'Afghanistan is uit me aan het weggaan.'

'Wat bedoel je?'

'Ik vergeet dingen. Ik weet niet meer wat voor soort bloemen ik op mijn vaders graf heb geplant. Op een keer had ik die bloemen tussen de bladzijden van zijn koran geperst en hem erg kwaad gemaakt. Hij zei dat ik Allah onteerde. Ik zei dat ik hem een bloemenhulde bracht. Daar moest hij om lachen. Mijn vader kon nooit lang kwaad op me blijven.'

We drinken onze middagthee in de kantine, de verslaggevers mijdend, die geleidelijk aan weggaan. Francis Hague en Shawcrofts advocaat zijn nog steeds niet terug en Forbes ook niet. Zou het kunnen dat ze kerstinkopen zijn gaan doen? Even voor drieën komt een advocaat van de openbaar aanklager ons halen. De verdediging wil met Samira spreken. Ik word meegevraagd.

'Ik wacht hier op jullie,' zegt Dave.

We gaan een reeks trappen op en worden door een deur geleid waarop ALLEEN RECHTBANKPERSONEEL staat. Een lange gang met aan weerszijden kantoren. Aan het ene uiteinde staat een eenzame palm in een pot met daarnaast een nogal geërgerd kijkende vrouw die op een stoel zit te wachten. Haar in zwarte kousen gestoken benen steken als verbrande lucifers onder een bontjas uit.

De advocaat klopt zachtjes op een deur. Er wordt opengedaan. De eerste die ik zie is Spijker, die er zelfs voor zijn begrippen deprimerend somber uitziet. Hij pakt mijn hand, kust me drie keer op de wang en maakt een lichte buiging naar Samira.

Shawcrofts advocaat zit aan de andere kant van de tafel, tegenover Francis Hague. Naast hem zit een andere man, die niet veel tijd lijkt te hebben. De vrouw in de bontjas zou zijn vrouw kunnen zijn, die buiten zit te wachten en had gedacht elders te zullen zijn.

'Mijn naam is Adam Greenburg,' zegt hij terwijl hij opstaat en Samira de hand schudt. 'Ik ben plaatsvervangend directeur van het parket van de openbaar aanklager.'

Hij verontschuldigt zich voor de benauwde atmosfeer in de kamer en bet met een zakdoek zijn voorhoofd.

'Ik zal u uitleggen wat mijn werk inhoudt, mejuffrouw Khan. Als iemand wordt gearresteerd voor een misdrijf, komt die niet automatisch voor de rechter en in de gevangenis. De politie moet eerst bewijsmateriaal verzamelen en de taak van het parket van de openbaar aanklager is dat bewijsmateriaal te beoordelen en te zorgen dat de juiste persoon wordt vervolgd voor het juiste misdrijf en dat alle relevante feiten het hof ter hand worden gesteld. Kunt u me volgen?'

Samira kijkt naar mij en weer terug naar Greenburg. Er zit een olifant op mijn borstkas.

De enige die zich niet heeft voorgesteld is de man die de rechtszaal binnen kwam lopen en de borgtochtzitting verstoorde. Hij staat bij het raam in een duur maatpak en heeft het profiel van een roofvogel en merkwaardig uitdrukkingsloze ogen. Desondanks suggereert iets in zijn houding dat hij van iedereen in de kamer een geheim weet.

Meneer Greenburg gaat verder. 'De beslissing om tot vervolging over te gaan bestaat uit twee stadia. Het eerste stadium is de bewijskrachttoetsing. Procureurs-generaal moeten ervan overtuigd zijn dat er voldoende bewijsmateriaal voorhanden is voor een realistisch vooruitzicht op veroordeling van elke beklaagde op elke aanklacht.

Het tweede stadium is de toetsing van het openbaar belang. We moeten ervan overtuigd zijn dat vervolging een publiek belang dient. Het parket van de openbaar aanklager zal een vervolging pas inzetten of voortzetten als een zaak alle twee de toetsingen heeft doorstaan, ongeacht het verdere belang of de ernst van de zaak.'

Meneer Greenburg staat op het punt tot de kern van de zaak te komen. Spijker durft me niet aan te kijken. Alle ogen zijn op de tafel gericht.

'Het parket van de openbaar aanklager heeft besloten de vervolging van de heer Shawcroft niet voort te zetten, omdat deze de toetsing van aannemelijk publiek belang niet doorstaat en omdat hij heeft toegezegd de politie volledige medewerking te zullen verlenen en bepaalde aannames gerechtvaardigd zijn ten aanzien van zijn gedrag in de toekomst.'

Een moment lang beneemt de schok me de adem en ben ik niet in staat te reageren. Ik kijk naar Spijker, hopend op steun. Hij staart naar zijn handen.

'Een zaak als deze roept serieuze morele en ethische vragen op,' legt Greenburg uit. 'Er zijn veertien zuigelingen geïdentificeerd als geboren uit onwettig draagmoederschap. Deze kinderen wonen in stabiele, liefhebbende gezinnen bij hun biologische ouders.

Als we de heer Shawcroft vervolgen, zullen deze gezinnen uit elkaar worden gescheurd. Ouders zullen worden aangeklaagd als medesamenzweerders en hun kinderen zullen in een kindertehuis geplaatst worden, mogelijk voorgoed. Door één individu te vervolgen lopen we het risico de levens van talloze anderen te verwoesten.

De Nederlandse autoriteiten staan voor een soortgelijk dilemma, waarbij zes kinderen van illegale draagmoeders betrokken zijn. De Duitse autoriteiten hebben vier geboorten vastgesteld, terwijl het in Frankrijk mogelijk om wel dertien gevallen gaat.

Ik ben net zo geschokt en ontzet door deze boosaardige handel als wie ook, maar wij dienen hier vandaag beslissingen te nemen die bepalend zijn voor de blijvende gevolgen die dit zal hebben.'

Ik vind mijn stem terug. 'U bent niet verplicht de ouderparen aan te klagen.'

'Als we ervoor kiezen te persisteren, zo heeft de raadsvrouwe van de heer Shawcroft aangegeven, zal zij alle betrokken echtparen laten dagvaarden die wettelijk en ethisch gezien kinderen grootbrengen die de facto iemand anders toebehoren.

Dat is de situatie waarvoor wij staan. En de vraag die wij dienen te beantwoorden is of wij hier een streep onder zetten of doorgaan en de levens van onschuldige kinderen ontwrichten.'

Samira hangt lusteloos onderuit in haar overjas. Ze heeft zich niet verroerd. Alles gebeurt met zo'n beleefdheid en zo veel gevoel voor decorum dat het geheel iets onwerkelijks heeft.

'Hij heeft onschuldige mensen vermoord.' Mijn stem klinkt hol.

Mevrouw Curillo protesteert. 'Mijn cliënt ontkent elke betrokkenheid bij een dergelijke misdaad en is niet aangeklaagd in verband met een dergelijke gebeurtenis.'

'En Cate en Felix Beaumont dan? En Hasan Khan en Zala?'

Greenburg heft zijn hand ten teken dat ik moet zwijgen.

'In ruil voor herroeping van alle aanklachten heeft de heer Shawcroft de politie de verblijfplaats van Brendan Pearl genoemd, een vermoedelijke mensensmokkelaar en voortvluchtige crimineel die nog altijd een voorwaardelijke straf heeft voor in Noord-Ierland begane vergrijpen. De heer Shawcroft heeft een verklaring afgelegd waarin hij stelt niet betrokken te zijn geweest bij de dood van de Beaumonts en zegt dat Brendan Pearl in zijn eentje handelde. Hij houdt ook staande dat hij geen rol heeft gespeeld in de smokkeloperatie die heeft geleid tot de betreurenswaardige doden in Harwich International Port in oktober. Een criminele bende heeft misbruik gemaakt van zijn naïviteit. Hij geeft betrokkenheid bij commercieel draagmoederschap toe, maar zegt dat Brendan Pearl en zijn kompanen het plan hadden overgenomen en hem chanteerden om deel te nemen.'

'Dit is belachelijk! Hij heeft de hele zaak opgezet! Hij heeft vrouwen gedwongen zwanger te worden! Hij heeft de baby's weggehaald!' Ik kan mezelf niet horen gillen, maar er verheffen zich geen andere stemmen. Terwijl ik mijn woede op Greenburg richt, gebruik ik woorden als 'rechtvaardigheid' en 'eerlijkheid', terwijl hij terugkomt met termen als 'gezond verstand' en 'openbaar belang'.

Mijn taal begint uiteen te rafelen. Ik noem hem laf en corrupt. Hij wordt mijn woedeaanval beu en dreigt me te laten verwijderen.

'De heer Pearl zal worden uitgeleverd aan Nederland, waar hij terecht zal staan in verband met prostitutie, mensensmokkel en moord,' legt hij uit. 'Daarnaast heeft de heer Shawcroft ermee ingestemd alle betrokkenheid bij zijn stichtingen en het New Life Adoption Centre te beëindigen, met onmiddellijke ingang. De vergunning van het centrum om adopties te coördineren is ingetrokken. De Commissie Liefdadigheidsinstellingen stelt momenteel een persbericht op. Ik meen dat "vervroegde uittreding" de gekozen formulering is. Het parket van de openbaar aanklager zal daarnaast een verklaring doen uitgaan waarin staat dat de aanklachten wegens gebrek aan bewijs zullen worden ingetrokken.'

De zin heeft iets definitiefs. Zijn taak zit erop. Terwijl hij opstaat trekt hij zijn jasje recht. 'Ik had mijn vrouw beloofd met haar te zullen lunchen. Dat zal nu wel een dineetje worden. Dank u voor uw medewerking.'

Samira schudt me van zich af, wringt zich langs mensen heen en loopt struikelend naar de lift.

'Het spijt me, Alisha,' zegt Spijker.

Ik kan niet reageren. Hij heeft me hiervoor gewaarschuwd. We zaten in zijn kantoor in Amsterdam en hij had het over de doos van Pandora. Sommige deksels kunnen beter gesloten blijven, vastgelijmd, -gespijkerd en -geschroefd en onder twee meter aarde begraven.

'Er zit een zeker logica in, weet je. Het heeft geen zin de schuldigen te straffen als we daarmee de onschuldigen straffen,' zegt hij.

'Iemand zal hiervoor moeten boeten.'

'Er zál ook iemand boeten.'

Ik staar over de bestrate binnenplaats, waar duiven de standbeelden met muisgrijze uitwerpselen hebben bedekt. De wind is weer opgestoken en jaagt naalden van natte sneeuw tegen het glas.

Ik bel Forbes. Windvlagen happen aan zijn woorden.

'Wanneer wist je het?'

'Rond de middag.'

'Heb je Pearl?'

'Dat is mijn feestje niet meer.'

'Ben je van de zaak afgehaald?'

'Als publieksdienaar ben ik niet hoog genoeg om dit af te handelen.'

Ineens zie ik de stille man voor me die bij het raam aan zijn manchetknopen stond te plukken. Hij was van MI5. De geheime diensten willen Pearl. Forbes is gedwongen teruggetreden.

'Waar ben je nu?'

'Arrestatieteams hebben een pension in Southend-on-Sea omsingeld.'

'Is Pearl binnen?'

'Hij staat voor het raam te kijken.'

'Hij zal niet vluchten.'

'Daar is het te laat voor.'

Er verschijnt nog een beeld. Dit keer van Brendan Pearl die het pension uit wandelt met een pistool in zijn broekband gestoken, klaar om te vechten of te vluchten. Hij gaat hoe dan ook niet terug de gevangenis in.

Samira. Wat ga ik haar zeggen? Hoe kan ik dit ooit uitleggen? Ze heeft gehoord wat Greenburg zei. Haar zwijgen sprak boekdelen. Het was alsof ze al die tijd al wist dat het hierop zou uitdraaien. Verraad. Verbroken beloften, dubbelhartigheid. Ze is hier eerder geweest, heeft deze plek al bezocht. 'Sommige mensen worden geboren om te lijden,' zei Lena Caspar. 'Voor hen houdt het nooit op, geen seconde.'

Daar staat ze nu, vlekkerig door het natte glas, bij het beeld, met Hari's jas aan. Ik wil haar over de toekomst vertellen. Ik wil haar de kerstverlichting in Regent Street laten zien, haar vertellen over de krokussen in de lente, haar echte dingen laten zien, waarachtige dingen, geluk.

Er is een donker gekleurde auto gestopt die langs de stoeprand wacht. Fotografen en cameralieden komen de rechtbank uit stromen, achteruitlopend en elkaar wegduwend voor een plekje. Julian Shawcroft komt naar buiten, geflankeerd door zijn advocate en Eddie Barrett. Zijn zilverkleurige haar glimt in de tv-lampen.

Hij maakt geintjes met de verslaggevers, ontspannen, joviaal, meester van het moment.

Ik zie Samira in een zigzagbeweging zijn kant op lopen. Haar handen zitten diep in de zakken van haar jas gestoken.

Ik heb het op een lopen gezet en ontwijk op de gang links en rechts mensen. Ik geef een klap op de knop van de lift en kies in plaats daarvan de trap, slinger me over elke tussenverdieping en ga uiteindelijk de dubbele branddeuren op de begane grond door.

Ik zit aan de verkeerde kant van het gebouw. Welke kant op? Links.

Sommige baanatleten zijn goede bochtenlopers. Ze hellen over naar binnen en verschuiven hun zwaartepunt in plaats van de middelpuntvliedende krachten te bevechten die hen eruit proberen te gooien. De truc is om je niet tegen die kracht te verzetten, maar er gebruik van te maken door je pas te verkorten en tegen de binnenrand aan te blijven lopen.

Een Russische coach vertelde me ooit dat ik de beste bochtenloopster was die hij ooit had gezien. Hij gebruikte zelfs een video van mij om zijn jonge lopers op de academie in Moskou te trainen. Op dit moment heb ik geen schuin oplopende baan en de straatstenen zijn glibberig van de regen, maar ik loop deze bocht alsof mijn leven ervan afhangt. Ik hou mezelf voor dat ik de bocht moet volgen en kom er als een pijl uit een boog uit tevoorschijn. Afzetten. Afzetten. Alles schrijnt – mijn benen, mijn longen – maar ik vlieg.

De tweehonderd meter was mijn handelsmerk. Ik heb de longen niet voor de middenafstanden.

Voor me zie ik de persoploop. Samira staat er vlak buiten; ze wipt van de ene voet op de andere als een popelend kind. Dan baant ze zich toch een weg naar binnen, schouders opzij duwend. Een verslaggever ziet haar en doet een stap achteruit. Een andere volgt. Meer mensen maken zich los; ze voelen dat zich hier een verhaal aandient.

Samira's jas hangt open. Ze heeft iets in haar hand dat het licht vangt: een glazen olifant met kleine spiegeltjes. Mijn olifant.

Shawcroft is te druk om haar op te merken. Ze omhelst hem van achteren, slaat haar armen om zijn middel, drukt haar linkervuist tegen zijn hart en haar hoofd tegen het midden van zijn rug. Hij probeert haar van zich af te schudden, maar ze laat niet los. Een sliert rook kringelt op tussen haar vingers.

Iemand schreeuwt en mensen duiken weg. Ze zeggen dat het een bom is! Wat?

Het geluid van mijn schreeuw verdwijnt in de knal van een explosie die de lucht beetgrijpt en hem doet sidderen. Shawcroft tolt traag om zijn as, tot hij mijn kant op kijkt, met een niet-begrijpende blik. Het gat in zijn borstkas heeft de grootte van een soepbord. Ik kan zo naar binnen kijken.

Samira valt de andere kant op, met haar knieën uit elkaar. Haar gezicht raakt als eerste de grond doordat haar linkerarm de val niet kan breken. Ze heeft haar ogen open. Een hand strekt zich naar me uit. Vingers zijn er niet. Er zit helemaal geen hand.

Mensen rennen rond en schreeuwen, brullend als verdoemden, hun gezichten bezaaid met glassplinters.

'Het is een terroriste!' schreeuwt iemand. 'Pas op!'

'Ze is geen terroriste,' antwoord ik.

'Er kunnen nog meer bommen zijn.'

'Die zijn er niet.'

Over de lengte van haar armen zitten stukjes spiegel en glas, maar haar gezicht en lichaam, die achter Shawcrofts rug schuilgingen, zijn aan de kracht van de ontploffing ontsnapt.

Ik had het me moeten realiseren. Ik had het moeten zien aankomen. Hoe lang geleden heeft ze dit gepland? Weken, misschien wel langer. Ze had mijn olifant van het nachtkastje gepakt. Zonder het te weten hielp Hari haar door modelraketmotoren te kopen die vol met buskruit zaten. De ontsteking moet op haar onderarm geplakt hebben gezeten: de reden dat ze haar jas niet uitdeed. Het glas en de spiegeltjes hebben de metaaldetectors niet doen afgaan.

De gerafelde voering van de mouw van haar jas smeult na en het verbrande poeder heeft het vlees rond een gekarteld stuk bot dichtgeschroeid. Ze draait haar hoofd.

'Is hij dood?'

'Ja.'

Tevredengesteld doet ze haar ogen dicht. Twee verplegers nemen haar voorzichtig van me over en leggen haar op een brancard. Ik probeer op te staan, maar val achterover. Ik wil blijven vallen.

Ik dacht dat ik alles wist over vriendschap en gezinnen: de blijheid, de eenvoud en de vreugde die erbinnen kunnen heersen. Maar toewijding heeft een keerzijde, die Samira begrijpt. Ze is per slot van rekening haar vaders dochter.

Om te zondigen is één hand genoeg. Om te redden is één hand genoeg.

EPILOOG

Afgelopen nacht droomde ik dat ik trouwde in een witte jurk in plaats van een sari. Mijn vader kwam, mij heftig toesprekend, het gangpad af stormen en de kerkgangers braken in een spontaan applaus uit in de overtuiging dat het een stukje sikh-variété was.

Samira was er ook, die Jasper omhooghield, die trappelde en kraaide en opgewonden met zijn armpjes zwaaide. Hari hield Claudia boven zijn hoofd om haar te kunnen laten kijken. Zij was veel serieuzer en leek klaar om in huilen uit te barsten. Mijn moeder vergoot emmers, uiteraard. Op dat onderdeel kon ze voor twee landen uitkomen.

Ik heb de laatste tijd vaak van dit soort dromen. Volmaakte levensfantasieën, vol ideale koppels en eindigend als een soap. Zie je wat een weekdier ik ben geworden? Ik was altijd een meisje dat niet huilde als het triest afliep en niet sentimenteel werd van baby's. Tegenwoordig moet ik op mijn lip bijten om de tranen tegen te houden en wil ik wel door het plafond zweven zoveel als ik van ze hou.

Jasper is altijd vrolijk en lacht zonder aanwijsbare reden, terwijl Claudia de wereld met bezorgde ogen bekijkt. Soms, als je er het minst op verdacht bent, produceert ze tranen van rampzalige triestheid en weet ik dat ze huilt voor degenen die dat niet meer kunnen.

Hun namen zijn gebleven. Dat gebeurt soms: iets krijgt een naam en het lijkt gewoon niet goed om die te veranderen. Ik ga de mijne niet veranderen als ik trouw, maar andere dingen zijn al wel anders geworden. Het was altijd Mij, nu is het Wij en Ons.

Ik rol op mijn zij en glij met mijn vingers over het laken tot ze Daves borst raken. Het dekbed zit om ons heen geslagen en het voelt veilig, beschermd, beschut tegen de wereld.

Hij laat inmiddels zijn haar groeien. Het past bij zijn nieuwe manier van leven. Ik had nooit gedacht dat ik verliefd zou worden op een man die visserstruien en zeilbroeken draagt. Zijn hand ligt tussen ons in. Er beginnen eeltplekken op zijn handpalmen te komen van het werken met de schoten en het hijsen van de zeilen.

Uit de kamer naast de onze komt een nasaal kreetje. Na een poosje hoor ik het opnieuw.

'Het is jouw beurt,' fluister ik terwijl ik Daves oor kietel.

'Jij staat toch op,' mompelt hij.

'Dat maakt niet uit.'

'Het is het meisje.'

'Hoe weet je dat?'

'Zij roept zeurderig.'

Ik geef hem een harde por in zijn ribben. Meisjes zeuren niet. En sinds wanneer wordt er onderscheid gemaakt?

Hij laat zich uit bed rollen en zoekt zijn boxershort.

'Hou jij het bed maar warm.'

'Altijd.'

Hoewel het nog maar zes weken geleden is, zijn de gebeurtenissen van die dag veranderd in een surrealistisch waas. Er was geen strijd om de voogdij. Barnaby Elliot trok zich bruusk terug toen hij geconfronteerd werd met aantijgingen dat hij informatie voor de politie had achtergehouden en medeplichtig was door steun achteraf.

Rechter Freyne oordeelde dat Samira de moeder van de tweeling was, al bracht de DNA-test een nieuwe wending in het verhaal teweeg. De tweeling waren broer en zus en de embryo's waren afkomstig van Cate, maar ze waren bevrucht door een derde, iemand anders dan Felix. Er ging meer dan een rimpeling door de rechtszaal toen dat kleine stukje informatie openbaar werd.

Hoe was dat mogelijk? Dokter Banerjee oogstte twaalf levensvatbare embryo's en implanteerde er tien tijdens IVF-procedures. Cate nam het overblijvende paar mee naar Amsterdam.

Het kan natuurlijk zijn dat er dingen door elkaar zijn gehaald en dat het sperma van iemand anders het proces heeft verstoord.

Volgens dokter Banerjee was de belangrijkste reden dat Felix en Cate geen kinderen konden krijgen dat haar baarmoeder zijn sperma behandelde als kankercellen en ze vernietigde. In een andere baarmoeder, met krachtiger sperma, wie weet... Maar er was nog een kwestie. Een recessief gen waarvan Cate en Felix drager waren en dat een zeldzame genetische afwijking veroorzaakte, een dodelijke vorm van dwerggroei. Zou ze zwanger worden, dan was er een kans van vijfentwintig procent dat de foetus de aandoening zou hebben.

In de slaapkamer of in haar hart zou Cate Felix nooit bedrogen hebben, maar ze verlangde zo ontzettend naar een kind en nu ze al zo lang had gewacht en zulke risico's had genomen, kon ze zich een volgende teleurstelling niet permitteren. Misschien vond ze iemand die ze vertrouwde, iemand die Felix nooit zou ontmoeten, iemand die erg op hem leek, iemand die haar iets verschuldigd was.

Het is natuurlijk maar een theorie. Niets dan speculatie. Hij kwam voor het eerst in me op toen ik zag hoe de tweeling lag te slapen en ik boven hun hoofdjes naar de droomvanger keek en mijn vingers langs de veertjes en kralen liet gaan.

Ik betwijfel of Donavon enig idee had van wat ze van plan was. En als hij inderdaad de vader is, heeft hij zich aan zijn belofte aan haar gehouden en het aan niemand verteld. Het is beter zo.

Ik glip uit bed, rillend terwijl ik mijn sportbroek en een met fleece gevoerd topje aantrek. Tegen de tijd dat ik het huis uit stap wordt het al licht boven de Solent en het eiland Wight. Over Sea Road loop ik langs The Smuggler's Inn, sla links af over de parkeerplaats en kom bij een lange landtong van kiezelstenen die bijna tot halverwege de oversteek naar het eiland reikt.

Waadvogels stijgen op uit het drasland als ik erlangs ren en de lichtbundel van de vuurtoren flitst om de paar seconden, vervagend tegen de lichter wordende hemel. Het geluid van mijn schoenen op het dichte kiezeldek klinkt geruststellend terwijl ik de laatste anderhalve kilometer afleg naar Hurst Castle, dat de westelijke toegang tot de Solent bewaakt. Op sommige dagen, als noordoosters de zee tot een schuimend monster hebben opgezweept, kom ik niet tot bij het kasteel. Grote rollers met witte koppen buigen dan omhoog en slaan stuk tegen de zeemuur, waarna ze exploderen in een mist die de lucht ondoorzichtig en massief maakt. Ik kan dan nauwelijks tegen de wind in lopen en moet voorovergebogen het zout wegknipperen.

Het weer is zacht vandaag. Er zijn al zeilbootjes op het water en links van me zijn een vader en een zoon kokkels aan het zoeken in de poelen. In april wordt de zeilschool heropend. De zeilboten zijn klaar en ik ben een kei geworden in het repareren van zeilen. (Al die jaren dat ik mama achter haar naaimachine aan het werk heb gezien zijn toch niet helemaal voor niets geweest.)

Mijn leven is in de afgelopen acht weken ingrijpend veranderd. De tweeling laat me niet langer dan tot zes uur 's ochtends slapen en sommige nachten neem ik ze bij me in bed, hoewel alle deskundigen zeggen dat ik dat niet moet doen. Ze hebben me van mijn slaap beroofd, me helemaal in beslag genomen en me laten lachen. Ik ben betoverd. Mijn hart is twee keer zo groot geworden om plaats voor ze te maken.

Als ik de strandkant van de landtong nader, zie ik op een omgekeerde roeiboot een gestalte zitten met zijn laarzen in de kiezels geplant en zijn handen in zijn zakken. Naast hem staan een canvas vistas en een hengel.

'Ik weet dat je niet slaapt, meneer, maar dit is belachelijk.'

Ruiz tilt zijn haveloze pet op. 'Je moet vroeg opstaan om een vis te vangen, sprinkhaan.'

'Waarom zit je dan niet te vissen?'

'Ik heb besloten ze een voorsprong te geven.'

Hij slingert de tas over zijn schouder en loopt met me mee de rotsige helling op.

'Heb je ooit weleens echt een vis gevangen, meneer?'

'Gaan we brutaal doen?'

'Het lijkt of je geen aas gebruikt.'

'Dat betekent dat we als gelijken van start gaan. Ik geloof niet in oneerlijk voordeel.'

We lopen in stilte voort terwijl onze adem de lucht in dampt.

Vlak bij huis stop ik aan de overkant van Milford Green en koop een krant en muffins.

Samira is in de keuken, in een pyjama en mijn oude ochtendjas met de op de zak genaaide uil. Jasper ligt in de holte van haar linkerarm genesteld aan haar rechterborst te snuffelen. Claudia ligt in haar wiegje bij de haard, fronsend alsof ze het er niet mee eens is dat ze haar beurt moet afwachten.

'Goedemorgen, meneer Ruiz.'

'Goedemorgen.' Ruiz neemt zijn pet af en buigt zich over het wiegje. Claudia schenkt hem een allergelukzaligste glimlach.

Samira keert zich naar mij. 'Hoe waren ze vannacht?'

'Engeltjes.'

'Dat zeg je altijd. Zelfs als ze je vijf keer wakker maken.'

'Ja.'

Ze lacht. 'Bedankt dat je me hebt laten slapen.'

'Hoe laat is je examen?'

'Om tien uur.'

Ruiz biedt aan haar een lift te geven naar Southampton, waar ze aan het City College haar middelbareschooldiploma probeert te halen. De examens zijn pas in juni en de grote vraag is of ze ze zal maken zoals het Hare Majesteit behaagt of in een gewoon klaslokaal met andere scholieren.

Haar advocaten lijken er vertrouwen in te hebben dat ze een geval van niet-volledige verantwoordelijkheid of tijdelijke ontoerekeningsvatbaarheid kunnen bepleiten. Gezien wat ze heeft doorgemaakt zal niemand erg enthousiast zijn als ze gevangen wordt gezet, zelfs niet meneer Greenburg, die zijn emoties moest wegslikken toen hij haar vertelde dat het Openbaar Ministerie de aanklacht wegens moord doorzette.

'Wat is hier het openbaar belang?' vroeg ik sarcastisch.

'De mensen hebben het op de BBC zien gebeuren, op primetime. Ze heeft een man gedood. Ik moet het voor een jury brengen.'

Samira is op borgtocht vrij dankzij Ruiz en mijn ouders. De inspecteur is als een grootvader geworden voor de tweeling, die in de ban lijkt te zijn van zijn verweerde gezicht en het diepe rommelen van zijn stem. Misschien is het zijn zigeunerbloed, maar hij lijkt te begrijpen wat het is om op een gewelddadige wijze de wereld binnen te komen en je aan het leven vast te klampen.

Mijn moeder is de volgende die betoverd is. Ze belt vier keer per dag voor het laatste nieuws over hoe ze slapen, eten en groeien.

Ik neem Jasper van Samira over en hou hem over mijn schouder terwijl ik zachtjes zijn rug wrijf. Ze neemt Claudia op met haar rechterarm en biedt haar een borst, die ze gretig besnuffelt, tot haar mond de tepel vindt.

Een ontbrekende hand lijkt niet eens een handicap als je haar zo met de tweeling bezig ziet. Ze is volkomen stapel op ze en is dagelijks bezig met dingen als wassen en voeden en luiers verschonen. Ze is een slimme, knappe tienermoeder van een babytweeling.

Samira praat niet over de toekomst. Ze praat niet over het verleden. Vandaag is belangrijk. De tweeling is belangrijk.

Ik weet niet hoe lang ze bij ons zullen blijven of wat de volgende stap is, maar ik ben gaan beseffen dat we zoiets nooit kunnen weten. Er zijn geen zekerheden. Het einde van het ene verhaal is het begin van het volgende.

DANKWOORD

Dit verhaal had niet verteld kunnen worden zonder Esther Brandt en Jacqueline de Jong, wier hulp van onschatbare waarde was bij mijn research. Via hen ontmoette ik Sytze van der Zee, Leo Rietveld en de opmerkelijke Joep de Groot, mijn gids door de beroemde Amsterdamse Wallen. Verder ben ik dank verschuldigd aan Ursula Mackenzie en Mark Lucas voor hun vriendschap, advies en vertrouwen dat er verhalen in mij schuilen die het waard zijn verteld te worden. Voor hun gastvrijheid ben ik Richard, Emma, Mark en Sara dankbaar. En omdat ze me jong houden, alhoewel grijs, dank ik mijn drie dochters Alex, Charlotte en Bella. Maar wederom is het Vivien die de meeste lof verdient. Mijn researcher, meedenker, lezer, recensent, minnares en vrouw: zij is míjn liefdesverhaal.